KU-565-158

IN A LAND OF PLENTY

Also by Tim Pears

In the Place of Fallen Leaves

For Hania

WESTERN ISLES LIBRARIES

Acknowledgements

The author gratefully acknowledges the financial support of a writer's bursary from Southern Arts.

For information and advice, many thanks to Tinker Stoddart, Mandeep Dillon, Atlanta Duffy, Mr Peter Teddy, Alison Charles-Edwards and Mariella de Martini.

   Special thanks to Bill Scott-Kerr at Transworld for his work on the final version; to Greta Stoddart for her support and acumen when most needed; and to Alexandra Pringle, without whose editing the author would have been flummoxed.

Contents

PART ONE

THE HOSPITAL (1)

'WHEN I GO BACK TO THE BEGINNING I HAVE NO SINGLE EARLIEST memory of you, James,' Zoe said. 'Rather, a series of quick-cutting images of you, running. In and out of rooms and along the corridors of the big house; racing your brothers, chasing your sister, fleeing from your father across the lawn. That's how I see you, an anxious, laughing child. Dashes at sports days, tearing after a football, imagining yourself as someone else: skittering like Hawkeye in and out of trees in a corner of the garden.'

James lay unmoving, an effigy of flesh and bone, attached by a drip to liquid food and by wires to machines gauging the echoes of his vitality.

'You always loved to run: like you had a discomfort, an impatience with yourself; you were happier running than walking, got off on the high of out of breath, gasping laughs of air. It began running through the house.'

In the ward office the ward sister watched Zoe talk to James. 'He can't hear her,' she told Gloria, the staff nurse. 'He can't hear a word she's saying.'

'Maybe,' Gloria said quietly. 'Maybe not.'

13

*

Zoe took her cigarettes out of her bag and was about to light one when she saw the sister march towards her, remembered where she was and put them away.

'Visiting times are over,' the sister said. 'You'll have to leave now. We've got to check his drip and catheter.'

'I'll be back tomorrow,' Zoe told James. She squeezed his hand before letting it go, limp once more upon the bedspread, and made her way out of the ward.

1

CRICKET ON THE LAWN

SATURDAY, 7 JUNE 1952, WAS THE HAPPIEST DAY OF CHARLES FREE-man's life. It was three weeks before his wedding.

'I've a surprise for you, darling,' he told his betrothed, Mary Wyndham, when he picked her up from her parents' house in Northtown in his pre-war Rover. Instead of turning right and heading up Stratford Road, as Mary had expected, Charles drove back towards the centre.

'I thought we were going to see the vicar,' Mary frowned.

'Change of plan.'

'Where *are* we going, then?' she asked.

'Can't tell you; it's a top-secret surprise,' Charles replied. 'You'll have to quell your anticipation for a few short minutes,' he said, in the odd idiom he employed.

'If you don't tell me I'll tickle you,' Mary warned, 'and you won't be able to defend yourself because you're driving.'

'I'm not ticklish.'

'But I want—'

Mary was silenced by her fiancé's thick forefinger pressed against her lips. She grasped his hand, snarled and bit his finger. Charles smirked at the road before him; he drove along as if he owned it.

15

Mary held his hand in her lap — both hands lifting together when he had to change gear. She relaxed into the leather upholstery of the Rover as they skirted the town centre, and gazed at her husband-to-be.

Charles Freeman was a large, powerful man — his wide shoulders accentuated by a double-breasted jacket — with ink-black hair, thick eyebrows, the dark-brown eyes of a gypsy, a proud nose and greedy lips.

'Getting warmer,' he announced with a grin that introduced one ear to the other as they drove over South Bridge and through St Peter's, and up the hill. 'You just have to contain your excitement,' Charles murmured. He had a rotund and plangent voice that came rolling from deep in his lungs, as if his words had already been tried there before being issued forth. Charles Freeman was thirty-four years old and was a man entering his prime, with an energy whose engine was the sense of his own worth, and destiny.

At the top of the hill Charles indicated and turned left through wrought-iron gates.

'I know who lives here!' Mary exclaimed. 'Those sisters, what are they called? The Misses Fulbright. They're Papa's patients. Except they're never ill. "The Sprightly Spinsters", he calls them, neither of them need him from one year to the next. He has to visit and insist on giving them a check-up just so that he can justify his fee.'

'Well, they may not fall ill,' Charles informed her, 'but the older one died last month.'

'We're going to make a condolence visit?' Mary asked. 'That's considerate. I didn't know you knew them.'

'Put a sock in it, for God's sake. Don't spoil the surprise.'

The drive led for a hundred yards directly to the front of the house, through a garden of lawns, umbrageous trees, lime walk, a herb garden and rampaging roses within a high surrounding wall. The two-storeyed Queen Anne façade of the rectangular house had single bay projections at each corner, with a one-storey bay added to the west side. In the centre Ionic pilasters supported a pediment above the front door, like an arrow pointing upward; above it, from behind an unadorned parapet, rose a steep pitched roof of stone tiles — perforated by dormer windows — enclosing the third, attic floor. The severity of the house's geometrical façade was softened by its golden Cotswold stone.

Charles steered the Rover around the parking bay and brought it

16

to a satisfying halt on the crunchy gravel. They got out and Mary climbed the fanned flight of steps to the front door.

'I'll ring the bell,' she said.

'Go ahead,' Charles agreed, from the other side of the car.

Mary drew the bell-pull, released it and heard a distant dull clanging. No other sound came from inside the house. Charles was gazing at the garden, with his back to her. Mary rang again, and waited.

'No answer, eh?' Charles said, joining her on the steps. 'How odd.' He put a hand in his jacket pocket and produced a large key, with which he proceeded to unlock the front door. He put his finger to his lips and winked at Mary, pushed open the door, and then before she knew it he'd bent towards her and scooped up her slender body in his arms.

'Charles! Put me down!' she screeched. 'Someone'll see! They'll tell Papa. Put me down!'

Charles ignored her and carried Mary over the threshold.

'This is bad luck, whatever's going on!' Mary protested.

Holding her effortlessly, Charles looked Mary in the eye. 'I shall honour and protect you from everything, my darling, including superstition,' he pledged in his leonine voice, before setting her down in a large, square-paved entrance hall. A wide staircase with twisted balusters climbed around the walls to a landing above them. Doors led off on either side and straight ahead.

'Let's explore,' Charles suggested, and Mary followed him through the ground floor of the house, from the large drawing-room in the extended bay on one side of the entrance hall to the library on the other, through the dining-room to the kitchen and damp, dank larder and pantry beyond. It was like walking through a museum inhabited by squatters: the drawing-room was an Edwardian clutter of plump sofas, tattered armchairs and battered leather settees scattered with frayed velvet cushions and petit-point worked pillows; of sagging pouffes and embroidered stools covered with magazines on threadbare Oriental rugs; a vase of dying flowers dropping their petals on a grand piano by a window; faded chintz curtains and ruffled pelmets. The room had an air of exhausted wealth, and it was the same in the musty library of leather-bound books in built-in bookcases, and the dining-room with its scuffed herringbone parquet floor, oval mahogany table and scratched Regency chairs.

Mary kept expecting to surprise a deaf old lady snoozing over her sewing in a deep reading chair, who would jump up and offer them

tea, and was unable to accept the obvious answer to the riddle Charles
had set before her, until they came back to the bottom of the curving
staircase.

'Well, what do you think?' Charles asked.

'It's yours, isn't it?' Mary ventured.

'No, darling,' Charles corrected her. 'It's ours. Death duty,' he
explained, as they climbed the stairs. 'The younger Miss Fulbright's
gone to live with her nephew. I bought it lock, stock and barrel for
cash. She moved out yesterday.'

Mary was bemused. 'I thought we were going to live in St Peter's.
You've already paid the rent.'

'Change of plan.'

Upstairs was different from below because the two sisters had
evidently inhabited only their respective bedrooms and one shared
bathroom. Charles and Mary opened doors upon airless rooms with
a faint smell of lavender in which it seemed all that had occurred
in two generations was the accumulation of a layer of grey dust. It
had settled on four-poster beds, embroidered linen, lace-covered
dressing-tables, porcelain ewers and basins, writing desks and tilting
mirrors, oak chests and walnut dressers.

Mary found she had only to blow and dust lifted from velvet
curtains and quilted eiderdowns to reveal the colours it had protected
– rich reds, greens, blues – of another age. Gradually, though, her
enchantment at papier mâché tray tables, Chinese vase lamps and
carriage clocks that had stopped ticking in another century gave way
to an awareness of how much there was to be done.

'We've three weeks to get everything ready,' she protested.

'I'm afraid not, darling,' Charles told her. 'I don't have any more
money,' he admitted. 'Apart,' he said, emptying his pockets of
change, 'from this: two pounds . . . fifteen shillings . . . and
threepence.'

Mary slumped on a bed, releasing a cloud of dust that enveloped
her.

'What are we going to do? Move into an empty house?'

Charles pondered for the merest moment. 'Not at all,' he declared.
'We'll leave it as it is. We'll brighten it up with a splash of paint here
and there. A spot of dusting and polishing. But otherwise we'll call
it all our own. Pretend everything's been in our family for generations. You know: like a doctor buying goodwill when he takes over
a practice. Come on,' he said, taking Mary's hand, 'this is marvellous.'

They carried on, and Charles showed her the master bedroom, for them; suggested which room could be Mary's boudoir and which their dressing-rooms; how they would put his ageing parents here and house guests there. Up on the third, attic floor above the west wing they entered a nursery, intact with rocking-horse, doll's house, tin animals and lead soldiers, building blocks, a rocking chair and battered stuffed toys that must have belonged to the Victorian children in photographs on the wall.

'I've got another surprise,' Charles revealed. 'Guess who I telephoned today. Can't guess? I'll tell you, then: I got hold of Robbie Forsyth. Remember, the March-Joneses told us about her? She was his old nanny. Battle-axe, they called her. Miss Syrup-of-Figs. Sounded to me like a wonderful woman. She's agreed to come and work for us.'

'What are you talking about, Charles?' Mary demanded.

'She said she needed to give a year's notice to her present employer. I told her she was an old-fashioned fuddy-duddy, but that it didn't matter, a year would suit us fine; we'd be sure to have some work for her by then.' Charles smiled slyly. 'So the point is, my sweet, we have to find her some work. Trouble is, I can't think what, exactly. The only clue we have is that she's a nanny. But,' he murmured in her ear in a voice that reverberated down through Mary's body, 'I'm sure we can come up with something, as the actress said to the bishop.'

Charles drew Mary towards him, squeezing her in a bear-hug of an embrace, and pressed his hot mouth onto hers.

'Not now, Charles,' Mary gasped, struggling for breath. 'Not here.'

'Don't resist me,' Charles said, tightening his grip. 'I want you now. I want you here.' Mary could feel his temper as well as his ardour rise as she squirmed against his strength. 'It's all right, darling,' he said, fishing in the same jacket pocket from which he'd produced the front door key. 'I brought along a French letter.'

He began undoing her garments as he lowered her to the dust-covered floor. A musty lavender cloud rose around them. Mary felt Charles' thick fingers caress and mould her. Before they'd removed half their clothes he was ready: he entered her with a groaning sigh. She opened her eyes; Charles loomed above her.

'Do you know how many rooms there are in the house?' Charles asked. 'Twenty-eight. After we're married we can make love in every *one* of them,' he gasped. 'Where do you think he'll be conceived? In the library?'

'And be a writer?'

19

'Not ruddy likely! Let him choose. Let's give him every option. If not the library, then the next day,' and Charles thrust forward, 'the *drawing-room*.'

Mary murmured, shifting her position.

'And if not *there*,' Charles grunted, 'then the *dining-room*. On the dining-room *table*. All laid out for twenty fucking *guests*. And they can all *watch*, oh, Mary, sweet fucking *Mary*, we'll fuck in every room in the *house*, oh, God, slow down, stay there . . . mother . . . Mary.'

And as she felt his body shudder across her Mary cried out in anguish, a wordless cry Charles didn't hear as, collapsing, he tried his best not to sneeze in her face.

Afterwards, they climbed a short ladder out of a room at the east side of the attic floor up on to the roof, and picked their way carefully around the parapet. From the back of the house they looked down across a public park towards the middle of town.

Charles produced a hip-flask from another jacket pocket, and two small leather-bound cups. They sipped whisky, and Charles embraced Mary from behind, in a tender version of his bear-hug.

'When this pile was built,' he told her, 'it was a manor in the village of Hillmorton. Over time the town's spread out and enclosed it. Do you know what? If you look at a map of the town, the house is now in its dead centre. This is my town now,' Charles said in a faraway voice; and then the voice changed, as he squeezed her tight and whispered in her ear: 'I love you, Mary. I want you with me. This is *our* town, darling.'

Convinced that he was right, Mary pressed Charles' hands tight against her belly, feeling her own destiny safe in his arms.

The town that lay below them was shaped just like a spread-out, upturned left hand – they stood at the tip of the forefinger. The forearm was the northern side of town, down which two parallel roads ran, like the radius and ulna, surrounded by stalwart late nineteenth- and early twentieth-century houses. These roads converged at the wrist in a wide boulevard flanked by proud municipal buildings; with parking spaces, on either side between wide pavements and rows of plane trees, which were cleared of cars for the annual fair on the first weekend each September. The rest of the palm was filled with the shopping centre.

The new comprehensive school and its playing fields lay either side of the thumb, which then continued as a link road across marshy pastures to reconnect with the town at the forefinger, at the side of a hill of houses and a public park on the top of which stood Hillmorton Manor.

At the end of the middle finger lay Charles Freeman's small factory, and mushrooming in the fields around it was the council estate, where most of the factory workers lived. The third and little fingers were roads sided by town houses less grand than those in the northern part, leading to suburbs.

The railway line ran along the outer edge of the little finger and the side of the palm and wrist; beyond it a meadow stretched across the valley towards wooded slopes and, beyond, the pastures of the wolds, in which nestled Mary's sister Margaret's small farm.

Between these fingers of roads and houses lay green: playing fields, allotments, parks, and patches of wasteland. In the centre, too, there was a certain amount of space around buildings, in the wide boulevard and squares and a park just north of the centre. It gave the town an airiness that was accentuated, in soft evening light, by the warm brown sandstone of many of the buildings.

Mary Wyndham was eighteen years old and had, like Charles, grown up in the town, though their paths had only crossed for the first time a year before. Her father was a doctor in general practice with a mixture of private patients and ones on the National Health Service – whose introduction he had vehemently opposed; he had inherited his father's surgery, and was a member of the middle class that felt its status diminishing in the postwar years, under a government one of whose Ministers said: 'We know that the organized workers of the country are our friends. As for the rest, they don't matter a tinker's cuss.'

Dr Wyndham was a gloomy physician who'd diagnosed his own condition as migraine, exacerbated by melancholia. Once or twice a month he retreated into glowering silence, and his wife draped beige cloths over the lamps and hushed her children if they laughed too loudly. His private patients grew old and he failed to impress new ones; he seemed weighed down by the stethoscope around his neck.

Thomas Wyndham had been born in 1900. 'This century's in decline,' he liked to say, 'and so am I.'

Mary's mother was a gentle, timid woman who did her best to provide her family with palatable food from tasteless, meagre rations,

21

to wash and clean with rationed soap, to improve the inferior clothes available; she spent hours in queues clutching a buff-coloured book of coupons and filled in endless forms for tickets for bread, petrol, coal.

With two much older sisters, Mary was an almost-only child who grew up during the war and the age of austerity that followed. A remote and vacant girl, she neglected chores, failed to materialize at meals on time because she was lost in some corner reading, and addressed her family as if they were strangers. Once she disappeared for two days and the police found her dawdling in a street on the other side of town.

'Why did you run away from us?' her mother cried.

Mary smiled brightly back at them. 'I didn't. I was just following the sun, and then the moon.'

'Her head's in the clouds,' her father lamented. 'She's floating.'

It didn't help that she was the plainest of the girls, and therefore had no excuses. Her otherworldliness was that of a young heifer, with large brown eyes, who wandered around the house, grazing on whatever she found in the kitchen when she was hungry, or else stared at the sky with a vacant expression.

And then Mary entered puberty. Her oldest sister Margaret, back from the war, had become a brawny, solid woman; Clare was homely and busy. Mary looked certain to follow them into unprepossessing womanhood. Instead she was transformed, over a period of months, into a slender, graceful willow of a woman with a delicate, oval face; the prettiest not just in her family but in her school and social circle. All she had in common with the child she had once been were her large brown eyes.

What had once been Mary's vices now became virtues: her laziness was revealed as delicacy, her poor time-keeping as originality, her nervous sporadic high spirits as charm, and her vacancy as evidence of a melancholy nature absorbed in matters of the spirit: she acquired the allure of beautiful youth.

Boys queued up to court her, but she barely noticed them. She dreamed through her time at the girls' high school, excelling only in English and Latin, and her father didn't mind because the subjects he regarded as important for his daughters were poetry and domestic science, plus a working knowledge of the human body, useful preparation for a good marriage as well as an interim occupation as a nurse. It seemed to Mary that she spent her youth reading in a pool of yellow light in the joyless house, either to herself or − when he was able to withstand the noise of another person's voice – nineteenth-century poetry out loud to her father. She couldn't recall enjoying a single meal, putting on a dress that fitted her or hearing music in the family home; her memories of childhood were all dimly coloured, khaki or olive.

Charles Freeman entered Dr Wyndham's surgery one evening in the spring of 1951 for a check-up demanded by BUPA for his medical insurance policy. He explained that it was nonsense, of course, there was nothing wrong with him, he was fit as a fiddle, this was a ruddy annoying piece of red tape for a man as busy as himself. The morose doctor had to ask Charles to be quiet a moment so that he could time his pulse, test his reflexes, feel his glands, peer into his eyes and listen to his lungs. He told the young industrialist that he was right, he was in dauntingly good health; it was clear that his high blood pressure signified nothing more than the pounding heartbeat of his ambition.

In the hall on the way out of the surgery, Charles saw Mary coming down the stairs. Dr Wyndham introduced his daughter, and Mary felt Charles' dark eyes bore into her and heard his voice pour through her like honey. He shook her hand and she realized that if he didn't let go of it soon she was going to faint.

The following evening Charles reappeared in the surgery, complaining of a headache. Dr Wyndham searched in vain for further symptoms, and Charles brushed it off. Mary heard his voice in her room above, and happened to be passing through the hall when he left. Again they shook hands and exchanged pleasantries.

The next day Charles returned suffering from indigestion, the day after that it was breathlessness, and by the end of the week he'd come up with a complaint which was genuine, that of insomnia, because by then he was lying awake at night thinking about the doctor's daughter, with her oval face and wide brown eyes.

'I don't have a clue what's wrong with you,' Dr Wyndham admitted in exasperation. 'You seem to have declined from vitality to hypochondria in the five days you've been my patient.'

'With all due respect, doctor,' Charles told him, 'the cure is under your nose.'

Charles' parents had a small electrical engineering firm, along with an old foundry making metal castings, lampposts and iron railings, and odd agricultural machinery. Their only son joined the company straight from school and had barely completed an apprenticeship – as his mother Beatrice called it – of the management of the firm by September 1939.

The outbreak of war found the Freeman Company largely an assembly business using outside components for products designed for the electrical distribution market. The collapse in the volume of new work there brought a near standstill. The workmen joined the services, leaving behind a depleted, idle workforce of boys from school, old lags and a few women. Profits fell to their lowest for years and the search for work was handicapped by the lack of new equipment.

With his parents dispirited, Charles effectively took over the firm at the age of twenty-two. The first thing he did was to threaten the chief engineer with the sack unless he was able, within a week, to make a simple belt-driven lathe that could turn out shells. With it Charles got his first contract from the Ministry of Supply and threw his energy and the company's fortunes into war work.

As the country was cut off from its import markets, the need to recycle metals into munitions became crucial. In July 1940 a campaign was begun to turn saucepans into Spitfires, calling upon the public to hand over everything from old keys to industrial safes. A mania for collecting swept through the town: libraries handed over old iron bookcases, children purloined their mothers' kitchen utensils, Mary Wyndham's primary school collected a ton of scrap metal, the council tore down street-lamps, iron staircases were dismantled leaving people marooned in the air, and patriots proved their virtue by removing railings from the tombs of their ancestors. By the autumn the town had generated a thousand tons of scrap iron.

Much of the scrap was delivered – some of it was being *returned* – to the Freeman Company foundry, and after being melted down there was moved on to an increasing number of production lines manufacturing bombs, aircraft parts and mine sinkers for contracts from the Air Ministry and the Admiralty. As the war continued, so Charles ordered his engineers to adapt and diversify. The foundry roared and hammered day and night, and the factory site expanded with blackened glass-walled buildings filled with lines of lathes at which men and women made machine-gun mountings, rocket-firing apparatus, parts for Bren gun carriers, tail units for Horsa gliders, depth charges, torpedoes, motor scythes and trenchers, and bulkheads for magnetic mines.

'Flexibility was the key,' Charles would later tell Mary. 'We were

24

small, but with the foundry we could make our own components. And by God's good fortune the Luftwaffe never hit us.'

By the end of the war the Freeman Company had been transformed from a dwindling family firm into a thriving manufacturer; and then the vast salvaging machine had to be thrown into reverse: Spitfires had to be turned back into saucepans. The limited housing programme in the town concentrated on expanding the estate around the factory site as returning soldiers took jobs there, and Charles instigated both an intensified programme of mechanization and the setting up of a single fine toolmaking department. There they made the jigs, fixtures, moulding, press and other tools upon which the rest of the factory depended, and trained the skilled apprentices upon whom the future would be built.

'This is my town,' Charles Freeman told his fiancée, on the roof of the house he'd just bought them, three weeks before their wedding.

He had courted her on a number of dates, accompanied by chaperones, in between which boxes of luscious chocolates, sparkling jewellery and huge bouquets of flowers were delivered to brighten up the drab Wyndham home. Then at the end of the summer, Charles took Mary on their first date alone: he drove them down the A1 to London to the last day of the Festival of Britain, the celebration of the country's recovery from war.

At the South Bank Exhibition and Pleasure Gardens in Battersea Charles and Mary visited the television pavilion and the Home and Gardens exhibition, they drank coffee in a piazza beside the Thames and ate lunch in a brightly coloured restaurant, they marvelled at murals and modern sculptures, had rides on the Emett railway and the Mississippi Showboat.

After darkness fell they laughed at Richard Murdoch and Kenneth Horne, danced on the Fairway to Geraldo and his orchestra, and joined Gracie Fields and a crowd of thousands singing 'Auld Lang Syne' and the National Anthem.

Exhausted and in love, Mary leaned on Charles' broad shoulder walking back to his Rover, where he produced a small box from the glove compartment. He snapped it open to reveal a diamond ring, with which he proposed, and before she fell asleep on the drive home – with Charles' voice resonating around the car as he enumerated his plans for expansion – Mary felt a blissful reassurance that the man beside her was taking her out of her colourless childhood, and into a bright new future.

25

It took a year of married life for Mary to conceive their first-born, though not for want of trying. She couldn't be sure where it happened but she rather hoped it was in the third guest bedroom, because they made love there one dark Sunday afternoon and took their time. Her pregnancy was an easy one, and the only odd thing about it was that as she grew larger so too did her husband. He kept pace with her pound for pound, whether out of sympathy or competition it was hard to say. After their son, Simon's, birth, Mary reattained her slender figure, but Charles continued to swell. He had an insatiable greed and the petulance of a child if he was hungry; freed from rationing, he demanded four square meals a day, and helped himself to snacks in between. By the time the last of their four children was born, he was a giant.

Charles' sexual appetite too was a regular, irresistible need: he marched into his and Mary's bedroom in an altered state and approached her making animal noises. He clambered across their wide bed with a body gone soft, liquescent with desire: the fearsome charisma and willpower that made his great frame resemble that of a swarthy bull had left him, he was a skeleton surrounded by a sea of helpless flesh, his body gone soft around the part – grown hard, and he poured himself over Mary's unresisting body, sought her out, thrust with rolling waves and came with a grateful, groaning shudder that made her fear for the bones of her rib-cage.

Simon was born in 1954, and was followed at two-yearly intervals by James, Robert and Alice. Simon had dark, floppy hair, brown eyes, a sensual mouth and puppy fat that made him look like a miniature version of his father. He also had an older sibling's smugness. One autumn morning at the age of five he woke after a chesty cold, recovered except for the fact that when he opened his mouth he spoke with a husky voice.

'Sing us "Lili Marlene"'!' Charles told him.

Simon liked his croaky voice so much that he decided to keep it, and he spoke slowly too, as if thinking each word as it came out; added to the already cute appeal of a tubby boy, Simon's voice drew people towards him.

Simon was a hypochondriac child. 'My tummy bones hurt,' he complained. 'I've got hay fever in my knees, Mummy.' He was brought low by a change in the weather, and got a nose bleed if he climbed the stairs too fast up to the children's third floor. He got all the usual illnesses – chicken pox, mumps, measles – but, failing to acquire immunity like normal children, suffered again with each of his younger siblings when their turn came.

Mary fretted over her first-born: she kept him home from school on the slightest pretext, took his temperature every hour and provided him with regular doses of medicinal chocolate milkshake. The only thing she forced him to do was to stay in bed reading the latest comics ordered by special delivery from Mr Singh's Post Office Stores and Newsagent, or else sink into a nest of cushions and blankets downstairs on the sofa in front of the television; measures which provoked the envy of the other children and reconciled Simon to his delicacy.

James too looked forward to being ill, since it was when their mother was most concerned with them: she wrestled the children's welfare away from their nanny. Robbie considered Mary's pampering bad for the bairns, convinced that looking after people when they were sick would only make them weaker. She recommended that illness be severely dealt with: a plain diet supplemented with cod-liver oil, enforced sleep, and solitary confinement in a cold room sealed from draughts and distractions.

Mary floated into James' room one morning when he had a flu-bug fever that Robbie announced was looking set to break the thermometer.

'What's the matter, little man? Are you all achey?' Mary asked him. 'Go and buy some starch or something, Nanny,' she told Robbie. 'I'll look after James.'

Robbie grimaced and muttered under her breath, 'I'll have a word with Charles about this,' as she left the room.

'Have as many words as you like,' Mary called after her, and James swooned back on the pillows. James was a funny, intense child with sandy hair that the sun bleached blond and almost white; he had freckled, pale skin and sticking-out ears, so that in summer he resembled a scurrying, anxious albino bat, but one who would stop every now and then to watch what was going on around him through a pair of spectacles that were invariably held together with tape. He was born a wall-eyed child, looking in two different directions at once, until corrective spectacles gradually brought his divergent visions into alignment.

Mary turned up the heating, opened the curtains, brought him Lucozade, a hot-water bottle and a draughtsboard and pieces, she

27

stayed and played with him, which made him forget that he'd ever been in pain.

'I don't want to get better, Mummy,' James told her. 'I want to be ill all the time. Then you can stay here for the rest of my life.'

'Oh, let me hug you,' Mary soothed. The smell of her perfume made him feel better than Miss Syrup-of-Fig's hideous medicines.

The trouble was that the children rarely recovered quickly enough, and Mary began to lose interest. She had more important things to think about, even if it wasn't clear what they were.

'You're so sweet, James,' she said. 'I'll see you later, little man.'

'Where are you going?' he croaked. 'It's your move, Mummy. You're in a good position: you might win this game.'

'I've got things to do, sweetie-pie. I'll tell Robbie to come and look at you.'

'There's no need,' he pleaded, in vain.

Robbie reappeared with her self-satisfied straight back, and James saw her rub her hands with glee before she unplugged the wireless, removed his teddy bear ('a *perfect* place to harbour germs') and searched his body for a plaster she could rip off with relish.

Simon was the one most often ill, and no one could understand why he was closer to his father than his mother, because Charles had no patience with Simon's fragile constitution. He believed that illness was simply another word for malingering; he imagined that employees phoning in sick were making fun of him, they were probably digging the garden or off to the seaside, laughing to themselves at 'getting something for nothing', as he put it, which he imagined to be the main aim in life of most members of the working class.

'Don't you dare bully Simon. He's a sensitive boy,' Mary told him. 'You must remember having measles yourself, for goodness' sake.'

'Me?' he replied. 'I was never ill, woman, I've told you that. I didn't miss a day's school throughout my education. For all the good it did me.'

Simon appealed to his grandmother Beatrice for help in the matter, shortly before she died, since it was quite clear that his father's memory was defective. But Beatrice had never taken any notice of her offspring's ailments.

'How do you think I could have run the business if I was constantly blowing his nose and wiping his bottom?' she demanded of her grandson.

*

James could just remember his grandmother, Beatrice; he was four when she died, and he remembered her as a tiny old woman who seemed to have shrunk in her old age to the same size as his older brother, Simon. He remembered her as a decrepit dwarf crawling like a snail through the house, cursing the children who swept past her like the wind and forced her to clutch hold of furniture to save herself from being knocked over. He remembered how she moved so slowly that no one ever knew where she was, and they had to search through the house for her at mealtimes: she left a trail behind her, a scent of ammonia and face-powder which they were able to follow, and they knew they were getting close when they heard her frail, bitter curses. The children found her, and led her through to the dining-room.

He could remember her in the small drawing-room in her suite of rooms in the east wing of the big house, perching forward from the seat of a vast armchair. On the coffee table before her were scattered black-and-white photographs: accumulated in odd boxes over the course of her busy life, now grandmother Beatrice was attempting to order them into albums. It was clear, however, that the task was beyond her: Beatrice picked up photos, stared at them, tried to match them with others as if playing a cruel game of Pelmanism. She filled the first page of one album with a picture of herself as a toddler beside another of her wedding, and continued in such a manner to paste a senseless mosaic; she had lost touch with the chronology of her own life.

Much later, James would remember his early years as a group of photographic images. He had a poor memory. Friends would recount their earliest recollections – of things seen from a cot or pram – and he couldn't believe they weren't deluding themselves.

James' memories were photographic partly because photographs were a literal substitute for actual memories. They provided confirmation of other people's recollections. 'No wonder James can't sit still!' his father roared when James was itching to leave the dinner table and go outside to kick a football in the dying light; 'he spent his formative years in a ruddy wheelbarrow!' Sure enough, there were black-and-white photos in the family album of James being steered by the gardener, Alfred, in a heavy wooden wheelbarrow, or standing on his unsteady toddler's legs and leaning against the barrow while Alfred mulched the roses.

The first time he saw Garfield Roberts, walking up the drive hand in hand with Pauline, Stanley the caretaker's sister, apparently James ran through the house shrieking: 'Robbie! Robbie! Come and see! It's Little Black Sambo!' The doll (of which James had no actual recall) responsible for his response to the first black man he encountered at the house was there in a photograph of Simon and himself sitting with their mother in the drawing-room, clasped in James' hand.

He studied another photograph: a hot high-contrast summer's day; Simon standing on the edge of the pond grinning inanely towards the camera (with their father's grin and his double-chin, too;) himself, James, shielding his weak eyes from the sun behind the camera, looking like he was talking; the unidentified shadow of the photographer thrown up across the lawn from the bottom of the picture; Robert, off to one side, on his face . . . what? a scowl? a grimace?; on the other side little Alice, naked except for a halter around her chest attached to a rope that trailed across the grass to a stake, allowing her to reach only as far as the edge of the pond.

Their mother sat on the wall of the pond, close to Simon, one hand resting in her lap, the other hovering in the air between herself and her son, as her smile revealed not only its remoteness but also a nervous flickering of her lips. She was looking at the camera but was also aware of her chubby, grinning son wobbling on the low wall, with the water behind him. Mary wore a white blouse and a long, black pleated skirt, and a slide around her brown hair. She looked like a young and lovely maiden aunt of these children around her, enjoying their company for the day, not quite at ease with them.

But where was his father? He was surely there, for his presence was evident in the others' postures: in Simon's wheedling enthusiasm; in his, James', self-protection; in Robert's sullen distance; in Alice's proscribed activity; in their mother's uncertain smile. James could even hear his voice now, cajoling Simon: 'That's my boy, my simple pieman,' his rich voice, laughing. 'Dance, my belly boy, my dancing jelly baby.' And Simon grinning back, stepping unsteadily on the wall around the edge of the pond.

He was surely there, James could hear him, he could feel him. And then he saw him: their father was *taking* the picture; the shadow swelling into the frame was the shadow cast by the 18-stone bulk of the man-in-charge.

The originals in the family albums of these photographs were usually disappointing: they were snapshots grabbed by amateurs, essential details blurred or cut off at the edge of the frame, and they had inessential paraphernalia − a hedge, part of a car − leading one's eye astray. Studying them years later James would find himself closing his eyes and recomposing them − improving the subjects' arrangement, changing gestures − as if retouching them in the darkroom of his mind.

Robert was born with his left arm wrapped around his head, which was squeezed during his passage through the birth canal: when he opened his eyes they had vivid red splotches. It made him look furious with the world; and it turned out that he was. In his cot he didn't cry for milk like Simon and James before him so much as bleat, like a tiny, disgruntled goat. As soon as he was replete, however, instead of snoozing in Mary's arms Robert started bleating again and only stopped when she put him back down.

When Mary blew raspberries into his tummy, played peek-a-boo and made silly faces that had amused her first babies, Robert just stared at her with a grim, disconcerting expression. What *did* make him laugh was when his boisterous father, home from work, picked the baby boy up and threw him high in the air. Robert loved such treatment, the wilder the better, giggling helplessly as he spun perilous cartwheels in the air.

Robert came out of the womb nursing a grievance; his eyeballs were bloodshot with envy, and it was exacerbated by the unwelcome arrival of both a real sister, Alice, and what would prove to be a surrogate one, Stanley the caretaker's and Edna the cook's daughter Laura, in the same household in the same month when he was not quite two years old.

From then on Robert's childhood was coloured by rage at others' preferential treatment. He couldn't stand to lose out or be left out: he scrutinized portions of dessert at mealtimes, and snatched the biggest plate for himself; when one of the other children was given a present, he threw a tantrum and tried to break it.

'He's got a chip on his shoulder, that one,' Edna told Stanley.

'I don't blame him,' said Stanley, 'with two brothers above and like two sisters below.'

Mary tried to reason with him. He listened with hunched, resentful shoulders, a brittle countenance and wary eyes, making no response, until she left the room. At which point he sprang to his feet and attacked those he blamed for spilling the beans. But then when Mary returned and ordered Robert to apologize he reverted to his posture of an aggrieved statue, and proved perfectly capable of withstanding solitary confinement in his room, missing his favourite TV programmes and even Robbie's stinging slaps, rather than say the word 'sorry' to a brother or sister.

Charles tried a different approach, that of ridicule. If Robert found Alice and Laura playing some soppy girls' game with dolls or paint or teddy bears it reduced him to a state of befuddled rage, since he couldn't bear to be excluded even from something he had no wish to be a part of. Charles found Robert trembling on the verge of violence, and started laughing.

'Our little hornet's buzzing!' Charles mocked. 'Our tiny Tartar's having a temper tantrum!' he teased – ignoring the fact that it was one trait he'd clearly bequeathed Robert himself.

Far from pacifying Robert, his father's ridicule only enraged him further, and when Charles tickled him Robert became so furious that he turned purple, and Mary had to intervene to save him from bursting a blood vessel.

The trouble was it was impossible to discern exactly what Robert wanted: when someone else got too much attention and Robert yanked them out of the spotlight it was only to stand dumbly centre-stage; if any adult hugged him for more than a moment he struggled free ungraciously, wiping avuncular kisses from his face with distaste.

'Don't worry yourself, darling,' Charles reassured Mary. 'He'll grow out of it.'

'Do you think so?' she doubted. 'You haven't.'

'He'll have to, won't he? He can't beat up the whole world.'

Robert was tough. Afflicted by childhood ailments, he refused to succumb: as if they were rites of passage, challenges to his infant masculinity, he wrestled with them. He coughed and groaned through thick sinusy nights but emerged, bad-tempered and unbowed, at breakfast – to Robbie's delight, who held him up as an example to the others; he was her favourite, which he didn't mind, since with her such preference didn't bring with it unwelcome tenderness or intimacy.

By the time Robert started school he was as tall as James, his next oldest brother (and would even catch up with Simon, although he would eventually be overtaken again by both of them). But no one would have mistaken James and Robert for twins. Robert had dark, hooded eyes and his mother's finely carved features; he appeared entirely unrelated to James with his unruly haystack of sandy hair over sticking-out ears and a spattering of freckles passed down from farming ancestors. And while James was as verbose as and more articulate than Simon, Robert was taciturn and grimly charismatic.

'It's all yackety-yack with ye, is it not, James?' Robbie told him. She was right. James chattered away, asking interminable questions or telling never-ending, inconsequential stories that no one could listen to for more than thirty seconds without their attention wandering, while Robert rarely opened his mouth except to eat. Yet James overheard Charles informing Mary:

'Did you hear what Robert said today? Stanley told me. He heard Simon explaining to him why I've got so many people working for me, and Robert said: "People are stupid. They don't deserve any better." Isn't that smart, darling? The boy's not six years old.'

Robert said little but it was remembered; he smiled seldom, but when he did then his smile lit up a room. James was disappointed that his mother at least couldn't see through Robert, being impressed as everyone else by his disdainful words and begrudging affection. Whereas James knew that *he* made little impression on people; no one disliked him, but he was no one's favourite, really. Mary made him feel special when she needed to, but weeks went by when she hardly noticed he was there.

As well as taking on a nanny for the children and retaining the Misses Fulbright's gardener, Alfred, Charles had also employed a caretaker for the house and a cook. Mary found herself adrift in her own home. The household and her children's welfare were taken care of, and Mary withdrew from the hubbub.

The preoccupied child had inherited her father's periodic depressions, but in inverse proportions. She stayed in her dressing-room, writing poetry at a table by the window, or just staring out of it, and the children learned not to disturb her.

'Can't you see? Your mother needs time to herself,' Charles told them. 'I don't want you upsetting her, buzzing around like ruddy flies.'

The children acquired patience, and it was rewarded: every two or three weeks she emerged with her brown eyes burning bright and an ironic smile playing around her lips, to tease and divert them like a flirtatious older sister.

On Wednesday evenings Charles went to Round Table meetings, and Mary invited two friends round to discuss each other's poetry in her dressing-room. Then one Friday night when Charles was away on business, shortly before bedtime Mary whispered to James: 'Get your coat and meet me at the back door in five minutes. And don't tell anyone.'

'Don't worry about James,' he heard her tell Robbie. 'I'll put him to bed. He wants me to read him a story.'

A few minutes later they were driving away in Mary's Zephyr, James brimming with anxious excitement.

'Where are we going?' he whispered.

'That's a surprise,' Mary laughed. 'You're here to give me confidence, little man.'

James tried to remember if he'd ever been driven late at night before. It felt different from a dark afternoon. Car headlights zoomed into his eyes as they passed, then into country darkness like a long tunnel opened up by the Zephyr's lights.

'Where's this?' James asked, as they re-entered urban landscape.

'We're coming into Birmingham,' Mary told him. 'Don't you recognize it?'

They went into a huge room above a pub, smoky and loud and crammed full. They sat down on the floor against a wall. James couldn't see any other children. There were men wearing donkey jackets and duffel coats, and women with cropped hair and men's overcoats that made them look elegant in the same way as his mother did. Mary got herself a beer and let James have a sip: it tasted of soap.

Then a man stood up at the front of the room and introduced another man, and *he* stood up when everyone started clapping. He had a big, bushy beard and was wearing sunglasses indoors. Mary squeezed James' arm, and he looked up at her, but she was looking at the man with the beard, who then read out poems in a voice like a cowboy's.

James drifted in and out of the evening, dropping off then being woken by applause or shouts of approval, slipping between brief, curtailed dreams and the sweaty, smoky room. After the American had finished, people in the audience were invited to read poems of their own. James was woken by Mary squeezing his arm again, and he stirred to find her standing up. He was just about to follow, assuming it was time to leave, when she began reading out a poem. It was something about blood and ice. When she'd finished there was silence, then everybody clapped her and Mary sat down again beside James, her cheeks flushed, breathing hard. She put her arm around him and pulled him tight. James leaned into her, and felt her ribs heave against him through her clothing.

Stanley was five years younger than Charles, who'd taken the welder aside on his factory floor and offered him better wages and free accommodation to come and look after the house. He was the one man that Charles never shouted at. Coming home in a foul temper he strode into the hall yelling at everyone in sight or – since they scurried away along corridors and up stairs – what he knew to be within earshot, for his deep voice chased them: 'Where's my ruddy smoking jacket? What have those children been up to? I've never seen such a mess! What time's dinner? I'm hungry, damn it, bring me some food!'

If Mary was in the hallway then she shouted back at him to: 'Grow up, Charles! What kind of an example are you?' and they yelled at each other until all of a sudden Charles shouted even louder:

'I'm sorry, my darling, I'm a galumphing boor, you're right, come here. Let me hold you. Forgive me.'

More often, though, she couldn't be bothered with Charles' storms, and simply closed the door of her dressing-room.

Those like Simon or Edna or Robbie who rushed to fulfil his demands only made Charles more mad, and he reduced people to tears with his careless humiliations. When he reached Stanley, however, Charles quietened down, he stopped quaking and his voice returned to a human level. If they were outside then Stanley rolled a thick cigarette as he told Charles what had been done and needed doing in the house and grounds, and Charles listened in unnatural silence.

Stanley and Edna were married a couple of years after she came to be the cook, and there was nothing surprising about their union – much the same age, they worked and lived together – except for their physical dissimilarity: Stanley was a short, wiry man with a composure that made him seem more compact than he actually was. His nakedness would never fail to surprise Edna, for in daily life he possessed a manly stature far outweighing his actual frame. She, on the other hand, though no taller, was big-bosomed and wide-girthed, broad-beamed and thick-thighed, twice his width and weight, my roly-poly pudding of a woman, as he came to call her.

They moved through time at different speeds. Stanley was precise, quick, sharp, making only relevant movement to perform the task of the moment. He often looked like he was snatching at things. Edna, on the other hand, was slow but flowing, for anyone watching her in the kitchen there seemed no discernible break between one task and another: while doing one thing she was already planning the next, clearing a space (first mental, then actual) on the table for the mixing bowl, reaching flour from the cupboard but remembering there was only half a pound left in that bag, moving towards the pantry for more.

She liked Stanley from the beginning, attracted to his calm authority and his stony countenance. It took him longer to notice her, but she was always there at the end of the evening, they seemed to find themselves alone in the kitchen, discussing the events of the day or just drinking tea and sharing the quiet twilight of the busy house. Stanley would not be able to remember exactly when companionship grew into courtship, and Edna had to remind him of a look exchanged – eyes seeing, searching, finding something new in a familiar face – of holding hands one Sunday evening, of a goodnight kiss in the doorway of her room.

By the time Stanley realized he'd been seduced it was too late, but he didn't mind. He came to love her amplitude, the generosity of her flesh a perfect physical expression of a strength he knew he lacked himself, and he would never lose his gratitude towards her for saving him from the loneliness of a hard man.

While Stanley roamed freely around the house and garden, his territory extending to the perimeter wall, Edna was confined within the large kitchen. The floor was paved with great flagstones, on which the girls played hopscotch, and there was a large oblong table in the middle of the room. That was where James sat, surrounded by measuring jugs and cold joints, and ingredients in various stages of preparation. If he was lucky a bowl of cake-filling had to be licked clean (*if* he got there before Simon). James sat on top of the table, entranced by the dexterity of Edna's chubby fingers as she chopped vegetables with percussive precision or rolled sheets of pastry like sails on the table beside him – scattering flour over his bare legs – and cut intricate shapes to be laid across the tops of pies. Sleeves rolled up revealing the great white hams of her forearms, beads of perspiration beneath the brow of her white cap, Edna moved smoothly from one task to the next, six different pots muttering on the stove and more in the oven, her eyes full, never glazed, always checking this quantity and that texture.

Edna's size was an oft-remarked oddity among the inhabitants of the house, a running joke at every meal, for she had the appetite of a sparrow: she'd serve them all and then put no more than a spoonful or two on her own plate. And even then she left half of it uneaten. But James knew better: for Edna was constantly testing and tasting her cooking throughout the day, adding herbs or spices or sugar or salt when necessary, because she was insecure and didn't trust her recipes. The result was that, without realizing, her eating habits were not those of a normal person but a grazing animal, and she consumed twice as much as anyone else in the steady accumulation of tiny mouthfuls.

If at bedtime James was absent from the nursery Robbie knew where to find him: sitting on the table with a milk moustache or else on the window sill, setting sun behind, a tired silhouette with translucent orange ears. She got fed up with traipsing from the third floor of the west wing down the stairs to the kitchen to fetch the boy, so she asked Stanley to install a bell between her room beside the nursery and the kitchen. When it rang, three sharp times, Edna lifted James off the table in her fat arms.

'Bedtime, James,' she said, and he smelled the sweetness of her perspiring flesh as she lowered him to the floor and pointed him in the direction of the door, through which he obediently, cheerfully ran.

Stanley and Edna both agreed, when they married, that they wanted many children, but they managed only one. Laura was born just a couple of weeks before Alice, and she shared Alice's and the boys' lives from the beginning.

Little Alice had white skin and autumnal hair, rich auburn, a miniature pre-Raphaelite, and her eyes were odd colours – one green, one blue – which added to the impression that Alice perhaps belonged to some place or time other than this one. She was both a solemn and a spontaneous child with a vigilant demeanour, who watched her brothers running around or scrambling up trees in the grounds as if searching for clues in their behaviour as to how she should act herself, only to wander off in another direction entirely. She developed something of the distracted air of her mother, entering a parallel world of her own invention, occupied by fantasy companions. But just when someone began to worry about her Alice burst into action with effervescent energy and ran with the boys for hours,

37

winding herself up with excitement until she just as suddenly collapsed like a broken spring.

It was as well that Alice had another friend in the house.

Laura was practical, and tended to look after her absent-minded semi-sister, because left to her own devices Alice neglected her own well-being. At the beginning of every summer she took her clothes off at the earliest opportunity, exposing her pale skin to the sun with painful results: the sun's hot breath turned her pink, and Edna had to soothe her with calomine lotion, her gentle hands feeling the heat radiating from the sobbing child's scorched body. But Alice never learned: each year she suffered the same ordeal, and the rest of the summer Laura had to keep an eye on her – plonking sun-hats on her head, rubbing Skol lotion into her face and shoulders and leading her forcibly into the shade when she noticed that Alice had been out in the open too long and had a look of disorientated excitement.

It was the same in winter. Alice declined to use her umbrella with Walt Disney characters on it because she didn't want Pluto to get wet, and neither did she wish slushy snow to ruin her new gloves. Even when Laura did manage to wrap her up before Alice got out of the door, she turned out to possess the innate talent of an escapologist: scarves unwound themselves from around her neck and trailed in her frosted wake, her squashed auburn hair sprang woolly hats into the crisp air, and tightly buttoned jackets popped free and shimmied themselves loose from her limbs. Laura followed a trail of winter garments through the garden to find her surrogate sister with her ears red, nose running and teeth chattering, a shivering pixie oblivious to the reason why.

Alice would prove to be the most intelligent of the Freeman children; or at least the most academic. She was just incapable of making certain connections. And she had to pay the price, a snuffly, bronchial child, spending half the winter under a towel over a jug of steaming water, inhaling Friar's Balsam.

Laura, in contrast, had a calm, controlled relationship with her body: whereas Alice was always caught out by her own sneezes, which came upon her suddenly, Laura had plenty of time to find a handkerchief, raise it to her face and 'aachoo!' with perfect manners; when she had an upset stomach she felt a warning swim through her body well in advance, and recognized it for what it was.

'I'm just going off to be sick, Mum,' she told Edna matter-of-factly, and calmly made her way to the bathroom. She learned to take her own temperature – and Alice's too – at an early age, went to bed when she was tired without having to be told, and helped herself to Disprin when she had a headache.

The only odd thing was that at family and other social gatherings it was Alice, not Laura, who volunteered to look after even younger cousins, playing with them, feeding them, and staggering around with a paunchy toddler on her slender hip; while Laura preferred the company of children older than herself, with whom she could have a sensible conversation. To her annoyance, she ended up having to rescue Alice from a chaos of wailing, unfed babies, and restore order.

'You know what?' Alice asked Laura one day. 'I'm going to have masses of children when I grow up.'

'Don't be stupid,' Laura told her, 'you can't even look after yourself.'

'I know,' she replied, unbothered. 'But that's different.'

Laura accomplished the remarkable feat of beginning her journey through childhood as her mother's daughter and somehow ending it as her father's. She had his almond eyes, which assessed the world before her, unruffled, prepared for whatever might come her way. Otherwise, though, as a child she was plump, moon-faced and open-hearted like Edna, with the same strange combination of clumsiness and grace, and the same awareness of others even when she appeared fully absorbed in what she was doing: Alice or James would come up behind her as she helped her mother core apples from Margaret's orchard or painted at the kitchen table; they stood beside her for a moment, silently, and Laura, without saying anything or looking up or indicating in any way that she was aware of their presence, raised her hand and touched them on the arm, reassuringly, letting them know that she knew they were there and were welcome, and could join in whenever they wanted.

She developed so gradually that no one noticed, but by the time she became a woman she would have the boyish figure as well as the eyes and shape of her father's face. She would also have his self-reliance, his hard and lonely grit; which was just as well, for the time was going to come when Laura would need them.

Back then, James loathed and adored his father in equal measure. Charles came home from sacking workers and intimidating secretaries, and went straight to the nursery to play with his children. There were times when he brought home distinguished visitors with whom he was in some business negotiation and promptly forgot them behind him as he saw his sons on the lawn and rushed towards them, removing his jacket and loosening his tie on the way. The VIPs watched their formidable opponent in the boardroom, renowned pugilist of the manufacturing world, roll around on the grass with his children, just another fat daddy, oblivious to the chlorophyll stains on his Summer Island cotton shirts and his Savile Row trousers, scuffing his hand-stitched shoes from Jermyn Street, until they had little option but to join in.

The fact was that Charles was more childlike than the children. He organized croquet tournaments on the lawn, asked Alfred to make a football goal out of raspberry netting at the back of the orchard, and ushered everybody outside for cricket after Sunday lunch, games of Children against Grown-ups that were sure to end in tears, because Charles was an even worse loser than Robert.

Mary was designated wicket-keeper, with a pair of gardening gloves – though no one could tell whether today she'd be in the mood to catch everything that came her way or ignore the ball disdainfully. Robert demanded first bat and slugged away, aiming for the windows with a grin. Alice wandered around the unmarked boundary, losing interest, while Laura kept score from silly mid-off. Simon gamely persisted, with a tubby child's surprising agility, producing wonders beside cousin Zoe in the slips. Edna bowled generous underarms.

Alfred the gardener, a tall, rangy man who still bit his nails at the age of sixty-five, bemoaned the damage done to his grass. But Charles bellowed at him to: 'Returf it, man!' He even persuaded Alfred to join in; only for everyone else to regret it, because Alfred had played in his distant youth and kept a frustrating straight bat, content to stay at the crease without scoring any runs, a strategy suited to the opening day of a Test match but hardly an impromptu children's game on the wide lawn of the house on the hill. Instead of having a quiet word, though, Charles joined him for an unbudgeable partnership, twisting his mouth with satisfaction in imitation of young Geoffrey Boycott as they reached the half-hour mark standing at nought for no wicket.

So that tempers inevitably rose, as Robert bowled aiming less at the stumps than at the man, and James saw his increasingly desperate spinners met with Alfred's stonewalling straight bat and, copying him at the other end, Charles' too.

And it had to end in tears because when James finally produced a

40

googlie that sent his father's middle wicket flying, Charles yelled: 'That wasn't fair! I wasn't ready! It's not cricket!'

'I got him fair and square, Mummy!' James pleaded.

'Grow up, man,' Mary told him. '*Walk*, Charles!'

'Not out!' came a Scottish voice from the front steps.

And then all hell broke loose, the game evaporated in a mayhem of shouting and sulking, with adults stalking off and children being sent to bed.

One Saturday Charles bundled the family into his Rover for an impromptu trip to Oxford, an hour and a half's drive away, to celebrate Midsummer's Day. He dragged them around the centre, pointing out the college a great-uncle had been to ('Maybe *you*'ll come here one day,' Mary whispered in five-year-old Alice's ear) before reaching the river and hiring a punt. The six of them crammed into it, pushed off, and there was no escape.

Charles was in his element. Having steered the punt in circles for a while he let the boys have a go and lay in the middle broadcasting advice on correct poling technique. With his voice like a fruity fog-horn he regaled other punters passing by, as well as people lounging on the bank, as if they were guests invited to his party, as if they were there only because he was.

'Marvellous day, isn't it?' he boomed. 'Ruddy useless gondoliers we've got,' he laughed. 'Oops! Direct hit, Robert, you big booby!'

Mary put on her dark glasses, lit a cigarette and ignored him. The children shrank inside the low sides of the punt – apart from Simon, who copied Charles' conviviality, his voice a husky echo of his father's. But even the others couldn't help but appreciate that, despite the horror of being addressed by a stranger – by this clear breach of English etiquette – those whom Charles addressed appeared honoured to be so, such was the charisma of his self-importance.

Charles was so gregarious that when he saw his sons go into the lavatory he was reminded of his own needs and followed, to pee into the toilet bowl beside them, chatting away unnervingly. When he had more serious business he kept the door open, engaging anyone who passed by along the corridor in conversation. He organized surprise parties for the children, invited their friends himself, and then laughed at their embarrassed ingratitude. He was an overpowering father, who had no idea what he was doing. And his wife, their mother, couldn't quite be bothered to compete with him.

As the children grew up, so for a transitory period between nursery and outside interests of their own they shared much of their parents' lives. They had their supper with Robbie at the kitchen table at six o'clock each evening, but on Wednesdays they sat on the landing watching through the banister rails as Mary's guests arrived. Her friends had brought other friends until soon there were too many to fit into her dressing-room, and so they began to meet in the drawing-room.

'Keep out of the way,' Mary ordered her children. 'My friends don't want to be distracted by you lot.'

The children were enthralled by the sight of lugubrious, underfed strangers in polo-neck pullovers and threadbare jackets and women wearing denim trousers, and also by the air of secrecy surrounding the event: the poets always skulked out shortly before nine thirty.

Then one Wednesday Charles arrived home early, and found the drawing-room door not only closed but, to his astonishment, locked. He stood there for a moment, stupefied, and then the door opened. A cheerful, middle-aged man wearing a sailor's cap and smoking a pipe emerged.

'Who are you?' he asked Charles.

'Who am I?' Charles wondered. 'WHAT THE RUDDY HELL DO YOU MEAN, WHO AM I?' he exploded, 'WHO THE HELL ARE YOU?'

'I'm Brian,' the man said cheerfully. 'Who are you?'

'GET OUT OF MY WAY!' Charles commanded him.

'Wait a minute, friend,' Brian smiled. 'You can't come in without a poem. Do you have a poem? That's the rule here.'

James and Simon on the landing knew they had a moral duty to warn the unfortunate Brian. Neither moved a muscle.

'*I* MAKE THE BLOODY RULES HERE!' Charles shouted. 'THIS IS *MY* HOUSE, YOU RUDDY IDIOT.'

'Oh, well, in that case, my friend,' Brian smiled, 'can you tell me where the toilet is?'

'I'M *NOT* YOUR FRIEND, YOU MORON!' Charles yelled. He knocked Brian's cap off his head, pushed him out of the way and strode into the drawing-room, where he proceeded to bellow at the uninvited guests as he threw them out of his house one by one. When he'd finished he came back in and confronted Mary.

'What the hell's the meaning of this?' he demanded. 'Who were these layabouts? Where have they come from? Why wasn't I invited?'

Mary looked at Charles coldly, stubbed out her cigarette, stood up and walked past him.

'Where are you going? COME BACK HERE!' Charles shouted. But she carried on across the hall and up the stairs, where the children crouched stock-still as she passed them, and Charles came after her, crying: 'COME BACK HERE, WOMAN!' even as he followed Mary to her dressing-room.

'What's going on?' Charles exclaimed. 'I demand an explanation. What do you think you're doing?'

Mary took no notice of Charles as she calmly took clothes from her wardrobe, folded them and put them in a suitcase.

'Look, hang on a minute,' Charles told her. 'TALK TO ME! All right, darling, I was a bit hasty, I can see that, but will you tell me who those people were? I thought they were burglars. What do you think you're doing, damn it? STOP! NOW!'

Mary continued to ignore him, and came back down the stairs, past the boys in the exact same postures as before, and through the hall, with Charles behind her saying: 'Darling, look, I was out of order, yes, I know that now, I'm sorry, it won't happen again. Ever. I can see your point, darling. Where are you going? Speak to me, for God's sake! *Please!*'

Mary walked out of the front door and across the crunchy gravel to her car. She threw in her suitcase and got in herself, followed by Charles' now pleading voice. 'They're your friends, darling, I realize that now, it's clear to me. They can come whenever they want, they're welcome here, of course they are. They can *sleep* here if they want, I'd like that. Just *speak* to me, woman. Darling. Tell me what you want. I love you, Mary, I need you. I'm lost without you. I should be horse-whipped. Look, I'm on my knees. On this bloody gravel.'

Mary looked at Charles once more, still coldly, but nodded, and got slowly out of the car. She hauled her suitcase out too and took it back to her dressing-room, where she drew the curtains and shut herself in for the next three days.

From then on Mary's Wednesday poetry group became a regular and above-board event, although the door remained firmly closed to outsiders. Charles sometimes stood outside it, fuming: like his youngest son, he couldn't bear to be excluded even from something he had no wish to be a part of (and Charles had no interest whatsoever in poetry) and he found it insufferable to accept that his wife had a world which had nothing to do with him.

Once, he came home and found two beatnik idlers browsing through the ancient books in his study while drinking his whisky, but Charles controlled his natural impulses, smiled obsequiously, and asked if they'd like him to fetch them some ice. He never made a fuss again. He could cope with Mary's cool distance, and he could ignore her need for solitude, but he couldn't stand to lose her.

The weekends were very different. Then Mary joined forces with her husband for extravagant cocktail parties to which were invited his business associates, town councillors, newspaper proprietors and editors, bank managers, solicitors, lawyers, the mayor, the local Member of Parliament, doctors, surgeons, churchmen and other worthies of the town. The children bolted their supper down and raced upstairs to help their parents get ready, Simon and Alice drawn to the perfume, lipstick and rustling dresses of their mother, while the younger boys ran to Charles' dressing-room. James cloaked himself in his father's voluminous jacket and shuffled around in his huge shoes, before Robert took over and polished them in silent concentration.

'Robert! Haven't you done those ruddy shoes yet?' Charles demanded. 'By God, you'd make a good squaddie.'

Then James joined Simon and Alice in their mother's dressing-room, where they watched her apply make-up at her mirror, and inhaled the intoxicating scent of her perfume.

When the guests arrived they were received by the whole family, whose younger members stayed a while on their best behaviour as the adults drank cocktails in the drawing-room. Before the children were spirited away by Robbie they watched their gigantic father hold court, and they watched their mother, resembling on those social occasions some European princess. Women who approached her seemed by their movement to be fighting off a strange impulse to curtsy; she turned young men into speechless idiots and had to use all her charm to elicit normal conversation, while old men visibly shed their years in her company. Few of the pictures that appeared in the local newspaper of Charles at that time failed to include Mary at his side, the beautiful wife of the man-in-charge.

When James was seven he and Simon shared a room. Despite their proximity, once the boys fell asleep they entered different worlds. James had prosaic, reassuring dreams, inhabited by people he knew in familiar places, so that he readily confused them with reality: he asked Alfred in the morning why he'd laid out the tools on the lawn like that, and told his mother that he liked her experiment of having everyone sleep squashed up together in one room, only maybe the drawing-room would be a better choice than the downstairs lavatory.

Simon's dreams, in contrast, were invariably fantastic. He was an untroubled child who laughed as much as his father while lacking his bad temper. Once he fell asleep, however, his dream world took over and it was either frightening or fabulous, with nothing in between. In the morning he told Robbie of journeys through fairy-tale lands of glass palaces and mythical beasts. But sometimes she found him in James' bed, huddled up beside his younger brother, and she knew he'd had another nightmare.

Simon became scared of the dark, insisting upon the door being left open; he woke up in the middle of the night and stumbled around the house switching on lights, seeking to dispel the alien worlds of his own mind. Sometimes he bumped into his mother in a doorway, and they startled each other, because while Simon was recovering from a nightmare, Mary was sleepwalking.

It only happened when she was depressed, and everyone knew it was coming, because their elegant mother became pale and inert, with slack cheeks and dead, puffy eyes, and withdrew to her dressing-room for days on end. Her poetry group was cancelled, Charles had to have his personal assistant, Judith Peach, stand in for her at the cocktail parties, and the children spoke in whispers when they passed her door.

On the evenings of James' parents' cocktail parties the drawing-room became a strange, enchanted place. He was always disappointed the following morning. His dreams were so often extensions of what he'd experienced in the hours before sleep that he woke up thinking the party was still going on. But when he went downstairs he found everything already cleared up, and Edna finishing washing-up in the kitchen.

The library, on the other hand, had a different, consoling effect on him: he was only really happy in there when he was alone. It was his father's study, where Charles entertained his own important visitors, or where after smaller dinner parties the men retreated for port and cigars around the fire. Once or twice James eavesdropped on their dirty, guttural laughter, their brittle intimacy, their loud assumptions.

He preferred to sneak in there after school, to get away from the crowd. At the far end, between two tall sash-windows, was Charles' enormous desk. The fireplace was in the middle of the left-hand wall, surrounded by armchairs and small tables mushrooming out into the middle of the room. Bookcases filled the alcoves either side of the fireplace and lined the entire right-hand wall, while either side of the double doorway hung a single large painting, the same size, by the same nineteenth-century artist, of views of the town.

The leather-bound books of the previous owners still filled the shelves, and were only ever opened to be dusted. Except, occasionally, by James. He perused those books no one else read, took one off the shelf, inhaled its musty smell – which would ever after trigger feelings of solitary, almost forbidden activity – and lost himself in the adventure stories of Arthur Conan Doyle, H. Rider Haggard and James Fenimore Cooper, despite vast numbers of words he couldn't understand, deaf to noises from outside the library door and oblivious to the passing of time.

So that James didn't hear his father sweeping into the house, even when he burst straight into the library and strode over to his desk to make phone calls there. And neither did Charles notice his middle son curled up at the bottom of a bookcase, engrossed in some wondrous tale, less in the room than lost on some other continent. James was invisible.

Usually Charles would complete his calls and sweep out again. But sometimes he stayed a while longer, enjoying *his* few moments of solitude, fiddling with a row of pendulous balls which, set swinging, thumped against each other and sent their momentum right through the row, so that the ones on each end kept clacking in and out, ad infinitum.

Charles sat there, brooding on some new product he was planning, unaware of his invisible son; while James, wrapped up in a story, was sealed off from Charles at his desk; until eventually the click-clack, click-clack of the pendulum – its rhythm aping and perhaps aiding the thump and punch of Charles' thought – awakened James. Coming groggily out of another world he stood up, the book hanging from his limp hand, and Charles saw him for the first time.

'James!' he yelled. 'How long have you been hiding there, you little joker? Put that ridiculous object down: you'll damage your eyes and soften your brain! Didn't you hear the gong? Edna rang it twice already. Come on, race you to the kitchen, you scoundrel!'

*

Charles regarded reading as a waste of time, that most valuable resource, and made no secret of the fact. He didn't mean to antagonize Mary, or belittle her. He did his best to be supportive of her writing; he just didn't make the connection between writing and reading, assuming that her poetry was a hobby Mary pursued cloistered in her dressing-room when she was in a bad mood, or else exchanged aloud with fellow enthusiasts on Wednesday evenings.

When her first slim volume of poems was published that year, 1963, by a small local press, Charles held the copy she signed for him and stared at it, as if waiting for its significance to magically reveal itself. He turned it over in his hands until he saw the price, five shillings, written on the back.

'How many have been printed, darling?' he asked.

'Five hundred,' she told him.

'That's a hundred and twenty five pounds,' he said instantly. 'What's your cut?'

'Look, Charles,' she said, 'if we sell them all we'll cover the costs, OK?'

Charles frowned. 'I don't get it,' he puzzled.

'When I think about what a barbarian I married,' Mary told him, 'I try to remind myself why. And do you know what?'

'What, darling?'

'I can't remember.'

Still, Charles provided the champagne for a party to celebrate the publication, at which Mary's bohemian friends mixed with Charles' business acquaintances, because he was loudly proud of her.

'Yes, there are one or two about me, I believe,' he told the mayor. 'But of course they're metaphorical, you know: that's the fashion in poetry these days.'

Mary gave James a copy, too, which she inscribed: *To my little man, who helped me speak out loud.*

'The poem on page twelve,' she told him. 'It's the one I read out that night, remember?'

He didn't tell her he couldn't recall the poem, that what he did remember was Mary's arm squeezing him tight, and her ribs against him as she recovered her composure.

Charles was both generous and acquisitive – with a huge appetite for both: generous with what he had, greedy for what he hadn't. He gave extravagant presents that he sent his personal assistant Judith

Peach out to buy; no one could reciprocate in scale, but Charles didn't mind. On his forty-fifth birthday Mary gave him a dictaphone, a fantastically tiny tape-recorder with a built-in microphone.

'You can record your thoughts on the spot,' she told him; 'whenever you want, wherever you are.'

'Thank you, darling,' he said as he kissed her. 'I've got some thoughts right now,' he whispered hoarsely. 'But I'd like to record them in your ear. In private. You remind me of Christine Keeler in this light, and I don't want to leave any evidence.'

Charles was such an impractical man that by the time he worked out how to operate the dictaphone – being shown how to by Simon – he'd forgotten what it was he wanted to say. So he tossed it into a corner and forgot all about it, until a few days later he came across Simon in Mary's dressing-room making an inventory of his mother's wardrobe.

'Hey, that's mine!' Charles exclaimed, grabbing it from his nine-year-old son. He took it straight downstairs to his study and spent the next half-hour recording ideas on his intentions to investigate drilling equipment that might be required for a project such as a Channel tunnel. Except that he pushed rewind instead of record, spoke for ten minutes with the pause button on, and finally succeeded in taping something only to try to listen back to what he'd said and in doing so erased the entire thing. At which point Charles lost his temper and hurled the dictaphone against the door, smashing it into plastic smithereens. The man for whom technology made money was defeated by it himself.

When the first domestic record players that had separate speakers were manufactured the Freeman Company provided parts and assembled them in the factory. Charles took one look at the finished product and ordered one record deck and twenty-eight pairs of speakers. When they were delivered to the house he had Stanley wire up two in every room, all leading back to the record player in his and Mary's bedroom, for the simple reason that Charles loved to share the good things of life. He took to putting a record on when it was time to get up in the morning – and if *he* had to get up, why should anyone else laze around all day? – and then he hollered in the bath along with one of Mary's Beatles records or, better still, 'The Ride of the Valkyries', his pleasure amplified fiftyfold by the knowledge that the rest of the household were being thrilled by the same bombast blasted into their rooms.

It was a habit Charles carried on for many months, long after Mary had adopted the use of earplugs, and everyone else had worked out how to snip the wires to their speakers.

The only things Charles really understood, in truth, were numbers. They had more reality for him than letters: he couldn't spell, and was unable to write more than the incomprehensible memos of an angry dyslexic, which his PA translated into the English language. In the boardroom he unnerved opponents by doodling while they were talking to him, scribbling columns of figures in various currencies, which he could mentally convert into sterling quicker than any abacus and add up in an instant.

Charles regarded himself as a pragmatic man with his feet on the ground, immune to the temptations of abstract thought or the dangers of introspection; his chief measure of things in life was the effect they had on the stock market.

'Wealth is built on mud and silt!' he proclaimed. 'Money is round, and rolls away!' he warned. 'If you've got a good harvest, never mind a few thistles,' he advised.

The more eager of his employees seized upon these home-made proverbs as if they were complex acrostics and discussed them in the staff canteen, attempting to decipher their true meaning.

Charles Freeman, bullying guru in a suit and tie, addressed the world in abstruse generalizations. He spoke in specifics to his accountant, his general manager and his personal stockbroker, and then not in their native tongue but in monetary units.

He liked to move his managers around in a game of musical chairs that left most of them with higher salaries and less responsibility. His personal assistant would stay with him until the day of her retirement (the day of *his* bankruptcy) thirty years later, but ordinary secretaries changed with horrendous regularity: a constant supply of them arrived with a confidence born of glamorous efficiency, only to be seen tottering away on their high-heels with make-up running down their cheeks, having taken dictation of their own letter of dismissal.

Charles had no more sympathy with feminine complaints than he did with back pains or influenza: 'We work daily shifts here, not monthly rotas!' he declared when one of his periodical secretaries phoned in poorly.

'If women can't work to the same routines as men, they shouldn't expect to get the same wages!' he exclaimed.

'We don't,' Judith Peach quietly reminded him. Her surname was descriptive: Judith was not yet thirty, and there was something over-ripe about her; she was both louchely attractive and matronly, and she was Charles's most loyal confidante.

The one legitimate cause for time off, in Charles' opinion, was an accident at work. When there was an industrial accident in the factory, however small, the manager responsible for that section was sacked on the spot, and an investigation into its causes ordered. The embarrassed victim found himself visited in hospital by the boss: in Charles burst, full of apologies and encouragement, to autograph the plaster-cast, berate the nurses and plump up the pillows. And then flowers, chocolates and toys were delivered by his chauffeur, not just to the patient but to his family as well, with everyone's names on gift-wrapped labels. And their next pay-packet showed an impromptu increase in salary.

'But we need proper procedures for this sort of thing,' the chief shop steward complained. 'You can't buy off my members with back-handers, Mr Freeman. What's more, it mucks up our differentials.'

'Tommyrot!' Charles declared. 'Any man gets injured working for me, I'm going to see he's all right.'

Charles had an uplifting effect as he marched along corridors, through offices, across the factory floor, his transient secretaries and humbled mandarins flapping in his wake. He could give his voice the peculiar bark of a megaphone; when he addressed somebody more than two feet away, everyone else within a radius of half a mile stopped what they were doing and looked up, afraid they were being reprimanded.

He also had the habit of standing a little too close to people, invading their personal territory with his laughter, his smell, his energy; and if they took a step back he merely followed, keeping them enclosed within his orbit. Charles treated everyone the same, as a stupid yet vital colleague on a joint venture of huge importance, and would stop at a welder's bench or at Garfield Roberts' side to tell a joke, ask after the kids, make an off-the-cuff suggestion. He could dress shirkers down with his arm around their shoulder, tear them off a strip grinning as he did so, while if he was in a good mood then he might suddenly embrace them in an almighty bear-hug, squeezing them so hard he caused the victim to both belch and fart at the same time.

He became known for reducing distinguished men to tears; for facing down lesser bullies than himself; for firing people on Tuesday and reinstating them on Thursday in a higher position; for commending workers in public and then transferring them to oblivion; for entering negotiations for a wage rise and striding out of them after four sleepless days and nights having agreed an across-the-board pay-cut, only to announce a week later a universal salary increase greater than the union had initially demanded.

Charles' extraordinary self-confidence surged through the work-force and productivity increased steadily. The workers, despite his reliance on caprice and whim, regarded him paradoxically as a good boss, hard but fair. The white-collar workers saw him as a still youthful promoter of talent, of their own potential. And, once he'd got rid of the last few stuck-in-the-mud old-timers, the management team saluted him as their captain on an exciting voyage into clear, uncharted waters – the only question each had was whether he'd throw them overboard on the way.

One Tuesday after school that winter Simon took his cousin Zoe to his father's factory out at the edge of town between the railway line and the canal. It was a wet, dark afternoon and she suspected that Simon, who'd become a server in the local church, was punishing her for making fun of his religious piety. He led her round the site, past slag heaps and through oily puddles, jumping out of the way of lorries, fork-lifts and dump-trucks that appeared to thunder out of nowhere through smoky, sulphurous air.

Simon pointed through filthy windows at blast furnaces with orange raging flames, at rivers of white molten metal, at showers of purple sparks from arc-welding torches, at huge hooks like anchors swinging on wires thick as pythons, at great squat engines whose insides whirred and strained as if furious at their immobility.

Zoe stared at men in greasy overalls with owls' eyes, their black faces flashing white-toothed grimaces that looked like inexplicable smiles, the soot and grime of their working day steadily erasing racial differences. They shouted at each other desperately above the hammering torrent of noise in which they stood. She thought this must be hell, and wondered what crimes those men had committed to be sentenced to work there.

The entire way home Simon reeled off a list of items the factory produced, a list Zoe couldn't hear because her ears were filled with the roar of internal combustion engines. Gradually, though, as if approaching from far away, Simon's voice joined up with his lips.

'We make manhole covers, Zoe, iron railings, precision tools, door handles, hinges, buckles, nails and screws.'

The strange expression on Simon's chubby face – fat rolling over his schoolboy's collar – turned out to be pride. 'We make staples, parts for cigarette lighters, spectacle frames,' he continued, counting them off on his hands till he ran out of fingers and started again. 'We make coathangers, keys, hairgrips, drawing-pins, needles. See, Zoe, father makes everything. Things that people need so he makes millions of them. There's going to be something of ours in every house in England one day. We make tie pins, rubber-holders for the ends of pencils, and the wires holding in the eyes of children's teddy bears. Now you can understand,' Simon concluded, smiling benignly, 'why we're going to be so rich.'

Once all her children were at school, Mary thought the time had come to take an interest in the house, only to discover she was too late: Charles had already made the decision to spend some of his wealth on their home.

Stanley took care of maintenance, repairs and decoration with a minimum of fuss. Mary woke one morning to find there'd been a discreet invasion of their home: the sound of many people talking in low voices far away drew her to the east wing, where she found men in paint-splattered white overalls. Some were stripping paint from doors with blow-torches, others scrubbing ceilings with sugar soap, still more scraping off the old wallpaper, and they were working on every floor. Mary climbed the stairs – upon which the youngest, the apprentices, were sandpapering the banisters, the most fiddly and tedious job of the lot. Mostly they worked in silence but occasionally they leaned towards each other and quietly conversed: it looked as if they were passing on instructions, their whispers were like a stream rippling through the rooms and down the staircase, a whispering fountain of words containing advice and commands. Mary weaved her way up the stairs following those susurrations to their source on the top, third floor, where she found Stanley calmly giving orders.

'That's right, the moulding a different shade from the ceiling,' he informed the foreman of the decorating firm. 'Royal blue the dado, then scumble up to the picture rail, that's what the boss wants. And none of your watering down the beer, Jocky, we don't want none of your grinning through around here.'

Mary went outside and accompanied Alfred on a walk around the grounds, whose every square inch was carefully divided up: rose beds and ornamental ponds, avenues of acacias and rock gardens, creeping plants and flowering shrubs, a walled vegetable garden and a croquet lawn were all plotted on an architectural map hanging on one wall back in Alfred's potting shed. He took Mary over to another wall covered with gardening tools hung on large nails, and he lifted off a small pair of red-handled secateurs.

'These could be yours, Mary, and no one else will use them,' he suggested. 'You can prune the roses whenever you feel like it. I've just bought some lovely weeping standards: this morning I planted a Félicité Perpétuée by the gateway to the west.'

Mary then made the mistake of coming up with suggestions of her own. She went shopping for children's clothes without Robbie; cut a recipe out of a women's magazine for Graham Cracker Chocolate Pudding and cooked it herself in Edna's kitchen; bought some decorators' stencils and began painting Rococo patterns on the wall in the hallway; and ordered bulbs and seeds from a Sutton's catalogue which she planted right under Alfred's nose.

Stanley, Edna and Alfred began to treat Mary with an icy politeness, and Charles found her in her dressing-room with the curtains drawn.

'They think you're criticizing them,' he explained. 'They feel undermined. Anyway, those are menial activities, darling. You know I hate to see you upset. I can see you might be bored. Why don't you speak to my friends' wives? Join them in golf, shopping, charity work, that sort of thing.'

Mary shrugged. 'I don't like your friends' wives,' she told him blankly.

It was soon after that that Mary had an accident sleepwalking. Usually she was found standing in some doorway, hovering, as if on the verge of escape but not quite able to make up her mind. But then one night Mary got confused inside her dream and thrust a door open, only to find that in reality it was a window that she'd smashed her arms through. Thirty-five stitches seemed to cure her; and for the time being, they did.

In the mornings the children set off together to go to the same primary school, halfway between their house on the hill and the factory (which was where most of the other pupils' fathers, and a good many of their mothers, worked). Mary had assumed that her children would go to the twin private establishments – a boys' and a girls' preparatory school – in the north of town, but Charles wouldn't hear of it.

'If there's one thing I can't abide,' he told her, 'it's privilege. The old school tie, the old boys' network; it's been the ruin of this country, an aberration, a divided nation, Mary. The playing fields of

Eton, the Oxbridge connection, we're having none of it.' He grew red in the face and his eyes bored into her.

'Look at me!' he said, using himself as exemplar of what he most admired. 'I went straight to work, I never learned a ruddy thing at school. No, darling, I got my education on the factory floor. I raised myself up by my own bootstraps, through my own efforts!' he proclaimed, choosing to ignore the fact that his mother owned the firm in the first place. 'If Simon expects to take over,' Charles concluded, 'he'll have to prove himself just as I did. *And*,' he added with an emphatic grin, 'he'll have me to contend with.'

Mary watched the children go off to school each morning. One day she followed them a short while later, and marched into each of their classrooms. 'There's been a crisis at home, I'm afraid,' she told their teachers, as she rounded them up and packed them into her Zephyr saloon and drove away.

'What's wrong, Mummy?' James asked anxiously.

'What's happened?' Simon demanded.

'You won't be young for ever,' she told them brightly. 'You don't realize it yet. But that's the tragedy,' she explained, as she swept them off on a mad adventure: they drove all the way to Brighton on the south coast, where she gave them her allowance to lose as gaily as she did on slot machines on the pier, they got sick on toffee apples and candy floss, and watched her strip to her underwear before following her example and chasing her into the sea.

Until suddenly Mary said: 'Simon! James! Look at the time! Quick, hurry! Find Alice! Robert, come here! We've got to get back. And don't *anyone* tell your father. It's our secret, OK?'

The children took a long time to fall asleep that night, despite the sea air in their lungs, intoxicated still by their mother's high spirits, and their illicit behaviour.

The primary school was a small brick building with four classes, each presided over by a woman, and the children graduated from one teacher to the next: Miss Shufflebotham in the infants' class was insanely unpredictable, flipping from tears to fury to rapture throughout the day; Miss Edwards was stern and lovely, and when she first smiled she released a wave of bliss through the classroom; Mrs Beech – the headmistress – was absent-mindedly affectionate, and caused many generations of her pupils to confuse her memory, in later life, with that of their mother; and Mrs Claiple was a statuesque matron with no sense of humour, angrily mystified by the rude puns and innuendoes children competed with each other to insert into their answers to her questions.

Competition was the common factor in James' experience of primary school: seeing who could piss the highest in the outside, open-roofed urinal, saving it for the afternoon break when their bladders were so full that sometimes one of the boys managed to send his stream right over the wall and into the playground; races at summer sports days James always won; autumn conker fights he always lost; walking in orderly crocodile formation to the swimming pool on the link road and then leaping, yelling, into the chlorinated water (James got stinging eyes, gulped in water and felt sick, and hated it when Robert's class came too, for his younger brother ploughed up and down, totting up impressive lengths); prolonged, shifting winter snowball fights; and the lunchtime when Eleanor Patterson, a girl in Mrs Claiple's class above him, invited him inside her classroom while the others were all out in the playground and, unable to think of how else to articulate their mutual attraction, they decided to arm wrestle, during which he was startled by his first erection.

James was called the Bat at school on account of his sticking-out ears, and his habit of hanging by his knees from the climbing-frame, enjoying the sensation of blood filling his head and the sight of the playground turned upside down. He didn't mind the nickname because there was a *Batman* series on TV, and he turned the ridicule to his advantage by coming to school one day in a black cape he'd stolen from Robbie's trunk, as well as bringing a home-made mask he gave to Eleanor, explaining that she could be Catwoman. They swooped around the playground during dinner-break, and James went from being an oddball to the coolest kid in the class as the others queued up to convince him of their credentials for the roles of Robin, Penguin and the Riddler.

As for education, James most enjoyed Mrs Beech's impromptu oral arithmetic tests, because they made his brain fizz, his hand the first to shoot up and then waving it desperately, high, bursting with his knowledge and the glory. It was the only time in class James could remember not being bored. He preferred to be outside, dashing around the playground playing any kind of sport, although the one he liked most, from the very beginning, was football.

Once a week the headmistress's husband, Mr Beech, came in to take the older boys for football. He divided them into two teams, handed out different-coloured bibs, and proceeded to referee. He was such a stickler for the rules that it appeared as if the game itself were a side-issue to the more serious subject of discipline: if anyone questioned one of Mr Beech's decisions with so much as a quizzical frown, he made them shiver on the touchline for five minutes; and if the game flowed freely for more than a minute, Mr Beech grew visibly frustrated, until he was unable to restrain himself from blowing his whistle and then having quickly to invent some offence.

The only thing that allowed the game to continue without interruption was if Mr Beech got carried away shouting instructions.

'Get rid of it, lad!' he yelled. 'Don't mess about with the ball, Hayhurst! Leather it!'

He shouted himself hoarse and − if the boys were lucky − too breathless to blow the whistle.

'Get stuck in, lad! Back! Back! Thump it, you great softie! Put the boot in, boy! Go on, don't be scared, hit him! Show some character, Freeman!'

And then one Wednesday Mr Beech announced that the following week they would be playing not each other but a proper match, against a primary school on the other side of town. It was an unprecedented event and the whole school began to buzz with excitement, because everyone was to be given the afternoon off lessons in order to cheer the team on.

Mr Beech declared that he would be considering his players during the intervening days and would announce the team via a sheet of paper pinned to the school notice-board the day before the match. James was certain he would be selected, because he was one of the best two or three players. He wasn't so sure, however, about his best friend, Lewis; and on his account he began to worry.

Lewis was the first-born son of Garfield, the immigrant, and Pauline, Stanley's sister. Garfield worked on the assembly-line in the Freeman factory. He was only in this country, he often told James and anyone else who cared to listen, by mistake: he'd just come to visit a friend before going on to settle in America. Garfield never quite got used to the fact that he was still here, and would maintain throughout his life that he was 'on me way to 'Merica, James'. He'd taken temporary work in the factory, met Pauline there, and before he knew it he had a wife and a son, a permanent job and a council house on the estate that sprawled out of the east side of the town.

Garfield was a fine cricketer, almost as good a batsman as Harry

Singh's father, proprietor of the Post Office Stores and Newsagent, with whom he shared the opening partnership in the East Side Social Club cricket team, and he never really forgave Lewis for reneging on endless patient coaching in the back garden and preferring soccer to cricket – especially when Mr Singh's son was such a promising youngster, and had recently fielded for their team when someone was taken ill.

Harry was in the same class as James and Lewis. He thought football was a rather undignified, scrambling-around-in-the-mud sort of sport, a game for barbarians and almost as primitive as rugby.

'People should never begrudge the Empire,' Harry's father had told him, 'because it gave cricket to the world.' It was one of the few things they agreed on.

Lewis, though, loved football. He just wasn't very good at it. He was gangly and awkward, his limbs – giving notice of the height he would achieve in maturity – long and uncontrolled, like the young shoots of some wild plant. No one could remember a time when Lewis wasn't a full head and shoulders taller than his friends. His mother Pauline's memories of him even as a toddler were of staggering around like a spindly giant. She did know (it was a recorded fact) that he'd been a normal enough weight at birth – 8½ lb – and so she came to the conclusion that, although it hadn't made an impression at the time (since after all he was her first and she hadn't been sure what to expect), he must have been born a long and skinny baby. And she imagined him before that with his limbs curled up tight inside her, like a string of bony sausages in her womb.

Lewis had the intelligence of an athlete but his body let him down. It wouldn't do what he wanted: he couldn't trap the ball to save his life, it bounced off his shins, and he was unable to pass it in a straight line, putting an unintentional spin and curve to its direction. He also had, already, a certain sense of personal elegance which made him unwilling to head the ball and mess up his hair or to get his long legs muddy by slide-tackling an opponent.

In fact, if James were honest, he wouldn't pick Lewis if he were choosing the team, at least not on merit, which both his father and his teachers – and certainly Mr Beech – clearly regarded as the only basis for selection in such matters. James, however, was aware of another consideration: Lewis was his best friend.

'We'll both score three goals each, Jay,' Lewis told him. 'I dreamed it last night: one with each foot and one with my head.'

'You *must* have been dreaming, Lew.'

'Oh, I wasn't really asleep, exactly.'

By the weekend, though, he began to think that Lewis's selection in the team was more important to him than to Lewis himself. While James was becoming more and more excited, Lewis appeared to be losing interest, and kept changing the subject. On Friday afternoon they walked together after school to Lewis's house, discussing their geography project on the rivers of the African continent. Garfield was at home, having worked the early shift, and was bouncing Lewis's baby sister Gloria on his knee.

'Just look at these hands, man,' he told James; 'she's a born wicket-keeper.'

Lewis took a bottle of milk from the fridge and was pouring them a glass when his father said: 'I hope you're not frettin' like this son of mine over so stupid a thing as a *football* team. At least when I was your age and forcin' me way into the Bridgetown Boys Eleven I didn't bite me nails.'

James saw Lewis's eyes blaze.

'I didn't go losin' sleep like this here misguided son of mine, wide awake when I'm off to work at five in the morning. I hope you're not so foolish, boy.'

'No, Garfield.'

'Good. Well, have a word with him, then.'

'Yes, Garfield.'

Of course James didn't. He tried to persuade Lewis to test him on statistics from his *Rothman's Football Year Book*, or to go outside and let loose his rabbits in the back garden, or even to discuss the stupid geography project. Anything to get Lewis out of his silently fuming mood. But Lewis just dumped himself down in front of the television and glared at the screen, and James let himself out of the back door.

James walked home, racking his brains for a way to make sure Lewis got picked. He even considered writing Mr Beech a note saying *he*'d play only if Lewis did too, but he suspected that Mr Beech was impervious to blackmail and would perfectly happily drop James, as a matter of discipline. And James wasn't sure that he was ready for quite such a sacrifice. It was then that he thought of God. He knew – or at least he'd been told – that God was everywhere, saw every action and could hear every thought (if, that is, he existed at all, the one detail over which adults tended to disagree). James closed his eyes and tilted his head up, disregarding passing pedestrians or motorists who might think him insane.

'Please, God,' he said inside his head, 'please, if you're there, and if you'll do something for me – and I've never asked you for anything before so I don't see why you shouldn't – please, make Mr Beech put Lewis in the team for Wednesday. If you do, I'll . . . I'll . . . put back Simon's Action Man he thinks he lost.'

On Tuesday morning James approached the notice-board in the school corridor in a confident frame of mind, and stared at the note pinned up there with horror and dismay: Lewis's name was on the list, but he'd been named as substitute, twelfth man.

So, God, you won't listen to me, won't you? James thought to himself, in his first crisis of faith; but he didn't dwell on it because the real problem was more pressing than a religious one, and James wasn't yet ready to concede defeat.

The solution when it came to him, halfway through science later that morning, was simple: to put one of the other players named in the team out of the picture. And the means of doing so made James feel both inadequate and evil.

Robert was two years younger than James but he was just as big and was the most feared boy in the school. His entry into a game marked the beginning of its end. The most popular one involved boys and girls taking turns to catch prisoners and drag them to a base at the centre of the yard, where those caught had to submit to kisses. The game's viability rested upon the children's agreement that once caught they had to give in to their captors. Robert, though, was uncivilized. He kicked and yanked himself free or else, if held by two or three girls, went coyly limp and waited his chance till he felt a girl's hold on his arm go slack, and then he'd wrench it free and punch her and the others, and make his escape leaving behind pain, tears and a game in ruins.

Robert was eight years old, and everyone knew not to cross his path. He tended not to bother anyone as long as no one called him dumb or stupid, and few made that mistake: other children sensed that Robert had little compunction about hitting someone, about inflicting pain. Nor indeed (what was truly unnerving) about receiving it.

Now, as soon as the bell for dinner-break was rung, James went to look for Robert, having decided upon the most suitable candidate for intimidation on the team list. When he found his brother, James simply said: 'Come and help me a minute.' Robert didn't ask what he wanted, he just followed James, and they cornered Gary Evans at the back of the playground.

'If you tell Mr Beech that your knee's bad, and your mum says you can't play tomorrow, I'll give you all my spare bubblegum cards,' James told him.

'That's not a fair swap,' Gary bravely replied, his bottom lip quivering, less at James than at his younger brother looking over his shoulder.

'You'd better take it,' said James in as forceful a voice as he could muster.

'What if I don't?' Gary asked.

'If you don't,' James said, as calmly as he could, 'we'll beat you up.'

Gary knew that the *we* meant *he*. He might be prepared to have a ruck with James, but not his surly brother. He could feel both lips tremble.

'All right,' he agreed. 'Give us your cards.'

James handed them over. 'Don't forget to tell Mr Beech,' he added. He and Robert turned and walked away.

'I didn't even want to play anyway!' Gary called after them, preparing to dash towards Miss Shufflebotham in the opposite corner of the yard should this defiant gesture provoke reaction. But Robert carried on walking away as if he hadn't heard.

The game was a disaster. They lost 13–0 – the official if possibly approximate score – against what turned out to be the other school's third team, even though that school had much the same number of pupils: the difference, it transpired, was that a coach with the town's professional football club came in once a week and gave them lessons, not in discipline and character so much as passing and movement. James and Lewis and their team-mates spent the entire match running around in a shapeless, enthusiastic pack after the ball, as they did every week (with a slight hesitancy due to the fact that they kept expecting the whistle), while the opposition players kept by and large to their positions on the field and passed the ball from one unmarked player to another, unhindered, scoring at will in front of a hostile crowd that began the game in noisy support of James' and Lewis's side, but ended in philosophical silence.

James and Lewis walked home with their muddy boots over their shoulders. James was in a state of bewilderment. He asked Lewis his opinion of what had befallen them but Lewis declined to answer: he just walked with his head down.

'What's the point of it all?' James wailed. 'What are we going to do now? Oh, God, what if my dad finds out? Or yours for that matter? They're *bound* to. How did Eric let that tenth goal in? He *dropped* it.'

But Lewis just walked with his head down. James had made sure he didn't let slip that it had been his efforts that got Lewis into the team, but he was nevertheless exasperated by Lewis's silence: he knew it didn't make sense, and wasn't fair, but he couldn't help feeling Lewis was being somehow ungrateful. When Lewis failed to acknowledge him for the umpteenth time, James had enough.

'Bloody hell, Lew,' he blurted out. 'What the bloody hell are you so angry about *now*?'

Lewis came out of his trance and looked down at James with a faraway, mystified expression. 'I'm not angry, Jay,' he told him calmly. 'I'm thinking.'

James was a gregarious child who loved to run and shout. Forced to sit still for too long (other than on the floor, secretly engrossed in a book, in his father's library), his body began to squirm even before he himself realized he was bored. His face remained blank but his bottom shifted across the chair, his legs twisted around each other and bent themselves into awkward angles, his arms reached backwards over his shoulders as his fingers tried to scratch an impatience that was itching somewhere just beyond reach in the middle of his spine. They looked to his worried teachers like the symptoms of some slow-motion St Vitus's Dance, until they recognized a more common condition, that of a child with an overactive brain.

James was really only happy, it seemed, when he was on the move. If he was stuck in the same place he talked non-stop, because the energy inside had to come out somehow.

He wore out clothes before he had time to outgrow them: his jumpers frayed at the elbows and trousers ripped at the knees; underwear sustained holes as if moth-eaten; socks were simply lost, leaving him with a drawerful of odd ones; while he kicked and scuffed his shoes until they fell apart on his feet.

James didn't progress from the adventure stories in his father's library to more serious literature on other shelves, as might have been expected; he would stop browsing there once he went to the comprehensive school, the library's only legacy a taste for solitude. And, having given up on her husband, Mary seemed to have given up on her children too, making little effort to bequeath them her own pleasure.

By the time James left school he was, his cousin Zoe would despairingly tell him, practically illiterate. There was no doubt about where he got whatever aesthetic sensibility he possessed from; there was only one possible place: the Electra Cinema run by his great-aunt, Agatha Freeman, his cousin Zoe's grandmother.

Agatha had had the cinema built on Lambert Street, north of the town centre, at the end of the First World War. The ninety-nine-year-lease on the site still had seventy-five years to run. By the time James and his brothers and sister began going to the children's matinées on a Saturday afternoon, almost fifty years later, Agatha was a legend in the town. She ran the cinema almost single-handed, assisted by an unseen projectionist who'd been there nearly as long as she had and had never been known to take a day off, much less a holiday, other than Christmas Day and Easter Sunday. She chose the films, put up the posters, changed the lettering on the neon-lit façade, punched the tickets, sold ice-cream in the intermission and cleaned up in the mornings. Her severe expression had hardened over time and she was so stubborn that regular customers of all ages considered it their duty to try to force a smile from her. They never succeeded: she hadn't been seen to smile in years. But often after a film had started she would lock the glass doors at the front of the cinema, creep into the auditorium and stand at the back to watch a film for the umpteenth time. And if it was a comedy, then the audience were likely to hear one person laugh louder than anyone else, old Agatha at the back, laughing like a drain, in the dark.

Every Saturday there was a children's matinée and Simon and James and Robert went to most of them, along with Lewis and, once they were old enough, Alice and Laura. They were joined in their row of seats by Zoe.

'Matinée: it's an interesting derivation,' Zoe told James. 'It means an afternoon performance; from the French *matin*, meaning "morning". What a stupid language. I don't see why I have to learn it at school. I'll pick it up much better when I go travelling with Dad anyway.'

No one knew who the father of Agatha's son Harold was. She never told anyone, not even Harold himself. He grew up an only child in the tiny flat above the Electra, as would his daughter. Zoe was two years older than Simon. She would soon start accompanying her father on his travels, but back then she stayed with her grandmother above the cinema, and she saw every film that was screened. And Zoe had an added interest in those films they watched each Saturday: Harold had gained revenge on Agatha for not telling him who his father was by refusing to shed light on the identity of Zoe's mother, having brought her home as a baby after two years' working and travelling through the United States. The only detail he'd let slip was that she was some kind of actress, and Zoe came to conceive the notion that she might see her mother in one of those Saturday matinées. Maybe she knew it was an absurd illusion, a game she needed to play, but the others couldn't be sure because she certainly appeared to take it seriously.

Robert liked the monosyllabic gunfighters in Westerns, dressed in black, while Laura's favourites were Walt Disney cartoons – especially *101 Dalmatians* with Cruella de Ville – because, she claimed, they were the most realistic. Zoe preferred the epics – as did James and Lewis – because their women were the most noble and tragic, not to mention exotic, and therefore the most likely candidates for her parentage. Despite inheriting the dark hair and olive skin of her father's line she became convinced that her mother was Russian after seeing the blond Julie Christie as Lara in *Doctor Zhivago*. When *The Vikings* was shown (after which Robert wore a demonic scowl and an eye-patch for three weeks in imitation of Kirk Douglas, which made him look grimmer than ever) Zoe was certain that her mother was Danish and bore a close resemblance to Janet Leigh.

Lewis liked the epics best because there was always a chance that Woody Strode would be in them: whether set among the gladiators of Rome, Barbary pirates or in Jerusalem at the time of Christ there was invariably a brave, bald black man in an important supporting role. He was sure to be killed, but at least he was equally sure to have a courageous life and a valiant death, and afterwards Lewis would torture himself trying to summon up similar courage and shave his hair off.

'*I'll* do it for you,' Laura volunteered.

'My dad'll kill me,' Lewis worried, biting his nails.

'We could keep your hair in a bag, and if he gets too cross we can stick it back on,' James suggested, trying to be helpful. They never quite managed it, though they came closest after seeing Yul Brynner in *Taras Bulba*, when James impulsively suggested they could *both* shave their heads in a double pact of friendship, and share whatever punishment might come their way.

'All right,' then,' Lewis agreed, biting his nails.

'Actually,' James ventured, after considering the idea a little longer, 'I'm not sure. I think I preferred Tony Curtis *really*.'

They saw a different film every week, emerging from the cinema with a new identity that lasted at least halfway home, by which time James and Laura had usually started arguing about some aspect of the film, since James was the one who loved the films most and Laura was the one who most enjoyed an argument. They nearly came to blows walking home from *Cheyenne Autumn*: James, profoundly moved by the injustice portrayed, was upset by Laura's jeering ridicule of American actors made up with paint and wigs to look like Red Indians, and of anyone else stupid enough to be taken in by them.

Sometimes they even began squabbling with each other while the film was still in progress, and then before they knew it their Great-aunt Agatha, making no allowances for kinship, would lean over them from behind, pinch their ears and frogmarch them outside as she had seen it done in a hundred silent comedies, and which clearly gave her an inordinate amount of pleasure.

In actual fact, when James looked back, he recalled that Simon was as obdurate a philistine as their father. ('Money,' Charles told Mary when he cancelled the piano lessons after school she'd enrolled Simon in, 'money, not music, is the international language.') Simon didn't like the cinema, and only ever went when he had nothing better to do. And Alice was only allowed to go when she was a hundred per cent healthy – she had first to pass a medical of glands felt and temperature taken – because on one thing their mother agreed with Robbie: that cinemas were horribly unhealthy places, all those children squeezed together, all those germs gestating in the dark just waiting for a frail little lassie like Alice.

James was sure that there were just the five of them – Lewis and himself, Robert, Laura and Zoe – in their little group when they watched *Helen of Troy*, in which Zoe got her grandmother's Greek ancestry mixed up with her unknown mother's identity and convinced herself that she was the daughter of Rosanna Podesta, whose face launched a thousand ships and spellbound ten-year-old boys.

What James couldn't have imagined was that a shot of their hypnotized faces, in the watery light spilling from the screen, would make a crucial early image if there were ever a film made of *hi* life, since he had no way of knowing that the five of them (plus a child whose birth was still a long way off) would turn out, despite a fifteen-year effort to leave his childhood and everything in it behind, to be the principal protagonists of his life's story.

2

GROWING PAINS

THE HOUSE ON THE HILL WAS THE CENTRE OF THE FREEMAN children's world. At ground level it was sealed by the garden's surrounding wall, in a lagoon of privileged existence. A person rising through the house, though, could see the town spreading out below. And it was possible to ascend from the third floor to the roof: it was only a service ladder to give access for repairs, there was no roof garden or anything on top and the children were cautioned by Robbie never to go up there.

'A high wind'll sweep ye off,' she told them, 'and ye'll be *dashed* to pieces on the ground below.'

But sometimes, when she wasn't around, they dared each other to creep up and, hugging the tiles, crawl along wooden struts on lead alleyways between the pitched sections of the roof. As they got older, and bolder, they ventured further, Robert at least as far as the edge, the stone balustrade that ran around the whole of the roof. James occasionally went up on his own: pulled by the vertiginous drop, he kept well back from the parapet, but he could still see everything. On the hill leading directly down to the canal (over its bridge the town centre beyond) was a large open public park, with runners and dogs, families kite-flying and solitary walkers. The slope on either

65

side was more gradual and coiled with twisting cul-de-sacs and private lanes to detached houses in hedged gardens like satellites of the big house itself. The smells of hops fermenting in the brewery in town sometimes rose up from below.

Behind the house the town stretched across a plateau through acres of housing, in which were studded the primary school, Lewis's house, Mr Singh's Post Office Stores and Newsagent, the town football ground. Beyond them his father's factories were clustered by the ring-road, around which sprawled the housing estate with its single tower block.

It was best up on the roof at night. It felt more dangerous and forbidden, for one thing, but it felt also like not just the centre but the top of the world too, with sights and sounds more vivid in the dark: the discontented murmur of traffic, cars' lights probing a way through congested streets; the brilliant floodlights of the football ground and the disembodied roar of the crowd that burst as if from some underground monster into the night sky; beyond, in the distance, the smoking chimneys and tiny fierce flames of the factory; down in the town centre the house and street lights, and the lit-up face of the main church, and people blurred dots of movement in and out of shadow.

It was the top of the world and James could have stayed up there all night, if it wasn't that he was soon cold and hungry. He descended, shivering, into its warm heart down on the ground floor, and asked Edna for a mug of hot chocolate – whipping it with a whisk as it heated, the way she always did, which made it taste so creamy.

James added sugar. 'Don't stir with a knife, it's sure to bring strife,' Edna warned.

One hot afternoon in the late summer of 1965 Mary burst bright-eyed into the school.

'Death in the family,' she told the teachers.

'Oh. I'm so sorry,' they sympathized.

'No, don't be,' Mary assured them. 'No one important.'

Mary rounded up James, Robert and Alice before remembering that Simon was at the comprehensive now. So she drove over there and dragged him out too. Zoe saw their car and jumped in.

'This better be good, Mum,' Simon warned her. 'It's different here.'

'It will be,' she exclaimed. 'It is. Look!'

They peered out of the car windows, and realized that their mother

66

had brought them out of school just because warm showers were falling from a blue sky, and rainbows materialized on every horizon.

'See? I couldn't let you miss this,' Mary said. She drove them out of the west side of town and parked in the gateway to a huge field, where the river flowed beyond it. They got out of the car and Mary said: 'Race you to that cow over there. Winner gets a bar of chocolate.'

They ran across the grass. James won the race but Mary turned out to have chocolate for everyone. Alice skipped off to one side, into a world of her own, and Simon went after her, held her by the wrists and twirled her round. She sang as she flew, and her voice sounded like a strange bird's.

Mary grabbed Robert's hands and danced with him, and the others clamoured until she let them in and made a circle, and they spun till they were giddy, and collapsed on the wet, slippery grass.

The rain was sparkling and James thought they might all dissolve in it. They walked across the field till they were drenched. Robert gave Alice a piggy-back. Simon told some swans that he was a swan in another life and they hissed at him.

'Hey, little man,' Mary said, pulling James to her. He could feel her ribs through her sopping shirt.

Mary had brought swimming costumes, towels, blankets and a picnic. The children swam in the river. Simon was a porpoise, pulling Alice with her red armbands. James jumped from the branch of a willow tree laughing, splashing whoever he could. Robert disappeared downriver: anxious voices called him; a dog barked back; Robert returned, ploughing upstream unperturbed.

They swam across the river in the afternoon, and soft rain speckled the surface of the water, and then passed away across the fields.

The sun went down. Zoe floated on her back in the middle of the river. Mary sat on the bank, gazing over the children's heads, smoking; she held a cigarette like it was heavy. The town glowed orange across the horizon behind her. Then she called them out: sudden goose-pimpled flesh, trembling children peeling off tight wet swimmers, towels rubbing hair dry.

They shared tartan blankets, sandwiches and chocolate, hot drinks, on a warm summer night, and Mary gathered them to her, tired, sleepy, drawing them round her, her children accretions for her comfort; and there, with Zoe too, all fell asleep.

Zoe woke, shivering, in white clouds. She stood up, rose out of the mist and watched it forming from the water and rolling out across the fields. Her shoulders were above the mist, she couldn't see the others any more asleep around her feet; could see only the disembodied tops of trees, the orange glow of the town and a million stars fixed in the blue-black summer sky; high alone above mist in the moonlight.

Breakfast was the most chaotic meal in the kitchen, because everybody was always late. Charles would already be getting distracted by the phone, James had lingered under warm sheets dozing for too long, Robert was lost, Alice searched for her clothes and her satchel, having forgotten where she left them yesterday, Laura would be locked in the bathroom, Stanley be cleaning the grates, Robbie complaining: 'Ah called ye all *hours* ago!'

Only Simon was at the table in plenty of time to consume his breakfast calmly, and digest it properly, because eating was his number-one priority.

At the age of six and a half Alice declared one morning in the middle of that chaos that she was a vegetarian. She addressed it to no one in particular, in a tone less of conviction than surprise – 'I'm a vegetarian now, you know,' she said, as if it were something obvious she'd only just noticed, or else the first half of a joke whose punchline she neither remembered nor fully grasped the need for, a habit Alice had that drove her older brothers insane.

'What do you get if you cross an elephant with a telephone?' she'd asked Robert the day before.

'I don't know,' he responded. 'What *do* you get if you cross an elephant with a telephone?'

Alice merely shrugged her shoulders.

'But what's the *answer*?' he demanded.

'*I* don't know, Robert,' Alice replied.

'But you *must* know,' he complained. 'What's the point of asking if you don't know?'

Alice looked at him sadly. 'Well,' she improvised, frowning, 'you get a telephone with big ears.' And she walked off, her mind drifting onto other things already, as Robert clenched his fists in exasperation and yelled: 'I'm not *stupid*, you know!'

So when Alice quietly announced that she was a vegetarian no one took any notice in the hubbub of half-asleep brains and panicking gulpers, of crackling, crunching cereal, sizzling eggs and bacon and spilt tea. It was only afterwards, when adults had disappeared and children had run cursing late for school, after the kitchen had ceased to shudder with the echoes of raucous voices, that Edna, clearing away the table, found an untouched sausage and a rasher of limp bacon pushed tidily to the side of Alice's plate. And later that morning, when she made herself a mug of milky coffee for elevenses, Edna began copying out vegetarian recipes from her shelf-ful of cookery books, with each quantity of ingredients amended so that they made up single portions.

That evening at supper the rest of the family tucked in to a steaming steak-and-kidney pie, while Alice had her own small dish of mushroom croustade. Robbie couldn't quite understand what was happening: she could only stare at Alice's plate with a look of stupefied consternation. It was one of the first signs that Robbie was getting old.

'I'm not sure we should indulge Alice,' Mary ventured to Edna afterwards. 'It's only a child's fad; the sooner she snaps out of it the better, instead of wasting your valuable time.'

'It doesn't take me a moment,' Edna assured her. 'The child's got to have her protein. She won't get it from vegetables and pie-crust.'

Over the following days what was, at first, greeted as a joke soon drew other responses.

'Who's been putting these ideas in your head, young lady?' Charles demanded at dinner. 'Have you been listening to your cousin Zoe and her father's crackpot eastern theories? She's perfectly happy to eat our Sunday roast, Mary, and then I suppose she goes upstairs and tells our children to eat nuts and lettuce!'

'No one's told me anything, Daddy,' Alice told him calmly. 'I'm just a vegetarian now, that's all.'

'She's so soppy her guts can't cope with real food,' said Robert.

'I suppose you think you're better than we are, Ali,' Laura said, offended.

'There's Bushmen, I believe, in the Kalahari,' old Alfred ruminated, 'who live like beachcombers in the sands of the desert on dried fruit and roots and groundnuts . . .'

'Really?' Alice asked.

'Oh, yes,' he continued, 'and bulbs of plants and wild berries; and caterpillars and grubs . . .'

'Oh, no,' she retreated.

'And tortoises and ostrich eggs and snakes. And *then* they go hunting.'

'She's right in a way,' James opined. 'Maybe we should only eat meat from animals we've killed ourselves.'

'We can soon fix that, lad,' Stanley told him. 'I'll tell you next time I go shooting.'

'Thanks, Stanley,' James whispered, aware that Stanley could discern his squeamishness.

'Mmmm,' Simon murmured, polishing off his own plate of shepherd's pie, and then, seeing there were still some leeks in cheese sauce on Alice's dish: 'Are you full up, Alice? Do you want me to finish yours off?'

To the universal jeers of those around him Simon exclaimed: 'Well, I don't see why someone shouldn't be half-carnivore, half-vegetarian, actually.'

'Half-gannet, half-pig, more like,' Robert replied.

'Half-fat, half-lard,' Laura laughed.

'There's no need to be cruel, children,' Charles declared, grinning widely himself.

There were various responses to Alice's meat-free diet, but the one thing they all had in common was that it took everyone years to fully appreciate that Alice's vegetarianism was more than a passing whim. Everyone, that is, except Edna, who alone — and from Alice's first proclamation — took her seriously, somehow perceiving that that enigmatic, elusive child had meant what she said. No one else took her seriously because there was nothing obstinate or stubborn in her nature, and in a household of powerful personalities Alice made her own way among them like a benevolent elf. But Edna alone was right: at the age of six and a half Alice had acquired a moral conviction as naturally as a new tooth, and it was one she would stick to for the rest of her life.

Alfred the gardener rarely joined the family for supper, and then only in the depths of winter. He couldn't bear to come inside when there was still daylight outside and still things to be done. He could be seen in the garden after darkness had fallen, working by the somewhat erratic light of a bulb Stanley had connected to a lawnmower for him.

During school holidays, when James was at home in the middle of the day Edna gave him a plate of sandwiches to take out to Alfred for lunch, since he usually forgot to come and collect them himself. James crept between the flowerbeds and approached Alfred from behind, hearing his mellifluous voice as he drew closer.

'Now you get your roots down well, my lovely,' he heard. 'I'll just nip these shoots off here, don't fret now, you'll flourish all the better without them.'

As well as talking to his flowers Alfred also sang to them. Or rather he sang, quietly, of his own accord and they, perhaps, heard him; whether they reacted in the same way as human beings, who can say? His repertoire was limited in genre, alternating between torch-songs and patriotic ditties. 'Easy come, easy go,' Alfred sang, and 'Cocktails and laughter, but what comes after?'

Or else: 'It's a long way to Tipperary,' and 'Pack up your troubles in your old kit bag'. Alfred's problem (a problem too for anyone within earshot) was that he didn't know all the words to a single song in the history of music: he crooned little snatches of songs (and even the snatches were wrong) as he worked, with the briefest of pauses in between.

> There'll be blue crows over
> The white cliffs of Dover . . .
>
> It won't be a stylish marriage
> You can't afford a carriage
> But we'll look sweet
> Upon . . .
>
> I get a kick from cocaine
> That kind of thing doesn't thrill me at all . . .
>
> But smoke gets in your eyes.

The other thing about Alfred's horrendous medleys was that he was unaware he was performing them. Edna would hear him near the back door and say: 'Oh, go on, how does that tune go?'

'What tune?'

'You know, that one you were just singing.'

'Me? Singing?' Alfred asked.

It was an unbearable habit, and what made it worse was that it was compulsive listening. Members of the household who wandered unsuspecting into the garden found themselves hypnotized and waiting for the next strain of music to emerge from Alfred's mouth, to see what it would be and whether he could finish it this time. He never did, but stopped short (unaware of someone not far away unable to tear themselves out of earshot) before starting on another one:

71

Give me the moonlight
Give me the . . .

But much, much more than this
He did it my way.

And when they did finally manage to wrench themselves away it was only to find the same tunes stuck in their heads for the rest of the day.

Alfred spoke to his plants years before the practice came into common use because he liked talking, and there were no people to speak to. He liked people, and he liked talking, but for some years he'd refused to take on an assistant because, he claimed, he couldn't stand to see a job done cack-handed.

'There's perfectionists and bodgers in this life,' he told James. 'If a job's worth doing, and all that, that's what I say.' He worked all day long every single day of the week. When he was forced, by an unavoidable social occasion, to take time off he enjoyed himself more than anyone; Alfred was a naturally gregarious man. But then he went straight back to work, because there were always a hundred things that needed doing before the weather changed. 'Time and tide, and all that,' he said, taking his leave.

'People are either fixers or prevaricators, doers or meddlers,' Stanley, on the other hand, declared. 'Me, I'm a fixer. There's too much needs doing around here to hang about. Make it work and move on.'

Robert, standing close by, nodded in silent agreement. 'Look at it this way,' Stanley concluded: 'Would you rather have a car up on a ramp being tuned like a bloody piano, or out on the road, taking you from A to B?'

James wondered which he'd turn out to be when he grew up. Perfectionist or fixer? The fact was he already knew: he was a bodger, because he was basically lazy; and it bothered him only because he had no wish to align himself alongside Stanley, at least not opposite Alfred.

When Alfred mowed the lawns James gave a helping hand, despite Alfred's making it clear that James was a lot more trouble than he was worth. Alfred used a wide, ancient roller mower that cut the grass, 'closer than the centre court of Wimbledon', according to his boast. He steered the mower to and fro in unnervingly straight lines,

72

pausing at each end to empty the bin into a wheelbarrow. When the barrows were full he – or James, shakily returning bits of grass to the perfectly cut lawn on the way – pushed them to the compost heaps in a corner of the vegetable garden: piles of new-mown grass, their fresh, zestful smell, heady with petrol, intoxicating; tiny stalks of grass stuck to sweaty skin; older grass beneath, sometimes slipped into, mulchy rank and yellow.

Alfred mowed the lawns with particular concentration one Thursday in July 1966. 'That's a damn sight better turf than Wembley, that is,' he told Charles, as the marquee arrived.

It was the first wedding James and his brothers and sister had ever been to and was the last of their parents' generation.

Jack and Aunt Clare, Mary's sister, had certainly taken their time, having been engaged for many years, but they were both cautious people who didn't want to be rushed into anything. Jack Smith had inherited his family's farm to the west of the city, where the river valley began to slope up into the wolds. It was a farm composed almost entirely of stock: mostly sheep, and a small herd of Jersey cows.

'I can't be doing with this grain and beet and barley and what have you,' Jack, a big, bluff man, told Stanley, who was a distant cousin of his, at the stag party Charles threw for him. 'They're all too unpredictable. No, you give me animals, I can understand them all right.'

Jack finally decided to press ahead with the wedding only when someone pointed out to him that until he did so there'd be no sons to inherit the farm – it would pass directly to his younger brother's daughters – and it was a good thing he did because Clare could have gone on for ever without making up her mind. Her younger sister Mary had got married to the man in charge almost as soon as she was legally allowed to, while Margaret, the eldest, disdained the institution.

Neither Jack nor Clare was a believer, but they agreed that only a church service represented a proper wedding, and they took advantage of Clare's church-going sister and brother-in-law's good offices to get married in their church.

The parish priest was a young man with a righteous air and a propensity for giggling. Old ladies – widows and spinsters and women who'd found themselves wedded to heathens – made up the majority of the congregation, and they thought the vicar a man of rare and enchanting spirituality. Of the rest, even the children, who had to go to Sunday school each week and rejoin the adult congregation for the end of the family service, found it difficult to take him seriously.

It was a High Anglican church, a Victorian Gothic building, where the churchwardens, the sacristan and the choirmaster together ensured that the young priest did things the way they'd always done them, which seemed to suit him anyway. They waved incense and rang bells of various sizes and sounds, sung the responses and recited prayers in Latin. Different verses of each hymn were sung without warning in completely different ways: men abstained from a verse; then the women sang descant; and in another the entire congregation refrained, leaving it to the choir alone, according to a complex formula people could only grasp if they'd been worshipping at that same church since childhood, and which caught out unwitting visitors.

It was 1966, and the Parochial Church Council had recently acknowledged the fact that they'd entered the twentieth century by voting by a majority of one to admit females to the choir, a local schism being averted only through the young vicar's charm in placating the irate old ladies. Alice was the youngest among the first intake of girls and Simon was one of the servers, dressed in a ruff-collared surplice, with a special responsibility to ring a bell during prayers.

James was going through that stage of a boy's development when his parents fear their son's some kind of idiot savant: he was obsessed with statistics, and could reel them off like the memory man on TV. In James' case they were ones related to football; far from being the irrelevant arcana they appeared to others, however, they actually broadened his mind and enlivened his interest in the subjects at school that had bored him. Aided by the supernatural memory of a ten-year-old English schoolboy, James developed an awareness of his country's geography by mentally dotting the map with the ninety-two Football League grounds; he began to discern the significance of history through memorizing the dates of each club's foundation; and he understood the different populations of towns and cities, and their demographic shifts, by studying ground capacities and crowd attendances.

When the date for the wedding was fixed – for 30 July – the

74

previous winter, it had occurred to no one to check the date of the World Cup final, to be held in England for the first time, nor indeed that England's own team might reach the final. But they had. James and Lewis (whose family had also been invited) had been trying all week to work out how to slip away from the reception at the big house just for a moment – well, just for two hours. Robert regarded their fearful planning with scorn.

'Just go ahead and do it,' he sneered. 'The worst you'll get's a whack from Dad.'

'That's easy for you to say,' James replied. 'You don't *like* football.'

'Yeah, but if I did, I'd have the guts to take it. And you know I would, too.'

The boys got no sympathy from their parents. Charles dismissed sport. 'Life's a game,' he told James. 'Life *is* competition. You're a winner or a loser in *life*. Competition's too important to play games with. Don't waste your ruddy energy on *sport*, James.'

Lewis's father was no more helpful. 'This here's your mother's second cousin gettin' married, boy. It's about time you knew: family is more important than sport and all that.'

'What if it was the final day of the fifth Test between England and the Windies?' Lewis demanded of his father.

'And don't be talking to your elders in that tone of voice, boy,' Garfield told him.

Mary saw that James was becoming obsessed with missing what even she could appreciate was a special event, and it increased her own anxiety. One of the few responsibilities she embraced was the behaviour of the children in public.

'Imagine you're watching a film,' she told James on the morning itself. 'Imagine you're in the cinema.' It crossed her mind to ask the vicar if Agatha could come and distribute ice-cream and popcorn during one of the hymns.

It must have been the idea of the cinema that gave Mary the inspiration of a camera. She rushed someone off to buy one and showed James how to use it in the middle of getting dressed herself. 'Whenever you feel yourself getting bored,' she advised him, 'just think about taking a picture of Jack and Aunt Clare up at the altar with the vicar and Daddy, who's giving Clare away, and Ben, Jack's best man. But only click it,' she added hastily, 'in the middle of a hymn.'

The house was full at that moment of an extraordinary hustle and bustle. Guests from out of town dumped their suitcases and changed

75

their clothes in the spare bedrooms, Edna supervised a team of caterers in the kitchen, Stanley and Alfred set up chairs and tables in the voluminous marquee that had blown up like a balloon on the lawn the day before.

Charles was striding around bellowing at people in a good-natured way. He came into Mary's dressing-room, said: 'My God, you're going to upstage the poor bride, darling,' and had his hand on her bottom before noticing James fiddling with the camera on the floor. 'I hope you're ready, James,' Charles told him. 'Don't distract your mother,' he ordered, and left the room.

James practised clicking the camera, taking pretend pictures of his mother putting on mascara at her dressing-table mirror. 'Is this going to be like your wedding was?' he asked her.

'You're not like him at all, are you?'

'Who?'

'Ours was a mistake,' she said distractedly.

'What?' he asked.

'I mean ours was much bigger, James,' Mary said. 'We had *hundreds* of guests. Run along now; make sure the others are ready.'

On his way downstairs James was overtaken by Robert chasing Alice and Laura – one already in her choirgirl's surplice, the other in her bridesmaid's dress – along the corridors until he tripped Laura up and ripped her dress, which Simon mended for her with his own needle and thread.

'Stop trembling, Laura,' he told her, 'I don't want to stick the needle in your leg. Stop crying.'

'Yeah, you're not *hurt*,' said Robert.

'Shut up!' she replied in a sniffly voice. 'I'll get you.'

'Ha!'

'Go away, Robert,' Simon pleaded. 'You're only making it worse.'

James was on the telephone when Mary rounded them up to drive down the hill to church. Lewis had rung because he just had to, because he was sure they were going to lose without Jimmy Greaves in the team. It made him feel sick, he said.

'Don't worry, Lew,' James tried to reassure him, although Lewis had infected him with the same queasy feeling. 'Stanley says we beat them at Dunkirk and we'll beat them at Wembley.'

'We didn't beat anyone at Dunkirk,' Lewis's confused voice replied.

'JAMES!' Mary's voice, unnaturally loud, echoed through the house.

'My mum's calling, Lew. You sure you organized the TV?'

'Yes, we're going to Harry Singh's, I told you. His dad'll be working in the shop and his grandma can't get out of her chair.'

'JAMES! WHERE ARE YOU?'

'I've got to go. See you in a minute.'

'See you in church.'

'Bye.'

'James! There you are! We'll be late! Come on! Where's your carnation, for goodness' sake. In your pocket? It's all crumpled! Give it to me, James. Have you got the camera? Well, go and get it then. Hurry up. Your father's waiting in the car. RUN!'

From the moment they reached their pew and settled down, James became aware of something in the air that he'd never associated with church. In fact he'd never associated it with anywhere, because he'd never sensed it before and he didn't know what it was.

Jack and Ben stood up at the front in black- and grey-striped trousers and long-tailed jackets. The choir took their positions in a rustle of surplices and sheet music. The vicar whispered something to Simon. The church was filling up. James forgot about Lewis, who with his parents and little sister Gloria had sat down a few rows behind James and was waiting for him to turn around so that he could give him a look that communicated the depths of their mutual anxiety about the forthcoming match. But when the organist hit the first notes of 'Here Comes the Bride' and everyone stood up, James turned round and didn't see Lewis at all, he only saw Aunt Clare in white on his father's arm proceeding down the aisle, followed by Zoe holding her train and Laura and the other two bridesmaids carrying small bouquets of flowers.

James felt his throat constrict and his ears grow hot, and his eyes prickled but they also opened wide as he watched the ritual unfurl before him.

It passed with the speed and the continuity of a dream. James sat as still as Robert, to his mother's amazed relief. So much so that she felt towards the end a twinge of annoyance at his absorption, and during the final hymn leant down and reminded him in a curt whisper of the camera she'd bought to avert a social disaster. James wrinkled his brow in irritation and said: 'Sssh!'

In the marquee afterwards Charles congratulated Mary on controlling their fidgety son and she told him it was nothing to do with her, James was just engrossed in the occasion.

'Boys aren't supposed to *enjoy* weddings, they're supposed to *endure* them,' he declared. He frowned. 'For God's sake, Mary, we've not got one of those for a son, have we?'

'Don't be an idiot, Charles,' Mary replied. 'I think it's rather appealing in a boy.'

Charles, still frowning, marched off towards the bar. James, meanwhile, was finding that the reception promised to be as engrossing as the wedding service itself. He was watching Jack and Clare greet the last in a long line of guests when Lewis sneaked up behind him and whispered in his ear: 'Come on, Jay, it's time to leave.'

James didn't even look at him. 'You go on ahead, Lewis,' he replied. 'See if Robert wants to go.' And before Lewis could say anything James marched into the crowd inside the marquee and disappeared.

Lewis was devastated. He stayed where he was for some minutes, rooted to the spot, released from his trance only by his father's hearty slap upon his back.

'*Here's* my boy! We're on that table over there, Lewis. Look at these eats! What a spread! Get yourself over before I gobble yours up.'

Lewis slipped away from his father and, in order to find time and space to think, into the big house. He was wandering through the empty house in a state of abject loneliness when he heard the sound of a number of men groan in unison. Lewis carried on, past the kitchen, and found Charles' chauffeur, the best man, one of the marquee bar staff, a dozen already inebriated wedding guests, and the vicar, all squashed into Stanley's and Edna's sitting-room around a small black-and-white television set. Haller had just scored the opening goal for West Germany.

Two hours later there were more men packed into that tiny room than in the vast marquee. Sat and stood and knelt and crouched in nail-biting silence. Alfred's head poked around the door.

'The bride and groom are ready to leave,' he announced.

'Hang on, mate,' a single voice – the chauffeur's – replied.

'*The fans are on the pitch!*' declared the commentator. '*They think it's all over . . . IT IS NOW!*'

The men spilled out of the house, the vicar dancing like Nobby Stiles, wishing he had dentures he could remove in imitation of England's toothless hero. The chauffeur dashed over to the Rover and brought it, tyres squealing, to the side of the lawn just as Jack and Clare were saying their final goodbyes – to be driven away through a whole town that seemed to be celebrating their wedding.

At the very last moment James remembered the camera in his pocket, just in time to take one single photograph. It would have an original composition, the world tilted at a forty-five-degree angle. In the bottom left-hand corner half of Jack's body and most of Clare's were climbing into the back of Charles' Rover in a blizzard of confetti. In the bottom right-hand corner was a forest of guests waving goodbye, leaning over like trees in a terrible storm, as if bidding farewell to two of their fellows uprooted and blowing away for ever. In the top left-hand corner, above the car, Lewis was turning a cartwheel on the grass in the belief that he'd been transformed into Alan Ball, except that because of the camera angle he resembled more a levitating starfish. In the centre of the picture Mary, out of focus, stood with one arm raised. While in the top-right hand corner, on the green grass in front of the dangerously teetering white marquee, Robert was chasing Laura, her dress torn from the hem to above the knee. Owing to James' photographic inexperience those two occupied the only area of the image that was in focus, and despite their small size, and the fact that it looked like they were attempting to fly, it was possible to make out the expression of panicky excitement on Laura's face and the blazing determination in Robert's eyes.

That evening James wound the film off and gave it to his mother to have developed. A few days later he contrived to pick it up himself, and so hid from her the fact that it had only one image on it. But that skew-whiff photo was to be the first in a secret album, which James would never show to anyone. Until, many years later, a small girl discovered it, and would use it to help mend her broken life, containing as it did pictures of her history.

It was in the following spring, of 1967, that the children woke one morning of their own accord, because no one had called them: they found Robbie in her room, lying on the floor in her night-dress. Her jet-black hair, which she only ever wore in a tight bun, was spread out around her in weird disarray; some strands were startling white. She was as formidable in death as she had been in life and they were loath to disturb her. Robert, though, plucked up courage, leaned forward and touched her cheek.

'She's cold,' he said, frowning.

*

The following afternoon James, alone on the third floor, heard the sound of crying coming from Robbie's room. He crept towards the open door and peeked around the corner, to sigh with relief when he saw it wasn't Robbie's ghost but only his mother. Mary was kneeling on the floor by Robbie's wardrobe, stopped in the midst of putting her clothes into a suitcase, her shoulders shaking. She didn't hear James come into the room and started when he put his arms round her shoulders.

'What's the matter, Mummy?' he asked. 'Are you crying because of Robbie?'

'Yes,' she said, blowing her nose. 'Yes, that's right, James. Of course it is. Give me a hug, little man.'

Charles and Mary decided not to replace their nanny, but at least to get an au pair for the summer, for Alice's sake in particular. Pascale arrived in June. She was seventeen years old, and spoke a few words of English with a thick accent, in a low voice that made the boys want to die. They stared at her with open mouths and weak knees, unaware that they were doing so, until Alice took her by the hand and led her upstairs to show Pascale her room.

James fell helplessly in love. His voice was beginning to break in a haphazard way, his balls had dropped and his limbs were gangly, his whole body become awkward and intense, and Pascale sailed into the first confusion of his puberty like a French Helen of Troy. He lusted after her with a dreadful intensity: at first he had to keep out of her way because even the sound of her voice in the next room or the faint smell of garlic she left in corridors gave him an instant erection he found difficult to conceal; to actually find himself in her immediate presence provided a rush of blood that amounted to a medical crisis, and he fainted. The trouble was he couldn't keep away. He followed her round the house in a state of servile agitation, opening doors, carrying her bags, making the tiny cups of bitter coffee she drank sweetened with six spoonfuls of sugar, running her bath and providing fresh towels until she pushed him backwards out of the bathroom, his hard-on aching towards her, the last of him to leave.

Pascale couldn't help being provocative. She smoked thick, white, foul-smelling cigarettes the boys devoted much energy to stealing from her pockets and which made them retch. Within a fortnight of her arrival her command of the English language was such that she was able to render anyone unwise enough to enter into debate with her speechless, through a combination of skittishness and Gallic rationality, confusing everyone with logic. When she sunbathed on the lawn James and Robert came to blows for the privilege of rubbing Ambre Solaire into her brown skin.

Robert was just as imprisoned as James by Pascale, only he didn't break out. He scrutinized Pascale with a look less of passion than of mistrust, as if resenting the impression she made upon him that he could not deny. His response was furtive: he tried to spy on her in the bathroom through the keyhole; he crept into her room and fondled her underwear, unsure whether he wanted to suffocate in it or rip it to pieces. He lowered his guard rarely: once when they went swimming Robert dived into the pool and swam underwater towards Pascale and grabbed her legs; he pulled her under and wrapped his limbs around her body, oblivious to their need for air, a limpet of pre-pubertal fascination. It took all Pascale's strength to struggle to the surface and reach the side, where she hauled herself out of the water with the boy still clinging to her.

Simon, too, was helpless. Pascale flirted with everyone, not on purpose so much as with the abstract self-confidence of her youth. Only with Simon did Pascale flirt openly – maybe she knew it was safe. The way she kissed him goodnight, fluttered her eyes at the door and blew kisses across the room made him laugh, and he copied her, returning her seductive gestures, throwing them back at her, and that made *her* laugh. He did funny walks, he aped her smoking her sickly cigarettes, he told silly jokes. What Pascale liked most of all was Simon's mimicry of his brothers in their attentions towards her: both James and Robert were too intense for irony, theirs was a desperate, humourless passion and ripe for caricature. Of course they knew it, and they knew too when they were being made fun of, they'd hear Pascale's laughter just a little out of control and they traced it through the house to where they found their older brother mimicking their hopeless, helpless desires. And Simon would become aware of them too, their fury escaping from them like smoke, but he carried on in a state of mounting elation, because the happiness he got from making Pascale laugh was greater than any fear he might have to pay for it later.

James, however, was her favourite: his flattering adoration, more innocent than Robert's, was ultimately more welcome even than laughter.

'You are my little prince, *non*?' she told him. 'You must grow up queek, Jams,' she demanded 'so's I can marry you, *non*?' He knew she was kidding and tried to tickle her, so she tickled him, and soon they were wrestling. Pascale needed little encouragement to join in. It was a voluptuous game with her: she didn't hurt him, she wasn't clumsy like Simon, who was likely to crush him with his weight; neither did she fight underhand like Robert, who in a good mood could start a mock fight playfully enough but as soon as he got the worst of it responded with a jerky kick or flailing fist.

Pascale was different. She embraced him and he embraced her and then they struggled and strained for supremacy. It wasn't really fighting at all; James realized that this was a kind of artful pastiche, not just of wrestling either but of some other struggle too. He loved the smell of her, of sweat and garlic. He loved the feel of her breasts through her jumper, squashing beneath his weight. They rolled over slowly, as if in a medium thicker than air, she rolled him over with a great effort. All his limbs strained but he couldn't quite resist her. He loved the colour in her cheeks and the sweat on her upper lip, and the grimaces and grunts she made as if it were mortal combat when really he knew she was stronger than he was and she was only feigning.

The game drew towards an end when she raised herself up and pinned him down. Then she started to tickle him and to laugh: 'I'm the winner, Jams, zis ees the end, you can never escape me,' as he spluttered and wailed and begged for mercy.

It was a time of civil war among the children. And it wasn't only the boys who'd been afflicted. Alice thought she must have been living in a vacuum before, because Pascale arrived and filled her life. She was a big sister, best friend, protectress, wise counsellor and heroine, rolled into one. Pascale taught her the French words for bodily functions, lent her clothes, and taught Alice that summer to write in joined-up handwriting, in strangely chequered rather than horizontally lined exercise books; Alice would for ever after cross her sevens, in the French style, in a repeated act of unconscious homage.

It was a difficult time for Laura, who found herself cast out. She was the only one immune to Pascale's charm and kept out of her way; she wasn't immune to jealousy, though, and waited impatiently for Alice to return to their friendship.

Despite the season Alice was struck down that summer with several of her minor illnesses. Pascale joined her in bed and sang Rolling

Stones songs with a tuneless, husky accent, and stroked Alice's forehead to help her sleep. Robert, who'd always withstood sickness with Stoic grit, now feigned it, only to be sent packing because he couldn't fake the symptoms. Assuming Alice had only been doing the same, but successfully, he cornered her one day by the fruit trees. Pascale caught him twisting each of Alice's limbs in turn: she grabbed a stick and gave Robert a furious beating which caused even him unaccustomed, squealing tears that brought Mary outside and almost cost Pascale her job. She was only saved from being sent straight back to France by her capacity for rational argument: a long discussion took place in Charles' study, within a silent house in which four children all held their breath, at the end of which a compromise had been reached whereby Pascale promised not to strike anyone with a sharp or indeed a blunt instrument, in return for the children to refrain from bullying, sarcasm and mimicry, a once-and-for-all truce that lasted a whole day.

The object of the boys' desire was short, with a slightly bent nose, eyes close together, olive skin and the close-cropped hair of a gamine, and she was as sexy as they thought she was. When she took the children to buy sweets in Mr Singh's store young men of the neighbourhood gaped from a distance.

'What eez wrong wiz Ingleesh boys?' she asked seven-year-old Alice. 'Zey don't even know 'ow to whistle.'

They did, though, rack their brains for excuses to visit the house on the hill, and Stanley and Edna got fed up with answering the back door to obscure offers of assistance or purchase. Did they need anyone to mow the lawn? Would they like to buy this used rabbit hutch for the kids or that second-hand radio in perfect working order? Edna pondered those offers at length, but Stanley soon cottoned on, and told them to bugger off.

When the children went back to school Pascale left to take up her place at the University of Rennes. And the house was plunged into a period of mourning, as if to make up for the fact that such had failed to occur after Robbie's death.

From that day James, as if in psycho-metabolic response to his first love's departure, began to put on weight.

'It's only puppy fat, little man,' his mother tried to reassure him. 'I think it's sweet.' He thought she might prove this by kissing his pudgy cheek or hugging his chubby body, but she was floating past him.

'You're getting slow!' Lewis yelled at him on the football field when James failed to reach a miscued pass up the wing.

'You'd better drop back into midfield,' the games teacher at their new, comprehensive, school told him.

'What's wrong with not being a scrawny skeleton anyway?' Simon complained at tea. Simon had *always* been tubby.

'He's right,' Edna agreed. 'Anyway, your body's got to find its own size, and at your age it tries out different shapes to see what suits it.' She set plates of sandwiches and soggy cake on the table and poured glasses of milk. James noticed her wedding ring squashed in place by the flesh of her fingers.

'But it hurts sometimes, Edna,' James told her. 'In my legs.'

'Oh, that's growing pains, child. Everyone has them. You'll be shooting up tall before you know it.'

Maybe she said that because she recognized James' envy of his best friend: Lewis was growing taller, and even thinner, by the day.

'What a waste,' Garfield moaned. 'The Lord done *made* you for fast bowling.'

One Saturday James and Lewis were cycling slowly home from a boys' football game, along the wide cycle path beside the link road connecting the north of town where their school was with the south-east where they lived.

'What are you going to be when you grow up, Lew?' James asked.

'*I* don't know,' he replied indignantly, as if the question were totally absurd. 'A politician, I suppose. Or music something. *I* don't know.' He carried on cycling in silence, but he couldn't think of any other options, so he asked James:

'Why? What about you?'

'I want to be a footballer of course,' James replied emphatically.

Lewis laughed, indulgently. 'That's your problem. You're a dreamer, Jay.'

Lewis was probably right. James didn't enjoy being at a bigger school. He hadn't joined any of the gangs that formed, broke up and reformed every few weeks; he made friends with other boys and girls independently, some of whom only spoke to each other in his neutral company, until he was a kind of loner but with an alternative, part-time gang of his own. The lessons bored him as much here as they had at primary school, and he lost the superiority he'd consoled himself with in mathematics, as other children were either brainier than he was or else caught up and overtook him. He found his mind drifting in the classroom, the teacher's voice becoming distant, the text-book going out of focus, the hard desk-seat and everything else in the physical world softening, receding, disappearing, as his mind drifted into space. The lessons passed him by. He was unengaged. He didn't know why.

'I know, I've noticed,' Charles agreed with the headmaster, at the beginning of James' second year. 'Like his mother. Don't be afraid to use discipline, you have my full support.'

Fortunately for James, discipline was going out of fashion. It was the end of the summer of love, when force was met with flowers. Zoe's father dropped her off home from a six-month trip to India and she appeared in Simon's class – her absences setting her back two years at school – smoking flat cigarettes that smelled like bonfires and wearing a bandanna and beads. Instead of sending Zoe home and telling her not to come back until she was wearing the school uniform, her form mistress, a young woman newly arrived from teacher-training college, only asked if Zoe could get her a caftan dress like hers.

Even Charles surprised everyone with his tolerance. When a free music festival was held one Saturday afternoon in the park on the hill below them, and then continued all night, keeping everyone awake, Charles came down to breakfast not in a foul temper, as expected, but in high spirits.

'Young people should enjoy themselves while they can,' he announced. 'Responsibility comes soon enough.'

Simon, emboldened by his father's unpredictable indulgence, asked Alfred for a bouquet of marigolds, and he entwined them in his hair. Since, encouraged by Zoe, he'd recently dispensed with a tie and given up tucking his white school shirt inside his trousers, the garland gave him the look of a young and decadent Roman emperor. Charles came home from work one day and saw his chubby eldest son sitting by the pond with two of his friends: between them they were strumming a guitar with one string missing, blowing a harmonica and beating a tambourine, while singing a song in loud tuneless voices. '*Come, mothers and fathers throughout the land . . .*'

Alfred in the rose beds, Edna at the kitchen window, James and Alice coming at that moment out of the front door, and his chauffeur: all watched Charles jump out of the back of the car and stride across the lawn.

'*Then don't criticize what you can't understand . . .*'

The witnesses could tell from the abruptness of his movement and his hunched shoulders that the man in charge had blown a fuse, and was about to throw one of his tantrums.

'*Your sons and your daughters are beyond your command* . . .'

Simon and his two friends, however, were playing and singing with their soulful eyes closed, so they didn't see Charles coming, and they didn't interpret the tremor of his furious footsteps making the ground tremble beneath them, until it was too late.

'*Your old road is rapidly ageing.*'

Charles grabbed the harmonica out of the mouth of a ginger-haired boy and tossed it in the pond. Then he picked the boy up and threw him in after it.

The tambourine man, a short, bespectacled and spotty boy called Rupert, leapt to his feet. In a moment of panicked inspiration, as Charles strode over to him, he threw the tambourine into the pond himself, perhaps hoping by such an act of propitiation to escape the same fate himself. If so, he was wrong. He landed with a spreadeagled splash out of all proportion to his size.

Charles turned to Simon, who was in a state of shock, his constitution unable to cope with the plethora of abject emotions with which his father's behaviour had besieged him: fear, shame, confusion, ridicule. Charles came right up to Simon. But he didn't touch him. Instead he inclined his head towards Simon's and proceeded to bellow in his face.

'If I ever find you wearing flowers, playing a ruddy guitar, singing those songs, mixing with these morons or in any other way making fun of your father, you won't know what hit you! Understand?'

Simon didn't respond. He was dumbstruck.

'Good!' Charles declared, and he strode across the lawn and into the house. It was the first act of rebellion of Simon's youth; and also the last.

Mary was furious with Charles' disgraceful behaviour, but maybe he had his own reasons beyond those of a tyrant. He'd been in a strange mood all that week, since the previous Sunday lunch, at which Alice had revealed the awareness of her own mortality at the age of eight, in a moment of illumination. She'd been absent from the conversation for some while, with that faraway look of hers that showed she was thinking of something else, when she suddenly snapped back to reality and interrupted her father:

'Daddy, I'm going to die one day, aren't I? We all are.'

Most people apprehend the inevitability of their own demise through their children, whose very existence reveals the inexorable cycle of birth and death, but in a benign fashion. So it was for Charles, except that in his case his fourth child opened his eyes not through the simple fact of her being but rather with a direct statement.

'I'm going to die one day, aren't I?' she said. 'We all are.'

Charles looked at her. 'Are we?' he asked. Then he collected himself and said: 'I'm not.'

'Yes, you are, Daddy,' Alice assured him. 'I just worked it out. You see, we live with angels for a long time, then one day they say: "You! Go and live with that family down there!" And so we're born. We live here. And then we die again.'

'Then what?' Charles asked, disarmed by his daughter's matter-of-factness.

'I don't know,' Alice admitted. 'We might go back to the angels or we might just go to sleep for ever.'

'Oh,' Charles replied.

'It's a bit sad I suppose but it doesn't really matter, does it?' Alice proposed. Then she asked Edna if there was any more summer pudding.

At primary school the children had little conception of what their parents did, or their parents' relationship to each other. In his second year at comprehensive, however, James began to realize that a good many of his fellow pupils' fathers – and mothers, elder brothers, aunts and uncles – worked in one capacity or another, in this or that department, for his father's company. It was something none of them spoke of. Just occasionally he interrupted a conversation from which stray words informed him that they were discussing his father, swapping some story of the generosity or the wealth or the temper of the man-in-charge. They would stop what they were saying and clumsily change the subject, more out of embarrassment than any kind of resentment, since apart from the odd father sacked on one of Charles' whims they were mostly grateful to him for providing an increasing number of jobs: it was a boom time. The business was expanding in all directions and Charles was investing in new plant and machinery, and building new workshops and warehouses. The factory site was coming to resemble a small industrial village.

When the students from the college of further education in town tried to follow their successful sit-in of the principal's office with a march to the gates of the factory and a declaration of solidarity with the oppressed, put-upon workers, whom they proposed to join in a strike designed to turn that purgatory of capitalist exploitation into a co-operative of the proletariat, they stood shouting all day until their voices were hoarse. When, at four o'clock, they heard the blare of a hooter, and saw hundreds of men in overalls carrying lunchboxes walking and cycling towards them, they thought for a brief moment that the workers, inspired by their clarion call, had mobilized themselves along the assembly lines.

It was a brief moment indeed. The gates swung slowly open by remote control and the factory workers poured out and, setting off home at the end of their shift, succeeded in entirely ignoring the fifty or so long-haired students, who were left lying disillusioned in the road, placards broken, noses bleeding from stray elbows. They happened to be studying in the wrong town.

Things were also changing in the big house on the hill. They seemed to see more of Charles' face in the newspapers, and hear his resonant voice on the radio, than at home. He was always having meetings in London and other cities, sometimes travelling in a helicopter that took off from the lawn.

The children weren't sorry: when Charles was away Mary was more relaxed. Not that they saw much more of her – when he was gone she spent even more time in her dressing-room, which had recently developed beyond being a study. Mary created a bedsit inside her own house by moving a divan in there.

James came up to ask her for extra pocket money for a new pair of shin-pads and found her sat staring out of the window. Her jowls were pasty, he saw creases at the sides of her eyes and grey hairs he hadn't noticed before in her long brown hair, and it struck him that his mother was growing older.

'Mummy—'

'Zut!' Mary jumped. 'You shouldn't creep up on people, James,' she said, recovering. 'You startled me.' He could smell her sour whisky breath.

'Mum, why have you got a bed in here now?' he asked her. 'Do people need more sleep as they get older?'

'Don't be so rude!' she gasped. 'Look, it's quite normal. You know I find it hard to fall asleep in the first place, James; I have to take pills to help me. If your father wakes me with all his snuffling and snorting, then I can never get back to sleep. I get scared he'll crush me.' Mary laughed and lit a cigarette. 'Be off with you, little man. I'm working.'

Charles, not wishing to lose face, moved a bed into *his* dressing-room, hoping to convince the children that it was a mutual arrangement. When Charles was at home Simon came in in the mornings and joined him, sitting on Charles' bed as his father talked back to BBC newsreaders and politicians on the radio while he shaved.

Without Charles' loud and blustering presence the large house was quiet and empty. Simon came home from school alone and went straight to his room, where he stayed until he heard Edna bang the gong for supper. And afterwards he returned there.

'Hey, Simon,' James asked him, 'do you want to play darts in the scullery with me and Lewis?'

'Lewis and me,' Simon corrected him.

'Yeh, OK; Lewis and me. Do you want to or not?'

'No.'

'Why not?' James persisted.

'Homework,' Simon told him. Charles had given Simon his own telephone for his fourteenth birthday; Simon's friends who knocked on the door and asked for him were directed to the phone in the hallway and told to dial his number.

'What are you doing?' they asked. 'You want to come out?'

'I'm busy,' he told them, and replaced the receiver. Since his father had thrown his friends into the pond he didn't seem to want to see them any more. He had a television in his room, too, and James and the others often saw the sad blue light seeping out from under his door.

Robert's friends from school weren't the kind to spend time playing in each other's houses. He achieved intimacy with boys he'd fought with; once they'd bruised and bloodied each other then they could embrace in the afterglow of combat, blood brothers, and then indulge in delinquent acts in wastelands and derelict buildings.

Robert's companion when he was, rarely, at home was Stanley. Robert followed him as James had once followed Alfred around the garden, though less in his case a gabbling distraction than a small, silent shadow.

Stanley was a practical man. He took the view that every man-made device could, since it had been designed and assembled by other men, be understood by him.

'All you need is common sense, lad,' he told Robert. 'Don't be scared to have a go.'

Stanley could take apart any broken machine, study its mechanism, isolate and replace the defective part and put it all back together again in full working order. Whether it was a combustion engine, an electric device or a plumbing unit made no difference: nothing daunted him. He laid an old sheet out on the floor and placed upon it nuts and bolts, washers, wires, screws, pistons and gaskets, committing their connections to each other to memory as he did so. His fingers, flattened and thickened by physical labour, closed around a spanner or screwdriver, his knuckles large as walnuts.

It wasn't in Stanley's nature to be openly friendly with anyone. He didn't invite Robert to give him a hand when he got out the long ladders to clear the gutters, and neither did Robert ask if he could. He just stepped forward and placed his small, steadying weight on the bottom rung. Theirs was an almost wordless relationship. They could drive in the pick-up to the builders' yard to pick up sand and cement or wood and nails and drive all the way back again without a word exchanged between them.

When James saw how engrossed his brother was he suspected he was missing out on something. It was obvious that Robert's silence was not lack of curiosity but pride, a reluctance to display his ignorance of how things worked: all they said, under the bonnet of Mary's Zephyr, were things like: 'Pass the big daddy, lad,' or 'Do you want the adjustables or the mole-grips, Stan?'

So James squeezed between them and annoyed them both by asking a stream of questions: 'What's that do? What makes it bob up and down like that? Why's the plug so small? Maybe there's a leak. Why don't you just hit it with a big hammer?' He left, though, before they had to tell him to, because in the event James found a car engine utterly captivating for about two and a half minutes, and then he found himself yawning with boredom.

Although it would have been difficult for anyone else to tell, from his stony expression, Robert never got bored. He loved the smell of grease and oil and hot metal, of a blowtorch on flux, the feel of a ratchet-spanner tightening a nut, the sound of an idling car engine improving as he adjusted the points. He marched around the house in a cut-off pair of Stanley's old blue overalls carrying a screwdriver, pausing to check and tighten loose things like doorknobs and saucepan handles. Outside, in the back yard, delivery men sometimes mistook the ten-year-old son of the man-in-charge for a midget mechanic.

When Stanley needed to do some welding the blue-purple flame and the showering sparks entranced Robert. Stanley told him not to look at the flame, but when he saw that the boy clearly couldn't help himself he gave him a helmet of his own, punching extra holes in the headband, and it hung like a shield in front of Robert, covering most of his torso.

Edna sent Laura out with mugs of tea and bacon butties for 'the men', as she called them. When he heard that, Robert was unable to stop his stony face from cracking into a fleeting smile.

Having recovered from Pascale's brief intrusion, Laura and Alice at nine were more like sisters than ever. Although they looked quite different – Alice with her porcelain skin and rich auburn hair, slight and fragile, Laura still resembling more her mother than her father, robust and bouncy, with short brown hair – they spent so much time together that for a time they took on the same rhythms, had the same thoughts and adopted each other's mannerisms. Alice would stroke a brother's arm absent-mindedly at tea, while Laura acquired Alice's habit of suddenly being seized with some strange idea and running off to do whatever it was had sprung into her head: her dolls needed to be taken outside to enjoy the evening air, or she had a compulsion to check that the goldfish in the pond hadn't been eaten by a neighbour's cat. They often slept together, Mary or Edna finding them in one or other of their bedrooms and seeing no point in moving them.

James was closer to the girls than to either of his brothers. Simon hadn't minded James joining in, when he was bored, the impromptu parties of which Simon was host and ringleader. His sudden withdrawal was unequivocal, and he didn't like being pestered when he was, he said, trying to do his homework in front of the television in his room. And neither did James find common interest with Robert, who liked hunting animals and taking machines apart, and thought football was for idiots running around like demented rats.

Lewis had to pick up his sister Gloria from primary school and look after her till his parents came home from work, and often Garfield would then dragoon Lewis into accompanying him to his allotment between the football ground and the cemetery.

'Come along, boy, you're not too young to start earnin' yer keep with a few chores,' he told him.

'*Dad*,' Lewis moaned, 'me and James have got to practise keeping the ball up.'

'And if James wants to help dig a few spuds he's welcome.'

James and Lewis exchanged pained looks. 'See you tomorrow,

Lew,' James told him with a twinge of guilt: there were limits to friendship, and gardening was one of them.

So, since he derived little pleasure from his own company, James found himself spending time with the girls. At first Laura's presence tempered his enjoyment: her being there emphasized his being the older brother at a loose end, trying to worm his way into their games; and there was also something in her manner, her self-confidence and composure, that he felt reproached by. He couldn't pretend he didn't know why: it was because she made him feel immature, which he knew he was. He was impatient, for one thing: he could never suck a sweet for more than a few seconds before biting and crunching it up and swallowing, no matter how hard he tried not to; while Laura could make hers last for hours, and would stick out her tongue to reveal a shard of barley sugar still undissolved upon it. And James still loved running along the corridors of the house for no reason, just for the sake of it, although growing pains were a regular ache in his hips. And he enjoyed pretending to have nose-bleeds with the aid of tomato ketchup, and telling terrible jokes.

'What's the difference between a buffalo and a bison?' he asked at tea in what he imagined to be an Australian accent. They all ignored him.

'You can't wash your hands in a buffalo!' James declared.

'Arghh,' Simon groaned.

'It's not funny, you idiot,' Robert said, as James laughed at his own joke.

'It's not *that* funny,' Simon agreed.

'What's the joke? I don't get it,' Alice complained.

'I'm going upstairs,' said Simon.

Only Laura smiled, wanly. 'I think it was very clever, James,' she told him. And that shut James up. He preferred being ignored to Laura's patronizing indulgence. Still, it was a small irritant. He liked showing them the best trees to climb in the garden and how to hide in the pile of autumn leaves and jump out and surprise old Alfred the gardener wheeling another barrowload towards it. He liked helping them shell chestnuts for Edna at the kitchen table.

'Why have you got red hair, Alice?' Laura asked her. 'I've been thinking about it.'

'Robert told me I was found in a dustbin in Gath,' Alice replied, unperturbed.

'Don't take any notice of *him*,' Laura reassured her. 'He's horrible.'

They played endless games of Monopoly on winter afternoons in

Laura's room, games in which Alice lost interest: she went off to the lavatory and forgot to come back, so James and Laura finished on their own. James taught her to play chess with a set Mary had once given him when he was ill, and their relationship found a happy balance: Laura was engrossed by the game, while James was gratified by the fact that he could beat her, and so discarded his inferiority complex in her company.

Once or twice thirteen-year-old James fell asleep on Laura's bed, with the chess set scattered between them; when Alice found them there she yawned, and joined them.

'Well, I think it's sweet,' Mary assured Charles, having made the mistake of telling him.

'Sweet?' he repeated. 'He's not a bloody *girl*, woman! At his age he should be trying to crawl into bed with nineteen-year-old women, not nine-year-old girls! And his own sister at that! Can't anyone keep an eye on things when I'm away?'

Charles gave all three a dressing-down and they were forbidden to share a bed, but the next morning Alice was found in *James*' bed, which was a first. They were worried that she'd inherited the sleepwalking propensities of her mother, but it was just that she couldn't understand what it was they'd been doing wrong and her father's tirade had only upset her. Simon had to explain that it wasn't wrong, just a question of custom, which Alice accepted. She didn't do it again; she wasn't a sleepwalker. That particular characteristic would, as it turned out, jump a generation.

It was a Saturday afternoon in October 1969, a quiet weekend. Charles was away. Stanley had taken Robert with him, in matching flat caps, on a shooting expedition, after rabbits on Jack's farm: Robert was too young for a shotgun like Stanley's, but he had his own air-rifle. The girls had gone to the children's cinema club and been invited by Zoe to a farewell tea afterwards in Agatha's flat above the projection room. She'd come to the house in the morning, just to say goodbye to James. He was confounded by the compliment.

'Why me?' he beamed.

''Cos you're my favourite, sweetheart,' Zoe told him, taking a drag of her herbal cigarette. 'Didn't you know that? I mean, you lot are all hopeless, with that bully of a father and your strange mother.'

'Strange?'

'But you're the best of the bunch, James. Anyway, I've got a favour to ask you.'

'What?' he asked, while wondering whether he should tell Zoe that just about everyone at school thought *she* was the weirdest person anyone knew. She never did any school work, but was always reading odd and forbidden books.

'Keep an eye on my grandma, James. She won't admit how old she is and she won't stop working twenty-four hours a day. Dad's useless, he doesn't notice anything, but I have. And if she goes too batty, you write and tell me. I'll give you my address.'

'Where are you going?'

'The Pyrenees. It's in France. Dad knows some groovy people on a commune there. He just wants to check it out, but I might hang out for a while.'

'What about school, Zoe?'

'I'm seventeen now, James. I don't have to go any more if I don't want to. And I don't.'

When she left she gave him a hug that smelled of caftan and patchouli. Her bracelets tinkled and she had to extricate her glasses from his curly hair.

'Take care of yourself, sweetheart,' she told him.

James forgot to point out to Zoe that he didn't go to the cinema much any more, since the Saturday matinées clashed with football.

Garfield drove James and Lewis to their game that afternoon against the Northtown Boys at the top of Stratford Road. James wasn't looking forward to it. He loved football more than anything else in the world, and he found it hard to admit how much he'd come to dread their Saturday matches. Within two years he'd been transformed from the star player in their primary-school team, the fastest runner, a boy for whom walking was unnatural because he had impatient limbs and his body would rather be running, into a tubby, slow, ungainly lurcher in almost permanent discomfort. And not only was his no longer the first name put down on the team sheet, he knew that if things carried on the way they were, soon he wouldn't get into the team at all.

Lewis, ironically, was moving in the opposite direction: he'd not improved as an athlete but he'd learned to compensate with anticipation, using his brain to get to where the ball was likely to arrive before boys quicker but less intelligent. He was also so much taller than opposing attackers that it never occurred to them that he didn't know how to head the ball, and they rarely challenged him. Above all, though, he'd already begun to display the qualities of leadership: without its being obvious how, or why, it just began to happen that other boys would follow his advice, gather round him in the playground, and generally seek his favour. The games teacher, Mr Rudge, wisely perceived Lewis's standing and made him captain above more gifted players, and thereby Lewis's place in the team was assured.

James knew – his father had warned him – that he had gone from being a big fish in a small pond to a small fish in a big pool. Charles exhorted him to work as hard as he'd once done. 'Life's a race, James,' he continued in language he thought James would understand. 'It's vital to get an early start.'

James also knew that the fat that swelled upon him was bound to have slowed him down. 'Look at the two of you!' Garfield chuckled at James and Lewis. 'You growin' in opposite directions. Slow down, boys!' he laughed. 'Funny thing is,' he added, 'you'll prob'ly end up the same size.' Which was no consolation to a boy trapped in the present.

But these were minor factors, he knew above all, compared to what everyone called his growing pains. Since they'd begun a year or so before they'd been getting steadily worse, changing from an occasional ache into a permanent one, and recently he'd been startled by stabbing, breathtaking pains that shot out of his hips. At the previous Wednesday's training session after school they had begun with the circuit-training Mr Rudge had brought with him from the army, a punishing series of push-ups, press-ups, jumps and squats, which ended with twenty sit-ups: each one made James wince with pain. By the time the others were completing theirs James had managed only ten. His eyes were closed and his teeth were clenched.

'I'm watching, lad!' He heard Mr Rudge's voice, and knew it to be directed at him. He'd positioned himself at the back, behind Dave Broomfield, their big goalkeeper, but Mr Rudge's eagle eyes could pick him or anyone else out among fifteen straining boys. James carried on: *twelve, thirteen.* He could hear the noise of the other boys' exertions cease around him; now only the gasping of them getting their breaths back. *Fourteen.*

'Come on, lad, put some effort into it!' He could tell from the voice that Mr Rudge had come forward and was standing above him. James had his hands clasped behind his neck. He touched the ground behind him and he took a deep breath and thrust his head and torso up and forward towards his knees. The sharp pain – a raw nerve pincered between bones – attacked again and he let out a brief whimper.

'Oh, we're crying now, are we, lad? Did you hear that, boys? It must pain poor James here more than it does any of you.'

James did another sit-up and it hurt even more, but he bit his lip to stop any sound escape his mouth. *Sixteen.* His eyes were shut fast inside his clenched face, but he felt tears seep into the sweat running down his cheeks.

Seventeen.

Mr Rudge, who missed nothing, saw them too. The boys' parents marvelled at his patience with their sons and they appreciated the discipline he instilled. He also had a way of both castigating and exhorting boys at the same time that let them know he expected more of them than they were giving. He believed in them, that they had more to give, and his imprecations generally stoked a boy's self-belief. But he was an old soldier, and the one thing that irritated him was weaknesss.

'The poor boy's suffering, isn't he, lads? Come on, James, that's it, push!'

Eighteen.

James didn't think he was going to make it, but even in the midst of the pain that engulfed him there was still something inside him shouting to be heard, not a voice exactly, not even a thought, but an inarticulate, unformed force at the centre of his being. If it could have spoken itself in this moment of crisis it would have been shouting: 'I can do it, I'll show you you big bullying FUCKER.' But it came out as a groan of anger through his clenched teeth: 'Aaargh!' *Nineteen*, as his torso broke through the wall of pain that it hit when it reached a certain angle in its arc towards his knees. His brow touched them and then went falling back.

'You're *soft*, lad, aren't you?' came the voice from outside. And the voice inside yelled back, 'Aaargh!' as James broke the pain again, the last time. He'd made it, his hands behind his head snapped apart and slapped the ground either side of his legs as he leant back, sweat pouring, heart pounding.

James opened his eyes: beyond his own two feet were two much bigger ones, spread apart.

'What's wrong, lad? What's the matter, eh? Why are *you* having so much more trouble than the others?' the voice boomed down.

James tried to catch his breath to answer, but it kept bursting out of him before he could grab it.

'I can't hear you, lad. I asked a question: what's the problem?'

James leaned back a little, still looking at the ground. He gulped a draught of air. 'It's my legs, Mr Rudge,' he spluttered. 'My legs hurt. Growing pains in my legs.'

'Ah, *growing* pains, is it?' Mr Rudge said with bombastic sarcasm. '*Growing* pains, again?' Then the voice abruptly changed. '*Every* boy has growing pains. Yours are no worse than anyone else's. You have to *fight* the pain, lad; that's what'll make you a man. Now,' he added as to James' horror he saw those two big football-boot-shod feet step forward and onto his ankles, the studs biting into his flesh, 'now, since you enjoy sit-ups so much, you can do five more for us. Give the other lads a *proper* idea of how it's done, eh?'

James wanted the ground beneath him to soften, soften, to gently give way and let him sink into it. The other boys were sitting and standing around, watching, enjoying this humiliation. They don't know, he thought. They don't *know*.

'Come along, lad, we're waiting,' Mr Rudge declared, grinding the studs of his boots a little into James' ankles. 'We don't have all day.'

James closed his eyes as he fell back, feeling his eyeballs slide upward in their sockets, and he clasped his hands behind his head. You're right, Mr Fucker, he thought, his willpower finding its inner voice. I'll do it, as his brain blazed. I'll be a *man*!

Now, as Garfield drove Lewis and James towards the game that James was dreading, he admitted to himself that on Wednesday evening he'd named his growing pains for the first time in months, and only then under extreme duress. Earlier he'd stopped complaining about them because no one took them seriously and he didn't want people to think he was a moaner. But they'd continued to get worse and at some point the *reason* he didn't mention them changed: he knew that something was going wrong inside him; something serious.

It was an undistinguished game. Mr Rudge put James on the right of midfield. 'You may not be fast, lad, but anyone can run up and down. Help out the defence, support the attack. I want to see some work.'

So James tried to work as hard as he could. But the play swirled around him and the ball was always running a yard away, just out of reach. And although the pain got steadily worse through the first half it only stabbed him once when he stretched to keep the ball in play, and once when he was forcefully tackled.

At least James was playing on the far side of the pitch from Mr Rudge, who as usual was pacing up and down the touchline and issuing a non-stop litany of barking orders: 'Don't mess about with it back there, Sean! Get rid! Good boot, boy! Now – up! Up! Move up! Ah, get stuck in, lad! Now back behind the ball! Back, Kenny! Get back!'

But in the second half he was right there, a few feet away, patrolling the touchline, and James could almost feel his raging breath on his neck: 'Get in there, James! Hit him, boy! Good lad! Now get rid! Not *backwards*, boy, hit it upfield! Give it distance! What's wrong with you?'

When James caught sight of the substitute Steve Halliday taking off his tracksuit trousers while Mr Rudge peppered orders in his ear, he knew with absolute certainty that he was about to be taken off. He'd never been substituted before. Wretchedness, anger and relief fought within him. Then he realized the ball was coming in his direction.

The ball was flying across the pitch, directly along and above the half-way line, tracing it like a plane about to land. It was just another miscued or thoughtless pass into nowhere. But it was coming towards him.

'Good boot, lad!' he heard Mr Rudge's voice calling. James could see that the ball was going to bounce on the half-way line and sail off into touch a few yards ahead of him, and he set off towards the spot. An opponent was approaching from the opposite direction.

I'm going to get it, James decided. I'm going to show him, as he ran with all his strength, tracking the flight of the ball as he did so, and seeing out of the corner of his eye the other boy running. The ball hit the ground and bounced up and continued on its mindless course. James struggled forward, the other boy got nearer, the ball was coming across from the side.

Time is elastic. When a football's pinging around the penalty box time's all panicky and rushed and there's no time to think. Now, though, time was expanding. Every muscle and sinew of James' body was straining to reach the ball before his opponent, just feet away now, but time slowed and his mind was lucid even as his lungs and limbs burst and he realized that, yes, he could reach the ball a fraction of a second before his adversary. The ball would be two or three feet up in the air but James could stretch his leg and toe it away; but, just as surely, a moment later the other boy's boot would come up and kick his from below. And because James would be at full stretch already, the impact would shoot up into his hip and bite like a clamp into his nerve-ends.

Time was elasticated. James could see clearly what was about to happen if he carried on. He had plenty of time to consider pulling out and in fact it wouldn't matter if he did, because not only was the ball in an insignificant area of the pitch, but also he − or indeed the other boy, whoever reached the ball first − would be unable to do any more than toe-poke it into touch for a throw-in to the other side and, anyway, he was about to be substituted. It even occurred to James that he could pull out at the last possible moment with a flourish, like a matador, exaggeratedly making it clear to everyone that he'd outsmarted his dumb, lunging opponent, and trotting smugly off to retrieve the ball for his throw-in. But that, he knew, would have been to fail to meet the challenge of the moment.

So James lunged forward, straining, stretching his leg out, urging his foot towards the flying ball as the opposing boy charged towards him. His toe just reached the ball before the other boy's boot came crashing up into James' foot: he felt a piercing, sickening jab of pain and he heard his own yelp of animal agony as the world spun out of control, and then he hit the ground.

Steve Halliday was already trotting onto the pitch when Mr Rudge helped James off.

'Good lad,' he said. 'Well played, son. Good tackle. That's what we like to see.'

James glanced back over his shoulder and saw one of the opposition take the throw-in: he hadn't even gained a free kick for the team for his moment of futile courage. Mr Rudge patted him on the head and turned back to the game, instructions resuming instantly, automatically, from his lips. James started limping towards the dressing-room. After a few paces he heard Mr Rudge's voice directed towards him.

'Where do you think you're going, James? Put Steven's tracksuit on to keep warm.'

James ignored him and kept on walking.

'Did you hear me, boy? You come back here and cheer the lads on!'

James gritted his teeth and carried on. He could hear Mr Rudge's voice filling up with anger, and the sound of it pleased him almost as much as it scared him.

'All *right*, then! You keep walking, James Freeman! You keep walking now and you walk right out of this team!'

James didn't stop and he didn't turn round, but he had the feeling – he wasn't sure – that the game itself had stopped and not only Mr Rudge but all the players, and the referee, and assorted parents and other spectators, they were standing still and watching him limp across the grass, away from the game he had loved and now hated, towards the dressing-rooms. When he realized that he was sobbing he didn't know whether it was from the pain or from the confusion. Behind him Mr Rudge was shouting something else but he couldn't hear what, the voice was getting smaller; he could hear his own voice telling himself, over and over whispering inside his head: 'I'm a man, I'm a man, I'm a man.'

James turned the shower on and by the time he'd peeled off his kit the water was running hot. He stepped beneath it. The water soaked his hair and ran down over his face, his neck, his shoulders, his front, his back, as he shifted position. It flowed down his stomach, hot water, over his genitals, his bottom, his thighs, knees, calves, feet, hot healing water. He wasn't sobbing any more, he was crying, shaking; but it didn't feel like crying, it felt good. The pain in his hips melted away, and the pain in his head, too. He found a bar of soap on a rack by the taps and rubbed it into his hair until there was a thick lather, which rippled down his face. Then he soaped his body all over, and when he'd finished he stood there till the hot water had washed all the soap away.

After he'd dried himself in the empty dressing-room – alone in that echoey chamber meant for a squad of athletes – he sat for a while fully dressed, his kit packed away, staring at nothing. 'Fuck you, Rudge,' he said aloud, and his broken voice sounded brave and resonant. 'I'm alive and I'm all right. Fuck all of you.' The resonance of his voice hovered and died.

'This isn't happening to me, God,' he whispered.

James left before the others came in and sat in the car with Garfield, waiting for Lewis. He was sure Garfield would say something, would give him some moral advice about how a boy should conduct himself; but Garfield didn't say anything.

Lewis was the first out of the changing-rooms.

'You've really upset Rudge,' he told James as he got in the car. The omission of the prefix 'Mr' was a small but brave act on Lewis's part: James saw Garfield's reaction, a disapproving glance at his son.

James knew the omission was for his benefit, a comradely gesture, and he appreciated it, although he didn't reply. They drove home in silence.

They dropped James at the gates of the big house. Lewis passed his bag to him, and caught his eye. 'It'll work out all right, Jay,' he said. James nodded, and turned to the gates.

He limped down the drive; his right hip hurt more than his left – it was hardly pain in his left, just something there that didn't feel right, like his right hip had been a year earlier. He considered what he'd do when he got in and he decided to take a bath, a deep, hot bath after football, and then he realized he only wanted to get more relief from the pain, already, so soon after his long shower. Time was running out. They were wrong; they were all wrong. It wasn't growing pains inside him, there was something serious the matter, it was getting worse, and it was time to tell someone.

But who? Charles was away, and that was just as well: his father would chivvy James along, maybe organize a party for him or take the whole family out to his favourite restaurant.

Of course, it was his mother he had to tell, and there she was, planting bulbs in the corner of the garden that was hers, bent over in an old mackintosh and wellies. He turned and limped across the grass in her direction. Mummy, I am sick, he thought, hold me and help me. Mum, I need you. And then he imagined her face cloud with remote anxiety. James stopped, forgetting his own self-pity for a moment, and he decided that he didn't want to burden her. He turned and walked back towards the house.

Why was Zoe leaving again? She would take him seriously, wouldn't she? He approached the house. At the left side the gate to the back yard was open: a grey Mini-van was parked with the bonnet open; most of the engine was on the ground beside it, with various disconnected leads and tubes spilling over the grille and wings, like a patient hideously abandoned on the operating table. Stanley was forbidding, he didn't like James, and *he* wouldn't ask someone for help, he'd take care of his problems himself and would expect anyone else to do the same. Edna, on the other hand, would sympathize. Maybe he should tell Edna. He stopped walking. She'd give him a hug and a mug of hot chocolate and cut him a thick slice of cake and make him feel a lot better; but he didn't think she'd do any more than that, she wouldn't really know what to do outside the kitchen. She kept a first-aid kit in the pantry, she was the one they ran to with a knocked elbow or a scraped knee. But now he needed more than a dab of Acraflavin or a plaster.

He resumed walking, not to the back door as usual but on past the front of the house. It was a shame Simon had retreated into his room; there was something kind about Simon and if he'd only be himself, instead of wanting to be like their father, he might have been the person to talk to. There wasn't anyone else, James accepted. Except, it occurred to him, for Laura, and sardonic laughter burst from his mouth: four years younger than he was, she was about the most sane and able person in the household; one person you could trust with your body *and* your frightened heart. And she was nine years old; it was ridiculous.

James' bitter laughter had died by the time he realized that he'd limped right past the front door. He was despairing of finding help and he was beginning to shrink inside, he wanted to hide, he wanted to curl up and be taken care of; he wanted to curl up into a small boy and be wheeled in a wheelbarrow away from his mutinously altering body. He walked between the rose beds, past heaps of compost and grass cuttings. A wispy column of smoke rose from a pile of leaves.

James reached the closed door of the large potting-shed. It was hung on sprung hinges, so that Alfred could push it open with his hands full, like a waiter. He kept the hinges well oiled: the slightest squeak would annoy him. James pushed it and it opened without a sound. He stepped inside. The door swung silently closed behind him. The great shed was dimly lit, window panes obscured by tomato plants trained up the outside wall.

James stood still, barely breathing, as his eyes became accustomed to the darkness. Along the side wall beneath the window ran a long, wide shelf covered with seed-trays and pots of cuttings and bulbs. The largest, back wall directly ahead held Alfred's tools, hung on nails. They emerged from the dark as James stood there, tools of every size and horticultural use, from trowels and secateurs, to spades and hoes, to rakes and scythes. They emerged each with their own specific, evolved shape; as old as Alfred himself, thought James.

On the brick floor of the shed were mowers and wheelbarrows and carts. The light seemed to spread across the shed to the far wall, along whose length ran Alfred's work-bench with its two − light and heavy − vices, sawdust, odd pieces of wood. But James didn't want his eyes to become accustomed to the darkness; he didn't want to see everything. He climbed into a cart, curled up and closed his eyes.

The surgeon at the orthopaedic hospital was a tall, dignified man with white hair and a bow-tie whom James recognized from his parents' cocktail parties. He manipulated James' legs at odd painful angles, murmuring as if in agreement with himself whenever he caused James to wince. He showed little desire to look James in the eye, as if the boy would be awkward to get into focus. Instead he addressed Mary: 'You two go and get an X-ray, and then I'll explain the problem.'

They waited in a large, bright, high-ceilinged room while a woman in a white coat ushered people behind a screen and stepped out to push a button: the machine hummed; she went back behind the screen for a few moments, reappeared and pushed the button, half a dozen times for each patient. The woman's movements in her work were jerky like Stanley's, methodical and accomplished. James watched her. He wanted Mary to hold his hand. He didn't like waiting.

Eventually it was his turn. The X-ray woman didn't look at him either, but ordered him onto a table and positioned his limbs with one hand while manoeuvring the huge X-ray camera with the other. Each time she disappeared, and the machine hummed, like some animal hypnotizing its prey before striking, James closed his eyes and wished that he could disappear.

Back in the surgeon's office they looked at the X-rays pinned to a light-box.

'Your son has a slipped femoral epiphysis,' he explained to Mary, pointing at the ghostly images. 'The top of the thigh-bone fits into the hip-socket, and with a small number of children — about one in a hundred thousand — when the bones are soft in puberty the femur slips and grows out of place.'

'How bad is it?' Mary asked.

'The right one's rather advanced. We'll have to cut the femur, alter its position, and put a plate in to clamp it in place. The left is much better; we'll just insert some pins. Then have James back in in a year or two and take out all the hardware.'

James scrutinized the ethereal X-rays of his damaged bones. It was hard to believe they were his bones. They looked all right to him, but then he had nothing to compare them with.

His mother asked practical questions; she sounded like someone else. 'How long will he have to stay in hospital?'

'Two or three months, Mary. Maybe a bit longer.'

'When do you want to operate?'

'Bring him back in tomorrow, and we'll operate the day after.'

That night back at home James lay in bed with his teeth chattering, but he also felt relief that he was going to be dealt with. He found that he was almost able, by concentrating hard, to detach himself from his body (he couldn't quite detach his face, for some reason, which was why his teeth chattered) and in his imagination he gave over his body, a willing sacrifice, to the surgeon's knife.

The hospital smelled of anxiety and antiseptic. The boys' ward had sixteen beds. Two or three held recent arrivals from the operating theatre, drowsy and moaning. The rest looked both bored and alert: they were trapped in their beds, with legs in plaster, or hooked up in traction, or inert beneath cages that kept the weight of the bed-linen off their limbs. One small boy with bent legs hopped from bed to bed on a tiny pair of crutches.

'You been in before?' he asked when he got to James. His voice was gritty and cheerful. 'This is my ninth time. One for every year. I'm nine, see.'

'Right.'

The boy didn't look big enough to go to school. 'It's not too bad here. The teacher's a dragon but the food's all right.'

'I'm not allowed to eat anything today,' James told him.

'Well, you don't want to be sick when you're being operated on, do you?'

James thought about it, and agreed. 'What's wrong with you?' he asked the boy.

'It's my legs this time. I've had them done twice.' He leaned on his crutches and swung his legs. 'They're the wrong shape, see? I've had the lot done,' he added proudly. 'Hips, kidneys, bladder, knees. I'll probably have more after this. What's your name?'

'James Freeman.'

'I'm Graham Wrigley. Well, James, I better be off to say hello to the girls. They're only through that door, see? That's another good thing about this place.' He turned and hobbled away towards large double doors.

A male nurse from another ward took James to a small, grubby bathroom. 'Got to shave you for the operation,' he said. James couldn't work out what he meant.

104

'Hygiene. Drop your pyjamas.' He used a safety razor, warm water and no soap. His fingers were thick and clumsy. James watched him shave the pubic hair that had recently grown and he tried to rise further away from his body. I'll float away, to the clouds, he said to himself.

The surgeon visited him on the ward with four attendants half his age and half his height. His gaze was again averted from James, and he addressed his subordinates, as he marked each of James' thighs with a red felt-tip pen.

James woke up from the operation in a dim room feeling as if he were immersed in a thick, poisoned liquid. The pain was hot and deep, and although they gave him painkillers at regular, lengthy intervals it only went away when he slept, fitfully. The next day he woke up back in the boys' ward. Gradually the stupor of the anaesthetic wore off and he realized he couldn't move: he was encased in plaster from his right ankle to his upper chest; only his left leg and groin were free. The plaster kept him prone.

A nurse passed his bed. 'I need to go to the lavatory,' James whispered.

'You need a bottle or a bed-pan?' she asked. To his blank response she added: 'Do you want to pass water?'

'I suppose so,' he whispered.

She brought him a glass bottle and he lay it between his legs and inserted his penis into its neck. Nothing happened: his bladder remained full. He didn't know what to do. Peeing wasn't a mechanical action, it was just a thought from which the action followed. Flowed. But now it didn't, and James had no idea what to do. The nurse came back.

'I haven't finished yet,' he whispered, and she went away again.

Panic and embarrassment made his skin prickle. Eventually he took the empty bottle from between his legs and placed it on the locker beside the bed, with its paper bag over it. An hour later he tried again. Again nothing happened when he wanted it to: his muscle, gland, whatever it was, failed to respond to his thought. It was visiting time: the ward was filling up, families clustering around the other beds. He lay with the bottle in place.

I want to leave this body, but I can't, he thought. I just want to be a passenger, but the machine's no good. He'd planned to render his body superfluous, not really there, the plaster cast in effect hollow, but it hadn't worked. He couldn't escape.

In the end, when he'd given up and was thinking about something else entirely, urine trickled into the bottle, and his bladder emptied.

Time passed slowly. James had never realized how long a day lasts. They were woken briskly by the night nurses at six a.m., washed, given a drink, and then left to lie there like fish beached by the sea of sleep for hours before breakfast.

Being an orthopaedic hospital, with children in for lengthy periods, there was a school. The teacher turned out to be a solid, middle-aged woman with a hearty disposition and a dragon's bad breath. She sat on the beds of children with no means of escape – tied down by traction pulleys, weighed down in plaster – and breathed her breath at them, wilting the flowers visitors had brought and sending the more sensitive children into inexplicable relapses. Maybe that's what Graham meant, he wondered, but he couldn't verify it because Graham had left.

'I'm going home. I don't mind,' he'd told James.

'Are you going to need another operation?'

'Of course I will. I always do, see? Why are you whispering?'

'I'm not whispering,' James whispered.

'Well, there's no point in trying to keep secrets in here,' Graham advised him.

Mary visited James with one or other of his brothers and sister. Simon was sometimes unable to resist the temptation to sidle away from James' bed and watch the television that was on a high shelf in the opposite corner of the ward, but generally he was as talkative as he used to be; he seemed to be recovering his old friendliness.

'Father took me to Munich for the weekend,' he told James one Monday. 'I spent all day in the hotel.'

'What on earth did you do?' James asked.

'Everything! I watched lots of TV, they had loads of channels, and I ordered room service when I was hungry, and explored all the floors. The porters told dirty jokes to teach me German. What did the elephant say to the naked man? I'll tell you in English, of course.'

'Don't know, Simon. What did the elephant say to the naked man?'

'The elephant said: "How do you manage to eat with one of those?" You get it? Uh-oh, here's Mum. I'll tell you another one next time.'

106

Robert didn't say much more than usual. He sat eating James' grapes, spitting the pips into a plastic cup. One day, though, Robert appeared with a present, something heavy wrapped in an old comic, which James tore open to find some kind of crowbar. He studied it a while, then looked up to see Robert grinning slyly at him.

'What's this for?' James asked.

'It's a jemmy,' Robert told him. 'So you can break out if you have to. I couldn't stand it, cooped up in here.'

'Well, thanks,' James said.

'You know what I read?' Robert asked. ' "You've got to be planning your exit even when you're making your entry." ' He flashed his stony grin at James.

'That's good,' James nodded.

'Yeh. But also,' Robert exclaimed, 'jemmy's a nickname for James, see?'

'Really? I didn't know that.'

'It was in this dictionary.'

'Hey, that's clever, Rob.'

'Yeh, well, people think I'm stupid, but I'm not. I'm not stupid. I've got to go now.'

Charles wasn't sure where James' condition lay between sickness and injury; he couldn't work out whether his middle son was a malingerer or a heroic victim. He would visit three days running only to berate James for lying in bed all day, or else not make an appearance for weeks but then arrive with a boxful of presents to make up for his absence. There were so many toys, games and sweets that James distributed them among his fellow patients after Charles had left. He hoped his father wouldn't recognize his gifts in another boy's hands, but he needn't have worried: Charles didn't even know what they were, having sent Judith Peach out to buy them.

'I trust my boy's not giving you any trouble?' Charles boomed at the nurses.

'Don't worry. We tickle his feet if he does,' they told him.

'By God, James, I wouldn't mind being in your position myself!' he declared, before leaving.

Mary, though, visited every day. Sometimes she came floating in smiling gaily, and older boys in the ward ignored their own visitors to watch her. More often she looked tired and worn in the harsh light. She brought James small, practical things like tissue-wipes, a long straw and a pen whose ink defied gravity so that he could write lying on his back. She conferred with the surgeon and the ward sister and the teacher; but when it came to talking with James they ran out of things to say.

'You're a brave boy,' she told him. 'Sister says you're recuperating quicker than we could have hoped for.'

'Thanks, Mum,' James whispered in reply. He knew that there was lots more he could say, that he was frightened, and he couldn't work out why this was happening to him. What had he done wrong? Had he done something to deserve it, or was it someone else's fault? Would he be able to walk again, to run, to play football? And when could he go home? If he asked the first question, confided the first anxiety, then the rest would tumble out, all his brave bottled-up wretchedness. But then all questions would have to be asked, and there were things he needed to ask her. He wasn't sure what they were, but there was something wrong, and he didn't want to know what it was.

'I'm trapped here,' he said once when she appeared, frustration at his immobility overcoming his reticence. 'I'm trapped here, Mum.'

'I understand, James,' she said, 'I know that feeling,' and her face clouded over as it did on those days she retreated into her dark room; James wondered who was visiting who. He almost asked her, then: 'What's the matter, Mum? What is it? What's wrong?' But instead he lay back and stared at the ceiling and she sat in her chair in silence, while the ward bustled and echoed around them.

Despite such awkwardness, however, James enjoyed his visitors, because the days were so long and tedious, and he and his fellow patients shared only a desultory comradeship. Edna brought him bouquets of flowers from Alfred that he was too busy to bring himself and also paper bags with doughnuts and biscuits and cream pastries she'd made. She looked around the ward surreptitiously before handing them over.

'They don't feed you properly in here, anyone can see that,' she told him. James didn't have the heart to tell Edna he didn't want her home-made delicacies: he decided that the weight he'd put on over the last couple of years had contributed to his condition and that he'd prefer to be thin again. He declined the desserts from the hospital food trolley, ate all the fruit visitors brought, and despatched Alice to the girls' ward with the boxes of chocolates he was given, along with Edna's pastries.

I'll leave this bed thinner than I got into it, he told himself. His diet helped in other ways, too.

'Have you had any motions yet?' a nurse asked him, scrutinizing her clipboard.

'What?' he whispered.

'Have you had a bowel movement?'

It wasn't easy to lying down, and he went for days without being able to, his body filling up with food. They gave him laxatives and inserted suppositories up his backside, but nothing happened, partly because if he strained, the stitches in his hips screeched with pain. What a way to die, he thought, turning to shit from inside. Eventually they drew screens around the bed and administered an enema. He felt the soapy water gurgle and flood through his rectum, and with a gorgeous relief he felt the compact mass in there break up like a huge frozen river thawing and flow wonderfully out of him.

The only person he didn't much like to visit was his best friend. The rest of the time he was impressed by how well he was coping with his immobility, but whenever Lewis came in they discussed football gloomily, since that was all they knew what to discuss, and James' invalidity was a shadow across every word of the conversation. It was as hard for Lewis as it was for James.

'You'll be out soon,' he told James on his first visit, two days after the operation. 'Won't be long now, Jay,' he said the next time.

Lewis did, though, bring James a pair of water-pistols. James, like all the boys in the ward, fell in love with the junior nurses. Much of his sedentary time he spent wondering which was his favourite, beguiled by their sensitivity, sophistication and common sense. The only thing he disliked was that they tickled his toes whenever they passed his bed. There was nothing he could do about it except curse, which only encouraged them, and he was so ticklish that he couldn't help wriggling inside the plaster, his hips flaring up hot. So he asked Lewis to get him water-pistols and he waited until his two favourite nurses passed by the end of his bed.

'I just want to warn you, that's all,' he whispered. They didn't hear him, so he said it again louder, rediscovering in that moment his normal voice: 'I'm just warning you,' he said.

They stopped. 'Warning us what?' they asked.

'Just don't tickle my feet again, that's all.'

'I wasn't going to,' said one, taken aback.

'Good. Just as well for you.'

'What if we do?' asked the other one, bolder.

'You'll find out. Just you try it,' James challenged them. They looked at each other, grinned, and stepped towards the end of his bed. His hands were under the blanket, fingers gripping the handles of the water-pistols.

'I just thought I ought to warn you,' he reiterated. 'Don't say I didn't.'

They lifted the end of the blanket and took a foot each, and James waited a second or two before drawing his weapons and firing. He hit them both with thin jets of water. Shocked, they dropped back for a moment, but then rushed him, giggling, one each side of the bed, braving the oncoming water. They grabbed his arms and the three of them tussled. James was surprised by how strong he was: he wouldn't let go his finger on the trigger and water sprayed on their uniforms and faces and into the air. They all three saw the ward sister at the same moment: she was standing in the doorway of her office, glaring. The nurses let go of James' arms and scampered away.

Alice was the only one to whom James' incarceration seemed nothing out of the ordinary, the most normal thing in the world, and although it wasn't, of course, her denial of reality made it bearable. Alice took James' condition in her stride, as if it were as natural coming to visit him here after school as popping into his room at home: she told him what she'd been doing, tidied his bedside cabinet, and swapped the latest jokes and riddles, until at some point her attention shifted, she'd have that look that said she was thinking of something else, and she rushed off. She became a regular visitor to the girls' ward next door, and as well as sharing out James' surplus chocolates and sticky buns she assumed the role of go-between, delivering messages of greeting and declarations of love between immobile admirers.

Laura came with Alice, and when Alice set off to tour the beds of children without a visitor of their own Laura stayed with James. They played chess, her hand absent-mindedly stroking his arm. She smiled when he made a good move, and he noticed for the first time that when she smiled two tiny dimples appeared above her cheekbones.

'I'll beat you one day,' she promised.

'It's a shame you're not older, Laura,' he told her.

'Why?' she asked.

'I don't know, really,' he admitted.

'Yes, you do,' Laura stated. 'You wouldn't say it if there wasn't a reason. You ought to think about it.'

'You're right,' he said. 'Don't be so grown-up. Come on, it's your move.'

James dreamed of a wedding in the ward. The nurses were brides-maids in their uniforms and the patients in their beds were the congregation, except that they were mostly members of his own family: Robert was in the bed next to his, staring at him, and Simon was on the other side, speaking rapidly, nonsensically, with two male nurses. The teacher came over and bent towards him.

'I'm your best man,' she told James, enveloping him in her bad breath. He grimaced and closed his eyes, and leaned forward to accept her lips. They began to kiss but were interrupted by music: the sister was playing an organ in a corner of the ward, glaring around the room as she struck the keys. In a bed opposite James his mother was moaning with pain.

'She's only just come out of the operation,' he said loudly. 'She shouldn't be here yet.'

No one took any notice of him. They were all watching Alice, who was running around the empty centre of the ward shouting out: 'Where is she? Where is she?'

The bride, apparently, had disappeared. Everyone was mortified. James was filled with fear and shame. Then he felt something on his arm and looked across to find Laura there beside him, calmly gazing out of the huge glass doors at the green lawn, and softly patting his arm. Suddenly something struck him and he discovered that Robert was shooting a water-pistol at him, except it wasn't water that came out but hot urine. It splashed on his face. He couldn't move to escape, and didn't want to take his arm away from Laura. As if as a form of protection, the teacher began caressing his face, and then his neck and chest, smothering him with her hands and her bad breath, and he realized that he'd had a bottle between his legs for a long time, unable or unwilling to piss. Now he felt it rush out of him in a fitful stream of relief, hot and pleasant, and he woke up from his first wet dream, his pyjamas damp and sticky.

By the time they took off the plaster, after three months, James was squirming inside its shell. They hardly needed to saw it: he could almost have sloughed it off on his own. His clothes looked comically baggy on him at the same time as being too short at the wrists and ankles. He was given a wheelchair in which he raced another boy along the corridors until the sister caught them at it and threatened them with being kept in hospital an extra week. He had physio-therapy sessions in the pool, and from the wheelchair he graduated to crutches: James was well balanced on them, agile, and he felt, strangely, more athletic than he had for two or three years. The day before he was let out of hospital – four months after entering it – Mary came in and went with him back to the surgeon's office.

'You're a very fortunate young man,' he told James while pointing at the X-rays on which they could see clamps and pins inserted into James' femur and hips, clearly defined metal in the ghostly bone.

'If this had happened fifty, a hundred years ago,' the surgeon continued, 'you'd be crippled. Thanks to modern orthopaedic surgery, you can look forward to a normal, reasonably active life. Of course,' he added, 'you'll be restricted in some ways: no contact sports, and keep off bicycles, I should. But otherwise, you're fine. Come back in a couple of years and we'll take the hardware out.'

Mary pushed James back to the ward in a wheelchair, along endless echoey corridors that had exhausted him on his crutches on the way there. James felt like Odysseus in a film he'd seen in the cinema – wounded but defiant as he was carried to safety by Menelaus from the battle on the Trojan plain, holding his crutches like spears.

James got into bed.

'Would you like us to get the nurses a big box of chocolates?' Mary suggested.

'Yes,' he agreed, 'and some flowers. They're always putting flowers into vases for other people. It'd be nice for them to have some of their own.'

Mary smiled at him. 'You'll be all right,' she said, nodding. 'You'll be OK, James. You're a little man, now. And you'll soon be free again, that's the important thing.' She poured him a glass of orange juice. 'I've got something to tell you,' she said.

'What, Mum?' he asked, matter-of-factly, his question followed by a flush of anticipation as he realized that she was about to announce some special treat to make up for his ordeal. Maybe a holiday or some extravagant present awaited him. Her face was serious.

'James, I'm not going to be there when you get home.'

This was a complicated gift. Maybe a riddle had to be solved first? She'd have to give him a clue, though.

'What do you mean?'

'I've stayed while you've been in hospital. I'm going away, James.'

James could feel the blood draining from his head. It didn't make his mind any clearer.

'Are we going on holiday?' he whispered.

Mary chewed the inside of her cheek for a moment, and frowned.

'James,' she said intently, looking him in the eye, 'I'm leaving.'

'But you can't,' he whispered.

'It'll be best for everyone, for all of you, in the long run, I'm sure.'

'What's he done?' James blurted out.

'Don't blame your father, James,' Mary said. 'Don't blame him. None of you must do that.'

James lay back on the pillow.

'It's not an easy decision,' Mary was saying. 'I've thought about it for a long time.'

James stared at the ceiling and tried to lose himself, but he couldn't shut out the sound of her voice.

'It's something I have to do, James. I don't expect you to understand. Not yet, anyway. Maybe one day.'

There was silence. James wasn't sure whether he'd succeeded in blocking out the sound of his mother's voice or whether she'd finished. Maybe she'd just leave now, just slip out without another word, that would be best. But then he heard her again.

'James?' she said, and paused. 'I'm sorry, James.'

'Go away,' he said, without knowing he was going to.

'You know—' she began.

'Go away,' he interrupted, whispering this time because words were bricks in a dam, each one spoken escaped and loosened it, and it mustn't loosen now, in front of her, no, sir, no way. Hold on.

There was a long silence. Eventually he heard her chair squeak back across the floor, her clothes rustle and her footsteps receding.

He wondered if he could disappear inside himself. Sometimes on the edge of sleep the ward expanded and he felt himself tiny, minute in a corner of the vastly enlarged space. Maybe now he could achieve the same effect by willpower and then instead of living as his body he'd live deep inside it, and spend his life exploring its tunnels and caverns, rivers and caves and chambers. No. That was silly. Better to leave his body altogether. He didn't want it, he didn't like it. Fly away through the ceiling. Then the frightening thought came to him: I might find myself left behind. I'm not ready to die. I'm scared to die. I am my body. I am what I don't like.

It grew dark outside. The lights came on in the ward. Visitors left. James didn't move. He was pretty sure one or two people asked or said something to him but he ignored them and they must have gone away.

Maybe then, he thought, I can stay here just like this, still, barely breathing, and time can carry on without me.

Unlike the rest of the boys in the other beds, James didn't notice the commotion of energy that swept into the ward until she'd identified him and come over to his bed.

He smelled patchouli oil a moment before he heard her voice.

'Well, sweetheart, I've had to look through every single ward of this bloody hospital to find you.'

James opened his eyes. It was Zoe, but he hardly recognized her: her hair was cropped, her skin was brown, she was dressed in flowing silk.

'We just got back from Goa. Harry – I don't call him Dad any more, James, it's so *passé* – ran out of bread. They said you'd been here for *months*, poor baby, I didn't have a clue.'

Suddenly a middle-aged staff nurse was striding towards them.

'You can't be here now, young lady,' she exclaimed. 'Visiting hours are long over.'

Zoe didn't even bother to look at her. 'Stuff it, sister,' she said over her shoulder.

The nurse stopped in her tracks. 'I *beg* your pardon?'

'He's my long-lost cousin. I haven't seen him for *years*. Go away and leave us alone.'

To James' surprise the nurse turned around and scuttled off.

'Well?' Zoe said. 'Are you pleased to see me or what?'

James wanted to smile but his bottom lip was unstable and if he smiled he knew the dam would burst.

'Blimey! You could at least say *some*thing before I give you a great big hug, James Freeman.'

James could feel his whole face trembling.

'What's the matter, honey?' Zoe asked him, her grin vanishing. She leaned closer.

'What's wrong, sweetheart?' she asked again, reaching both her arms towards him. One hand touched his shoulder and the other touched his cheek and, groaning with the surrender of his willpower, James both pushed himself up and collapsed forward, letting the dam burst, into her arms.

3

THE SWIMMING POOL

THAT NIGHT MARY RESUMED HER SLEEPWALKING. AT LEAST, THAT was the official version. It was what Charles told everyone, and maybe he believed it himself. It was accepted by the coroner: death by misadventure, a tragic accident. Perhaps it really was; James would never be sure. He didn't repeat what she had told him, even though they found a suitcase in her dressing-room, half-packed with her clothes.

They found Mary's body in the back yard, broken glass and splintered mullions all around it. She'd gone straight through her dressing-room window on the second floor and had escaped for good.

Charles watched undertakers drive Mary's body away. When they'd disappeared through the wrought-iron gates he turned around without a word to anyone and made his way to his study. There he lit the open fire and sat down in an armchair facing it, and proceeded to stay there the rest of the day, staring at the flames, stewing with what appeared to be a mixture of stupefaction and rage.

One person after another came to ask or tell Charles something but his brooding presence was so forbidding that no one dared disturb him, except for Robert, who in the late afternoon went in and sat on the arm of his father's chair, leaned on his shoulder, and stared into the fire for a while beside him.

Charles stayed where he was through the evening and into the night. He left Edna to comfort his grieving children and stirred himself only to put more coal on the fire. The members of the household went to bed upstairs while he sat with his anger and sadness churning inside him.

In the morning Edna found Charles in the same armchair, staring at the dead embers of the fire. She made him a mug of tea and placed it on the reading table beside him: he failed to acknowledge Edna and ignored the tea, upon whose cooling surface a white film settled; Charles remained immobile, as his heart turned to ashes.

The rest of the family gathered for breakfast, mourning and leaderless, and remained around the kitchen table. Until, around ten o'clock, there was heard in the silent house a sharp intake of breath, an armchair seat's springs reasserting themselves and the approaching footsteps of an 18-stone man.

Charles appeared in the doorway of the kitchen and looked around those assembled. They looked back at him, awaiting his lead. Without a word Charles knelt on one knee and opened wide his arms, and the three of his children who were there rushed towards him.

Charles Freeman moved into action. He sought out royal undertakers who came up from London with their own team of manicurist, beautician and dresser, with the last of whom Charles spent hours sifting through Mary's wardrobe. Ignoring the vicar's advice on Anglican custom, he had Mary laid out, adorned in her wedding dress, in an open coffin: the drawing-room was filled with scented candles and a botanical garden of flowers; mirrors were draped and voices hushed as relatives, friends and acquaintances filed through the makeshift mausoleum to pay their respects.

The morticians succeeded in removing the crow's-feet from Mary's eyes, her odd white hairs, the resignation from the sides of her mouth and her anxious frown, leaving her looking in death like the teenage bride she'd once been. The visitors took one look at Mary and burst into tears at her tragic, futile demise. When they'd recovered they reminded themselves that she was also a thirty-five-year-old mother of four, and they wept again with pity for her poor children and her courageous husband.

Charles stifled the sobs that shook his own great frame to comfort them, offering mourners a grief-stricken version of his bear-hug, squeezing and shaking them at the same time. 'Yes, yes,' Charles snuffled, 'yes, you let them fall.' In his embrace the visitors – habitués of cocktail party or poetry group – let go of their own noisy sorrow.

James was brought home from hospital by Charles' chauffeur, and he watched people he was sure had hardly known his mother weeping in Charles' arms; he couldn't bear to be in the same room as his father.

The others were swept along in Charles' wake, taking turns in the drawing-room, accepting condolences. Simon stayed close to his father, both copying him and, in the manner of an eldest daughter rather than son, filling the space where Mary had been. He took it upon himself to embrace those visitors unable to face his father's bear-hugs.

Robert shed no tears, as if their mother's death were another childhood affliction whose symptoms he fought, and people understood his stoicism as evidence of deep feeling. As for Alice, she was taken under Edna's wing, moving between the drawing-room, where she grew faint in the fragrant, emotional atmosphere, and the kitchen, where she recovered.

James only crept in after everyone else had left. He lit his own candle for his mother each evening and sat silently beside her coffin. He wondered whether he'd left some part of himself behind in the hospital bed, because he felt frozen. It was as if *he* sleepwalked through those days, and woke up at the funeral.

It was a grand affair that Charles organized with more panache than any of his parties. The church was packed. The choir was augmented by singers from other churches, who sang requiems fit for a queen. Carefully chosen readings, prayers and hymns were followed by a eulogy from the diocesan bishop, who completed the impression that the deceased had been an extraordinary wife, a marvellous mother, a special friend, a rare, talented poet, a both exquisitely sensitive and unusually happy ray of sunshine in the mortal shape of a woman.

James sat fuming, and those who glanced in his direction saw not an angry child but a boy bravely holding back tears with a supreme effort.

Charles retained a solemn dignity throughout, but it was clear to all, from his ashen pallor, the hollow rings around his eyes and his crumpled shoulders that he'd neither eaten nor slept in his grief of these past days. As the coffin was carried out to the graveyard Charles, holding little Alice's hand, followed behind his three sons, the middle one poignantly hobbling along on crutches.

It was that picture that appeared in the local newspapers: the man-in-charge seemed to take on the dimensions of a mythic figure, even as he suffered tragedy like any other man.

'Your mother has left us,' Charles told them, gathered in his study back home. 'We'll all have to pull together and get along. I've considered employing another nanny or au pair but decided not to. Edna will look after us all, especially Alice. It's best for us to try and carry on as if nothing has happened. Any questions?'

'Can we go now, Dad?' asked Robert.

They reacted in different ways except that they all followed Charles' advice and copied his example. Simon spent more time with Charles than anyone else, without either of them mentioning Mary's suicide: they thus achieved an equality of denial as they drew closer together, giving each other comfort without realizing it. Simon went straight to Charles' office after school and helped his secretaries with their filing. They liked him because, unlike his father – whom he was coming increasingly to resemble, since he was now almost the same height as well as weight, and wore, even to school, the same dark suits, white shirts and silk ties, and the same short-back-and-sides haircut – his charm and humour were not erratic but constant. At first they were kind to him, knowing his mother had just died, but he was such an easy listener that soon they found they were telling him about their boyfriends or husbands or children; and before anyone knew it they were listening to and even acting upon the soundest advice they'd heard outside the columns of newspaper agony aunts.

The sixteen-year-old son of the boss, a carbon copy, a clone, rediscovered the charm of his childhood. Charles came across his son in the typing-pool telling the women there what men really wanted, and he didn't mind that it was only two o'clock in the afternoon. He ruffled Simon's hair when they got into his car at the end of the working day.

'You'll get into trouble, you will, my boy,' he said approvingly. 'I like to see you at the factory, Simon. See how it all works; pick it up in good time. You'll learn more here than they teach you in school. You've got to stand on your own two feet. Here's a fiver.'

*

Robert was so uncommunicative, so much his own person, no one noticed that he entered and left the house according to an ever more sporadic timetable of his own invention. He never told Edna when or whether he'd be in for tea or other meals.

'Leave the lad alone,' Stanley advised her. 'He knows how to look after himself.'

She tried to entice him with favourite foods, but since he'd never expressed an opinion of dishes laid before him – apart from bacon butties and mugs of tea – she realized it was a fruitless exercise, and they came to a tacit understanding that he was free to raid the larder whenever he was hungry.

Instead Edna lavished her attention on Alice, who began to spend so many nights in Laura's bed that they woke with cricked necks and stiff joints from squeezing their growing limbs into its space, until Stanley got Robert to help him carry Alice's bed downstairs and cram it into Laura's room. When the girls were together and Alice referred to Edna she occasionally dropped the 'your' from 'your mum'. The absent-minded slip irked Laura. She knew it would be cruel to tell Alice off, to point out that Edna happened to be *her* mother. But it clearly irked her: her eyes narrowed and there would follow a period of frosty silence between them of which Alice was quite unaware but that gave notice to everyone else that Laura was changing from her mother's daughter to her father's. Edna herself, though, didn't seem to mind at all: she was large enough in both heart and body to take on another, twin, child.

Others, too, stepped into the breach: Garfield told Lewis to keep an eye on his friend.

'You can invite him to stay the night if you want to,' he said. 'We may not have a mansion house but it's a welcoming one.'

Mary's oldest sister, Aunt Margaret, drove in with a great baker's tray full of fruit. She handed it over to Edna and stayed for tea, and told the children they could visit her farm any time they wanted.

'If you want to get out of the town,' she said. 'Get some fresh air in your lungs.'

One Saturday in that spring of 1970 Lewis came round to watch the FA Cup Final on television, in which Leeds United tortured Chelsea but couldn't beat them. Afterwards he and James went outside and sat on the lawn – James with his crutches on the grass either side of him – and practised heading a ball to each other. Then Lewis ate

119

two or three of the cream pastries that James couldn't tell Edna he wasn't eating himself, and James peeled an orange.

'You know,' James whispered to Lewis, 'they said I can't play football again.'

'It's not the only thing in life, Jay,' Lewis replied, with a voice that conveyed both authority and a certain lack of conviction.

'I know,' James agreed.

'You'll just have to think of something else to be when you grow up,' Lewis told him.

Being grown up seemed a long way away, but then on Sunday morning Zoe appeared. The others were all up and out already, and James was still in bed. Zoe burst through the door in a flurry of colour and the smell of musk.

'Out of bed, lazybones!' she exclaimed.

'Nnnnrgh,' James replied, pulling the covers over his head as she opened the curtains and light washed over his bed.

'What a mess in here!' Zoe cried.'How can you *live* like this? I'm going downstairs to make some tea. If you're not washed and dressed when I come back in *five* minutes, I'm going to tickle you into imbecility. Can you hear me, sweetheart?'

'Nnnnnnn.'

Sipping tea and orange juice, James told Zoe of his feelings of weightlessness while he was trapped in his hospital bed, of being there yet not being there, of the occasional sensation of being on the ceiling, looking down at himself and everyone else.

'I'm not surprised, James,' she responded, less impressed than he'd hoped she would be. 'Lying in bed like that so long, your astral body must have loosened its bonds with your physical one. Probably flew around a lot. Mine does too. Hey, if we'd thought about it we could have met up on the astral plane. Did you have any weird dreams as well?'

'Weird dreams?' he blushed. 'Um, no, not really.'

'I have a lot of weird dreams, James. I think I've got an unsettled psyche. You know.'

'Yes. Of course,' he whispered.

Simon and Alice came back from church and joined them, and listened to Zoe's stories. It turned out that she and her father had gone to the Pyrenees, stayed one night, then sped down through Spain and trekked around Africa for four months. Then they'd hitched a lift on somebody's boat to Goa, only to get on a plane and

120

come straight home, and not just because they ran out of money ('We never had any in the first place!' Zoe laughed) but because Harold had decided to become a student, something he'd overlooked at a more conventional time in his life, since he'd already set off on his travels.

'He's going to write a thesis in comparative religion,' Zoe told them proudly.

'What's a thesis?' Alice interrupted.

'Like an essay, stupid,' said Robert, who'd slipped into the room unnoticed.

'Well, I'm *so* sorry for not knowing,' Alice told him, making a face.

Laura appeared in the doorway. 'Lunch in ten minutes. Oh, hello, Zoe.'

Zoe reached her hand out to Laura. 'I'm just telling the others about Harry. He's going to compare English clergy with voodoo priests in Benin. Hey, you know,' she paused, looking at Alice and at Simon, 'he might want to visit your quaint church.'

Zoe joined the family for Sunday lunch, which Charles had decided was to become more than ever the focal point of their week. Whatever his own business commitments, he made sure he was home on Sundays, in the belief that sharing roast beef, Yorkshire pudding, roast potatoes, greens and gravy was the best way to keep the family together. As well as Stanley, Edna and Laura he invited relatives, like Aunt Margaret and her friend Sarah, Jack and Clare, and he told Zoe she would be welcome any and every Sunday.

'Thank you, Charles, I might take you up on that,' she replied.

After lunch, back upstairs, Zoe opened a canvas shoulder bag and handed round presents: she gave Alice and Laura bright Rhodesian scarves, Robert a rude fertility symbol from Mozambique, James a sandstone elephant from Somalia, and she let Simon smoke the thick joint she rolled in an elaborate ritual before their fascinated eyes.

'Are you going back to school?' Simon asked her, looking pale.

'I don't know yet. I don't have to. I may do.'

She told them stories of her travels, country by country, and they couldn't believe she was the same only slightly older cousin who'd sat next to them in the cinema a few months before. Simon staggered downstairs to fetch a jug of lemonade because his mouth had gone horribly dry.

Zoe took a sip and said: 'There was one day, in South Africa, we set off at five in the morning to walk up Table Mountain. We climbed all morning as the sun got hotter and hotter. We reached the top at midday; the sun was directly above. It was sweltering, we were pouring sweat. There's a café up there, they sold icy apricot juice. You know,' Zoe said, closing her eyes, 'it was like drinking gold.'

Charles told James that he didn't have to go back to school until the next academic year began in the autumn, as long as he did enough work at home to ensure that he wouldn't have to drop back a year.

Freed of the mindless routine of the hospital timetable, James stayed in bed till long after the others had left for school, but when he got up he didn't know what to do. He didn't *have* to do anything, and he began to suffer twin conditions of existence that would become his companions and which, later on, he would fiercely guard: freedom and loneliness.

James was disconcerted by what he'd found when he returned home to his own room. His possessions, his toys, were strange, alien objects that belonged to someone else, the child he'd been and left behind while encased in plaster. Not that he was anything like a man. He didn't know what, or who, he was. He hobbled down the stairs at 11 a.m. for breakfast and then climbed back slowly. He didn't miss running along the corridors, it was amazing how relative health and athleticism were: he was content to feel himself getting stronger and faster on his crutches.

Back in his room James sorted through cupboards and drawers and filled cardboard boxes with clothes, toys, books (save one of poetry), posters, Airfix models and albums of football stickers. Owing to his lack of mobility and his new-found patience, the task took several days, and James enjoyed every minute. When he'd finished his room was almost bare. One of the few things he didn't throw away was the camera his mother had given him that wedding day four years earlier, and which he'd forgotten about since. He snapped off the lens-cap and looked through the viewfinder. He scanned around the room and stopped, moved his head and stopped again, framing small sections of the empty room.

'This is interesting,' James whispered to himself. He hung the strap around his neck; the camera bumped against his chest with each step as he descended the stairs to ask Stanley to put the boxes with the jumble-sale pile in the garage and Edna to buy him a roll of film next time she went shopping.

*

122

The summer came. James graduated from crutches to walking sticks. His heading ability improved almost as much as Lewis's, but he doubted whether he'd ever actually kick a ball again. Lewis came round to watch the World Cup games on television, but although he sat spellbound by the beauty of the Brazilians James knew it was a sacrifice: Lewis would be better off watching with the boys he actually played with, with whom he could attempt to put the lucid geometries that they saw into practice themselves on the recreation ground.

James was happier with the more sedentary, mental geometries of chess that he played with Laura in a quiet corner of the house where no one would disturb them.

It turned out, meanwhile, that Zoe and Harold had got back just in time. Local residents and regular patrons of the Electra Cinema were so used to Agatha's fierce eccentricities that no one had noticed the signs; and the only one briefed to look out for them had been trapped in a hospital bed.

Agatha kept a blue Morris Minor in a garage at the back of the cinema. A local lad polished it once a week, and on Sundays Agatha drove it to church. She was a small, indomitable woman who peered at the road ahead through the spokes of the large steering wheel. Strangers wandering along Lambert Street on a Sunday morning did double-takes at the ancient, immaculate car that appeared to be driving itself, crawling along the sleepy street at a snail's pace, as if operated by remote control, until they looked closer and saw the top of Agatha's head, a dwarf at the wheel.

Agatha would have been a safe driver, except that she'd never quite mastered this fiddly business of left and right, and came close to causing a hundred accidents during her years of weekly, half-mile journeys: she either indicated left and then turned right (a cinematically comical sight that created the illusion of making the car appear to suddenly speed up) or else she operated the lever on the wrong side of the steering column, so that the indicators remained still, unblinking, as she turned the wheel, but the windscreen wipers scraped across dry glass.

Locals, despite the infrequency of Agatha's expeditions, had grown used to her unpredictable manoeuvres: they knew that a beep on the horn probably meant she was about to park, that a jet of windscreen-washing water spraying backwards over the roof heralded an abrupt lurch into St Hilda's Road where the church was. So they kept their amused distance. Strangers, on the other hand, had to dig deep into Sunday-morning-sluggish reflexes as, in front of them, a driverless Morris Minor came to an emergency stop for no reason at all, entirely without warning.

And yet, watched over by angels – perhaps because she was always and only ever driving between church and cinema – her car's bumper was not once dented, her blue polished paintwork never scratched.

When Agatha stopped driving to church people heaved a collective sigh of relief. They assumed she had accepted the inevitable frailty of her years. It never occurred to anyone that she'd forgotten where it was she kept her car; and then that she had a car at all.

In fact Agatha was as physically fit as ever. She had taken a daily spoonful of cider vinegar for years, to ward off arthritis and nostalgia, the twin curses of old age, which it did; only to give her another, which was to make her more crabby than ever.

When Agatha shouted out to the queue in the foyer that today's film not only had sound but it appeared to be in colour, too, they took no notice. Nor when she interrupted a screening with an unexpected interval and proceeded to clip people's tickets for the second time. Nor on the occasion she asked whether anyone had seen the piano player, and, come to that, where was the damn piano? When her projectionist arrived for work one day to be told, 'You can't come in here without a ticket,' even he took no notice because he'd had plenty of time to become accustomed to her rudeness. She'd been threatening every evening for a year or more to sack him if he couldn't get the film in focus and shouting at him to turn the volume up, even when people were coming out to complain that it was so loud their ears were hurting. So he'd learned to ignore her.

Harold and Zoe, though, were shocked by her decline: it was clear that not only her senses but her faculties too were disintegrating all at once. Zoe was unable to conduct a coherent conversation with her grandmother because she got tripped up on a word, the wrong one, and repeated it fixedly as if the movie had got stuck in a projector in her mind.

'Just like your Great-aunt Georgina, my sister, you are,' she told Zoe. 'You've got her spoons.'

'Her what, grandma?'

'Her *spoons*,' Agatha repeated, emphatic but frowning. She pointed at her own eyes. 'Just like hers, the same green spoons.'

Or else she spoke sentences whose parts came out in the wrong order, as if the reels had got mixed up in their cans.

'It's a popular ice-creams in the tray,' she said, when Zoe volunteered to be an usherette. 'Make sure you put lots of film tonight.'

It turned out that the projectionist, while hardly realizing he'd been doing it, had been covering up Agatha's forgetfulness for a long time – putting up the posters, ringing the local newspapers with the programme details, and ordering the popcorn. Finally, Agatha forgot herself: a few days after Harold and Zoe's return she looked in the mirror and failed to recognize the old woman staring back at her, because the passing of the last fifty years had slipped her mind.

Zoe made her a cup of tea and Harold suggested as kindly as he could that she might consider retirement.

'What did you say?' she asked, staring at the wall a couple of feet to his left.

Harold repeated himself.

'WHAT DID YOU SAY, WILLIAM?' Agatha shouted. He knew that was the name of one of her cousins, long dead, and assumed her poor sight and memory had combined to confuse her because of a family resemblance. He didn't realize how much of a resemblance; he didn't realize that she'd inadvertently revealed, for the one and only time, the identity of his father. So he said softly:

'It's all right, mother.'

'WHAT DID YOU SAY, WILL?' she yelled at him.

After a lifetime of severe self-control Agatha Freeman was coming apart at the seams, unwinding, unravelling. That night Harold and Zoe heard noises downstairs and descended from the flat above the cinema, and found Agatha in the auditorium shouting: 'BRING UP THE LIGHTS! WHERE AM I? WHERE AM I?'

She told Harold to go back to the farm and only calmed down when Zoe took her hand and led her back upstairs.

'Where are we going, Dorothy?' Agatha asked.

'We're going to follow the yellow brick road, Grandma,' Zoe told her.

'Oh, good,' she said. 'Oh, good. I am glad.'

Agatha's funeral was small and quiet, attended by those members of the family who'd not taken her rudeness personally, plus a cluster of film buffs grateful to her for introducing them to the French New Wave. They seemed at ease inside the church during the service taken by the vicar (a little older but still giggly) but when they stood outside around the grave with their sunglasses and pale skin they looked as much frightened as mournful. James wanted to take a photograph of their shoes, which all had holes in them, but he was too timid to remove the camera from inside his buttoned-up overcoat. He decided he preferred weddings to funerals. One of the film buffs threw a flower onto Agatha's coffin in the grave.

'The Sixties are over, man,' he confided in his nearest companion.

Zoe overheard him and gave him a scornful look. 'Don't be stupid,' she told him.

James carried his camera with him everywhere, although the first photographs he took with the roll of film Edna bought were so disappointing that for a long time he didn't ask her to get any more. He was content just to look through the lens, to get used to the world reduced to separated rectangles. For a while he was over-whelmed by the infinity of possibilities: there was no fixed, ideal framing for any subject; whenever he clicked the shutter (which he did even *though* there was no film in the camera) was an arbitrary choice. He found it difficult to keep the camera still; rather he moved it around, tracking the world before him – which itself was rarely still – as if he were holding a ciné camera.

The rest of the family asked him what he was doing. 'I'm practising,' he whispered.

They left him alone to practise, fed up with having to bend closer to hear what he was saying, especially since he didn't look at them when he whispered, he looked at the ground, so they couldn't even lip-read. The garrulous child, the gregarious boy, had withdrawn.

James spent whole days exploring the house through his view-finder. Furniture didn't move, and in the guest rooms, unoccupied for months on end, it seemed that time had stopped, and he was able to arrest the wavering movement of his roving eye. The closer he moved in, the easier it was, quietly approaching a vase on a window sill, a pillow, the panel of a door. The more he reduced the world, the more paradoxical depth he discovered, the more elements of texture, colour and light, of surfaces on different planes, of line. Sometimes he was unnerved by the fragility of things: he wondered how it all held together. Then he'd hear the gong for supper resonate from far below, or Alice's voice rend the silence of a room: 'There you are, James! Come on, it's time to go to the cinema.'

It took him a moment to remember how to form words. He blinked. 'You go on. I'm busy,' he murmured.

He looked out at the world, at little corners of the world, through his lens. It felt like looking out of a bubble; he was protected behind his camera. He was safe. He discovered that it was possible to get through the rest of the time in another kind of bubble. When he finally returned to school in the autumn he sat in the middle of the class and the teachers, unable to hear what he was saying, left him alone there. During the games periods – from which he was exempt – he inspected the quiet classroom, clicking his empty camera at aged inkstains and old graffiti scored in the wooden desks.

At home he sat silent at mealtimes but no one complained. James discovered that if you didn't demand anything from other people they demanded nothing of you; if you didn't speak they rarely addressed you.

'I'm just going off to practise,' he whispered, lurching away from the supper table: he got rid of the walking sticks but was left with the rolling gait of a seaman on dry land.

'What shall we do with the drunken sailor?' Charles boomed after him, chuckling, and James heard his father lead the others in a tuneless rendition of that childhood song as he climbed the stairs.

> 'Weigh hey and up she rises
> Weigh hey and up she rises
> Weigh hey and up she rises
> earli in the morning.'

James rose away from them.

> 'Put him in the scuppers with the hosepipe on 'im
> Put him in the scuppers with the hosepipe on 'im
> Put him in the scuppers with the hosepipe on 'im
> earli in the morning.'

The surgeon had been right: James could walk perfectly well. But he didn't venture far. He rarely went to the cinema with Alice and Laura, despite its being an opportunity to see Zoe.

'Someone's got to help Harold through college,' Zoe told him when she came to Sunday lunch, and so instead of going back to school herself she took over the running of the cinema. 'It's a home of my own, James,' she said. 'I've had enough of travelling for a while. And once I'm established, I'll be able to fund my own travels.'

The old projectionist retired and Zoe hired a man she'd met on the road to Marrakesh, but otherwise she did everything herself. She put the popcorn to one side and restocked the sweets counter with flapjacks, hazelnut bars and chocolate brownies from a wholefood co-operative on Factory Road. She found Agatha's mint-condition blue Morris Minor in the garage: those antique cars were just coming back into fashion, so Zoe took lessons, passed her test and drove it round town herself, almost as dangerously as her grandmother once had.

Every time she parked it in the garage, though, she thought it was a waste of space when she could leave it in the street for free. I could use this for something else, she thought, but it hadn't yet occurred to her what.

She took out a bank loan and replaced the once comfortable but now decrepit cinema seats with new, smaller ones that cramped tall men but allowed an extra row to be fitted at the back of the auditorium.

'I've got a plan to get the place going,' she told Charles another Sunday.

What Zoe did next was to inspect the programme, which consisted – as it had for years – of one film (plus supporting short) shown four times a day for one week. Then she walked outside and stood in front of the cinema, and watched the pedestrians walking along Lambert Street for a few minutes, before returning inside and ordering by phone every film distributor's catalogue.

What Zoe Freeman did before her time was to discern different audiences within the provincial town for different kinds of films, and to show old ones alongside the new: she organized mini-seasons reviving the Ealing comedies, Bible epics, science-fiction fantasies, a whole delirious night of the Marx Brothers, Shakespeare on film, and cinematic versions of whatever else was on the school syllabus, as well as Disney cartoons during half-term.

She initiated late-night screenings: on Fridays of pornographic films she was at first too young to legally watch, never mind order, herself (using her father's name on official forms) and on Saturdays of Sixties landmarks like *Zabriskie Point* and *Easy Rider, Woodstock* and *Valley of the Dolls*, at which hippies and Hell's Angels warily shared flapjacks and marijuana. The film buffs – who came to everything and whom Zoe teased, telling them the only films she needn't show were horror movies, since they were so like vampires themselves – rubbed shoulders with pensioners on Mondays, schoolchildren on Wednesdays and housewives on Thursday afternoons, squeezing their handkerchiefs while watching Rock Hudson and Doris Day. Zoe greeted them all, listened to their suggestions and complaints, and worked sixteen hours a day, until she was as well known in the town as her grandmother had been.

James missed that little revolution: he had his hands full with his still photography. He finally summoned up courage and took the huge step of putting film in the camera. He shot a number of rolls of film that Edna delivered to and collected from Boots when she went to the Wednesday market. He didn't want to show them to anyone else but he wasn't forceful enough to withstand Simon's, Alice's and Laura's demands to see them: James had been walking around clicking that stupid camera for over a year, when he looked at them it was invariably with one eye closed and the other hidden by the camera (as if their poor brother wasn't crippled but blind, and it wasn't a camera but a miraculous new medical aid). The truth was they possessed normal human vanity and expected to see snapshots of themselves; they were disappointed and perplexed by the close-ups of bedposts, chaircovers and a corner of the drawing-room carpet.

Simon turned them on their sides and upside down sympathetically. 'After all that,' he commiserated with James, 'there's something wrong with the bloody camera. I suppose the guarantee's run out by now?'

'There's nothing wrong with the camera,' James whispered. 'That's what I meant to take. They're called *still-life details*.'

'But they're so boring,' Simon frowned. 'There's nothing in them.'

Alice for her part looked at her brother pitifully. 'You're *strange*,' she told him; and then she remembered something she ought to have done earlier, and ran off.

'I think they're very interesting, James,' Laura said, but he could tell she was making an effort for his sake.

James looked at his photographs on his own. He studied them through a magnifying glass. He was as baffled as Simon, but for the opposite reason: there was *too much* in them. He realized he'd been overambitious. It crossed his mind that he'd be better off aiming to achieve the simplicity of X-rays.

'Of course,' he whispered to himself. 'That's it. Black and white.'

James asked Charles for some extra pocket money, Stanley converted one of the unused guest bathrooms into a darkroom, while Robert, in return for a 20 per cent commission, in cash, volunteered to procure all the equipment James needed direct from the warehouse at half-price.

'That's really good of you, Robert,' James responded in a surprised whisper.

'Yeh, well, I've got contacts,' Robert confided. 'Used notes, mind,' he added.

James spent hours in the darkroom. At first he was daunted by the discovery that the printing of photographs was a demanding art form in itself, especially with no teacher, but he soon found that actually there was nowhere he'd rather be than in the infrared, womb-like isolation of the darkroom with a DO NOT DISTURB sign on the door, and he had to spur himself on to take enough photos to develop in the first place. After a while, though – and perhaps in contrast to the hermetic cell of the darkroom – he ventured outdoors with his camera and explored the garden with the same detailed scrutiny as he had the house: he spent some weeks on a systematic project to photo-graph the petals of Alfred's roses, at various times of day and in successive stages of bloom and decay; then he selected one of the beech trees he'd once taught Alice and Laura to climb and took a sequence of pictures, taking a step backwards for each one, from a macro-close-up of the bark to a full-length study.

When he got to the end of a roll James trotted, swaying, into the house and up the stairs to the darkroom. He put the film, a take-up spool and canister and a pair of scissors into a changing-bag, and stuck his hands into the elasticated sleeves. He closed his eyes and saw images of what his fingers felt, and enjoyed the skill of a technician that he was acquiring.

What he loved most of all, like any budding photographer, was the emergence of an image on white paper in the developing tray, a moment of magic that never failed to excite him.

Some things change, and other things stay the same for ever. And then you realize they've changed too and you hadn't even noticed.

Simon had sat and failed most of his O-levels and promptly left school, on his father's advice, to embark upon an apprenticeship of business around the various departments of the company. Simon was becoming a self-confident and popular young man. He and James had swapped places: the boy battling with his worthlessness in the sad blue light of the television had made a deal with life, while the friendly child who'd preferred running to walking and couldn't stop talking had retreated into an infrared room.

Robert, meanwhile, came out of puberty even grimmer than he'd entered it. His voice when he used it was harsh, he stopped growing taller but his body took on the dimensions of a man, with wide shoulders and a powerful chest, and he slipped in and out of the back door at random: he would pass unseen among them, the only evidence of his presence a vaguely delinquent aroma of oil and sweat.

At weekends he went on shooting expeditions with Stanley, in identical flat cap and jacket, having graduated to a .22 rifle. Robert was like the son Stanley didn't have, they had the natural closeness of a silent master and his protégé. But even if they'd been by nature loquacious their relationship couldn't be spelled out, it had to remain unspoken, informal, because Robert, after all, was the son of the man-in-charge.

The one school activity that Robert took part in with any regularity was an extra-curricular one: on his thirteenth birthday, without telling anyone, he joined the boxing club run by the biology teacher in the school gym on Tuesday and Thursday evenings. Robert loved it at once: the sounds, the smells, the sweat, the pain, as twenty boys walloped punch-bags, shadow-boxed, performed punishing callisthenics and hit a thick pad held by Mr Bowman.

On that very first evening, after Robert had felt waves of nausea from doing press-ups, sit-ups and jump-presses, Mr Bowman handed him a skipping-rope and said: 'Now skip for five minutes, lad.'

Robert was dumbfounded. He'd never heard of *any* boy over seven years old skipping, still less a boxer. He didn't know *how* to – he'd never done it at any age. He quickly summoned up an image of Laura skipping in the back yard, whom he'd watched many times, and imagined his own limbs going through the same contortions, and then by a miracle of willpower and co-ordination Robert set off skipping around the walls of the gym.

Twenty boys of different ages who were grimly pounding punch-pags or lifting heavy medicine balls on and off their chests all stopped what they were doing in the same astonished moment, the sounds of leather on canvas and the boys' grunting and panting subsided into silence, as they watched Robert skipping around the gym.

And then their laughter started: smirks and snorts and suppressed guffaws burst forth into the open, echoey space and became shrieks and howls of glorious derision that bounced off the ceiling and rattled the climbing frames.

But Robert didn't hear any of them. He was locked into concentration on keeping his arms and legs co-ordinated: he was doing well, he thought with relief, keeping his eyes down, but he knew that if he relaxed a fraction then his steps would falter and the rope would get tangled up in his feet. So he didn't hear the boys who were falling on the floor in delighted abandon, including Docker Boyle, the fifth-form heavyweight, who was wetting himself, or the others who were whistling and whooping in his direction with tears streaming down their faces.

Robert had completed three laps of the gym when he wondered whether Mr Bowman would tell him he could finish or whether he should stop of his own accord, and that was enough for him to come out of his trance, sufficiently to become aware of the cacophony around him. And when he came to a halt and looked around, he realized it was directed at him.

'Don't stop, nancy boy! Keep going!'

'Yeh, go on, yer woofter, it's brilliant!'

Robert felt shame surge through him, and then anger too. He scanned the grinning faces before him, working out which one to hit first. And then, in an action so inspired, and so against his nature, that even Robert knew he hadn't thought of it himself – he didn't know *where* it came from – Robert pursed his lips into a cute, kissy smile, held the handles of the skipping-ropes out to the sides as if they were the hem of a skirt, and curtsied. And then he kicked up his heels and set off again, performing an imitation of a flapper girl he must have seen some time on TV. The boys in the gym fell about all over again, but this time with affection mixed in with their derision.

Docker Boyle lumbered over and ruffled Robert's hair with a boxing-gloved hand. 'You're all right, nancy boy,' he said. 'You're all right, son.' Robert was established.

There was no one else from his form there, and it was the one place where Robert was actually popular. While he played truant from classes with impunity, he never missed a boxing session.

Fortunately for Robert, once Mr Bowman adjudged him to have proved his commitment in shadow-boxing and exercises and let him actually start sparring with the other boys, the 'nancy' didn't stick, because Robert, despite his lack of height, could flatten almost every one of them (except for Docker, who merely absorbed the most fearful punches like a sponge, and Weasel Tanner, a flyweight who was so tall Robert couldn't quite reach his chin). But the 'boy' did,

132

and he started boxing against lads from other schools under the name of Rob 'Boy' Freeman.

Robert was born for combat, but the truth was he had the wrong shape for boxing: in the ring he came up against stringy boys the same weight but a foot taller, who kept his swings at bay with their long arms and wore him down; although when he *did* catch one of them they didn't get up in a hurry. After one defeat he said to Mr Bowman: 'Maybe I should find a wrestling club, sir. Maybe that's what I should do.'

'Wrestling?' the teacher replied. 'Wrestling's for *girls*, Rob, boy. No, you stick at it. You've got character.'

Robert felt no apparent need to share his hobby with the family. He never told them when his bouts were coming up, still less invited anyone to come and support him. They only knew they'd taken place afterwards, when they would meet Robert in the house with puffed-up eyes and skin bruised to hideous, fascinating colours.

Laura, with a sensitivity that showed she hadn't lost all her mother's qualities, contrived to enter puberty that spring at the same time as Alice. At supper in the kitchen, on one of the rare evenings that Charles was present, Edna whispered to him that their girls were young women now.

Charles loved to share things, and secrets were the best things of all to share. He thumped the table and got to his feet, declared to the assembled company that champagne was called for, and dragged Stanley off to the wine cellar.

Laura had a smug, pleased-with-herself grin on her face, Alice had her hand on Edna's arm, as they waited for their fathers to return.

'What's going on?' James whispered to Simon. Robert, his hearing attuned to the low level of James' speech, overheard.

'They've started bleeding, dumbo,' he told James in his grating voice. 'See, James,' Robert continued, 'our little girls here have grown up. Nice.' He stuck his tongue out at Laura and swivelled it between his lips, and did the same at Alice before Edna could stop him. Laura stared straight ahead in a blank state of shock. Alice burst into tears. Robert jumped up from the table and walked towards the door. Simon rushed after him:

'Come back here and apologize!' he shouted.

When Charles reappeared a few moments later with his hand on Stanley's shoulder, each holding a bottle of Dom Perignon champagne, returning to the kitchen they'd left moments before in a state

133

of celebration, they found Alice bawling her eyes out, Edna trying to persuade Laura to open the locked door of her room, Simon and Robert wrestling on the floor by the back door, and James swaying towards the stairs and the refuge of his darkroom. They looked at each other in bemusement, neither the man-in-charge nor the do-it-all fixer having a clue what to do. So they opened the champagne in the vague hope that their mad offspring would be calmed down by the popping of the corks, and toasted each other.

It took James the whole of the winter and spring to satisfy himself that he'd photographed the garden in sufficient detail, and then he tackled the outside of the house, covering it from every angle and in every detail. And then he had a dream.

He was standing at the top of the stairs on the landing above the hall. On the floor below people sauntered and jostled. Too many people. One of them, a man whom he didn't recognize, spotted him on the landing behind the banisters, and called up: 'Ah, there you are!'

Others around the man looked up too and began to chant: 'Speech! Speech!' and clap their hands. James turned and rushed away.

He went to the darkroom – or rather, to be precise, he rushed from the landing and abruptly found himself inside the darkroom – pulled the light-string that with a click bathed the room in infrared light, and stepped over to the developing tray. A white sheet of photographic paper floated in the developing fluid. He stared at it, aware that that was what he had to do in order for the image to appear: just stare. And what gradually emerged was a photograph of what was going on outside, he knew, at a moment just passed.

His mother, Mary, was dancing with Simon inside a white marquee. He could barely tell that Mary was dancing, she was just standing straight with one foot lifted inches off the ground, her leg bent slightly at the knee. But Simon was dancing: he had hold of her hand with one outstretched arm and was leaning right away in an extrovert pose, his other arm reaching out on the other side, his whole chubby body face on to the camera, one leg kicking the air.

People, both familiar and unfamiliar, stood around them. They looked as if they'd just stopped dancing themselves in order to enjoy and applaud Simon's exhibitionism. They were watching Simon and Mary, all except for one, who was Robert, and he was staring directly at the camera. The picture kept on developing, gradually, darkening. James wanted to take the print out and wash the chemicals off, but he couldn't move: he watched the image disappear into black.

When he woke up, after he'd got over the shock of seeing his mother so vividly, James realized that it was another wedding dream. He recalled the earlier one (in a hospital ward) and had a presentiment that they might become what Zoe, who knew about such things, called a recurring dream. And he would turn out to be right: it was his second wedding dream in a series that he would have at periodic intervals over ensuing years and which from then on would all end in the same say. And James, who had a pedantic streak in his nature and a fondness for puns, described them to himself not as a recurring but as a developing dream.

It was strange to dream a photograph of people: that was the last thing James wanted for a subject. He did, however, feel it was time to venture beyond the garden walls, and so he spent the next Saturday in town studying the shops and other buildings. It was a nightmare: he came back shaken up by children making faces for him, cyclists ringing their bells as they passed and shoppers cursing because he got in their way. He realized that, far from disappearing behind his camera, it only made him conspicuous.

I'm not going back there again, he decided.

One hot summer Saturday after James' O-levels they all jumped into Simon's VW Beetle – Alice nabbing the passenger seat and Laura squeezed between James and Robert in the back – to go swimming in the baths next to the school in Northtown, on a rare excursion together.

By the time they arrived James already regretted being persuaded to leave the darkroom and come along. He was self-conscious about his body: he wore Bermuda shorts rather than swimming trunks in order to cover up his scars, but he couldn't cover up his sunken chest or his skinny legs. So he trotted from the changing-room into the echoey, shimmering chamber and jumped straight into the shallow end. Then he remembered that he didn't even like swimming: he'd never been very good at it, for one thing. He wasn't comfortable in the medium of water the way some people, especially girls, seemed to be – which was a shame because it would have been a good exercise, one from which his wonky hips didn't exclude him. As it was, the limited articulation of his joints made swimming simply more frustrating than it already had been. Neither had he ever got to grips

135

with how you were supposed to breathe while swimming: he was always out of breath after a few strokes of the crawl and had to flip over to complete a length of the pool floating on his back, gasping for air.

Robert, though not a fast swimmer, had at least mastered the ability to breathe properly. He walked slowly towards the edge of the pool – looking even more anthropoidal in his trunks than when fully clothed, with the compact body of a weightlifter – glanced around the pool with hooded eyes, and dived in over the heads of two surprised small children. He then proceeded to plough a steady furrow up and down the length of the pool, brushing aside anyone unfortunate enough to get in his way; he progressed on even strokes with his head submerged and odd ones with his mouth emerging to one side gulping air; powerful, slow and rhythmic. James watched and tried to copy his younger brother. It looked easy enough, but he couldn't manage more than a few yards before losing the rhythm or else getting a mouthful of chlorinated water from some passing swimmer.

Simon couldn't swim very well either but it didn't bother him in the least: he was a lunging, clumsy porpoise in the water. In normal life he wore tailored suits and jackets – bought on Saturday shopping expeditions with the typing-pool girls, among the rare occasions he actually took other people's advice – clothes of expensive fabric and elegant cut designed to disguise the underlying shape of his body. In the swimming pool, though, in a pair of outrageously skimpy trunks meant for someone half his size, Simon's true dimensions were revealed and he looked more than ever like an overgrown baby with his barrel chest, floppy stomach and dimply thighs. He rolled around in the water rather than swimming lengths, or even widths, laughing at himself, pausing only to advise mothers on how to encourage their children to doggy-paddle or teenage boys on how to displace the maximum amount of water with bomb-jumps even as the attendant stalked around the side of the pool to reprimand them.

By the time Alice and Laura emerged from the women's changing-room James was already thinking he'd been in long enough. He saw them make their way to the edge of the pool and was struck by how quite extraordinarily different they were – or, perhaps, had become. Laura had broken her unspoken pact with Alice of simultaneous physical and emotional growth, their sisterly partnership: first of all, she'd suddenly grown taller. Overnight she spurted upwards, higher than Alice, Edna, Robert. She was already almost the same height as her father, and still growing. She'd lost the last of her maternal legacy of fat, her almond eyes the only constant as her adult countenance emerged from her childish, puppy-fat face.

The 'twins' looked like different species: Laura, with short brown hair, a full head taller than Alice, her tanned, slim body in a black bathing costume, talking to Alice, touching her arm at the edge of the water, shoulders slightly hunched, aware of boys' eyes upon her. And Alice, looking as if shorn with her pre-Raphaelite head of auburn hair hidden under a white swimming-cap, her body already settled in her hips and white thighs, a woman's bosom contained in her blue swimsuit, not really looking at anything, aloof from the echoing shrieks and intent, scampering bodies around her.

Neither of them, though, jumped or dived into the water, but dipped their toes in gingerly and climbed in slowly, as if it might be too hot or too cold, too chlorinated or too dirty, or just too *wet*, thought James, as they shared a small display of feminine fragility. He flopped onto his back and kicked away.

Once the girls were safely in the water Alice relaxed: the stronger swimmer, she separated from Laura and swam breast-stroke lengths parallel to Robert's sturdy crawl. Laura paddled and dipped around the shallow end. James, bored, swam over. Laura was standing, leaning against the edge of the pool, elbows on the tiles, gazing at the watery reflections shimmering on the ceiling. James ducked underwater and despite the chlorine kept his eyes open, and kicked towards her legs, his stomach grazing the bottom of the pool. He grasped her calves, considered tugging them in an effort to upend her, and decided not to. He let go and came up for air, gasping.

'Hi,' he whispered when he'd got his breath back.

'I thought that was Robert for a second,' Laura said.

James stood facing her: it was strange how tall she'd looked beside Alice, when she was still inches shorter than he was. The water came up to their thighs.

'Your fingers are all wrinkled,' Laura said, smiling.

'I've been in too long,' he whispered. 'I don't even like swimming,' he added.

'It's all right,' Laura shrugged. 'But it's a bit boring. Unless you're as friendly as he is.' She nodded towards Simon, who a few yards away from them was wading backwards pulling a small girl with yellow armbands, who was kicking furiously. Laura watched Simon, smiling. James' eyes, though, only glanced at Simon and returned to Laura: her strong shoulders, her small breasts, their nipples pressed by

137

the black swimsuit, her stomach, belly button, the top of her thighs above the water, the mound of her sex. In the time it took to run his eyes down her body James realized he'd got a hard-on – above the water. He bent his knees and dropped his body below the surface. Laura turned back to him.

'What are you doing, James?' she asked. 'You're not going to attack me again,' she exclaimed, lunging forward. James was crouching on the floor of the pool, only his head and shoulders showing above the surface.

'No!' he whispered, as Laura put both her hands on his head and ducked him.

'No!' he tried to say again, instead of closing his mouth as he should have done. He took a mouthful of chlorinated water and came back up spluttering and choking, with his eyes closed. He waddled forwards with his arms outstretched and found the edge of the pool. When he opened his eyes again Laura was, mercifully, paddling away towards Simon.

James crouched underwater, waiting for his erection to subside. He kept his knees squeezed together to hide it from anyone drifting around underwater. He looked at the ceiling, and at the censorious attendant, and at a shifting spot of water some inches away, anywhere except at Laura, but his hard-on remained. It must be the water, James thought, the warm water: it would never go down until he got out of the pool. But he couldn't get out of the pool until his erection had gone. He imagined scurrying to the changing-room, hunched over himself; then he imagined strutting proudly across the tiles, his stiff prick pushing out of his Bermuda shorts – and blushed just picturing it.

Eventually he felt the blood ebb, his hard-on begin to wilt. But then, absurdly, horrendously, he was unable to stop his eyes from scanning the pool, roving among the many bodies: seeking Laura. He couldn't help himself. His eyes found her outside the water, half-way down the pool, bending over and saying something to Alice. Immediately his prick sprang up again. Then Laura jumped in beside Alice, and James looked away.

So James stayed there, trapped; twice he lost his lust but couldn't stop himself from looking at Laura again, which was enough to revive it. At one point Alice swam over, her white swimming cap bobbing before her.

'Are you all right, James?' she asked.

'Fine,' he whispered.

'You've been there for ages,' she observed. 'You haven't got cramp or anything, have you?' she asked.

'No, nothing like that. I'm fine, Alice.'

'You sure?' she persisted.

'Go away!' he said. 'Leave me alone!'

'Well,' Alice said, turning away, 'sorry for being alive.' And she swam off.

Robert left the pool first. He climbed out near James, saying, 'Thirty lengths,' in his gritty voice. Simon was down at the deep end, chatting with one or two of the bomb-jumping boys, and they all got out together and walked off towards the changing-rooms.

The girls soon followed.

'Hey, grumpy features!' Alice called to James as they walked past the shallow end. 'We're all going now, Mr Crinkly Skin!'

'I thought you didn't even like the water, James,' Laura called. James decided it would be best to ignore them. He closed his eyes.

'Looks like Zoe's been teaching him one of her yoga positions,' he heard Alice tell Laura.

'Water yoga!' Laura agreed. 'James is a water yogi,' he heard, her voice trailing away.

He opened his eyes. 'I am a camera,' he whispered to himself. 'I'm a voyeur.' And he stayed there a while longer, wondering whether his alarming and unwelcome lust for Laura, who was practically his sister, was incestuous; and hoping it would vanish as suddenly as it had arisen. He resolved never to go swimming with her again, ever, or even to imagine her in her tight black swimsuit, to picture taking it off, one shoulder, then the other, peeling it down over her breasts . . . and then he summoned up memories of that year's FA Cup Final, concentrating on the move that culminated in Charlie George's winning goal, until his capricious prick had returned to its normal size.

When James got to the changing-room Robert was still drying himself. James dried and dressed quickly. He yanked his T-shirt down over his shoulders.

'Come on, Robert,' he snapped, grabbing his bag, 'why do you always take so bloody long?'

'Thirty lengths,' Robert told him. 'Thirty lengths. I'll be doing fifty by Christmas.'

The following Saturday James spent in Alfred's rose garden photographing insects. Or at least trying to. He didn't have a macro-lens and so attempted to get in close enough using the end of his long zoom. Ladybirds, fruitflies and caterpillars crawled in and out of focus on wavering petals.

Alfred pottered around, singing:

'Have you been in love, me visor, have you felt the plain?
I'd rather be in love meself than be in jail again.
The girl I loved was beautiful, I'll have you all to know,
and I saw her in my garden where potatoes grow.'

James hummed Alfred's tunes to himself, an abstract refrain, as he looked through the tunnel of his zoom, and hours passed in contented concentration.

Saturday being Edna's day off, she was visiting her sister, and Laura and Alice took over the kitchen in her absence. They baked a cake in the shape of a fairytale castle and proceeded to cover it in icing of all different colours.

'If we combine saffron and strawberry essence we'll get the colour we want for the tower,' Alice suggested. 'It's simple chemistry.'

'You take care of colours, Alice, just leave the taste to me,' Laura told her. She was inheriting her mother's culinary skills, though less for pastries and pies than for more eccentric combinations. 'I think I'll roast these walnuts we're going to use for fungus on the roof.'

Robert swept into the kitchen and helped himself to a leg of chicken and a lump of Cheddar from the fridge.

'Greedy-guts,' said Alice.

Robert glanced at what they were doing. 'What a pair of babies,' he growled. 'It's about time you two grew up.'

'Oh, yeh?' said Laura. 'Who's been dropped another year in maths, Mr Mature? *Everyone*'s heard about it.'

'Piss off,' Robert told her as he made to leave.

'You're thick,' she told him.

Robert turned round. Alice saw his hands knuckle into fists.

'She didn't mean it!' Alice said. 'Did you, Laura?'

'It's all right, Ali,' Laura assured her with a note of impatience in her voice. 'I can look after myself.'

'I'm not bloody stupid,' Robert told Laura through clenched teeth.

'All right, then,' she said. 'Challenge you to a game of chess.' Robert's face greyed. Laura turned to Alice. 'He doesn't even know how to play it,' she told her with a sneer.

140

''Course I do,' Robert countered. 'Anyone can play that stupid game.'

'Go on, then,' Laura repeated, 'play me. And the loser has to stand up in the middle of lunch tomorrow and say in front of everybody that they're more stupid than the winner.'

Alice looked nervously at her brother: he glared at Laura through hooded eyes.

'I know where James keeps his set,' Laura said. 'And you come too and be judge, Alice. Make sure he doesn't cheat.'

They put the board on the floor in Robert's room. He took his time setting up his pieces, with an air of professional deliberation, sneaking the briefest of glances at where Laura put hers.

'*No*, Robert,' Laura said in an antagonistic tone. '*Queen* on her own colour. Go on, you're white, you start. I might as well give you *that* much advantage.'

'*You* be white,' Robert snapped. '*You* can bloody start if you're so clever.'

And so they began. Robert copied Laura for as long as he could, but then she checked him with a bishop and he had to start coming up with moves of his own. He took ages, searching the empty corridors of his memory to determine whether knights moved to the left and then forward or to the right and back. He made a noncommittal move of a quiet pawn and Laura grabbed it from the board.

'*En passant*,' she said, and Robert was jolted by panic. How many other things had he forgotten, or not known in the first place? He cursed himself for having accepted this challenge. If there was one thing he couldn't stand it was being called stupid. But he was beginning to admit how stupid he'd been to let himself be put in this position.

He was also falling prey to the chess player's fear that his opponent is reading his mind. Laura sat cross-legged with a smug, feline expression on her face, and she made *her* moves as soon as Robert had taken his fingers off his piece, which made him take even longer the next time.

Neither of them took much notice when Alice woke up from a doze, said, 'Back in a minute,' and slipped out of the room and off down the stairs.

Laura became complacent: so impetuous was her game that she was bound to make a mistake, and she was a piece down for some time. But she was soon on the attack again, pinning Robert's pieces

141

into an ever more constricting corner of the board. Robert tried to concentrate on his defence, but he was distracted by nausea at the fear of losing, and by a hatred of his opponent that churned in the pit of his stomach.

James finally finished his roll of film in the rose garden, with a centipede twisting up a stalk. 'I'm going in now,' he called to Alfred.

'See you,' the old man replied, without looking up. 'I see seas of green,' he sang to himself, 'skies of blue, and we all say, I love you.'

James got a glass of milk to take with him to the darkroom.

'That looks good,' he told Alice, who'd returned to her culinary castle on the kitchen table.

'Wait till you *taste* it,' she said. 'Laura's an amazing cook, James. It must be heredity.'

'Where is she? Have you seen her?'

'Laura? No,' Alice shook her head. 'Oh, yes, wait a minute. She's playing chess.'

'No, she's not,' James smiled at his absent-minded sister. 'I've been outside for hours.'

'I *know* she's not playing with you, silly,' Alice told him. 'She's playing with Robert.'

'Robert? Don't be— Where?'

'In his room.'

James set off. Alice called after him: 'James?'

He stopped in the doorway. 'What?'

'Don't be upset, James. I don't think he's very good.'

James clumped up the stairs, and halfway up the last flight from the second-floor landing to the third floor. But then stopped. He could see through the banisters into Robert's room, and he stared at Laura sitting cross-legged playing chess with Robert, who sat with one leg tucked under him and the other stretched out across the carpet. James' first impulse was to march in and grab his board and chess set that Laura had taken without his permission: how could she have done that? To play with Robert, of all people? But instead James silently raised his camera to his right eye, and zoomed in.

No matter how hard he concentrated, Robert couldn't see more than one move ahead before his brain dissolved into meaningless blurred shapes, and he had to start again. Until, that is, he left an unguarded rook that Laura nonchalantly picked off as if she were flicking a fly from her cheek. And then all of a sudden Robert saw clearly the next *three* moves, which led to an inevitable checkmate.

Maybe, though, Laura hadn't yet realized. Just maybe. Robert let out a groan.

'Cramp!' he gasped, and unbent his left leg from under him. 'Shit!' he exclaimed, as he accidentally kicked the board, sending the pieces scattering across the carpet. He lay outstretched, massaging his left thigh. 'Agh, damn, that's better,' Robert sighed.

Laura stared at him for a few seconds. 'Why, you bloody cheat!' she exploded. 'You bloody horrible cheat!'

That's right, James thought. That is not fair. But what did you expect?

'It was an accident,' Robert replied. 'Shit, you might sympathize, you cow. Cramp bloody hurts.'

Laura unknotted her crossed legs and moved forward on her knees to Robert's prone body. 'That's it,' she said. 'You're the loser, Robert. You can't get out of it like that.'

'I couldn't help it,' he claimed. 'I didn't *want* to, I was just getting into it. I had a tactic all planned you hadn't seen.'

'Rubbish!' Laura spat. 'I had you mate in three.' She knelt there, looking down on Robert, eyes blazing with frustration: she knew he was cheating, and she also knew she couldn't prove it.

James realized he was a witness; but he wasn't sure he wanted to intervene.

'I can get you mate in two,' Robert growled.

'What are you talking about?' Laura demanded.

Robert lifted his arm to Laura's breast, and squeezed it through her clothing. James focused the lens on what he was seeing; he couldn't work out why Laura wasn't moving.

'Check,' said Robert, and then he lifted himself up on his elbow and, moving his arm from Laura's breast to her neck, pulled her down to meet him. As they began to kiss they closed their eyes, and so too did James; he let his body slide down the stairs to the landing below.

4

WELCOME TO THE ARK

IT WAS A BRISK AND BLUSTERY AUTUMN AFTERNOON. LAURA AND Alice, home from school, were warming themselves with mugs of tea and hot buttered muffins in the kitchen. Edna rolled pastry on the table. Laura took a mouthful of muffin and raised her head.

'Look!' she gasped, scattering crumbs from her lips. 'Through the window. Look, Mum! It's snowing!'

Edna and Alice looked up and gazed at a swirling shower – not of snowflakes, but white and yellow rose petals. A multitude of them flurried past the window, and then were gone. Edna wiped her hands on her apron and took it off.

'Where are you going, Auntie?' Alice asked her, but Edna was already out in the back hallway pulling on her coat. The girls followed. Outside the back door Edna found Alfred's sandwiches and thermos untouched in the box where she'd put them for him that morning.

The girls braced themselves as they scurried after Edna, but as they came out of the back yard the wind dropped. They turned the corner of the house and saw the rose garden: every bush had lost its petals; each one was naked and frail. In the middle of them stood Robert, his school satchel (containing more tools than books) strung behind his back, staring at the ground. He turned when he heard Edna trotting towards him.

'I had a premonition,' he said.

Laura and Alice came around the back of Robert and Edna and found Alfred lying on his back, half-submerged in rose petals. There were some on his face too but it was possible to make out, in his fixed gaze and his downturned lips, an expression of intense disappointment.

After some moments Edna said: 'I'm going to call the doctor.' She rushed back towards the house, forgetting the children behind her.

Robert turned to Laura. 'Touch him,' he said. 'He's as cold as stone.'

James was in hospital when Alfred died, having removed from his hips the metal pins and plates which he was given and brought home in a small cardboard box.

At school, having scraped through O-levels, James enrolled for A-levels in history, physics and art, an absurd combination of subjects he chose ignoring all advice, and which he was able to select owing to a quirk of the syllabus by which none of the lessons interfered with each other.

'What the hell have any of them got to do with each other? Or with anything else, for that matter?' Charles demanded. 'You can do economics *and* business studies at your school, damn it.'

'These are the subjects I'm interested in,' James whispered, standing his ground.

'Well, it's your funeral, boy. As long as you don't expect me to subsidize you through college as well.'

'I don't, father,' James muttered, and limped away.

One pupil who *was* taking both economics and business studies was Harry Singh. He'd given up cricket to concentrate on his studies, which slightly worried his father, who wanted him, rather than his younger brother, Anil, to take over the shop; but Harry had other plans.

Harry regarded his father behind the post office counter, with his bruised eyes and air of weary responsibility, as the latest in a long line of clerks who'd been carrying the weight of the world's bureaucracy on their shoulders. And the last: from the very beginning Harry had made it clear that he had no intention of accepting such an inheritance. He saw himself as English, and even as a young child

145

had acted as though he were a house guest among his own family, accepting such things as their language, religion and dress as quaint rituals to be tolerated on account of their nostalgia, but nothing to do with him. Food was the only cultural entity Harry was forced to admit a fondness for; he enjoyed cooking with his father on a Saturday evening, and copied his habit of chewing cardamom seeds during the day. Apart from that aberration, though, Harry saw himself as having somehow been billeted with these unfortunate people, less for his own good than to help them survive in the mother culture.

Harry had entered primary school with a complete command of the English language, something which had proved beyond his mother, who took him to shop or doctor's surgery to act as her interpreter. His grandmother sat in a chair in the flat above the shop berating her family for bringing her to this land of drizzle and rickets, all grey, without colour, which she couldn't see anyway because of cataracts caused, no doubt, by the winter snow, and she watched television all day.

Harry knew he didn't fit in with them. You couldn't move across the world and pretend you were still at home. You had to plunge into the world you lived in; you had to assimilate. Not that this was anything other than a steady rationalization of his own taste and temperament: Harry felt at ease in the world he grew up in; it was only inside his own home that he felt out of place.

Although they took quite different subjects, Harry told James that he too was interested in photography, and James invited Harry to join him in his darkroom. James enjoyed having a companion, even if Harry was a somewhat inattentive colleague: his professed interest was hard to discern, as James explained what quantities of chemicals to mix and how to avoid scratches on the neg. They had long coffee breaks, and found how much they both looked forward to leaving home, swapping stories of their stifling home lives; although Harry didn't admit that despite their apparent agreement James' wishes made no sense to him at all. Why would anyone want to leave a house like this? It was exactly the kind of place he wanted to escape *to*.

Neither did James fully realize that Harry was bored stiff in the darkroom. He only enjoyed the journey through the house towards it, and afterwards away from it: for he walked slowly, peering into the rooms; and sometimes he was rewarded with a glimpse of Alice. He paused, breathless, in her doorway, waiting in vain for Alice to notice him too, until James turned to see where his companion had got to and Harry rushed to catch up.

Lewis, too, was taking entirely different subjects from James, and their friendship ebbed a little further. There were always people around Lewis, and James didn't want to be one of a crowd.

'You want to come out on Friday night, Jay?' Lewis invited him. 'A bunch of us are going to the Cave.'

'No, thanks, Lewis,' James whispered. 'I can't dance,' he shrugged.

'Neither can I,' Lewis laughed. 'I'll be helping out the DJ, racking up the records and that. You won't catch me on the dance floor. Come on, Jay, you'll like it, there's always Spanish girls there on a Friday.'

James looked at his feet. 'Thanks, Lew. I'll see, OK?' he whispered unconvincingly.

Lewis never asked James to come to the school team's football matches. A part of him knew how difficult it would be for James to watch what he'd loved but couldn't join in with any more, but another part figured that James might want to come and support them anyway, and he resented James' withdrawal.

'You've always been a dreamer, Jay, but at least you used to share them,' he told him.

James dreamed through the rest of his schooldays. History turned out to be a hoax: the past bore no relation to the present. Instead of getting some hints at least of where he fitted in the scheme of things, as he'd hoped, the subject was merely a grinding struggle for James to remember the names and dates of kings and queens and other rulers of Britain, who were shadows of real people. And apart from a brief period studying the properties of light and its perception by the human eye James found physics a frustrating combination of the banal and the impenetrably abstract. He watched, surprised, as boys and girls he'd considered less intelligent than himself showed an easy grasp of the increasingly complex concepts of science with which they were presented – as if their brains were expanding and his was not.

He took refuge in art, and although he couldn't draw, paint or sculpt as well as other pupils, when he turned every project into a photographic one his teacher, far from marking him down, as he feared, encouraged him instead.

'Since you clearly know what you want to do I won't stand in your way, James,' she told him. She was a large, elderly lady on the verge of retirement, with an aristocratic manner quite incongruous in the school, who frowned upon any attempt to copy what had gone before.

'Do you think they're good?' James whispered, showing her some prints he'd made of the garden pictures.

'They're wonderful, James,' she assured him. 'But rather life-like, don't you think?' She frowned. 'In photography a certain surface realism is a given, and is therefore that much easier to subvert.'

'But I *want* them to be realistic,' he objected.

'Well, I won't stand in your way, James. But do *think* about it. For heaven's sake don't just *snap*.'

The fact was he didn't think about a great deal else. He spent more time inside the darkroom than outside it; at supper time Edna stood at the foot of the stairs banging the gong until he opened the door and came swaying down the stairs.

'Jumping jellybeans!' Alice exclaimed, staring boggle-eyed at James' face as he came into the kitchen. They all turned and stared at him. 'Horrible haggises!' Alice cried. 'You've been so long in there your skin's infrared!' she teased. They all laughed and James blushed, obligingly turning her joke into reality.

'What's that infernal smell?' Charles demanded.

'It's those bloody chemicals,' Robert said in his sandpaper voice.

'They're probably poisonous, James,' said Simon.

'There's no need to swear at the dinner table,' Laura told Robert.

'Best wash your hands, dear,' Edna suggested to James.

'Ouch!' Robert exclaimed. He'd tried to stamp on Laura's foot under the table, but she'd been attacked enough times to know when it was coming, and Robert had stubbed his heel on the floor instead.

Charles ignored him. He nodded to Stanley, who produced an already opened bottle of red wine from nowhere.

'I want us to drink a toast tonight,' Charles loudly proclaimed. 'Dilute the girls' with water, Edna, if you will.'

'That's not fair, Daddy,' Alice complained. 'What about him?' she protested, pointing at Robert.

'Now, now,' Charles scolded. 'He's fifteen, he can cope with a glass of wine.'

Robert flashed his stony grin at Alice and Laura. When the glasses were filled Charles stood up and said: 'I'd like to propose a toast to Simon, here. He doesn't know it yet, but he's about to be promoted: junior manager in the Marketing Department. Everyone tells me he's doing his father credit down there. We're *proud* of you, boy!'

Charles chinked his glass against Simon's, and everyone else did likewise, including Robert, who slammed his against the others', each one a little more startling, until when he reached Simon there was the sound of shattering glass and bits sprinkling into a bowl of Brussels sprouts.

'Oh dear,' said Edna.

'*Now* look what you've done,' said Laura.

'It's only a glass,' James whispered.

'It's only blood,' said Robert, inspecting his cut finger.

'Congratulations, lad,' Stanley told Simon, scolding his protégé Robert by ignoring him.

'Oh dear,' said Edna, picking shards of glass from among the Brussels sprouts.

No one was surprised by Simon's rapid promotion. Quite apart from the fact that it was inevitable – since despite Charles Freeman's demands of the various heads of department of his business that they should treat Simon exactly the same as any other young trainee, they each came to the same conclusion: that it was safer to grant favour than to deny it to the pleasant young son of the man-in-charge. Apart from that, James could see for himself Simon's own development. His ability to listen to other people with a tolerant smile and to then afford them the benefit of his advice hadn't deserted him; in fact he'd developed it into a personal trait, except that he found he needed to listen less and advise more: Simon (and everyone around him) discovered he possessed an opinion on any subject that arose and revealed himself to be an expert in all fields of human endeavour.

'You'd do best to plant the begonias over there in the shade,' he told one of the team of three gardeners that had been required to replace Alfred. 'Train clematis up a west-facing wall, if I were you, and bed those tulips down in July.'

'Yes, sir,' the gardener replied.

'Take a left, then a right, and straight on over the roundabout,' Simon told a car-load of late, lost German tourists who'd meandered down the drive by mistake one Saturday afternoon. 'Right at the lights, keep going for half a mile, and it's there on your left,' he continued.

'*Danke*, sank you,' they nodded, frowning, as they reversed away.

'That won't take them anywhere *near* the museum, Simon,' James frowned.

'If you don't understand something, James,' Simon told him, 'if you're not sure, make it up.'

James eyed his older brother sceptically, but Simon waved his objections aside.

'It's better to be wrong than confused,' he explained. 'Remember that, James. It makes people feel safer.' Simon had a certainty of always being right, presumably copied from his father, and it was a confidence rarely dented by error. He came upon Alice and Laura conducting a chemistry experiment in Alice's room with a set she had been given that Christmas. Simon watched from the doorway for between three and four seconds before striding over.

'What on earth are you two trying to do?' he demanded.

Alice explained that they were combining hydrogen and sulphur. 'Mr Hughes said we wouldn't be able to do it at home,' she told Simon, 'but I'm going to prove him wrong.'

'Well, your tubing's too long for a start,' Simon said, grabbing hold of it. 'This bit here should be shorter,' he said, twisting it. It split like a peapod.

'Simon!' Laura exclaimed.

'Er, yes, that's *much* better, you see, cut it off there,' he told them. And then, when they'd done it, he advised: 'You need more heat, the Bunsen's on too low.'

'How do *you* know?' Alice demanded.

'Oh, we did all this sort of thing in fourth year,' Simon assured them, turning up the flame, which changed from yellow to blue and white and attacked the retort suspended above. The glass shrieked and then cracked and exploded apart, pouring liquid onto the naked flame and filling the room with a sudden putrid smell.

'Simon!' Alice yelled.

'Look,' he said calmly. 'See? *There's* your problem,' he said, backing out of the room, holding his nose. 'Your beaker was too thid. Why od earth did't you use a stronger wud?'

It wasn't just in the small, practical details of existence that Simon was an expert. He understood the deeper mysteries of life as well, and in those early days he provided answers to people's problems with a mixture of astrological wisdom gleaned from women's magazines and Edna's kitchen aphorisms.

'I suspect that a fear you've had in the back of your mind since childhood,' he told one of the girls from the typing pool, who'd followed him home for some further, more private advice, 'could be a contributory factor, Debbie, to the history of a certain complaint.'

She thought about it for a while. 'Our dad was a womanizing drinker,' she told Simon, nodding. 'Mum always put up with him.

She was so stupid. You think I'm repeating her mistake?'

'Or else you're looking for the same behaviour in your boyfriend, Debbie, finding things that aren't there.'

'I'm *sure* he's seeing someone, I can *feel* it,' she said vehemently. 'I know he's lying.'

'Get him to make you toast for breakfast,' Simon advised her. 'Watch him. I always say: if a person can't cut bread straight, it's a sure sign of dishonesty.'

A few people in the company's departments thought Simon possessed an oracular wisdom. Some were merely perplexed by this precocious, overweight sage. The truth was, though, that *most* people called him Bullshit Simon, at first behind his back (since no one was stupid enough to antagonize the son of the boss), until gradually it emerged that the other thing Simon enjoyed was having the mickey taken, and what saved him from being unbearably pompous was that he didn't take himself seriously, and even the young men of his own age who derided him quite liked Simon at the same time.

The one thing that Simon did take seriously was his health. The hypochondria of his childhood afflicted him still in adult life. In the morning he staggered downstairs clutching the banisters with his eyes glued together like a baby's, unable to open them until Edna had administered a mug of strong coffee; but he then went the rest of the day without having another cup because even if he drank it for elevenses it kept him awake at night with heart palpitations. He was unable to enjoy cheese after dessert because it played havoc with his dreams, while after-dinner chocolates made him wake up in the middle of the night with a migraine – and when *that* happened he'd spend the following day mooning around the house in his silk pyjamas and dressing-gown, confusing his father later on with a request for the compulsory (and in this case parental) sick-note.

Despite his size – the same as Charles', who had an iron constitution – Simon was fragile.

'We are what we eat,' he chided Robert, who was pausing to shovel into his mouth whatever was on the sideboard as he passed.

'Sugar rots the brain,' he told Alice, who was able to consume a box of chocolates within the duration of a single soap-opera episode.

Simon believed that diet was the key to healthy living. He was constantly *on* a diet, which he stuck to with unwavering discipline, except that it was always a different one, changing constantly. For a time he ate nothing but fruit that Edna had to order in bulk from the market.

'You must have a *varied* diet,' Edna tried to convince him.

'You're absolutely right,' he replied. 'Maybe you could get hold of some cumquats?' And she had to give further orders to the immigrant greengrocers on Factory Road.

At supper, instead of the normal meal everyone else shared (allowing, of course, for Alice's vegetarian dish and the fact that Robert was most likely somewhere else), Simon piled up a small mountain of plantains, raspberries, oranges, mangoes, apples, pomegranates and pears, a pyramid of fruit from behind which he lectured the others on the beneficial effects of cleaning the system with food that was a combination of water and sunlight, that was all, becoming visible as he ate his way through it from the top down, leaving a plateful of peelings and pips.

'And look at that, you see,' he rounded off: 'all good stuff for the compost heap.'

A couple of days later Simon announced that fruit was all very well but too much of it gave you acid, and also caused a person to pass wind more than was strictly necessary (a fact that had already been pointed out to him, but which he had ignored). They assumed Simon had seen sense, only to be informed, with equal conviction, that the body knows best what it needs and therefore a person should eat exactly what they like most, when they crave it. For the next few weeks he drove Edna mad by swooping into the kitchen at odd hours of the day and requesting *coq au vin* for breakfast, *pâté de foie gras* and champagne for a mid-afternoon snack, and a full grill of 'sausage, chips, bacon, eggs, tomatoes, beans, black pudding and fried bread, please, Edna,' for supper.

It was an unpredictable diet that Edna managed to provide without complaint, thanks to her unfailingly servile generosity and a good deal of assistance from the deep freezer she'd recently had installed in the pantry.

'Bloody hell, Mum! Let him make it himself!' said Laura, who regarded Simon's demands as beyond the bounds of reason, and disliked seeing her mother being taken advantage of.

'It won't take me a moment, dear,' Edna told her.

Even so, Simon's whimsical diet had pushed even Edna close to the end of her tether when he abruptly announced that in fact there was nothing wrong with what they normally ate, it was simply a question of moderation, and furthermore most of the major problems people encountered in their day-to-day well-being could be traced back – as recent research showed – to the fact that everyone swallowed their food too quickly.

The rest of the family breathed a sigh of relief as Simon rejoined them for meals and ate the same as they did, and what did it matter that he made sure Edna only served him with minute portions of everything? 'One thin slice of chicken breast, please, two carrots, thank you, half a potato, yes, twenty-five peas, please, no, not thirty, twenty-five, and a soupçon of gravy, that's it, a touch more, *stop*! Thank you, Edna.'

That was fine, there was nothing wrong with such behaviour, they welcomed Simon back into the culinary fold. Except that he then insisted upon chewing each small mouthful fifty-two times.

'You all gobble up your food, you see,' he told them. 'You don't give your stomach time to tell your brain it's full. And then when it complains later you're surprised.' Simon shook his head. 'People are *so* silly.'

It took Simon so long to finish his food that gravy congealed and vegetables sagged, but that didn't affect his appetite: he nibbled his way like a tenacious rabbit through to the last pea, while the others had to watch, having finished their much larger portions ages before but unable, owing to the etiquette of table manners, to begin to clear away until the last person – Simon – had put down his knife and fork.

The other children lobbied their father for a change in the unwritten rules of dinnertime, and he was about to succumb when Simon discovered a new diet.

'We are not sheep!' he declared. 'We are not cows! We are *human beings*! Carnivores, that's what we are. How about a barbecue, anyone?'

And so it went on, Simon promiscuous but utterly dedicated to each new diet. Whether it was the period he refused to come to table without a pocket calculator, in order to count the calories, or when he ate nothing but grapes two days a week, Simon stuck to it with a fastidiousness and willpower altogether absent from the rest of his life, and left his family fuming – and wondering how it was that the only thing that *didn't* change was Simon's size.

'The thing is, James,' Simon told his brother, 'some people like someone to tell them what to do, and other people like to pretend they don't ever listen to anyone else. But we all end up in the shit.'

James admired his brother's confidence, and envied it, but he couldn't make him out. There was something clearly parodic about Simon's counsellor's posturing, both an apprenticeship for their father's actual power and a pastiche of it. Except that Simon rarely broadcast his wisdom without utter conviction.

'You don't know anything, Simon, why are you always pretending you do?' James whispered. 'Why do you tell everyone how to live their lives?' he demanded.

'You might well ask,' Simon replied. 'Pearls before swine. I mean, it doesn't matter what you plant if it doesn't rain. A complete waste of breath. I *do* sometimes wonder why I bother.'

'You know what I mean,' James persisted.

'Haven't a *clue*, James.' Simon shrugged.

He had his reasons, James reckoned. Quite often girls spent the evening in the old nursery that had been converted into a sitting-room up on the third floor. Simon read them their horoscopes or quizzes from the women's magazines he bought, and advised them on their make-up.

'They're a good smokescreen,' Simon confided cryptically in James. 'They'll keep Dad off my back. Stick around, James,' he continued, 'Cheryl'll be here any minute. And Sue. I think she likes you. Come back! You can hide in your darkroom any time.'

But James didn't enjoy their company. For one thing, none of the family would see more of Robert for days on end than a brief, blurred glimpse of him grabbing a handful of fruit and nuts on his way in or out of the house; but whenever Simon's friends from the typing-pool dropped by and were directed by Charles, with a conspiratorial wink, up to the third floor, then Robert would appear out of nowhere.

'He just smells their perfume, that's all,' said Alice.

'He's got very good hearing,' said Simon. 'He can even hear what *you* say,' he told James.

'He spies on people,' said Laura.

Most of Simon's young women visitors ignored James. They appreciated Simon's gnomic advice, and they enjoyed the way he made them giggle when he read from articles outlining what real men really want or how to be an independent woman and still have a satisfying relationship. James could see that his big brother was like a big sister to them. Whereas he, James, was just a little brother. When he plucked up the courage to whisper something they lost interest before he'd got halfway through. So if he hung around at all, then he just sat back in a corner of the room, and contented himself with composing imaginary photographic portraits of Simon's young women.

Robert, however, changed the chemistry in the room, just as he had with Pascale years before. He sat cross-legged in an opposite corner of the room, fiddling with a padlock with oily fingers: he smelled of old engine oil and fresh sweat. And the young women stopped joking freely with Simon, they turned serious, said less than ever and let Simon read whole articles without interruptions other than his own, and now and again their eyes would glance into the corner and meet Robert's with an almost perceptible, abrasive sound. Occasionally at the end of an evening one of them would get up to leave and then lose her sense of direction making her way down the three flights of stairs and along the corridors and through the hallways, and by some fluke end up not at the back door but in Robert's room, right next to the old nursery.

James was the middle son and he was lost somewhere between Simon's camp self-confidence and Robert's sexual allure. He realized he didn't need to hide behind a camera to be invisible. He could be in a room for half an hour and someone would bump into him and jump: 'James! Where did you come from?' At school, teachers questioned his absence the day before, having failed to notice him in the middle of the class. Yet he also felt intensely self-conscious, that *unless* he kept a low profile he would stand out for his ugliness and awkwardness.

'I've got no centre,' he whispered to himself; I'm hollow, he thought. He saw other people's purpose, the solidity of their being, and wondered how they'd acquired it. He saw they were at home in the world. He saw them change, and lose nothing.

Just before Christmas of 1972 the art teacher organized an exhibition of her pupils' work, including four of James' photographs: under pressure from Miss Stubbs he'd experimented with long exposures and each picture was of a different, apparently empty classroom, except that when you looked closer you could make out the faint ghosts of teacher and pupils.

Every artwork was on sale at £10, the proceeds to go towards a new pottery kiln. When Charles arrived at the private view he studied the results of his son's photography for the first time, and was unable to work out why anyone would want to waste as much time as he knew James did on make-believe jiggery-pokery, as he described them to the headmaster. Until, that is, he noticed the red stickers on the wall beside them. Although Charles had never been to an art exhibition in his life he realized immediately what they meant, and ordered a set for himself.

'I only paid for these because I had to give something,' Charles told James when they got home. 'From now on I expect one framed photograph a month, James. We'll put them up in the hallway. Impress our guests, eh?'

James wasn't sure whether to be flattered or angry. 'Hang on, Dad,' he whispered. 'I only printed those for Miss Stubbs. I don't plan to print any more for a while.'

'Nonsense, James,' Charles countered, hand raised. 'Simon was earning his living at your age. I support you: therefore, strictly speaking, the photographs are mine.'

And Charles marched away, brooking no argument, leaving James silently fuming.

There was only one person who could stand up to Charles. Sunday lunch at the house on the hill had become the family tradition Charles demanded it be. Judith Peach sometimes came, as well as relatives like Jack and Clare, and Zoe.

Zoe usually arrived early, spending time with James while others were at church or Laura was helping Edna in the kitchen; and then, once lunch was served, it was only a matter of time before Zoe engaged her uncle in argument.

Zoe still believed in the power of love, that flowers were stronger than bullets, that innocence is more truthful than experience, and that the best cure for capitalists like Charles Freeman would be to take their clothes off and smoke home-grown grass in the summer sunshine. She had, however, been impressed by German radicals and South American revolutionaries she'd read about (and whom she wished she could meet travelling) who, instead of quietly dropping out or growing disillusioned, as most of their generation had done, had gone just a little further and then found themselves at the opposite extreme, advocating the carrying out of ruthless acts of terrorism in the name of love and justice.

So that Zoe's arguments, however heartfeltly expressed, tended always to be somewhat confused.

'The people who *create* wealth aren't you and your kind, Charles,' she told him, 'it's the workers who *make* things, and while you and your fellow shareholders live in the lap of luxury they're like animals in cages in that disgusting factory.'

156

'My dear, you're old enough to have realized by now,' Charles replied, 'that most people are like sheep, they need leadership, they're only worried about their home and their hobby and if it wasn't for men like me we'd still be in the Stone Age.'

Charles conducted those arguments over roast beef and Yorkshire pudding in good humour: he found the idea of discussing politics with his niece faintly absurd, and so he argued with a big grin on his face, which only made Zoe furious.

'I can't help noticing,' Charles smiled, 'that you're perfectly happy to come and eat this capitalist exploiter's Sunday lunch, young lady.'

Zoe dropped her knife and fork and pushed her plate away.

'And I believe, according to various authoritative sources,' Charles continued, nodding in the vague direction of his children seated around the table, 'that you keep up the sordid tradition of charging people money to come and watch films in your picture palace.'

'That's the whole bloody *point!*' Zoe spluttered. 'We all have to operate by your rules, and that's why we're going to change them. We'll have a world with*out* money one day.'

'That's a very good idea,' Charles agreed. 'And, what's more, it's going to happen before too soon, I'm sure of it. Money's a waste of paper and other resources, you're absolutely right, Zoe. There's a computer revolution coming: in twenty years' time we'll all have digitally coded credit cards, and there'll be no need whatsoever for grubby notes and dirty coins to change hands.'

'But, but,' Zoe stammered, flustered and infuriated, '*that's* not what I'm talking about at *all*. And you *know* it's not.'

No one else joined in those heated sessions. But James was enthralled. Usually he hated the tensions around the dinner table, they drove him to his darkroom, but Sundays were different. He loved the way Zoe stood up to his father, undaunted by Charles' bulk, his power or his temper. James wanted to enter the argument but he was far too shy, even in his own home, and besides whenever he *did* think of some pertinent point, by the time he'd formulated it into a coherent sentence the two main protagonists had moved on.

Once or twice James managed to interject some stumbling opinion, in support of Zoe, to which Charles responded with ridicule, his teasing treatment of Zoe moving up a gear to deal with his own son.

'Zoe's right, father,' James hesitantly ventured. 'Everyone can be responsible if they're encouraged to be. It's leaders who *make* people into sheep.'

'Oh, it is, is it?' Charles replied, leaning back in the chair and arching his eyebrows. 'I see,' he continued gravely. 'In that case, James, perhaps you would be so kind as to explain. You're clearly an expert. Might you furnish us with the relevant data, young man, make us party to your sources of research? We're *dying* to hear. We await your words of wisdom with bated breath, James. The floor is yours.'

James sat there flushed with tongue-tied frustration, surrounded by his siblings' nervous giggles and embarrassment, until Zoe came to his rescue. She had little reason to thank James for his support, though, since his humiliation only made her angrier and Charles more smug.

But just occasionally she found the weak spot in Charles' armoury, his own Achilles' heel.

'If you're so wonderfully responsible for all those poor souls,' she proclaimed, 'then presumably it's your fault when someone gets injured or maimed or even killed.'

'Nonsense!' Charles declared. 'I set great store by our safety standards. As everyone knows.'

'Oh, I'm sorry, Charles, I forgot, you are a caring capitalist after all. It's a shame about that poor man who was *squashed* in the recycling plant last month.'

'I've ordered a full enquiry!' Charles bellowed.

'I'm sure it wasn't your fault,' Zoe sympathized, becoming calmer. 'I know you weren't responsible for the shoddy machinery; you've got your balance sheets to think of, after all, *you* can't go around repairing faulty hydraulics, Charles. You've got your profits to protect.'

'I do everything I can!' Charles roared.

Zoe leaned forward across the table. 'Profits killed him, *you* killed him, you shouldn't be surprised that people call you a murderer—'

'What?'

'—because he died for the sake of profit, pure and simple, money killed him and it's your money, Charles, and it's got his blood on it.'

'How dare you!' Charles thundered, pushing back his chair. 'You ungrateful ragamuffin! Coming here to insult me!'

Zoe relaxed, half-closed her eyes at Charles, and in her ascendancy made a dismissive – and obscurely obscene – gesture at him that she'd learned in Zanzibar. At which point Charles' face went a puce colour and he turned on his heels and strode out of the dining-room, cursing all the way, leaving a table of relatives and offspring looking like embarrassed statues, except for Zoe smiling to herself and Alice saying, 'What happened? What happened?' as she struggled to find out what she'd missed, adrift in a world of her own.

'I should get out of here; out of town,' James whispered to himself. 'I should go to the country, and photograph . . . animals.' And then he remembered his bluff Aunt Margaret's invitation to them all to visit her farm. He rang her up and asked if he could come out one weekend.

'What did you say?' she shouted down the line. 'Speak up, boy, I can't hear a word you're saying!' James had to pass the receiver to Alice, who acted as interpreter.

One Saturday morning in March James caught a bus that passed within half a mile of the farm. The driver dropped him off on a country road in the middle of nowhere, opposite a narrow lane, and James lurched along it and then down a track marked RUGGADON FARM. He found his way into a yard blocked by a gaggle of geese hissing at him. There were eight or ten of them and they rushed waddling across the muddy ground, webbed feet slapping, flapping their wings. James was terrified and backed away; the geese followed after him only so far, to an invisible line that marked the edge of their territory.

James stiffened his resolve and stepped forward, but the geese arched their necks towards him and stuck out their hissing tongues, and he retreated again. Surely, he thought, someone will have heard this racket and will come to my rescue. ‑

'Help!' he cried, but he knew it came out as little more than a murmur. He wished he had a tripod with which he could defend himself; he considered trying to hide behind his camera in case it worked as a better camouflage with animals than with human beings. He took it out from beneath his jacket and raised it to his eye, and immediately felt safer. He took a step towards the geese and they again threatened him, but he knew he had to advance. He hadn't loaded the camera yet, so he decided to adopt his old habit of taking imaginary pictures, in order to at least take his mind off the danger. He got the boldest goose, the one nearest to him with the longest neck, in focus, clicked, and marched forward.

James lost focus immediately and had trouble readjusting on account of his own progress and the flurry of the geese's wings and serpentine necks, and so it took him until he was right in the middle of them to realize that they were actually pecking at his legs. At that moment Margaret and her two farm girls emerged from their coffee break in the farmhouse, and they were rendered instantly helpless by the sight of a thin, hapless youth dancing awkwardly across the yard towards them with one eye closed, taking photographs of the geese that were biting him.

Eventually one of the farm girls recovered herself and took pity on him, grabbing a stick and swiping it at the geese.

'Shoo! Get away!' she shouted. 'Scat! Get!' They hissed and waddled off resentfully.

James stopped jumping. He refocused the lens and found himself being stared at by a blond young woman with a mud-flecked face. He lowered the camera. She scrutinized him a moment longer and then turned over her shoulder to the others and shouted: 'Looks like we've got a right townie here, Miss Marge.'

Margaret's was a small farm with a limited number of most species of breedable animal, assorted fruits and a variety of crops dispersed across her few acres, not because she was spreading her risk or was a believer in agricultural diversity, but rather because performing any activity for more than a couple of days at a time bored her. As a result she was unable to afford labour-saving machinery, and drove herself and her farm girls – a different pair of whom moved in every year for work experience between leaving school and going to agricultural college – like slaves. Their one compensation was that they got at least a little of just about every experience they were likely to need in the future.

They introduced themselves to James.

'Welcome to the Ark,' said Joanna, his blond saviour from the geese.

'Welcome to Maggie's Farm,' said Hilary, who was shorter and thinner and had dark-brown hair.

'Go on inside, James,' Margaret told him. 'Get Sarah to give you a coffee. We've got some mucking-out to do, haven't we, girls? See you at lunch.'

The ancient farmhouse was a long, narrow, stretched-out building: there was a tool-shed at one end and a storeroom with an apple loft above it at the other; the living quarters were in the middle, entered through a wooden porch to the left of the centre of the wall full of muddy boots and a rack of torn and frayed jackets and coats. It gave

160

onto a small hallway, with a staircase up one side, that ran straight through to the back door; on the left of the hall was a dining-room full of the best furniture, a dresser with what looked like an unused dowry of an immaculate dinner service and, around the walls, hundreds of unidentified rosettes of various colours.

On the right of the hall was a huge kitchen. It took up two-thirds of the length and all of the width of the ground floor, and was the cooking, dining and living room all in one. The kitchen area was at the far end, with an Aga against the wall that kept the tool-shed beyond, where Margaret's dogs slept, warm all winter. In the middle was a solid round table; while in the corner to the left of the door was Margaret's desk laden with receipts and bills, and to the right a TV encircled by a sofa and armchairs that looked like they were gradually sinking and spreading towards the floor, their morale broken, submitting in defeat to the human beings who sat on them.

The inhabitants of the house woke up slowly drinking tea around the Aga, ate their meals at the table, and spent their evenings in the comfy chairs playing cards and Scrabble, doing the newspaper crossword, knitting and reading, and drinking home-made wine. At night they dragged themselves upstairs out of the dozy warmth reluctantly, wondering if they couldn't organize sleeping arrangements in the big room as well.

Sarah, Margaret's wartime comrade, presided over their female ménage: she was cook and housekeeper. She wore colourful aprons over floral dresses and rarely stepped outside the front door because she didn't like getting muck on her polished shoes, and however much work there was to do on the farm Margaret never coerced her partner into helping, she just went out earlier and stayed out later herself.

In fact it was some time before James realized that Sarah took complete responsibility for the back garden – a vegetable patch, flower beds and lawn. In complete contrast to the front of the house, it was neat and tidy, the soil as clean, the grass as manicured, as a suburban garden, not a farm in the middle of the country. It was kept in such good order that Sarah didn't even need to wear gardening gloves to protect her delicate skin and painted nails, she just used a pair of yellow plastic kitchen ones.

Sarah was as slight as Margaret was solid, and she treated their farm girls with a maternal fussiness, making sure they'd eaten their greens and wrapped up warm before she let them outside.

'Don't fuss so, woman,' Margaret berated her. 'I've a hard enough time toughening them up when they get here without you spoiling them.'

'Don't be silly, Mig,' Sarah told her. 'They're just lasses away from home, not tough old boots like you.'

She was right. Margaret dressed in thick cords and what appeared to James to be about five layers of cardigan, and a tweed jacket that'd lost its buttons and which on windy days she tied with baler twine. She treated the girls with an older sister's presumption, when she wasn't driving them like feudal serfs. When she came inside, though, Margaret left her authority along with her wellies in the porch, she spoke in a reasonable voice instead of barking, and she took neither issue with, nor indeed any apparent interest in, the household management, which she left to Sarah. Instead she sat in her chair, lit a cigarette and waited for tea.

At first James found it hard to follow Margaret and the girls outside with his camera because Sarah urged him to stay indoors, saying, 'What a skinny boy you are, James. Doesn't anyone feed you properly at home? Look, I've made you some walnut cake, have another cup of tea, goodness, you don't want to go out there, it's blowing a gale.'

The girls smirked and winked at him, and he was too polite to refuse Sarah's kindness and go with them. As the weather grew warmer, though, he slipped out more easily and he drifted around the farm, Margaret granting him permission to take whatever pictures he wanted to. His preferred method – after the long apprenticeship of taking pictures with an empty camera – was simply to study his subjects through the lens before actually photographing them, and so he spent hours watching the various animals. James was entranced. They'd never had pets in the big house on the hill, not even gerbils or hamsters, and he gaped like a six-year-old at the self-important stupidity of guinea fowl, the humour of pigs, the awkwardness of ducks on dry land, the clumsy dignity of the cows, the prickly intelligence of the two horses, the timidity of the sheep, and the schizophrenia of the sheepdogs: meek supplicants after human affection, transformed when it was time for work into dervish persecutors of sheep.

By May James knew every inch of Margaret's farm, its fields either side of a meandering stream through a valley in the lowland wolds. All except for the furthest field, because across the fence lay the pine wood at the edge of Jack's farm, where Robert came shooting some

Saturdays with Stanley. James had never actually seen Robert there – and he preferred to catch the bus rather than ask Stanley for a lift, he preferred to keep them separate – but he'd *heard* them: the throttled cry of pheasants rising, their wings beating like old football rattles, and the dull cracks of the guns.

James kept away from there. Partly because, although he couldn't see in he knew people could see out, and he didn't like the idea of Robert watching him. He could, though, see far enough into the woods to make out the carcasses of magpies hung on wire.

'It's horrible,' James whispered to Joanna, 'warning the birds to keep away like that; it's like bullying.'

Joanna looked at him pitifully. 'You don't know anything, James,' she told him. 'They hang them up for maggots, then the maggots drop and the pheasants eat them. It's food, that's all.'

James spent the daylight hours of his weekends on the farm when he should have been revising for A-levels, and when the exams were over he spent every day of whole weeks there, finally loading a film in the camera one Tuesday in July: he no longer startled animals every time he entered a field – birds panicking into the sky, bolting rabbits swallowed by the ground – and was able to skirt around the women at their work without them stopping to watch what he was doing; he was no longer under the illusion that he was invisible, but at least hoped that he was inconspicuous. In reality, whenever any of the women saw him prowling around with one eye closed, they were reminded of the pantomime of his first arrival, and had to stifle their laughter.

Gradually, though, his absorption in his ridiculous hobby, and his persistence, won them over, and they found him more endearing than absurd.

'Are you sure you're a Freeman?' Margaret asked him. It was no secret that she didn't much like the rest of her relatives. 'You're not a bad chap at all, really,' she told him approvingly. 'And I'm sure you'll find something better to do with yourself eventually,' she added to encourage him. She never referred to his mother Mary, her sister. She'd never understood her sister's marriage, or how anyone could stomach being yoked to someone else like that for more than a week. And as for bringing up children twenty-four hours a day, they were more trouble than turkeys, with their moods and illnesses. Not that Margaret was quite insensitive enough to share this opinion with James; it did, though, mean that she had little sympathy with him, and she treated him with the same straightforwardness as she did everyone else.

'What are you wasting your time for, James, taking snaps of *sheep*?' she demanded as he got in the way while they were bedding the sheep down the night before shearing, not on straw but on stinging nettles, which wouldn't catch in their fleece. 'Sheep are all the same, they've got no character. Why don't you go and photograph the pigs? Now *they're* worth it.'

The two sows were Margaret's favourite animals. She wouldn't let Joanna or Hilary go near them, insisting on looking after them herself.

'A dog looks up to you, James. A cat looks down on you. But a pig is equal. Scratch her behind the ears like this, that's what she likes.'

James caught the bus out every day and walked into the farmyard. He'd bought himself a pair of wellington boots, which as well as keeping him clean also protected him from the ferocious beaks of the geese, whose aggression was unrelenting. They were the only animals he didn't like, and he gained a great deal of pleasure from standing still and letting them peck at rubber, as he looked around the yard. It was a mess. Odd pieces of rusting machinery poked through grass and nettles. Smoke rose from a pile of rubbish. Hens pecked at grit and dirt. He breathed in the sweet smell of silage from a mass of it underneath black plastic covered with hundreds of old tyres. It had mulched into a huge cake, from whose side moist bricks were cut to be loaded on a trailer and scattered across a field. There was something edible, something mouthwatering, about that mixture of shit and straw; it looked as soggy and heavy as Sarah's carrot cake.

'Can I do anything to help, Aunt Margaret?' James volunteered once at tea, thinking he should make some contribution for all the meals Sarah gave him. 'Shall I clean up the yard or something?' he asked.

'What's wrong with the yard?' she countered. 'Did you hear that, Sarah? What a cheek!'

'He's right. It's a shambles.'

'What?'

'We don't need a man's help around here, do we, Marge?' said Hilary.

'Of course not!' Margaret agreed.

'We don't need his either,' said Joanna, nodding towards James.

'You look like a strapping young man to me,' said Sarah, who noticed James' blushes.

'We're only fooling, aren't we, girls?' said Margaret. 'No, James,' she said, 'really, it's rather quaint to have a man about the place.'

The time when James had been frozen was coming to an end, although he didn't yet realize it. He spent a week photographing the horses: an old nag put out to grass and a temperamental mare Margaret was looking after that some local girl couldn't handle. Joanna rode her most evenings, and James took his first photographs of a human being under the pretence of capturing an airborne horse flying over a jump in the horses' field.

'Go on, lie right under the beam, James,' Joanna called to him. Having saved him from the geese, now she wanted to trample him to death. 'Don't look so scared,' she shouted, 'I'll clear it easily.'

'I'm not scared,' he whispered, his finger trembling on the shutter release.

'I'm coming!' she yelled, as the horse's hooves grew louder.

Joanna was tall and strongly built, and she smelled of milk. She and Hilary were the same age as the nurses back in the hospital ward, and they were just as brusque and just as sophisticated. It always sounded strange when Margaret or Sarah referred to them as the 'girls', but James loved it when they did; it made them appear a bit less intimidating.

Joanna looked after the cows: it was the closest thing to a full-time job on the farm, because apart from the fruit trees – whose produce diminished each year, since Margaret never made time to prune and replant properly, but which still provided a crop of pears for perry and apples for a local chutney factory – the small dairy herd was the only thing that earned any real income. Joanna brought them in for milking twice a day – or, rather, they came of their own accord, loping across fields, their heavy udders swaying, and into the yard.

It was Joanna who, when it was time for calves to be weaned, took their mothers to the furthest field on Margaret's land, where it butted up against Jack's much larger farm, beside their pine copse.

'Why are you bringing them all the way over here?' James whispered.

'You'll find out soon enough,' Joanna told him. She was right. The cows mooed constantly, a bathetic chorus. By lunchtime the next day, even though he was photographing the farmyard cats basking in the sunshine outside the farmhouse porch half a mile away, James couldn't stand it any more.

165

'I ought to get back and process some of these films,' he told Joanna. 'I think there's a bus in half an hour,' he whispered.

She peered at him, her face muddy. She leaned her mouth to his ear. 'They'll do this for another two days, and then they'll forget all about their calves and stop,' she whispered back. She smelled of milk and sweat, and made James nervous. He lurched away.

'Don't forget to come back,' Joanna called after him.

'Is my sister-in-law turning you into a country bumpkin?' Charles boomed at the breakfast table the next morning, 'now that you're coming home smelling of manure instead of chemicals?'

Simon and Robert chortled.

'Talk to the animals, do you?' Robert asked him.

'Shut up, Robert,' said Alice.

'Ee-ore. Oink, oink. Baaa,' Robert mimicked, but in a whisper. Laura, who was sitting beside James, put a hand on his arm and the other over her mouth. When she'd recovered herself she glared at Robert. His eyes narrowed. He leaned across the table towards her and made obscene snuffling noises.

'Now, now, *children*!' Charles declared. 'Cut this nonsense out.' Charles was always disconcerted by how much less servile his children were than his employees.

'Do you want a game of chess later on?' Laura asked James after breakfast.

'Not today, I can't,' he replied. 'Sorry. I've got to go into school. I've got to pick something up.'

James waited till the *next* day, Saturday, before taking his A-level results to his father's study before lunch: he'd passed each exam with the minimum grade, and he thought Charles might be in a better mood at the weekend.

'My God! Three Es!' Charles roared. 'Is that the height of my son's achievement? My God! It's just as *well* I don't set much store by education.'

Alice was turning out to be the only academic success among the children. She was top of her class, gaining straight As without really trying, without any apparent ambition. At the age of fourteen she tried to explain the thirty-two proofs of Euclid to her older brothers, who each came up as best they could with hurried excuses: 'I don't have time now, Alice, I'm late, yes, of course I understand, I remember doing these when I was your age, a bit younger actually, but I've got to run now.'

She did well enough in arts subjects, but it was in science that she really excelled. Charles was confused. He'd always assumed that one of the boys would be good with numbers, a girl with words or pictures. Eventually he accepted that it was possible for Alice to have inherited his head for figures and his business acumen, except that he could see from brief perusals of her homework that the algebraic equations, formulae and periodic table that engrossed her were in fact quite different – with their strange symbols, and letters mixed in with the numbers – from the columns of accounts that represented money.

Robert, on the other hand, had failed most of his O-levels; but then no one had expected him to pass any. They all knew he'd been no more than a fleeting visitor to school and had already started selling the old cars Stanley towed into the yard for him and which he repaired and then tested at high speed up and down the drive in noisy exhibitions of black smoke and burning rubber.

'Look at Robert!' Charles boomed at James in his study. 'Hardly learned to *read*, poor boy. They've barely taught him the shadow of a shade. But,' Charles tapped his skull, 'he knows which way's up. He might be uneducated but he's not stupid, I don't care what anyone says. But you, young man, what are *you* going to do?'

James wasn't sure. His art teacher hadn't been much help. Miss Stubbs was so surprised that he'd been given a pass at all for his weak drawings and his straightforward photographs that when he'd bumped into her at school the day before to find out his results she hugged him to her ample bosom.

'Well done, you stubborn boy,' she cried.

James extricated himself gracelessly from her embrace. 'What should I do now?' he asked. 'Should I go on to college, do you think?'

'You should have thought about it last year, when everybody else did,' she told him. 'Still, taking a year out's a good idea, in my opinion, as you know. I certainly wouldn't stand in your way. But you must do what you want to do, dear boy. As you surely will, no matter what I say.'

'I don't know,' he whispered. 'If I go to college, Father's too rich for me to get a grant. But I don't want him to support me.' He shook his head. 'I just want to take photographs.'

'I should hope so,' she replied, 'after avoiding my life-drawing classes for two years. Just don't *snap*,' she begged. 'And study the great painters,' she added as she turned towards another pupil approaching them, another student to congratulate or console.

167

'What? You mean the great photographers?' he murmured after her.

She turned her head without breaking stride. 'The *painters*, dear boy. Turner, Vermeer, Caravaggio.' She waved her hand as if pointing them out among the group of pupils a few yards away. 'We've been struggling with light for centuries. You snappers have only just started.'

'Yes, *you*, James!' His father's voice now boomed into his thoughts. 'What are you going to *do*?'

James felt his heart racing and his cheeks burn; he was fatally unprepared, but he couldn't, he wouldn't, admit it. He swallowed.

'Well,' he whispered, 'I've been thinking, Father. I should go to London. And Amsterdam. And Florence. To take photographs, study the painters, look at the light—'

'All right, James,' Charles interrupted. 'Stop your gibberish. I don't understand a word you're saying. You want a holiday, is that it? Fine.'

James' cheeks burned deeper. 'You don't *listen* to me,' he hissed. 'You never listen. It's not a *holiday*.'

'When you get back, I suppose you'll be wanting me to see you through college, eh? Rely on your old man to see you through? The thing is, James, I can't see the point in supporting you now you're old enough to earn your own keep, when you don't even *like* studying to judge by these lamentable grades.'

'I'll get a job then, Father,' James whispered.

'Rubbish!' Charles proclaimed. 'I want at least one of my sons to get a decent education. You should go to university. Anyway, who's going to *give* you a job? I know I wouldn't't!' Charles laughed heartily. 'Do you want a whisky, James? I'm going to pour myself one.'

James could feel himself trembling with impotent rage. 'No,' he whispered.

'Please yourself, boy,' Charles yelled from the drinks cabinet.

'No,' James repeated. 'I'm going to be a photographer, Father. I'm going to get a job as a photographer.' He turned and made for the door, swaying.

'Fine!' Charles called after him. 'Good! But where are you going to *study*? Which college do you want to go to?' he shouted. 'I need to know if I'm to help you get in.' But James was already limping up the stairs.

*

James went straight to the darkroom and stayed there, processing negatives and then making a print of the temperamental mare, except that instead of printing the whole frame he blew up a detail, excluding the horse entirely apart from a few hairs of her mane. He was left with a grainy, soft close-up of Joanna's face: she looked so calmly concentrated that anyone would have thought she was sitting in a chair watching TV and not on an unstable horse flying through the air.

It happened to be one of the hottest days of the summer, and James missed most of it, shut up in the infrared light of the darkroom. While the prints were washing in the old guests' bath he went outside for some fresh air, and the light was so glaring he could hardly even squint for some minutes.

'It's too bright out here,' he said.

'James!' Simon's voice called. 'There you are. Bring your camera over here. I've got you some work. Robert wants some photos.'

Alice and Laura still went to the cinema on Saturday afternoons, though less often now to watch the children's matinée than to copy Zoe's clothes and her gestures and listen to her stories on the flat roof of the Electra, where she sat on warm afternoons sharing good Lebanese black with the projectionist, while the film drifted in and out of focus on the screen below. When Zoe heard from the girls about James' impending travels, which news Charles had immediately shared over lunch, she gave them a lift home from the cinema, excited by the possibility that someone else in the family had inherited wanderlust genes. And she suspected that James could do with some traveller's tips, since he'd be too shy to even ask directions, and anyway if people couldn't hear what he was saying in English, what chance would he have in Italy?

'So James is setting out on the yellow brick road,' she said, accelerating dangerously past a double-decker bus up the hill. 'The Tin Man's setting off on his own.'

The boys were round the back of the house in a rare tableau of fraternity: James had agreed to photograph a couple of Robert's resurrected rattletraps for the *Midlands Trader*, while Simon advised him on the most flattering angle, as well as telling Robert how to give the small engine of some tin lizzie a fruitier noise. The girls had to close their eyes and brace their knees as Zoe careered her Morris Minor around the side of the house, accelerated towards the yard, and came to a crunching halt a few inches from the scrapheap Robert was working on. Robert was the only one who stayed where he was:

Simon and James picked themselves up from the ground where they'd flung themselves, and the girls opened their eyes, as Zoe got out of her car.

'How much you want for this old banger?' Robert asked her in his gritty voice, tapping her bonnet.

'It's not for sale, mighty mouse,' Zoe said, going up to him. 'And another thing: my ticket seller said she caught you trying to get into the X-film again on Thursday night. I've told you before, you little squirt, I could lose my licence. I'm warning you, Robert, don't do it again. At least,' she added, 'not until you've grown a few inches.'

The girls tittered. Robert scowled. He grabbed a spanner and ducked back under the raised bonnet, banging his head.

Simon finished dusting off his elegant jacket and trousers. 'I thought all those drugs were meant to relax you, darling,' he told Zoe ruefully.

'Don't be simple, Simon,' Zoe replied.

'And what *is* that extraordinary animal on your back?' he continued. 'You must let me take you shopping some time.'

Zoe was wearing clogs, loon pants, a cheesecloth shirt, two rainbow scarves around her neck and one round her ringleted hair, and an Afghan coat. She raised her chin at Simon and stroked it with her thumb in a gesture of disdain, without breaking her stride towards James, whose face was split in two by a huge grin: their cousin Zoe was the only woman he knew who was neither charmed by Simon nor impressed by Robert, who even seemed to actively prefer his, James', company.

'Hi, sweetheart,' she said, kissing him three times on the cheeks. 'What's all this about you hitting the open road, you sly mole, you?'

They drank tea by the pond and James tried to smoke one of Zoe's multi-coloured Sobranie cigarettes.

'Why haven't you been to my cinema lately, you rotten stay-away?' she demanded. 'Hasn't Alice shown you the programme? And don't tell me you're put off by subtitles, or I'll throw your cake in the water.'

'What are you talking about?' he asked. 'I thought you didn't really like films.'

'Not any more, James,' she told him. 'I've been converted. I just saw a print of this film some idiot was raving about on the radio.' It was the first time Zoe had sat through an entire film without falling asleep, she admitted, since the last time she'd watched *The Wizard of Oz* as a child in her grandmother's cinema, wondering whether her mother bore any resemblance to the Wicked Witch.

'It's called *Solaris*, James.'

'What's it about?'

'I haven't a clue; I couldn't understand a single moment,' she told him. 'I was just hypnotized. I thought it must have been some kind of trick. I mean, it's meant to be science fiction but it's not. That night I couldn't sleep. Images from the film kept running through my brain.' She shook her head deliberately, as if trying to realign the pictures in her mind's eye. 'So,' Zoe continued, 'I went back the next day and saw it again.'

'And?' James whispered.

'Well, the veil was lifted. Like Siddhartha at the river. I felt like I was watching my own life. Or, to be more precise, my own dreams. It was uncanny, James. I always thought I was running an entertainment arcade, a penny peep-show. I didn't realize films could show the human soul. I'll book it for the cinema. And more like it. You just wait and see.'

Over the following months and years Zoe would become what she'd been only pretending to be: a connoisseuse of world cinema. She varied the programme with an ever widening variety of films, some of which she was the first to bring into Britain. She not only showed them at the Electra but, in order to cover the costs, also sold them to other cinemas around the country. Within a short time Electra Pictures would become a significant distributor and Zoe an expert in Japanese masters, the banned masterpieces of the Soviet Union, and the new South American cinema. The ciné buffs greeted her films as if they'd been sent from El Dorado, with gold in the piles of round cans.

'Instead of travelling, I'm going to bring the world to me, James,' she told him by the pond. 'I'm sorry, honey, but I'm afraid photography's been outgrown by its bastard child. You ought to get rid of that outdated box around your neck and buy yourself a movie camera.'

James smiled. He lacked the wit to argue with Zoe, even if he didn't agree.

'The thing is,' she continued, 'cinema can show *time*, James. *You* can only take snapshots, little moments, glimpses. Films can describe

171

the movement of the soul, think of it, they could show bilocation on a split-screen, or by using cross-cutting effects.'

'Maybe you should be a film-maker yourself,' James whispered.

'Don't be absurd, sweetheart,' she said, brushing the suggestion aside. 'It's hard enough to *watch* a film properly. You must need to be a genius to make one. Anyway, I've got other things on my mind: did I tell you about my new teacher?'

'Gurdjieff's godson?'

'That was *months* ago.'

'You mean the chanting group?'

'No, James, we had a row. No, my *new* teacher. He's a hundred years old. Maybe even older. He's visiting England for the first time, and he's teaching us Dream Yoga. It's a technique for learning to stay in the state between being awake and sleeping, and directing the course of your dreams.' Zoe glanced at her watch. 'I'll tell you all about it when you get back, sweetheart, I've got to go and get ready for this evening's screenings. I can only afford to pay a part-timer.' She got up with the tea-tray. 'Tell me when you're going. I've got lots of maps and stuff you can have. Here, start with this. It's a *Teach Yourself Italian* tape.'

Charles had organized a family holiday in the Dordogne for a fortnight in August, but James excused himself and was allowed to stay behind.

Stanley and Edna and Laura went away with Stanley's sister Pauline and her family – Garfield, Lewis and Gloria – to adjoining B. and B.s in Weymouth.

'He'll be all on his own here,' Edna worried. 'Who'll make sure he eats properly?'

'I'll be all right,' James whispered. 'I'm going to stay out at the farm.'

'You can always come with us, I'm sure,' Laura suggested when they were on their own. 'I bet Lewis would like that. I don't think he's looking forward to it.'

'Forget it, Laura,' James told her. She looked hurt. 'I'm sorry,' he whispered. 'I know you're only trying to be helpful.'

Fortunately Margaret and Sarah never took a holiday. James went back to the farm with a rucksack and a new, long lens on his camera. After Sarah showed him the guest room Margaret and the girls embarrassed him back in the kitchen by adjusting the zoom back and forth.

'It's obscene,' Margaret declared.

'Typical men's invention,' Hilary agreed. She pointed it out of the window and zoomed in. 'Shoot!' she cried.

'Don't you take any notice of them,' Sarah told him. 'They don't know anything about photography, dear. Here, James, have another mug of tea.'

'It's so I can take wildlife pictures,' James whispered, blushing.

James kept the zoom lens on his camera most of the time: he took a number of shots of small birds, one or two of rabbits, a heron, and even a fox, crawling after it through the pear orchard one hot blue afternoon. Mostly, though, he used it as a telescope to spy on Joanna, pretending to himself that he was studying her physiognomy in preparation for a portrait of a human being, the next projected stage in his photographic development. He watched her push the sheep's heads under in the dip, he watched her forking straw when they burned the stubble (and wondered whether he was ready to make the jump back to colour film), he watched her swilling out the milk churns.

'Looks like Mr Snoopy Lens has found his subject,' said Hilary loudly behind him. James abruptly lowered the camera.

'There's a sparrow flapping around in the milking shed,' he whispered, flustered. 'It's looking for a way out.'

'It's not the only thing, then,' said Hilary curtly. Then she looked over at Joanna and they both laughed.

The weeks went by and James forgot about going home. One Friday in the middle of September Joanna and Hilary brought in the last of the hay. They set up a conveyor belt from the trailer up to the hayloft: Hilary heaved the bales onto the belt and Joanna took them off at the other end, grabbing their twine and swinging them round with her knee. Hilary had to stop loading the conveyor belt every once in a while to let Joanna stack the bales further back in the loft, but the last few Joanna just let pile up around her. When Hilary had emptied the trailer she drove away, leaving Joanna to finish stacking.

James watched her from the kitchen, where Sarah had enticed him in to taste the Parkin cake she'd made for tea.

'It's too soggy, isn't it?' she asked worriedly from the sink.

'It's scrumptious, Sarah,' he reassured her with his mouth full, looking out of the window.

'No, it's all claggy,' she maintained.

173

'It's delicious, Sarah,' he whispered, cleaning sticky bits off his teeth with his tongue, gazing across the yard. He lifted his camera to his eye and zoomed in on Joanna, a shadowy figure inside the hay loft, stacking the last of the bales. It couldn't have been a great year: there was a lot of space between them and the loft door.

'Photographing the geese again, are you, dear?' he heard Sarah ask. He could tell from the sound of her voice that she'd turned to face him. His heart jumped, but he quickly realized that she couldn't see what he saw, from where she stood on the other side of the kitchen.

'There's a couple of, er, redwings outside,' he said.

'That's nice,' Sarah replied distractedly. He could hear her slapping dough on the work surface. 'We don't usually see them around here at this time of year,' she continued. 'They don't usually arrive for another month or two, I believe.'

It was eerie to look at something on the full zoom, with your other eye squeezed tight shut: it was because the image was, despite being apparently so close, *silent*. Of course he could hear things – like Sarah's voice – but he couldn't hear the swish of the hay sweeping across the wooden boards or the gasping breath of Joanna's exertions. She was isolated and unreal. She must have finished then because she stepped forward and leaned her forearms against the top frame of the loft doorway and, bent, peered out from beneath them. She looked around abstractedly. For a few seconds her gaze seemed to fix on James; again his heart thumped but he remained still, looking at her, gambling that she couldn't make him out with her naked eye. Or perhaps hoping that she could. And then she pushed herself off the door-frame and walked backwards a languorous pace or two, paused . . . and then she just *fell* back into the dark.

James stared, unable to believe his own eyes. Had she really just done that? Fallen, spreadeagled, backwards? Was she right now lying flat out on the dusty floorboards?

There was no movement there whatsoever. She's fainted, James thought. He lowered the camera and scurried to the door, besocked feet sliding across the tiled floor.

'Sure you've had enough, dear?' Sarah called after him, but he didn't reply. 'No,' she said to herself. 'Too much honey.'

James yanked his wellies on in the porch and swayed across the yard. One sock was already slipping down over his heel as he entered the barn and slowed down. He stopped and listened, and breathed silently. He couldn't hear anything from the hayloft above. He stepped over to the ladder, paused, and then began to climb it.

Shafts of light poked through the patchy roof. Particles of chaff and dust corruscated in the sunrays. James' skin prickled. There was complete silence, not broken but rather accentuated by the distant sound of Margaret's gruff commands to her sheepdogs. His eyes became accustomed to the light and he clambered up onto the wooden boards and stepped around the side of the newly stacked hay: Joanna lay on her back with her eyes closed, breathing peacefully. If she *had* fainted, then a scrappy carpet of loose bits of hay, scattered across the boards, had cushioned her fall a little. But she didn't look uncomfortable, she looked relaxed, as if she were sleeping.

James stood over her. She was dressed in scuffed short riding-boots, blue jeans and a dirty white shirt. Her short blond hair was streaked blonder from the sun; there were flecks of mud on her tanned face. Her mouth was open slightly and her cheeks were slack with puppy-fat she hadn't lost. She was tall – as tall as James – and big-boned.

It was hot up there in the hayloft, hot and itchy. James stared at Joanna's spreadeagled body and back at her face. He could hear his blood thumping. He raised his camera to his right eye, closed his left eye, and felt himself calm down, distanced from the reality of her body. He lowered himself onto one knee, framing her all the while, closing in on her face. A thin stem of hay, he saw now, lay across her bottom lip, adhered to her saliva. He adjusted the focus, having to withdraw an inch or two because he'd been too close for the zoom lens's focal length. And then, without a conscious order from his mind, the index finger of his right hand clicked the shutter release.

Joanna's eyes opened slowly, blinked, and widened through comprehension, surprise, anger. James was petrified. And because he could only see, through the viewfinder, her face, he never saw her hands coming: they grabbed his collar and he found himself being flung across her twisting body. He let go of the camera: he landed on his back and the camera – attached to its strap around his neck – swung after him, missed his face and struck the floor beside him.

'What the bloody hell you think you're doing?!' Joanna shouted at him. 'Sneaking up on people like that! You little bloody perv! Jesus Christ!' She was getting up as she shouted, glaring at him with raging eyes. James stared startled as a rabbit back at her.

'Jesus Christ!' she said, and turned away. She looked out of the loft door, not *at* anything, just away, calming herself. 'Jesus Christ!'

James recovered himself, became aware of his body: his dry mouth, his coldly sweating armpits, his trembling fingers. Then he felt the strap around his neck and lifted it over and looked at the camera: the force of its impact with the boards had sprung it open, twisting the door on the back and denting the zoom lens, as well as wiping out that roll of film which had included his first proper portrait of a human being.

'You've broken the camera,' James whispered, bewildered.

Joanna spun round.

'Fuck the camera,' she said. She came over to him, and stood above him as he'd just stood above her. 'Fuck the bloody camera, James,' she said. And then she kicked his foot. It wasn't hard enough to hurt, it was just a gesture of annoyance. She was standing with the open loft door behind her, James had to scrunch up his eyes to look at her. He was leaning back on his forearms and elbows. She stared at him.

'Just keep away from me,' she said. She didn't move. Instead she kicked his foot again, harder, and James grimaced.

'All right?' she demanded.

James raised his torso up to a sitting position, drawing his feet in at the same time, but Joanna quickly kicked again before he'd got them out of range.

'All right!?' she yelled, and he yelled back:

'Yes!'

'All right, then,' Joanna said. 'Just keep away from me, that's all,' she said, and she turned slowly and started to move towards the ladder in the far corner of the loft, looking about her as if searching for something she might have dropped, and brushing bits of hay off her shirt.

James watched her. And what then infuriated him, what seized him with sudden rage at that moment, was how slowly she was moving away from him. He pushed himself up and was at her in two or three strides and she only had time to half-turn before he caught her waist, and they both fell.

'Urgh!' Joanna grunted when she hit the boards. James landed with his face on her stomach and he clambered up her body, his hands grabbing her shirt for leverage, which ripped loudly apart.

She smelled of milk and sweat, and her hot breath came on his. At first she rolled from side to side to get him off her, but he clung on like a limpet and then he felt her wet tongue in his dry mouth. She undid her bra and her breasts spilled out and he gnawed one with his lips. Her fingers were undoing his jeans, his groin was bursting. He attacked her mouth. They were both silent and furious

176

and overwhelmed. Joanna's jeans and pants were round her ankles. His prick came out too late, he felt it hot and surging, and, groaning, saw his spunk come shooting onto her thigh and onto the dust and strands of hay on the wooden boards.

They didn't say anything. Joanna pulled her jeans up, James zipped up his. They sat there, recovering as if from a sudden accident. Joanna gave James a quick, fierce hug, then climbed down the loft ladder.

James took his battered camera to his room in an unsure mood of despair and elation. He didn't know whether Joanna was frustrated or satisfied; whether she liked him or thought he was an idiot. He hoped that whatever it was that had happened things would go further, and that he was safe in Joanna's hands. It didn't occur to him that she had little more idea what she was doing than he did.

The next day, Saturday, the district agricultural show took place in a large village a few miles deeper into the wolds. James produced from his rucksack a pair of framed photographs of Margaret's favourite sow.

'Just a small thank you,' he said quietly.

'What a marvellous boy you are!' Margaret proclaimed. 'Look at these, Sarah, aren't they beautiful?'

'Indeed they are, Mig,' Sarah replied, glancing at them. She was filling a hamper with sandwiches and other things. 'We need more ice, Hilary,' she said, 'it's going to be sweltering today.' She was clearly anxious, she had other things on her mind: Sarah had a big day ahead.

'Could we have them on the wall in the dining-room, do you think, dear?' Margaret asked her.

'Of course we can, Mig.'

'I'll put them up when we get back, if you like,' Hilary volunteered. 'So you were snooping on the pigs after all, you wily fox,' she told James.

'Not bad, James, not bad,' Joanna told him. He stared at the tablecloth, overcome with modesty – and also embarrassment: he could hardly bear to look at Joanna, his body hummed with desire, he was convinced the others could hear it. He sat with his legs crossed, praying that she would leave the room.

'I'll fetch the car up to the front door, Sarah,' Joanna suggested, nodding at the hamper and bottles on the table, answering James' prayers.

The show was held in a huge, sloping recreation field below the village hall. Sarah went straight to the produce tent and stayed there all day: she'd entered jars of jam, marmalade, chutney, pickles, home-made wine, cakes, scones and biscuits, as well as vegetables from her garden in any category where they were judged not for their size but their taste. All were now wilting in the heat of the tent. She inspected her rivals' superior wares and decided that this year she wouldn't win a single rosette.

Margaret hadn't entered any of her animals in competition: she knew she didn't have a prize bull or ram or even bantam among her motley assortment of animals.

'They ought to have a prize for the biggest number of different animals from the same farm you can fit in one pen,' said Hilary. 'You'd have no competition, Marge.'

Margaret wasn't bothered. She roamed among the other farmers' pens and joined them in the beer tent.

James found himself following Joanna around, trailing in her wake: she was being dragged by Hilary through the crowded field, through the attentions of young farmers all bigger and stronger than he was. She glanced over her shoulder at him but Hilary's influence was greater than his, and when James saw his Uncle Jack and Aunt Clare with their two sons, Edward and Thomas, he went over to say hello and tagged along with them. Jack and Clare kept stopping to greet people and the boys were restless in the hot sun.

'Leave them with me,' James volunteered. 'I'll look after them if you want.'

There were stalls all around the edge of the field and James was glad of the excuse of chaperoning the two boys to have a go at everything on offer: trying to get three darts in the same playing card; guessing the weight of a pig (which he made a note of to tell Margaret, sure she'd win it); skittles; a coconut shy; passing a ring over a twisting, electric wire without it buzzing; a white elephant stall at which he bought an ancient wide-angle lens for fifteen pence; a bran tub and a tombola; a bottle stall at which he bought six tickets, one after another, to win the champagne or whisky there but succeeded only in encumbering himself with jars of piccalilli and tomato ketchup and a bottle of lime squash; and an air-rifle shooting range. James mistrusted guns, but Edward wanted a go and then Thomas had to follow, and in the end James decided he didn't want to be left out either. He found his aim was steady and enjoyed the soft thud of the trigger, and his six pellets all hit the square paper targets: he went back three times during the day, improving his score each time, and won the third prize of a five-pound note.

They all met up for lunch together around Jack's pick-up, on spread-out tartan blankets: butter melted and ran, Margaret knocked over her cider, Edward and Thomas argued over the last of Sarah's chocolate brownies, Hilary distanced herself and Joanna from the family group and a couple of young men invited them to the beer tent. James watched, squinting from the sun, and resolved to buy himself a pair of dark glasses.

In the afternoon the roped-off space in the middle of the field was used for sports of all kinds – humans first and then animals. James drifted around on his own, observing. He watched the two boys fall over each other in the children's three-legged race and Joanna and Hilary go tumbling in the sack race. He watched Jack fumble with the veterans' egg-and-spoon and Margaret win the women's tossing the hay bale, planting her feet apart, swinging the long fork up and then flicking it with a grunt to send the bale soaring over the bar.

James was surprised by how content he was, how little he missed being there on the track inside the ropes, running, stretching, gasping. The boy who'd run and yammered had changed into a quiet observer; he'd moved from the centre to the outside; and right now he didn't seem to mind.

James swayed drifting through the crowded field, his ears filled with ponies' hooves thundering and their riders' hard breathing as they veered around the racetrack, his nose filled with the smell of grease and hot metal and burning coal from the traction engines displayed in a corner. But most of all he saw: he forgot his limp and his shyness and became a pair of roving eyes.

'I am a camera,' James said to himself, seeking out moments and framing them in his imagination: a line of men pissing behind a screen of canvas; a dark, gypsy-looking man mocking a squat stallholder until they traded blows, the gypsy laughing even as their fists were flailing; three judges tasting sips of someone's carrot whisky, the competitors eyeing them with the same fearful resentment as the mortals did the gods of Mount Olympus in a film he'd once seen, their entire fates in their hands.

It's time to take pictures of people, James decided.

*

179

They drove home hot and listless, the car smelling of beer and damp, sour clothes. James was squeezed in the back seat between Margaret, dozing, and Hilary staring blankly at passing cars and rushing hedges. Joanna drove, and beside her Sarah cradled in her lap a pile of blue and red and yellow rosettes to add to her collection in the dining-room.

They persuaded Margaret to lie down on the sofa in the kitchen, and while James for once helped the girls with the chores Sarah prepared a barbecue in her back garden. She cooked enough baked potatoes and skewered kebabs for twice as many people, so they all ate more than they needed to, and then sat in the warm dark, gazing at the rising moon, replete and supine. Eventually Sarah started clearing away, refusing all offers of help. Then Margaret stood up and said:

'Well. That's the end of another summer. You've been good girls, you two. And it's been nice having you around too, young man.'

Hilary soon followed them off to bed, yawning. James' and Joanna's hands reached tentatively into the dark between them. They pulled each other up and went without a word to the hay loft. There they kissed for a long time; when they paused they caressed each other's faces, necks, his stomach, her breasts.

'You're a good kisser, James,' Joanna told him.

'Thank you,' he whispered. He thought it was the nicest thing anyone had ever said to him. Emboldened, he almost asked her if he was the very best of all the men she'd kissed, but decided not to push his luck. He wanted to compliment her too. Possibilities skipped through his mind: I'm in love with your breasts, Joanna, your flesh is edible, I could become a cannibal, you're like milk, you make me feel like I'm drowning. None of them sounded right.

'You're gorgeous,' he whispered. Joanna took her clothes off and James took off his, releasing his eager erection into the open air, but he knew it was safe this time, his body was restraining itself.

They kissed again, calmly, their hands exploring the strange terrains of the other's body. Joanna smelled of milk and beer and mushrooms. She opened and took him, and he realized he *was* drowning, and he collapsed across her, shuddering with relief and happiness as he lost what was left of his virginity.

The next morning James said goodbye to Joanna, before Margaret and Sarah drove her and Hilary home. They kissed and hugged and swapped addresses.

'I'll write,' Joanna told him.

'I'll phone,' he told her, knowing that neither would keep their word.

Instead James telephoned Lewis, to see if he could come and pick him up from the farm. He had too much stuff to carry on the bus, but he also wanted to see Lewis again.

'I can't wait to see you, Lew!' James told him.

'There's no need to shout, Jay,' Lewis said.

'I'm not shouting!' James replied.

James took a last walk around the farm, smiling. 'Time to go back to town,' he told himself. He breathed the country air deep into his lungs; he felt hollow, and elated.

Once they got out of the lane and onto the main road Lewis drove his father's car so much over the speed limit that the chassis shook and the engine moaned and his hands on the steering wheel reverberated like an old drunkard's.

'Bloody thing won't go any faster,' he apologized. 'I can't wait to get my own wheels, Jay.'

That was about all Lewis said for the rest of the journey because he was unable to interrupt his friend, who to his surprise had shed his whispering reticence, and proceeded to regale Lewis with an account of what he'd been doing in an entirely new voice: James hadn't spoken above a whisper for years, so that Lewis now had the impression that James' voice had belatedly broken at the age of eighteen.

'The thing about women, Lew, is that you never really know what they're thinking. But that's OK, you see, that's the whole fun of it, you'll find out, mate. Anyway, Joanna's friend, the other girl, was called Hilary. She was probably more your type, I mean she was pretty cool, you know, she wasn't friendly at all. This one day she was driving the tractor over to the orchard, right, and . . .'

Lewis hardly took in a word of what James was saying. He wasn't listening. He was waiting for James to talk about what had happened at home. And gradually it dawned on him that James didn't *know* what had happened.

'How long have you been out here?' Lewis managed to interject. 'Has anyone rung you?'

'No,' said James, and he resumed his prattle.

Lewis realized that he had to explain, he had to prepare James for what he'd find. James, however, showed no interest in what had been going on in his absence, rambling on instead with the story of how he'd spent his summer which, if Lewis *had* been listening, would have certainly bored him into falling asleep at the wheel: deprived by his shyness of practice in telling a story, James now included every extraneous detail, failed to exaggerate when necessary, and laughed out loud at the bits that were least funny, deaf, or oblivious, to Lewis's silence.

When they joined the ring road, Lewis eased his foot off the accelerator pedal to give James time to shut up, to ask how his family were keeping. As they circled the town, however, Lewis had to accept that his nice, troubled childhood playmate had grown up and been transformed by one brief summer into a self-important bore.

'I took fifteen rolls of film of the pigs, can you believe that? They're Margaret's favourite animals, and I wanted to do her a favour. You know what she says? "A cat looks down on you, a dog looks—" '

'James!' Lewis interrupted. 'Listen, James, there's things I ought to tell you, things have happened while you were away. In your house. In your family.'

'Save it, Lewis,' James told him. 'I want to surprise them. I don't want to spoil *my* surprise. Anyway,' he resumed, 'I think I'll come with you to the Cave on Friday. Now I know how to handle myself, see—'

'James!' Lewis tried again. 'You don't understand, you dumbo, something's happened, I ought to tell you.'

'Has someone died?'

'No.'

'So relax, Lew. Don't worry, man. I don't want to hear it. It's just great to see you again. I can't wait to show you a photograph of Joanna. I mean, I've got to print them first, right, then I'll give you a call.'

At which point Lewis gave up. He drove round the roundabout and off the ring road onto London Road, and cruised slowly along it towards the white house on the hill.

'Drop me outside, Lew,' James told him. 'I want to walk up the drive.'

James pulled his rucksack out of the back seat and set off, jeans and T-shirt and torn jacket flapping around his skinny, limping frame. Lewis watched him go.

I've failed you, you dumb prick, Lewis thought to himself. I'm stronger than you, you obstinate idiot, he said in his head. I should have *made* you listen. He put the car into gear and pulled away.

Don't ever let that happen again, Lewis chastised himself, little realizing then that the same challenge would one day arise again, nor imagining how much harder it would be.

There was no one outside and all was quiet as James approached the house. His footsteps led him straight round to the back door. As he opened it he understood where he was going: he wanted, most of all, to see Laura.

Something was missing. As well as no sound, there was no smell either, of Edna's food in the ovens wafting through the back corridor from the kitchen, the enticing smells of pastry and herbs, spices and meat slowly stewing, smells softly sighing: 'Supper's nearly ready.'

But James didn't pause. He went straight to Laura's room, thinking as he approached it, She probably won't be here, she'll probably be with Alice somewhere, upstairs, outside, not here. He knocked on her bedroom door and, without waiting for a reply, turned the handle and stepped inside. Laura was sitting at her small table by the window, staring out, her back to James. His heart ballooned in his chest and into his mouth and he felt glad and anxious.

'Laura,' he said in his new voice. 'Hi. It's me.'

She turned slowly. James awaited the sight of her almond eyes, her pretty face, her indulgent smile, with two tiny dimples at the top of her cheekbones.

She turned slowly, and as she turned a wave of nausea and disbelief rose through James, draining the blood from his legs and his head all at once, collecting it in his throat. He slumped back as he saw . . .

She turned slowly. Laura's face was blue, black, purple; disfigured, misshapen, one eye closed, puffy, the other barely open, just her pupil and a bit of bloodshot white exposed; her cheeks were swollen, and her lips too, and her nose was bent, broken.

James staggered backwards, unable to breathe, and floundered as if through water along the corridor.

He lurched through the kitchen, knocking over a chair and an empty pan that clanged on the tiles.

He stumped up the stairs like a zombie to the third floor and swayed along the corridor to Robert's room past the old nursery, at the far end. He threw the door open and there Robert sat cross-legged on the floor, a record-player in a hundred pieces on newspaper pages spread around him. James flung himself on his brother, who was taken by surprise and was unable to defend himself. James grasped Robert by the throat with both hands and collapsed astride him, pinning his arms with his knees. Despite his superior strength there was nothing Robert could do, overpowered by James' fury, as James squeezed his brother's throat with all his might.

Afterwards, they were too frightened to contemplate what would have happened if Simon hadn't been in the old nursery with two of his girlfriends: whether James would have strangled his own brother to death. The three of them pulled him off, but it took all of their strength: James was groaning as he throttled Robert, in a state of rage beyond appeal other than that of greater brute force. With Simon wrenching James' neck they finally prised his arms loose and dragged him backwards, grunting, out of the room, leaving Robert barely conscious, gasping, on the floor.

Next door, James gradually calmed down. Simon dismissed the girls and made him drink a glass of wine.

'I've seen what that fucker did,' James spluttered.

'It wasn't him, James, he didn't do it,' Simon told him. 'Easy, James, take it easy.' He sat and held his shoulders to soothe him, gave him a tissue to blow his nose.

'That bastard!' James cried.

'He didn't do it,' Simon repeated.

'Of course he did.'

'No,' Simon declared. 'It was Stanley. It was her father, James.' He paused, poured more wine. 'Listen, I'd better tell you about it.'

So Simon explained: Laura had got pregnant; she'd told Edna, who'd told Stanley. Stanley had beaten her. Not just because she'd got pregnant, but because of who it was she'd let herself get pregnant by. He'd just blown a fuse, Simon said, 'Like you just did,' he added.

James listened with his head in his hands, his heart thudding. 'So who made her pregnant?' he asked, finally, knowing the answer.

'Well, Robert, of course,' Simon told him. 'Who else?'

She'd had an abortion three days ago. The worst thing about it, though, was Edna: she'd had a heart attack and though she wasn't in any danger, she was still in hospital.

James stood up. 'I'm going out,' he told Simon. As he turned to leave the room Robert appeared in the doorway. He didn't look at James but addressed Simon:

'If that crazy cunt ever tries anything like that again,' he said, 'I'll kill him.'

James pushed past him down the stairs and out of the house.

*

184

He caught a bus across town, to the cinema. He bought a ticket for a film that was half-way through and crept into the darkness. When the film was over he stumbled out to the foyer and joined the next queue, bought another ticket and watched the same film again. Then he went outside to the back of the line standing in the rain for the late-night film and sat through that one as well. The smell of wet, warm clothes and alcoholic breath lulled him. James was absorbed by the film: it engrossed his mind entirely. At the same time it passed through him, undigested, unremembered, the images and sounds sliding over his eyes and ears like water. In the middle of whatever the film was he fell asleep, and proceeded to dream his recurring dream for the first time in many months.

People were dancing in a white marquee, disco dancing, the music pumping dense and rhythmic and unbelievably loud. Lights – blue red green – flashed and splashed around the crowded tent. People were all dancing differently, doing their own thing, as if they all heard different music. Zoe was hopping, springing from one foot to another; James himself had no sense of rhythm, he knew he was jerking around but he didn't mind, he was grinning and drenched in sweat; Alice danced with her eyes closed, in a world of her own. Lewis was at the mixing desk. Children kicked balloons. Laura was dancing with her back to James. She was lovely to watch, her hips and shoulders in tune to the music, as if the music were improvised, fitting itself to her movement.

Then the lights changed to a strobe effect, people became isolated, clockwork mannequins. Laura's white dress was luminously purple. James tried to move around her, to get in front of her, but he couldn't because she moved in sync with him – as if she had eyes in the back of her head – keeping her back to him always, her face from him. He kept on moving in an arc around her as he danced, and the tent strobed, and she kept moving her face away from him as she danced in violet isolation.

The strobe stopped and the purple light turned red, only James was no longer in the marquee, he was up in his darkroom. In the infrared glow he was staring at a white piece of paper in the developing tray. Gradually grey appeared in or through the white, as if through snow; shapes grew; the image appeared to be struggling to come through, only disconnected parts of it did – a head, an arm, hands, feet; parts of people or a person. Until James realized it was not the image itself but rather his mind that was struggling, to make sense of it, and all of a sudden it *did* make sense: a child, a young girl, was running towards him, and she was wearing a white dress that, all told, took up over half of the frame. He looked at her face: it was both familiar and unfamiliar. Was it Laura? And was she laughing or was that panic in her face? But he couldn't make up his mind, because the image just carried on developing, fading into black.

James woke up with a jerk as seats around him flipped back: credits were rolling, people were leaving. He sensed he'd been slobbering and wiped his chin. The auditorium emptied; the film finished and the lights came up. The last spectators stirred themselves and left. A breath of silence filled the cinema.

James was immobile. He heard doors swing open, and a voice: 'We're closing up now.' It was cheerful. 'It's time to go home.' The voice was Zoe's. There was a pause.

'James!' The sound of her footsteps and jangling bracelets. 'James, you devil!' Her footsteps shuffling between the seats towards him. 'You're home, you sly mole, creeping in here without saying hello. What are you thinking of?'

She was standing beside him now, above him. He didn't look at her. And then her voice, serious: 'Come with me, James,' and her hand taking his.

She took him upstairs to her flat above the cinema and ran a deep, hot bath, infused with geranium oil. She came into the bathroom unabashed with an armful of her father Harold's clothes.

When James had got dressed Zoe gave him a brandy and then she rubbed his hair with a big blue towel, slowly, massaging his scalp as much as she was drying it.

When James' hair was dry, Zoe dropped the towel but carried on stroking his scalp with her hands. Music from her record player drifted into his head.

> Queen Victoria,
> do you have a punishment under the white lace,
> will you be short with her,
> make her read those little Bibles . . .

Eventually James said: 'I'm never going back there again.'
'You can stay here,' Zoe told him. 'You know that.'
'I'm never going back there again,' James whispered.

PART TWO

THE HOSPITAL (2)

ZOE CAME INTO THE HOSPITAL WARD IN THE DEPARTMENT OF Neurology, and made her way to James' bedside. She bent to kiss him – carefully, since as well as the wires and drip attached to him, he had also been put on a ventilator – but then she saw that there was now a bandage across his throat covering a scar, with a metal object inserted into the wound.

'It's quite normal,' a voice behind Zoe said. She turned. It was Gloria, the staff nurse. 'A tracheotomy. With this his body will ventilate on its own again.'

Zoe nodded. 'Thank you,' she said, and Gloria left them.

Zoe threw out flowers from a vase on the bedside table and put others in their place: yellow roses, whose peachy smell she hoped might reach him. She sat down and took his hand, and held it for a long time lost in thought.

'We sat on the roof of the cinema on warm summer evenings after the last film had started. We sipped white wine, ate olives, smoked. A mouthful of wine held before swallowing, a drag on a cigarette.

Talking about nothing, time going by. A black olive; a segment of orange. On the roof on a warm summer evening.'

'I want to show you something.'

Zoe realized she was being addressed, and turned round. It was the ward sister.

'Look,' she said. 'The patient is unconscious. He's in a persistent vegetative state. He can't hear a word. His body maintains its heart beat, blood pressure, ventilation and respiration, but that is all. Occasionally he blinks; that is all. His only response to the world is a mechanical one.' She struck James' midriff through the sheet, and his limbs flexed rigid. 'He didn't feel that,' she explained. 'He's comatose. But,' she added, as she turned to go, 'it's your breath you're wasting.'

Zoe sat a while, to recover her composure. Then she squeezed James' hand goodbye, and made her way out of the ward.

5

CLARITY

JAMES STAYED WITH ZOE FOR SOME WEEKS, CONTRIBUTING TOWARDS his food and board by selling tickets and ice-cream in the cinema, and wearing Zoe's father's cast-off clothes, which hung loosely on his skinny frame. Then a vacancy appeared for a trainee photographer on the local newspaper, the *Echo*, and Zoe helped James fill out the application form, type a CV and prepare for his interview over mid-morning breakfast in her tiny kitchen: smoking French ciné-philes' cigarettes and drinking foul cups of herbal tea, Zoe read out questions she'd prepared the night before, after James had gone to bed, that drove him to equal extremes of inferiority and irritation.

'Do you agree with Auden, James,' she asked, 'that photography brought a new sadness into the world?'

'A new *sadness*?' James struggled.

'OK: is photography inevitably less an aesthetic medium than an anthropological tool?'

'*I* don't know,' James complained. 'Ask me about f-stops,' he suggested. 'I know what f-stops to use.'

'Look, James,' Zoe said, exasperated with her cousin's obtuseness. 'Think about it. As Lévi-Strauss said, history is the source of our greatest anxiety: the past, once harmonious, now broken and

191

crumbling before our eyes. We seek consolation through knowledge, and yet that knowledge gives us no hope, no optimism, only, if we're lucky, a certain detachment. Right?'

James stared dumbly back at her. 'Yes?'

'So: in photographs we see, above all, the past. Whether a photograph's of a person, a building, a landscape, whatever, more than anything else it's a record of something we *know* – as Lucretius pointed out – has since changed, decayed. Which in turn reminds us of our own state, and fills us with pessimism.'

James frowned. 'And that's what Auden was on about?'

Zoe waved her cigarette impatiently. 'No, no, James, he meant something else, he was referring to the way photographs force us to look at what in life we have the freedom to turn away from. Anyway—'

'But, Zoe,' James interrupted, 'they'll just want to see if I know the different grades of printing paper and stuff like that. Here, test me on my depth of field tables.'

'If they *don't* ask you these sorts of questions,' Zoe responded, her voice rising, 'they bloody well should do. *You* should ask them. They're fundamental. Don't you ever *read*, James?'

Zoe went up to the house to retrieve James' own clothes and most necessary possessions – which mostly meant his camera equipment – as well as his boxes of prints, from which, spread around the floors of Zoe's small flat, they selected a portfolio of his best work. For the first time Zoe saw the evidence of what James had been doing with his hermetic youth and was impressed, if not by the derivative and banal pictures themselves, then at least by his commitment.

'You're really doing this thing, aren't you?' she said, perusing the prints.

'Sure I am,' James replied quietly.

James got the job, after a disconcertingly brief interview with the chief photographer, a stooping man called Roger Warner. He barely glanced at the portfolio, his main concern apparently less James' aptitude than his contract.

'We don't want a lad who's looking to head off to London as soon as we've trained him,' he told James.

'I've got no plans of that sort,' James reassured him honestly.

He offered James the job on the spot, start Monday, and on the way out he asked him: 'You related to *Charles* Freeman, James?'

'Yes,' James replied curtly, hurrying away.

The flat above the cinema which Zoe had inherited from her grandmother Agatha was a suite of tiny rooms. 'Of course I'm twice as big as she was,' Zoe told James. 'Or maybe human beings required less personal space in those days. It's no wonder Harold went travelling: he was probably suffering from claustrophobia.'

Those cramped quarters seemed to James, who'd grown up in the big house on the hill, like a miniature museum whose curator, rather than opening it to the public, had chosen to live inside it. It was stuffed with artefacts Harold had brought back as presents for his mother and then Zoe had carried home for herself: a Makonde carving, Kenyan sandstone sculptures, a voodoo mask from Haiti, Tibetan bells, a wooden statue from Benin, a pot-bellied Buddha and a shrunken head from Borneo. They crowded in upon each other, totems from distant cultures jostling among themselves for breathing space.

The walls were covered with Turkish rugs, an Aboriginal hide-painting and Indian miniatures illustrating episodes from the *Kama Sutra*, all of which left little room for the hundreds of dog-eared, travel-worn paperbacks Zoe owned. She read them at great speed but couldn't bear to throw any away, no matter how frayed they were, and so, with no space for bookshelves, she'd discovered places other people would have overlooked in which to stack them: on the stairs, either side, leaving a narrow funnel up which to climb; on top of the toilet cistern; underneath chairs; and wedged in the window frames, which, as she explained to James, provided insulation from wind and noise and also saved money on curtains.

'But they block out the light, Zoe,' he pointed out.

'You may not have noticed, sweetheart, but I'm a nocturnal animal,' she told him. 'I'm a night-owl.' It was true. After locking up the cinema at eleven in the evening – or one in the morning when she had late-night screenings, Friday and Saturday – Zoe sat up half the night reading. She lit a joss-stick, poured herself a glass of brandy and rolled a joint, which she shared with James but which made him feel even sicklier than the incense did: it gave him a dry mouth and a headache, and the way it loosened his moorings to reality made him feel anxious rather than relaxed. So Zoe let him roll them for her; the ritual gave him more pleasure than the drug itself. He stuck three papers together to make a large taper; broke up

193

an ordinary cigarette and spread the tobacco; held a flame to Zoe's block of Lebanese black until it crumbled easily.

'Hurry up, James,' Zoe berated him, 'I'm waiting over here.'

James rolled the joint up, licked the paper and eased it tight. He twisted one end, and tore a tiny strip of cardboard off the cigarette packet to insert in the other. Then he handed it to Zoe. She held the crooked, wrinkled reefer in front of her.

'Keep practising, kiddo,' she sighed.

'Shall I try it again?' James asked eagerly, reaching a hand towards her.

'No way,' Zoe replied, snatching it away from him. 'I'm not *that* patient.'

Zoe lit the joint and took a deep drag, holding it in her lungs – looking as if she'd been assailed by some painful memory – before exhaling: the intoxicating smell mingled with incense.

'It's like coffee,' James opined, 'it smells better than it tastes.'

They talked more about the family. Zoe told him what she learned when she went up to the house for a subdued Sunday lunch: that Laura was healing; Edna was out of hospital; everyone was lying low, hoping it would all blow over. What else could they do?

'It's a bad place,' James said. His anger was all confused. He hated Stanley, and his father, and Robert; and he knew he hated Laura for having got pregnant – with Robert – without actually admitting that he did, and he didn't understand any of it. Zoe listened patiently; she told him that families screwed up, sometimes, and that there would always be a refuge for him here.

They read together. It was a habit Zoe had acquired on travels with her father, she explained: as studies showed, travellers spend 15 per cent of their time on the move, 5 per cent searching for places to eat and sleep, and 80 per cent waiting in railway stations, docks, airports and at the sides of roads. So she'd read voraciously, swapping books with fellow travellers.

'Listen to this,' she said. 'Orwell kept a childhood photograph of himself on the mantelpiece, right? He says: "I have nothing in common with the boy in the photo, except that he and I are the same person." Good, eh, James?'

James had never seen anyone read as fast as Zoe. She scanned one page, then the other, and turned over to the next. And whenever he looked to see what book she was reading, it always seemed to be a new one. James, who was trying to follow her lead, only found himself watching *her*, her speed-reading a hypnotic spectacle.

'How can you take anything in?' James demanded. 'I don't see how you can.'

'Well,' Zoe pondered, 'I suppose as you get older, you find that you sort of know what you're looking for.'

'So you've just gradually speeded up through practice?'

'Who, me? No. I've always read this fast.'

Zoe often forgot that James was present, and talked back to the authors.

'Oh, bollocks!' she announced.

'What's the matter?' James asked, startled. 'Did I do something?'

'What? Who?' Zoe responded dreamily. 'Did you say something?'

'No, you did,' he told her.

'But why did you start?' she asked.

'I didn't, you d— Nothing,' he said. 'Forget it.'

Or else he heard her murmur: 'That's a nice way of looking at it. Interesting.'

'What's interesting?' James enquired.

'God, you must be psychic, James,' Zoe informed him. 'I told you you might be. I was just reading this: "He who has a true idea at the same time knows he has a true idea, and cannot doubt the truth of the thing . . . As the light makes both itself and the darkness plain, so truth is the standard both of itself and of the false." '

James smiled. 'You were talking to yourself again, Zoe.'

'No, I wasn't,' she replied. 'I was speaking to Spinoza.' As if it were quite natural that her only intellectual companions had died, some hundreds of years ago.

When James had read a chapter of *his* book (borrowed from Zoe's library) he closed it with a yawn and went to bed. The first nights he stayed there Zoe put a sheet and blankets on her small sofa for him. He awoke every hour with a different joint aching, and Zoe found him in the mornings half on the sofa and half on the floor, contorted and snoring; eventually she took pity and shared her own bed with him. It was big enough, a double mattress that took up most of the floor space in Zoe's bedroom, leaving only room for a shallow chest-of-drawers. That in fact was the most surprising thing about Zoe's entire flat: James imagined she must own a huge wardrobe, because whenever he saw her she was always wearing something different. In reality Zoe only ever wore one of two pairs of jeans or a cotton skirt, with a blouse and pullover, and the apparent variety of her attire was an illusion created by scarves, bandannas, beads, bracelets and rings.

James slept soundly in Zoe's bed. She informed him in the morning, with unusual bad humour, that he'd snored, snuffled, tossed and turned all night, waking her up every fifteen minutes. He apologized profusely, and she forbore from banishing him back to the sofa. The only things that woke James were scented steam wafting through from the bathroom in the middle of the night, or noises from the kitchen, where Zoe made herself the snacks of an insomniac.

Now that he had a job, though, it was time for James to find a place of his own. He took Zoe's invitation to stay as long as he wished as generosity; he didn't like imposing on her, and he felt clumsy in her tiny flat, where he was always knocking his head or elbows, and endangering her Third World antiques. He knew he must be restricting her life, a life filled with ticket sales, deals with distributors, special screenings with invited guests – actors, directors – she appeared to know well. Even though she was only twenty-three years old she seemed much older than he was and he assumed he was getting in her way. So that James didn't wonder whether, if he wasn't there, she would be reading and smoking alone in her small flat above the cinema.

'You can stay as long as you like, sweetheart,' she told him. 'It's nice having you around, James.'

'Thanks, Zoe,' he said, looking through his own paper's 'To Let' ads.

Back at the house, meanwhile, it was true what Zoe told James: Robert kept a low profile, rarely sleeping in the house; Laura *was* healing, remarkably quickly and well. Edna was out of hospital, her heart no longer fluttering – instead it was hardening inside her. And there was much that remained unsaid.

Edna was so straightforward and matter-of-fact a woman, and Stanley so naturally taciturn, that no one except Laura realized that after Edna came out of hospital she resolved never to speak to her husband again. She was unable to forgive his assault on their daughter, who thenceforth became their go-between. The first message Edna gave her was to instruct Stanley to arrange separate sleeping arrangements: so he swapped their marriage bed for two single ones from a distant guest room. What Edna had meant was that she wanted separate rooms, but she didn't want to enter an argument, or even a negotiation, via Laura, and so she accepted the arrangement, and from then on she and Stanley slept on opposite sides of their bedroom.

Stanley too had been stunned by the ferocity of his anger, but he was too proud a man for it to occur to him to apologize to anyone. Edna refused to speak to him, and *he* couldn't say the words he had to say – 'I'm sorry'.

The strange thing was that Laura understood him – both his brief, sudden violence and his pride. She knew that deep inside he felt contrition, but had no way of expressing it, and she forgave him: his entire subdued demeanour she perceived as an apology. But Stanley didn't know that. He carried on with his work, he took his seat at mealtimes, he watched television in their small sitting-room in the back quarters, and he made his way to a single bed across the room from Edna, who sometimes woke to the sound of her husband weeping in his sleep.

As for Laura, the only physical evidence that remained of the beating was a slight twist in her nose; the gynaecologist assured her there'd been no damage to her reproductive organs. There seemed to be no lasting damage to her personality, either. If anything, she grew closer to her father once Edna stopped talking to him, the role of go-between forcing her into a kind of pitying complicity; and she spent more time with her mother, too, helping her in the kitchen after school. Since neither mother nor daughter knew how to articulate their feelings directly, they did so through the medium of food. Edna's hardening of her heart towards her husband had not yet extended to other people, and she taught Laura her basic recipes, imparting the knowledge that cookery is a scientific process relying on precise quantities, preparation and cooking time; while Laura in turn made her mother appreciate that after you've made a dish once it's fun to experiment the next time.

It took James a while to find his way around the newspaper offices because, due to his shyness, he was content to remain inside the photographers' department filing negatives, developing film and assisting the printer, Keith, in the darkroom, where he had to learn the procedure.

Keith was a tubby, enigmatic young man with a pale, lardy complexion who peered at the world through tinted spectacles, with the look of an anxious bat. James soon realized, having spent most of the waking hours of his youth in a darkroom of his own, both that he was a far better printer than Keith *and* that this was irrelevant:

Keith had acquired the necessary craft for grading prints for reproduction in the newspaper.

'What are you doing?' he demanded as James used a piece of cardboard as a mask to give part of a print more exposure to the light.

'I'm burning in the building there, Keith,' he explained.

'No, you don't, mate, no, don't mess with the neg like that,' Keith admonished him. 'Mr Baker doesn't like anything fancied up.'

Otherwise, though, Keith was a good teacher: he got on with his work and left James free to watch him, to ask questions when he wanted to, and make his own mistakes. James learned habits of scrupulous cleanliness and of systematic order that he didn't have. In the office, they would go through James' own negatives and prints with a magnifying glass, and James went back into the darkroom on his own, after the others had left work, and kept developing till late at night.

'There's a family of compositors on this paper,' Keith told him in the office one afternoon, 'who can trace their line back to the time of William Caxton.'

'No, really?' James replied, as gullible as he was shy.

'It'll all change,' Keith averred. 'They've got it sewn up down there, mate,' he said, pointing through the floor. 'It's a closed shop. But it'll all change.'

'You don't know what you're talking about, Keith,' Roger Warner interrupted. 'Take no notice of him, James. Nothing's going to change. We work together, the paper comes out on time every day, the punters buy it. It works: don't fix it.'

'It doesn't bloody work,' Keith muttered.

'Roger'll have you believe the whole ship runs on sweetness and light,' Derek, one of the staff photographers, declared dismissively. 'The truth is you've got the union downstairs and the bosses upstairs. If they could produce the paper with robots, the bastards would. It's only the union being strong that safeguards everybody's job, yours included, son. Know which side you're on.'

'Hey, you,' Roger said, 'the lad's not been here five minutes and you're putting ideas in his head. Leave him alone. Our job, Jim boy, is to take photographs. Good ones. Leave politics to the father of the chapel. And as for you,' he added, addressing Derek, 'shouldn't you be down at the council chambers?'

'I'm on my way,' Derek said reluctantly, draining his mug.

'They've got dogs fouling footpaths on the agenda: the shit'll hit the fan today.'

James thought that was meant to be a joke but he held off smiling because nobody else did. You could only tell when Derek was trying to say something funny by the fact that he said it with even more clipped vehemence than he said everything else.

James felt as out of place on the newspaper as he had at school or at home, but it wasn't a problem because it was clear that the other photographers did too: they were misfits who had nothing in common except their work. It couldn't have helped, he thought, that they were all different ages: Roger Warner was sixty-odd, and the other two staff photographers, Derek Moore and Frank Spackman, were around fifty and forty respectively, while Keith, the printer, was in his late twenties. James realized that he'd stepped onto a conveyor belt, but that didn't bother him either because all he wanted was to take photographs.

Gradually James was sent on errands: submitting contact sheets to the subeditors for their perusal, taking prints down to the composing room where they were transformed into plates for the presses, and seeking information from the cuttings library. There were three floors: on the ground floor the printing presses, behind the front desk where the public were dealt with; on the first floor the journalists; and upstairs the management and administration with committee rooms that James never saw.

The middle floor was split by a long corridor lined by partitions of brown metal and frosted glass. On one side ran offices, with the editor, Mr Baker, at one end and the typing-pool at the other. In between were two long open-plan offices in which the reporters and the subeditors worked.

On the other side of the corridor were the toilets, the photography department, the cuttings library and, at the end, the office of the *Echo*'s weekly sister paper, the *Gazette*.

James hardly said a word to anyone outside the photographers' office during his first days, intimidated by the institution, the noise of the presses churning in the bowels of the building like the engine of an ocean-going liner, the hectic deadlines, but above all the people. The subeditors were the worst; strange monsters deranged by the fact that their day was split in two: in the mornings they were tyrants of furious temper and concentration, shouting at the typists, bawling at the journalists and rubbishing the photographers as they rewrote poor copy, brainstormed banner headlines, cut and pasted pages, and rolled up articles and inserted them in missiles which they popped into pipes to shuttle down to the typesetters below.

Every morning was a mounting crisis of last minute telephone calls, traumatized egos and shredded nerves right up until, shortly after midday, the first edition had gone to press. And then the office emptied, the subeditors disappeared, every last one, and James walked into an eerily silent room in which echoing curses were dying into silence as if onto the bridge of a ship marooned with no survivors. The first time he dashed back to the darkroom.

'Everybody's gone,' he told Keith. 'There must be a fire and we haven't heard the alarm.'

Keith smiled behind his tinted glasses. 'They've gone to the pub,' he explained. 'They're a bunch of drunken sods,' he added.

The subeditors returned an hour or two later, transformed by their liquid lunch into avuncular jokers and jesters, having sailed once again through the storm into calm waters. They scrutinized the fresh day's paper with blackening fingers, and then spent the remaining hours of their working day updating later editions with incoming news in an altogether more relaxed mood, as well as flirting with the secretaries and swapping crude jokes with the typesetters without showing any regret for their diabolical behaviour of only hours before.

To James these monsters were all too familiar, scaled-down versions of his own father. When one of them shouted at him to reprint this fucking photograph, you can't tell the bloody mayor from the fucking statue, and have it back on my desk in three minutes flat or you can fuck off back to whatever pit you climbed out of, he had to develop the photo with trembling fingers, in a state of shock.

'What's the matter with you?' Keith asked him, and James explained that he'd only been here a couple of weeks and he'd already made a mortal enemy.

Keith grinned. 'Don't take it personal, mate,' he said. 'They're like that to everyone. It's part of their job. No one takes any notice.'

Keith was right. There existed between the subeditors and the rest a daily battle followed by mutual amnesia and then conviviality. Except, that is, for the reporters, with whom they shared an uneasy truce.

The reporters were a less volatile breed, divided, James discovered, into two kinds: the younger, ambitious journalists for whom working on this provincial paper was a stepping-stone to one of the nationals, seeking stories with which to make their name; and older hacks each with their own network of contacts (among policemen, council employees, publicans and others around the town) whose mastery of the newspaper's style meant that, unlike their younger colleagues crouched over their typewriters, they were able to dictate entire articles to the typists off the top of their heads, making it up as they went along, down to an exact word count. They referred only cursorily to the mysterious hieroglyphics of their notebooks – in which each had evolved their own personal shorthand, less for reasons of speed than because the one thing they had in common with the younger reporters was the conviction that every other bastard was after their scoop.

The typing-pool was a small room with three bored young women who painted their nails and did crosswords until the phone rang or someone rushed in with a deadline a minute away: then the girls stubbed out their cigarettes and spat their gum into the bin and, to James' amazement, their slender fingers hammered the heavy keys of ancient typewriters, not like the reporters stabbing with two fore-fingers, no, rather making the keys dance, their feet leaving effortless footprints on the white paper, as if the girls were reading an article that was writing itself, which they had nothing to do with. James knew theirs was a mechanical skill, anyone could do it really; but it *looked* magical, the typographical equivalent of an image appearing in the darkroom, and he loved watching them. If they ran out of things to type, though, they lit up cigarettes and teased the gauche young man about the girlfriends he was surely keeping secret from them, and he made stammered excuses and headed back to the darkroom, where no one could see him blushing.

Downstairs were the presses, constantly clattering and churning, and you had to shout to be heard. The men – they were all men down there – carried on elliptical, sporadic conversations as they worked, yelling a few words to each other at their machines during momentary pauses which only made sense with reference to another such sentence broadcast a quarter of an hour earlier. It could take two men working side by side all morning to discuss the previous evening's football.

James felt uneasy among grease and ink and heat, and the smell of burning metal (especially since people were always shouting at him.) He fancied Robert would be comfortable down there, but it made James feel out of place. It was the ground floor but (with the windows all painted over for some inexplicable reason) it felt like the basement, the bowels of the building, those presses not printing newspapers but powering the building itself, the engines of a ship. As he went downstairs to the plate room he wouldn't have been surprised to see water spilling down the steps or puddles swilling across the floor as he, his father's drunken sailor, swayed between the machines.

At the end of his second week on the paper James received the first pay-packet of his life, a square brown envelope containing a pay-slip detailing gross wages and deductions for income tax, national insurance and voluntary trade union contributions as well as, in cash, his net pay of £27.80 one week in arrears. He persuaded Zoe to leave her part-time usherette in charge of the cinema for the evening and took her out for a Chinese meal.

Zoe, who apart from the film reviews never read newspapers, was unsurprised by James' descriptions of alcoholics, clock-watchers and brutes.

'Well, sweetheart,' she sympathized, 'you know, you won't work there for ever. You don't even have to stay there now. There are other places.'

'What do you mean, Zoe?' James asked. 'It's great. I'll be taking photos soon, too.'

She had to admit he looked happier. 'Have you made any friends yet?' she asked, brightening up. He told her about Keith and the lugubrious Derek.

'The trouble is,' she told him, 'you and me, we're two of a kind. We're both loners, really.'

James answered a number of ads in the 'To Let' section of the paper: having inside information, he was the first to reply; landlords sometimes returned from placing their ad at the newspaper office to find their phone already ringing. Zoe accompanied him, advising caution, and James took her advice. He rejected rooms in shared houses both with students near the college of further education ('Studying stops you growing up, sweetheart, you can tell they take their washing home to Mummy; and with non-smoking professionals in Batley ('Petit-bourgeois anal-retentive types, James; you'd be screaming in a week').

They saw a minuscule apartment off Blockley Road ('There's not enough room to swing a cat in here,' Zoe sniffed. 'No pets!' said the landlady. 'I thought I put that in the advert! No pets allowed!').

They dismissed grease-stained, paint-peeling bedsits, let by absentee landlords, whose squalor even the letting agent apologized for. And a garret in Northtown in the house of a widow who, rather than money, wanted someone to weed the garden and read aloud to her in lieu of rent.

'She'll have you listening to her life-story and escorting her to the cemetery,' Zoe assured James. 'She won't leave you alone. You can forget *that* one.'

'It's clean,' James protested. 'It's quiet.'

'It won't do at all, silly. Come on, let's get back and have a cup of tea.'

Eventually, though, she had to let him go. At the end of October James moved into a room in a large house less than half a mile out along the road from the cinema.

The house had three storeys and a basement and had been divided into eight bedsits, each plain white door fitted with its own Yale lock. The hallway was bare except for a telephone that only took incoming calls and a permanent litter of junk mail and letters addressed to long-gone tenants, which built up against the wall behind the front door. It was picked up and thrown away once a week by the cleaning lady, a short, intimidating young woman who muttered imprecations and curses beneath her breath as she hoovered the carpets, cleaned the windows and scoured the bathroom. She didn't speak to the residents but rather scowled at them instead, responsible as they were for grimy rings around the bathtub and the dust, human hair and flakes of skin that filled her vacuum cleaner. James assumed she couldn't speak English, since she looked like a disgruntled Spanish peasant, and he kept out of her way.

There were no mirrors in the hallway and only a single mirror-tile in the bathroom, glued to the wall above the sink. The bathroom was bare, as the tenants each kept their toiletries in their rooms, passing each other on the stairs like migrant workers carrying sponge-bags containing individual toothpaste, toothbrush, shampoo, soap and even toilet-paper.

There was no communal sitting-room or kitchen, just eight separate bedsits each with a sink and a small stove, the bathroom on the first floor, and an extra lavatory in the basement with a shower that dripped. The house had a desolate and unloved atmosphere, but behind the eight locked doors were eight solitary little worlds. James felt at home. He tiptoed through the hallway and up the stairs with a bag of groceries; he let himself into his first-floor room and boiled some plain rice with vegetables, not craving at all the rich meals of his childhood; and he spent content evenings listening to John Peel on the radio and reading paperback books he borrowed off Zoe: he chose mostly nineteenth-century Penguin Classics, and, encouraged by the alienated youths of Tsarist Russia, James suffered for a short time the illusion that he might be a central character in his own life-story, rather than a peripheral observer. His life was getting under way.

It was weeks before Charles noticed James' absence from the big house on the hill; he hadn't noticed his brief *return*. No one had elected to tell him that James had left home, vowing never to come back. That was one of the problems of being a tyrant: when you were in the habit of shooting the messenger, people declined to give you unwelcome information. Finally, in the middle of November, Charles said to Simon: 'I say, it's high time we had a party, and Judith tells me it's James' birthday this week. Where is our helpless hermit? We need to sort out a guest list.'

'He doesn't live here now, Father,' Simon revealed.

'Because when you're part of a family,' Charles continued, ignoring Simon, 'you have certain responsibilities. One of them is to throw your fair share of parties – even when you're a recluse in your own home.' He paused. 'What on earth do you mean he doesn't live here any more?'

Simon courageously explained that James had moved down town, and got a job on the local newspaper.

'Why the hell didn't anyone tell me?' Charles demanded, and Simon feared the worst. 'I could have had a word with the proprietor. *And* the editor. How does he expect to get anywhere without my help?'

'You didn't need to, Father. He got the job anyway.'

'Are you sure?' Charles asked. 'Well, good for him,' he decided. 'He's obstinate. If he wants to stand on his own two feet, I admire him for it.'

Relieved at Charles' benign reaction, Simon recounted James' return from the farm, his assault on Robert, and even his vow never to return home.

'Well, he's made his bed, as far as I'm concerned, and he can ruddy well lie in it,' Charles decided. 'It's a shame,' he concluded. 'We could have done with a party at the moment.'

*

Charles had some excuse at least for being so out of touch with events in his own household during that time (as well as for wanting a party). His iron rule of the company was being challenged by the union, subverted by foreigners and, he declared, undermined by an incompetent Cabinet. In protest at the Conservative Government's prices and incomes policy – freezing wages and prices in an attempt to curb inflation – power workers, coalminers and railwaymen had gone on strike. The Government responded by declaring a state of emergency: within a matter of weeks soldiers, trained to kill for their country and die for each other, found themselves doing the very jobs they'd once escaped from, delivering coal to power stations and trying to produce the nation's energy. Middle Eastern countries had, meanwhile, halved their supplies of oil – the other main source of power – while quadrupling prices.

Everyone was affected. Bank lending rates rose, credit controls were tightened and public spending was cut. Cars formed long, fuming queues for petrol that could only be bought a gallon at a time with ration books, and when they got out onto the open road they found a speed limit of 50 mph had been imposed. Robert found his trade in second-hand cars badly hit.

Television blacked out half-way through the evening (which finally weaned Simon off the habit for good) and families were told to only heat one room and spend the rest of the winter together inside it. Children were sent home from school to save heating classrooms – which would have an important consequence for Alice – while hospitals operated on emergency generators, and police stations by candlelight.

In the New Year a three-day working week was introduced.

'My workers – or shirkers – do three days and I have to work seven to make up for it!' Charles thundered.

The Prime Minister called a general election in March, so that the country could help put the unions in their place, asking: 'Who Governs Britain?'

'Not you, you ruddy idiot!' Charles yelled back at the television.

'He's doing his best, father,' Simon suggested. Simon admired a politician who was not only a bachelor but appeared to regard politics as a dutiful diversion from more worthwhile pursuits, like racing yachts and conducting orchestras.

'Well, it's not bloody good enough, then!' Charles exclaimed. Enough of the rest of the country agreed to give the Labour Party victory.

'Now that's really buggered us up!' Charles pronounced, as the miners were given a 35 per cent pay rise.

The power cuts that disrupted public-sector schools provided Charles with the excuse he needed to forsake his meritocratic principles without admitting he was doing so. The fact was that Alice was the most academically gifted of the children; she actually seemed to enjoy school, which was a novelty. Charles owed it to himself to see at least one of his offspring go on to university, and he owed it to Alice too, so he enrolled her at a girls' public boarding school whose exorbitant fees impressed him almost as much as their examination results.

'They've got a fully equipped laboratory,' he told Alice.

'I suppose you think we should have gone to a public school now,' Simon ventured.

'Codswallop!' Charles replied. 'Single-sex education should be compulsory for girls, because they get distracted so easily, but it's catastrophic for boys,' he explained. 'As everyone knows,' he added.

'Yes, Father,' Simon concurred, as he usually did. Having done well in marketing, Charles had ordered another promotion: Simon now had his own office with a sign on the door saying Assistant Manager of Personnel.

'You're a very lucky girl, Alice,' Simon told her.

'Yes, Simon,' she agreed.

'It's an opportunity none of the rest of us have had,' he continued. He knew he was only repeating his father's opinions, and unless Charles was in the immediate vicinity it was an act difficult to maintain. 'Anyway,' he added, 'have you seen the uniform? Maroon: it'll set off your colouring nicely.'

Everyone else offered sympathy. Zoe found out when she came to lunch the following Sunday, and took Alice aside.

'You poor thing,' she said, stroking Alice's auburn hair. 'Boarding school. It's like going into the army.'

'Yes, Zoe.'

'The most important thing is to remember who you are, Alice. If they grind you down, just find a quiet corner and tell yourself: "I am an individual. I am Alice Freeman." Like a mantra, kind of.'

'Thanks, Zoe.'

Laura was the most put out of all, and the night before Alice left she cried on Alice's shoulder. 'At least you'll come home at half-term.'

'Of course I will.'

'And we can write letters to each other. You can even phone me when you get too lonely,' Laura sniffed. 'It's just not *fair*,' she wept.

'I know,' Alice agreed, trying to conjure up tears of her own. The truth was Alice looked forward to boarding school. She wasn't daunted by the things that other people were worrying about on her behalf: a military regime, the loss of privacy, dormitories, cold showers, compulsory games in bad weather and the intimidating prospect of being the only new girl in the middle of term. None of these things bothered Alice because she lived in a world of her own, and anyway they paled by comparison with what she looked forward to: she'd become bored at school, yawning over her homework because it was too easy, unable to discuss chemistry experiments with her classmates because they were still grappling with basic formulae while she was keen to repeat the more advanced experiments of Marie Curie, whose portrait was pinned to the wall above her bed where other girls had Marc Bolan and David Cassidy. Alice wasn't distracted by boys – she hadn't been distracted by Harry Singh – but she was bored. She looked forward to more rigorous study under teachers who might inspire her, or at least whom she could treat as equals.

Harry Singh, meanwhile, was deeply unhappy. Unlike her family in the house on the hill, Harry had already been pining for Alice for months. School had broken up back in June, so he didn't see her there any more, and then James had gone to the farm for the summer, robbing Harry of the excuse to visit her home. In September Harry himself went off to university in Manchester, to study economics. There'd been no question of Harry taking a year off: he didn't have time to waste because he already knew what he wanted from life and where he was going. The trouble was that one of the things he wanted was Alice. He'd made his choice – or, rather, his choice had been made for him by fate, by her being alive and their paths crossing – and when Harry Singh had set his mind on something he was constitutionally incapable of considering other options.

Going to university entailed leaving home, going away to study in a strange town, and it served a dual purpose: part education, and part learning to establish the relationships and the independence of adulthood. Harry was able to fulfil the first, having been a straight-As pupil in school; he may not have had his beloved's intellect but he was single-minded and studied, wrote essays, read text books, revised and took exams with a clear-eyed method and a minimum of fuss. In the second, however, he was adrift: all around him his fellow students got drunk in the subsidized bar; got stoned on poor-quality grass; lost themselves in the blistering shadows of dinning discos, in slippery kisses and befuddled couplings; then found themselves in demonstrations for free contraception and civil rights in Northern Ireland, and engaged in vehement argument about the meaning of life that lasted all night in small, crowded rooms, where they would wake at noon in the arms of unexpected lovers.

To all this activity Harry was a well-dressed spectator (he wore a suit at college, and was constantly taken for a particularly young lecturer or member of the administrative staff), a wallflower at the discos, a passive smoker of marijuana, a bookworm in the library while others waved placards, the only student in the accommodation block who slept every night in his own bed, alone. He didn't even have the consolation of alcohol, since he was a teetotaller, not because of his upbringing but because he'd tried it once and it made him feel unsure of himself; Harry Singh *needed* by his nature to be clear-eyed. Right now, however, he was *too* clear-eyed: all he could see was Alice Freeman. Her image floated before him, just out of reach. She left him alone to study but the rest of the time tormented him: for she was what he didn't have.

Harry wasted the entire Christmas vacation of 1974 back home in the town sneaking glimpses of Alice. He even went to church on Christmas morning, and felt so uncomfortable, so alien, in the traditional heart of the culture he regarded himself as being a part of but not knowing when to stand up or sit down or kneel, always one step behind those around him, that he almost bolted during one of the hymns. But he forced himself to stay, and such was his sense of purpose that when Alice (seated two pews in front) joined the queue for communion he jumped up and followed her, and took bread and wine for the first time in his life, without a hiccup.

He also went to the temple with his father and brother, and realized to his dismay that he felt a twinge of envy for his conformist, hide-bound brother, Anil; the same patient, unambitious brother who by the age of eight knew the price of every item in the shop, who preferred stacking shelves in the evening to watching TV, who had risen without complaint at dawn to do a newspaper round before school. For Anil had agreed, at the age of ten, to his parents' arranging a marriage for him, with a distant cousin in India. He'd gone over with his father a couple of years later and the two children (she was three years younger) had been introduced to each other, and got on awkwardly but well. Thereafter Anil carried a passport-size photograph of his betrothed with him at all times, a photograph updated every year; the *out*dated ones he stuck in a small album that showed her growing up, growing towards womanhood, towards him.

It had been agreed that Anil would go over for his wedding, and return with his bride, when she was eighteen and he was twenty-one. The date was still five years off, but Anil was a patient man. So, Harry thought, was he – it was one of the few qualities he shared with his brother. He too could wait, as long as he knew that what he awaited was certain.

Alice's graceful carriage in a Christian church, along with one or two other glimpses, saw Harry through the holidays, but once back at college his melancholy returned. He bit his fingernails, found himself wide awake in the middle of the night, ate bad food and put on weight.

February came, the most gloomy month, but right in the middle of it St Valentine's Day. Harry's accommodation block was awash with amorous intrigue and rumour. Home-made and shop-bought cards appeared in pigeon holes, single red roses were propped against doors in the white corridors, cryptic messages were pinned to notice-boards, infantile announcements (Bunny Baby Bear be my Valentine love Blatty Wuffles) appeared in the campus newsletter, and a huge banner was hung from the rafters of the refectory during the night so that everyone at breakfast could see that

SUE 👁 ♥ U KEV.

At the sight of which Harry lost his appetite.

The following weekend Harry took the train home. On Saturday morning he walked up the drive to the big house clutching a small bouquet of early primroses. Laura answered the door and recognized Harry Singh, head boy at school, from his readings at morning assembly, as well as his occasional appearances in the house with James; though he'd always been clutching a cheap instamatic camera on those occasions, not flowers.

'Didn't you know?' she asked. 'James doesn't live here any more. He lives down in Gath. I can get you his number—'

'No,' Harry interrupted. 'I came to see Alice.'

'Alice?' Laura frowned. 'Well, she doesn't live here either. She's at boarding school.'

'Oh, no,' Harry replied, sagging. He took a step back, then forward again; then he turned round, and slowly descended two or three steps; then stopped again. Laura stood still, entranced by his confused indecision. After some moments she saw his back expand as he took a deep breath, and his crumpled shoulders rise. He turned back to face her.

'Is Mr Freeman in?' Harry asked.

'Mr Freeman?' Laura queried. Who *were* these flowers for? she wondered.

'Her father,' Harry confirmed. 'Charles Freeman. Is he at home, or has he left as well?'

Laura led him to the library and left him there. It was a room he'd sneaked glimpses of in passing and always wanted to enter, and now here he was; maybe it was that satisfaction that countered his heart's thumping, because he didn't feel at all intimidated as he surveyed the stacks of unread books, the formidable portraits, the immense, engulfing armchairs, the Persian rugs and, at the far end, Charles' vast desk. Instead Harry Singh – whose family's whole flat above the shop, he reckoned, would fit into this room – looked calmly round and thought to himself: This is good, this is what I've imagined; this will do for me, although personally I don't like the colour of those curtains.

Suddenly the double doors burst open and Charles Freeman came striding into the room, his 6-foot-2, 18-stone frame causing the hundreds of books on their shelves to nervously giggle, like an approaching steamroller as he marched over to Harry, demanding good-naturedly, 'Well, young man, what can I do for you?' until he came to a stop a few inches short of Harry's face, as was his imposing habit.

Harry, though, didn't flinch. 'I've come, sir,' he stated, 'to ask for your daughter's hand in marriage.'

Charles made no response. His broad smile died away and he remained blank-faced for some time. He looked like Harry's grandmother after many hours in front of the television. Was he even breathing? It didn't look like it – his eyes had lost all sign of life. But then the lips moved.

'I beg your pardon, young man?' they asked, all on their own in a face of stone. 'I beg your pardon?'

'I'm asking for permission,' Harry replied, his heart hammering but his mind clear, 'to marry your daughter.'

'My daughter?' the lifeless lips intoned.

'Yes, sir. Your daughter Alice.'

'I see,' said the lips. And then Harry Singh received first hand, for the first (and indeed the last) time, one of Charles Freeman the man-in-charge's full-in-the-face, legendary tongue lashings. Without warning and without build-up Charles switched from impassivity to fury in an instant and proceeded to rage at the unfortunate youth a few inches in front of him.

'Why, you insolent, idiotic imbecile! You jumped-up juvenile delinquent! You backward brown bloody booby, how *dare* you? HOW DARE YOU? Spotty, wet-behind-the-ears, poverty-stricken son of a shopkeeper, you Asian upstart, *you* have the gall to ask *me* for my one and only adorable daughter's, my *fourteen*-year-old daughter's, hand?'

Charles railed, his eggs-and-bacony breath, flecks of spittle and the heat of his rage cascading down upon young Harry Singh's face, and he could have carried on for ages – he *would* have – except that the thing that always happened wasn't happening: young Harry Singh was not withering beneath the onslaught. In fact, Charles realized disbelievingly, the boy seemed to be *smiling*. And, robbed of his victim's customary capitulation, the tyrant's tirade dried up, his bully's bile petered out.

'Feather-brained . . . foreign . . . feckless . . .' Charles, his trembling bulk heaving, heard not his oaths and curses but only his laboured breathing. He also became aware of the smell of cardamom on the young man's breath.

'Foppish . . . foolish . . . *fiend*!' Charles blurted out, before his invective finally ground to a halt.

Harry wiped his face with the back of his hand, without either taking his eyes off Charles *or* subduing his mild, friendly smile.

'Have you finished, sir?' he asked respectfully. And when there came no reply he continued, calmly (even though *he* could hear his heartbeat pounding in his ears): 'Thank you for your time, sir. I'm glad we've had a chat, and I appreciate your provisional response. I assure you that I shall prove myself a worthy suitor to your daughter, for whom I hold the most honourable feelings, as well as the greatest respect for your family.'

With that Harry nodded and turned to make his way around the gargantuan frame before him and towards the door. Then he stopped.

'Oh,' he added, passing a crumpled bouquet of primroses into Charles' astonished hand, 'and these, sir, are for your wife.'

'My *wife*?' Charles spluttered. And although under normal circumstances Harry's idiotic mistake would have been enough to set Charles off again, this time he was unable to do anything other than watch the young man's departing figure leaving the room with a jaunty stride.

At the *Echo*, the photographers' days – unlike the subeditors', split in two, or the journalists', out chasing leads – were unpredictable but on the whole relaxed on that provincial paper. They were sent out either accompanying a reporter or, as often as not, on their own to cover an event with no more than a photograph and a brief by-line.

In between times they drank tea and ate sandwiches in the office, and said little as they collated prints and loaded their cameras. They never went to the pub.

'You might be able to type with trembling fingers, Jim boy,' Roger Warner told James, 'but you can't expect to take a decent photo unless you're stone-cold sober. You'd best keep away from the pen-pushers if I was you,' he advised. 'A photographer needs three things: an eye, nerve and a steady hand.'

James also received advice from the editor. Mr Baker (no one appeared to know, let alone use, his Christian name) was a dour, scrupulous man who rarely came out of his office. He hated sloppy journalism, was a stickler for detail, and had been known to keep the presses waiting and, later, the distributors' vans ticking over, news-agents nervous, street sellers impatient and delivery boys and girls kicking their heels all over the town while he scrutinized a con-troversial article – sometimes with the aid of a lawyer from upstairs – checking the facts were correct. Once he was convinced that they were he ran the story, no matter how scandalous it might be. His clarion call was not so much truth as accuracy.

Mr Baker disliked ornate description, sloppiness and irrelevant detail much more than partiality, because that could be balanced by an article in the next issue, whereas fudge and vagueness couldn't be redeemed, they left a woolly impression in the reader's mind and that was that. And photographs had, in the house style, to be similarly unfussy.

Shortly after James had completed his apprenticeship in the darkroom and was being sent out to take photographs, early in 1975, Mr Baker summoned him to his office. He'd discovered James was the son of Charles Freeman, who as well as appearing regularly in the newspaper as a prominent local businessman, member of the Round Table and pillar of the community, had also been the subject of one or two articles about aggrieved ex-employees and disgruntled business rivals. Mr Baker wanted to set his mind at rest, and soon established that this stuttering young man was no troublemaker, at least. When he asked James what his ambition was he replied:

'I just want to take pictures, Mr Baker.'

'And I hope you'll take plenty of good ones for us,' the editor affirmed. 'Nothing flashy. Our readers are ordinary people. They deserve a clear picture, and that's what we try to give them.'

James had, meanwhile, gradually got to know the other bedsit residents, or at least gained a nodding acquaintance, since there appeared to be an unwritten rule that they didn't invite each other into their rooms or presume so to trespass. Instead they met on the stairs or, leaving the house at the same time, exchanged a few polite words about the weather. Once or twice during an evening the telephone would ring loudly in the front hallway and whoever was passing or was nearest answered and yelled up the stairwell to whoever it was for – usually one of the two students at the top of the house.

On the first floor next to James' room was Jim – which might have caused some confusion except that Jim never received phone calls. He was a middle-aged man who by coincidence worked in the Freeman factory and set off across town at dawn for the early shift on his bicycle, which he carried up and down the stairs and kept in his room, along with a spare pair of boots, a change of clothes, five library books, the food of a parsimonious diet, and a shelf-ful of notebooks in which Jim recorded his reflections and observations of life.

'I'm going to publish them one day,' he confided in James. 'Keep it to yourself, mind, I haven't told anyone else.'

'Right,' James agreed.

'In a single volume. I'm going to call it "Journal of a Simple Man".'

'Sounds good,' James encouraged him.

'Well, it's modest,' Jim told him. 'And ironic, mind,' he added. 'It'll shake a few people up, I don't mind telling you.'

The students at the top of the house – on the floor above James and Jim – unlike the other residents, shared a sink, stove and kitchen cupboards on their tiny landing. It was just as well they were on the top floor: the fumes of charred toast and burnt pans rose mostly upward, along with the sounds of three records, *Dark Side of the Moon* and *Yessongs* and *Tubular Bells*, which they kept flipping over and playing again.

Below James was a young woman, Pat, who spent days in her

room but always emerged from it in a hurry, so that it took James some months to discover that she was, as she put it, an activist – at which he nodded sagely and wondered what that meant. She knew Zoe because she spent her dole money on seeing every film that showed at the cinema. She also told James about the man in the basement below her: a porter in the mental hospital at Middlemore. He suffered from insomnia, and when he couldn't sleep he sawed wood in his room.

'Doesn't that keep *you* awake?'

'Sure,' she said, shrugging her shoulders and frowning at the same time. 'I told him to pack it in, but he said if he couldn't saw wood he'd go mad and what did I want, an occasionally noisy neighbour or a madman in the basement? And then he gave me a wad of cotton wool to use for fucking earmuffs.' She shrugged again. 'You get used to anything.'

Unlike Jim's room, Pat's was packed solid; a true bedsit, thought James, glancing through the door she'd left open to answer the telephone, because it looked like a houseful of rooms crammed into one: one wall a kitchen, another for clothes, on a third shelves of books above her bed, and against the fourth, beside the door, a desk covered with typewriter, files, papers, pens. Shoes were stacked on top of the wardrobe, cassettes scattered across the floor.

Next to Pat, in the room at the front of the house beside the front door, lived a woman whose name no one knew since she received not only no telephone calls but no post either. She was referred to by the other tenants as the Plant Woman, because her sill was filled with window-boxes and from the curtain rail hung not curtains but pots of hanging plants, and the only things inside the room that could be spied through the foliage were even more green leaves of various shapes and profusion. She was a middle-aged woman of immaculate appearance but she rarely stepped outside her room and so was seldom seen; although from the silent hallway she *could* sometimes be heard, her voice a pleasant murmur in some one-sided conversation.

Below the Plant Woman in the basement (beside the wood-sawing lunatic) was Shirley, a large woman of similar age to the Plant Woman but who in complete contrast appeared to be in a state of disarray: she dressed in clothes that were either too tight or else absurdly loose for her amplitude, as if she'd put on a large amount of weight overnight and had had to borrow other people's clothes in a hurry. She greeted James cheerfully from the very beginning, although he never saw her before midday. Shirley was the most sociable of all the tenants: she went out every evening and staggered back late, unsteady on her feet but assisted by furtive men who shushed her as she giggled down the basement steps.

James was content with the nodding acquaintance of his fellow tenants. He preferred to construct imaginary pasts and present activities for them, these secondary characters in his own developing life-story: Jim, some exiled intellectual; Pat, a dangerous revolutionary; the Plant Woman, a genteel lady fallen on hard times; Shirley, a drunken prostitute; the nutty porter, one step from being a patient; and vapid, chaotic students on the top floor. The one thing they all had in common was a respect for each other's privacy.

James liked living in one room; there was plenty of space. He had a chest-of-drawers for his clothes and a large bookcase for his photographic equipment, which consisted simply of cameras and lenses — he didn't need a darkroom because he could use the one at work in the evenings. As for books he didn't require any more space than the few built-in shelves above his bed. Unlike Zoe, he couldn't see the point of keeping books you were never going to read again; the ones he read were borrowed from her or the public library, and the only ones he actually bought were photographic collections that he pored over for hours, while listening to Zoe's *Teach Yourself Italian* tape.

In imitation of the Plant Woman he got a couple of pot plants, but their leaves soon went brown and withered, however much he watered them or fed them with Baby Bio. He felt guilty smoking, but not enough to stop, and eventually gave up on plants and began what would become a life-long habit of buying a bouquet of flowers after work every pay-day. It would still be a while, though, before he bought them for someone other than himself.

When he started on the newspaper James was paid an apprentice's wages. Ten pounds a week went on rent, and after other expenses only a little was left over for a repetitive, loner's diet of porridge for breakfast, cheese sandwiches for lunch and a tasteless stew for supper. The fact that the only cooking facility was a Baby Belling, and that instead of a fridge he copied his fellow tenants and put milk out on the window ledge, was no problem at all for James. His one extravagance was Colombian coffee from the covered market, where a machine ground the beans and funnelled the coffee into tight white paper bags. Each Saturday morning he bought a pound first thing and put it in his jacket pocket, and the gorgeous aroma accompanied him through the town until he got home.

Once he became a staff photographer James was given a wage rise. He found himself with surplus income, and his standard of living rose: he shaved with Boots' foam instead of making a lather out of ordinary soap, and left his clothes at the launderette for a service wash rather than waste hours watching them spin. In the corner of the room that was his kitchen sunflower oil became virgin olive oil, margarine was replaced by butter, orange squash became fruit juice. His staple of apples proliferated into a varied fruit bowl. He bought croissants from the French-style patisserie that had just opened in Gray's Road and wine from the deli near the cinema. James lived contentedly within his means. On account of his press pass and his camera, he got in free to music gigs, football matches and first nights at the town theatre. He rolled his own cigarettes (he'd got better with practice; Zoe no longer complained at the joints he rolled when he visited her) and shopped in jumble sales and charity shops.

One evening there was a knock on his bedsit door. He opened it expecting to find Pat or Jim but instead there was Simon. He peered around the side of James' head.

'My God,' Simon exclaimed. 'What an absolute bloody rat-hole.'

James made them both coffee and Simon demanded to know how long James was going to keep away from the family. 'When you're in a hole, darling, stop digging for God's sake.'

'I'm not going back there,' James told him. 'I'm going to make it on my own. That's final, Simon.'

'You are a stubborn little shit,' Simon admonished him. 'And by the way,' he said, accepting that there was no more to say on the subject, 'how can you bear to dress in dead men's clothes?'

'Someone else has already worn them in for me,' James smiled.

'Next time I visit,' Simon said as he was leaving, 'I'm taking you out for a meal. You're like a bloody beanpole.'

It didn't take James long to establish himself in the team of photographers on the paper. Whatever he lacked in self-confidence he made up for with his willingness to take on unpopular assignments, which initially meant the least exciting, bread-and-butter jobs of councillors planting trees, the façades of buildings in which stories had already taken place, and summer traffic jams around the ring road. Soon, however, they included early-morning stories and emergency call-outs in the middle of the night – which necessitated James installing a line for the newspaper inside his bedsit room after complaints from the other residents. The only jobs he resisted were those involving his father, and Roger tactfully assigned them to someone else.

Through 1975 James came to know the town he'd grown up in. As a child there were places, and pockets around them (home, school, friends' houses, the swimming pool) and the routes out from home along roads and paths like bent spokes in a crooked wheel. Now, on a racing bicycle, his camera bag stuffed in a pannier, he got to know all the streets of the town and the flow of traffic as if he were a taxi driver, as well as the cycle- and footpaths, the towpath along the canal, a hundred short cuts.

He learned the geography of the town as a series of maps of particular significance that he could mentally plant like grids over a straightforward A–Z of the town, each imaginary map with appropriate places marked in one arbitrary colour: green for the parks and football pitches; red, blue and orange (and later another, darker, green) for the homes of the town councillors; yellow for schools; purple for the various local artists – writers, painters, singers, musicians; black for the darkness of pubs and clubs; and brown for the vantage points from which to get good views of that town in the valley.

Early on James acquired a nickname among his fellow photographers. Roger stooped over James' contact sheets, pointing out mistakes he considered James was making and advising him on how to improve framing and composition in line with what was required, which was chiefly, as Mr Baker had once explained, simplicity. It was Roger who noticed that on almost every sheet there'd be at least one image slightly askew; and they were always ones taken in haste, captured on the run.

'Look at the way he walks,' Derek Moore pointed out. 'See how he lurches. No wonder they're skew-whiff. You'd have thought they'd *all* be.'

And so in those early days they called him Lurcher, scrutinizing his rolls of film for odd frames to corroborate the evidence; when they found a glaring example Keith printed a large blow-up and they pinned it on the wall of the office and then discussed it over tea in tones of mock-serious criticism.

'You see the way Lurcher's composed this one,' said Frank; 'tilting the frame so that the mayor looks like she's about to slide out of the left of the frame.'

'Aye,' Derek agreed, 'a subtle reference to the fact that the end of her term of office is approaching.'

'And also, I reckon,' said Keith, 'a guarded criticism of the whole paraphernalia of pomp and ceremony. Isn't that right, mate?'

'It's subversive stuff, Lurch,' they told him. 'It'll never get past Mr Baker, but it's a good try.'

James took it in as good heart as he could, smiling wanly, while concentrating on each assignment to eliminate this unwelcome quirk from his craft. At first the badinage – and even more the reason for it – upset him, and he confided in Zoe.

'All I can say is: forget that advice I gave you,' she said when she saw some of the lopsided prints.

James frowned. 'What advice?' he enquired.

'To give up stills and make films. They'd be all over the place, James. Unless, of course,' she faltered, her gaze drifting away, 'unless you didn't do any hand-held. Hey, maybe Bresson's a lurcher, too.'

'You're not being very helpful,' James complained, but Zoe didn't take any notice.

'And Ozu as well,' she continued. 'On the other hand,' she mused, 'that doesn't explain why he shot everything from knee-height.'

'What are you on about, Zoe?' James moaned. 'You're not listening.'

'Of course I am, sweetheart,' she said. 'Look, James. Don't worry what people say. Or at least take Cocteau's advice: he said an artist should listen carefully to the first criticisms of their work, and note what it is the critics don't like; it may be the only thing in the work that's original and worthwhile.'

James frowned. 'I'm not an artist. Anyway, who's Cocktoe?' he asked.

Zoe slapped her forehead. 'Oh, the ignorance of the young! *You* are going straight downstairs. I'm showing a fabulous new film from Greece, about a travelling theatre company. It was only in the London Film Festival last week.'

'I've got to go, Zoe, I'm meeting someone.'

'Rubbish. You're going to watch this film if I have to chain you in your seat.'

It was probably because they were too busy scrutinizing his photos for tilted frames that the other photographers took a long time to realize that James' pictures, during those first couple of years, were growing bolder. Under the influence of the masters whose books he studied in his bedsit, he took close-ups of local politicians and other dignitaries in harsh light or half in shadow, depending upon what he perceived of their self-importance and mendacity, in the manner of Arbus or Brand; sent out to get stock shots of the town centre, he roved among shoppers and workers for hours, keen-eyed as a bird, seeking the significant moment of Cartier-Bresson; covering children's sports days, he snapped the prize-winners perfunctorily but then hung around hoping to capture an image with the charm and humour of a Doisneau. His photos were still derivative; but in the context of the provincial newspaper they were radical.

It was Mr Baker who first questioned the orthodoxy of the prints James chose to submit to the subeditors. He summoned James into his office: three recent editions of the paper were laid out across his desk, opened at pages displaying three of James' photographs. Mr Baker proceeded to explain once again his precepts for providing what their readership wanted – clarity and simplicity – and James listened calmly, politely, grateful for the correction, not saying a word until the editor had finished and James said: 'Thank you, Mr Baker, I appreciate it,' before leaving the room.

Since everyone knew that a summons from Mr Baker meant a mild rebuke, but one delivered in such a way that a sterner one would not be needed, it meant toe the line or look for another job, the other photographers became aware of James' nonconformity. They assumed, however, that it was a youthful phase both spotted and put a stop to by their vigilant editor. It wasn't. James had neither the courage nor the confidence to be a rebel, but the one thing he was – throughout those years of freedom and loneliness – was stubborn. His lurching was forgotten as his colleagues scanned his contact sheets instead for surreptitious images that, sure as eggs is eggs, were not the way things were done around here.

'You'll never get that past Mr Baker,' Keith told him, staring at the wet print of the local Member of Parliament, on a long lens, addressing a garden party of his more loyal constituents, positioned with the sun directly behind him, creating a sardonic halo.

Keith was right on that occasion, but James wasn't stupid: he always covered himself with more straightforward pictures. There was no point in being out of work; he had no intention of returning to his earliest adventures, with an empty camera. But he was sure his bolder pictures were better. As time went by he covered himself less and less.

It wasn't until the long hot summer of 1976 that the inhabitants of the house on the hill began to notice how Edna had changed, because she'd never complained or made a fuss about things, coping over the years with no more than a raised eyebrow with the children's whims, Charles' impromptu parties, Simon's fads and the endless unpredictable comings and goings that meant she never knew from one day to the next how many people would sit down to supper. Her quartermaster's ability to eke out the contents of the larder while satisfying tastebuds with a mastery of pastries, puddings and pies, with unfailing good humour, was so unostentatious that everyone took it for granted.

It took even Simon – with his super-sensitive palate – a while to notice that Edna's food was losing its flavour. He was unable to mention it to Edna, less because he was worried about upsetting her than because she had become unapproachable: he was so used to greeting her at breakfast or requesting a particular dish and being met with her fat woman's compliant smile that when she stopped, it gave him a feeling of sad dread in his stomach. So he took Laura aside, and informed her of the tastelessness of her mother's cooking.

'I know,' Laura agreed. 'I think she's stopped eating.'

'That can't be it,' Simon said. 'She eats the same as she's always done,' he maintained, because Edna still sat down to supper and dished out for herself the usual meagre portion of a sparrow. Laura had to point out to him that Edna used to eat more than anyone else, consuming mouthfuls of whatever she was cooking, without realizing she was doing so, simply checking the taste.

'She's stopped doing that,' Laura explained. 'She just works automatically now, measuring and weighing from recipes. She doesn't even *smell* the food. When I try and tell her it could do with more garlic or coriander she tells me to go away.'

Laura decided to mention it to Stanley. She told him Simon's observation of the loss of flavour, and that Edna no longer nibbled her way through the day. Stanley was relieved.

'That explains why she's losing weight,' he replied.

'Don't be silly, Dad,' Laura told him, 'she's not lost a pound.'

Laura was right, but Stanley's misconception was understandable: something was happening to Edna and whatever it was bore a distinct resemblance to the symptoms of a fast: deep shadows appeared around her eyes, which took on a haunted look; her movements became blurred, as her once flowing limbs moved momentarily later than they should have done; and they would come across her in the kitchen sitting on a stool and staring into space, a mixing bowl in her lap, after a lifetime's perpetual motion.

Gradually others began to notice too. 'Auntie Edna's face is all red,' Alice – back home for the holidays – told Laura. 'Is she all right?'

One of the gardeners told Stanley he'd seen Edna stumble on the way to the compost heap, and then his sister Pauline called round because she'd heard that Edna had to be helped to a taxi at the open market that morning. Even Robert – who stayed most of the time God knows where and limited his apearances at home to Sunday lunch – telephoned the next day. As luck would have it, Laura answered.

'Hello,' she said.

There was a pause. 'Is Simon there?' came the familiar gritty voice. Laura too paused, briefly. 'I'll go and see,' she replied.

Simon came down and picked up the receiver.

'You know my mate Radko?' Robert asked him.

'No,' Simon replied. 'Should I?'

'Well,' Robert explained, 'he delivered dry-cleaning to the house today, he's been doing it for years, he said Edna didn't recognize him. She used to give him one of her pastries and come out to say hello to his dog in the van, but she didn't recognize him.'

'Thanks, Robert,' Simon told him, surprised by his brother's loquacity.

'Is she all right, Simon?' Robert asked.

'She's fine, Robert,' Simon assured him. 'I'll let you know, I'll look into it.'

'Good. See you Sunday.'

It was a Sunday morning in the Easter holidays of 1977 when Charles asked Alice to gather everyone she could find, except Edna, for sherry in his study. When they'd all – including Zoe and one of Simon's secretary friends – congregated there, Charles declared to Stanley that he had the feeling that Edna had been working too hard recently.

'I thought you and I,' he continued, 'might impress upon these young people that we should all value her a bit more and demand of her a bit less. We've been taking Edna for granted.'

Charles finished his brief speech of a man-in-charge, and was disappointed to discover that the rest of the household were well ahead of him. But at least his leadership brought them all together in the same room, and in the ensuing half-hour of shared concern, observations and memories they began to realize, too late, that that cheerful, chubby aunt had been a mother to them all, not just since Mary's death but before it as well.

They were interrupted by the emphatic ringing of the gong in the hallway, Edna calling them in to Sunday lunch. The conversation never let up throughout the meal, right through the main course of chewy beef, soggy roast potatoes, heavy Yorkshire pudding, insipid peas, bland parsnips and watery gravy, a conversation full of forced joviality and shrill expressions of appreciation they directed at Edna without looking her in the eye. She prodded the few peas on her plate with her fork, cleared the table, served up the dessert, sat down, and then suddenly slammed her bowl down and stood up.

'For God's sake,' Edna said breathlessly, 'do you all think I'm stupid? Can't a woman suffer a little heartburn without it being the talk of the town?'

They all stared at their plates with expressions of anxious embarrassment; only Charles and Laura were actually looking at her.

'This is one meal too many, Charles,' Edna declared. She turned to Laura. 'Do take that stupid look off your face,' she told her. 'And tell your father to get the car out. I'm going back to my sister's.'

She marched towards the back door through to their quarters. Forgetting himself, Stanley blurted out: 'Why do you want to go there?'

Edna turned round and addressed not Stanley but Laura. 'Tell your father I haven't seen my sister in too long, and it's about time I had a holiday. Tell him Laura can take over the cooking,' she added, confusing herself in the absurdity of their zig-zag communication. 'If she can't cook properly by now, she never will.'

Edna left behind a taut silence as she went to her room and packed a suitcase. I've had enough, she decided; I've had it up to here with this place, with that bossy buffoon, who does he think he is, Winston Churchill? With those sons of his, young Robert, I don't trust him and I never have, and that pompous Simon treating me like a slave. What a bunch, feed them all day, every day, it goes in one end comes out the other without a word of thanks. For what? I've had it with that silly, feckless girl, how could she do it? She didn't deserve what she got but how could she be so foolish? Alice wouldn't let such a thing happen, poor girl, she should have been mine, Laura's his, you can see that: just look at her, it's clear enough; the bastard, beating our child for his own wounded pride, just because it was the boss's son, and then crying himself to sleep every night, he's had two years to say he's sorry and he still can't do it, how did I ever love him?

Bloody hell, she thought, I've just about had it with these ridiculous palpitations. Calm down, woman, you're not a calf, breathe easy, that's it, sit down, push the suitcase on the floor. I've had it up to here with this hammering inside, like a muffled gong, boom-boom, at least no one else can hear it, but perhaps they can, boom-boom, boom-boom, boom-boom.

Back in the kitchen Laura was clearing the table while Simon did the washing-up for the first time in his life. Zoe and Simon's friend dried up in silence. Stanley was reversing the pick-up out of the garage. Charles and Robert remained seated at the table. No one said a word.

It was Robert who suddenly pushed his chair back and made his way with unfaltering stride to Stanley's and Edna's bedroom. He poked his head around the door and felt a great sense of relief: Edna was simply taking a nap. She lay peacefully on the bed, her hands crossed on her stomach. Robert began quietly to withdraw, but then he realized that he couldn't, that the evidence in front of his eyes was less reliable than his own grim premonition, for he'd just – while seated at the kitchen table – felt the same burning sensation in his forehead and seen the same momentary and indescribable change in the light that he had walking home from school years earlier, on the afternoon he found Alfred's body in among the moulting rose bushes.

'Shit,' Robert said to himself. I don't want this, he thought.

Robert dragged himself reluctantly back into the room, and walked over to the head of Edna's bed. Her bruised eyes and her twisted mouth were both slightly open, and on her pale face was an expression of surprise.

Robert didn't grin this time; but neither was he intimidated by death. He closed her eyes, moulded her mouth into a more contented shape, and hoped that it wouldn't fall open again, before stepping outside to break the news, first, to Stanley.

The first James knew of Edna's death was at work the next day, because none of the messages Simon and Zoe left at his bedsit to call home reached him. It wasn't until the next morning that he found out, when one of the typists downstairs rang through to the photography department and related the death notice delivered from the house on the hill. James sent a note of condolence to Laura, and went to the funeral with a wreath, but stood at the back and slipped away before having to commiserate with Stanley or anyone else.

*

223

Nineteen seventy-seven was the summer of the Queen's Silver Jubilee. By day James took photographs for the newspaper of street parties in her honour as the town, along with the rest of the nation, celebrated their monarch's reign. Men climbed ladders and criss-crossed their streets with bunting hung from the gutters, and Union Jacks fluttering in the breeze. They blocked off cars and set up trestle tables, while the women prepared picnics of sausage rolls, potato salads, coronation chicken, paste sandwiches, vol-au-vents and trifles, jellies and fizzy drinks. Children stuffed themselves and became manic with sugar, fidgeting through pompous speeches and running in the streets as their grandparents had once done. Neighbourly feuds were forgotten, elderly people who'd been cast adrift by bereavement found themselves insisted back into the swing of things, and families that had disappeared behind DIY walls and garden hedges came out and conversed with each other, saying: 'It's for the kids, really, isn't it?' before standing unsteadily for the National Anthem.

Her Majesty's image was everywhere: on posters, plates, coffee mugs and coins.

Pat, the tenant on the ground floor below James, was in the hallway when he got home. 'It's bloody depressing, isn't it?' she said. 'Do you want a cup of tea? Come on into the Republic of Gath.'

She was the only one at home: there was a party in *their* street, and weaving rapidly through it James was surprised – and dis-appointed – to discover that his eccentric fellow residents had joined in, and looked as normal as everyone else.

Nineteen seventy-seven: it was the summer of the Sex Pistols. By night James went into one or both of the two dingy pubs in the town where local garage bands and very occasional touring punk groups played. Youths with startling hair and safety pins through ears and noses, wearing mohair sweaters, torn army fatigues, ripped T-shirts and laddered tights, with expressions of sullen condescension, stalked in from hidden corners of the town to those two pubs, the Oranges and Lemons by South Bridge or the Queen's Head near the railway station.

The bands all thrashed their instruments, torturing them into divulging noise in tuneless bursts, brief songs of angry, compressed energy. The audiences greeted them not with applause but spittle, a shower of gob that splattered the guitarists and increased their anger. Gradually, though, if they stood their ground, the bands won over their listeners, who squashed together and leapt into the air like demented salmon, pogo-ing, a dance of frantic liberation.

All through that year James took along an old camera and a battered lens. He snapped both the bands and the fans – for photos some of which he sold to the music press but mostly gave away, either to the proliferating fanzines of that era or to the bands themselves – and then he deposited his camera behind the bar for safe-keeping and threw himself into the heaving mass of bodies. He couldn't dance, had hated the various discos to which he'd been occasionally coerced, owing to his dodgy hips and a clumsy sense of rhythm. The pogo, however, was different. Anyone could do it. It looked ridiculous and felt wonderful. James pushed through as if into a crowded goalmouth and jumped on other people's shoulders to gain height, bumped against their hips and shoulders, sweat spraying through the dark air from shocked hair in that asexual dance of sexual energy, in a din of music and feedback shrieking from the speakers, leaping into oblivion.

One evening early in the autumn of 1978 the council allowed the town hall to be used for the first and last time for a punk rock concert: a triple bill of Suicide – two lugubrious Americans in suits, sunglasses and synthesizers – a raucous female band, the Slits, and, headlining, the Clash.

The hard-core punks of the town were hugely outnumbered by a mish-mash of students, rastafarians, unrepentant hippies, greasers and, in the main, townies of no tribal affiliation, who included Laura and Alice – in that last summer between school and college – and Lewis, who was providing music in between the acts with his own mobile disco.

The concert was a pre-sold sellout. The only youthful clan who didn't seem to want to attend were skinheads from the southern estate, but they came into town anyway in order to attack the more flamboyant punks, buzzing them like irate wasps from out of the alleys around the town centre, until police vans arrived. And then a few of the skinheads, though without tickets, managed to shove their belligerent way through the front doors, up the wide municipal stairs and into the hall, where they scowled around and provoked the odd scuffle here and there, until they too were sucked into the fraught, anticipatory atmosphere.

The wide staircase led straight up to a landing and across it, through double doors, was the main hall. On either side were other doors which gave onto stairs leading up to a balcony that ran around the back and sides of the hall. These stairs had been roped off: the doors couldn't be locked because there were also stairs leading *down*, for emergency fire exits.

When the first band played a lot of people remained in the bar back across the landing, or else were still arriving, and there was plenty of space in the hall. The audience was enthusiastic only in their spitting. A shower of gob increased in quantity until the unfortunate American musicians wilted behind their synthesizers – they looked as if they might be crying behind their dark glasses and left the stage in mid-song, looking fit to fulfil the promise implicit in their name (James took a photograph of their phlegmatic siege that was published in the following week's *New Musical Express* alongside an editorial condemning a practice it had once championed, under the clumsy headline HAWKING FORBIDDEN).

By the time the Slits came on, after a long, unexplained interim, the hall was heaving. The hall wasn't used to such numbers as were there, or at least to them displaying the exuberance that would soon manifest itself. Concerts *were* often held there, but they were of classical music, brass bands, and the town choir singing carols at Christmas. The floorboards were gently tested at Wednesday afternoon tea dances, and a little more vigorously at professional wrestling bouts, less by the wrestlers (their canvas ring was raised above the ground) than by handbag wielding spectators enraged by villains fighting dirty.

It transpired later, however, that although the balcony was closed off for the evening, as many tickets had been sold as if it were being left open as usual. So that latecomers and boozers from the bar, barely able to squeeze into the back of the hall, let alone get a decent view of the banshees shrieking on the distant stage, began to step over the ropes and climb the side stairs to the balcony. There were too few stewards in that area to stop them and they soon gave up trying, using their initiative instead and unhitching the rope entirely so that at least no one would trip up.

The dancing started at the front, towards the end of the Slits' set, which had proceeded in tuneless disarray but none the less sustained the knife-edge atmosphere through the incessant hammering of the male drummer, the cool detachment of the guitarist, and the unpredictable yells of the singer, a striking schoolgirl with the hair of a Medusa.

When the group left the stage Lewis's sound system pumped out reggae at a deafening level, the bass turned right up so that it prowled around the hall and thumped against the walls. The sweet smell of cannabis mingled with sweat and spilt beer, and from the balcony James – who'd gone up to get a new angle – saw the music insinuate itself into people's defenceless bodies and a slow, sinuous movement ripple through the audience: the crowd was loosening itself.

The chief steward at the town hall that evening peered over the tops of heads, through the smoky haze, from the hall doorway up at inebriated youths and raucous girls leaning over the balcony. If he'd done anything, it should have been then.

James had come back down into the hall and wormed his way to the side of the stage by the time the Clash appeared. They burst from the shadows with guitars strapped to their shoulders and plugged them in without a word or a look or any kind of gesture that indicated their awareness of the expectant audience. One of them spat into the microphone: 'One-two-three-four,' and furious music leapt from the speakers and ignited the audience: instantly the hall became a cauldron, bubbling and seething.

By the third or fourth song the mayhem had spread to the balcony: there too people leapt and bounced and ricocheted against each other, shedding their sense of mortality in the liberating noise.

The chief steward stared up at the balcony in terror: it was vibrating insanely, and he realized that a catastrophe of hideous proportions was looming. He turned from the hallway. He felt for a moment the urge to run down the side, emergency, stairs and hide somewhere deep down in the basement, but he resisted the temptation and instead rushed down the main staircase and into the street, where he found the most senior police officer on duty and dragged him back up to the hall.

'We'll have to clear the building!' he blurted out as they climbed the stairs.

In the doorway of the hall the chief steward stared again at the quaking balcony; the police officer, however, was studying the pulsating, surging audience. His main experience of crowds of hyped-up youths was at football matches, in those days of barbaric hooligans; and *they* never looked as frenzied as these.

'If you think I'm telling this lot their party's over,' he yelled in the steward's ear, 'you don't know a thing about crowd control. They'll rip the place apart.'

They both studied the balcony. It sat on beams projecting out from inside the wall, and was supported by massive brackets, which were now vibrating; plaster dust and loose flakes floated from the wall.

'Well,' the steward hesitated – although he had to shout at the officer – 'it *might* hold.'

'Will it or won't it?' the officer yelled back.

The chief steward felt extremely lonely. 'I don't bloody *know*!' he cried.

They split off, each to inspect opposite sides of the hall, and reconvened on the landing at the top of the stairs. 'Well?' the officer yelled, because even out there the noise ground the air at a deafening volume.

'My side *seems* secure,' the steward ventured.

'Mine too,' the officer declared. 'I think it's going to hold.'

And so they let the concert carry on. The steward was quaking almost as much as the balcony. The officer felt the strange elation of power withheld, of letting chaos free. He was more attracted by disaster than the thought of preventing it and then some engineer coming in the next day and saying: 'This balcony was built to take such pressure, of *course* it was. Who the hell cancelled the thing? What moron was responsible for the riot?'

The crowd was oblivious to the danger. The crowd included James, who, once he was satisfied he'd got enough photos, had hidden his camera behind a speaker and pushed his way into the mass of bodies, where there were no longer any individuals but a writhing organism of ecstatic devotees of oblivion, provincial dervishes in Little England. When he found himself at one point leaping beside – and into – Laura, he didn't quite register that she was real; and then they were swallowed up in different directions.

The balcony held. The Clash pumped out their intense, compassionate fury for two hours. Eventually, after cheering and clapping and stamping their feet for a third encore, the lights came on and the crowd began to drift out, zombies, drained of all malice. James retrieved his camera and made his way out. Condensation streamed down the whitewashed walls. His stride was unsteady, his mind was empty, his ears were ringing, and he stepped out into an uncanny night.

A few nights later, death came to visit James.

He went to bed and lay on his right side, waiting for sleep. He closed his eyes, and his head started to slowly spin inside its skull.

He hadn't drunk anything during the evening except coffee. He opened his eyes and the spinning stopped, but he knew it hadn't gone away. A ripple of nervousness spread through his body, until it reached the sweat pores in the skin.

James shut his eyes, and again the spinning started up, gently, with an easy rhythm. He could make no sense of it; it worried him only slightly, and he lay there, letting it happen, studying it. Then he realized it was no longer only his head that was acting strangely: he felt himself moving, as if he were liquid, yet his body lay beneath the sheets, quite still.

Then he stopped moving, and just stayed a few inches away from his body, hovering, suspended, as if treading water, but with no effort involved at all. Yet it was not an *I* who was now detached from a *me*. There was no subject and object. He knew he had only to open his eyes, or lift the hand from his thigh, to return to his normal state. He had control over this. And he had only to submit himself, to let go, and he would leave the body completely.

The choice was his, but how could he make it? He wanted to know whether he would have the option of returning once he had left, or whether it would be for good. And he wanted to know where he would be going, anyway. He was aware only of Death's trembling fingers. Perhaps it would pluck him from his past and cast him down. He had no proof of an afterlife. But what, on the other hand, did he have to stay for?

These thoughts flooded his mind. They were questions he knew would not be answered, and he let them sink beneath him. Having emptied his mind, he then tried to release his other senses: perhaps they could help. For a few moments, nothing; then the distant sound of an aeroplane made its way to his ears. It got louder, and seemed to be passing directly overhead. The people inside have never known me, he thought, and never will. Some perhaps are sleeping, others thinking of the welcome awaiting them when they land. All strangers, their lives will continue whatever I decide. Won't they?

The sound of the plane's engines grew fainter, as it passed on, until eventually it disappeared for good, and once again there was silence. James remained motionless, until the stillness of the silence began to prickle, and he knew there was no point in waiting any longer. He had an eternity in which to decide, but such empty time would bring him nothing new.

His hand moved up from his thigh, across his stomach, and lifted the sheets. He opened his eyes, and switched on the light. Whether it was out of fear, arrogance, whatever, he had declined the offer.

Needing to affirm his physical return, he masturbated, washed, smoked a cigarette, and soon fell into a deep sleep.

While Alice went off to university in Oxford in the autumn of 1978, Laura did the opposite: she anchored herself more firmly in the house on the hill, by accepting Charles' offer to be their cook. During the year and a half since Edna's death he'd had to hire a succession of women who couldn't cope with his family's unreasonable demands and never lasted more than a couple of months. As for Laura, it was a strange decision: none of the other members of the family, or her friends at school, could understand why she didn't get away – if she wanted to do that kind of work, why not take a catering course?

What was clear was that here was as much of a family as she had left. After Edna's death Stanley had gone into his own decline: now he had a double guilt that he had to suppress, and the effort seemed to suck out his energy. He aged visibly, slept twelve-hour nights, and lost his grip on the maintenance of the house: paint peeled, carpets curled, a banister came loose and stayed so, a cracked window was taped over and simply left.

Before Charles had to have a word, though, Stanley was dead, less than a year after Edna. No one was surprised, and not even Laura grieved for very long.

Laura's first months in the job coincided with Simon's conversion to vegetarianism. As if the idea were a novel one – as if Alice hadn't already been abstaining from meat for the last twelve years – Simon declared that red meat was what made people aggressive, that meat eating was an historical aberration, an error of evolution. He cited famous vegetarians in history, from the poet Shelley to the pacifist Gandhi. When Robert mentioned Adolf Hitler, Simon was unfazed. 'The exception that proves the rule, dear boy,' he replied.

At first Simon ate only raw vegetables, consuming mountains of carrots, cucumbers and cabbages as he'd once done fruit, but with less pleasure. Even that banal diet was too rich really, he explained, misty-eyed, as he recounted with what sounded like nostalgia the insubstantial, purifying flowers and spices upon which the gods in Elysium had lived. How Simon knew such arcane ephemera was a mystery. Nothing he'd been told in school had ever registered, and the only books he read were manuals of self-help written by psychologists with suspect degrees. But he had a magpie's eye for the glittering detail and the pithy anecdote, and picked them up along the way.

Simon's passion for raw vegetables was the briefest of all his diets, because he could never deny his sensuous nature for long, but luckily vegetarianism had many variations, and Simon discovered a succession of national cuisines whose complexity Laura explored. When his demands were unreasonable she told him to cook the food himself, but in fact it was an enjoyable period for Laura, as she spread the aromas of India and the Middle East through the big house on the hill, cooking dishes so delicious that even when Simon himself grew bored and moved on, the rest of the family requested them.

It was a combination of Lebanese hors d'oeuvres presented as an alternative at Sunday lunch and Simon's citing of Pythagoras' advocacy of vegetarianism that converted Zoe. The smoked aubergine pâté and home-made humous were mouth-watering, and anyway she already respected Pythagoras' doctrines concerning transmigration of the soul.

'I think I was always *meant* to be a vegetarian,' Zoe told Simon. 'I wouldn't kill an animal myself, so it's cowardly to let someone else do it for me.'

'Don't worry about dumb animals, darling,' Simon replied. 'That's not the point at all. It's a question of purifying the body.'

Charles and Robert were less easily impressed. When Laura tried making nut cutlets that looked like rissoles and using soya protein in cottage pie, Charles took one bite and said: 'I should try a new butcher right away, Laura. Your mother would never have let them get away with this.'

On the whole, though, it was an easy period of initiation. The house was emptier than it ever had been; the only full-time occupants were Charles and Simon (although since Stanley's death Robert stayed more often). It would soon fill up again – the chaotic years had passed, but the crazy ones were coming. But by that time Laura would be in complete control of her kitchen; she would become, at least locally, famous for her cooking.

While Laura spent her first year as cook in the big house developing her culinary skills, James was taking the next course in his sporadic apprenticeship in the difficult art of love.

One Saturday in June of 1979 there was a march through the town organized by the Anti-Nazi League which culminated in a rally in the south park, with speeches followed by music. James shot off two rolls of film.

On Monday afternoon he returned from another assignment to find his colleagues handling the contact sheets of the rally over their mugs of tea. When James walked in they jeered and hooted at him.

'Friend of yours, is she?' asked Derek.

'You've got taste, you dirty devil,' added Frank.

'What are you on about?' James demanded. 'Let me see those!'

He snatched one of the contact sheets away and looked at it: in fourteen of the frames the main focus of attention was a young woman, long dark hair swirling about her, dancing in front of the stage. It was the same with the other sheet.

'Bloody hell,' James blushed. 'I had no idea.'

'Yeh, yeh,' Derek jeered. 'It's about a thirty mill. lens, you must have been right in close.'

'Well, I remember her,' James admitted, 'but I don't remember taking so many. Maybe four or five, but not as many as this.'

'Why didn't you get more of Tony Benn?' Keith complained.

'You better not let Roger see them, let alone Mr Baker,' Frank advised.

'We can't use a single one of these,' Keith agreed.

'Why not?' James demanded, recovering his composure, studying the photos now for their compositional qualities. 'This one here's really good,' he said. 'You've got the band on stage behind her. And *there's* Tony Benn in the corner, see, standing over there.'

'Look at her T-shirt, dummy,' Keith told him. 'Front and back the same, in case we didn't get the message.'

'Oh, shit,' said James, blushing all over again. The words FUCK ART, LET'S DANCE were emblazoned, black on white.

'And don't even *begin* to suggest me burning it out,' Keith warned. 'Mr Baker'd have my guts for garters.'

That evening after the others had gone James made a print for himself of the dark-haired dancing woman, and back home he pinned it on the wall. If I see her again, he vowed to himself, I'll talk to her.

The following Thursday evening James was in the cinema, watching, on Zoe's recommendation, Fellini's *Casanova*. It was a peculiar film with a tone all of its own, but James was unable to concentrate. For at inappropriate moments during the film a woman seated directly behind him laughed out loud. It was a husky laugh that was part mocking, part dirty and part uninhibited pleasure; the sound of it made James' hair stand on end; it both annoyed him and gave him a hard-on.

When the lights went up he stood and turned around and right there was the dancing woman from his photos; she was with a whole group – a row – of friends, and they were speaking in Italian. James fumbled with his jacket, glancing at her as often as he thought he could. Their eyes met for a moment, and she smiled as she looked away, and joined her friends filing out.

James watched her leave in the crowd. You promised, you spineless idiot, he berated himself. What have you got to lose, you useless prick? he cursed. He pushed forward, squeezing through the bodies shuffling into the foyer, and caught up with her on the pavement outside. At least she wasn't holding hands with any of her friends, he noted. James' heart was thumping, his armpits sweating.

'*Scusi*,' he exclaimed, and had to take a deep breath. '*Mi permesso*,' he stuttered, as he discovered that he was unable to utter more than four syllables unaided.

The woman had stopped and was looking at him, as calm as James was flustered: there was no expression of either suspicion or interest on her face, only a faint blank smile as she waited for James to declare himself.

'*Sono* James,' he announced, 'James Freeman.' He took another breath, but before he could continue she interrupted:

'I am Anna Maria Sabato,' she said, proffering her hand. 'Please to meet you, James James Freeman.'

'I'm a photographer,' James explained, 'on our local paper. I recognize you because I took a bunch of photos at that rally last Saturday, you know, in the park, and you were in some of them.'

'I were?'

'Yes, and, er, maybe you'd like to have one, to see them?' James' heart was thumping loudly. The woman looked at him, weighing him up, for what seemed an eternity, although it might have been closer to two or three seconds.

'That is very awful,' she declared eventually.

'What?' James asked, flummoxed.

'To see peectures of me. Very awful photographs.'

'Oh, no,' James disagreed. 'They're very good. I don't mean because I took them,' he stammered, 'but because you're in . . . I mean, they're good, you'll like them.'

'Well,' she decided. 'I shall have them, and then I destroy the negateeve.'

'Oh, I'm not sure you can do that,' James said. 'I mean, you know, they belong to the paper, but—'

'No problem,' she cut him off. 'Where do we meet, James James Freeman?'

He gave her the name of a pub and they fixed a time the following day, and Anna Maria walked off along the road with her friends. James returned into the now empty foyer, opened the door leading up to the projection booth and Zoe's flat, and slumped on the stairs.

Anna Maria smelled of the sea, although she was a long way from her home of Naples, here to study English in this small town in the middle of a foreign island. James met her at the end of June and he was dazzled – whether by her or by the summer sun, he wasn't at first sure. She had dark-brown eyes that absorbed the sun's rays, while James' pale-blue eyes of some woodland creature, his troglodytic, northern eyes, blinked and ached and watered in the sun. He hid beneath hats and behind polychromatic shades that blazing July but still had to scrunch up his eyes as if he were frowning at her, his papery skin creasing with incipient crow's-feet at the age of twenty-two.

Only at night, when the sun had gone down, was James able to look Anna Maria full in the face and verify her beauty. And she *was* beautiful, even if only through a strange harmony of disparate elements: Anna Maria had large eyes close together, a nose that managed to be both flat and crooked, a mouth pushed slightly outwards by jutting teeth, and a square jaw. But put together – with her Neapolitan's brown hair, skin and eyes – those components made Anna Maria as lovely a woman as James thought he'd ever seen.

She was also six inches shorter than James, although he would be surprised whenever he saw them together, in reflection, standing side by side, for somehow the proportions of her body created the illusion that she was taller than she really was. And James' height was just whatever it happened to be: 'A person doesn't feel their height,' he told her; 'you just knock your forehead now and then against the lintels of low door frames; *things* tell you you're too tall!'

But he wasn't too tall – *she* wasn't too short – for them to kiss without undue discomfort. She came to his bedsit that first evening after the pub, chose music from his small record collection (selecting, to his surprise, his one classical record, Tchaikovsky's *Swan Lake*) and sat on his bed.

'So, James James Freeman, thees is your palace. Some time you show me round it, yes?'

'I'll give you a guided tour,' he replied, pulling the cork from a bottle of red wine with a slide and plop.

'We have seen Stratford, we have seen the Tower of London, we have seen Oxford and Bath. I have done the tourist, James James. It is not my cup of coffee.'

They looked through other photographs. When they'd drunk half the bottle of wine they kissed. Her breath was warm and heavy. Their teeth bumped and Anna Maria laughed. They undressed and she smelled of the sea. On the brink of intercourse, James lost his erection. It was an extraordinary thing, sudden and inexplicable. They lay side by side for a time, then James went to the lavatory, down in the basement. The shower dripped. He sat on the toilet contemplating his options. One – the most obvious and attractive – was suicide. The other . . . he couldn't quite think of another. The draughtless cubicle was dank and damp still with condensation from a shower someone had taken hours earlier; James' self-pitying curses were amplified in it in an almost sardonic way.

'Fuck this,' James said to himself, and returned to his room. Anna Maria was still there. He decided to enlist her help.

'Look,' he said, 'it's not you. And it's not me either, it's nothing to do with me. I've got an enemy, you're beautiful, I don't know what it is, but I can overcome it if you help me.'

'Of course,' Anna Maria told him. 'No worry, James. It happens. Always.'

'Really?' he asked. 'To you?'

'To me? Are you joking?' she replied. 'Of course it happens,' she added. 'In Eetaly, yes, of course.'

She soon fell asleep in his arms. He followed her much later, into a thick and dreamless sleep.

James awoke with a gasp, into sensory confusion, a few moments before Anna Maria slid him inside her: not long enough for the hard-on she'd discovered upon waking to realize it was being taken unawares. He thrust up out of his dreams; they possessed each other wide awake.

'See?' she said, moving astride him, 'no problem, James. Anyway, to make love it is better in the morning.' She put her hands on his chest and he closed his eyes.

'Thank you,' he murmured, when he felt his come approaching from a deep distance.

James had no more such problems. From then on he had only to have Anna Maria brush past him, to smell her, to see her, to be aroused. He wanted her all the time. They both conspired to pretend, however, that an enemy of impotence was lurking and had constantly to be outwitted: she taught him to kiss with their fingers in each other's ears ('Kisses are keys, James'). They made love blindfold ('Every sense that you rob, James, it makes the others more big'). And, just to make sure, Anna Maria squeezed his throat ('Like the Americans, James'), on condition he did the same to her.

Anna Maria bought a second-hand Vespa that quacked like a duck as she rode it without a helmet through red lights. At the weekends James raced her on his bicycle a couple of miles out of town, to a bend in the river where it came winding close to the reservoir that fed the valley, as if the waters were attracting each other there.

They swam in the river by a willow tree, made love in the grass, and then Anna Maria sunbathed with coconut oil which James rubbed into her skin, while he hid beneath shirts and towels, hats and sunglasses.

'If you do a beet at a time, James,' Anna Maria assured him, 'in the end you become brown. It is the science.'

'Not me,' he apologized. 'I can only turn pink like a lobster. You can have me white or pink, but not brown. Limited colours available. Sorry.'

'And how do you call yourself a photographer when you see the world through sunglasses only?' she chided him.

'All the great photographers wore shades,' he assured her. 'They've all had weak eyes.'

'Oh, yeh?' she said.

'It's a well-known historical fact,' he lied. 'Otherwise they'd have invented colour photos to begin with, wouldn't they, instead of sepia? There's the proof. Think about it, Anna.'

He suffered, he told her, from photophobia: an aversion to light. An ironic condition for a photographer, to be sure, but one that would one day put him, he said, in celebrated company. He'd be compared with the deaf composer Beethoven; with the crippled footballer Garrincha; the blind painter Alan Benson; the stuttering poet Charles Lamb.

'Idiota,' Anna Maria murmured. She lay on her stomach with her back browning as James, hidden in the shade of his wrappings, got carried away with his thesis: he wouldn't produce his eventual masterpieces until the ailment had reached an advanced stage and he was living entirely in the shadows, and his photographs would take on the added poignancy of his condition – of his human fragility, his fragile humanity – and people would *weep* with the poignant pity of it. Until even, he proclaimed, the infrared lamp of the darkroom would be too bright for his eyes, and he would retreat for ever into darkness.

'My last pictures will be black,' James declared. 'But what a black! Beyond the black of death, mere mortality, a black that holds a consciousness of consciousness.' He paused. 'Or maybe of unconsciousness. You see what I mean, though, right?'

But from Anna Maria there came no reply, for she'd fallen asleep in the sun.

Anna Maria stayed more and more often with James in his cramped bedsit, until she was practically another lodger in the house. In fact she spent more time there than James, and she soon knew the other lodgers better than he did. The Plant Woman gave her a chrysanthemum in a terracotta pot, Jim repaired a puncture on her scooter, and she even extracted a smile from the young cleaning lady.

'I like the Eenglish,' she told James. 'They are not nosy.'

'I hope not,' James replied; he thought that if his landlady found out about this extra tenant she might double the rent.

Anna Maria soon had more of her clothes in the room than James did, in a heap on the floor. He squashed all his clothes into one of the two deep drawers in the chest. 'This other one's free now,' he said, 'you can put yours in here.' Anna Maria stuffed them in, but within a couple of days most were scattered across the carpet again.

'It's such a small room,' James ventured, 'maybe we should try and keep it tidy.'

James was both irritated and enchanted by Anna Maria's habits. She hung her washing on a spider's web of string outside his first-floor window. She only bought cigarettes in packets of ten because she was going to give up tomorrow, smoked the last one two minutes after the shops shut, and filched his tobacco all evening – so that they *both* ran out before midnight. She never bought a lighter, for the same reason, and put dead matches back in the box, and they were the ones James picked out when he tried to light a cigarette in the dark.

When Anna Maria hankered after an *espresso* she made an entire super-strength jug of coffee (so that James had to rush into the market in the middle of the week) and whenever she cooked she somehow managed, despite the size of the bedsit Baby Belling, to make massive, wasteful portions, because she only knew how to cook in the generous quantities of Neapolitan hospitality.

And she was always late for their rendezvous, because she neglected to wear a watch, claiming that something inside her ('my magnetic feel, James') broke them within a week.

'Carry a clock in your bag, then,' James pleaded. 'I'll *give* you one.'

But Anna Maria declined the offer. 'It's only my body that does the thing that I want to do,' she told him. 'Why should I live with somebody else's time?'

'It's *my* time,' he moaned, to no avail.

Anna Maria brought many of her habits to bed – although maybe it only seemed that way because they spent so much time there. She cut her toenails, the clicking of the clippers putting James' teeth on edge. She was also capable of forgetting to eat all day; then, after making love, just as James was drifting off to sleep Anna Maria's tummy would rumble, and she sprang from his arms, returning with a plate of crisps, fruit, cheese and biscuits, which she munched beside him, sprinkling apple pips and crumbs in the sheets.

When James *did* finally get to sleep he kept waking up at intervals through the night, woken less by specific noises or movements Anna Maria made than by the novelty of having another human being beside him.

'I'm sure I never had that problem when I slept with Alice and Laura,' he told her in the morning (*before* he'd told her much at all about his family).

Anna Maria managed to bite James, get dressed, throw the chrysanthemum pot at him – it shattered on the wall above his bed – and break his only classical record, all the while cursing him in incomprehensible lingo, before James had the brains to realize what was going on.

'They're my sister and my . . . *nearly* sister,' he yelled from behind a pillow. 'They were *eight* years old.'

Anna Maria stopped her tirade for a second to gasp and glare at him. 'Then you're a feelthy, disgusting Eenglish *pork* as well,' she exclaimed, before storming out.

James spent the day in agonies of remorse, as well as stupefaction. That evening he found her in the pub where her fellow foreign students hung out. He had flowers for her, and a speech prepared of explanation, and apology for his stupidity. To his surprise, Anna Maria had a record for him, of Puccini's *Madam Butterfly*.

'Opera is better than *balletto*, James,' she said, kissing him. 'Italian is better than Russian.'

James was bemused. He thought he'd made a mistake, and would have to make up for it now with a siege of her pride and affections. He didn't know what to do, exactly, but he thought it would be difficult, and might take some time. In fact Anna Maria was in such a hurry to be reconciled that within half an hour they were back in the bedsit; within another five minutes they were back in bed. James thought they'd hardly begun to get to know each other, while for Anna Maria they were already intimate enough for lovers' quarrels. From then on they flared up twice a week, on the slightest pretext.

'You bastard,' she cursed as they left the house together one morning.

'Eh?'

'I see the way you look at that cleaner girl,' Anna Maria told him. 'How long has she cleaned up *your* rubbish, you two-time Eenglish goat?'

'Are you crazy?' James wailed. 'The woman *scares* me.'

'I shall not take your nonsense no more,' Anna Maria told him firmly as she unlocked her Vespa. 'Find another stupid foreign girl to spoil,' she called out as she pulled away.

'*You* scare me,' James whispered after her departing figure, his heart thumping with shocked anxiety, caught unawares by her outburst.

A few days later she was in a grumpy mood with him all day, and when he'd had enough and ask what the matter was, it transpired that she'd had a dream in which James had stolen her study books.

'You're blaming me for your *dreams*?' James demanded. 'Your insane psyche is *my* fault? That is the most *un*reasonable thing I've ever heard.'

Anna Maria was twenty years old, two years younger than James, but she was more like a child. And she made *him* feel middle-aged: stodgy in his placidity, peppery in his trivial irritations. But a middle-aged man who knew nothing of the mystery between men and women.

The next time they went out to the river there was another group of people in their favourite spot, so they camped a little further along. The interlopers were climbing the willow tree that branched over the water and jumping in, and one girl among them was topless. James realized that Anna Maria saw him watching her, but this time he was ready: he already looked forward to the fight, and to an angry reconciliation among the reeds, as he said: 'I should have brought my long lens.' He grinned. 'That's not a sight a man sees every day. Not in this part of the world.'

He turned cockily to Anna Maria, ready for her furious onslaught. Her expression, though, was not one of attack, but rather that of a distraught child, and before James had had time to reassess the situation Anna Maria burst into tears.

He'd got it wrong again. Except that he hadn't, entirely: an hour later, after a parallel river of tears, a cascade of soothing words and caresses and a reservoir of promises, they *were* making love just out of sight of the rest of the world, among reeds by the slow-moving river, as the sky above them clouded over.

James never knew what Anna Maria would do from one moment to the next, but he did know that he was in love. In the absence of parents he sought Zoe's approval of his beloved, inviting himself and Anna Maria round for supper, a meal Zoe began with hors d'oeuvres containing liberal quantities of hashish. James spent the rest of the evening in a stupefied silence, while Zoe and Anna Maria giggled together till after midnight.

The next day James phoned Zoe from work.

'Yes, she's great,' Zoe assured him. 'I liked her a lot. A summer romance, it's just what you needed, sweetheart.'

'I think I'm in love, Zoe,' he ventured.

'Of course you are,' she said. 'You *should* be.'

Anna Maria met him after work and they walked home through warm softly falling rain.

'It is grizzling, James,' she said.

'You're right,' he agreed, squeezing her hand.

She made him his favourite of her Italian dishes on his Baby Belling, a creamy *carbonara* with pasta, and they drank red wine, and she asked him if he thought the course had improved her command of this ridiculous irregular language of his.

'I love the way you speak,' he said. 'I loved the way you spoke when I met you.'

'Well, it is your fault I didn't get more good, James. I spend too much time with you. You're too naughty. Of course I could not concentrate in the class.'

James smiled. Anna Maria's flunking her course seemed a

worthwhile measure of *his* worth. 'Wait a minute,' he clicked. 'You mean it's over?'

'Of course,' Anna Maria replied, without looking at him. 'Last day today. Did I no tell you?'

'Well, no,' James replied.

'I am sure I did,' she murmured.

'What *now*?' he ventured bravely.

'The flight back is the day after tomorrow,' she told him. 'From Heathrow.'

It was James' turn for tears, now – and then for anger, too. *And* there was another reconciliation – the most emotionally confused sex of their brief history together – before, finally, in the early hours of the morning, reality.

'I'll come and visit you, soon,' James said. 'I'm due a holiday. I'll come to Naples,' he suggested. 'Will I?'

'Maybe not, James,' Anna Maria replied. 'Maybe it is not a good idea.'

'You don't want me to come. You don't want to see me again.'

'Don't spoil it now, James. I shall never forget you.'

'Of course not,' he scowled.

'Will you forget me?' she asked.

'Oh, Anna,' he groaned. 'How can you even ask that?'

'Well, James James,' she said, 'you're my Eenglish boy. When I dream of you, I blow a kiss across the ocean.'

'If you dream of me, just don't be angry, that's all,' James relented.

'And you blow a kiss to me sometimes, James.'

'Kisses are keys,' he said, and kissed her. The rain, harder now, splattered against the window. Anna Maria was the first to fall asleep. She smelled of the sea. And as James drifted off, he thought he heard, in his small bedsit in that town in the middle of England, the remote murmur of the ocean.

6

THE ASSIDUOUS COURTSHIP
OF HARRY SINGH

BACK IN 1975 A WOMAN HAD BECOME LEADER OF THE CONSERVA-tive Party, and now four years later she led them to victory in the general election. Her father was a shopkeeper; she knew Napoleon's dictum — that England was a nation of shopkeepers — and she took it as a compliment (although she wasn't stupid: she knew it had been *meant* as an insult, and she never forgave the French nation).

The new Prime Minister was a woman of unforgiving conviction and unwavering resolve. She reminded James of Robbie, the Freeman children's old nanny, and it was true that she aroused in people's hearts a nostalgia for the certainties of childhood: she answered the tiresome questions of journalists with patience and forbearing beyond the call of duty, treating them like infants; her opponents in the House of Commons and her own Cabinet she intimidated with a combination of feminine charm and masculine force; as for the electorate, as well as telling them what she intended to do, as other leaders did, she told them off as well.

After a generation of consensual politics, the Prime Minister provoked two extremes of response, enmity and adoration, and she thrived on both: the first strengthened her convictions, the second her presidential aspirations; she was a nanny with regal pretentions.

She split every political constituency down the middle – the aristocracy, the working class, white-collar workers, women, men, pensioners, students and housewives.

She split the inhabitants of the house on the hill as well. Charles was a huge admirer; he hadn't been so smitten by a public figure since the death of Marilyn Monroe. Robert liked her; but then he'd been Robbie's favourite, so it wasn't surprising. Laura thought she set a good example for women (Laura also shared her mistrust of foreign neighbours, because she had a different Frenchman's jibe Blu-Tacked to the wall by the stove: 'England has one hundred religions, but only one sauce'). Many years later, Laura's daughter would ask whether a man was allowed to be Prime Minister, which might have been seen to vindicate Laura's initial opinion, except that by then she'd long since changed her mind. Alice for her part even then disagreed with Laura – Alice wasn't sure she was a woman at all.

Simon, doubtless taking his lead from Charles, admired the Prime Minister, although (and maybe because) he never imagined she was serious. He didn't believe anyone could possibly possess convictions of such intransigent certainty, and he thought she was play-acting; being himself a pastiche of a businessman, he assumed she was parodying politicians, especially when she delivered a homily on finance likening the economic affairs of the country to a housewife's weekly budget.

'She's taking the piss, darling, don't you see?' he told Alice. 'Can't you see the glint in her eye?'

'Of course I can,' Alice replied. 'It's madness, Simon.'

Alice was going through her radical phase at university. She had thrived at the boarding school – or ladies' college, as it was misleadingly called. It was made up of a cluster of Georgian buildings – plus a modern science block – surrounded by a green sea of playing fields, and it was a cross between a military academy and an orphanage, presided over by a remarkable headmistress. Miss Lipton was a short, doughty woman well into the relieved middle age of a respectable spinster, prim and proper, and the only thing wrong with her was that she looked somehow too small for her own body, as if she'd been inadvertently squashed at some point in her life. And that, in fact, was just what *had* happened many years earlier: as a young teacher she'd fallen asleep at the wheel of her Morris Oxford and woken up in a hospital bed with one kidney, one lung, and one foot less than when she'd got into the car, and her skeleton was all bunched in on itself. But Miss Lipton had overcome these infirmities, acquiring the resilience of the disabled, and no one in the entire school suspected that her left foot was made not of flesh and bone but of plastic; generations of teachers and pupils, including Alice, would only find out years later, when reading her obituary in *The Times*.

Miss Lipton had both the zeal and the resolve of a true pedagogue, born as they were of a basic mistrust of parents, who, she believed, lacked the slightest idea as to what was best for their daughters: she refused to divulge fine details of the curriculum in advance because as far as she was concerned parents entered into a contract whereby they handed over all responsibility for their children's welfare along with the extortionate fees; and such was the reputation of the school that places were always oversubscribed. Parents sent their beloved little girls away to boarding school and they returned in the holidays as strangers – but such clearly intelligent, composed and well-mannered ones that no one felt able to complain.

Alice settled in immediately, thriving on the strict timetable, supervised homework, intense friendships, crushes on teachers and vigorous sports. (Her brothers would have been astonished to see their frail and clumsy little sister participating in the most violent of games, hockey and lacrosse; fortunately the girls' maroon uniforms matched their ever-present bruises.) Alice sang in the choir, learned ballroom dancing in the gym (taking turns in the man's role) and after a short settling-in period moved to the top of the class in her science subjects.

When Alice had first come home in the holidays Laura asked a hundred questions ('Do you have to wear uniform at weekends? What's the food like? Is there a tuck shop? Who's your best friend? Is it true there are communal toilets without doors? Is there bullying?'), none of which received a satisfactory answer, because Alice had learned to confine secrets to her school dormitory. Laura's last question – 'Where do you meet boys?' – received a dismissive shrug.

'Who needs boys? *We* don't, Laura,' Alice replied. She'd acquired the art of walking past the youths who hung around the school gate with her nose in the air, ignoring them completely.

As for Harry Singh, Alice no longer ignored him: now that she was aware of his interest, she laughed at him. Laura had told her all about his intrepid visit and his outlandish proposal, and the two girls mocked him all through Alice's first Easter vacation – rediscovering thereby their sisterly bond.

'You should have seen your dad after Harry left. He's brave, that's for sure.'

'Sounds stupid to me.'

'He's dishy, though. Don't you fancy him?'

'He's a big booby, Laura. Like all boys.'

From around that point on, however, Alice began to receive weekly letters from Harry Singh. She passed them around her dormitory for weekly sessions of reading aloud, scornful hilarity, and she never once replied. But the letters kept punctually arriving, and pretty soon the rest of the dormitory looked forward to them; and so too, at some point, did Alice.

As well as learning the waltz and the Charleston by dancing with each other, the girls also practised more modern steps in the dorm after dark. Since any noise was forbidden, on pain of being sent to Coventry, one girl would listen to a disco record through headphones and begin dancing. The other girls picked up the rhythm from her bodily movement and distributed it among themselves, jiving sinuously rather than energetically so as not to shake the floorboards, dancing in the silent darkness.

Many things were shared in the dormitory. Moods, periods, homesickness and jokes came and went in communal waves. It was the healthiest time of Alice's life, or at least it seemed so to her, because illnesses too were scrupulously shared: instead of suffering alone, as she had at home, Alice was merely one of a whole row of girls sitting in their beds of a winter evening, inhaling aromatic steam beneath towels. And the next day, instead of having to stay in bed, she went to classes as usual and snuffled determinedly through lessons, because Miss Lipton refused to regard being a little bit poorly as an authentic reason for a young girl to have to miss out on study.

'You girls are the élite,' Miss Lipton told Alice's year at their final assembly. 'You have privilege and responsibility,' she proclaimed (sounding misleadingly like Alice's father). 'Above all,' Miss Lipton told them, 'you have a responsibility to yourselves. When you leave here you won't need anyone to support you. My girls graduate as self-sufficient, independent women.'

Alice left school with five A–levels, and a grade A in each of them. She was a demure, modest young lady, as Charles had hoped she would be; but that was just on the outside. Underneath, her views

245

were rather different from what he might have wished; it was just that she felt little need to publicize them. Four years under the influence of Miss Lipton's combination of tradition, discipline and sisterly self-reliance had enabled Alice to sail through the choppy waters of adolescence without undue distraction, and she reached adulthood with her innate character intact. At eighteen, she was in many ways the same six-year-old child who'd one day announced without any fuss that she was a vegetarian, and stuck to it for the rest of her life.

Alice duly fulfilled her father's wish that one at least of his children would go on to university, taking a chemistry degree at Oxford, enrolling – on Miss Lipton's advice – in one of the last women-only colleges. It was, gratifyingly, much like a continuation of school, and although there were boys around they didn't present too much of an intrusion, in their sexless white coats, in the science laboratory where penicillin had once been discovered.

As for exercise, Alice gave up violent sports and joined the rowing club, but as she was the smallest of the new recruits she was immediately designated a cox. It didn't last long: Alice lacked the aggression to shout at other human beings. Even with a megaphone she failed to pass muster: it amplified the volume of her voice, but couldn't make it any more authoritative. Alice's resolve was internal and she could apply it to what she took *in* – stopping the intake of meat or studying more books – but not to what came out.

After a brief career on the river, Alice took up jogging. She didn't particularly enjoy it, but perhaps she knew she'd have a tendency to put on weight and some form of exercise was necessary for her. Every day in the early evening Alice put on a Sony Walkman and listened to tapes of whatever she was learning to sing in the college choir. Others with headphones passed her, but while they pounded the ground to drumbeat rhythms Alice jogged across university parks to the accompaniment of Thomas Tallis and William Byrd, oblivious to the occasional heads she turned: as well as having avoided, in the seclusion of her boarding school, the emotional crises of adolescence, Alice had skirted the physical ones as well. Unlike many pretty children, she'd survived to become an attractive woman, too, with her pre-Raphaelite auburn hair, her different-coloured eyes, her delicate features and pale skin.

Alice knew she was pretty. It bothered her that – as she also knew – she wasn't sexy. She'd had plenty of time to come to terms with this, since it was evident from the moment she and Laura had first begun to try on her cousin Zoe's clothes, to play with lipstick, to see themselves in the mirror as females, years – half a lifetime – ago. Laura's sexuality was apparent long before puberty, whereas long *after* hers there remained something otherworldly and remote about Alice.

Alice had the habit of greeting someone by extending her graceful neck towards them while tilting her head away, kissing the air some inches from them while allowing her cheek to be brushed against. Since her rippling auburn hair fell at the sides of her face, friends and acquaintances were used to coming away with strands sticking to their moist lips. Alice kissed like a duchess wary of physical contact: she thrust her head forward with friendly intent but then seemed to change her mind and turn it away; and that's how she was. Alice was affectionate at a distance. She didn't invite men's advances, and they, on the whole, withheld them.

In her second year a fellow chemistry student, a tall young man with owly glasses, asked Alice out for a beer.

'I don't drink, thanks,' Alice told him.

'Don't you?' he replied disbelievingly.

'Well, not for pleasure,' Alice said.

'I guess there's no other reason, is there?' he said, and walked away in his white coat. Alice was a blue-stocking despite herself. In fact she longed to be different, she ached for sexy clothes to look sexy on her. But she knew her one black dress, even while it showed off her generous bosom, looked faintly absurd, like fancy dress; she knew that mascara, far from enhancing her eyes (one green, one blue) only made her look blowzy and overblown.

No one else, though, would have imagined that Alice Freeman was troubled by such matters, she appeared so calmly self-reliant and at ease with herself, not even her best friend at university, Natalie Bryson, a tall cockney and fellow member of the college Women's Action Group. Alice never mentioned it to Natalie, because they were too busy handing out free mirrors so women could know their own bodies, marching through the city reclaiming the night, and picketing the Ashmolean Museum for displaying misogynistic representations of women.

'A woman without a man is like a fish without a bicycle,' Natalie told Alice.

'A good dump is better than bad sex,' one of their friends declared.

So Alice kept those few of her thoughts to herself, but she shared the rest as she had back in the school dormitory. Although Natalie had come to Oxford from a Hackney comprehensive, she shared Alice's views on privilege and responsibility: they made a vow to each other that they wouldn't waste their lives, that they would use their intelligence and learning to better the world of their sisters, both now and for those to come. At the beginning of her finals year Alice cut her gorgeous hair as short as Natalie did, although she only managed one session of the self-defence classes that Natalie ran for female students, because they gave Alice the giggles.

Natalie was an androgynous tomboy, to whom people were always saying 'Thank you, young man' and 'Certainly, sir.' She had a series of girlfriends, most of them not students but secretaries in the city. Just once Natalie asked Alice – late one night in Alice's room after a fund-raising disco for Solidarity with Nicaraguan Women – if she wanted to kiss.

'Sorry, Nat,' Alice demurred. 'I love you, but I don't fancy you.'

'You don't seem to like men,' Natalie opined.

'I think I do,' Alice told her.

'You poor cow,' Natalie sympathized. 'The crap you've got coming your way.'

'We'll see,' Alice replied.

'What are you going to do afterwards, anyway?' Natalie asked her. 'Have you decided yet? You're not really going to do that teacher-training course?'

'Yes. I like children,' Alice replied.

'You're nuts,' Natalie told her.

And so Alice spent her university years attending lectures, writing essays, choir-singing, jogging in the parks, engaged in feminist activism and debate, and in white-coated days in the chemistry labs; but, just like Harry Singh, she remained aloof from experiments in a more human chemistry.

Harry's letters, meanwhile, had followed Alice from school to university, despite his having made no attempt at contact during her vacations. Alice literally hadn't seen Harry since the last time (she had no *particular* memory) he'd been in the house on the hill with James, carrying his decoy camera, plodding upstairs to the darkroom. He just carried on writing his letters every week without fail; by the time she graduated (with a first-class honours degree) Alice reckoned she'd received around three hundred and fifty letters (she only stopped throwing them away when she went up to Oxford; the first two hundred – scorned in dormitories, laughed at with Laura, dropped into waste-paper bins – were scattered to oblivion), yet he'd made not a single attempt to see her. How strange men are, Alice thought, how very strange; until it dawned on her that he might just be waiting for a reply.

Harry Singh's letters to his beloved were friendly, one-sided conversations, in which he informed her (in the impersonal tone of a child's thank-you letters) of his life. They were like succinct diary entries, a list of the mundane, told banally, for the record. He made no mention of marriage nor a single declaration of love, gave no hint of emotions of any kind, and ended each letter, at the bottom of the second page: 'Respectfully yours, Harry Singh'.

The letters told Alice of Harry's life. He'd left university and returned home, and got a job in an estate agent's.

'I thought you wanted to go places,' his brother Anil mocked him. 'I thought you always told me you were going to be your own man,' he sneered. 'Get-rich-quick, Flash Harry, that's what you were going to be. Estate agent!' he snorted. 'At least *I'm* self-employed. I've got a licence to sell alcohol now.' Anil shook his head. '*I'm* not a nine-to-five man, Harry.'

His father, though, was impressed. 'Now that is a good, sensible line of work,' he said when Harry told him. 'Property in this country's a stable market. And people always need a roof over their heads. Good for you, my boy.'

'Thank you, Dad,' Harry responded.

The estate agent's paid for Harry to take a day-release course in surveying, which also entailed hours of study in the evenings. Between the course and his employment Harry learned about damp courses, attic insulation, loft extensions, crumbling foundations, planning permission, supporting walls, preservation orders, listed buildings, boundary markers and elevated views (as, in turn, did Alice through his weekly missives). Within a year Harry's name was top of the list in the back office; at twenty-three he was the highest paid agent in the firm.

Harry's secret was hard work: he did his homework; he knew the difference between impressive and notable houses, between elegant apartments and superbly presented flats, open countryside and rural views; between unspoilt and well-regarded villages, restored, converted or reconstructed barns. He didn't hoodwink his clients with flim-flam and humbug, though; he escorted them around properties providing a commentary in a phlegmatic tone of voice – similar to the tone of his letters to Alice. He explained the architectural, decorative and structural qualities of the house, while also adding other things he perceived they might need to know: reliable local builders, shopping facilities, school catchment areas, the prevalence of baby-sitters in the neighbourhood and local crime statistics. And to every question they asked he gave a truthful answer.

Harry Singh was good-looking in a jowly way, with a neat moustache and dark, tired eyes that gave him a rakish air. He had the appearance of a well-fed, unimaginative son who knows he'll never have to make much effort in life because there'll always be women to look after him; and it was deceptive. He moved and worked at a sluggish, stolid pace, it was just that he never stopped. Harry was as assiduous an estate agent as he was an epistolary suitor. He was unpopular in the office: his colleagues regarded him as being a workaholic drudge who had nothing to say unless it was about bloody buildings, since he didn't watch TV, come out for a drink after work or play a sport at the weekend. All he did was bore people into buying houses they probably didn't want and then go home to work his way through the sixteen encyclopaedias required to understand the finer points of conveyancing.

In fact Harry's colleagues were only half right. Far from taking up all of his time, Harry regarded his job as a temporary apprenticeship that gave him pocket money, personal contacts and a basic expertise in the buying and selling of property. He'd already embarked upon his real work: shortly after coming home Harry had taken out a mortgage on a delapidated terraced house in Easttown and moved in. With a further bank loan he paid young plumbers, electricians and other artisans, from within the Asian community, cash in hand to renovate the house 'from top to bottom and inside out', he wrote to Alice. It took three months and he then sold it at a 25 per cent profit – to a fellow Asian – bought another, moved in and started again. He employed bricklayers and chippies one at a time to work only in the evenings and weekends and he assisted them, both to save money and to learn how to do the work himself, 'because you can only be ripped off if you're ignorant', as he told Alice.

Harry Singh was a diligent man. He worked as an estate agent till six in the evening, as a building labourer on his own houses till midnight, studied till two, and slept till eight. Neither his colleagues nor his employers knew of his double life because he only bought from and sold to Asians, and employed illegal immigrants

– and also because every night he used copious quantities of Swarfega and Boots' moisturizing cream to 'transform the hands of a working man, into those of a pen-pusher', as he put it in one of his letters to Alice.

The only time off Harry allowed himself was on a Sunday evening. He downed tools at four in the afternoon to go and visit his family, stopping off at the Indian deli on Factory Road on the way over to pick up food, and he spent three hours cooking; it was Harry's one and only hobby and relaxation. He cut vegetables and ground spices with his father and ate with the family (soon to be joined by Anil's bride-to-be) in the flat above the shop. They didn't have much to say to each other but they didn't need to, they were content to savour the *massallas* and *muktaajs*; all except for Harry's grandmother, who had lost her appetite in recent years and preferred to sit in front of the television, popping bubble-wrap.

Then, when he returned to his temporary accommodation in some house in the midst of renovation, Harry wrote a once-a-week letter to his beloved, surrounded by builders' rubble. Far from being the perfunctory ten-minute chore it appeared to Alice, it took Harry many hours and many rejected, crumpled-up sheets of Basildon Bond paper to say exactly what he wanted to say, on two full pages precisely, in the perfectly appropriate tone, in his assiduous courtship of the woman he'd chosen. On countless Sunday nights he crawled into bed in the early hours of the morning, exhausted at the end of another week, to obtain far less than his customary six hours' sleep. But Harry always emerged on Monday morning with renewed, if phlegmatic, vigour for the week ahead. Like the man-in-charge in the house on the hill, Charles Freeman, his intended father-in-law (to whom he'd foolishly proposed eight years before he would eventually manage to bring up the subject with Alice herself), Harry Singh was an empire builder in the making.

In the last letter Alice received at Westminster Teacher-training College in Oxford (which was the last but one letter she would ever receive from him) Harry informed her that he'd handed in his notice at the estate agent's; that he had eight properties in various stages of renovation; that he was worth £372,428 on paper, although he actually possessed, he wrote (such was his honesty) £180 in his wallet; and that he would be a millionaire within two years. As well as, of course, that he remained 'Respectfully yours, Harry Singh'.

*

In 1982, during the Falklands War, Charles had a flagpole erected on the lawn of the big house, from which he flew a large Union Jack. Zoe came home from Sunday lunches there still fuming after fruitless confrontations that were cut short because farming Uncle Jack's and Aunt Clare's son Edward was serving on HMS *Sheffield*, and whatever people's political opinions familial disloyalty was taboo.

'I can't call my cousin cannon fodder, even though it's the truth,' Zoe despaired, having tea with James back at the cinema.

'Forget it,' he advised her. 'The lunatics have taken over the asylum, Zoe. Ignore them.'

'But she'll win the next election on the strength of being a war leader, a Boadicea, bloody Churchill in a skirt.'

'Just ignore them, Zoe. We've got enough problems of our own without letting politicians add to them.'

'What problems have *you* got?' she demanded. 'You're not still pining after your Italian inamorata, are you?'

'I wasn't thinking of me,' James protested. 'I just meant in general. Anyway, I know I was an idiot. I won't fall in love again.'

'You, James, will *always* be falling in love,' Zoe scoffed.

'No, I won't,' he averred, his jaw set hard. 'Not again.'

'Oh, God, I forgot,' Zoe remembered, 'you're a stubborn little bastard. Don't go and hide your heart away, now.'

'It's *my* heart,' he told her.

James had other things on his mind at that time. He'd joined the town's Artists' Group – twenty-odd people who included three photographers – which met once a month to buy materials at wholesale prices, to lobby the council and other bodies for grants, and to provide each other with moral support. Their immediate project was the creation of an Artweek (inspired by a member's visit to Boston, USA) during which sculptors, painters and craftsmen and women would open up their studios to the public. A special map for the purpose was being designed, and James volunteered to take photographs for publicity material, less to ingratiate himself than because the photographers who already belonged to the Group refused to use their cameras for such menial purposes.

James found his free time over the following weeks filled with visits to studios. Having advertised for participants, the Group was overwhelmed by the response: every street, it transpired, had a watercolourist or a weaver or a potter working away in quiet isolation; they emerged from obscure avenues and hidden cul-de-sacs and every day James was given a new address to visit.

'There are artists all over the town,' he told Zoe, showing her the first proof of the special map with little red dots clustered all over it (which corresponded to a new mental map in James' head).

'Artists?' she queried. 'That's a big word, James.'

'There's over a hundred of them,' he maintained.

Not that James considered himself one ('I can't very well open the photographers' office, can I?' he said); he was content to get to know the other photographers in the Artists' Group in the pub after their meetings. At first he was disappointed to discover that, instead of discussing their work, the main topic of conversation was money, since they were all broke. James felt some guilt at being the only one with a salary: the other three scraped a living doing odd-jobs, teaching, picture-framing, driving, as well as claiming whatever benefits were available.

As the Artweek approached, though, he saw their work. Karel, a big, shambling Czech refugee, made exquisite still-lives of bottles, wood, flowers, and naked women; Terry had found fame in the Sixties but retreated from its glare into dark alleyways of his own imagining, where he photographed minute details of life that people couldn't understand too clearly but which they discerned as indications of a baffling integrity; and Celia created long 'narrative sequences', as she called them, of unpopulated photos until, in a massive step, she took a single one of an unmade bed, recently vacated. When she saw it framed (in the Artweek's co-ordinating exhibition in the Tourist Centre) Celia felt naked, exposed, she'd revealed too much of herself, and, resolving never to do so again, returned to the inanimate.

As James got to know the Artists' Group photographers they softened towards him after their initial suspicion; he felt as if he were undergoing a second apprenticeship as they revealed their mentors and lent him books (he discovered there were great Czech photographers during the Prague Spring as well as the film-makers Zoe had already alerted him to; Terry convinced him of the blurred clarity of Robert Frank; Celia showed him the work of Eugene Atget), although none of them became any more forthcoming about their own work, still preferring to discuss the finer points of claiming tax back for working clothes and the possibilities of joining the Enterprise Allowance Scheme, the new employment programme, by which you could get £40 a week for taking pictures and still do odd jobs without having to deny them to the DHSS.

*

James kept his new friendships secret from his colleagues at work. To Roger and the others photography was a job. They sought no aesthetic dimension in their images beyond clarity. But it was an honest living. The occasional views of the town or surrounding countryside they took to fill a space in the Saturday edition were an indulgence they allowed each other, but that was the limit, as they made clear whenever the arts page listed an exhibition by one of James' new acquaintances.

'We've got one of those clickers in again,' said Frank. 'Look, he couldn't even get the flicking thing in focus.'

'Piss-artists, the lot of them,' said Derek.

'I'd like to see him try and do a proper job,' said Frank.

'He can cover for you next time you have a holiday,' said Derek.

'Wouldn't last a bloody week,' said Roger.

The newspapermen scoffed at those aspiring artists whose work no one bought, who were not just amateurs but pretentious with it, walking around with holes in their shoes and noses in the air. Their existence was the only thing that really annoyed Roger; it was the one time James heard him swear.

'They do what they bloody want, that's the problem,' he told James. 'Not like us, boy.'

'You're right,' James agreed. 'I can see that.'

What his colleagues would have made of the other artists emerging from anonymity around the town James shuddered to imagine. They might have approved of one or two of the elderly watercolour painters and would respect the furniture-maker in Otley and maybe the potter in Northtown. Most of the rest James himself couldn't understand, composed on the one hand of Sunday painters and on the other of young people stumbling through dust raised by the avant-garde elsewhere. Some took their materials from scrap-yards and skips. Others held joint exhibitions with titles like *Work in Progress, Marks on Paper* or *Forms in Space*. They were deluded but undaunted, James thought, talentless but obstinate; they didn't really have anything to say but were determined to say it anyway. He took Zoe and Simon on a tour of the studios on the opening day of the Artweek.

'At least they've got the courage to show their work,' Simon argued.

'You've got to start somewhere,' James agreed. 'They can only get better.'

'It's mostly crap, but as long as we recognize the fact, who cares?' Zoe said. 'When are you going to show us some of *your* pictures?'

'Oh, I'm not ready yet,' James protested.

'My feet are killing me, dears,' Simon complained. 'What say I treat you both to a cream tea in Rosie's?' he offered, linking arms with Zoe and James and leading the trio to tea.

In the middle of the week James dragged Zoe to a screening of films made by members of a Film Co-op in the Old Fire Station. 'It's *my* turn,' he said gleefully. 'Come along, cousin.'

Three minutes into the first film Zoe hissed in James' ear: 'I've sat through Andy Warhol, Michael Snow and Alfred Hitchcock in my time, honey, and I don't need *this*.' She got up and left, and although she might have been the first she certainly wasn't the last. Even close friends of the film-makers sneaked out before the end. They left bent forward at right angles to the ground, whether so as not to block the projector or in imitation of Groucho Marx it was difficult to tell.

All in all, though, that first Artweek was a success, if not in artistic (never mind commercial) terms, then at least in social ones. The solitary sculptors and painters felt less illegitimate and alone in the world, and their neighbours tended to like the idea of an artist living in their midst, an artist-in-residence in their own street, and from then on they greeted each other in shops and post offices with a new camaraderie.

Alice returned home with a teacher's diploma shortly after the end of the Artweek ('I always said you had fate on your side, Alice,' Simon told her) to take a job teaching chemistry to eleven to thirteen-year-olds in the comprehensive school on the edge of the housing estate. She'd applied for the job in secret; it was the only job she'd applied for.

The school was a sprawling mass of concrete-and-glass buildings in the shadows of the twin tower blocks. Across the rutted playing fields stood the Freeman factory buildings, in which most of the school's pupils would expect to get work.

'I always said you were quite mad, darling,' Simon proclaimed. 'Now everyone else can see I was right.'

'I've been living in ivory towers all my life, Simon,' Alice told him. 'What's wrong with a bit of reality?'

'You don't *need* it, dear, that's what's wrong,' he replied.

Alice moved back into her old room on the third floor of the house.

'I never thought you'd come back here,' said Laura. 'I thought you were up and away, Alice.'

'I was,' Alice assured her. 'I am. I'm not going backwards, I'm going forwards. Anyway,' she added, 'I love this town.'

'You don't *know* this town,' Laura mocked her.

'Well, all right, Laura, the truth is I came back for your cooking. That's why I came back.'

'You're such an enigma, Alice,' Laura said matter-of-factly. 'Hey, you remember Harry Singh? He used to write you those letters?'

'Used to?'

'Look, he's in today's *Echo*.' She unfolded the paper and handed it to Alice: there was a photo of Harry shaking hands with the local Conservative Member of Parliament and holding an enormous cheque, beneath a caption that read 'Young Businessman of the Year'.

'James took the picture, see?' Laura pointed out. 'I'll say one thing for Harry Singh: his suit's a lot sharper than the politician's is.'

'I thought we had a Labour MP,' Alice mused. 'He used to come to Daddy's parties.'

'Not any more, Alice. God, where have you been? This one's true blue. Your dad doesn't like him very much, I don't think, even though they agree about everything.'

'Well, it looks like Harry likes him!' Alice said.

'I think *I'd* like someone giving me five hundred quid,' Laura agreed.

The next day, when no one was looking, Alice took the newspaper off the pile in the pantry and cut out the picture in question. It would turn out to have an ironic historical value: it prefigured the same situation being repeated over ensuing years, except that the cheque would be worth rather more each time, and it would also be going in the opposite direction.

Charles, meanwhile, was delighted to have his daughter home again, but he was also dismayed that she was no more than a secondary-school teacher.

'You always told us we had responsibilities, Daddy,' she reminded him.

'Quite right!' Charles declared. 'And I'm proud of you, Alice. The thing is, though, times change. It's a rough old world out there; it's time for the strong to be strong, it's what's needed.'

'What about the weak?' she demanded.

'The weak don't want to be mollycoddled any more,' Charles claimed. 'They're sick of it. They need incentives, initiative, industry. It's a time for the lean and fit to survive.'

Alice grinned at her enormous father.

'I'm speaking rhetorically, young lady, as you well know!' he boomed. 'You're not too old to put across my knee.'

'Don't be silly, Daddy,' Alice laughed. 'You never did that when I was young. Anyway, there's a proven link between being over-weight and heart problems. And what with your temper as well, I'm only thinking of you.'

'Don't you worry,' Charles assured her. 'I'm as strong as an ox.'

The other thing Alice did, soon after she came home, was to send a brief note to Harry Singh, informing him of her return and inviting him out for a drink. Harry read and reread the note a dozen times, unsure what it meant. He stared at it for an hour or more. Was it a riddle to be deciphered? A hoax, God forbid? A joke? His letters had been unanswered for so many years that at some point he'd stopped expecting a reply, and only carried on writing them out of a mixture of willpower and habit. (In addition, although his daily postbag was often too large for the letterbox, they were all typed, official documents to do with property and money; Harry couldn't remember receiving a personal, hand-written en-velope).

Finally, though, Harry accepted that the note probably meant what it said, to meet Alice in Diego's Wine Bar at seven thirty on Thursday evening. He picked up the telephone to confirm he'd be there, but found the receiver trembling in his fingers. So he wrote a reply instead. He only meant to reciprocate Alice's note with a succinct memo of his own, but such was the discipline he'd attained through eight years of weekly letter-writing that he was unable to stop himself from stretching it to include his latest news and fill two pages (with a number of aborted attempts crumpled up in a bin beside him) and ending, as ever,

'Respectfully yours, Harry Singh'.

By seven thirty on Thursday evening Harry had calmed down: it had been as much surprise as amorous trepidation that had unnerved him. Alice was equally at ease. They sat in a corner and told each other what they were doing and what plans they had. Alice found that Harry was much as she had expected him to be: she wasn't conversing with a stranger; she knew him. There had been nothing extraordinary about his letters (apart from their unbroken regularity), they'd contained no great insights nor offered revelations of Harry's inner world. But as she'd read them so she'd been drawn into Harry's phlegmatically self-confident view of the world and his place in it. Which, so it appeared (though he hadn't actually mentioned it), included her somewhere beside him.

Now, as he spoke, leaning towards her because of the noise from the speakers, his breath smelling of cardamom (she wondered whether there had been a trace of that smell on the Basildon Bond paper), Alice found both the content and the tone of Harry's speech reassuringly familiar.

'The thing about property,' he was explaining, 'is that it's a fetish with us Brits. An Englishman's home is his castle, we push prices up and people follow. It's nothing to do with supply and demand *per se*, you see, in the accepted sense, it's a strangely arbitrary market, which is what most people don't realize—'

'Harry,' Alice interrupted him, smiling, 'you're just as pompous in real life as you are on paper.'

'I am?' he frowned.

'Don't worry,' she reassured him. 'It's sort of endearing.'

'It is?'

As for Harry, as he listened to Alice describing her plans he realized that *he* knew nothing about *her*. She was a complete stranger, an unknown entity. He was also somewhat devastated by the fact that she'd cut off her auburn hair. As she spoke it slowly dawned on him, with icy advance, that for eight years of his life he'd been sending letters into a void.

'We made a pact when we left, Harry, that we'd do what we were most qualified to. "Footsoldiers of feminism," Natalie called us. She's got a job in the women's refuge, yes, she's coming to live with us, you know, a lodger in the house, what do you think of that? You'd like her. Or maybe you wouldn't. You're such a huckster, Harry.'

'I am?'

'But you've got the same haircut as her,' Alice laughed. 'With plenty of gel.'

'It's important to look your best in my line of work,' said Harry, unsure whether Alice was encouraging or teasing him. 'I have my clothes tailored,' he continued. 'My clients have to have complete confidence in me. Clothes make the man, Alice, it's old but true.'

'You'll get on well with Simon, anyway,' Alice told him. 'He's as pompous as you are.'

'I'm serious, Alice,' Harry replied. 'I know what I want, and I'm going to get it.'

'What do you want?' she asked him.

Harry paused. 'I want you,' he answered.

'How can you be sure?' she demanded. 'You don't know me.'

'I know that,' he told her. 'I know.'

Alice took another sip of her cocktail. 'This White Russian is delicious,' she said, changing the subject. 'You want a sip, Harry?

'I don't touch it, thank you.'

'Neither do I much. But I could start now.'

Harry drank mineral water. Alice sipped her cocktail through a straw. She had no idea whether she should feel insulted or flattered by Harry's single-minded choice of her, whom he hardly knew. But what she did feel was a strong sense of reassurance.

For his part, Harry felt no assurance at all. What if, as he did get to know her, he didn't like her? She was lovely, of course, but that was the basis for the fumblings of his fellow students and colleagues at work: his correspondence had raised the stakes to some quite different realm. What an idiot I am, he thought. I'm just like all the rest, I just want to screw her, that's the truth; my bloody little brother's right, chase the white girls and marry our own; my parents are right, damn it, I should have let them choose.

Harry had rejected an arranged marriage only to arrange one of his own; and maybe, he conceded for the first time, matchmakers were better qualified than he was. It was a gamble, that's what it was; and Harry Singh didn't like to gamble unless he knew the precise odds. And all of this conjecture presupposed that Alice would succumb to his advances anyway, when he got round to making them, which, of course, she wouldn't; he was mad, she was only here for a laugh, just for a closer look at this mental defective who'd been sending her unsolicited mail all these years. Damn it to hell, he thought, sipping his Perrier. What am I doing? He put the glass down and looked at Alice. She was gazing at something else in the bar; she raised her eyebrows and sighed, then lifted the straw to her lips and took another sip of her cocktail, which slurped among the ice-cubes at the bottom of the glass. Who is this woman? Harry wondered.

'I don't drink,' Harry broke the silence. 'But I do eat.'

'I'm very glad to hear that, Harry,' Alice assured him.

'What I mean to say is that I cook. Pretty well, if I say so myself. Might I invite you to my house next week?'

'That would be very nice,' Alice replied. 'I should warn you, though, that I'm a vegetarian.'

'That,' Harry told her, 'will be no problem at all.'

*

259

And so Harry Singh's courtship of Alice Freeman entered its second phase. They met at first once a week, just as they had by letter, and it suited them both because Alice was as busy as Harry was. She loved teaching. She'd been warned at the teacher-training college not to smile in front of her new class for six weeks, because they'd perceive it as weakness; after such a period a smile would come across as warmth. Alice, however, didn't need to rely on such tactics. The boys fell in love at once with their pretty teacher who looked younger than some of the sixth-formers, and desperately sought her approval, while the girls soon followed. She was an impartial teacher, with no pets, but she gave the younger girls particular attention, reasoning that she had a short time to get them hooked on a science subject before the distractions of adolescence came along.

Alice was also popular because, unlike other teachers, she bore no grudges against rude or unruly pupils. In reality she simply didn't recognize insolent behaviour, never having displayed it herself, and it soon disappeared from her classroom. The only punishment she doled out was to mock silly or lazy children, but in such a teasing manner that, just like Harry Singh, they weren't sure whether they were being belittled or flirted with by their chemistry teacher, and quickly mended their ways so as not to fall out of favour.

Evenings Alice spent marking books and preparing lessons, and weekends in the company of Laura and of Natalie, her friend from university and now a lodger in the house. It was a time when people were waking up as if from a dream and realizing that they were surrounded by American airbases; there was one ten miles west of town. Planes came crashing out of nowhere over the tops of houses, to send dogs scurrying inside yelping and induce catatonic trances in old people. Children would look up to see them fly so low that they could make out every metal plate and rivet in the undercarriage, and the image would stay with them for ever.

'They're our allies,' Simon tried to explain. 'They're our friends.'

Alice and Natalie went out on Saturdays with food, clothes and encouragement to a small group of women camping outside the base, and they joined in demonstrations that to Natalie's frustration were based on the principles of passive resistance.

Natalie wore a crew-cut and men's clothes, and she accompanied Alice wherever she could, like a bodyguard, although it wasn't as often as she would have liked because *she* was busy too. The women's refuge was oversubscribed with battered women and their anxious children. The refuge, a four-storey terraced town house, was both a closely guarded secret and open twenty-four hours a day to any woman suffering domestic violence. Natalie often spent the night on a sofa in the office when one of the women's husband was looking for her, because Natalie was the best qualified to meet force with force. She was already running a self-defence class in the community hall off Factory Road.

'This woman who came in last night, married nineteen years,' Natalie told Alice and Laura one evening after supper, 'she's lovely-looking, forty-odd, could be younger. Her husband's beaten her once a week, every week, since two years into their marriage. He'd sit her down and review the week's events, pointing out what she'd done wrong – a meal five minutes late on the table, the car not filled up with petrol, shit like that, and there's always something, right, if you look for it? And then he'd punch her. Always in a different place, and just enough to bring up some good bruising, but hidden, you know?'

'Who would do something like that?' Alice asked.

'And he always told her: "I'll never touch your face, your beautiful face." It'd be her thigh, and then her shoulder, or her back, wherever. But that's not so strange. What was weird was that he made their son watch. And he'd say: "You see what your mother's done? Now she's got to be punished." Of course, the boy, he's come to accept it as normal. The husband would ask the boy where his mother should be hit this week.'

'Jesus,' said Alice. Laura listened intently, but in silence; Laura knew men could go berserk.

'What made her come to you now?' Alice asked.

'They've got a daughter, too. The woman's always made sure she'd been sent to bed before these sessions. Last week the girl had her first period. A couple of days ago they were watching telly and the man switched it off, sat down by the girl, and started reviewing the week's events: "You were late back from school on Tuesday. Overslept on Thursday." He winked at the boy as he said it.'

'Oh, Jesus,' said Alice.

'And did he?' Laura asked.

'No. Not this time. But the woman says she was sitting across on the settee, shaking. Just shaking. He finished by saying: "Well, don't be a bad girl, now, because bad girls get punished," and then he grinned, and switched the TV on again. So the woman came out yesterday, with her daughter. She wants to move, to start up somewhere else where no one knows them, but she doesn't know how. She said she took it all those years for the children; well, for the girl. Is there any more tea in that pot, Laura?'

'Sure.'

'I get scared, sometimes, that if one of these guys finds us and comes in for his wife, if he gives us any shit, I might just lose it. I mean you hear these stories, these women tell you these things and they're just so beaten down, you know, just so terrified and empty. I think I might find it hard to stop if I got started.'

Natalie shook her head and gulped down some more tea. Laura wondered whether she'd ever tell Natalie about *her* beating; she wondered whether Alice had already mentioned it.

'I can't imagine Harry ever doing something like that,' Alice said.

'Come on, Alice, don't be so naïve. You wouldn't believe some of the things that go on in the Asian community.'

'You can't tar all men with the same brush, Nat.'

'All men are potential batterers, Alice, that flash friend of yours included. The least you could do would be to learn some self-defence. If you're strong, you can't be a victim; you can only be a victim if you're weak and afraid.'

'I'm surprised you've not given up on me yet,' Alice laughed. 'You are persistent, Nat.'

Despite her failure in Oxford, Natalie still attempted impromptu sessions on quiet evenings in the house on the hill, which Alice was still unable to take seriously. The idea of bending back the little fingers of someone pretending to strangle her, stamping on their shin, or grabbing their scrotum only made her giggle nervously, especially when the assailant was a woman. Laura paid more attention to Natalie's instruction, but when Simon volunteered to play a mugger and grab Laura in a bear-hug, Alice, watching, fell on the floor at the sight of her roly-poly, Billy Bunter brother smothering Laura, who struggled in vain to find something she could get hold of to hurt. Natalie had to halt the exercise, with a martial arts shriek of her own that stunned them, to save Laura from fainting.

'You stupid walrus,' Alice cried, tears streaming down her face. 'You great big bully, Simon.'

'But I wasn't doing anything,' Simon protested.

'He's just so *big*,' Laura gasped, getting her breath back. 'He's just so *fat*.'

'He's *soft*, Laura,' Natalie told her. 'He's easy. You've got to mean it.'

'Er, right, OK, I suppose I better be going now,' Simon suggested.

'It's like being squeezed by an enormous octopus,' Laura explained.

'I told you I was taught by an ex-commando,' Natalie said. 'A couple of us used to stay behind, and he showed us his *real* tricks. If Simon wasn't a friend I'd show you; I'd drop him in two seconds.'

'Well, I'll leave you girls to it, then,' said Simon, retreating through the door.

'The bigger they are, Laura,' Natalie concluded, not wasting any more advice on Alice, 'the harder they fall. When you get rid of fear, nothing can hurt you.'

'I'm sorry, Nat,' said Alice, who'd recovered somewhat. She came over and put an arm round Natalie's shoulder. 'I'm just no good at defending myself, so I'll simply have to keep you close by to protect me, won't I?'

Natalie softened, and returned her friend's embrace. 'I'll have to be there, then, sister, won't I?'

'Me too, Natalie,' Laura joined in. 'Alice'll be all right; no one's going to hurt her. I'm the one who'll need your protection.'

'You too, then,' Natalie agreed. 'I'll look after you both, you useless bloody women,' she said, as Laura hugged her as well.

Laura was twenty-three years old. She worked as hard as her mother had but made sure she was no put-upon slave. She combined work with leisure, and liked to go walking alone in the country: she spent hours poring over maps plotting complicated routes along foot- and bridle-paths whose focal point was a trout farm, a cheese-maker, a breeder of rare pigs or an organic vegetable grower, from whom she could order direct. Or else she carried baskets with her and paused to pick blackberries, mushrooms, hazelnuts and sloes, and came home with scratched hands and stained fingers.

She became a doyenne of jumble sales and charity shops, though, unlike James, Laura dived into them in search of not clothes but Kilner jars, in which she preserved plums and pears, apricots and blackcurrants she'd gathered at pick-your-own farms. She stored them on free-standing shelves; on sunny winter days they refracted a syrupy light around her ordered kitchen.

Natalie wanted to chaperone her friend when she went out with Harry Singh, but Alice declined the offer. Natalie would, though, have approved if she'd been able to overhear their conversations, in which Alice patiently explained to Harry the changing role of women in modern society, and made clear to him her own independence.

She stated so categorically that men were no longer hunters and women submissive prey, they were equal in every way, a woman was free to make advances without being considered a hussy and a tart, that he was too daunted to make any of his own; he assumed she was telling him that she would make the first move when she was ready.

It was the summer of 1983. Having completed her first year of teaching, Alice enjoyed the long vacation.

'This is why she took the job,' Simon told Charles at breakfast while Alice was sleeping in three floors above. 'She's not so stupid after all.'

'She's recharging her batteries,' Laura told him. 'If they didn't have long holidays they'd get burned out, facing thirty little hooligans every day.'

'I face *three hundred* of them,' Charles objected. 'They're getting worse by the year. But some are going to have to take extended holidays before long.'

Charles was in an ebullient mood at that time. The Conservatives had just won another general election. Zoe had been right: following the Falklands victory the contest was portrayed as one between a war leader and a pacifist, and although more people voted against the Prime Minister than the last time, they didn't quite trust a conchie either, and so voted for a third party, the Liberal–Social Democrat Alliance, thus splitting the opposition vote. And now the Prime Minister was looking around for new adversaries, with a glint in her eye.

Simon was still unable to take her seriously. She had struck up a special relationship with the American President: 'They're a great double-act,' Simon told Alice. 'He tells the jokes, she's the straight man. It's a difficult role – look at Ernie Wise, look at Margaret Dumont. She's very good.'

In the town, however, local elections had followed a pattern opposite to the national one. As if by some compensatory reflex a Labour majority had been elected, and so on a local level a parallel political culture developed: while income tax was being slashed, rates – particularly for businesses – remained high, and the revenue was spent in ways that delighted some and enraged others, further polarizing wards, streets and households.

The council provided a second house for the women's refuge, and Natalie shuttled between them to provide the security of her karate and a listening ear for further horrendous stories. It extended street lighting, and placed skips at various points around the town for the recycling of glass and paper. It initiated a park-and-ride system for shoppers and commuters and restricted parking within the centre to discourage cars, giving Robert reason to curse as he tinkered with his resuscitated wrecks in the back yard – he was already furious at the recent imposition of compulsory seat belts. At the same time, bicycle lanes were marked out on some of the roads, which made James' progress around the town even faster.

Zoe, meanwhile, came to an arrangement with the council whereby pensioners and the increasing numbers of unemployed people could, on production of a Recreation Card, get into afternoon screenings at the cinema for £1, just as they could to the council's own sports centres, tennis courts and swimming pool. That last tempered Robert's bile: he got hold of a card for himself – although *he* certainly wasn't unemployed – and used it for his daily clocking up of fifty lengths of the pool.

It was the year that young people on Job Creation schemes planted 4,500 daffodil bulbs all along the bank beside the Wotton Link Road, which Robert passed test-driving one of his reconditioned cars from the house to the swimming pool, and which brightened up the journey for commuters and schoolchildren. Schools were also encouraged to plant flowers: a similar Community Programme scheme employed mostly ex-pupils to plant beds of roses around the concrete classrooms of Alice's comprehensive.

'What an extraordinary waste of money,' Simon opined.

'Don't talk drivel, man!' his father responded instinctively. 'Unemployment's a curse, an indignity. Every man should have the right to labour.'

'But, Father, we all know they're not real jobs,' Simon persisted.

'That's true,' Charles agreed. 'But then again, Simon,' he said, appearing to remember that he'd changed his views recently, 'they have to do something about the figures. People are sheep, but they'll only stand so much before bleating turns to something worse.'

'I suppose so, Father,' Simon accepted.

As housekeeper, Laura got into the habit of hiding the *Echo* when it was delivered in the afternoon, before Charles came home from work: in contrast to his pleasure at breakfast, checking his share prices and reading the Prime Minister's speeches in the *Financial Times*, the local paper made his blood boil.

'This ruddy council!' he raged one Tuesday. 'They've declared the town a nuclear-free zone! What the hell sort of piffle is that?' he stormed, ripping the paper to shreds on his way to his study.

Alice, as it happened, spotted the headline on a hoarding outside the Singhs' store, and bought her own copy; she and Natalie had spent the Sunday before at a demonstration against Cruise missiles. As if specifically to antagonize her father, Alice cut out the offending article and stuck it on the wall in the downstairs lavatory. Charles was halfway through his business there the next morning when he spotted it, pulled it off the wall and tore it up all over again. So Laura started placing the newspaper underneath the *Radio Times* in the drawing-room instead of on the table in the hall.

On some things central and local government came into direct conflict. Council-house tenants were encouraged to buy their homes, well below market prices. Far from flooding the market, as might have been expected, they only helped to stimulate it; Harry Singh was amassing his first million so fast he barely had time to count it. On the other hand, local authorities were prohibited from spending the proceeds from such sales on further council-house building. Like the revenue from North Sea oil, at its height at that time, the money seemed instead to disappear into thin air.

'They're using it to subsidize these tax cuts, of course,' Zoe suggested at lunch that Sunday in the house on the hill – to which Alice had invited Harry, for the first time, hoping Charles would have forgotten his last visit. 'To cushion the blow artificially,' Zoe continued. 'When the oil money runs out, and the changes they're planning hit the welfare state, they'll have taxes so low it'll be unthinkable to hike them back up to reasonable levels.'

'I'm sure we're all most impressed by your grasp of economics,' Charles needled his favourite adversary. 'I hadn't fully realized running a cinema was quite the complex operation it clearly must be.'

'You can be as facetious as you like, Daddy,' Alice told him. 'But people are worried. The mood in the staffroom at school was like being under siege, waiting to see if the next pay offer was as low as we suspected it would be. The holidays came just in time.'

'Teachers have had it easy for years, Alice, we all know that,' Simon told her.

'Most teachers are bloody idiots,' Robert made his contribution.

'The voice of reason speaks,' said Laura.

Robert glared at her. Natalie glared back at him on Laura's behalf, while Laura got up to clear the table and serve dessert.

'Frankly, I don't know what you're worried about,' Simon addressed Alice. 'You can always make up your income with some evening work: there are hundreds of adult education classes nowadays, everything from macramé to bridge for beginners.'

'I do wish you wouldn't belittle us, Simon,' Alice told him, as she went to help Laura fetch things from the kitchen.

'I'm not,' Simon exclaimed. 'I've been looking through the brochures myself, for a meditation course. It's the latest management thing in the States. And the fees are very reasonable too, you know, they're all subsidized.'

'I don't think they had you in mind, somehow,' Natalie pointed out. 'They're subsidized so that working people, housewives, the unemployed, can improve and educate themselves.'

'With all due respect,' Harry, who'd been politely silent till then, suddenly spoke, 'if they could, the loony left would subsidize breathing.'

'Hear, hear,' Charles concurred.

'My cousin Kapil has just started a football team,' Harry continued. 'He applied to the council for a grant on the grounds that it was a multicultural venture, and they gave him two hundred pounds for a complete kit.'

'You've got to admire his enterprise,' Simon remarked.

'I don't see what's so strange about it,' Zoe said. 'It sounds rather enlightened to me.'

'Well, for one thing,' Harry informed her, 'my cousin's the only non-white in the whole set-up. Even if he is the manager.'

Another of the council's initiatives that summer was to organize four Sunday events they called Fun in the Park, held on the hill below the house. Each one had its own theme – sport, international, music – and that day there was one devoted to health, so after lunch Zoe, Simon and Natalie accompanied Harry and Alice on a visit. Robert declined, while Laura said she'd like to but she had things she needed to prepare for the week ahead.

Not that Natalie derived any pleasure from chaperoning Harry and Alice for the first time. She had no idea how far Alice and Harry's relationship had or hadn't developed – it was one thing she and Alice didn't discuss – and she was unable to shift her attention from them, watching for signs of intimacy: for fingers touching, a whispered private joke, a surreptitious kiss. And although she saw none, that only reinforced a conviction that Alice was holding back out of tact, not wanting to hurt her.

At one stall Simon undertook a fitness test, in which his blood pressure, lung capacity and heartbeat recovery rate were monitored, and the results fed into a computer. The council officer studied the read-out and told Simon that he had the body of a nineteen-year-old.

'Blimey,' Zoe exclaimed, 'I bet he was glad to get rid of it.'

'No, that's brilliant, Simon,' Alice approved. 'That just shows, all your diets are worth while.'

Instead of being overjoyed that despite his weight he was as fit as someone ten years younger, Simon was most put out. 'There must be something wrong,' he told the man. 'Maybe you didn't measure my pulse rate properly.'

'It's perfectly accurate,' he was assured, but Simon continued the grumbling of a hypochondriac as they strolled on.

'If you think about it, they're only testing the heart and lungs, that's nothing. What about the other organs? You could be suffering from some fatal disease and still do well on that stupid test. It's irresponsible, that's what it is.'

'Stop bellyaching,' Zoe told him. 'You're like an old woman.'

'Zoe!' Natalie exclaimed, lowering her guard of a jealous chaperone for a moment. 'We don't need that sort of sexist remark.'

They wandered through the crowd in the hot afternoon, and after a while Zoe suggested they split up, and the group separated: she and Simon went one way, Alice and Harry the other – followed by Natalie. Zoe nipped after her and took her arm.

'Hey, Nat,' she said, 'let's look at this Twai-kan-do demonstration; you can tell me what it's all about.'

Natalie let herself be led reluctantly away; she blanched when Zoe whispered in her ear: 'Let's leave the lovers alone for a while, eh?'

'My feet are killing me. Time to go home,' Simon soon suggested. 'We've left Robert and Laura on their own long enough.'

'Robert and Laura?' Zoe asked. 'What have they got to do with each other any more?'

'Use your *eyes*, darling,' Simon told her.

Harry had been almost as oblivious to his surroundings as Natalie. Increasingly when with Alice he found himself wondering what to say or do, and that was an uncomfortable situation for Harry to be in, since in every other part of his life he knew exactly what to do.

They left the park, had tea in a café in St Peter's, and walked back up the hill. In the warm evening they dawdled along the drive to the house. Not far away believers were being called to Evensong by church bells pealing, the notes chasing each other round and round – they saw Simon dash towards the side door in the garden wall. Robert was gunning the engine of one of his cars in the back yard. Laura was visible in the rose garden in a gaberdine mac, gathering petals to fill a bowl, till she was cut off as they approached the front door.

The house was floating in the soft evening light. Harry felt his footsteps plodding far below him. They reached the front steps.

'Well, boo-boo,' Alice said, 'do you want to make me a passanda some evening this week, or what?'

Harry looked across the garden towards the sunset. 'Alice,' he replied, frowning, 'I want to kiss you.'

Alice followed his gaze across the lawn. 'Well, go on, then,' she told him. He stepped forward and she turned towards him. Their lips met and remained pressed together for some time, in a long, passionless kiss. Eventually they withdrew.

'You certainly took your time,' Alice declared.

'Me?' he replied. 'What about—'

'But it was nice, Harry,' she interrupted. 'See you on Thursday?' She reached forward and kissed him again briefly, smiled, and let herself inside.

Harry involuntarily took one step after her, although Alice had closed the door without a backward glance. So Harry took a step back – the same step, as if retracting it – turned, retreated down the steps, paused and looked back over his shoulder at the blank white door, before setting off at a thoughtful pace down the drive. He was repeating the indecisive choreography of nine years earlier, the day he had asked Charles Freeman for his daughter's hand, and it would be ever thus: in the ensuing years Harry Singh would walk in a straight line towards his fortune, except that occasionally he would be halted, and turn a little figure of eight of vacillation, on account of his wife.

It took Harry a further six months of courtship – during which time their kisses became passionate and their trysts more frequent, including Sunday suppers with *his* family – before he summoned up the courage to propose. And then he needed a great deal more, as Alice proceeded to lay down a long list of conditions that would have sent a man with less perseverance running straight back into the arms of an arranged marriage, which, his parents occasionally assured him, it wasn't too late to reorganize.

'Number one,' Alice explained, 'is I'm not giving up my job. It's as important as yours even if it's not so well rewarded materially, that doesn't mean a thing, it just shows what a corrupt society this is. I'm not giving up my career, Harry, I'm not going to be dependent on you or any other man. In fact, number two is we keep separate bank accounts.'

'Is this a yes or a no?' Harry tried to interject, but Alice had her far-away look and ignored him.

'Number three is I don't want any children. Well, not yet anyway. Maybe never. I don't know and I don't want to commit myself. There's no point in staking a claim to freedom and then becoming a slave to bawling babies, is there? It's only fair to warn you.'

'There's enough children in the world already, I suppose,' Harry bravely accepted. 'Except I thought you liked them.'

'Number four,' Alice continued, oblivious to his accord, 'is we share all the household chores: I'm not being your put-upon housewife, Harry Singh, no way, I've seen your mum run around after you lot of ingrates. Cooking, housework, gardening, everything: we'll draw up a contract.'

'A contract?' Harry asked, his conviction faltering.

'Not a legal one, fish-face! Don't be silly! I mean between ourselves. We can change it around as we go along, if we want, by mutual consent. Like, you might want to do all the cooking – in fact, you'd better. I can't bear cooking, in case you hadn't noticed. If you want *me* to cook you'll have to sing for your supper. Get it?' Alice chuckled.

'Get what?' Harry asked, bewildered.

'Singh for your supper, silly,' Alice repeated, but, getting no response, she continued, 'anyway, you might do all the cooking and I'd do all the cleaning. As long as it's fair.'

'I'm sure it should be,' Harry agreed. 'But are you saying yes or no?' he asked

'On the other hand,' Alice digressed, 'we shouldn't just assume we'd live together. I've often thought the ideal relationship was the one between Simone de Beauvoir and Jean-Paul Sartre. I don't really want to not live here, it's a big house, you know.'

'You're right, Alice.'

'And number . . . five,' she said, counting her fingers, using them as an *aide-mémoire*, since she'd had many months to rehearse her list of conditions. 'Number five is I'm not changing my name. I'm not going to be your chattel, Harry, an appendage to another patriarchal lineage. We can be Singh-Freeman, or Freeman-Singh, or just keep our separate names. I'm not sure yet. It's up for discussion.'

Harry wanted to weep. 'But what do you *want?*' he groaned. 'Do you want me?' he demanded.

Alice looked at him with a smile. 'Of course I do, boo-boo,' she said.

The following evening the family were finishing supper when Alice, who'd spent much of the meal discussing with Simon the nutritional and spiritual value of ginseng, said abruptly: 'Hey, everyone! I almost forgot: Harry finally asked me to marry him last night.'

The table went quiet. Everyone was waiting for Charles' response.

'I'm going to marry Harry,' Alice – oblivious to her father's temper tantrums – chuckled. The others braced themselves.

Charles smiled. 'He's a bright spark, that young man,' he announced. 'Good business sense. I like him. Good for you, Alice. He'll go far,' Charles said. He didn't yet know *how* far.

Everyone breathed a sigh of relief, and toasted Alice and her absent intended with a Beaumes-de-Venise Laura fetched from the kitchen.

Charles telephoned Mr Singh, put engagement notices in *The Times* and the *Echo*, and encouraged Alice to start planning their wedding with as much help from him as she required, not just because he was making up for Alice's mother not being around but also because, as ever, the man-in-charge liked the idea of a good party.

Alice and Harry were married on a hot Saturday in the middle of 1984, with a wedding in the same church in which Alice had once sung in the choir – with the same giggling priest – preceded by a blessing in the Singhs' Hindu temple.

Harry took a ring from Simon, his best man (as Alice had predicted, they'd become friends, and Harry didn't have any others) and placed it on the third finger of Alice's left hand. And then, in his phlegmatic tone of voice, Harry repeated after the vicar, 'I Harry take thee Alice to be my wedded wife, to have and to hold from this day forward, for better for worse, for richer for poorer, in sickness and in health, to love and to cherish, till death us do part, according to God's holy ordinance; and thereto I plight thee my troth.' Alice had to fight off an attack of the giggles, because she thought Harry was going to conclude: 'Respectfully yours, Amen.'

Charles Freeman gave his daughter away with a light heart. His youngest child was the first to be married, at the age of twenty-four, and he was genuinely glad for her; despite his wife's death, Charles regarded marriage as an appropriate condition for men and women to live together.

'It's about time you bucked *your* ideas up,' he'd told Simon some weeks before, on Simon's thirtieth birthday. 'It's all very well, these women of yours floating in and out of the house, but you ought to think about settling down with one of them,' he advised. He had no idea.

The church was packed. Harry had a large extended family who filled the first six pews on the groom's side and he had a great number of acquaintances, who could be defined as people with whom he'd exchanged money, property or favours.

James came with his camera. Outside the temple, where just the closest family had attended, he took a photograph of Harry and Alice blurred by a blizzard of rice. They had to shake it out of their hair and clothes before going into the church, only to be assailed again on the way out, this time with confetti. Before leaving for the reception at the big house on the hill in Charles' chauffeur-driven Rover, Alice threw her bridal bouquet over her shoulder. It landed right in the arms of her chief bridesmaid, Natalie (who'd refused to wear a dress, and was attired instead in a page boy's outfit). Displaying great presence of mind and quick reactions, Natalie promptly pushed it up in the air again without catching it, like a volleyball, and this time it fell into Laura's hands; she *did* grasp it, to be greeted with a chorus of whistles and cheers. Laura glanced involuntarily towards Robert, who responded with a surreptitious smirk.

Using a rapid shutter-release, James caught that sequence in a series of photographs, but then instead of going to the reception he went back to his bedsit.

'I know you vowed never to return there,' Zoe had argued with him a couple of days before. 'But this is your sister's wedding, for God's sake.'

'I'm not going back,' James replied, hunched up in her small kitchen.

'You only *made* the vow to yourself,' Zoe cried. 'It's not even like

272

you're going to lose face with anyone. What do you achieve by being so stubborn, James?'

'Bad things happened there. If I go back, they'll happen again, so I'm not going.'

'What *are* you talking about?'

'If they were having the reception anywhere else, I'd go. They didn't have to have it there.'

'Jesus, James!' Zoe cried, exasperated. 'I can't talk to you now, you're so unreasonable. I'm going downstairs. Let yourself out,' she told him, adding: 'You are the most obstinate person I've ever known. *Including* my grandmother.'

Harry and Alice spent their honeymoon in India, first visiting Harry's family home in the city of Bombay. Close relatives he'd barely heard of, never mind knew, queued up less to meet Harry for the first time than his English wife. After a week of incessant hospitality – from which Harry found respite in daily, hour-long international phone calls back to his office, because he didn't trust his small staff to make decisions – Harry had to drag Alice away for their holiday proper.

'Your Aunt Padma invited us to her place, Harry. We get on so well.'

'She's a gossiping housewife, not your sort at all, Alice. I don't get it. Anyway our train tickets are booked.'

'And your Uncle Javed's such a flirt, Harry.'

'He's a dirty old man, Alice.'

'And the twins are so sweet. Granny Singh said I was the only one except her who could tell them apart.'

'They're ill-mannered brats, if you want my opinion. They let them run around shouting the house down. How on earth are we going to transport all this extra luggage? What with their presents and your shopping expeditions, I'll have to send it separately.'

'Don't be grumpy, Grandpa. Although on second thoughts you're right: it'll give the airline the freight of their lives.'

'With what they'll charge us they *should* be happy,' Harry stated, either ignoring, or more likely missing, Alice's awful pun.

They spent their final week in Goa, which had been Harry's idea, although by the time they got there he was itching to get back home to work, assailed by the mounting conviction that without him at the helm his business would crumble. His daily phone calls stretched to two hours and he arranged for a delivery of photocopies of all

273

recent transactions and contracts, as well as copies of the *Financial Times* and *Property News*, to be brought over by one of his team of piecework labourers, who got a free flight out of it.

'Sounds like a good courier opportunity for the guy,' Alice remarked.

'It's just a one-off, Alice,' Harry told her.

'Do you think a sense of humour's a genetic inheritance or a cultural acquisition?' she asked.

'Probably a combination of the two, I should think,' Harry replied.

Their first two days in Goa were not happy ones. Harry was unable to relax on the beach or swim in the sea for more than ten minutes at a time before returning to his papers, to reread the small print of house-exchange contracts. Which was about as long as Alice could spend there too: her pale skin burned and she had to retreat into the shade.

'*Relax*, Harry,' Alice implored. 'At least one of us should enjoy this paradise.' He rubbed the strongest sun-tan lotion into Alice's shoulders: it blocked ultraviolet rays but didn't help her skin actually go brown.

'Stop it, Harry,' Alice told him. 'I'll do it myself: your fingers are all fidgety.'

Yet despite everything it was in Goa that Alice and Harry did finally relax with each other; they would return home from their honeymoon having replaced the tentative, exploratory negotiating of newly-weds with the easy intimacy of a long-standing couple.

On the third day Harry and Alice ate the same food and were struck down by a virulent case of food-poisoning. Until then they had remained modest with each other – unsure whether to be in the bathroom at the same time, undressing either side of the bed and sliding under the sheets towards the other's nakedness.

In the middle of that night, however, Alice awoke from a repulsive dream in which, swimming in the warm Arabian Sea, she found herself surrounded by jellyfish. Undulating their tentacles, they floated around her. After initial terror, however, Alice realized that none of them were coming any closer: they didn't wish to sting her. And she understood suddenly why: she was not a victim but, rather, somehow their incubator – they were guarding her, because they had laid their eggs inside her. Inside her the gelatinous bodies of baby jellyfish were squirming and growing.

Alice awoke from a nightmare sea into a nauseous reality. She staggered out of bed and into the hotel-suite bathroom, to discover Harry collapsed over the toilet bowl, already doing what she had to do within the next two seconds. She reeled to the shower unit, dropped to her knees and let go a jellied splurge of vomit.

Harry, meanwhile, though still heaving, had managed to push himself up in order to sit on the bowl, because no sooner had he emptied his stomach than his bowels had erupted too, and molten lava poured out.

Eventually Harry's stomach and rectum stilled. Breathing hard, he became aware of the world beyond the boundaries of his own body: Alice had crawled into the shower, and lay curled up in her own mess. Harry made his way giddily over.

'Alice. Are you OK?' he croaked.

She was whimpering, her eyes closed. Without opening them she whispered: 'Help me, Harry.'

He helped her get up and take off her soiled T-shirt, and turned on the shower. When the water had washed away Alice's evacuations, they held each other under the warm water until they were clean. They barely had the strength to dry themselves before collapsing back on the bed.

For the next twelve hours Alice and Harry felt the waves of warning swim through their bodies (sometimes taking it in turn, sometimes with exact synchronicity) and wearily turned aside the bedsheet and staggered unsteadily, moaning, back to the bathroom, where against all logic the malevolent bacteria uncovered further undigested food from the recesses of their intestines and expelled it.

They also took it in turns to nurse each other – laying a warm flannel across the other's forehead, moistening vomit-soured lips. Harry stroked Alice's arm, which made her feel secure against the isolation of illness because it was an action repeated from her childhood, something Laura used to do.

When, at last, the vomiting and diarrhoea were over Harry and Alice, empty and exhausted, slept for twenty-four hours curled up together, refugees from a violent storm of sickness. They awoke healthy and ravenous, ordered six portions of traditional English breakfast and three pots of tea from room service, stuffed themselves without repercussions (other than noisy belches and burps) and slept again. And then eventually they woke up slowly, in the dawn or possibly the dusk of some unidentified day, and they made love with an abandonment neither had imagined was possible.

275

For the rest of their holiday they left their suite only to have dinner, dressed to the nines, in the restaurant downstairs, during which time their sheets were changed and trays of dirty dishes cleared away, before returning to the bedroom; there they divested themselves of their formal attire, and explored the realms of sexual pleasure.

Harry put their flight back another week, and by the end of their extended honeymoon Alice knew Harry's body better than her own; Harry was suffering from a pleasant amnesia about anything to do with the English property market; and they had begun a habit that in years to come would cause half their children to recoil with embarrassed disapproval (and the other half to hoot with delight): that of lying in bed, silently, side by side, and taking it in turns to fart with as great a variety of tone, duration and under-the-sheets malodour as they could manage, awarding each other marks out of ten. It was a habit through which, moreover, Alice discovered the last secret of Harry's body to reveal itself, the location of his funny bone, because he laughed even louder than she did, hooting like a guilty schoolboy.

Harry and Alice Singh-Freeman (as they'd agreed to call themselves) returned to take up residence not in one of Harry's acquisitions, as might have been expected, but in the east wing of the house on the hill. Harry had succeeded in going along with the idea Alice had first mooted among her list of marital conditions − agreeing that there was nothing to be gained from a place of their own, he wasn't a proud man, and there would be plenty of privacy with a wing to themselves − without ever revealing that from the day he'd asked Charles for her hand it was his dream to live in this very house.

Their crate of gifts had already reached the house before them, and at an impromptu homecoming party they handed round the presents Alice had bought: camelskin slippers for Charles; a stone roller-grinder for Laura, along with a cache of rare spices; a statuette of the elephant god, Ganesh, for Simon ("Cos he's fat and wise like you,' Alice explained); a Sikh warrior's dagger, its hilt encrusted with emeralds, for Natalie; turquoise packets of *bidi* cigarettes for Robert; and a gorgeous silk sari for Zoe, which she would wear thereafter every time she showed an Indian film, like *Pather Panchali* or *Piravi*, at the cinema, and which felt like a sad substitute for the travelling days of her youth.

*

276

While Harry went off to reacquaint himself with his business, Alice, in the remaining fortnight of her summer vacation, set about refurnishing the east wing, which had had little human occupation in recent years; and it hadn't been decorated for over twenty. Once again a team of decorators was hired, working to instructions not from the man-in-charge this time but from his youngest child.

Alice took Laura with her on a whirlwind tour of the home showrooms on Otley Road, the curtains and fittings sections of the department stores in town, and the carpet warehouses outside the ring road. To make way for their delivery Alice hired three skips for the old furniture that was to be discarded.

Natalie came home at midday from her night shift at the women's refuge and found the skips overflowing with mattresses, rugs, cupboards, ripped-out shelves and worn-out armchairs. She stormed through the east wing shouting for Alice with such ferocity that the decorators pinned themselves to the walls to let her pass. She found Alice making notes in a distant room on the second floor.

'What the *hell* do you think you're doing, throwing out all that perfectly good furniture?' Natalie demanded.

'Oh, I've ordered lots of new stuff,' Alice smiled.

'But, *Alice!*' Natalie shouted, 'You've been to the refuge. That stuff in the skips is like Louis Quatorze compared to what we've got.'

'Well, that's true,' Alice agreed. 'I never thought about it,' she said brightly.

'Don't you think maybe you *should* have?' Natalie demanded. 'How could you be so insensitive all of a sudden? And what are you wasting so much money on all this for anyway?'

'These'll be the guest bedrooms on this floor,' Alice explained.

'Guests?' Natalie spat. 'What guests? Don't be evasive, Alice, you're nest-building. You're building the biggest bloody nest in this iniquitous town.' She turned round and marched out of the room. Alice followed and called down the corridor after her:

'You're welcome to get things out of the skips, Nat.'

'I bloody well intend to!' she shouted back without turning round.

It became a chaotic afternoon. Natalie found Robert drinking cans of beer with a couple of his mates in the garage and demanded they volunteer the use of a Luton van Robert had just renovated, as well as their labour.

'I'll give you both a fiver,' Natalie told the leather-jacketed friends. 'A bit of beer money.'

'What's in it for me, babe?' Robert asked her.

'Well, Robert,' Natalie said, 'think of it as doing your bit for the community of single mothers, whose numbers you work so hard to multiply.'

One of the greasers laughed.

'Shut it, Weasel,' Robert told him. 'What do you know?' he demanded of Natalie.

'You can shun responsibility, mister, but you can't run away from rumours,' Natalie told him.

'Ah, come on, Rob,' the other greaser said. 'Let's do our bit for fucking charity, eh?'

The decorators periodically brought further items of furniture outside, which they placed on the drive instead of throwing them into the skips because Natalie and her unlikely colleagues were hauling out of them any tables and cabinets which were still intact.

Then the *new* furniture began to arrive: lorries came crunching down the gravel drive, and maneouvred around the skips and each other and Robert's box van; delivery men swung open their rear doors and began carrying carpets and wardrobes into the house. Alice felt like a policewoman on traffic duty, particularly as, since she had an aversion to raising her voice, she found herself making hand signals.

Just then, though, Simon came home from work and decided to join in. He was perfectly happy to raise *his* voice, especially in the interests of giving advice. He took off his jacket, rolled up his sleeves, tucked his tie between the buttons of his shirt, and took over before anyone could co-opt him into doing something useful.

'Back it up over here!' Simon yelled to a newly arrived lorry driver, 'You've got *plenty* of room, duck, left-hand down and straight back. Weasel!' he shouted, 'you missed that standard lamp! Put it in the Luton. Carpets!' he cried, 'Where do you want carpets, Alice? First floor? Rightio, up to the first floor with them, sunshine, mind out, they're bringing down an old dresser there, hang on, I'll just sort them out. Turn it on its side!' he commanded, 'That's better, that's fine, ease it round the corner. Yes, a bit further. You've got plenty of room. Oops! Right. Well. Look, you're stuck now. Watch the paintwork, boys!'

Laura brought respite to the chaos with trays of refreshments, including bacon butties for Robert's mates.

'They're not for you, they're for your friends,' she told Robert.

He drew her to him and whispered his reply into her ear. Laura shrugged herself loose and returned to the kitchen, re-emerging minutes later with tea and cake and biscuits. Before anyone had a chance to pass them round, so the men could partake on the hoof, without wasting time, Simon bellowed: 'TEA BREAK, LADS!' at the top of his voice, and he directed Laura with her trays towards the lawn.

Twenty men and three women were sitting on the grass around the pond when, five minutes later, the Rover came cruising down the drive. Charles leapt out of the back seat and strode towards them.

'Oh, my God,' said Simon, who had a sudden attack of *déjà vu* that made him begin to tremble. 'He's going to start chucking people into the pond again,' he whispered, and promptly curled up into a foetal position and pretended to be asleep.

'What's going on here?' Charles roared. 'Who on earth ordered a tea break for so many lazy labourers?'

Heads slowly swivelled, eyes turned, towards a gargantuan baby dozing in the sunshine.

'Top marks!' Charles exclaimed. 'Good show! How about some for the old man?' he asked Laura. 'How's it all going?' he asked Alice.

Harry didn't get home till after dark; the decorators and deliverers were long gone. After supper Alice took him to the east wing: the floors were covered with plastic sheets and their footsteps rustled. Most of the windows were open but the air was still thick with the fumes of oil and emulsion paint.

'I'm so happy, Alice,' Harry told her. They went up the stairs hand in hand. 'Well done, my wife, you're so clever,' he said. 'I knew it was best to leave it to you.'

'I've had a *little* help, silly,' she admitted.

The rooms were mostly empty: the new furniture had been deposited in two rooms on the first floor, until the decorating was completed and they could be put in place. They reached the first of these rooms and Harry let go of Alice's hand.

'What's all this?' he asked quietly, stepping forward, moving between items of furniture, his hand trailing across them.

'They're the new things I bought today, for—'

'This won't do at all,' Harry interrupted her. The icy quietness of his voice made Alice catch her breath. Harry shook his head. 'No, this isn't right, we'll have to change it.'

Alice forced herself to breathe. 'What's wrong, Harry?' she managed to ask.

'Nothing, my love,' he replied. 'Except for this furniture. It's all new, you see. Any Tom, Dick or, or, *anyone* can buy this, off the shelf. It's simply not special enough; for my wife, you see? For us. We want genuine antiques, Alice.' He'd returned to face her. 'That is what we want.'

'You're angry, Harry,' she said.

'Me? I don't get angry, my love,' he assured her, in the same flat tone of voice. He took her hand again and led her back into the corridor and towards the stairs.

'But I've paid for all these things,' Alice told him. 'I can't take them back.'

'That's no problem,' he replied. 'I'm thinking of moving into the letting business, you know, I've just bought some flats off Stratford Road. I can move these things in there. Anyway, don't you worry, my love, leave it to me. Now, let's go to bed. I've been thinking about you all afternoon,' he told her, his hand roaming across her backside.

'Who were you thinking about this *morning*, Harry?' Alice demanded. 'Harry, my horny husband,' she teased him, grasping with relief and gratitude the distraction from their power struggle that Harry had just provided; avoiding confronting the fact that, although she could tease and cajole him into suppliant confusion whenever she wanted, it was all no more than a game. Beneath his pompous, phlegmatic surface, horny Harry, droopy-features, fish-face or whatever she called him, was as unremitting as a glacier. And as they made their way back into the main house, to their temporary bedroom on the third floor, giggling and poking each other, in reality Alice knew she was stepping out of his way.

After they had made love Alice lay with her head on Harry's chest, and he asked her: 'Was I dreaming this morning, before I woke up, or did I hear you throwing up in the bathroom?'

'I did a bit,' she affirmed. 'I was a bit queasy.'

'You don't think it's a recurrence of that damn Indian food-poisoning, do you?' Harry wondered.

Alice chuckled. 'Don't be silly, fish-face,' she told him.

7

THE FREEMAN TEN

JAMES HAD BEEN SO BUSY MEETING OTHER PHOTOGRAPHERS AND ARTISTS in the town that he'd lost touch with the music scene, and when he had more time on his hands to get into gigs again for free and take pictures of new bands, he found that there weren't any. Venues had stopped providing live music because they were tiny stages at the back of pubs, and pubs were going through a period of trans- formation: all over the town breweries had bought out free-house publicans and brought in builders who specialized in working twenty-five-hour days to gut public bars and refurbish them in a style somewhere between an Edwardian country house and a motorway service station, in various shades of red. Local beers were replaced by mass-produced lager (which research showed was drunk in greater quantity, though no amount of research could find out why). Coffee machines appeared below the spirits bottles and kitchens were renovated in accordance with EEC hygiene regulations: the idea was for pubs to become continental cafés, English alehouses and fancy restaurants all in one. Dominoes and shove-halfpenny were banned, old men who'd been propping up a bar since the war vanished like smoke, while single women felt able to go out drinking alone for the first time. At lunchtime the beer gardens were invaded by whole families; and at night live music was scrapped in favour of karaoke, because what was the point in paying unknown bands to make a racket if the customers preferred to do it themselves?

One evening after meeting with the Artists' Group Karel persuaded James to join him on a visit to the nightclub below the theatre in the middle of town.

'A lot of bloody foreign women go there,' he told James.

At the nightclub Karel bought himself and James a beer, rolled a cigarette, and then leaned against the bar, watching the dance-floor. James realized he'd already been forgotten. After a while Karel moved forward, and James watched him making his way through dancing bodies less towards any one woman in particular than into the midst of mutual glances and reciprocal movements.

James followed. The period of pogo-ing to punk bands years before had robbed him of his inhibitions, but also any chance he might have had of acquiring a sense of rhythm. He entered the orbit of various women but paid more attention to imitating their dancing than making contact, and they seemed to leave the floor before he'd succeeded in accomplishing either. So James closed his eyes, let thumping disco music enter his body, and wheeled around in a world of his own.

James didn't notice Karel leave. He stopped intermittently to have a rest and a glass of water, and carried on dancing, oblivious to the bodies around him and the passing of time, until suddenly the music stopped. In the deafening silence the nightclub rapidly emptied. James walked up the stairs and into the dark, cold morning: the night exerted a chill grip on his sweaty torso, and a sound like a thousand cicadas rang in his ears. He'd had no more than a couple of beers but he reeled home, drunk from dancing.

A few days later, after working late in the darkroom, his neck stiff, his eyes tired, James went back to the nightclub on his own. He entered past the thick-necked, bow-tied bouncers, paid at the kiosk, descended the crimson-carpeted stairs, checked in his jacket at the cloakroom and ploughed through the crowd to the bar. Sipping his first beer of the evening, he watched the pulsating dance-floor, multi-coloured lights cascading across it, a heaving sea of bodies; and then he caught sight of the DJ: it was Lewis.

James made his way over. When Lewis saw him he beamed, leaned over the console and extended his long arm in greeting, and said something not a word of which James could make out over the din.

'WHAT?' he shouted. Lewis gestured to him to come around the side of the stage and join him.

Between changing records Lewis and James conducted a difficult conversation, in which James couldn't hear himself speak and so wasn't absolutely sure he was saying what he meant to say; fortunately Lewis appeared able to lip-read. From Lewis's utterances James managed to glue together dislocated syllables in the deafening din and decipher the fact that Lewis worked in the club four nights a week; he was one of two resident DJs. But James found it such hard work to make out much else that he swapped assurances with Lewis that it was good to see each other and they'd talk again, and then returned to his original mission, which was to lose himself on the dance-floor.

Despite his ineptitude, James loved dancing. And he loved walking home at one or two in the morning, along deserted streets. The only people he passed were lost drunks or workers on their way to an early shift, bicycling blindly, heads down. The pubs, restaurants, even the burger vans had shut up shop and gone home. The one place still functioning was the bakery a couple of hundred yards short of his bedsit; the bakers worked all night. The smell of bread baking would greet him at some point along the street and entice him gently homeward. He'd stop off, and buy whatever was most recently out of the oven – a hot doughnut, a warm roll – off one of the bakers who gave change with floury fingers from a plastic bowl by the door. And then James would get home and eat it with a mug of tea, coming down off the buzz of dancing to far-too-loud music, before sleeping like a log.

James had never been so fit, bicycling around town, dancing till dawn.

All through that winter and spring of 1985 James went to the nightclub at least once a week. He always went alone; and usually left alone, too, although a couple of times he found himself emerging with a partner. One was a young Spanish woman: he walked her to the YWCA, and they communicated less on the empty pavements than they had in the cacophonous crowd; she spoke little English and he spoke no Spanish. They said goodnight and *buenas dias* at the door of the hostel and he never saw her again. Another was an American who took him back to her hotel near the station, made fast and furious love, and promptly fell asleep in his arms. James extricated himself and walked home, grinning at the streetlights reflected in drizzly puddles, and wondering why English women didn't like him.

James resumed his friendship with Lewis – he left the club more often with Lewis than with a woman and went back to his house on the small, modern estate by the northern ring road, where they wound down with cups of tea, ignoring both the fact that James had to go to work in the morning and also the occasional girlfriend awaiting Lewis upstairs.

'I better be off, then, Lew,' James volunteered when he'd drained his mug.

'Relax, man,' Lewis told him. 'Stick around. Women like to be kept waiting, it does them good. They shouldn't feel they're too much in charge.'

Lewis's house was a bachelor pad. Apart from a small kitchen (whose only oven was a microwave) the whole of the ground floor consisted of a large, sprawling sitting-room with a thick-pile carpet and a sofa and armchairs of such inviting absorbency that people's pulse rate and sense of purpose subsided as soon as they sat down: in Lewis's pad people hung out for hours, and there were always some there, men of various nationalities and races he'd met in the club and who had time on their hands. Lewis seemed to speak most of their languages. Many of them barely said anything, in any language, but were happy to lounge around, listening to music and watching TV.

Lewis was one of the first in the town to have a satellite dish attached to the outside of his house, and the only thing he watched was one of thirty channels of sport from around the world; and the only sport Lewis liked was football. At any time of day or night he could sink into an armchair and channel-hop with the remote control from one game to another: James realized that it was through football that his friend had become a polyglot.

Lewis was still a leader, though of what sort James wasn't sure. He was like a priest of an invisible religion. Visitors had to remove their shoes at the door, so as not to scuff the carpets; smoking was forbidden; and although alcohol wasn't, neither was it available, since Lewis rarely touched it himself. James liked it there – for brief, occasional visits, respites from his own energetic but, he reckoned, equally aimless life.

'There's time for everything that needs it,' Lewis told him. 'You wear yourself out if you want to, I don't intend to. Look at my

284

old man, poor sod, frazzled by his responsibilities. It's not worth it.'

'You're probably right,' James agreed. 'I'm not arguing.'

'You were always a dreamer, Jay. I admired you, you know.'

'You did?'

'Sure. I still do. But when are you going to show me some of your pictures? I don't mean the newspaper ones – your own.'

'I'll bring some round, really.'

'Don't forget.'

'I won't.'

Running a manufacturing company that employed three hundred workers was an incredibly demanding operation, especially for a man who thought delegating responsibility was, as he told Simon, 'just another word for shirking it'.

'Once you let other people make decisions for you,' Charles advised his son, 'they'll end up deciding they don't need you.'

Simon was in awe of his father's leadership, of the forthright way in which he made light of the countless aspects of business that had to be studied, predicted, weighed against each other and somehow balanced: profit and loss, market forces, research and development, salaries, insurance, raw materials, transport, new plant, wear and tear, redundancies, retirements and measures for the prevention of accidents in the workplace.

Having completed his management apprenticeship of six-month stints in each department, Simon had stayed – at his own request – in the smallest, Personnel, which, being the son of the man-in-charge, would have been risible, except that, Bullshit Simon being the sympathetic man he was, no one thought it too odd. So there he stayed, assistant director of personnel. He listened to employees' work-related grievances and personal concerns, had monthly meetings with department heads and shop stewards, and ironed out as many awkward wrinkles as he could without recourse to the boss, his father.

Simon hoped that one day he'd succeed Rupert Sproat as director of personnel and that would be that. He had a passable understanding of the workings of each department; but how they meshed together in a functioning – indeed thriving – whole was beyond him. He had his father's physical frame, his gregariousness, and the same blithe self-confidence; the difference was that with Simon that last quality was a front, his own *modus operandi*, whereas with Charles it was the rock from which he was hewn.

285

That, of course, was the secret of Charles' leadership. He did weigh up the mass of imponderables involved before coming to any major decision, and he did listen to advice. Sometimes he came to a decision based on a finely detailed study of sales projections, research and statistics; sometimes he relied on gut instinct. Sometimes he was right, sometimes he was wrong. But whatever he decided he did so with such conviction that his decisions carried a preternatural authority.

This was the reason it took people at the Freeman Company a little longer than elsewhere to realize that, by then, the summer of 1985, a conversion had taken place at the top. Or perhaps it was a revelation. It took people a while longer to realize what was happening because Charles' leadership had always been tyrannical, but had produced wealth and wellbeing for the benefit of all (and if that benefit had been somewhat unequally distributed, it was only the odd dotty Communist – unskilled shop-floor workers all – who'd ever complained; the union was as committed to differentials as management was). And by the time they did realize what was happening, it was too late. Perhaps it would have been anyway.

Not even Simon realized, despite being the one person apart from Judith Peach with whom Charles shared his revelation.

'I never quite understood how simple it is,' Charles confided. 'It's about money, Simon; it's about profit.'

'Of course it is, Father,' Simon replied. 'You've told me that a hundred times. I was listening, I promise you.'

'No, you bloody fool,' Charles told him. 'I mean that's *all* it's about. It has to be the basis of every single decision, at all times. Everything else has to find its own place in the scheme of things.'

'Of course it does, Father,' Simon agreed. 'I know.'

'You don't know a bloody *thing*, you idiot!' Charles roared, and stomped out of the study.

Unemployment was rising every month. 'Good,' Charles told the chief accountant. 'Cut the wages.'

'No more apprentices,' he told the recruitment officer. 'Unsound investment in times like these.'

The head of research was summoned to his office. 'Your assistants are fired,' Charles told him. 'Oh, yes, and you are too,' he added.

A group of machinists were being retrained in computer skills. 'We'll have to let them go,' Charles ordered. 'Offer the jobs to their wives instead. Part-timers. Women. Lower hourly rates. Less national insurance. No sick pay.'

286

He marched over to the transport bay. 'Inform the drivers,' he told the supervisor, 'as from the first of next month they're self-employed. They can buy their lorries off the company through a hire-purchase scheme; we'll take the payments out of their wages . . . I mean, their fees.'

'What's all this overtime nonsense?' Charles asked the shop-floor manager. 'Time and a half after six o'clock?' he enquired. 'Double time after midnight?' he demanded. 'Treble time on Sundays and bank holidays *and* a ruddy day in lieu?' Charles smiled. 'No, no,' he stated calmly. 'No more overtime around here. Standard rates at all times throughout the works. There's plenty of people *prefer* to work at night. And plenty more who'd leap at the chance of a Sunday job.'

The shop-floor manager and his five equally senior colleagues besieged Charles' office.

'These are unheard-of measures,' they cried. 'They're ruthless.'

'Not ruthless but radical, yes, gentlemen. They're economically justifiable and therefore necessary.'

'But what are we going to tell the workforce?' they wailed.

'You can tell them any ruddy thing you like,' Charles replied. 'That's your job.'

'They won't stand for it, Charles,' his accountant – the eldest among them – warned.

Charles laughed out loud. 'Not only will they stand for it, Peter,' Charles told him, 'in a year's time, when they see the bonus in their pay-packets, they'll queue up outside that door to thank us.'

'The ones that are left,' muttered David Canning, the young head of sales, quietly.

The others' heads all turned towards him and, in the silence, back to Charles. The veins in his face began to fill and turn his complexion a familiar shade of purple and they awaited the explosion with sick anticipation, pitying their impetuous colleague.

Instead, though, Charles restrained himself, the red mist in his eyes receded, and he smiled. 'Quite so, young man. But it can't be helped, you see. Good day, gentlemen.'

Less than twenty-four hours later it was the turn of the chief shop steward of the union to pay a call to the office of the man-in-charge.

Garfield Roberts had never had much of either political ambition or ideological conviction. Some five years earlier his name had been put forward as a candidate in the ballot for the union position, which had fallen vacant with the retirement of the then incumbent – a radical Welshman who long ago had walked to the town from South Wales in search of work. The other three candidates were all politically motivated idealists belonging to a different party – a Communist, a Workers' Revolutionary and a Socialist Worker – and Garfield was nominated by workers who thought the politicos would be better left arguing with each other than with the boss.

Having worked there over twenty years already, Garfield was known to everyone. After ten years on the assembly line he'd become the safety officer (a full-time post specially created, on Charles' orders) and his job took him all over the works. He had the uncanny ability to remember every one of his three hundred colleagues' names, addressing the most junior apprentice or secretary by their first name without a moment's hesitation, just as he did the senior managers, and indeed the boss himself. It was a feat rendered possible by the fact that Garfield made no attempt whatsoever to remember anyone's surname (the only surnames Garfield knew were those of his fellow players in the cricket team, of which he was opening bat, captain and secretary).

Even the most racially prejudiced workers were unable to find a bad word to say against Garfield. The word that *was* used most often was solid. It described both his build and his nature. He combined a first-name-terms friendliness with a certain aloof dignity. Three hundred colleagues regarded Garfield as a comrade – and could rely on him to get a faulty machine-cover or fuse-box fixed exactly when he said he would – without any of them being his buddy. Most men had one or two particularly close friends, men they worked alongside, with whom they also went drinking, watching football, and on holiday with their wives.

'You know Alan,' someone would say, 'he's Danny's mate,' which identified him. No one ever said: 'Garfield? He's my mate.' But everyone could say: 'Garfield? He's all right. He's solid.' And so five years earlier Garfield had been elected shop steward in an open ballot by an unprecedented show-of-hands majority. In fact the only hands raised for each of his far-left rivals belonged to *their* mates.

Now Garfield came into Charles' office and sat down across the wide desk. They got on well, and always began, whatever their business, with asking after each other's families.

'Well, Charles,' Garfield said, once the pleasantries were over. 'I have to tell you you're stirring up a hornets' nest this time. I'd appreciate it if you'd explain to me what it is you're doing.'

Charles went through the various radical measures he'd come up with, ending with the imposition of pay cuts.

'Labour's a commodity like any other,' he proclaimed, 'and right now there's a large surplus. If there's a surplus of any kind of goods or services on the market, the price comes down. It's the same with wages. Logical, is it not? If we're to beat our competitors all our costs have to be kept down.'

Garfield never answered (other than a greeting) instantaneously. Whatever was said to him he pondered a moment before giving his reply. He did so now, and then responded: 'I can see your logic, Charles, but you must also see that I can't possibly sanction a cut in my members' wages. You've always agreed that the very minimum we'd accept is a rise in line with inflation.'

'Quite so, Garfield,' Charles agreed, 'but surely you see that's all in the past? These are hard times, man, with new conditions. We all have to adapt or go under.'

'Well, I'll put what you propose to my members, but I'm telling you now they won't like it,' Garfield told him gravely. 'And neither do I, Charles,' he added.

There followed the most heated meeting of union officials since the imposition of a three-day-week over ten years earlier. Garfield, who'd had nothing remotely like it during his tenure, tried to restore order.

'I hear what you say, brothers, and I'll take your points back to the chairman. I'm sure he'll be reasonable.'

'He's taking the piss,' cried Steve Innes, Garfield's deputy steward. He was a young electrician and was known as the Wire, both because of his profession and because of his skinny build and jagged temperament. He was also a militant trade unionist. 'A bastard like that doesn't listen to reason, he only understands force. It's about time we showed him some.'

'I believe you're wrong,' Garfield maintained. 'We've always reasoned things out before.'

There followed days of negotiation between Charles and his two most senior managers on one side and Garfield, the Wire and their branch secretary on the other, with the director of personnel, Rupert Sproat, perched unconvincingly in between.

Charles Freeman was at his most implacable, stone-walling worst, but in contrast to his furious days of old he conducted these

289

negotiations in an unnatural state of calm, because things were so much clearer to him now. To every objection to his plans he smiled: 'If any of you gentlemen can come up with better ways to save money, I'd be only too pleased to hear them.'

Negotiations carried on into the night, neither side able to glimpse a possibility of compromise. Eventually Garfield persuaded his colleagues to accept the reclassification of HGV drivers as freelance instead of salaried employees, only to find no equivalent concession forthcoming from the management. He could feel the Wire seething with indignation and nervous energy beside him; he sometimes demanded a toilet break and dragged Garfield into the Gents with him, where he kicked the cubicle doors in his anger.

'He's taking the piss, man, I'm telling you,' the Wire exclaimed. 'We've got to go out,' he declared. 'We've got to go out.'

Garfield struggled to restrain his colleague, retain his dignity, and keep the negotiations going. No one really knew how much he suffered at the time, because he had no real confidants at work, and he didn't want to bother Pauline at home; it was bad enough that they saw so little of each other. Garfield kept his feelings to himself, bottled up inside, placating his secret stomach ulcer with surreptitious pills, while on the surface his black African hair turned greyer by the day.

The last thing Garfield wanted was a strike. He abhorred the idea that justice could be achieved by force. Maybe once, long ago, it was the only way, but surely no longer. He'd brought up his children, Lewis and Gloria, in the belief that the basic human values of respect for your elders, hospitality to strangers, care of the weak, self-respect and faith in God would bring about a better world; it would change through courtesy and good manners.

The day the research and training department closed down – with the loss of twenty white-collar workers – they'd still made no headway. That evening during negotiations the Wire called for a toilet break and instead of nudging Garfield he dragged the branch secretary – an old, almost retirement-age fitter – off to the Gents instead. After a few minutes Garfield realized he actually did need to empty his bladder. Approaching the toilets he heard the Wire's overheated voice: 'We've got to call a strike ballot tomorrow. *You* can see that, can't you? He's going to give us nothing. Uncle's too soft, he can't see it. The bastard's rolling him over and tickling his tummy.'

'Yes,' the old secretary agreed. 'We have to stand up now. You're right. Just one thing, Steven,' he added. 'Don't let me hear you call him uncle again. You're a mean little runt, but I'm not too old to box your ears.'

Garfield slipped into the unoccupied Ladies next door to relieve himself. He leaned forward and rested his head against the wall above the cistern as he peed. He felt weary.

'You should have carried on to America,' he told himself.

The open ballot in the canteen produced a clear majority in favour of an all-out strike, with immediate effect. The Wire addressed the workforce from his table-platform with rousing words, led them in a tuneless rendition of 'There is Power in Our Union,' and finished by holding his fist high in the air and proclaiming: 'Solidarity, brothers and sisters!'

There was a loud cheer, and clapping. Followed by silence. 'What do we do now?' a lone voice piped up, articulating the question of many, because only a very few people could remember the last time they'd gone on strike and no one was quite sure of the procedure: did they turn their machines off, tidy up paperwork, put tools in racks and switch off the lights, as if it was the end of a normal working day? Or simply walk out of the gates there and then? Eventually Garfield climbed onto the table, and explained to them that the working class was not a rabble: he designated lines of communication for the strike, and the factory was closed down in an orderly fashion.

The union waited for management to contact them. After some days they hadn't heard a word, so the branch secretary made a tentative phone call, to be told that the chairman had nothing to say until the workforce was back at work.

'Of course he's not going to give in immediately,' the Wire declared. 'We've got him by the short and curlies, but it'll take time to squeeze them.'

After a week the two sides were still standing off.

'The Government's behind it,' the Wire decided. 'They've struck a fucking deal: they want him to break the union here in return for Government contracts when it's over. Just you wait and see.'

'Some people can't afford to wait and see,' Garfield pointed out. They'd been informed by their National Executive that the strike, being unofficial, couldn't be subsidized from central coffers. Even on half wages the local branch could only afford three weeks' strike pay for the workforce. And that would clean them out.

'People have got kids to feed, mortgages to pay,' Garfield worried.

'They shouldn't have gulped the carrot and bought their council houses!' the Wire railed. 'Next thing you'll be telling me they're having to cash in their stocks and shares.'

Garfield pondered a moment, as was his habit. 'That's true,' he said.

Garfield wrestled with his conscience – as well as his brain – for a further week of stalemate, during which time worrying rumours circulated among the striking workers: an entirely new work-force was being recruited at that very moment in the mining villages of Yorkshire; the army was about to be brought in to keep the machines rolling; Charles Freeman was unavailable for discussion because he wasn't even there, he'd already sold the factory to the Japanese.

That Sunday after church Garfield made his way to the house on the hill. His niece, Laura, opened the back door.

'Get me to Charles' study without being seen, girl,' Garfield requested. 'Tell Charles I'm there. And Laura,' he added, 'don't tell anyone you saw me. I mean *anyone*.'

'Garfield!' Charles cried, after he'd locked the door behind him. 'Sit down. Have a sherry!' It was as if the last time they'd seen each other was at the annual works social and the only gap in between was a day lost to a hangover. Fortunately Garfield had expected nothing different. Charles sat down and Garfield slowly and pedantically enumerated a list of proposals that he believed could get them out of the current impasse.

Unlike Garfield, Charles rarely pondered. 'Excellent!' he responded. 'I'm with you. Now let's sort out how to put these into practice in the proper manner. Otherwise, old man, you'll really be in the shit.'

At five to one they'd finalized their plan, and it was time for Charles to attend the customary family Sunday lunch. At the door of the study Garfield took Charles' hand and shook it.

'You know, Charles,' he said, 'I always knew you were a reasonable man. I told them you and I could reason things out.'

'I know you did,' Charles told him cheerfully. 'We had a microphone in the toilets.'

Garfield paled.

'I'm only joking, old man.' Charles laughed. 'I'm just quite sure that you did. I said much the same thing about you.'

'You know,' Garfield said, recovering his dignity, 'it means a lot to me to bring this business to an end. A great deal. Thank you, Charles.'

'Don't thank me,' Charles declared. 'Thank yourself, if anyone. They're your ideas, and every one of them makes sound financial sense. It's a shame, Garfield,' he observed. 'You should have been in management. You've got an acute grasp of economic reality, which is rare among my so-called executives. We could have done good things together.'

'I hope we did already,' Garfield replied.

On Monday morning the union representatives were politely invited to a meeting at which Rupert Sproat reiterated the company's proposals and the Wire outlined the union's position.

'To business, gentlemen,' Charles declared, and for the next half an hour, to the silent astonishment of those who witnessed it, he and Garfield set about each other in a furious barrage of argument and counter-argument, bargain and counter-bargain, demand and concession and compromise, a verbal ping-pong in which neither appeared to draw breath, never mind leave a moment's pause for interruption from anyone else.

Within an hour they'd concluded the negotiation. While a mutually agreed wording was drawn up, Garfield's pre-arranged lines of communication sent word to the workforce to meet at the factory gates at three o'clock that afternoon: men and women were contacted, via spreadeagling word of mouth, and brought in from fishing on the river, decorating the kids' bedroom, nursing half a pint through the pub lunch hour, gardening, dozing on the settee, taking jewellery to the recently opened pawn shop on Factory Road, and other activities to which they'd resorted in those days of enforced idleness.

The Wire told the crowd it was a stitch-up and a sell-out and advised them to stay out until all their demands were met, every last one, which this pathetic compromise proved was bound to be soon forthcoming because the management were clearly losing their nerve.

'Let future generations say: *this* is where the workers made their stand,' he shouted, 'and *this* is where the capitalist exploiters began their final capitulation.'

Then Garfield read out the list of proposals – pausing before each one, as if he were pondering them anew – and then, by a greater majority than had voted to go out on strike, the workforce voted to go back to work. All but a very few of them could see that Garfield Roberts – in a meeting whose drama was soon known to all – had attained undreamed-of concessions from the man-in-charge.

They went gladly back to work, accepting without qualms the £500 in cash per person prepared to sign a special no-strike agreement; the new productivity bonuses that would soon make up for the cuts in basic pay; the voluntary redundancies on offer to men over fifty; the privatization of the company-subsidized canteen; the exchange of overtime rates for annual, profit-related pay-outs; an extra day's holiday per person per year; the abolition of company cars for executives, who only left them in the car park all day as a sort of provocation (Charles' Rover being, as everyone knew, his own); and the enforced redundancy of those who'd been working there less than six months and thus hadn't completed their trial period of employment, a clause that had long been in everyone's contract but until then had been generally regarded as a formality.

The few who failed to appreciate Garfield Roberts' concessions were the machinists being retrained in computer skills: their change of job description had necessitated new contracts, and now they fell into the category of those made redundant because of not having fulfilled their trial period. It was one point on which Charles had proved inflexible, because no one could possibly convince him that it made sense to employ men on their old wages of a skilled machinist (made even higher by incremental bonuses reflecting their years of employment) tapping away at a computer keyboard when with a week's training young female part-timers could do the same job more efficiently.

At first everyone – both those back at work and those let go – accepted the reality of the situation, and the works resumed production with a new mood of determined optimism. There were so many workers made redundant here and there – apprentices at one end and men taking early retirement at the other, and various people in different departments (in their present jobs less than six months) in between – that it was more than a week after they'd collected their cards that it became clear one group was different.

Ten of the transferred machinists – now redundant computer operators – had been working for more than five years. The other twenty or so had accepted their lot, joined the dole queue and looked for other jobs. But the ten, enraged at their situation, came back to the union.

'All right, Mr Wonderman,' the Wire asked Garfield, 'what do you propose we do about these comrades? I say we demand their reinstatement with the threat of a one-day stoppage in the first instance, and go on from there.'

Garfield thought about it. 'We won't do anything, Steven,' he decided at length. 'We've signed an agreement and now we're going to honour it.'

'You've got to be kidding!' the Wire exclaimed. 'They've been shafted. The trade-union movement is under no obligation to honour a dishonourable deal. No way.'

Garfield remained calm. 'We've reached agreement with the management, Steven. Our members voted for it. The dispute is over. That's that. We could have a whip-round for these men,' he suggested; 'we can organize a fund-raising event to help them get started again. But we cannot contemplate further industrial action on their behalf. It's out of the question.'

The Wire stood up. 'I don't know what you and that bastard have cooked up together, but it's a stitch-up, uncle. Those poor fuckers are the scapegoats of your pact with the devil. I'm having no part of it,' the Wire proclaimed. He gathered up his things, went off to empty his locker, and walked out of the gates at eleven o'clock in the morning.

The next day the Wire was back, with the ten redundant ex-machinists. They stood outside the gates, a small, unofficial picket line, trying to persuade people arriving for work – by car and bicycle or on foot – to turn back.

That picket was the visible legacy of the brief strike and the deal that ended it. And it didn't go away. Every day through the autumn of 1985 and into the winter the men camped outside the gates. They brought folding chairs and a brazier to keep warm on chilly days, unrolled banners, and put up a big sign beside the road saying, 'HONK IF YOU SUPPORT US,' to passing motorists.

The Freeman Ten, as they came to be known, were featured in the local and national media. Pat, the activist in James' bedsit, made a campaign video that was shown around the country at fund-raising meetings. Supporters shook buckets in the town centre. The Ten caused a great deal of embarrassment: to the trade union, which had

295

to explain why it refused to recognize the dispute; and to erstwhile colleagues who shuffled into work with their heads down, trying to ignore the shouts of 'Scab', 'Blackleg' and 'Lackey' that besieged them. Garfield always cycled to work: he'd done the right thing, he was sure of that. He kept his head up as he cycled through the gates; but he kept his gaze straight ahead because he was unable to look the Wire in the eye. Garfield's conscience was clear but his ideals were broken.

The only man not at all embarrassed was Charles Freeman. It was a shame about these men, he told the media, but his job was to make the company more efficient and productive. With luck as soon as the recession was over he'd expand, and could even hire them back. But in the meantime, the agreement he'd reached with the official trade-union representatives – and which that troublemaking Trotskyist shouting the most loudly outside had been a signatory to – was vindicated.

It was a time of guilty optimism for the many and acrimony for the few, whose daughters and nieces had indeed taken part-time jobs in their place because someone had to pay the bills. Not only acrimony but also confusion. Picketing men's daughters passed them on the picket line, while some working men's wives joined the verbal barricade on principle, to yell, 'Scab,' at their own husbands. In addition to embarrassment there was private bitterness and tears. But that was all there was.

Alice suffered from morning sickness for two months, having conceived on her honeymoon 'in the classical manner', as Harry put it, delighted. Their first child was born in April 1985; her name was Amy Padma.

It would be the same with their next two, Sam and Tom (who were also Taureans, Alice's fecundity turning out to be of a clockwork nature). Perhaps their English names were some kind of trade-off: Alice had initially taken six months' maternity leave but when it was over she decided not to return to teaching, and gave up her career without regret. At the same time, following her final pay-cheque, she closed her own bank account and Harry's became a joint one; she didn't do more than her fair share of household chores, it's true, but then neither did Harry, because they employed a cleaning lady five mornings a week; and she didn't have to do any cooking, either, because there was already a cook in the house, Laura, and it would have been unthinkable not to eat all together. The only change was that once a week, on Saturday evenings, Harry made an Indian meal for everyone.

In fact Alice, of her own accord, tore up their verbal contract; she gave up all her conditions of marriage to Harry Singh, including the last; when she filled in Amy's baptismal certificate she gave her his name – Amy Singh – and from then on used it for herself as well as her children.

'I just want you to explain to me, that's all,' Natalie demanded. 'Just explain why it's not yet another capitulation.'

'It's no big deal, Nat,' Alice assured her. 'It's simply avoiding a lot of hassle, for me *and* for them.'

Natalie was unconvinced. 'I suppose it's hormonal,' she said glumly to herself.

'No, it's not, Auntie Nat,' Alice replied, 'it's logical. Anyway, what do you want to get worked up about the name Freeman for? It's only my father's name, after all. And his father's before him.'

'I suppose so,' Natalie conceded. 'Except we've got to start *some*where, Alice,' she rallied. 'And I wish you wouldn't call me Auntie. I hate that.'

'But you are, silly,' Alice assured her.

It was no wonder everyone wanted to eat Laura's food. She was a far better cook than Edna had ever been, with a curiosity of mind and palate and an eagerness to experiment. She took off on foreign holidays alone in search of new gastronomic experiences and came home with ingredients and recipes, and the kitchen was turned into a culinary laboratory.

She served braised skate wings that had so many bones in them they took three hours to eat, and a coffee ice-cream so concentrated that everyone left the table twitching. She produced an exquisite meal of French *nouvelle cuisine* on large white plates, with five tiny portions on each: Alice fetched a magnifying glass with which to locate them, which Laura didn't seem to find very funny, so they didn't tell her that afterwards Charles gathered the others together and went off in his Rover to get some fish and chips on Factory Road.

Another time Laura tried stuffing mushrooms: after two and a half hours she realized she was losing the will to live, threw them away and made a quick pesto in the liquidizer instead, using nothing more than olive oil, parmesan, basil, garlic and salt, that, to her chagrin, became her most requested dish for some months.

It was a time of experimentation, and the kitchen came to resemble

Alice's bedroom when she'd been a schoolgirl chemist. After a trip to Barcelona Laura made a gazpacho soup that was so delicious people didn't notice how much garlic was in it until after they'd finished, whereupon they watched each other levitate an inch or two from their seats. The next day, on Judith's advice, Charles cancelled his meetings. Harry attended *his* meetings, but only by virtue of chewing a mouthful of cardamom seeds throughout the day.

He wasn't so fortunate, however, the time Laura entered his territory with a meal as might have been eaten by the maharajah of Madras. She warned them about the lime pickle, but Harry said:

'Nonsense, Laura, I grew up on this food, don't forget, I'm used to it,' as he swallowed a few cheerful spoonfuls just to show off, smiling smugly. The next moment he went rigid, stared at a spot a foot from his nose and clutched the table, frozen except that he was weeping profusely, tears pouring down his cheeks. Then he sprang to life, grabbing everybody's glass of water and emptying them down his throat, followed by the water jug too. He gasped with breathless relief.

'Wow, Laura, that's pretty hot stuff,' Harry sighed. 'It's lucky I'm used . . .' Harry was unable to finish his sentence, as he realized that drinking water had only made things worse. He broke out in the sweat of some tropical fever, clutched his throat, and promptly ran outside. Everybody else looked at each other and then ran after him, just in time to see Harry perform a perfect belly-flop into the garden pond.

Notwithstanding the occasional hiccups of her experiments, Laura had inherited her mother's ability to provide for whoever turned up at the table, and the house on the hill was filling up again. As well as Alice and Harry and the family they were beginning, Charles invited colleagues and competitors to dinner for the first time since Mary's death, along with Judith; Simon brought back people from his meditation class to try out Laura's latest dish; Natalie brought home her girlfriends; and Robert was in the house more now than he'd been since childhood.

Laura's relationship with Robert was something everyone knew about but skirted around like a guilty secret. Whether it was a legacy of Laura's abortion and beating over ten years earlier or simply a habit they'd locked into was hard to tell, but Laura was as strangely furtive as Robert was predictably so, as if she were denying to the world a desire she'd rather have denied herself, but was unable to. They never went out in public together and kept clearly apart at social gatherings.

But everyone knew that in the middle of the night, when the house was silent, Robert slipped down the dark back stairs. It was the way they both seemed to want it.

In his spare time James took off around town with his camera. Taking photographs for a living hadn't jaded his appetite. Far from it. He felt naked on the streets without his camera, and what's more whenever he lacked the means to capture them, he always saw brilliant images, and kicked himself.

James saw the purpose of such activity as twofold: whether his photos ended up in the newspaper or in the exhibition he was beginning to plan towards, he was producing a chronicle of the life of the town and its people; but it was also a personal exercise, his own way of trying to make sense of the world and his place in it. The first was a worthy enterprise, the second was doomed to failure: how could he fill the hollowness inside him by taking pictures of other people? The fact was James was looking for clues. No one else was hollow like him, that was obvious. He had only to look at other people – any of them, big or small, young or old – and he could see they had substance. They moved, acted, spoke, even breathed with purpose. And at some level James hoped that he would capture in his photos the secret of their sense of purpose, their solidity, their right to fill their allotted space on this earth. Maybe that very search, he realized, that may never be fulfilled, was *his* purpose.

And so James tracked the streets of the town. In the early morning he snapped the eccentric street-cleaners in their orange overalls and then the crowd walking, running, cycling and driving over South Bridge to work. He came to know the people of the streets: police and traffic wardens, including the fearsome witch who bawled out visitors dumb enough to drive into the pedestrianized High Street; the street hawkers who filled the air with the aroma of flowers and coffee and, in winter, roast chestnuts; the transitory buskers and the permanent one, who wheeled a barrel organ into the town centre: he wound a handle and clockwork figures jerked unconvincingly to a monotonous jingle that irritated shop assistants and delighted children.

James came to recognize the madmen who were sane enough to travel the same streets as he – and who, unlike James, appeared to have too *much* purpose in their lives. He gave them names: the Walker, a dark-skinned man with a black beard and a thick duffel coat in all weathers, whom James saw all over town striding along with a wodge of old newspapers under his arm, as if heading for the nearest recycling skip in a one-man environmental crusade. There was Spider Woman, an anorexic transvestite; and Mother, who pushed an empty pram along with an expression on the verge of tears that never came; and Jock, who stood motionless in full tartan outside Marks and Spencer. When the hour chimed on St Andrew's church clock he broke into a few steps of a Scottish reel, before reassuming his ghostly, shop-dummy stance.

James photographed them, in their freedom and loneliness.

When James dropped into the cinema after one of his sessions on the streets Zoe could always tell, from the look in his eyes. They were strangely vacant − as if the emptiness he'd tried to fill, through his eyes, had instead become visible through them.

'You'll wear your eyes out, sweetheart,' she told him. 'Your eyes will be worn out from looking,' she warned.

'I took a brilliant one just now,' he told her. 'Some guys were having a kickabout after work in the park, two teams, right? Eight or nine a side. But they all had different-coloured tops on, every single one, Zoe. I mean, it looked utterly bewildering, complete chaos. But *they* knew who was on their side, see, it's a kind of magic the brain performs. It took a full roll but I think I captured it.'

'Captured what?'

'*That.* What I just said. The order within the chaos, within the players' minds. A pattern. I *think* I got it.'

'Good,' Zoe said. 'Well done, kiddo.'

'Yeah, well, I better get going. Got to get some more while it's still light and there's people out. Thanks for the tea, Zoe. See you.'

'See you, sweetheart,' she called after his departing back. She watched him lurch doggedly along the street. 'Why don't you open your eyes?' she whispered.

The streets of the town were filling up with more than commuters and shoppers, which might have pleased James except that it was with people who should have been indoors: they weren't outside of their own choice. Onto the streets in those days came winos and beggars, homeless children, deranged schizophrenics yelling inexplicable curses, travellers forced off the road sleeping with their dogs in shop doorways. It was a strange period in the town: people had their clothes stolen off washing-lines and the police announced the arrest of shadowy, Fagin-like figures who ran gangs of ten-year-old pickpockets and bicycle thieves.

Jock, Spider Woman and the others found themselves jostling for space on the pavements with unemployed youths drinking cans of lager and burping belligerently at strangers; with evangelizing guerrillas from the Jesus Army, carrying a symbol not of the cross or the lamb but rather a sword; with Middle Eastern exiles persuading passers-by to look at Polaroids of torture victims and donate money to the cause of their release.

Campaigners, beggars, bums, they all saw James coming; even the most derelict and destitute could pick him out in a crowd from a distance, a soft touch. He didn't mind. He was protected by his camera: he had a bargain to strike; he gave money in exchange for a photograph, and they entered his chronicle of the town in his time.

There were two people James saw often, whose photograph he *didn't* take. They were an odd couple: a young black boy and a stocky white woman with white hair. The boy walked on crutches, fast, gazing straight ahead like a sprinter. The woman was fit, though, and kept up with him with no apparent difficulty, with equal single-mindedness. James saw them often, striding up or down Stratford Road. The odd thing was that whether the weather was blazing hot or freezing cold the boy always wore the same clothes: trainers, a pair of shorts and a bicycle helmet on his head, with his powerful torso bared to the elements.

This constitutional was clearly a physical therapy for the boy, although it *looked* rather more like punishment, like the dour, unsmiling woman was frogmarching him along the pavement; if he slowed down she might slap his bare back or legs; as if it were punishment, indeed, for his disability.

Each time James saw them he wanted to get off his bike and ask what their story was, and to take a photograph of them. He never did. He couldn't quite bring himself to interrupt their determined progress. And he thought, when he was honest with himself, that to request a snapshot of them would be an affront to their hermetic dignity.

And that was strange, he realized: he was a photographer, and the people on the streets of his town he most wanted to photograph he sensed he would somehow diminish by doing so.

James met Sonia in the nightclub – their eyes met on the dance-floor – and whenever they went dancing again, which would be often, he wondered whether the human being who first thought of moving their body to music had somehow had Sonia in mind as some distant ideal. She was tall and slim, dressed in a red sequinned dress, and she danced all evening with the energy of an aerobics instructor and the sinuous grace of a belly dancer. Sonia's only regret in life, she would tell James later, was that she wasn't a black back-up singer for Diana Ross or James Brown.

James spent much of that first evening glancing in her direction and then closing his eyes. His dancing was probably more askew than ever; but it couldn't have been *too* awful because some of the times that he did open his eyes he saw hers looking back; and they exchanged brief smiles.

Sonia was with a group of friends, one of whom James knew, and he accepted their invitation to leave with them – early for James, around midnight – and go back to Sonia's house for coffee.

There were half a dozen of them, and when they went into Sonia's house she let a teenage girl out, and ushered them into the sitting-room. It was a large, airy room with sanded floorboards and stripped-pine doors, and Habitat furniture that looked as if it had been arranged by a window-dresser.

James left the others in the sitting-room and went through to the kitchen, where Sonia was making coffee.

'You want a hand?' James asked.

'I don't think so,' Sonia replied. 'Well, you can reach that bottle of Bailey's down.'

'I've been wondering,' James said, 'whether we've met before.'

'I don't think so,' she said. 'Where? In court?'

'No, no. I wasn't there. I've got an alibi. Why, are you a judge?'

'Of what?' Sonia asked. She had X-ray eyes that appeared to assess his body under his clothes.

'Coffee,' he said. 'What is it? Smells good.'

'Viennese. With figs.' Sonia made a jug, and put it on a tray with half a dozen mugs.

'It's a nice place, this,' James said. 'So close to the centre of town. A couple of minutes from the railway station.'

'It does us OK,' she told him.

'Us?'

'I've got two kids. The three of us.'

'Are you joking? It's so neat in there,' James said, gesturing towards the sitting-room. 'No toys or anything.'

'They know if they leave anything downstairs I'll throw it in the dustbin. So they don't. They've got their den.'

On the crowded dance-floor James had opened his eyes while dancing and sought her out. Here in the small kitchen, with just the two of them – her friends' chatter next door both close and far away – he fought equally hard *not* to look at her. In the bright unpleasant glare of strip-lighting, James could feel his body being pulled towards her.

'You know something?' he asked.

'What?' she replied.

'I'd like to kiss you,' he said.

'I was thinking the same thing,' she replied, and they moved together. Their lips met, and then he felt her tongue in his mouth. He closed his eyes, and the glare of the strip-lights was imprinted on the inside of his eyelids.

'Where's that coffee?' came a voice from next door.

'Shush! You'll wake her children,' came another fast on its heels.

In the kitchen Sonia broke off their embrace. 'Better go through,' she told him.

James was the first to leave, an hour later, because none of Sonia's friends showed any signs of shifting; he didn't want to hang on until he was exhausted. She saw him to the door and they kissed again in the hallway; and they swapped phone numbers and promised to call.

James came round a few days later with a bottle of wine after Sonia's children had gone to bed. They sank in her sofa and smooched, and drank glasses of red wine, and told each other who they were. Sonia and her husband had split up four years earlier.

'We didn't love each other,' she explained. 'I realized I didn't need him, so we divorced. It was pretty clean-cut. The boys see him at weekends.'

On their second date she told him: 'Listen. I don't promise anything, OK? I don't want to get involved. You understand?'

'Yes,' James said; 'I understand.'

Sonia was a solicitor. She told him more about the complexities of the office politics than cases in which she was involved, which he assumed was due to professional discretion.

At first James cycled over to Sonia's house most evenings around nine, straight from the darkroom or some event he was covering. She made love with an eagerness that took James' breath away, and waited impatiently for him to recover sufficiently to start again, until he discovered what she wanted, so that their love-making could be conducted in unison.

Sonia had long, black, tumbling hair that she usually wore stacked up on the top of her head, with odd strands falling down around her face: she was elegant, with a glimmer of dishevelment. She had delicate features and deep-set eyes that when she was tired made her look exhausted; she was one of those people, though, for whom a few hours' sleep were enough to refresh her. And she had a long thin scar up the side of her torso.

'Is that from a Caesarean?' James asked her.

When she'd recovered from laughing Sonia explained that it was a childhood operation for a defective kidney, when she was thirteen: the same age as James when he had his operation. Her scar wasn't unattractive, which made his own feel less conspicuous.

The bearing of children had left no lasting impression on Sonia's body. James wondered whether they'd come out of her at all; maybe they were secretly adopted. She had a flat stomach and small breasts, and was fitter than he was; she went dancing at weekends and to twice-weekly aerobics classes; from which she came straight home without getting showered or changed, to allow James the pleasure of divesting her of her sweat-soaked leotard.

At first James left early the next morning, before her sons had woken. But that meant really early: David, the younger one, never slept later than seven. James let himself out of the front door, disturbing a flock of ducks by the canal across the road, who waddled around squabbling like indignant gossips: 'Look, look! There he is! The bugger's sneaking out! Quack, quack!'

Then David woke much earlier one morning and came crawling into his mother's bed. James was too sleepy to feel embarrassed and Sonia didn't seem to mind, and after that it was just plain silly to try to avoid the children. He stayed and breakfasted with them and they all left the house together, James on his bicycle, Sonia in her Peugeot to drop the boys off at school on her way to work.

Sonia worked long and irregular hours, and afterwards she went to drinks parties and dinners to which she took James; she had a tendency to slip off her shoe and fondle his groin under the table, and to drag him into strange kitchens for brief, deep kisses. He felt out of place, but she showed no interest in meeting his bohemian friends, or going to films or exhibitions. Her children were looked after by a child-minder after school and a baby-sitter in the evenings. The weekends they spent with their father and his new wife.

'They must have lots of semi-maternal relationships,' James ventured. *He* felt more like a big brother to them than a substitute father, the idea of which made him uncomfortable.

'I know, it's good, isn't it?' Sonia replied. 'They won't be too dependent on their mother as they grow up. Boys shouldn't be. You're quite right.'

'I wasn't exactly saying—'

'Hey, James, they'll be with their father tomorrow night. Let's go dancing.'

'Yeh, let's do that.'

James felt guilty for distracting the boys' mother. It was clear, though, that they adored her, with a particular adoration that James recognized.

It was hard not to be selfish. Sonia derided James' dress sense, and forced him to buy new clothes. She helped him choose a double-breasted suit, as well as white shirts, a silk tie and a pair of brogues. To James' surprise not only did they not bankrupt him, they made him feel more masculine, and he walked with his shoulders out and back straight after a lifetime of stooping modesty.

Sonia bought him her favourite aftershave, and that Saturday took him to her own hairdresser. When he saw her smiling at him in the mirror he felt proud that such a gorgeous woman was with him, and decided that they weren't such an odd couple, after all. He was surprised to find how easily he slipped deeper into their relationship. The rest of his life, which had always been busy, contracted here, opened up there, as he spent more and more time with Sonia. He saw less of other people, lost contact with acquaintances and stopped doing things he used to do alone. Including taking photos. James hoped it was just a coincidence that he'd decided he had enough photographs he was happy with to try to mount an exhibition.

James stayed behind in the newspaper at night in the darkroom, making large prints from his own negatives; none from his press work. He'd decided on that. That was his job; this was his art. These were the pictures he'd taken in his own time, on the streets, in parks and clubs, even at friends' and relatives' weddings.

Those last he enjoyed most. Each time he studied the contact sheets, scrutinized negatives on the light-box, he chuckled to himself. With this exhibition he would bridge the gap between his colleagues on the paper and his photographer friends; he'd prove to each camp that it was possible to be in both. But what made him laugh was that his best photographs were ones taken at weddings. And if there was one thing the press and artistic photographers had in common it was a disdain for wedding photographers.

None of his serious friends – not Karel nor Terry nor Celia – made any kind of a living from their work. They took odd-jobs, manual work – 'Like being back bloody home, innit?' said Karel – and signed on. The one alternative, easy way of making money would have been to cover weddings. They'd only have to do one every Saturday to earn a basic wage and it could hardly be easier work.

'You could do it with your eyes closed,' James told them.

None of them, however, would dream of doing so. They considered the possibility but only in jest, in order to have a good laugh dismissing it, a running joke that was perpetually funny.

'Karel'd have to get himself a decent suit,' Celia pointed out.

'I've got a bloody suit!' Karel complained.

The thing was, it was a point of principle, and of pride. It wasn't like advertising, which would be selling your soul (and which they didn't laugh about but became angry). It was more the fact that they'd never be taken seriously again, by other people or indeed themselves.

Which was why James chuckled to himself now in the newspaper darkroom, because he couldn't wait to see their faces when they came to the exhibition he would soon have. Not that they were orthodox wedding photographs, groups of bride and groom and bride's father and mother and the rest. When he was asked to photograph friends' and acquaintances' weddings James always told them he would, gladly, but that they'd have to hire an official photographer too to get the compulsory groupings: he would take others, candid black-and-white snaps of them and their guests, the best of which he'd later put in an album and give them as a wedding present. The newly-weds would show those albums off to their friends, who invited James to *their* weddings. During the course of his twenties he'd been to over a hundred. It was his secret.

He didn't know why, but James was always in the mood at weddings. Just like the first time he was taken to one, Uncle Jack and Aunt Clare's, as an eight-year-old boy and his mother had bought him a camera because she was worried he'd fidget through the service, he was always affected by the occasion. He responded to the emotion inherent, if not on open display, within the formal setting. What he didn't know was why he slipped into the mode of taking photographs.

James sometimes asked himself whether he didn't take photographs to keep the world away. Every time he clicked that shutter he recorded people at a particular distance from him. If they came too close they went out of focus; he lost focus, the world came crowding in on him and he could feel himself losing definition. Sometimes taking photographs he forgot himself in a state of intense concentration and was aware only of what he saw: he became a pair of eyes – one eye, looking through the viewfinder – and the rest of him was lost to himself, as well as invisible to other people. When that happened (which was generally sporadic and unpredictable) he became attuned to gesture, stance, composition of people before him that (he hoped) betrayed in an instantaneous image some truth of their being.

And at weddings James entered that state and remained in it, an eye circling scenes, infiltrating groups, invisible, clicking the shutter and moving on.

Afterwards, exhausted, he came back to himself as if out of a trance, and found he was clutching a dozen rolls of film.

In October James took Sonia and her boys to his Aunt Margaret's farm to pick apples. He hadn't seen Margaret for years; he knew that since her partner Sarah had died five years ago she'd become reclusive (she'd long since stopped hiring farm-girls and let the dairy herd dwindle, as well as most of the other animals). Her sister Clare lived on the neighbouring farm and kept an eye on her but she was a tough old boot, as Sarah had often called her, content now with solitude and scornful of anyone's pity.

James wanted to show Sonia a part of his past life, and it was a good idea to let the boys run wild in a country field, outside the town in the valley. So he rang Margaret to propose a visit.

'What did you say!?' she shouted down the line, as if he were still whispering. 'Speak up! What did you say your name was?!'

'It's James,' he told her, 'your nephew, Aunt Margaret.'

'James!' she shouted. 'Of course it is! How's school, young man?'

The yard they drove into was just as scruffy as it always was, and although there were no bad-tempered geese to greet them there was a sheepdog dozing in the porch, and it stood wagging its tail in meek welcome. Margaret, too, as she stepped outside, looked unchanged. She even seemed to be wearing the same old cords and buttonless jacket, and she looked as sturdy and ruddy-cheeked as ever. Only her wiry hair had become the colour of mist.

Margaret came towards them. She took in Sonia and David with a glance but scrutinized John a moment longer, then James, then John again, before appearing to come to a decision: she reached her hand towards James.

'How are you, young man?' She clasped his hands. 'How nice to see you. Come on in. I've got some tea brewing.'

As he stepped through from the hallway into the big kitchen James' heart sank. The room had been transformed. Sarah's clean domestic scene was now a squalid mess of encrusted utensils, mouldering food, dirty clothes, dust and soot. The aromas he remembered of baking and roasting and fresh herbs had been replaced by a stale, crusty stink. James felt ashamed for his aunt, especially since she appeared unaware of the degradation and was fussing about with filthy mugs at the greasy sink. James realized that there was no way in the world Sonia would let a single morsel of anything in this room pass her sons' lips.

'Actually, Margaret,' James said, 'we've just had tea. Can we go outside? We've been cooped up in the car.'

'Good idea,' she replied. 'Let these lads run around, eh?' she said, slapping John on the back. As they left the room James glanced out at Sarah's old kitchen garden at the back of the house. The manicured lawn grew thick and coarse and the vegetable patch was overgrown with weeds, except for a line of blackcurrant bushes that looked as if they'd been capably pruned that spring and not neglected for the past five years.

The orchard had been neglected for much longer. When James had gone out to the farm fifteen years before they still picked apples worth sending to a local chutney factory, but that activity, too, had long since ceased. Walking towards the orchard, James took in the empty pastures, broken fences, eerie silence. It struck him that the old sheepdog in the porch was the only animal left on the farm – apart, no doubt, from rabbits and rats. At that moment Margaret stopped and put a hand on his arm.

'The other morning,' she said, pointing towards the stream beyond what had been the cow pasture, 'I saw soldiers coming out of the fog.' She took her hand off his arm. 'Down there in the valley,' she added, and set off again, into the orchard.

They spent two hours picking small, wrinkled apples that were quite inedible. It was a complete waste of time but James didn't want to hurt Margaret's feelings by abandoning the activity, and the boys were enjoying themselves climbing among the twisted, brittle branches. James exchanged glances with Sonia, hoping she understood, and played through the sad charade.

They carried carrier bags full of apples back to the car. Saying goodbye, Margaret said: 'Do come again, young man. Bring a loaf of bread next time, would you? I always seem to be out of bread and you can't buy flour for love nor money these days, you know.' Then she clapped the boys on their backs and they got into the car. James sat in the passenger seat and wound the window down.

'Goodbye, Margaret,' he said. He couldn't think of anything else to say.

'You know, James,' she told him. 'That was a very nice summer. You were here a lot, weren't you? Sarah was very fond of you. I think it was our favourite summer.' Then she stepped back, and waved them away.

'My God!' said Sonia. 'What a cornflake! It's a good thing I haven't got too attached before meeting your family.' She shook her head. 'What a fruitbat.' Only then did she glance at James.

'Oh, I'm sorry,' she said, 'I didn't mean it.' She took a hand off the wheel and tugged in one of her jean pockets, pulled out some crumpled tissue and passed it to him. James blew his nose. The boys in the back seat stared at him.

'She used to be so strong, she was a one-off, you know?' he said.

'What a shame,' Sonia said.

'Yeh. Well, I'll call Clare, her sister, when we get back. Although I suppose she is coping on her own.'

'Sure she is,' Sonia agreed. 'She's fine.'

That winter James spent so much time with Sonia he wondered whether he shouldn't pay rent to her instead of his landlady. In December he emptied the last jar of coffee in the bedsit and pulled plugs from the mains.

'Why don't you move in for good?' Sonia asked him.

'No,' James demurred. 'I don't want to feel like I'm edging you into something. I know you don't want to make a commitment.'

'Me neither,' she said. 'I mean, I don't. Still, the boys really like you.'

'I like them.'

'And anyway, if you're here I can keep an eye on you, right?' she whispered, fondling his crotch. 'And keep my eyes off other men.'

The weather turned cold right after that Christmas of 1985 and when they weren't invited to dinner somewhere they ate out at restaurants around town, compiling a Michelin star system of their own devising. For the first time in James' life he began to relax and let go of the twin conditions of existence he thought were in-escapable: loneliness and freedom.

Afterwards, weighed down with food and drowsy with wine, they went back to Sonia's airy house and made love slowly, into the early hours; sometimes neither of them came, and neither were sure whether it was because they wished to prolong the pleasure for the other or whether greater passion was drifting beyond them.

'You make me irresponsible,' she told him.

'I do?' he asked.

'Too much sex. Not enough sleep,' she yawned. 'And too much *wine*,' she added. 'I can't concentrate on my cases. I nod off after lunch. And then I think of you instead of the brief I'm meant to be writing. And *then* suddenly it's time to leave. I told you I'd be offered the partnership, but it's not actually a formality.'

'I'm sorry,' James said.

'We should go easy on the wine,' she told him.

The picket line at the gates of the factory struggled on through the winter. The brazier was lit every day, fuelled by coal donated by an ex-mining village in Wales. The picketing men no longer yelled, 'Scab', at those passing them; sometimes ex-colleagues dropped off sausages to roast in the flames on their way into work. Motorists still honked their horns, but a note of derision seemed to have entered the sound. James had got into the habit of stopping whenever he passed and taking a quick photograph, which he handed over to Roger back at the office: every now and then, when they had a space to fill, they put it in the paper. The last one appeared in February. By the end of that month the Freeman Ten were down to seven; it was clear that this was a lost cause.

They made their last day a Wednesday in the middle of March, and took away their banners, brazier and foldaway chairs, exchanging pathetic handshakes of solidarity in defeat. The next day, however, the Wire turned up on his own, just to show the world that *he* wasn't beaten: there was going to be no offer of either job or compensation but that, he wished to show, was no longer the point. You had to show defiance even when you'd lost.

For the first time in six months Garfield Roberts stopped his bicycle; for six months he'd seen the Wire as a blur at the side of his vision, and heard his rasping voice: 'Blackleg!'

Now Garfield stopped and looked the young man in the eye. The Wire looked back at him: the old colleagues become adversaries.

310

Perhaps in truth, Garfield considered, they were always adversaries; perhaps, thought the Wire on the other hand, they were still colleagues. He suddenly grinned.

'Well, uncle,' the Wire said, 'you've always come to work on that rusty old bicycle, I'll give you that. You never sneaked in, like some of them.'

Garfield pondered. 'You're a good man, Steven,' he said at length. 'What do you plan to do now that it's over?'

'Over?' the Wire exclaimed. 'You've got to be kidding.'

Garfield paled.

'Nothing's over, uncle. Have you not heard about this new Community Charge to replace the rates? This time they're really taking the piss: it's a return to a poll tax. They've smashed a union but they'll never break the working class. You wait and see.'

Charles, meanwhile, was thriving. The strike and its conclusion, and even the picket line outside his factory gates, seemed to have given him renewed vigour. Those who'd worked for the company all their lives said it was like the old days: the man-in-charge was once more a rampaging elephant. Evidence of his idiosyncratic behaviour abounded: on the last day before the privatization of all catering facilities secretaries from the typing pool had to push the tea-trolleys around the factory floor in their skirts and heels, because the boss had swept the four retiring tea-ladies into his Rover and taken them off to the seaside for the day.

A couple of weeks later Charles went to London for some meeting accompanied by two of his managers. One of them – David Canning, the young head of sales – disagreed with the boss about something (no one knew what, every account differed) and Charles ordered his chauffeur to pull over to the hard shoulder. Charles not only fired David Canning on the spot, he made him get out of the car at the side of the M1 and make his own way home.

It was true, Charles was reinvigorated. He'd long since made his fortune, and then spent twenty years doing little more than administer it. Now he had other plans. Having discovered the purity of making money as a single, simple priority, the complexities of life fell away and Charles' bombastic blood flowed freely through his veins; the zeal of a convert gave him the courage to trust his gut instincts. He began to buy up small rival companies in order to close them down. His managers told him it made no financial sense and he browbeat them into acceptance by claiming that it was time to diversify, he was killing two birds with one stone, exterminating competition and entering the property market in one fell swoop. Or else he bought strategic stakes in ailing companies that were in the midst of hostile takeover bids. Charles presented himself as an impromptu arbitrageur, a white knight; only to then offer his shares to both sides, encouraging them to bid against each other, to his profit.

Charles had never given a damn what people thought of him.

'Father? He doesn't give a flying fuck, darling,' Simon told Natalie admiringly.

'Sticks and stones, Simon,' Charles told his eldest son. 'Weak men's bones are broken by other men's tongues. They don't realize an insult's simply another form of flattery.'

His personal assistant, Judith Peach, had aged gracefully: she was now a middle-aged matron, but she retained the ripeness of her twenties and remained an object of fantasy for the clerks of the head office. Judith went through the newspapers each morning cutting out any articles about her boss and put them on his desk. The more vehement the criticism, the more ghoulish the caricature, the more Charles laughed. With the strike, the young entrepreneur of twenty years before who spoke in bewildering aphorisms was back in the national headlines. In February a member of a right-wing think-tank who was also a junior minister at the Treasury produced a confidential report proposing the introduction of Charles' paycuts into the public sector: the report argued that raising pay in line with inflation provided no incentive for workers to see inflation brought *down*; all they understood was money in their pockets. Whereas an annual *cut* in wages meant that curbing inflation was in everyone's interest.

What the report called Freeman's Dictum made Tory back-benchers and captains of industry swoon at its beautiful logic. The report was leaked to the media before the Cabinet had a chance to discuss its implications. In the resulting furore the junior minister was sacked, a senior minister resigned from the Cabinet complaining of a breakdown in constitutional government (the leak was traced as far as the back door of No. 10 Downing Street) and the Chancellor of the Exchequer was forced to issue a statement in the House of Commons making it categorically clear that such a lunatic proposal would never become the official policy of Her Majesty's Government.

Charles didn't mind a bit. He enjoyed the notoriety, even the vilification, which increased in May when he announced a massive pay rise for his senior executives and one of 73 per cent for himself.

'It's perfectly rational,' he told a television interviewer. 'It provides an incentive for others to work their way up. That's what they want. But what's more,' he emphasised, 'we've earned those rises by the profit the company's made.'

'But aren't they in part profits from other people's lost jobs?' the interviewer challenged him.

Charles frowned. 'Yes, we're more efficient now,' was all he said. He didn't seem to understand the question.

Charles enjoyed being in the news. He was puzzled by those tycoons who brought injunctions and libel suits against the media. He admired moguls prepared to promote free speech by becoming newspaper proprietors in addition to their other responsibilities, despite the fact that in making necessary technological changes they had met insufferable resistance from the trade unions; *their* strikes and demonstrations, outside newspaper buildings, gained a lot *more* coverage than Charles' own picket, the Freeman Ten.

They were national newspapers. Once the technological revolution was effected in London it would be the turn of the provincial papers. And one day Charles heard on the grapevine that the proprietor of the *Echo*, an old Harrovian who left editorial matters to Mr Baker, was looking for a buyer. He'd inherited the group from his father forty years earlier, and it had leached most of the family fortune; and what's more, unlike Charles Freeman, he was too old for revolution, too tired for conflict.

One Sunday lunchtime Zoe revealed her plan to renovate her cinema by splitting it in two, with separate screens.

'Expanding the market,' Charles realized. 'Excellent idea!' he enthused, and offered his niece a loan, because he didn't bear grudges and saw no need to let their political differences get in the way of a shrewd investment. Zoe, though, refused, preferring a bank loan.

'You're a hippy entrepreneur,' James told her that evening.

Zoe was indignant. 'No, I'm not,' she replied. 'I'm making money without meaning to.'

'Nobody does that,' James argued.

'I'm just doing what needs to be done,' she claimed. 'It's all a big gamble. I might be bankrupt tomorrow for all I know.'

She'd already proceeded with another gamble: films on videotape had entered the market place and achieved an instant popularity; Britain soon had the highest number of video players per household

313

in the Western world. Shops renting out cassettes sprang up in every corner of the town. Most of the tapes were trashy slasher movies and pornographic films, resurrected from studio vaults for a public beguiled by the idea of miniature cinemas in their own living-rooms. A generation changed their Saturday-night social habits overnight: instead of going out for the evening they ordered a take-away pizza and stayed in to watch a horror film instead.

Far from being dismayed at these events, as other cinema proprietors were, Zoe saw the opportunities on offer in the coming communications revolution. 'We've got cable television, satellite dishes here, more channels coming,' she explained to James. 'It's a novelty. In the future we're going to have unimaginable choice, which means there'll be plenty of room for quality as long as we provide it.'

And so Zoe started up a new company making tapes of her back catalogue of foreign films under the banner of Electra Video Classics.

'What about the cinema?' James asked her. 'You're helping them cut your own throat.'

'I don't think so,' she told him. 'I think it'll bring them *back* into cinemas. It'll develop the audience for quality films.'

'There must be a logic there somewhere,' James said.

'Look,' she said, 'we've got to capture the next generation's attention or we'll lose them for ever, to computer games and virtual reality and other moronic pursuits. All you see is what's in front of your lens, James; you don't see the future.'

It was, in fact, a difficult time for Zoe. She was busier than ever, but such activity was partly to cover up the itch to be off travelling, which brief holidays no longer assuaged.

'I've got cabin fever,' she admitted to James. 'I'm going crazy.'

'Sell up,' he suggested.

'Maybe I should,' she agreed.

The most avid reader anyone knew, Zoe found she no longer read books unless they were written by Eric Newby or Freya Stark. She began to fall asleep in films, something she'd never done before, and would have vivid dreams of places she'd never seen. And when she bought a newspaper the first thing she did was to check the prices of flights to Katmandu or Caracas, and then to study the small ads placed by brave and lonely souls seeking travelling companions.

And then the travellers suddenly came to her.

*

For some years Britain had been spawning new, dispersed groups of nomadic people who joined traditional gypsies on the road: old hippies; itinerant musicians, clowns and fire-eaters; Druidic mystics; home-owners who'd gained a mortgage then lost a job and found themselves driving around the country in a ramshackle home on wheels.

Gradually, though, they'd begun to coalesce, coming together at free festivals organized by the more enterprising among them: they'd camp on some common and spend a few days exchanging mechanical advice, battered copies of *Food for Free* and juggling skills. At nights they sat around bonfires singing, and smoking different weeds. And then the nomadic bands discovered that by coincidence they all shared a spiritual centre: Stonehenge, the prehistoric megalithic monument on Salisbury Plain.

That was when the trouble started: rag-bag convoys of travellers converged on Stonehenge for the summer solstice from all corners of the country. Wherever they stopped on the way they enraged the local population with their careless dirt and their dirty freedom. The further they travelled the more their psychedelic trucks and converted ambulances broke down and overheated in the summer sunshine. They took such enforced halts less as catastrophes than as opportunities to play guitars and tambourines on the verge, while queues of fuming motorists formed behind them. It was a problem not helped by the growing bands of nomads from the media who followed in their wake.

Not to mention the police: at first different constabularies escorted them to county borders and bade them good riddance with good humour. The Government, however, had other plans, promising to rid society of medieval brigands, just as those other threats to public decency and national security, the striking coalminers, had been seen off; often reluctant police forces were again coerced into operating under a co-ordinated strategy, against travellers to the Stonehenge People's Free Festival.

In the summer of 1985 a massive police operation deflected, diverted, blocked, turned back, impounded, arrested and, as a last resort, beat up the anarchic pilgrims, and Stonehenge was once more reclaimed for decent day-trippers and honest tourists.

Now, a year later, the travellers were less a Sunshine Circus, as they'd called themselves, than the stragglers of a ragged army in retreat. Some hardened into the violent ruffians they'd been portrayed as, and would give the police the confrontations that had been

315

predicted; others transferred their spiritual allegiance from Stonehenge to Glastonbury and the music festival held there; many, though, simply roamed the country as they had five years earlier, again isolated tribes, except that now their innocent optimism had been replaced by dispirited, tired cynicism.

It was one Wednesday in the middle of June that Zoe noticed men and women with dreadlocked hair, with rings through their ears and noses, dressed in army fatigues and faded floral skirts. They walked along the pavement past the cinema followed by crocodile lines of dirty children and sprightly dogs, and walked back the other way carrying food and cans of beer.

The next day Zoe found herself leaning on the ticket counter and staring outside, waiting for another one to enter her field of vision. Suddenly her elbows collapsed beneath her and she jumped up and ran out of the foyer.

'Luna!' Zoe cried at a woman who was making slow progress along the pavement, carrying a baby on her hips and a toddler on her shoulders while a third walked along with a hold of her skirt. 'Luna, is it you?'

'Zoe!' the woman responded. They embraced warmly, if awkwardly on account of the infants involved in the physical equation.

'Are these all yours?' Zoe asked.

Luna checked them over quickly. 'Yup, all mine,' she affirmed. 'Were you just coming out of the cinema? What a coincidence. God, I haven't been to a cinema in . . . hardly *ever*,' she laughed.

'It's mine,' Zoe told her. 'I own it.'

'You *what*?' Luna gasped. 'You own it? God, times change, Zoe.'

Zoe's father, Harold, and Luna's mother had been lovers in Casablanca many years before, and the two girls – single children both – had each had a sister for six months.

'I haven't seen you for, what, fifteen years? Twenty?' Luna guessed. 'You look great, Zoe. Listen, you've got to come down and see us, we're by that big meadow over there; meet my man, Joe the Blow.'

'I'd love to,' Zoe said. 'Is he their father?' she asked.

Luna looked over her children once again. 'Two of them,' she ventured. 'Yeh, the baby, and this one,' she said, gesturing to the toddler still sitting on her shoulders, who was staring at Zoe.

Luna and her friends had camped on the old rubbish tip, now landfilled and grassed over for a nature reserve, between the meadow

316

and the railway line. Zoe left her usherette in charge of the cinema and went there with Luna. Twenty trucks were parked here and there, oily men tinkering with some of them; other people were gathering and chopping wood; children were helping and hindering and dogs were dozing. Joe the Blow, a short, thick-set man with an angelic face hiding behind straggly beard and knotted hair, was working with a couple of others connecting amps on a small stage that fanned out of a trailer.

After introducing Zoe, Luna took her to their van, a Commer Walk-Through, in which another, older, child was reading.

'Caz, this is Zoe,' Luna said. 'I knew her when we were your age. Fancy making us some tea?'

The two women caught up with each other's lives.

'I can't tell you what I feel, seeing you again and being here, in all this,' Zoe said. 'I forgot what people really smell like!' she laughed. 'I feel like a mixture of nostalgia and excitement. And envy, Luna.'

'Don't,' Luna replied. 'We had it OK for a while, but it's become a life of endless hassle, Zoe. We used to think we'd be applauded for living a simple life, you know, recycling everything, I mean, the only bad thing we burn is petrol. And that's because the oil companies are blocking the use of solar-powered transport. But we leave a little mess in a lay-by and people call us animals.'

'People don't think about all the shit they produce because it's flushed out of sight, one way or another,' Zoe agreed.

'Have you seen your local pubs, and some of the shops? We only got here yesterday and they've already put signs up saying: NO TRAVELLERS. And the fuzz kick us around for fun now. Honest, Zoe, it's not worth the hassle any more. What we really want is to get our travelling theatre going; that's our dream. But it takes money. So I've told Joe we've got to look for a permanent place in the autumn. Get the kids in school and everything.'

'Is he into that?'

Luna laughed. 'He wants to go to Portugal for the winter, he says there's a scene down there. Mind you,' she said approvingly, 'he's on another planet.'

The night before, the strains of music and the smell of cannabis had wafted into the town, and word had got around. While shopkeepers and publicans put up bars, their children, after the sun went down, drifted over to what had become an impromptu, free, illegal festival.

317

James, whose bedsit was closer to the old tip than the cinema, was among them; he went over with his camera. He spotted and joined Zoe at Luna's campfire, leaving it sporadically to photograph faces flickering in the firelight and musicians on the stage.

'You see the guy on the flute?' Luna asked him on one of his returns. 'He used to play with the Incredible String Band.'

'Who?' James asked.

'No, really?' asked Zoe.

'Someone said so, yeh,' Luna replied. 'Joe reckons these guys are brilliant, but they won't take a record deal. They've all been ripped off before.'

Luna's children slipped off to bed of their own accord, but she went to tuck them in, and came back with baked potatoes and lentil roast she handed round before disappearing again with the offer of dandelion coffee.

James, who'd had the foresight to bring a bottle of whisky with him to the site, had plenty of swigs himself and was feeling sleepy; he didn't want to fall asleep, though, because he wasn't sure his camera would be there when he woke up. Music was being made around the fire now in a disorganized jamming session and James felt left out of it. He was thinking of going home, when suddenly Zoe beside him called out: 'Hey! Robert! Come over here!'

James jerked out of his drowsiness, glanced up and saw his brother: he wore jeans, a T-shirt and leather jacket; a bunch of keys dangled from his belt and bumped against his thigh as he approached. Then Robert saw James. He hesitated where he was, some feet away; James looked up at him, his heart thumping.

'What's up with you two?' Zoe demanded. 'What do you need, an introduction? Come and sit down, Robert.' Relaxed by alcohol and nostalgia, it had slipped Zoe's mind that the brothers hadn't spoken to each other since James had tried to strangle Robert over ten years earlier. They'd seen each other – at Alice's wedding, around town – but avoided conversation.

'You all right?' James asked.

Robert nodded. 'Yeh. OK,' he replied in his gritty voice. 'You?'

'Fine,' said James.

Robert sat down on the other side of Zoe. 'A couple of them needed parts for their trucks,' he told her. Then they whispered something to each other; Robert felt in his pockets and gave something to Zoe, and she handed him some money. Luna came out with a tray of mugs, passed them round and sat down beside Robert. Zoe introduced him.

'Another cousin?' said Luna. 'You didn't tell me about *them* in Morocco.' She laughed across Robert, giving him a sideways glance.

'They were little kids then, you idiot,' Zoe replied.

'You want some dandelion coffee?' Luna offered Robert. 'Here, you can have mine.'

'You're kidding, are you?' Robert growled. 'Isn't there anything stronger?'

'Have the rest of this,' said James, passing over his whisky bottle.

'Ta,' said Robert. He felt in his pockets. 'You want some Colombian?' he asked.

'Coffee?'

'Hash, you twat,' Robert smirked.

'Robert, won't you ever learn any manners?' Zoe, sandwiched between them, scolded him.

'You can have an eighth if you want,' Robert told James. 'Twelve quid. Well, ten to you.'

'I don't think so, thanks,' James replied. 'Wait. What, you're selling it?'

Robert put the packet back in his pocket.

'You're dealing this stuff?'

'Take that look off your face.' Robert glared. 'I had enough of that look when we were kids.'

'What are you doing, Robert?' James asked.

'It's only hash, man, I don't do gear or smack,' Robert said. 'Don't look at me like that. Zoe, tell him to stop giving me that superior shit.'

'You're dealing drugs.' James shook his head.

'Crap,' Robert countered. 'I buy and sell all sorts, cars, antiques, everybody knows that. *This* stuff should be legal anyway.'

'Sure.'

'What's it to you, anyway?'

'Oh, nothing, Robert. Nothing. Forget it.' James stared at the embers of the fire; then looked at Zoe. She was staring into the fire as well. 'I suppose you . . .' James started to address her. 'Is he your . . . ?' he tried to ask.

Zoe kept her gaze on the glowing embers. 'Don't be a prig, honey,' she said quietly. 'It doesn't become you.'

'Hell, you're right,' James whispered, picking up his camera bag and getting to his feet. 'What do I know?' he said, and walked away across the wasteland, home through the darkness.

Very late the next morning Zoe woke up in her flat above the cinema with the smell of woodsmoke in her hair. She showered and had a leisurely breakfast, looking through old photographs but finding none of Luna or her mother. She went downstairs at one o'clock to let the projectionist in: he was followed into the foyer by Luna, Joe the Blow and the children, and another small group behind them, all carrying whatever bags they could bear.

'What's the matter?' Zoe asked. 'What on earth's happened?'

The police, they told her, had descended upon the site earlier in the morning. 'No, it wasn't a dawn raid, I'll give your locals that,' said Joe. 'They were good-humoured throughout, the pigs.' They'd evicted the travellers from the reserve and then stopped them again as soon as they got onto the road, and inspected their vehicles, one after the other.

'They declared half of them unroadworthy,' Joe explained, 'and said we couldn't drive them another yard or they'd charge us. And if we tried to park up without written permission they'd arrest us for that as well.'

'What option did that leave?' Zoe asked.

'Too right,' Joe told her. 'None. Catch Twenty-bloody-two. They kindly offered to impound the vehicles.' He laughed bitterly. 'They've arrested our trucks and let the human beings go. Still, ours was on its last legs.'

'The others,' Luna interjected, 'have piled into the decent vans. They've been escorted out of your town. But there just wasn't room for all of us, Zoe.'

'Well,' Zoe said, 'come upstairs, if we can all fit, and let's have a think.'

It had been a squash in Zoe's flat above the cinema when James was a sole lodger, so there was no possibility of them staying there with her. She thought about asking Simon — there was plenty of room in the house on the hill — but wasn't sure how they'd all get on with Charles.

'He's such an old fascist he'd probably call in troops to evict you,' she said, in her tiny kitchen.

'Who would?' Luna asked. They were knocking up scrambled eggs and toast for the crowd squashed into the living-room.

'Who?' repeated Zoe. 'Oh, no one. I was just thinking out loud.'

'You know what *I* was thinking?' Luna said. 'What I'd really like to do? See a film! In your cinema. It'd be a real treat. If I can get Joe to look after the kids. What's on? Not that I care.'

'Luna,' said Zoe, 'you are a genius.'

'I am?'

'You can *stay* in the cinema,' Zoe said. 'You can *sleep* there. All of you. We'll find some camp-beds or something, and you can sleep in the aisles.'

And so it was that after months of dreaming vividly of far-off places, Zoe found herself giving shelter to a group of nomads in her cinema. During the afternoon the women and children picnicked on the meadow while the men busked in the town centre; in the evenings they crowded into Zoe's flat, except for Luna, who happily watched *Vagabonde* and *Year of the Quiet Sun* every evening for a week. And when the last screening was over they made up a huge bed of mattresses, cushions and blankets at the front of the auditorium, and fell asleep in one big litter.

A week was all they stayed, though. After only a couple of nights Zoe's customers began to complain about the smells of burning leaves and patchouli. The local shopkeepers and residents soon cottoned on to what was happening. Someone alerted the council, and someone else collected signatures in protest at the provision of bed and breakfast in a commercial property. Not everybody signed it, but many did.

'Next thing you know there'll be hundreds of them here.'

'Parking their trucks in the residents' parking spaces.'

'She's exploiting them, making money out of the homeless.'

'She's charging them?'

'Twenty pounds each!'

'Really?'

'Including the kids. And imagine trying to sleep in a cinema seat.'

''Course *they* don't pay. Claim it off the Social.'

'That means us.'

'Well, you don't feel safe, do you? I told Adrian to put a chair up against the door before he came to bed.'

'I heard they can't use a flush toilet any more. Or won't. They go down to the canal to do their business.'

'Oh, no. That's disgusting. I have to walk my dog down there.'

*

321

After five days an inspector from the environmental health depart-ment of the council called by and told Zoe, who didn't deny the presence of her guests, that they'd have to leave.

'But they're my friends,' she said.

'They can't sleep in the cinema,' he told her. 'It contravenes health and safety regulations, I'm afraid.'

'Well, next time someone nods off in a Tarkovsky film I'll give you a call,' Zoe told the council man as he left.

The travellers departed a couple of days later, watched by two bailiffs from the council. Zoe had bought them a new van – an old Black Maria, ironically, which Robert had reconditioned – and they piled into it eagerly, as if it were taking them away from prison and off on some seaside excursion. Which it probably was.

'I was looking forward to watching the new programme,' Luna said, nodding up at the plastic letters at the front of the cinema. 'Thank you, Zoe,' she said, embracing her friend. 'We'll drop by again one day,' she promised. 'Next time we're passing through.'

'You do that,' Zoe told her. 'Keep in touch.'

They left without fuss, and Zoe watched them go without envy. The episode somehow stilled her impatience. She'd enjoyed both offering hospitality and antagonizing some of her neighbours. Maybe she had found a happy medium for herself: as long as she didn't feel too much at home here, maybe she could stay with a certain contentment. She didn't know then that a few years later people would be dragged out of her cinema chained to their seats; that a large crowd held back by barriers would cheer them as they were loaded into modern-day Black Marias. Nor that Zoe herself would then leave the town for ever with a young girl who, unknown to anyone at all, was at that very moment having her destiny set in motion, as an egg fertilized by her father's sperm sought refuge in the lining of her mother's womb.

Another witness to the travellers' departure was James: alerted by Zoe, he brought his camera and took not the usual full roll of photographs but a single one. Back at the newspaper Keith printed it and put it, along with James' brief caption, in Roger's tray.

When James returned from further assignments that afternoon Roger confronted him.

'We can't use this,' he declared. 'Why aren't there any more?'

'I didn't need to take any more,' James explained. 'What's wrong with it?'

'You know what's wrong with it,' Roger told him bluntly.

The single image was of Luna handing the toddler to Joe the Blow already in the van. The child, who had just knocked his elbow on the van door, was bawling. Standing behind Luna were two donkey-jacketed bailiffs, whose expressions could be read as either bored indifference or heartless persecution.

'It's the truth as I saw it,' James declared.

'As you *chose* to see it,' Roger corrected him. 'This isn't reportage, James, it's an interpretation of events. You've been here over ten years, man, what are you doing pulling a stunt like this?' He shook his head. 'With my retirement less than a month off,' he complained.

'Well, I'm sorry to upset your final days.'

'No coverage,' Roger continued. 'It's so unlike you. Unprofessional. What's up?'

'Nothing's up,' James replied bad-temperedly.

'I can tell you this, James. Mr Baker won't like it. Not at all.'

'Oh, screw Mr Baker,' James declared, and stalked out of the office.

James planned to hang fifty photographs in his exhibition at the Old Fire Station in September 1986. Making the final selection was a bewildering task. Thirty or so pictures chose themselves, but as for the rest, he gazed dumbly at contact sheets of the same subject taken from different angles, eventually making up his mind only to change it again five minutes later. It was impossible.

Sonia was his saviour. She was a harsh critic, and had no compunction about telling her lover if she thought his work was rubbish, apparently unaware that even if he agreed, it hurt to hear it from someone else. Despite his discomfort, however, her adjudication was what he needed. He narrowed his choice of a particular subject to three or four variations and offered them to her, and Sonia pronounced: 'This one's the best. The rest are crap, James.'

She was usually right. Sonia was right about most things. She was down to earth and matter-of-fact, chasing her career, enjoying her social life, bringing up her sons, each day an itinerary that began with breakfast, ironed skirts and efficient briefcase, packed lunches and brushed teeth and leaving the house on time; days to be crossed to sleep on the far side with James for company. She made James feel normal, and he was grateful to her. She grounded him; she filled the emptiness inside him.

As the date of his exhibition approached James barely noticed what was going on around him. At the newspaper he dashed off to complete assignments in a rapid and perfunctory manner.

'Your work's been excellent lately,' Frank (who'd taken over as chief after Roger's retirement) told him. 'It's sharp and plain,' he said. 'At a time like this Mr Baker wants everything straightforward.'

James wasn't listening; nor did he join in the gloomy conversations over coffee in the office. He avoided the canteen, too, where printers and journalists exchanged worried rumours at lunch. James was busy in the darkroom at every spare moment and then rushing his final work-prints over to the Framing Workshop off Factory Road, where Karel tried to dissuade him from using the same plain ramin frame for every single picture.

'They're all different from each other,' Karel opined. 'Why you want the same bloody frames? We've got the whole range here.'

'It'll bring them together,' James insisted. 'It'll help make them one homogeneous group.'

'If the photos aren't homogamous the bloody frames won't make them that. Still, it's your money, innit?'

James had invitations to the private view printed, and leaflets advertising the exhibition which he distributed around town, calling in old favours and leaving small piles of them in shops and pubs, restaurants and cafés, the public library and the sports centre, as well as Zoe's cinema and Lewis's nightclub.

'Where have you been lately?' Lewis asked. 'You haven't brought that gorgeous woman of yours here for weeks.'

'Don't worry,' James shouted above the noise. 'We can't keep away for long.'

The Old Fire Station provided one large, airy room for a fixed fee plus a receptionist on hand to take payment for any work sold. Zoe suggested James ask Laura to provide catering.

'Ask the old man's cook?' James frowned. 'Are you joking?'

'No, didn't you know? Laura does that sort of thing, catering for dinner parties and stuff, as well as at the house. She's expanded.'

So James rang Laura up. They'd hardly seen each other in years, but she responded as if they'd spoken yesterday.

'Sure, James, sounds simple enough,' she replied. 'Why don't you pop in and we'll go through what you might need.'

'I can't come to the house, Laura,' James told her. 'You must know that.'

'Of course I do,' she said. 'I was just testing, to see if you're as obstinate as ever. Which you obviously are. So let's meet somewhere in town.'

A couple of days later they rendezvoused for coffee in a café in the covered market. James got there a few minutes early. When he looked up and saw Laura making her way between the tables towards him he felt his heart thud in his chest, constricting his lungs and making it difficult to breathe: because either the dress she was wearing was quite ingeniously unflattering, or else she was reacquiring the puppy fat of her childhood, turning *back* into her mother. Or else . . . Laura was about six months pregnant. James wrenched his eyes from Laura's midriff to her face, and stood up to greet her.

'You look wonderful,' he said spontaneously. 'You look great, Laura. The cliché's true about pregnancy: you are kind of glowing.'

Laura smiled and thanked him. He fetched her a mug of peppermint tea from the counter.

'No one told me!' James blurted out. 'I'm just shocked.'

'Well, everyone's a bit sheepish about it,' Laura said mysteriously. 'As I was coming down here, James, I was wondering: will he say anything when he sees me? I thought you wouldn't. And what do you do? Respond straight out. It means you've changed, James.'

'How?' he asked.

'Well, you're not a timid boy any more.'

'Thanks, Laura!' James laughed. 'You, however, are still like a patronizing younger sister, it seems. I'm thirty years old, you know.'

'We've hardly seen each other, have we?' Laura frowned. She'd put her hand on James' arm on the table. It was an instinctual gesture: she didn't even know she'd done it.

'I've hardly seen anyone,' James told her.

'Why be a stranger?' Laura asked.

James sighed. 'I know it sounds stupid, but I can't be in the same house as that man.'

'Your father.'

'Bad things happened, and whenever I've thought about them, they always come back to him.'

'James,' Laura said seriously, squeezing his arm. 'It wasn't your father that beat me. Or made me have an abortion, or anything that happened then. It was *my* father.'

'I know, Laura, but it wasn't just that incident with you. That was the breaking point.'

325

'I've always wanted you to come back.' She swallowed. 'I've always felt responsible for you being estranged from your family.'

'What?' James exclaimed. 'You're not serious, Laura. It's just between me and him, it's nothing for *you* to feel bad about.'

'Well, I did,' she replied, with her head bowed. 'Plus, of course,' she said, brightening, '*I've* missed you. I mean, you and me and Alice were little buddies, weren't we, and everyone knows what's happened to Alice, poor thing.'

'What's happened to Alice?' James asked worriedly.

'She's been turned into a Stepford Wife, that's what,' Laura informed him.

'Oh, that,' James said, relieved. 'Maybe she's happy,' he shrugged. He laughed. 'I thought we'd meet and discuss sausage rolls and cheese on sticks, Laura, and that would be that. I've heard you're very businesslike.'

'I am,' she replied, pulling a notepad and pen from her handbag.

'Hang on,' James said, putting his hand on *her* arm. 'So who's the man, the father-to-be? I mean, are you with someone, or what? You're not *married*, are you?'

'Don't you know?' Laura frowned.

'I didn't know you were pregnant, did I?' James said.

'It's Robert, James,' she told him.

James froze. Laura looked away. Then she said: 'We're not together or anything. We made a mistake. Well, *I* did, I guess, It's *my* body. And, well, here we are.'

She looked back at James. 'I'm going to be a single parent,' Laura told him. 'From what I hear, you wouldn't object to that.'

James blinked. 'No,' he said.

'I heard you're living with someone with two kids,' she resumed.

'Almost,' James replied. 'Practically.' He felt her hand on his arm again.

'So, are you in love, James?' Laura asked, smiling.

The child is the woman, James thought. She hasn't changed. She disarmed me then and, twenty years later, she disarms me now. It wasn't just that he wouldn't, or couldn't, lie to her. It was that Laura asking him the question made him know instantly the answer.

'No,' he told her. 'I'm not in love.'

Laura looked sorry she'd asked. She didn't *mean* to cut through his defences; she was only making conversation. James felt sorry he'd answered.

'So how about this reception, then?' he asked. 'What can you do?'

Laura picked up her pad and pen with relief, and they set to assessing quantities of olives and canapés.

The private view took place on the second Saturday in September, at seven in the evening. Despite his anxiety James slept like a log the night before and woke slowly, finding Sonia doing the same; they groped their way dozily out of sleep together. James was more readily aroused in the morning than the evening; he wondered whether that was true for most people, and if so why did they court at night? Sonia had only to snuggle herself up to him in her somnolence, draining the final luxurious dregs of sleep before reluctantly facing the day ahead, to turn him on.

It was warm under their duvet and cool outside it. They both had their eyes closed. James stretched and yawned and took Sonia's breast in his mouth; he licked her nipple. He felt her hand caress his body, and reach his erection.

'Are you sure?' he whispered drowsily. 'It's late.'

'It's Saturday,' Sonia murmured. 'The boys'll be watching TV.'

They kissed; her warm, sleep-stale breath assailed him. She eased him inside her. 'Let's do it quickly,' she murmured.

It might have been because he wasn't fully awake; it might have been the contrast with their customary leisurely love-making; but when James ejaculated the orgasm came like an electric shock and scattered his brain.

'Jesus,' he said, when he'd got his breath back. 'That was a real animal fuck.'

'It was great,' Sonia whispered.

'You too?' he asked.

'Mmm,' she said.

James spent most of the day hanging the photographs in the large, light room. He'd set aside Friday for the job, but he should have known, after his vacillation in selecting the images in the first place, how difficult it would be. Hanging fifty pictures in a room offered an infinite number of possible permutations, and his original plan to exhibit them in chronological order was clearly – when he leaned them against the walls on Friday morning – an unimaginative solution. So he spent the rest of the day arranging them according to subject matter: a cluster of music gig photos here, sports ones there, children together, wedding photos on the far wall. But when he surveyed *those* results, grouping them by subject seemed even

327

more banal than chronology, and he thought there must be a more appropriate order, a less obvious but more telling pattern to his work.

As before, he needed someone else's help to select his own work. He didn't want to ask Sonia – at least not outright. He did drop a hint on Friday evening when she asked how it'd gone and he told her that it was fine, no problems, only none of the prints were actually up on the walls yet, that was all; it was impossible to decide which ones went beside each other, but he'd sort it all out tomorrow.

'Sure you will,' Sonia assured him. 'Well, you'll have to, won't you?' she laughed, and failed to volunteer her services. On Saturday morning James phoned Zoe, and she joined him at the Old Fire Station at lunchtime. She rolled a cigarette, frisked herself for a light, and walked slowly around the room pondering the prints overlapping each other, leaning against the foot of the walls.

'Very good, James,' Zoe pronounced when she'd got right round, back to the door. 'Very good. Now, I'll just move them here and there and you tell me how they look, OK? I'm your curator's assistant. I'm at your service.'

And from then on it was easy. They hung the photographs on alternately long or short forks of nylon wire from a picture-rail that ran around the room. James was perfectly capable of making up his mind – Zoe only proffered three or four suggestions all afternoon – he'd simply needed someone else to reinforce his decisions, to nod or 'yup' agreement; even just to be there at all, allowing James to see through eyes other than his own.

James had tended to agree with Zoe that most of the other artists in the town whose work they'd seen, so desperate for attention they organized exhibitions long before producing the work to fill them, were trivial dilettantes. Having finished hanging his photographs, and surveying the result with one of Zoe's rollies, James concluded that he was one as well.

He didn't say anything to Zoe, but maybe she read his mind. 'One of my yoga teachers told me,' he heard her say, 'it's not what you're doing now that counts, it's what you're doing when you're fifty.'

'You think I need another twenty years?' he asked her.

'I think I was thinking of me, actually, sweetheart,' she smiled.

'Thanks for your help,' James told her. 'I really appreciate it. You've got me out of another hole. You've made a habit of it, you know. You're always there for me.'

'Well, you'll probably be doing the same for someone else some time. Now, you better go and get changed so you can be back here in time. It's almost six o'clock.'

The evening unravelled like a dream.

When James returned with Sonia and her sons Laura had already laid out red and white and sparkling wine, and fruit juices, and covered a trestle table with hors d'oeuvres: taramasalata, humous, coleslaw, guacamole, smoked salmon, sliced peppers, baby tomatoes, bowls of fruit, pitta and crispbreads, devilled eggs, galantines and other cold meats, salamis, sausages and pâtés, shrimps in avocado.

'What a banquet,' James gasped. 'They bloody better all come.' Sonia and the boys helped themselves. James couldn't: he was far too nervous, both sweating profusely and icy-cold with apprehension.

Lewis set up a mobile turntable and speakers: he'd volunteered to provide music, begging or borrowing an assortment of classical and world music to play in the background. Lewis greeted James with a Masonic handshake signifying membership of a nightlife underworld.

'Looks good, Jay,' Lewis declared. 'I like that one best,' he said, pointing to a photograph of twenty men in a public park all in different colours, every one of whom appeared to be hurtling in a different direction, each focused on an invisible football. There *was* a ball visible, suspended in the air above their heads, but they appeared oblivious to it.

James saw a small red sticker on the wall beside the print. He looked back at Lewis, who was grinning.

'Yeh, I wanted to be the first to buy one, Jay. It'll look great in my pad.'

Then the guests began to arrive; and more red stickers went up beside the pictures: James was selling them as runs of ten prints of each picture at £50 each. Zoe came back with a man she called Dog, and bought a photo James had taken at one of her matinées, of a group of children staring spellbound, open-mouthed, at the cinema screen.

'I'll hang it in the foyer,' Zoe told him. 'It reminds me of *Spirit of the Beehive*.'

'It reminds me of us,' Laura said.

'Who?' asked James.

'*Us*,' she reiterated. 'Don't you remember the arguments we used to have on the way home?'

The artist photographers arrived. They went straight to the food, Karel muttering that he wasn't to blame for the bloody frames. Then

329

the other photographers followed them in, James' colleagues. They and the artists seemed to recognize each other, so decisively did they avoid contact. Instead Keith the printer spent a long time staring at each photograph through his tinted glasses, shaking his head. While Roger, James' retired chief, congratulated him on the clarity of his images until they came to three photographs together of audiences in crowded, sweaty, smoky pubs dancing to music from some unseen band.

'Oh, dear,' Roger said, and James smiled and left him. His other colleagues were sticking together.

'Well done, son,' said Frank. 'You've not gone in for this arty crap like we were worried you might have.'

James was disappointed. 'Haven't I?' he asked.

'It's all *people*,' Frank told him.

'Aye, people all right,' Derek interrupted. 'There's good stuff here, Jim, I'm not saying there isn't, it's just a shame that when you were let off the leash you didn't do a bit more . . . well, you weren't a bit more critical.'

'I suppose you've already heard, son,' said Frank. 'We just heard this afternoon.'

'Heard what?' asked James.

'Well, the rumours turned out to be true,' said Keith.

'What rumours?' James demanded.

'Bloody hell,' said Frank to Keith. 'He's hard work sometimes. Your old man,' he said to James.

'What *about* him?' James demanded in exasperation.

The two men looked at each other, then back at James. 'He's taken over the paper,' Frank told him.

'What?' James asked, bemused. 'What paper? You mean . . . ?'

At that moment, though, Alice and Harry and their two babies plus Uncle Simon and Auntie Nat came in together. Simon clasped James in a bear-hug and said: 'Marvellous, James! Our little brother's a star! And such a well-dressed one! Who would've ever believed it?'

When Simon released James from his sponge-like grasp James took a few seconds to get his breath and balance back; but he couldn't feel bad towards his older brother since Simon had taken responsibility for making sure Charles didn't turn up uninvited – an intrusion quite within his capabilities.

Alice kissed James on one cheek and made to kiss him on the other, but on the way she spotted Zoe and left James' proffered lips in mid-air, to go and say hello to her cousin.

Natalie, who seemed to be official nanny for the evening, had Amy by the hand and Sam on her hip, and went over to introduce herself to Sonia. Harry studied the photographs, while Simon started introducing himself to strangers, and then strangers to each other, becoming, within two minutes of entering the room, self-appointed host for the evening. James, finding himself alone, watching his brother, felt a sudden rush of love for him, for those qualities James would never have.

Nerves making me tired and emotional, he thought to himself. He felt a touch on his arm: it was Laura, with a glass of wine.

'You look like you could do with this,' she told him, and then returned to behind the trestle table. He took a grateful swig as more people arrived.

Pat, political activist turned video-maker (the only one of his fellow bedsit tenants he'd become friendly enough with to invite), handed him a small sheaf of envelopes.

'Thought I'd bring your post,' she said. 'You might as well sublet your room the amount of time you're there. By the way, I won't be there much longer myself.'

'What, are you buying a house or something?' he asked.

'You're fucking joking,' she snorted. 'I'm so skint I'm shooting on tapes from a video rental shop's dustbin. No, I'm going to film school; I've been offered a place.'

'Congratulations,' James declared.

'Yeh, great, eh? And the same to you for all this. I'm only sorry I can't afford to buy one.' Pat's eyes, scanning the room, alighted upon Laura's trestle table, and lit up. 'Food!' she exclaimed. 'Yummy,' she said, and disappeared.

The room filled up with James' acquaintances, some of them the subjects of photographs, so that people kept doing double-takes between human beings and their photographic representations. The wine flowed and the room filled and chatter became an undifferentiated din. James trawled through it. He overheard Karel telling Natalie: 'You've got a wonderful head. I'd like to photograph you some times,' and James whispered in his ear that he was on the wrong track, he shouldn't waste his time. Karel whispered back: 'Push off.'

James saw that the photographers – artists and hacks – had joined forces at last by the far wall, finding agreement with each other at how pitiful it was that James had stooped so low as to take these wedding pictures. And so many of them! James, inebriated, grinned at their mutual stupefaction.

Harry came over and shook his hand. 'Well done, James,' he said. 'Very interesting. Bit of an eye-opener. I think I underestimated you.'

'Well, thanks, Harry,' James replied.

'Yes. Very interesting. Fifty pictures, ten prints of each, at fifty pounds: that's a possible twenty-five grand. Minus expenses, of course. Assuming you sold them all, you wouldn't need too many shows like this a year to make a decent living.'

'I won't sell them all, Harry,' James demurred. 'Nothing like.'

'I've bought one myself; that one of the plasterer and his mate standing by a freshly skimmed wall. It makes me nostalgic. I like it.'

'Thanks, Harry.'

There was also a red sticker beside a photograph from the time of the Freeman Ten picket line. It showed Charles Freeman, the man-in-charge, in the back seat of his chauffeur-driven Rover cruising past the protestors, Charles resembling nothing so much as a smiling Buddha; while through the window on the far side of the car was framed the furious face of the Wire, hurling abuse at his erstwhile employer.

Just then Simon appeared beside him. James flinched from what he thought was about to be another bear-hug, but Simon made do with an arm around James' shoulders.

'Of course, I had to do a deal with father,' he boomed in James' ear.

'A deal?'

'That's right, a deal. How did you know?'

'You're as pissed as I am!' James told him.

'I've only had a sip or two of wine, dear. Anyway, he commissioned me, in his absence, to buy one of your photographs.

'Shit, Simon, I want to be free of the old bastard.'

'Don't be such an uptight little turd, James. He's just another customer. Guess which one I've bought him.'

'Not this one in the car?' James grinned.

'That's the one!' Simon confirmed.

'He looks like an evil goblin,' James snickered.

'The Wire's blowing a fuse,' Simon hooted.

'He'll hate it.' James chortled.

'He'll love it!' Simon shouted.

'Stop it, Simon, I'm going to piss myself,' James blurted out.

'I already have!' Simon gasped, as they crumpled in the middle of the crowded room.

They were saved by Lewis: just then, at ten o'clock precisely, he turned the lights down low and the music up loud, and the private view became a private disco.

The older and the younger and the more staid of the guests departed, but most remained. A friend of Sonia's took her sons home.

'You're a success,' she yelled in James' ear.

'WHAT?' he yelled back. Sonia leaned close, stilled his dancing motion, and to an inappropriate beat they slow-danced in a perpetual circle.

Zoe danced with Dog, who was a lumbering bear of a man. Harry had taken his children home and left Alice dancing with Natalie. Karel had shifted his attentions to one of the newspaper typists. Simon was drinking with the press photographers.

James went off to find a lavatory. Instead of coming straight back he went over to a large bay window in the corridor, opened it and leaned out. The music's after-noise buzzed in his ears. He felt stupefied by alcohol and nerves, and lit a cigarette. After a while he heard footsteps and turned to see Laura coming along the corridor. She joined him at the window.

'Not dancing?' she asked.

'Just having a rest,' he told her. 'You?'

'I'm all packed up. People can help themselves to the rest of the booze. There's not much left. It's gone well. You must be pleased.'

'I am,' James replied. 'I've realized something important. Well, important for me.'

'What's that?'

James took a final drag of his cigarette and dropped it out of the window. 'That I'm not an artist,' he said. 'I'm just a snapper. I always wanted to be an artist, I thought I'd be one.'

Laura didn't disagree, she let him talk on.

'I'm just a chronicler of small events, recording them for a while; not even for posterity. They're too mediocre to last long.'

'You don't sound disappointed,' Laura told him.

'I'm not. That's funny, isn't it? But I'm really not, I suppose because it's the truth, and *that's* the important thing. To know who you are, what you're capable of. God!' He laughed. 'Two minutes ago I was sloshed, and lost in drunken musing. And now, talking to you, I'm lucid and seeing things clearly.'

'I have that effect on people,' Laura smiled. 'I sober them up. Ah!' she exclaimed.

'What is it?' James asked.

'The baby kicked. It doesn't hurt,' she assured him, seeing his worried look.

'Can I feel it?' James asked her.

'Sure,' Laura replied. 'You can try.' She took his hand and pressed it against her belly, through the material of her cotton dress. 'Here,' Laura said, loosening a couple of buttons. She slid his hand in onto her bare skin.

'It's a bit hit-and-miss. When or where he'll kick.'

'He?'

'Only boys kick and move around as much as this one does. Or so my Aunt Pauline tells me. There! Did you feel that?'

'Yes.' James pictured a tiny foot pushing through amniotic fluid into his palm. It happened again a few moments later, and then James withdrew his hand, and Laura buttoned her dress.

'Thanks for doing all the food, Laura, it was superb,' James said.

'It *is* my living, James,' she laughed.

'Of course,' he said hurriedly. 'You give me the bill as soon as you want. Now, if you like. I can give you a cheque right now.'

'Oh, no, it's all taken care of,' she told him.

'What do you mean?' he asked. 'I didn't give you anything up front, did I?'

'Your father's already paid me,' Laura stated matter-of-factly.

'What are you talking about?' James demanded. 'What's it got to do with him?'

'He told me last week to provide a five-star buffet, the best of everything. I assumed you'd agreed or something.'

'Laura!' James groaned. 'How could I have? You *know* I haven't spoken to him. You *know* I can't stand him.'

'Didn't you notice all the food tonight?' Laura demanded. 'You're not blind, are you? A blind photographer? We discussed prices and I was going to provide a few dips and some plonk. Didn't it cross your mind that the banquet was just a little more lavish than you expected?'

'Yes. I mean, no,' James replied. 'I can see maybe it should have, but—'

'I thought it would be better,' she interrupted. 'Your guests don't care who paid. I'd have thought you might *appreciate* it, James.'

'Jesus, Laura,' James responded. He was flummoxed. '*You* thought

334

it was better to let my father pay. *You* thought I'd appreciate it. Who do you think you are? Who do you think I am? My God, you patronizing . . .' James' voice trailed away. He shook his head. He felt disorientated, and drunk again. He ran his hands through his hair.

'I'm confused,' he said.

'You're ungrateful,' Laura told him coldly, and turned to go.

'Hang on, Laura, I'm sorry,' he called after her, but she kept going, and disappeared.

'Fuck!' James cursed himself. He felt anger fill his head and swirl around inside it, an inchoate, confusing rage. Confusing because he wasn't angry, above all, with Laura; or with his father; or with the fact of his own mediocre talent; or with his dumb colleagues or his superior friends. His anger was with none of them – it was with one who wasn't there, his brother Robert; and maybe it *was* too with Laura, after all. And with himself, somehow, in some way he didn't understand.

'Fuck!' he exclaimed. His hand was a fist. He drew it back, and punched straight through a glass pane of the window in front of him.

8

FREEDOM AND LONELINESS

WHEN SHE GOT HOME LAURA WAS STILL BERATING HERSELF. WHY DO I
do that? she wondered. I expect everyone else to be cool and rational.
But they're not. What's wrong with them? Why can't people just be
more reasonable, for God's sake? But it's not them. What's wrong
with me? Why do I do that? Oh, James, I'm so stupid. I'm not so
clever. Stop it. Don't agonize over what you can't change, woman.
Forget it. I smell of smoke, horrible. All those smokers.

After showering Laura passed her reflection in the long mirror in
her bedroom, and returned to it. Her seven-month bulge protruded
hugely forward, both a part of her and a grotesque, magical
malformation of her body. She sat on her bed rubbing oil into the
skin of her belly. She thought back over her life and the people closest
to her – of her mother and father, Robert, James, Alice – and was
confronted by the stark, sudden truth that she had never loved
anyone, not really. Maybe she couldn't; maybe it was just a natural
gift some people had and others, like her, lacked. She had never felt
so lonely, and she wept naked tears of self-pity that ran down her
face and onto her belly, tears that it dawned on Laura were less for
herself than for the child growing inside her.

*

The glass gashed James' hand. There was a lot of blood, and Simon rushed him up to the hospital. On duty in Casualty that night was Lewis's sister, Gloria.

'What happened to you, James?' she asked, unwrapping the blood-soaked towel.

'I tried to hit someone and missed,' he grimaced.

'Oh, this is nothing,' she said. 'You're lucky you didn't sever an artery; for a Saturday night this is a mere scratch. I'll just give you a few stitches.'

James asked Simon to ring Sonia – who'd gone back to relieve her baby-sitting friend – and tell her there was no problem. And then to take James to his bedsit.

'You want to be alone?' Simon asked when he dropped him off.

'I want to think a bit,' James said.

'That's a dangerous habit,' Simon told him. 'Don't overdo it.'

Gloria had given him a local anaesthetic, whose effects soon began to wear off. James had emptied his food shelf but he had left a half-full bottle of brandy. He carried it and a glass in the uninjured hand over to his one armchair, and stayed there until he was insensible.

James woke up with bruised lungs and what felt like someone else's raw throat. He was in bed, naked, with no memory of undressing, nor of crawling in there. His bladder was full: he got up to move, and simultaneously his dehydrated head was squeezed and his hand flared up with pain.

James moaned and fell back on the pillow. He cursed his inability to drag himself to bed while there were still cigarettes in the packet and booze in the bottle. The alarm clock said seven fifteen. He pissed in the sink and drank a lot of water and managed to gain readmittance to sleep's merciful domain.

When James woke again it was almost noon. His hangover was gone and his hand merely sore. He walked to the cinema.

'You need some breakfast,' Zoe told him. 'You're lucky, I'm not going to Sunday lunch today.'

She fried eggs, tomatoes, mushrooms, bread and beans, and made a large jug of coffee. James ate and was full, and he lit his first cigarette of the day.

'I came to beg you to lead me out of the wilderness,' James smiled. 'But now I feel human already without saying a word. I can see there's no point in suicide.'

'What are you talking about? What's the problem?' she asked.

'Apart from that wounded paw, what have you got to complain about? You're floating through, James Freeman.'

'I look in the mirror. I'm thirty years old. What do I see? An immature kid, the same one who was there fifteen years ago except this one's got lines in his face. Not to mention receding hair and a slack belly.'

'Sounds unique.'

'I wasn't even sure I *was* there. I'm not just invisible behind a camera. I'm insubstantial; I'm hollow. No, listen, Zoe, this isn't self-pity. See, other people, they live their lives, they're solid. Just look at the people in my family, in that house I left: my father, his ego rampant, bursting with money and power, and *thriving*. I've been determined, you know, not to run away, to stay in this town and make it mine, but I can't escape him. He's bought the newspaper, did you know that? Really. Obviously I'm going to leave it.'

'Maybe you *should* leave town now,' Zoe suggested. 'Go to London. Or somewhere.'

'No,' he said. 'It's my town, too. Anyway, that's not even the point. The others: Simon, he's a great fluffy bear, Zoe, and he's brilliant. I mean, he's making himself into something fake but he's got all this generosity inside, this generous spirit, and he makes people feel good, he really does.

'Alice, there she is with her babies, I don't know, maybe that was always her destiny and maybe she's fulfilled; she's with a man who's going to get what he wants. And then Laura and Robert, Jesus, all this time they've been screwing, I thought she hated him, but no, there's something between them I'll never understand. A realm of life I've never been a part of, like other people. Like they're living their lives, and I'm just letting mine be blown into whatever shapes fate moulds. And that's why I'm saying about Simon, he's pretending but it's still him steering the ship. Oh, Zoe, it's so hard to explain.'

James poured himself another, tepid, coffee, and lit another cigarette. He met Zoe's gaze and shrugged: she had a look that said she knew him, she knew exactly what he meant; or else that she *couldn't* understand what he was going through and felt powerless to help him.

'You're just about the most stubborn, determined, independent person I or anyone else knows, sweetheart. Sometimes you don't see what's right in front of your nose, that's all. But as for living your life . . .'

'It's an illusion, then,' James told her. 'Ever since I was a child I've felt these two conditions of my life: freedom and loneliness. Right now I feel neither and that's the problem. Maybe it's my destiny to be free and lonely and I shouldn't fight that, I should accept it, embrace it.'

Zoe shook her head. Her ringleted hair rippled and her brass earrings tinkled.

'James Freeman,' she said, 'maybe your destiny's a psychoanalyst. Maybe *I'm* not the one to help you out here.'

She got up.

'I've a film to screen,' she said. 'I've got a cinema to run. You can let yourself out after you've washed the dishes.'

She reached the door, and turned round. 'Nothing I say can make you accept yourself,' she told him. 'But I accept you. More than that. I . . . you know, I feel . . . Oh, shit.' She turned and went down the stairs. James took the plates to the sink.

James walked. Out of the cinema and down to the canal, along the rutted, muddy towpath, north out of town, and over to the meadow. It was a warm late-summer day. James was thinking, I am wretched; he thought, This is my town, and this is James walking . . .

Onto the meadow, five hundred acres of flat land, of space to breathe into on an overcast late-summer Sunday. There were blue crows, and the sun broke through: cows and horses slowly turned towards it; coal vans on the railway track flickered through the trees.

He crossed the meadow to the river thinking, I am worthless, but also seeing, and he wanted to see outside himself. A heron stood on the bank. A boat from the rowing club came, its cox a midget who shrieked at gasping men, their eyes closed, somnambulists locked into a dream of pain. Their oars smacked the water, then rose and beat the boat like a drum. And James was a sleepwalker too and he felt their pain, their athletic ecstasy of endurance.

Children's sailing dinghies, bright sails flapping and thudding, danced like fireflies around a sluggish barge. A mallard skimmed along the river; perhaps, James thought, he's really underwater and it's only his reflection in the air. There is always more to see. He walked back across the meadow. An anguished jogger in mulberry tights interrupted a flock of geese in silent meditation, grey on green grass. They cackled as they scattered, and rose with hollow wings and flew across the sun.

Beyond, a gardener scooped up horse manure, a kite ripped up the sky, men flew model aeroplanes, the drone of their engines inexplicable music. And two tired lovers walked barefoot slowly; the smell of mint, lifted by their footsteps, will always remind them of this moment.

He crossed the allotments. Wiry men and leather-skinned women with crooked backs put tools away in potting-sheds; onions overflowed the baskets of ancient bicycles. He took an apple from an abandoned tree, and there was no past or future.

He walked straight through the Infirmary, along its arterial corridor. He loved – despite or perhaps because of his own pubescent incarceration – the smell of hospitals, in the wards where miracles took place, where the afflicted gritted their teeth and prayed for return to the human race.

Outside, a bunch of people chatted around placards saying SUPPORT THE NURSES and SAVE OUR HOSPITAL and HANDS OFF THE NHS.

In the road a yellow-clad street-cleaner, his shovel a shrimping net, fished for rubbish in the gutter. A black man in a white car with a sunroof passed and music escaped like a trail, an aroma, tantalizing, thumping rhythm and thuddy bass and a voice saying, 'PUMP UP THE VOLUME, PUMP UP THE VOLUME, PUMP UP THE VOLUME, DANCE! DANCE!' The music burst through James' head and he laughed with the man telling the world he was alive.

Another driver threw litter out of his window. A boy and girl sat cross-legged on the pavement with their dogs, playing tin whistles. James emptied his pockets of change to the girl with plaited hair and a ring through her nose and he smelled sandalwood as he bent towards her. He walked by a man in his mid-fifties, preoccupied, worrying a cigarette with toothless lips; his trousers were too short: the cruel, thoughtless badge of institution. So many images. I am a camera. 'You'll wear your eyes out, James,' said Zoe in his head.

James entered the park, sounds came from all directions. A hesitant beat from the tennis court; small boys whose bicycles were really motorbikes changed gear with a guttural whine; the *cloc*, and *cloc*, from a bowling green where pensioners shed their years in slow-motion duels. Then he was lost in the trees on the far side, monumental trees, oak, beech, sycamore. The wind giggled; the trees whispered to one another. They sounded like the voices of young children.

The wide sky became blue and empty save for vapour trails of silent planes. Knees green with chlorophyll stains, two sisters turned cartwheels on the grass, pony-tails flying. A man and a woman lay side by side; it was hard for James to tell from where he walked whether they were crying or sighing. So much to see.

Children were running, a dog was barking. In an empty playground James swung higher and higher, his stomach laughing.

He walked up the hill, past the house on the hill, the walled garden of his childhood, walking in the dusk, and on out to the ring road and round to his father's factory on the edge of town. He didn't pause there but walked back in the dark along Factory Road. This is my town, he thought. I must see everything.

All the way into town along Factory Road past four Indian restaurants, two Chinese, one Jamaican, two Italian, five pubs, two greasy spoons, one kebab take-away, one fish and chips and a Kentucky Fried Chicken.

Past the Golden Scissors Hair Salon, the Tattoo Studio, Honest Stationery, Valumatic Laundry, Joe's Discount Store, Gala Bingo, Bilash Tandoori Take Away (We Deliver), Bombay Emporium, Fundamental Wholefoods, Good Gear Second-hand Clothes, the Inner Bookshop, Vinyl 1234 (We buy sell exchange CDs Tapes LPs), Bangladeshi Islamic Education Centre and Mosque, Chopstick Restaurant, Ashraf Brothers General Grocers & Halal Meat, Hughes Cars of Distinction, Star of Asia (Fully Licensed – Air Conditioned), Boots, Tesco, the parish church of SS Mary and John, and a hundred other shops and institutions all along the road. This is my town.

He was soon back beside the canal by the brewery behind the prison, and he followed it towards the town centre. The mud on the towpath had dried, ossifying push-chair grooves and horses' hooves, cigarette butts and bicycle ruts; here were a child's footsteps, immortalized, at least until it rained again. At that moment he felt soft drops kiss the skin of his face, and saw others alight upon the water.

He walked past Sonia's house and crossed the bridge into the town centre. A radio somewhere played the *Moonlight Sonata* and the rain in the streetlights was falling. He walked in the rain past pubs spilling out quiet girls and raucous girls, youths cheerful and youths belligerent with beer, and two down-and-outs begging still and staggering, their brains and bodies fused. Twenty yards away shattered glass scattered on the dazzling pavement.

He scrounged a can of Coke at a kebab van from an Arab whom he recognized from Lewis's house. He leaned against a wall in the falling rain and drank the Coke and smoked a cigarette till the cigarette was soggy. I am free and lonely, he thought. He felt empty, and he felt a sense of exaltation that made him tremble in the falling

341

rain. He walked on to the bedsit, took off his clothes, towelled himself dry and collapsed on his bed.

James handed in his notice at the newspaper. No one was surprised.

'I'd do the same in your position,' Frank told him. 'I wouldn't have worked for *my* old man.'

No one made a fuss of James' departure – no party, no farewell – because others were also leaving, including the editor, Mr Baker. It was said that he went upstairs to a meeting with the new proprietor, Charles Freeman, came back down to his office and cleared his desk without a word to anyone, not even his secretary.

James also gave notice to his landlady and, with Lewis driving a hired van, removed his possessions from the bedsit in one load and into a rented flat above a chemist half-way up Factory Road. It took another load to move his stuff out of Sonia's.

'What do you think love is?' she demanded. 'We were nearly there, you moron. I was never a bloody princess. You see me yelling at my kids, you see me tired and dirty. I know you think I'm superficial. How could I know what you want? Did you ever tell me? You never talk. You have to work at it, James.'

'I'm sorry, Sonia,' he said.

'Fuck your sorry,' she told him. 'You're so stupid. I thought you were serious. I should have realized you weren't. You're not grown up, are you? You don't know how it works, do you?'

Sonia didn't cry. She was too angry to cry, and she contained her anger. James packed up as quickly as he could as Lewis stood by the van outside, and he stayed just long enough to give his abrupt abandonment the finality he'd decided upon.

'You're a bastard, James,' Sonia told him on the doorstep. 'I hope for other women's sake you grow up.'

He thought she was probably right. He felt no guilt. Or at least, what remorse he did feel was outweighed by relief, and release. The flat was dirty and cheap, on the second storey above the chemist and another flat, and it comprised two large and one small room, plus a kitchen and a bathroom. The interior staircase had been boarded up, and the flat was reached by an iron staircase at the back. The metal stairs bent under the climber's feet and then sprang back a moment later, giving a person the impression they were being followed.

James piled his belongings in the middle of the large room overlooking the street and bought white paint, a roller and brushes.

He painted everything white – walls, ceilings, skirting-boards, windows and doors. The decorating took a week, and he played the same tapes over and over again as he worked: Vivaldi's *L'Estro Armonico*, Glenn Gould playing Bach's *Goldberg Variations*, Monteverdi's *Vespers of 1610*. The music swirled around; the flat became new, reeking of oil paint and emulsion.

He bought an answerphone and installed it with the message: 'James Freeman is unable to answer. Please speak after the long tone and I'll get back to you.' He let the phone ring and the machine click on, and then stood there listening to callers' faltering messages. He answered them assiduously, not with return calls but with postcards, half a dozen of which he had made from his own photographs, saying how busy he was and asking them to call again.

He also bought a half-size, second-hand washing-machine with a mind of its own. As it spun it bounced around the kitchen, and reminded James of pogo-ing nights lost in noise ten years earlier. Sometimes in those first weeks, indeed, he joined it, banging his head on the ceiling, giggling to himself the deranged laughter of a recluse, while the Clash roared at full volume inside his skull. Until finally his neighbours on the floor below – three students at the college of further education – introduced themselves all at once. They invited him downstairs and showed him where the plaster from the ceiling in *their* kitchen was snowing into their supper.

'I'll wedge the washing-machine in one place,' James promised. 'Otherwise I won't be able to complain when you have parties.'

'Don't worry about us,' they assured him. 'We won't bother you.'

'Why not?' he asked. 'You're students. You *should* do.'

'There's not much time for that kind of thing,' they explained. 'We've got degrees to get. We want good jobs.'

'You make me feel old,' James said. 'Or young. I'm not sure which.'

Laura was almost eight months pregnant when she moved into Alfred's cottage tucked inside the wall around the grounds. Each of Alfred's three successors in the garden was a specialist, so that Ron tended the flower-beds, Henry disappeared into the walled vegetable garden and young John mowed the lawns. They each owned their own battery of power tools – strimmers, chainsaws, rotorvators and Flymos – besieging the house with a whining, raucous racket of activity, while failing to meet the horticultural standards that pottering old Alfred had maintained to the end, because, as he'd often

343

explained, the secret to hard work is not showing off but working steady. The three gardeners drove into work from outside, clocking on (like the rest of Charles' employees) at eight o'clock each morning, and Alfred's cottage had lain vacant over the years since his death.

Laura woke up one autumn dawn with the baby kicking inside her after dreaming of her mother for the first time in many years. It was as close to a memory as a dream can be, Edna at her kitchen table surrounded by the Freeman children, smiling her fat cherubic smile as they demanded one cake or pastry after another, and each one she had somehow to concoct instantaneously from ingredients before her. Her fat fingers were lost in dough and jam and cream and sugar as she performed culinary conjuring tricks, producing an apple turnover for Simon, a jam doughnut for Robert, a meringue for Alice, sliding them in and out of the oven, all the while smiling her fat-woman's smile through a pale cloud of white flour. And yet, Laura knew, watching – in the dream – from across the kitchen, although her mother was smiling, was happy, was a willing, infinitely yielding servant, she was also dying.

Laura woke up, pulled on her dressing-gown, and walked through the empty, foggy morning across the garden to the vacant cottage. Alfred's furniture was more or less untouched after all those years and Laura made her way through the musty rooms, her mind racing, seeing little of what was there but rather how she could transform it.

At breakfast Laura told Charles she thought it was time she moved out of the house, and she asked him whether there would be any problem in her taking over the gardener's cottage by the south wall. Charles agreed. He treated Laura with more respect than he had her mother: he always checked first whether it would be all right if an Italian media magnate could be fed and watered this weekend, or extra people come to next Sunday lunch, rather than simply foisting such inconveniences upon her.

The cottage had stood idle and neglected for fifteen years only as an oversight, perhaps because it was so close to the house that no one noticed it. Charles congratulated himself on having kept it empty all this time for just such a need.

By the time she gave birth Laura had replaced most of the furniture in the cottage, redecorated from top to bottom, and completely redesigned the kitchen, planning to expand her catering business as soon as she'd recovered from maternity. Those around the big house shuddered when they saw her, in a headband and swollen dungarees, moving tables and chairs, scraping and sanding and filling walls from dawn to dusk, and waddling up and down a ladder to paint the window sills on crisp October mornings. But Laura knew she was strong. And she suspected that the boy growing inside her was even stronger.

That child was so active inside her belly that Laura thought he was trying literally to break free of his walls of confinement. 'Let me out!' he seemed to scream. 'I want to live out there!'

Robert stayed away, as he had throughout the pregnancy; no one had seen him, no one knew where he was, apart from occasional rumoured sightings around the town. And Alice's hands were full with her own offspring. But Natalie stayed close to Laura.

The contractions started when she was painting the ceiling of the last room in the cottage. She lay down on the floor, gasping, and suddenly Natalie appeared in the doorway, breathless herself. She dragged Laura to the car, despite her protestations that this was only the beginning.

'You can't go on what the midwives say,' Natalie told her nervously. 'We're not taking any chances.'

By the time they got to the hospital the contractions had receded and the doctor, after a brief examination, advised them to go back home.

'The head's nowhere near engaged,' she explained. 'I should get a good night's sleep if I were you. It's your first, you know you ought to be prepared for a long labour.'

On their way out of the doors of the maternity ward Laura told Natalie she needed the lavatory, so they turned round and went back to the Ladies. Natalie refused to leave Laura's side and followed her in. Laura entered a vacant cubicle and instead of sitting on the toilet seat, as she meant to, she abruptly squatted on the floor, her waters broke, and it was there that a short time later Laura gave birth to her daughter, Adamina, who came squelching and sliding into Natalie's astonished, unwavering hands before she could even call a nurse.

Zoe, who believed in reincarnation, had advised Laura that she should get someone to watch her baby closely when it was born. Adamina arrived, after months of shifting and kicking, in a state of calm. Her eyes open, she gazed at the people around her – as well as the walls and fittings of the ladies' toilets – with a look of curiosity, as if with a sense of *déjà vu*, ascertaining that things hadn't changed so very much since the last time she was here. But with a look also, Laura

345

maintained, of purpose, as if saying: 'Right. This time, you lot, we're going to do things *my* way.'

And *then* she opened her mouth and her lungs and let out a scream that echoed around those cubicles.

James had business cards printed saying: JAMES FREEMAN – FREELANCE PHOTOGRAPHER. He installed a darkroom in the small room of the flat, where he could develop black-and-white, and opened an account with a colour lab in St Peter's.

He began with postcards. Bulk orders of his six calling cards worked out so cheap that he had 500 printed of each, and hawked the surplus ones around shops to offset the printing costs. While doing so he noticed that there were hardly any postcards of the town itself; the same few appeared in every shop and looked like they'd been taken twenty years ago, judging by car number plates and people's clothes. Their corners curled in the stands like stale sandwiches.

'There's not much of a call for them,' one shop proprietor told him.

'I'm not surprised,' James agreed.

'It's not exactly a tourist town, is it?' she said.

'We get plenty of visitors, I'd have thought,' he demurred. 'Enough, anyway.'

All through the spring and summer of 1987 James woke to the alarm an hour before dawn, five days a week, and cycled to a different vantage point on the hills outside town. There he set up his tripod and waited for sunrise. When the day came grey and overcast he packed his stuff and went straight home, but often enough the sun made the brown sandstone buildings glow. The town's horizon was, James had to admit, nondescript; but church spires rose through morning mist in the river valley, and he used long lenses and colour filters.

Then he moved in, photographing the town across the river and the meadow and down from the hill by the big house. For the first time he seriously considered going back home: he remembered sitting up on the forbidden roof as a child, gazing at the town below, and he contemplated sneaking in and creeping up the back stairs. But he rejected the notion and made do with some shots from the park below.

When James first moved into the flat the noise at night – amplified, as if by the dark – kept him awake: drunken voices, car doors slamming, revving engines of thoughtless revellers emerging from places all around him on that busy road. He got used to it, though, as he did to getting up so early: he'd already reached an age when he no longer lay in in the mornings with any pleasure, and once he was out of doors in the pre-dawn he was grateful to be so, to see the light infusing the world, to hear birdsong and scattered sounds of humanity, sober versions of the night before, which would build towards the raucous symphony of rush-hour.

'It could become addictive,' he told Zoe. She had persisted longer than anyone with messages on his answerphone that became increasingly enraged with his smug announcement, and his infuriating postcards.

'I know you're there, James Freeman!' her last call had yelled. 'Pick up this bloody phone and talk to me!'

James' hand hovered above the telephone.

'Right! That's it, you little twerp!' Zoe declared and slammed down the receiver.

She came round one morning, early, so as to catch him still in bed, only to meet him at the door as he returned home with his camera bag and tripod. He made coffee and toast.

'So what is it?' Zoe demanded. 'You're turning into a crepuscular animal now?'

James shrugged.

'It means twilight,' she explained. 'It also means dim; not yet enlightened. So either way it fits you.'

'I'm sorry, Zoe. I've been really busy. I've taken any job I've been offered, and begged for others: I've done portraits, pets, publicity shots for amateur dramatic groups, that dance centre—'

'All right,' Zoe put her hands up, 'I've heard enough.'

'I've just got my first colour postcards printed. Look at these.'

He opened a box; Zoe flipped through them, wrinkling her nose in disgust.

'Our town doesn't look anything like this,' she declared. 'You've made it look like Bath, or Oxford. How have you hidden the factory? And the high-rise? And the pylons?'

'The camera never lies,' James laughed.

'Merchant–Ivory Postcards Incorporated,' Zoe said.

'Who are you to talk? I've seen the queues round the block for their films.'

'Just because I'm a pimp doesn't mean you have to be a whore. Especially not, in fact.'

'So I'm a hack,' he said. 'There's nothing wrong with that.'

Alice and Harry's Taurean children were quiet and well behaved from the very beginning. Wheeling her placid children around the stores, Alice drew envious, admiring glances from those whose offspring were chasing each other up and down aisles screaming. In fact, most people assumed that Alice was their nanny: she still had the pixie face of a child and was short enough to make people think she may yet grow some more. And she was still all arms and legs, unco-ordinated, as if she hadn't worked out the precise use of her own limbs. From a distance Alice looked like a child still trying to gauge the best way to walk; her older children looked more grown-up than she did.

While Alice was mistaken for her own children's nanny, her Indian *au pair* – a series of Harry's young female relatives came over for six months or a year each – was routinely taken to be their mother. Each of Alice and Harry's five children would be born with light-brown skin and dark-brown hair; if they had a trace of their mother's auburn, people only assumed that was due to the use of henna. They would also all have their father's curranty eyes; Alice's eyes – one blue, one green – would, through her choice of a partner who proved to have dominant chromosomes, be a genetic freak, a one-off, lost in the family history.

Having given up her career, Alice transferred her scientific bent and pedagogical training to the realm of motherhood, inventing gadgets and devices for her babies. She attached mirrors to the skirting-boards so they could locate themselves in the world; she created mazes with furniture, into whose centre she would lower them and which they had to crawl their way out of.

Alice also constructed wire cages in which she placed the children's food, but which could only be opened by pressing certain levers in the correct order, transforming mealtimes into tantalizing games.

'It's like being in a laboratory, poor things,' Uncle Simon protested. 'They're babies, darling, not experimental rats. Look!' he remonstrated, 'they'd much rather play with me.' Which was true: there was nothing Simon liked better than crawling around on the floor, letting his nieces and nephews clamber over his body. They adored him. He entered the east wing with his pockets filled, both with sweets and with scraps of paper on which riddles and jokes were scrawled.

'What do you get if you cross a dinosaur with a tangerine?' he asked Amy.

When he saw Simon crawling across the carpet with his children it made Harry feel slightly queasy.

'It's undignified behaviour,' he told Alice when they were alone. 'I worry it will spoil them.'

Harry doted on his children, but from a distance. Maybe he assumed they knew how wonderful he thought they were. They were miracles of creation. He would see in each of them small reflections of himself, in their appearance, gestures, character, and it moved him. Even better, though, he saw echoes of Alice, the wife whom he adored, and he loved them for carrying her on, reprises of her echoing in space and time.

Harry approved wholeheartedly of Alice's scientific experiments (even if he did ask her to confine her creations to the playroom, since however functional they were, they all *looked* hopelessly home-made and clashed with the antiques with which they'd ended up furnishing their wing of the house). Not only did Harry approve, he encouraged further ideas, having been impressed by what he'd heard of hot-housing in America: he brought a music tutor in to teach them on miniature instruments and enrolled them in Saturday classes in computer skills, gymnastics and chess.

Not that either Harry or Alice saw any reason to wait until their children were born before giving them the stimulus they needed to fulfil their potential. Alice continued with her cyclic pregnancies, her production of Taurean babies, taking them in her crab-like stride, and she and Harry bought cassette tapes with heartbeat rhythms, which Alice placed on her stomach during her afternoon naps, in order to energize the developing brain of the foetus inside her. They also recorded tapes of their own with messages saying: 'Mummy loves you. Daddy loves you. We can't wait to meet you. Have a nice day.'

'Our children are special,' Harry told Alice.

'Their children are creepy,' Natalie told Laura. 'And so are they.'

'Don't exaggerate, Nat,' Laura reproved her. 'They're just a bit overzealous, maybe.'

'Just make sure you keep yours out of their kitchen kindergarten,' Natalie warned.

'I don't think she'll need it somehow,' Laura ventured.

Laura had been warned, in her ante-natal classes, of the possibility of post-natal depression. But when it happened she forgot the advice she'd been given and sank into it. It was a physical condition, which dragged her down: she ceased to see the world around her in colour,

349

colours drained away leaving monochromatic vision. She became addicted to sleeping. When the baby slept, so did Laura; when awake, all she wanted was to slink back to bed.

Some days she didn't get dressed, and slopped around the cottage in dressing-gown and slippers, feeding herself and Adamina. The cook she'd hired for the big house got on with the job, occasionally checking things with Laura; otherwise she heaved herself out and down to the post office to cash her child benefit and buy groceries.

Alice had just had her third baby, Tom, and had her hands full in the east wing. Natalie dropped in, and so did Simon, but Laura told them she was fine and didn't need anything and she really wanted to grab some sleep while Mina was dozing, would they mind very much if she did?

Ever since her parents had died she'd regarded herself as removed from those around her; although when she thought about it she realized she'd *always* felt that way. She'd grown up as an only child but in the margin of that large family; and since her parents' deaths she'd stayed at the house, unsure whether she was an orphan, a parasite or, like her mother, the keeper of its heart, the only sane person in a house of fools whose role, or destiny, was to keep it somehow together.

Now, with a child totally dependent on her, Laura had never felt so isolated. From the day she'd confirmed her pregnancy Robert had said barely a word to her. Initial anger gave way to relief: it made things clearer. This was her child, her responsibility. She'd bring her up as she wanted, answerable to no one.

But it meant Laura was alone. She knew people saw her – had always seen her – as self-sufficient. And it wasn't altogether an illusion. She wasn't even sure she was lonely, in a way that others could be even when surrounded by people; Laura wasn't insecure. She was simply alone. And now, sunk in a depressive stupor, there was no one to drag her out.

Laura found her own escape route – through food. She began to spend a little longer preparing her meals, and used them to try out new recipes. Taste was the first of her senses to come back to life, she would one day tell James, followed by smell.

Laura began by experimenting with neglected recipes in the cookery books she'd inherited, adapting them, rediscovering forgotten flavours, substituting new ingredients for old, and it became clear how limited a cook she (and Edna before her) actually was:

Laura had served an apprenticeship of sorts under her mother in the mundane quartermaster's art of catering for a household, and then she'd assumed she had to go abroad for new ideas and ingredients which she brought back as formulae to be repeated in the kitchen of the big house.

Now an antiquarian bookseller in the High Street sent out requests along his grapevine and obtained for Laura the Victorian *Modern Cookery* of Eliza Acton and Alexis Soyer's *Shilling Cookery for the People*; Mrs Raffald's *Experienced English Housekeeper* and Hannah Glasse's *Art of Cookery* from the eighteenth century; and a facsimile copy of Robert May's *The Accomplisht Cook* of 1660.

Laura read the archaic cookery books while breastfeeding Adamina, but now instead of going back to sleep she put Adamina in her cot and went downstairs to the kitchen. Her world was reduced to a primitive realm but it was an exciting one, her kitchen a laboratory of rediscovery and reordering of essential ingredients: of meat and fish, fruit and vegetables, herbs and spices, flour, cheese and cream. Of chopping crisp vegetables, kneading dough, breaking eggs, baking cakes and roasting joints, blending juices and simmering stews, pounding meat and grinding spices with pestle and mortar, of sautéeing onion and garlic in hot butter, of coddling, boiling and seething.

The ends of Laura's fingers were always burnt or snicked but she didn't mind, as she spent hours making complicated dishes in minute portions, just to test and taste them, recording the results in a card-index system.

The task Laura found she was setting herself was so enormous and so absorbing that she simply forgot she was unhappy. She discovered that she wasn't altogether alone, either. Jane Grigson and Elizabeth David stood over her shoulder, encouraging or chiding her to throw away that corn oil, it's good for nothing; always make your own bouquets garnis, woman, don't be lazy, and don't forget lemon peel with fish, and try fennel, too, and how about tarragon? Don't be lazy, girl.

Laura got one of the gardeners to dig over a plot of land by the side of the cottage and she planted small quantities of rocket, lovage, orache, garlic, fenugreek, mallow, rue and tansy in a miniature medievel garden, as well as sorrel, parsley, chives, lemon, thyme, mint, carrots, onions, leeks, shallots and globe artichokes.

Indoors, she revived the sixteenth-century custom of burning rosemary, juniper or bayleaves as herbal incense, or simply strewing aromatic herbs on the kitchen floor and raising their fragrance with her footsteps.

Those aromas and the smells of her cooking emanated from Laura's cottage. Simon and Natalie came over ever more often but instead of sending them away she invited them inside to taste this mackerel in gooseberry sauce or that lamb with plums: is it as good as with laverbread, or should I stick to that ragoût I made last week? Whenever he dropped in Simon begged Laura for a pot of crème brulée and she got into the habit of having one on hand, even though each time she tried in vain to get him to ask for burnt cream.

'This is nectar,' Simon drooled. 'Those French know what they're doing,' he slavered.

'I've explained a hundred times, Simon,' Laura admonished him, 'it's English. It's an export, not an import.'

'Have you got any more of those Brazil-nutty mushrooms?' he asked her. 'Umbrellas or something.'

'No more parasols, but I found these field mushrooms in the park this morning. I'll do you some on toast with clotted cream. I think you'll like them.'

By the time Laura was back at work in the big house, six months after Adamina's birth, she had grounded herself back in reality.

Laura never blamed Adamina for her brief depression (now no more than a dim memory). Her daughter was easy; Adamina had seemed at home in the world from her first days. She responded to visitors with gurgles and smiles that put them at their ease, but she was equally content with her own company: she lay in her cot, cooing and sighing to herself as if reminiscing.

'She's been here before,' Laura told Alice. 'She looks around like she's taking stock, ticking things off on an inventory.'

'They're who they are from the word go,' Alice agreed. 'They come out of the womb with their characters formed. Every mother can see that.'

Adamina was so quiet and contented that Laura occasionally forgot she *had* a baby. She'd be surprised to hear the mobile in Adamina's cot tinkling, or to open a cupboard and find it full of baby food.

Laura didn't tell Alice that one day she decided to go shopping on the spur of the moment and threw on a coat and walked out of the door. She got into her car, turned on the ignition, and was half-way down the drive when she suddenly remembered that she was a mother with a six-month-old baby in a cot back in her room. Laura reversed and rushed in, to find Adamina softly sighing to herself.

Adamina was such an easy baby that when people sympathized with Laura about how hard it must be being a single parent she didn't know whether to agree, fraudulently, or contradict them with the truth. The only problems Adamina gave her mother came at night: she seemed to lack the ability to fall asleep. During the day she snoozed soundly enough between feeds, dozing off at the nipple, eyes glazing and closing and lips sliding off. Laura put her in her cot, and Adamina slept deeply – even if she did have the strange habit of turning her body round in her sleep, ending up with her feet on the pillow.

At night when Laura put her down Adamina gurgled to herself as usual, but gradually her utterances and behaviour became more agitated, until she ended up crying out of sheer tiredness.

'Put a tot of brandy in her milk, darling,' Simon advised when he visited one evening, yelling above the baby's bawling.

Laura carried Adamina around on her shoulder, cooed soothing sounds in her ear, rocked her to and fro in her pram in the kitchen with one hand as she held an old cookery book she was reading with the other, in an effort to help her daughter fall asleep. Before long, though, Laura discovered that the only place Adamina was guaranteed to drop off was in a moving car; and Laura lost count of the number of times she drove around the block until Adamina was asleep on the seat beside her.

'You know what that means?' Zoe demanded at Sunday lunch. 'It means she's a traveller.'

'It doesn't mean anything,' Laura replied. 'It's just the rhythm soothes her.'

'Everything means something, Laura,' Zoe assured her.

Late in the evening of Adamina's first birthday, in December 1987, there was a knock on the door of the cottage. Laura turned off her food processor, wiped her hands on her apron and opened the door. There before her were so many parcels wrapped up in the same red shiny paper, stacked one on top of another, that it took Laura a moment to notice someone standing behind them.

Laura looked from Robert to the pile of gifts, back at him again, then once more at the presents. Unable to resist a rush of gratitude at this display of generosity – it looked as if Robert must have walked into the Early Learning Centre and bought one of everything – Laura had to then collect herself.

'What is this all about?' she asked.

'It's our daughter's birthday, isn't it?' Robert smiled. 'There's stuff here I thought she might like. A swing. A paddling pool. Toys. Games.'

'Are you mad?' Laura asked. 'You've ignored me – and her – all this time, and now you bring all these? It's too late, Robert.'

'We can talk,' he suggested. 'Aren't you going to invite me in?'

Laura shook her head. 'No,' she said, as she reached behind her and closed the door. 'No, I'm not.'

Robert was undeterred. 'They're not all for her, babe. That one on top's for you.'

'I don't care,' she replied.

'I'll show you,' Robert said, and stepped forward. He picked up a small packet from on top of the pile and tore open the gift-wrap: inside was a jewellery box, and he opened that too, and held it towards Laura, so that she could see the twenty-carat gold chain he'd bought her.

Laura rubbed her forehead. 'It's different now, can't you see that? I've got over you, Robert. I don't need you, and neither does she. I've decided.'

'I decide when something's over,' Robert replied.

'Not this time, Robert,' Laura said. She turned round and let herself back inside, slipping the catch as she closed the door.

Half an hour later she glanced out of the window and saw Robert standing, immobile, not having moved an inch from where he'd stood. When she went to bed a couple of hours later she looked again and he was still there; she could see the red glow of his cigarette in the dark.

In the morning, however, he was gone, and his abundant gifts with him.

As well as being easy, Adamina was also precocious. She never crawled, for one thing, but watched Laura walking about the place and one day stood up and tried to copy her. Of course, she didn't succeed right away but, undeterred, stumbled and fell a hundred times rather than revert to the more conventional first stage of ambulation, crawling on her stomach like a porpoise on the beach.

'You *are* a sea creature,' Laura tried to reason with her. 'You can't

354

expect to change from swimming in the womb to walking upright on dry land overnight. Be patient, little one.'

Adamina took no notice. She pulled herself up the side of a chair with a look of intense concentration and launched herself forward for one or two doomed, ludicrous footsteps before crumpling to the floor in a heap, astonished. But when Laura reached towards her with a calming or a guiding hand Adamina only pushed it away, stood herself up unsteadily and tried again, determined to master this thing on her own or not at all. And maybe that's why it gave her so much pleasure: within a couple of weeks Adamina could totter clear across the living-room and she did so laughing with delight, happy to let Laura join in now, toddling across the carpet into her mother's arms.

It was the same with speech. When Adamina first began to utter the experimental syllables of a toddler Laura responded in kind, to encourage her.

'Coo coo pa?' Adamina asked, pointing out of the window.

'Coo coo pa, yes,' Laura agreed. 'Coo coo pa.'

But instead of appreciating this nonsensical solidarity Adamina glared at her mother, and clammed up. While Alice's children spouted streams of gobbledygook, from which odd words leapt, miraculous, Adamina remained mute. Not, however, that anyone imagined her to be backward: her sense of self-possession made clear that she'd simply chosen to bide her time because baby-talk was beneath her. And that was how it was: when her contemporaries finally managed to glue intelligible words together Adamina all of a sudden deigned to join them. The silent child learned to talk overnight, and the only eccentricity of her speech – which may or may not have been due to her unwillingness to learn by trial and error – was that she spoke for ever after with a slight lisp.

Adamina also mastered the art of falling asleep without having to be driven around the block, but developed a new habit of waking up half-way through the night and stumbling sleepily through to Laura's room. Adamina climbed into Laura's bed without fully waking her, and mother and daughter slept the rest of the night side by side.

It became such a routine that when Laura woke in the morning to find her bed empty she rushed through to make sure Adamina was all right. Sometimes, seeing her daughter sleeping peacefully, Laura was unable to resist the temptation to snuggle in beside *her* for a few more minutes of shared, luxurious comfort.

*

355

As Adamina grew Laura, instead of reducing her workload, proceeded to expand her business. She negotiated with Charles a raise in her salary and then subcontracted the woman who'd filled in during her maternity on a part-time basis. She was soon employing an occasional assistant in her cottage as well, after knocking down walls and converting the whole of the downstairs into one large kitchen, with her and Adamina's living space above. Laura prepared meals and took them out to dinner parties once or twice a week; and she specialized in traditional English cooking.

Laura had revealed her plans at one of the Sunday lunches – a lunch of roast beef, Yorkshire pudding, roast potatoes and fresh vegetables.

'This is the best meal in the world,' Simon proclaimed. 'But what about the other six days in the week?' he demanded. 'Not to mention breakfast and supper. You're quite mad, Laura.'

'I have to disagree, actually,' Harry chipped in. 'There's a great deal to be grateful for in our national cuisine, but as usual we knock it instead of celebrating it.'

'Ha!' Alice spluttered. 'What do you know, Mr Harry Haute-cuisine? The only thing you know how to cook is curry!'

'I thought you liked my cooking,' Harry complained.

'Of course I do, silly, it's my favourite. You're a Muglai magician, Harry, you're the chapata champ. You're prince of passandas, my love. But since when have you been an expert in English food?'

'There's lots of things, actually, for which these islands have a right to be proud: Welsh rarebit, cottage pie—'

'Roast parsnips,' added Simon.

'Fish and chips!' said Amy, catching on.

'I was thinking of more salubrious sorts of dishes,' Laura tried to interject.

'Cauliflower cheese,' Simon, ignoring her, continued.

'Ice-cream!' said Sam, slightly missing the point.

'Steak-and-kidney pie,' Harry resumed. 'Bread-and-butter pudding, bubble and squeak, beef stew with dumplings.'

'I say, Harry,' said Charles, who'd been unnaturally absent from the conversation. 'I think you're on to something,' he opined, having found an angle on the subject that interested him. 'We've spent the last hundred years importing other people's food. It's high time we started *exporting* our own.'

'Well, yes, actually,' Harry agreed. 'You see, Charles, we don't blow our own trumpet. We prefer hearing our competitors'. But think of the market out there.'

'Enormous,' Charles enthused. 'Untouched.'

'And chocolate sauce!' Sam shouted.

'Yes, *thank* you, Sam,' Alice told him. 'That's enough.'

'Thanks to *all* of you,' said Laura, standing up and clearing away the dishes. 'You're all very helpful, as usual.'

'Trifle!' Sam yelled.

'Shush!' Alice scolded. 'You'll wake the baby.'

'No,' Simon said, 'he's right. Trifle's a very good example.'

Adamina grew up, just like her mother before her, in the kitchen. Her first toys were pots and pans and the more robust vegetables; she explored shapes by cutting them out of pastry; she learned to count by adding up ingredients, and understood weight and volume through the use of a measuring jug; while the first books she learned to read were less often children's stories than illustrated recipes.

Laura's reputation spread and her clientele enlarged in an ever-widening circle around the town. One summer evening in 1989, when Adamina was almost three, Natalie rang to say a crisis had occurred at the refuge and she couldn't baby-sit. Laura put Adamina as well as her dishes in the car; she wasn't worried, she knew Adamina would entertain herself in someone *else's* kitchen. Tonight's clients lived some miles south-west of the town. As she drove Laura went over in her mind preparations for the meal: what had to be cooked fresh and what merely reheated, how to lay out the hors d'oeuvres. Adamina sat silently beside her, and Laura forgot that she was there (except that every time she braked her arm left the steering-wheel and hovered in front of Adamina's chest). So Laura didn't notice the puzzled frown on the child's face. When they were about half-way there Adamina asked: 'Mummy, have you been to their house before?'

'No, I haven't,' Laura replied.

Adamina was silent again, but ten minutes later she again piped up: 'Mummy?'

'What, Mina?'

'If you've never been there before, how do you know where to go?' Adamina demanded. For half an hour she'd been baffled at the succession of choices her mother was making, whether to go left, right or straight on, at every new junction and turn-off.

357

It took Laura a moment to realize what it was Adamina was oblivious to.

'Mummy knows everything, honey, don't you know that by now?' she laughed.

'No, you don't,' Adamina replied; she wasn't fooled. So Laura explained what signposts were.

'Don't worry, Mina,' she concluded. 'You'll soon be able to read them; you'll be able to find your way around.'

It might have been in response to Uncle Simon and Auntie Natalie's guarded criticisms. Or maybe even Alice thought it was going too far when Harry gave Amy her own personal computer on her fifth birthday, in April 1990. Whatever the reason, it was then that Alice went into town one day and came home with a dog.

'A companion for the children,' she told Harry. 'They'll grow up together.'

Neither Harry nor Alice had ever had a pet themselves. In fact it was the first domestic animal to reside in the big house.

'Are you sure it's a dog?' Harry asked. He was nonplussed. 'It looks more like a rat to me.'

'It's a puppy, silly,' Alice told him. 'It's less than a month old.'

'I suppose it's going to grow into a wolf and bite them, is it?' he wondered. 'This might be very irresponsible, Alice.'

'No, it won't, grumpy-features. It's a short-haired terrier. They're tiny.'

The children christened him Dick, and were captivated by their pet. They prodded and poked him; carried him around; bathed him; and they antagonized him with a long ribbon Dick chased in enraged circles, until he discovered his own short tail and chased that instead.

No one thought to train Dick, so he grew up with a mind of his own. The first thing to become clear was that he didn't like children. He began turning his nose up at them, and when they tried to ruffle his wiry hair or stroke his belly he snapped at their fingers. Dick treated beings the same sort of size as himself with utter disdain. The only humans he regarded as his equals were those looming high above him. He abandoned the children and trotted jauntily around the house in the footsteps of adults who had no idea he was there, and they stepped on and tripped over him, and kicked him out of the way.

The sad thing was that none of the adults liked Dick. Harry had been right: even when fully grown Dick looked more like a rat than a dog, with his short, wiry hair and an ugly snout. The children were above such superficial judgements but he pranced out of their rooms and into Alice and Harry's on a Sunday morning, walked up to the bed and, without preparation or warning, bounded vertically up in the air and landed on top of them.

'Agh!' Harry cried. 'Get off!'

Because he wasn't trained, Dick the dog only learned to do things he wanted to, thus acquiring the obstinate eccentricity of an autodidact. He liked to unwrap other people's Christmas presents with his front paws, to take a siesta at the back of the Aga like a cat, and to move people's shoes from one room to another – during which exercise he revealed a natural propensity for neatness by always making two trips in order to keep each pair intact.

Dick was, on the other hand, and for all his intelligence, neurotically insecure. When, on rare occasions, he found himself somewhere where another dog twice his size was being given attention he walked around in tight, disgruntled circles, cranking himself on a coiled spring of jealousy, until he unwound instantly with a suicidal snap.

Although Dick didn't like the people he was supposed to and the people he did like didn't like him, it never occurred to anyone to get rid of him. Except, that is, for Robert, who on his rare appearances in the house offered to dispose of the ugly little runt.

'Bash him on the head, drown him, bury him. Gone and forgotten,' Robert volunteered.

'Oh, how could you, Robert?' Alice rebuked him. 'Look, you've upset Sam.'

'Don't say I didn't offer,' Robert told her.

Harry was tempted by that option. Even-tempered in all other known circumstances, there was one thing that reduced Harry to primitive rage. Dick usually made no more noise than a low growl in some corner as he chewed an old tennis ball to pieces. Just occasionally, however, he toddled into the hallway and started yapping – an intolerable, high-pitched yap of exquisite unpleasantness. Irate people came rushing from all directions but Harry got there first, to grab Dick by the scruff of the neck, carry him outside and drop him in the pond.

'I do wonder,' Harry ventured the next time he found himself alone with Robert, 'whether anyone would miss him if he was quietly disposed of.'

'Just say the word,' his brother-in-law said.

'I'm not sure,' Harry prevaricated. 'You never know with children.'

'He's not trained, that's the trouble,' Robert stated.

'I know,' Harry agreed. 'It's irresponsible. And it's too late now.'

'It's never too late,' Robert told him. 'Tell you what. I'll take him next time I go shooting, if you like. He looks like a squashed ferret. If he's got a nose for rabbits, I'll train him up.'

Harry wasn't sure what Robert was on about, but it sounded like a generous offer.

'Thanks, yes, good idea,' he said.

From then on Dick would disappear from time to time, and when someone noted his absence someone else would say, 'He must be with Robert,' because Robert never told anyone, he just spirited the dog away. Sometimes he took him for a few hours, sometimes for a few days. And then Dick would simply reappear, again without warning – although with his behaviour altered. He lost interest in tennis balls, ceased yapping altogether, and spent hours in the hallway in a tensed posture with his ears pricked back, waiting. Until, after days – weeks – of neurotic patience, he heard Robert's whistle, bounced up and leapt like a hare through the dog flap.

James' postcards were on sale all over the town. The rose-tinted, sun-kissed pictures were coming to define the town's image. It was true that not enough tourists visited the town for them to sell in phenomenal numbers; instead, townspeople themselves bought them, to send to distant friends and relatives to prove what a lovely town it was they lived in. The postcards provided James with a staple income. In fact, it tended to be virtually *all* his income. He wanted to be a freelance professional, but when it came to it James lacked the skills necessary to secure work.

'You need to sell yourself,' Zoe explained. 'Letterdrops, portfolios, headed notepaper. And smarten up, James, that's what people do. You've gone and got scruffy again.'

His heart, though, wasn't really in it. Occasionally marketing agencies who'd seen his postcards tracked him down, wanting to advertise some product by giving it an image of idyllic English wholesomeness. To Zoe's surprise, James turned them down.

'I don't need to do that kind of work,' he explained. 'I'm not starving. I don't have a family to feed.'

'You've got to start somewhere,' she suggested.

'No, I don't,' he said.

James also received calls from people who wanted photos but couldn't afford to pay for them. They came from people he'd once taken them for for free: young actors and musicians of their shared youth who were now involved in campaigns, for AIDS research and against the poll tax.

'You'll have to pay for film and chemicals,' James stated (although he always found it difficult to remind people again) and he also explained that he hated demonstrations and would rather not photograph them.

'Why not?' he was asked. 'They're vital.'

'I don't feel comfortable with a lot of people I'm supposed to agree with,' he replied. 'I don't like being part of a crowd.'

'You won't be,' they assured him. 'You'll be outside it, wherever you are. People don't trust photographers any more.'

James' favourite work, though, was a project, also unpaid, of his own choosing. He'd grown up in the sealed-off house on the hill, then spent ten years in a bedsit in a quiet quarter of the town; now he lived in a flat on Factory Road. It was a vital artery of the town and more lively than the centre, because residents lived there, and most of its small shops and restaurants were worked by their owners, who also lived above them.

Soon after moving in James set up a tripod at his living-room window and took pictures of the busy street below, in the manner of André Kertesz, discovering that it's easiest to observe people from above because they never look up. He found it, though, a dishonest and unsatisfying activity; he felt like a *paparazzo* of ordinary people. So he left the tripod behind and took his camera down to the pavement. He wandered to and fro, watched the flow of shoppers, walkers, workers, children, parents; and took photographs; and realized that other people were watching him.

Photographers are shifty figures, James knew that. Ones like him, anyway, their whole purpose to capture, to steal, an image from the people they move among, stealthy as pickpockets, cold-eyed and heartless. In a crowd at some public event it doesn't matter: everyone, whether nominally performer or audience, being to some extent on show, on parade, by common assent.

In a residential neighbourhood, though, he found this wasn't so. James wasn't invisible behind his camera. He felt as conspicuous as he had that day, many years before, when he first ventured outside the walls around the big house to take pictures in town, only to be jostled and yelled at and to retreat home. It was the same thing now, because people weren't in this place for a special occasion – this was where they lived. Despite the bustle of traffic, shoppers, ghetto-blasters, bicycles, buses, children and dogs, residents and shopkeepers alike took in the life around them, and they took in the lurching man snapping photographs. James saw their suspicion and hostility.

It didn't take him long to find a solution. Unable to remain inconspicuous, he went up and down the road introducing himself to people who were, after all, his neighbours. And he asked whether he might photograph them because he was, he explained, chronicling his – their – shared neighbourhood. They all said yes. He photographed them standing in front of their shop signs, their trays of vegetables, their discount-price posters, their life-size, smiling butcher, their second-hand furniture, their racks of newspapers, the sallow-faced waiters in the burger joint, the bad-tempered Chinaman in his take-away, the nonchalant Greeks in their fish-and-chip shop, the friendly gangsters in the Lebanese restaurant, the melancholy Turk in his kebab van. Taking inspiration now from August Sander, he photographed them gazing steadfastly back at him in their aprons and caps and other working clothes. Someone called him the Camera Man and the nickname stuck: within a few weeks it accompanied him along the road. People waved and called to him but now in affectionate greeting, and invited him to photograph a new shop assistant or waiter or a relative who happened to be visiting.

James began to jog daily up and back down the road; he had breakfast most mornings in the Café Milano; he played football with kids on the grass in front of the Health Centre; he shared a can of beer with unemployed youths on the bench outside the Community Centre. Whenever he had spare time he descended to the street. And, having taken portraits, and given prints to the subjects, he found he was now free to take the spontaneous pictures he preferred. He had permission.

Lewis was one of those friends who'd left two or three messages on James' answerphone and then – receiving no more than James' vapid postcards in return – let it go. For a couple of years they didn't see or speak to each other. How large, James wondered, does a town have to be for familiar people to lead entirely disconnected lives?

Then one day in December James met Lewis on the street, and they arranged to go to a home game of the town football team that Saturday. Lewis picked James up, parked close to the ground, and joined bescarved fans on foot. Lewis walked with a lazy, reluctant-looking lope; James scampered to keep up beside him.

The team were in the fourth division of the football league. The standard of play was atrocious; the ball ricocheted around the pitch, players chased and hoofed it blindly, as if punishing it for its waywardness.

James and Lewis stood on the terraces in the main stand. There was one black player in the opposition team. Every time he gathered the ball the home fans made noises like excited monkeys. There were *two* black players on the town side, but it seemed that the colour of their skin was not apparent: the fans cheered or booed their contributions just like everyone else's.

After ten minutes Lewis stopped responding to the game. He became still and stiff, and guardedly alert. When the whistle blew for half-time he said: 'Let's go,' and James followed him out.

They walked to Lewis's car in silence, and he drove James home without saying a word. James invited Lewis in for a cup of tea but Lewis shook his head.

'They're morons,' James said, before he got out of the car. 'Fuck them, Lew.'

Lewis remained staring out of the windscreen. 'They're English.'

'Sure,' James agreed.

Lewis sighed. 'When I was tiny and Mum took me shopping, sometimes when we passed a group of West Indian women they clicked their tongues at Mum, and hissed at her. Only when there was a bunch of them, mind you. You know my sister's a nurse?'

'Of course. She stitched my hand.'

'A few months ago this patient was brought in, and she told the sister that she wasn't having that coloured nurse touching her.'

'Gloria? Jesus, what a dumb cow.'

'Yeh, and what's more, this patient was a middle-aged Asian woman.'

Robert never told anyone of his comings and goings. He was secretive by nature: when he wrote something, even signing a cheque, he cupped his other arm around his writing hand in the manner of a suspicious schoolchild. He was a ghostly presence in the house. He was the only one who still had the same room as in his childhood, up on the third floor. Around the time Alice married Harry, Simon had moved down into a large room on the second floor, where Charles and also Natalie already resided. Robert took over his siblings' old rooms, where he stored boxes of unknown content that came and went up and down the back stairs, and where invisible guests would stay for periods of mysterious duration.

Only Simon had the courage – and the persistence – to question his taciturn brother, when Robert made a rare appearance at breakfast.

'Those vans that woke us up last night, were they involved in some criminal activity?' he demanded. 'What on earth do you *do*, Robert?'

'A bit of this and a bit of that,' Robert replied, without taking his eyes from the toast he was spreading.

'And these footsteps we hear,' Simon continued. 'Are these people in hiding? Is our home being turned into a safe house of some kind?'

'A couple of mates,' Robert mumbled through a mouthful of toast and marmalade.

'Leave your brother alone,' Charles told Simon. 'Sounds like the ruddy Inquisition.'

None of the family entered Robert's domain on the third floor. They weren't invited. If they had to communicate they'd leave notes or, in urgent cases, telephone him on his private line, which had been installed at the same time as Harry's children's, by unanimous demand: Robert was the most taciturn of men, yet he was in the habit of hijacking the telephone and conducting endless inconsequential conversations with a nagging, playful undertone.

Even the cleaning lady stopped going beyond the second floor: she hoovered the stairs as far as the landing; beyond that the carpets had a tangled strip of hairy fluff at the angle of each tread and step.

Robert came and went as if he inhabited a parallel dimension within the house. Yet he would sporadically, suddenly, be there at Sunday lunch, or would appear at one of Simon's gatherings in an incongruous suit, leaning against a wall, eyeing the women in the room with guarded interest.

The fact was Robert moved between worlds. He was most at ease in the company of men on the roughest estate out on the west side of town that was notorious locally for its social degradation: statistics for unemployment, truancy, illiteracy, single-parent families, car theft and other crimes were batted back and forth across the council chambers from one side to the other in order to prove opposing arguments.

Many of the cars that Robert did up he bought from unemployed men with a wad of notes and towed home along with dubious vehicle-registration certificates and incompatible stereos. The men of the estate – some of them old comrades and adversaries from Robert's boxing days, like Docker and Weasel – were famed for their hardness. They had haircuts that would make a paratrooper blanch; wore T-shirts in the depths of winter without shivering; regarded a smile as evidence of homosexuality; and liked to display their machismo by taking as pets Dobermanns, Rottweilers and Pit-bull Terriers.

The hard men liked to accompany their women (who wore *mini-skirts* in winter) to the shops with their chests puffed out with pride, while casting glances around to spot any man who dared to look at the source of their pride. They neglected their illegitimate children, except to cuff small sons for displaying emotion or daughters who expressed an opinion. And they believed that art in all its forms was another sign of homosexuality, regarding the tattoos with which they adorned their bodies as an honourable exception, since they were unaware that every art imposes pain of some kind.

Robert felt at ease in their company, and after haggling over the price of the cars he joined them for a drink in the Long Barrow, the main pub on the estate, which consisted of one large, rectangular room. They conversed by means of insulting each other while drinking copious quantities of lager, until all of a sudden at a certain stage of inebriation – and to the accompaniment of Country and Western songs on the jukebox – all pretence fell away, and the hard men leaned on each other's shoulders telling filthy jokes, threatening violence to gain the right to buy the next round, and initiating arm-wrestling contests that no one minded losing because they ended in proclamations of undying friendship.

With women, too, Robert moved between worlds and seduced them in each. Introduced to those in his family's social circle, they took in his disdainful, hooded eyes and his rough, hard workman's hands. He didn't have to say anything, all he had to do was smile, and they vanished like magic soon after he did, to follow him up the back stairs to the third floor. With his friends, however – out-of-work mechanics, leather-jacketed bikers – women would see Robert's feet under a car and wait for him to come up for air so that they could listen to his anomalous accent, intrigued by the maverick son of the man-in-charge.

Robert's family knew more about his life from hearsay than from his own lips. He was still, it was said, fascinated by locks. He was able to break into a lover's house while she was out: she'd come home and go about her business in the privacy of her home, until she became flesh-crawlingly aware that an intruder was sitting in the dark, waiting for her.

What with Charles' complicated schedule, Simon's diets, Robert's fridge raids, Natalie's shifts at the refuge, Alice's vegetarianism, Harry's taste for spices and their children's whimsical palates, Laura had to develop her mother's flexibility in order to stay sane.

The most troublesome diet of all remained Simon's. He still seized upon some new fad as the panacea for the ills of existence – sometimes it was one he'd already tried years before and forgotten – unable to accept that his natural weight was that of a Sumo wrestler, or that, as his GP maintained, he was as healthy an individual as ever entered the surgery.

'I demand a second opinion,' Simon grumbled, and returned to a curative diet of his own devising. At night, though, he'd creep into the kitchen (where he sometimes bumped into Robert) and binge till he was sick. Then he'd go on week-long, contrite fasts that left him dizzy and disorientated, and gave his body the aroma of hot metal.

Simon was so sensitive that he was both the healthiest member of the household and the most often ill. He could feel every twanged muscle and twinged tendon, each approaching virus or impending ache; the faintest rumour of indigestion deep in his gut would send him anxiously to the bathroom cabinet.

It was perfectly obvious to everyone else how healthy Simon was. He had the physical radiance of wealth, because he spent a good proportion of his salary on eau-de-cologne, manicures and pedicures, and had his hair trimmed once a week along with a luxurious shave. He also went to the exclusive health club in Northtown whose customers paid by gold credit card. Simon paused in the doorway of the gym, broadcast exhortations of encouragement to the thrusting executives and the gorgeous, bored housewives submitting themselves voluntarily to machines based, he told them, on the designs of medieval torture apparatus.

'Confess!' Simon demanded as a parting shot, and tittered to himself all the way to the sauna, where he sweated impurities from the pores of his ample flesh, and from which he recovered with a full-body massage given by the resident masseur.

Simon swam in the warm pool, in a pair of outrageous swimming trunks, and then he returned home a glowing beacon of health, only to complain that he'd just caught a cold in that bloody club's draughty changing-room.

It was inevitable that sooner or later Simon would realize there was more than one way to skin a cat, as Laura indelicately put it: around that time Simon began to make friends of fellow hypochondriacs in the waiting-rooms of various clinics around town, which had opened in recent years; like Mr Smith, a skeletal man whose stomach didn't seem able to digest nutrition from food; or the bald woman, who wore a wig. The giggling secretaries became a thing of the past, to Charles' disappointment: Charles was still waiting for his son to provide legitimate offspring of the Freeman dynasty. Within a short time the sitting-room of the big house resembled a waiting-room as Simon's new friends came straight from the chiropractor or the homoeopath, the voice therapist or the spiritual healer.

Charles was infuriated to find his house infested with shirkers and malingerers (who reminded him of Mary's poetry group meetings), but this time Simon stood his ground, pointing out that most of them were respectable professionals like himself.

'Anyway, Father,' he explained, 'you can't get this sort of thing on the NHS: it might be alternative but it's also *private* medicine.' And since that was something of which Charles approved, he left his eldest son alone.

They met after work and swapped their experiences of Japanese shiatsu, Chinese acupuncture and Indian yoga – being joined, briefly, by Zoe, who was always keen to find out about new teachers, until she came to the conclusion that Simon and his cronies were less spiritual questers than cranks.

'The body is the temple of the soul, darling,' Simon tried to explain to her.

'Yes, Simon, and he that's born a fool is never cured,' she replied.

Simon was unabashed; though sensitive to the minutest change in temperature or pollen count, he was immune to slander. He returned to the sitting-room, where he was master of ceremonies, and his friends sat in a circle discussing parts and functions of the human body as if describing exotic places on foreign travels. And they *were* explorers, searching for the unknown sources of human ailments. One of them would make some new discovery and return to the house with the news that there were such things as meridians, invisible to the blunt instruments of modern medicine, which get blocked up with nasty knots of energy that cause illness; or that there are 70,000 nerve endings in the sole of each foot and only intensive massage can be expected to keep them in good condition.

Some of the group's discoveries were radical new cures, but most were ancient medicines from distant, purer cultures. As soon as the group were told about one they promptly felt the very symptoms it was supposed to cure, for the first time in their lives.

'Yes, it's true!' the bald woman remarked. 'I *can* feel my liver ache when you press there. It works! Do it some more!'

Just as Zoe had the habit of dissolving an aspirin in a cup of strong coffee, thus causing and curing the same headache, so Simon and his friends joyously greeted cures for ailments they'd never known existed.

Harry Singh was never ill – not at least since the food-poisoning episode of his honeymoon. Maybe he was protected by the cardamom seeds he chewed. Harry certainly didn't *look* healthy: he'd inherited his father's sad complexion, and the same bruised eyes. But he had the robust constitution of a workaholic; Harry simply didn't have time to be ill. He'd converted a Georgian house in a genteel neighbourhood in Northtown into offices, and moved his business there. The only evidence that the house was something other than a comfortable family residence was a small brass plate beside the front door saying: HARRY SINGH ASSOCIATES. Who his associates might be, or if they existed at all, no one knew.

Harry spent sixteen hours a day there. House prices had rocketed to unprecedented levels, and Harry sold his properties, realizing extraordinary profit. Then, however, against all common wisdom (if not advice, since he never sought any), instead of spreading his investment Harry not only spent his entire capital on buying *more* houses; he also negotiated loans from every bank, building society and mercantile credit company that would listen to him, in order to purchase every house on the market. And he didn't sell those ones or rent them or do them up. They just lay empty, while Harry went seeking further loans.

The only person Harry confided in was his brother, Anil, who ran the stores while their father still served behind the post-office counter at the end of the shop. Their mother had retired upstairs, succeeded at the till by Anil's Indian wife. Harry often dropped in on his way home from work to buy chocolates for Alice.

'You're mad,' Anil told him. 'Loopy. And irresponsible, too. You've got a wife and kids now, it's all very well going bankrupt and off to prison, but what about them?'

'I'm not going to prison,' Harry told him.

'Even I know property's reached the top. It's got to drop now.'

'I don't think so,' Harry confided.

'Totally unrealistic, these prices are. Everybody knows that. What makes you think they can keep rising?'

Harry looked away from his brother. 'I don't know,' he admitted. 'It's a gut feeling.'

Harry may not have known, but he kept his nerve; and he proved to be right. Prices kept rising, and Harry sold his second phase of houses six months later. Many were bought by people moving out of London, who commuted on the morning train, and other people desperate to own their own home whatever the cost: the more expensive houses became, it seemed, the more people desired to buy them, with a doomed and dangerous lust.

By the time Harry sold his last properties (keeping back half a dozen houses for accommodation to rent) prices *had* reached their peak. People hardly had time to catch their breath from the meteoric rise in their standard of living and social status than they found themselves sliding backwards, with equally breathtaking speed. Businesses closed, redundancies rose, shops all over town changed hands with inexplicable regularity. The flamboyant Chancellor of the Exchequer resigned – citing discord with the Prime Minister – just before everyone else realized what was happening: it was another recession.

Many of Harry's houses reappeared on the market the following year, their owners unable to keep up the mortgage payments. Harry resisted the temptation to re-buy them, despite the fact that he could have done so with loose change. Even after paying off his loans he was hugely wealthy, though his only concession to such status was to replace the plaque at his offices with one a little smaller and more discreet. This one said simply: HARRY SINGH. His mysterious associates had disappeared.

Over a whisky with Charles and Simon, Harry told Charles that his career as a glorified estate agent was over, and for the one and only time in his life – affected as he doubtless was by the watered-down whisky – ventured to offer Charles a word of advice.

'The future branches before us in unpredictable directions,' Harry declared with his customary (if swelled by alcohol) pomposity. 'Clever men might predict it. But men of destiny dictate it.'

It didn't occur to Charles (which was just as well, Simon thought) that Harry was addressing him in particular. Charles was accustomed to giving advice rather than taking it. In September of 1987 he ordered his investment brokers to switch 50 per cent of his equities into gilts and safe government bonds.

'Why?' they asked, bewildered at the gambler's change of heart. 'Safe, Charles?'

'Don't question my authority!' he barked. 'Just do it!'

Into October they watched unhappily the lost profits of their client's usual high-rolling investments; until on the nineteenth there came the sudden Stock Market crash of Black Monday, and as all around him lost millions Charles Freeman greeted the news with a hearty laugh.

'How did he know?' his brokers wondered. 'He's a magician.'

So that now Charles thought his phlegmatic son-in-law was merely offering an opinion, tossing it into the air.

'The thing is not to play the markets, but to create them,' Harry explained. 'Not to be at their mercy, but in command of them.'

'Poppycock!' Charles declared with relish. 'Boom, recession, boom, recession,' he said. 'This is the law of capitalism. Simple. As long as you remember,' he added, 'that there are ways to make money in a boom, and ways to make money in a crisis.'

Harry frowned, shrugged and let it go.

'From what I hear,' said Simon absently, 'poor James only knows how to *lose* money, whether it's a recession or a boom-time.'

'James?' asked Charles. 'Your brother made his choice a long time ago. If he ever needs my help he can come and ask for it. With his ruddy tail between his legs.'

After much persuasion from Alice, Harry took his wife and their by now five children (Amy, Sam, Tom, Susan and Mollie) on a month's holiday to India, along with both their latest au pair and Natalie, who didn't earn enough for such a holiday herself. It turned out to be a chaotic trip without serious mishap: Natalie was the only one who got mildly ill, Alice renewed acquaintance with relatives impressed by her procreative regularity, the children unwound, and Harry spent most of the time asleep, replenishing the store of energy used up in suppressed anxiety in recent years.

Harry returned to the fray as a property developer. He began to buy empty plots of land in unlikely spots around the town; if the land did have buildings on it – bought at rock-bottom prices off bankrupts and debtors – he knocked them down. While some of the sites lay empty, others Harry now developed, and what these had in common could be summed up in one word: tradition.

Employing architects who'd turned their backs on the Sixties,

Harry Singh told council planners, business executives and chain-store owners that the age of concrete brutality was over.

'It's time we rediscovered the humanity of architecture,' he explained, 'time we created a human environment.' He saw a future in the past, recognizing a language that was a ready-made marketing ploy. But then, Harry being Harry, he quickly came to believe his own rhetoric; he was such an honest salesman that the first person he convinced was himself.

'We've lost touch with our roots,' he said ('*You* have, mate,' Anil told him) as his first superstore went up outside the ring road.

'It has the dimensions of a Roman villa, you see, and uses local materials.'

'This is *local* plastic?' someone asked.

'And we've landscaped the surrounding slopes and planted trees in the manner of an eighteenth-century country house.'

'Very nice.'

Next, Harry developed an *old* shopping centre: along the Factory Road, at the edge of the large housing estate, was a zig-zag-shaped arcade of supermarkets and smaller stores, which turned in the slightest breeze into a wind-tunnel. Pensioners pulled their shopping trolleys leaning into the wind at a forty-five degree angle and young mothers had to keep hold of small children for fear of seeing them blown away. Dark corners stank of urine and stale booze, and in the evenings gangs of youths took over the precinct for glue-sniffing and skate-boarding to music from enormous ghetto-blasters.

'The Regency period had more than style,' Harry proclaimed to his associates – who were now for real. 'There was an understanding of people in relation to buildings, a mix of function and aesthetic.'

A new tiled floor was laid in the arcade, a perspex roof erected, and the entrances were covered with vast walls of glass, including heavy doors that were locked at night by security guards. Plants were potted and façades were added to shop doorways. The wind disappeared, and so did the smells, the dogs and the teenage gangs.

'We've neglected our ancestral traditions,' Harry explained, invoking the spirit of Wren, Hawksmoor and Capability Brown, as well as more recent, royal, opinion.

For some years the bus station and the weekly open market had jostled for space in a run-down area at the edge of the town centre, behind the Old Fire Station. It became the most prominent of Harry's developments: a great double crescent, in the shape of the letter E;

the bus station in one space, the market in the other, which became on non-market days a large pedestrian precinct with continental cafés, tables and chairs. The four-storeyed buildings had shops on the ground floor, offices on the first storey and flats above; using different coloured bricks, it resembled a fairy-tale castle, with turrets and towers, tiny windows in odd places, parapets and crenellations. The whole family attended the opening.

'It's a transformation,' Charles declared.

'Better than those concrete monstrosities,' Laura agreed.

'I wouldn't mind living in one of these flats myself,' Simon suggested.

'They're horrible,' said Natalie.

'At least they're on a human scale, darling,' said Simon.

'They're on a *doll's* scale,' Natalie told him.

'You see, architecture to me,' Harry told the local Member of Parliament, who'd cut the ribbon, 'is, well, frozen music, if you like.'

'That's very fine, Mr Singh,' the politician remarked.

Harry appeared, following this success, in a discussion programme on local television, but he made such a poor impression that everyone advised him (they didn't wait to be asked) not to repeat it: with his monotonous tone of voice and his weary expression Harry came across as even more pompous and humourless than in real life; the camera didn't pick up the silent, subterranean force of his personality that came across to those who met him. Nor indeed the smell of cardamom.

Not that Harry regretted so brief a media profile. He preferred to keep it low. When he gave a sizeable donation to Natalie for the women's refuge, he made sure only enough people knew about it for word to get around discreetly.

'I'm proud of you, Harry,' Alice told him. 'I'm glad I married a philanthropist.'

'It's not philanthropy,' Harry confided. 'It might be nepotism.'

'But that's bad,' Alice rebuked him.

'Not at all,' he told her. 'Natalie's one of the family.'

Harry recommended Laura's dinner-party catering to the wives of his business associates; it would be some time before Laura realized it was more than coincidence how many of her clients happened to know that fine man Mr Singh, who was doing so much in his quiet way for our town.

Harry made clandestine deals with Robert, in the corridors of the house, which appeared to concern the discreet removal of tardy or recalcitrant tenants from his rented properties. And then he paid a call on James.

'Is Alice all right?' James wondered.

'My beloved is as radiant as ever,' Harry told him.

'Your children?' James asked.

'Your nephews and nieces are all thriving,' Harry assured him. 'James,' he said, coming quickly to the point, 'I'm not much good at small talk. I've reached a position where I now require, I feel, a full-time photographer on my staff. It amazes me how many photographic images we seem to need; I suspect it's a combination of the times we live in — when presentation is all — and of our own success as a company. Anyhow, I want to offer you the post before advertising it. Simon tells me you've been reduced to hawking postcards and suchlike.'

'Harry,' James said, 'thank you for your offer. I couldn't possibly work for you.'

'There's no need to make a decision on the spot,' Harry counselled. 'Take your time. Think it over. Salary negotiable, but generous, that sort of thing.'

James grinned. 'Harry, we were classmates together when we were snivelling kids. You're married to my sister. How could I possibly work for you?'

Harry frowned. 'I'm doing my best,' he said mysteriously. 'If you have second thoughts, call me.'

'I will, Harry,' James nodded. 'I will.'

It was around that time that Harry began to invite guests to the east wing of the house. Once again, and for the first time since Mary's death twenty years earlier, cocktail parties took place in the house on the hill. These were more subdued occasions, since the host sets the tone, but at least the drinks were better: cocktails had swung back into fashion and Harry hired two barmen to mix and shake White Russians, Bloody Marys and Gin Slings for the new rich of the town.

In fact Harry derived little pleasure from his drinks parties. He felt uncomfortable in groups of people: he gave the impression that he'd rather be somewhere else, and tended to wander around his own parties with the look of someone lost; more than once people unaware he was their host kindly told him where the lavatory could be found.

The person who enjoyed them more than anyone was Charles, even if he was somewhat confused to have been invited to a party in his own house. Occasionally Charles forgot that he *had* been invited, and when it came time for guests to leave Charles saw them out, thanking them for coming and wishing them safe journey home. And then the *guests* were confused, saying thank you, lovely party, good evening, while peering around the bulk of the man-in-charge to at least *wave* goodbye to their real host and hostess, only to glimpse Harry standing on his own in a far corner and Alice rounding up her children. It was a confusing time, for everybody, in the house on the hill, and would only become clearer with the benefit of hindsight.

Charles, though he may have caused confusion, felt none himself, possibly because he was enjoying being able to see his views literally in black and white. He spent more time in his office on the top floor of the newspaper than at the factory, and moved Judith Peach in too. Despite, on arrival, promising editorial independence, Charles hadn't been there long before those who knew him recognized his imprint in the leader columns: every now and then one would appear more forthright and more contradictory than usual, like one of Charles' inter-departmental memos (and, just like them, the editorials' spelling, punctuation and grammar had had to be tidied up by Miss Peach).

In the autumn of 1990 the Prime Minister, unassailable at the head of her party for fifteen years, was dramatically ousted from office. The man chiefly responsible looked certain to succeed her but at the last minute another contender came modestly to the fore, the Chancellor of the Exchequer: although regarded as a protégé of the Prime Minister, he appeared, in stark contrast, to be a nice man with no views of his own. In an editorial that was unmistakably one of Charles', the Chancellor's claims were advanced because it was time for a rest from personality politics and he was the right man for the job; the economy was too important to be left to politicians, so it was appropriate for a Chancellor to be at the helm.

'Can a man be Prime Minister, Mummy?' Adamina asked Laura.

The modest Chancellor duly won the leadership contest to become the youngest Prime Minister of the century.

'What a nice man,' said Alice.

'He's a wimp,' said Robert.

'He's tougher than he looks,' said Harry.

'Dreadful dress sense,' said Simon.

'Let's see what he does about Clause 28,' said Natalie.

'They're all the same,' said Laura. 'You can't trust any of them.'

*

The *Echo* had been losing money for some time before Charles took it over, and to Charles, loss was anathema. He hadn't bought the paper primarily to make money, but to lose it could not be countenanced. The first change he made was converting the format from broadsheet to tabloid and using a clearer typescript: the steady drop in sales halted. Then he halved the cost of second-hand car adverts and incorporated tiny photographs of the vehicles on offer, and sales began to increase.

That became Derek's full-time job: going around taking pictures of the cars for sale. He met James on Factory Road one day and told him that it would see him through to retirement.

'I'm not saying it's not challenging work,' he told James bitterly. 'You've got to make sure the number plate's in focus. That's what the editor told me. "It's got to be clear," she said, like she was taking the piss out of Mr Baker. Can you imagine, Jim boy, I take a bottle of water and a rag round with me, to wipe the bloody number plates.'

As well as commandeering the paper's editorials, Charles also took an interest in the news. Meeting a journalist in the corridor, he asked where he was going.

'To see the County Education Officer about them shelving those plans for the new primary school in East Side, Mr Freeman.'

'Not interesting,' Charles decided. 'Come with me. I'm hosting a businesssmen's lunch at the Golf Club. You can report that.'

'But Mr Freeman, Eva told me—'

'Who pays your wages?' Charles thundered.

'Well, you—'

'Who's the boss around here?'

'You are.'

'Come.'

Charles decreed that from now on the assistant editor had to OK all expenses directly with him. One day the man explained that it was time for the two senior subeditors to have their company cars updated.

Charles studied the request. 'They won't need them,' he decided.

'They won't, sir?'

'No. They're fired,' Charles said.

His love of gadgets now combined with the need to communicate with his minions at all times, and Charles had installed in his office a telex, a fax, answering machines, a satellite link-up, a conference-call telecommunication system, and a bank of telephones as well as three

375

mobiles that he carried around with him and which crumpled the pockets of his Savile Row suits. Owing to his utter inability to master any form of technology himself Charles was constantly picking up the wrong receiver, photocopying a document instead of transmitting it to London or hurling a computer keyboard at the wall.

In the months that followed Charles gradually divided the paper into sections on different days, for leisure, property and home and garden improvement; incorporated colour photographs; cut out the weekly books page and replaced arts reviews with comprehensive listings; and added a weekly glossy magazine, free with the *Echo* every Friday. With each change sales figures shifted upwards.

'It's a ruddy doddle, this newspaper business,' Charles told Simon one evening at home. 'I like it. And I'm going to expand.'

At the second annual meeting after his takeover Charles announced that the newspaper company was being renamed the Freeman Communications Corporation, and was to be transformed into a multi-media, technology-based conglomerate. His report unveiled plans to buy a local cable television company that had laid cables in three towns in the Midlands a few years earlier and then stopped, with the advent of satellite; to buy a minority stake in the independent regional television company, and a majority one in the new local commercial radio station. When the sceptical wondered where the money for such expansion was to come from they had only to check the accounts: pre-tax profit growth had risen by 80 per cent; Charles Freeman's buoyant optimism was justified.

What no excited shareholder or dazzled analyst looked harder for was the unpublished fact behind the figures, which was that Charles was subsidizing the expansion of the public company, FCC, through the purchase of its shares by his private Freeman Company. As share prices rose, it was a tactic that could only benefit both sides of Charles' burgeoning local empire.

The new Chancellor of the Exchequer, meanwhile, was busily denying that the country was in the grip of a recession; before long, however, he changed tack and began claiming that owing to his policies recovery was just around the corner. He and his colleagues urged people to become active patriotic consumers and help the country to spend its way out of the crisis: New Year sales lasted all winter and summer ones carried on through the autumn, until they linked up, with red SALE stickers on permanent display. It provoked one of Charles' more coherent editorials. 'The manufacturing industry is the basis of every developed nation's wealth,' it read. 'We also need strong competitors, who can afford to trade with us.'

Charles had become so involved with the paper that he was neglecting his *own* manufacturing base – the basis of *his* wealth.

Harry invited Simon to his study for a drink. Harry had his own ambitions, but he didn't want to achieve them by default.

'There are very few things of intrinsic value,' he told Simon. 'Land is one. Property another. Not absolute value, but I mean as lasting as we can imagine, or predict. Gold too, of course. Alcohol, I would venture, is another.'

'Couldn't agree more,' Simon replied. 'Speaking of which—'

'Everything else is just a commodity. They fluctuate in value.'

'Very true,' Simon agreed. 'Of course they do. By the way, have you noticed the posters for the Chinese circus? It's coming to the park next week. Why don't I take Amy and Sam?'

'Please, Simon,' Harry beseeched him, 'I'm trying to tell you something. The point is, between you and me, I fear that Charles may have lost sight of certain things. That, for example, what the factory produces is no longer of intrinsic value; that he therefore needs greater flexibility than before.'

'Quite right, Harry. Of course he does. But that's why he's expanding in all directions. The old man will sail along, I'm sure of that.'

'But the base is underwriting the expansion, and the base is . . .' Harry began to speak again, and hesitated. I've done my duty, he thought to himself. It's up to Simon to think it through for himself and warn Charles, or not, as the case may be.

'There's something else,' he said. 'In the strictest confidence.'

Simon held out his arms and smiled. 'We're friends, Harry, as well as in-laws. I promise.'

'Good,' said Harry. 'Simon, how would you like to work with me? We both know what I'm like with people – and I have to deal with an increasing number of them. Most of them are stupid. I need a people person, as they say; a PR man. I think we would make a good partnership.'

'Partners?'

'In the metaphorical sense, of course,' Harry made clear. 'An assistant, I mean. Rather, an aide-de-camp. A right-hand man. Not to put too fine a point on it: a second-in-command. What do you say? You look surprised, Simon.'

'Well,' Simon said, 'I am. It's a hell of an offer, Harry, I'm quite sure. But the fact is, I wouldn't think of deserting the old man. He needs me.'

Harry frowned. 'I don't understand. This is a business proposition, Simon. A career move, that sort of thing. You would certainly benefit.'

Simon shook his head. 'No, Harry. I couldn't leave Father. But give me that other half. I could do with it.'

James had played football in a kick-around with Lewis and his foreigners, and then gone to the pub with them. He bicycled home unsteadily and lurched into his flat. Seeing his answerphone had recorded one message he pressed PLAY. He recognized the voice at once: it was Laura's. James hardly took in what she was saying.

'Sounds f-fluzzy,' James slurred to himself. He ejected the cassette and put it in his music stereo.

'James, this is Laura,' her voice intoned matter-of-factly. 'I wonder if you'd be interested in taking some photographs of food. Give me a ring when you can. Do you have my number? It's 436214. It'd be good to see you.'

'It'd be good to see you too,' he said aloud. 'I think,' he added. He wrote down the number and dialled it, and then found he had to sit down.

'Hello.'

'Laura? Id's James here.'

'Hello, James. Thanks for calling back.'

'I got your meshage. I was playing f-football.'

'You play football? I didn't know you could. What about your hips?'

'Well, I enjoy it szo I do it.'

'Are you OK? Did you get hit on the head or something?'

'I'm f-fine. How are you?'

'Well.'

'Good. How's your daughter?'

'She's well.'

'I haven't met her.'

'I know, James. You should do.'

'I'd like to.'

There was a pause between them. James stumbled into it.

'I can't remember why I rang you,' he blurted out.

'I rang you, James, because—'

'No, I'm sure I rang you, Laura. In fact,' he said triumphantly, 'I've got your number right here.' Waving it in front of the phone he said: 'I have in my hand a piece of paper—'

'James,' Laura's voice coolly interrupted.

'What?' he asked.

'You probably don't remember, but the last time we spoke was three years ago, and you were drunk then. Do you want to call me back when you're sober?'

A familiar wave of emotion rolled through James' body. Once it had passed he was stone-cold sober.

'No. I'm sorry, Laura,' he appeased. 'You rang about photographs,' he said in a business-like tone. 'Of food.'

'I'll cook some dishes and then have pictures taken of them. You think you could do that?'

'I've never photographed food as such. I could give it a go.'

'I'm not looking for someone to have a bash, James. I want some good photographs of my work.'

'Shit, Laura,' he exclaimed. 'OK, I'll take some good pictures. Of course I will.'

They made arrangements. He'd have to take the photographs somewhere where Laura could cook. There was no way James was going to Laura's cottage, so he proposed making a studio in his flat. They scheduled the session for the following Sunday. In the meantime James hired some lights and went to the library for research, looking through hundreds of photographs in cookery books: some made you lose your appetite they were so bad, others made you drool. James was determined not to mess up.

Laura had continued her research into traditional English cooking. In her spare time she unearthed old recipes and experimented at home, testing the results on the inhabitants of the big house and incorporating successes into her freelance dinner parties. Now she'd decided to print a colour brochure to advertise her services. She wanted three sumptuous images of entire meals laid out.

On Sunday morning Laura, having left Adamina in Natalie's care for the day, arrived at James' flat early, with her car crammed full of boxes and bags. James had been up since six, preparing his sitting-room, which he'd already cleared the day before. He hoovered the carpet and cleaned the kitchen. He checked the lights and reflectors and loaded his 5 x 4 camera and shifted the blackout material he'd pinned to the windows, and sorted through the boxes of props he'd bought or hired: bottles and goblets and cut-glass decanters, fancy cutlery, salt and pepper pots, tablecloths, flowers; and he was still nervous. He was going to do this well, damn it, he was going to show her.

They made a series of trips up the metal staircase, and Laura pondered the cramped kitchen.

'There's enough space?' James asked.

'Plenty,' she affirmed, unpacking an electric mixer, whisks, knives and other tools of her trade. James noticed felt-tip-pen stains on her skirt.

'Well, you can leave me to it for a couple of hours,' she declared. 'I prepared a lot yesterday but I still need to get everything ready.'

'You do?' James was surprised. 'Well, OK. Two hours?'

He bought some newspapers and went to the Café Milano.

'Where's your camera, Camera Man?' Fabrizio asked him. 'What you having today? Full English or Continental?'

James was too nervous to eat. He read through the supplements of two Sunday newspapers over three cups of coffee, until his eyes ached and his fingers had a caffeine twitch. He wandered down to the bridge and back, not looking too hard at the sleepy world around him, before returning to the flat.

'Good timing,' Laura told him. 'I'll be two seconds here.'

James fiddled with the lights. Laura came out of the kitchen.

'OK,' she said.

'OK,' he replied, 'let's work.'

And so they did. The day passed fast because they were both concentrating and found themselves in remarkable (and unexpected, as far as James was concerned) agreement as to the details of each shot. Laura made three complete meals, of dishes from the Elizabethan, Georgian and Victorian periods, and they garnished each photograph with appropriate props. James took a couple of black-and-whites.

'I only want colour,' Laura reminded him.

'You never know, they may come in useful some time,' he said.

The only moment of discord came early when, after an hour of preparation, Laura looked through the camera at their first set-up.

'It's upside down,' she announced.

'Damn!' James exclaimed, clutching his head with both hands. 'I don't believe it! We should have set the table the other way up. What a fool!'

Laura looked at him open-mouthed. 'You what?' she demanded with narrowed eyes, putting her hands on her hips.

James lowered his hands. 'It's *supposed* to be upside down,' he said. 'That's the way it works. I know what I'm doing, Laura.' He could see that she wasn't sure whether to smile or curse.

She relaxed. 'I'm sorry, James. Of course you do.'

When they agreed they'd taken the final picture – of mock crab, *poulet sauté à la plombière*, ice-cream puddings and Savoy cake in fancy moulds – it was seven o'clock in the evening. All around the spotlit table was chaos: reflecting material had come unstuck and hung down from the ceiling; the props were all jumbled up against the wall beneath the windows; bits of gaffer-tape were stuck to every surface. The room smelled of hot plastic and melting food. The kitchen was worse. James took his camera equipment and films into his bedroom, then tidied up while Laura attacked the heap of washing-up. She put surviving food on the sideboard.

'What's going to happen to that?' James asked.

'Are you hungry?'

He hadn't thought about it. All day long he'd been taking photographs of food and yet such had been his concentration that he'd felt no hunger – until now.

'I haven't eaten since yesterday,' he admitted.

'You must be starving. It'll take me two minutes, James. Set the table.'

Laura reheated portions of dishes. James brought furniture back from his bedroom, and the temporary studio reverted to a sitting-room. They started with eggs in mustard sauce and an oyster loaf.

'This is delicious,' James exclaimed.

He ate a capon in lemon sauce, and pears in syrup.

'My God, this is fantastic,' James said.

'You shouldn't eat with your mouth full,' Laura chided him.

'I shouldn't *eat* with my mouth full?'

'I mean . . . you know what I mean.'

'This is brilliant, Laura. You're a pioneer.'

'No, not at all. But I really enjoy finding old recipes, it's a kind of culinary archaeology.'

'And I suppose it's a sort of indigenous cuisine, right? Using ingredients that are found, or grown naturally, in a particular region? Part of a sustainable economy?'

'Well, hardly,' Laura corrected him. 'Apart from some staple peasant dishes, and fish, of course. Otherwise we've been importing food since before the Romans; spices were being traded before gold ever was. When I say "English food" people assume I'm after some pure national diet, free of foreign influence. But it's almost the opposite, James: the history of food is a history of trade, and migration. We've never been a little cut-off island.

'In the Middle Ages we imported oranges, lemons, currants and raisins, figs, dates and prunes, sugar, almonds, pepper. Of course, I'm talking of the rich here; and it was more expensive for the British to import spices because we had to buy them at markets on the continent. But we did because medieval flavour was dominated by their use: ginger and cinnamon, nutmeg, mace, cardamom, cloves. We mined or harvested from the sea our own salt, though, and grew mustard and saffron.'

James couldn't recall seeing Laura so enthused; not even as a child.

'Don't get me going, James,' she warned him. 'Actually I ought to *be* going, and release Natalie from captivity.'

'I think it's interesting, Laura. I'd like to hear more when you've got time. I'd like to *taste* more.'

'Sure,' she said, getting up. 'That'd be nice. It's been a good day. I've enjoyed it a lot.'

'You'd better reserve judgement till you've seen the results,' he cautioned.

'I almost forgot about that,' Laura laughed out loud. James had noticed through the day that Laura smiled seldom and uneasily; she now laughed, though, like a child playing a trick on someone and being caught out. She laughed throatily, and, in addition, he saw that dimples still appeared above her cheekbones.

'I forgot we weren't doing it just for enjoyment,' she said.

'I guess that's something we have in common,' James suggested. 'We're both lucky enough to be doing work we enjoy.'

'You like taking photographs?'

'Of course. At least, I don't know what else I'd do. I wouldn't *want* to do anything else.'

'Next time,' said Laura, 'I'll talk to you about food, you tell me about photography. Will you bring the photographs round when they're ready?'

'OK. Tuesday or Wednesday, I guess.'

'Thanks, James.' She touched his arm as she said goodbye. 'See you then.'

PART THREE

THE HOSPITAL (3)

ZOE CAME TO THE HOSPITAL WARD. GLORIA WAS WITH JAMES. SHE WAS removing his drip, and inserting a naso-gastric tube. Zoe hovered, watching, as Gloria proceeded to moisten James' eyes.

'They dry out,' she told Zoe. 'We put ointment on them to stop ulceration.'

Zoe sat beside James and took his hand in hers, and spoke to him for an hour and more, recalling his life.

In the ward office, Gloria felt the sister bristle beside her.

'What a waste of time,' the sister said. 'Talking to a man who can't hear her.'

'I don't know,' Gloria wondered. 'Why does she bother you so?' she asked.

'I can't stand the false hope of ignorance,' the sister replied.

'Suppose he can hear,' Gloria said.

'For God's sake, you've seen the scans: all those small haemorrhages. It's a deep coma.'

'So why hasn't he died? He's outliving his prognosis. He should have got a chest infection by now, or an infection of the urinary tract. Spreading to his organs. Suppose she's keeping him alive with stories. We don't know. It's like a question of faith.'

'Now I've heard it all,' the sister fumed. 'I'll be glad when I retire. Why don't you go and see if your patient's had a bowel movement. Go and see if he heard that, staff.'

Zoe squeezed James' hand to say goodbye, and made her way out of the ward.

9

THE HOUSE OF TROY

JAMES PICKED UP PRINTS AND COLOUR TRANSPARENCIES OF LAURA'S food from the printers. He didn't, however, take them to the cottage: he had no intention of going into the grounds of the house on the hill for any reason. He had them delivered, instead, by courier. Laura rang him that evening.

'James, they're brilliant,' she exclaimed. 'They're just what I wanted. Well, they're better.'

He tried to agree without sounding arrogant; though also without making them seem like one-off flukes. He told her her food looked so delicious it wasn't hard to photograph it.

'Why didn't you bring them round?' she asked.

'I was busy,' he lied. 'I had to be somewhere, and I didn't want to delay your getting them.'

'Well, let's do it again. Or just meet up anyway.'

'Sure. I'll call you, or you call me.'

'Right. OK. Thanks again, James. 'Bye.'

James *was* busy. His project was taking up most of his time. If he wasn't down on the street he was most likely in his darkroom; as well as cataloguing negatives and producing prints for what was a burgeoning archive, he was conscientious in providing copies for the subjects. They were appreciative, and indulged the Camera Man in return: he was rarely allowed to pay for coffees, or even meals, in the cafés and restaurants where he ate alone watching, his eyes a little wild, the people around him.

James' status along the road subtly changed, the longer his project continued. At first the inhabitants had accepted, and been flattered by, his attention. He'd proved that he was serious in his aim of chronicling life up and down that road, and they were glad to be included.

But how long, they would ask themselves – and then each other – does a man spend on such an enterprise? Six months? A year even? By now he'd photographed every establishment's owner and employees, most of the residents and a good many others who passed regularly along the pavement or – delivery drivers, customers, salesmen – through the various premises. But still he came out, the Camera Man, in good weather and bad, early morning or late evening, to stand watchful in shop doorways or stop people and ask for their portraits or just snap them as they passed.

James spent most of his meagre postcard income on film, paper and chemicals. As if regressing to his early days after leaving home he bought clothes at charity shops again, and ate little more than what he was given. He began to acquire the reputation – and the look – of an eccentric.

There were, after all, plenty of others: it was the time when hospital wards closing down in the town began to empty long-stay patients into the community; onto the streets. These dazzled evacuees could be seen most days on the bench by the play-park in front of the Health Centre; and James began to resemble them, in his obsessive endeavour, his ill-fitting attire and his keen-eyed interest in the crowd through which he passed.

In actual fact James had been questioning the project himself: he didn't know whether to spread out – perhaps into another road, a purely residential one, in the rabbit warren of streets behind his flat – or to carry on in Factory Road but more systematically. To chronicle it at specific times of day or season, and concentrate on particular themes over a given period.

He cycled to the cinema one evening to ask Zoe her opinion. Dog silently made them tea while Zoe looked through some of James' prints.

'What are you going to do with them?' she asked. 'Are you going to have another exhibition?'

'No. I suppose they're more an archive,' he said.

'I thought you'd given up on posterity.'

'I think I've changed my mind,' he admitted.

Dog left without announcement, and Zoe called after him:

'Have one for me, Dog.'

James thought he heard a grunt in reply.

'Do you ever talk to him, Zoe?' James asked.

'Of course I do,' she answered.

'I mean, does he talk to you?' he persisted.

'What do you mean?' she challenged him.

James hesitated. 'It's none of my business. But I wonder what he gives you.'

'You, James, are not allowed to ask that kind of question.'

'I'm sorry. It's none of my business.'

'It looks that way,' she told him curtly. 'Listen, I've got to go downstairs, get ready for the late-nights. Why don't you stay? We're showing *Withnail and I*.'

'Never heard of it.'

'It's a cult film, James. We show and sell it out every three or four months. Do yourself a favour.'

James would remember little of the film, apart from the fact that he couldn't understand why people found it funny, and also that they seemed to know the dialogue in advance and laughed *before* lines arrived, which irritated him. The auditorium – the larger of Zoe's two screens, holding a couple of hundred people – was full. As he was shuffling slowly out James saw Laura in the crowd ahead of him. He was about to push forward when he saw that she was with a tall, distinguished-looking man with silvery hair, who stood out among the young audience. Instead of greeting her, James stopped still; people pushed past and around him.

When each of their children was born, the next thing Harry and Alice did after registering their birth was to enter their names on the waiting-lists of prep schools near Harry's office in the north of town, and of boarding schools further afield – including Alice's ladies' college for the three girls.

By now Sam had joined Amy in reaching school age and the next two, Tom and Susan, were old enough to attend the pre-school kindergartens attached to the boys' and the girls' prep schools. Harry left the house early and Alice drove the children to school. In the afternoons she sometimes brought them by the office on occasional, pre-arranged days: not, as might have been expected, when Harry knew his diary was free, but rather when he was meeting an important client. He found it took the tension out of such meetings when his well-behaved children trooped into the office, showed their father drawings done in school, answered Harry's client's questions with impeccable politeness and left the office in a well-ordered line. His clients realized they weren't dealing with an awkward, obstinate stone-waller, after all, but a pleasant family man with a lovely wife and enchanting children; and negotiations resumed in relaxed fashion.

Adamina had started attending a local playgroup in the mornings. Picking her up at noon, Laura sometimes slipped in early and observed a while. She was surprised to see that her daughter was the bossiest child in the group: she created games, and then ordered other children into position and allotted them their roles, not by the threat of force but by some other power. She simply gave instructions in a quiet voice, with a slight lisp, and they obeyed her. When the playgroup leaders stopped the games Adamina created, or took children from her charge and back into their own, she didn't stamp her feet or make a fuss but frowned, as if disappointed that they were so stupid. And then she resumed playing on her own, just as content with her own company.

One afternoon Harry came home from work and found four of his children playing with Adamina in the back garden. Amy and Sam were older and bigger than Adamina, yet she was arranging them all in some unfathomable formation from which all five proceeded to walk or toddle across the grass from one place to another, stopping to perform a hop or a skip on a signal from Adamina. Harry watched them for a while, bemused by the mysterious choreography, and disconcerted by his own children's acquiescence.

That evening, when he and Alice were in bed, he said: 'You know, my love, I'd rather the children didn't play with Adamina.'

'What do you mean?' Alice asked.

'She's a little odd. Haven't you noticed?' Harry said.

'She's a little girl,' Alice pointed out. 'They're small children, Harry.'

'Well, I'm just giving you my opinion, my love. And to be honest, I'd like to give you something else.'

'You're mad, Harry,' Alice giggled. 'Don't we have enough by now?'

'It's all right,' he assured her. 'It's perfectly safe. It's June. You know you only get pregnant in August or September. It takes you all summer to become fertile, my love.'

'You're right *so* far,' Alice agreed.

'And I think I'm going to enjoy this summer,' Harry proclaimed, easing himself into his wife's embrace.

Simon took his annual holiday in June every year, and every year he set off, alone, for a Greek island, having spent winter evenings studying a brochure offering 'Holidays for the Mind, the Body and the Spirit'. Simon took a different option each time; this year he'd been dithering between 'Honouring the Child Within'; 'Astrology: The Logic and the Mystery'; and 'The Shaman's Path'. But he'd made a number of friends on the island over the years and during long telephone conversations discussed courses they'd done and swapped notes. In the end he set off for Heathrow Airport and the way of the Warrior of the Spirit.

Simon always returned from his holidays sun-tanned, fit and contented, free of the symptoms of ill-health about which he moaned the rest of the year. The only surprise was that he didn't proselytize: the family were so used to Simon's regaling them with the curative wonders of his latest diets and remedies, it was a miracle that he didn't bore them to death with details of the one course of treatment that even he had to admit clearly worked.

Only Natalie knew why Simon was so reticent. The others were too relieved by his silence to risk asking him what kind of a time he'd had, in case the floodgates might open. And so they didn't think to notice that the holistic holidays lasted for a fortnight, and Simon went away for a month.

Natalie was the only one to suspect that there was more to Simon's vacations than met the eye, because she had friends in her own community of women in the town who went to certain Mediterranean islands. Natalie's suspicions were confirmed that year by eye-witness reports, and the Sunday after Simon's return – in his annual state of being at one with the world – Natalie hauled him outside for a walk around the garden. Dick the terrier followed them, and scuttled along behind Simon on his tiny legs like an eager courtesan. The fragrance of honeysuckle drifted across the lawn.

'So you had a good holiday?' Natalie asked.

'It was marvellous,' he smiled.

'You look like the cat that's licked the cream. Did you make new friends?'

'Masses,' Simon declared. 'You should take a holiday yourself, Nattie,' he advised. 'Get rid of that wan pallor, darling.'

'Simon,' she said. 'You know it's the Pride march in London next weekend.'

'I'm quite sure no one can have possibly failed to notice the poster on your bedroom door,' Simon pointed out.

'Why don't you come along?' Natalie asked him. Simon stopped walking, and Dick bumped into the back of his calves.

'I know where you go, Simon. I know people who have been to the same island. You're hardly anonymous at the best of times.'

She was right: Natalie and Simon were much the same height; but he took up three times as much space in the world. Simon lifted his feet as if out of mud and resumed walking, without looking up from the ground.

'They said you were the life and soul of every beach party going,' Natalie resumed. 'Simon,' she said, 'I don't get it. Are you some kind of animal that only mates in season – in your case a fortnight in the second half of June? On a distant island in the sun? Why don't you come out? It's not like it would surprise anyone, for Christ's sake.'

Simon stopped again, and this time looked Natalie in the eye. 'I have no intention of upsetting the old man,' he told her. 'And I trust you won't either.'

'OK,' she conceded, 'he's the one person who might be surprised. He still imagines you're screwing half the typing-pool.' She laughed, and Simon's unusually solemn bearing began to lift. 'He thinks your hypochondria's just an excuse to seduce nurses,' Natalie joked.

'Taking care of oneself is not hypochondria,' Simon admonished her.

'Sorry,' she said. 'But you can't live for your father. Anyway, he knows I'm lesbian, Jesus, he doesn't care. It's 1991, Simon. And you're thirty-six years old.'

'Age has nothing to do with anything,' he said. 'You don't understand, Natalie, you're not family. He's my father and I'm not going to hurt him.'

'What about you?' she demanded. 'Being honest and open for *yourself*, instead of living a lie? I think the stuff about your father is bullshit, Simon. I think you're a coward.'

Simon straightened his silk tie and his gaze wandered around the garden as he pondered her accusation, as if a riposte might appear from among the roses or over in the fruit trees.

'I may be a coward,' he replied at length. 'But I've never hurt anyone,' he said, in a tone of voice that told her the conversation was over.

They strolled back to the house in silence, until Sam spotted Simon coming and shrieked, and the others joined him in running towards their portly uncle; Simon curled up in an ample ball on the grass and they launched themselves like miniature Cameroonian footballers onto his already chortling, trembling frame.

Harry and Alice threw one of their parties one Friday evening late in July. They planned it to take place outside, with croquet and flowers, and Pimms replacing the customary cocktails, but it rained all afternoon and so was held as usual in their drawing-room in the east wing.

It was summer rain, on what was a hot and humid day, and people drank more than normal. The barmen were kept busy, while trays of stuffed mushrooms and canapés carried around by the children were returned to the kitchen largely untouched. Laura threw them away before Natalie saw them, because she knew Natalie would want to put them into cardboard boxes and drive them to the refuge, or the night shelter in town, despite having only just knocked off after another of her non-stop working weeks.

Charles drank with the panache of a genial host, sweeping himself a glass off every tray that passed by, and exhorting others to do likewise. In actual fact he took no more than a perfunctory sip before putting the glass back down on the nearest surface: Charles managed to convey the impression of a merry dipsomaniac while imbibing no more than a single glass of champagne all evening.

Harry was practically teetotal, while Alice was unable to resist one or three White Russians. Natalie only drank beer and had to provide it herself, entering Harry's parties with a four-pack of Ruddles Bitter under her arm and drinking straight from the can. Simon, despite his size, became tipsy from half a glass of wine. He was known to vanish from social occasions and be found on his back, snoring, in some quiet room.

Robert, on the other hand, could take any amount of alcohol. He drank steadily, with no visible effect except that at some point he became even more silent than usual, standing in a corner, surveying the room with dark, unfocused eyes.

Charles restrained himself at the end of that evening and allowed Harry and Alice to see their guests off by themselves, soon after dark. In the kitchen, Laura let the barmen out and finished clearing up with help from Natalie.

'Pop over later if there's a good film on,' Laura offered on her way out.

'Thanks. I might,' Natalie replied.

It was a moonlit night. Laura walked over to her cottage, fifty yards from the back door of the house. She entered through the porch and straight into the large kitchen that constituted the whole of the ground floor. She walked through the ice-blue room and up the stairs. The light was on in Adamina's room: Adamina often put herself to bed, and Laura would find her talking to her teddy bears or already sleeping. It was one of the advantages of Laura's job and of living in the cottage, safe within the walled grounds of the house on the hill. Laura walked past the open door of the sitting-room and her own bedroom and into Adamina's: her daughter was asleep, curled up across the bed, her feet against the wall, half-way through the unconscious process of turning right around in her sleep, a habit she hadn't quite grown out of. Laura put her hands under Adamina's light little body and shifted her round so her head was back on the pillow; Adamina frowned, without waking, and Laura kissed her forehead.

Laura went into the bathroom opposite Adamina's room and peed, without turning on the light. She looked through into the darkness of Adamina's room: the moon's illumination faded before it reached the bed, but Laura was able to imagine her daughter's sleeping body there as clearly as if she could see it. The question that often came to her mind at this moment of the day did so now: she wasn't sure whether her life was one of enclosure or freedom. The cottage in which she lived with her daughter was like her own space inside a larger prison. Within a defined orbit she was free. She flushed the toilet and the noise was loud, then drained away in the silence of the cottage.

She went into the sitting-room. The moonlight was uncanny, making the familiar space and objects strange, casting them in a cool, blue light. It seemed a shame to disturb it with electric glare. She thought she'd like to lie in it a while, listening to music. To what? Miles Davis, she decided: *Concerto de Arunjuez*. Laura moved across towards her stereo, looked for the tape. When suddenly her heart slammed to a stop: she wasn't alone; there was someone else in the room. She lost co-ordination of her limbs but managed to reach to the light switch, fumbled it on and turned round.

Robert was sitting in the armchair: he had been sitting there – how long? – in the dark. He closed and lowered his eyes from the bright light, and then raised them again. His arms hung heavy either side of the chair and a bottle drooped loosely from one hand, its bottom resting tilted on the floor. His eyes were dead.

Laura got her breath back and spoke, in a voice she heard as higher and wilder than her own.

'What the hell are you doing in here?' she demanded. It was weird the words formed at all; her tongue and her mouth were spastic, she felt like a puppet.

Robert gazed at her. 'I came to see my daughter,' he said. 'I've been watching her sleeping.'

Anger swelled in Laura's throat. 'How dare you? Go away,' she told Robert.

'It's time we had a little talk,' Robert declared. 'Sit down.'

'Get out,' Laura said, with as controlled a voice as she could. She wanted to scream at him, but it occurred to her that the most important thing in the whole world was that Adamina didn't wake up. She thought of the open door to Adamina's room, and promptly went through and closed it, before returning to the sitting-room. Those few steps helped restore her equilibrium, and to still her hammering heartbeat.

'Get out of my house, Robert,' Laura said.

'It's not your house. I came to see my daughter and now we're going to talk.'

'You bastard,' Laura exclaimed. 'I told you: we don't need you. She's almost four years old and you come in here like a thief. Get out, Robert.'

'Are you going to sit down?' Robert asked. His eyes were dead and his gravelly voice was a drone.

Laura leaned a hand on the back of the sofa behind which she stood, and with the other rubbed her forehead and her closed eyelids.

'You fucked me like I fucked you,' Robert said. 'You may not like it but she's mine as much as yours. I want to see her. I want to give her things. I want—'

'*Get out!*' Laura screamed.

Robert pushed himself up from the chair, stumbled, got his balance back and advanced towards Laura. He stepped onto the sofa and lurched forward to grab her; she jumped aside as the sofa fell backwards and Robert rolled over it, landing on the floor and against a sideboard. Books toppled onto him.

Laura didn't know what to do; what could she do? She couldn't run and leave him there in the cottage with Adamina. She crossed to the other side of the room and stood behind the chair he'd just been sitting in. Robert staggered to his feet, breathing heavily, and came towards her again.

'You think you're so fucking clever,' he said.

'No, Robert,' Laura mumbled. She didn't know what to do and she realized she was about to cry. She began to prepare to shield herself from the blows to come, a submissive victim, she was fourteen again and her knees were giving way.

The first blow hit her hand covering the side of her face and sent her reeling. She prepared for the next. She could hear his footsteps, feel his body come close, smell his whisky breath, sense his hand withdrawing . . .

An incredible noise rent the air: a raucous, angry animal shriek that stunned both Robert and Laura. Their heads turned slowly to the doorway, and there stood Natalie, staring at Robert. Laura gasped with relief; it swelled inside her. She blinked her wet eyes and wiped them and stood up straight. When she looked again at Natalie, and then at Robert, she saw that neither of them had moved a muscle: both were locked into the other's gaze. The relief Laura felt began abruptly to drain away. She knew what both these people were capable of. She realized that the three of them were on the brink of something far worse than what might have happened a moment before.

Now, however, the fear didn't overwhelm her. Her mind instead became lucid, her body icy and under control.

'Natalie,' Laura said in an easy, welcoming voice. 'Hi. Robert dropped by for a coffee. Do you want to see that film on TV?' She spoke warmly, normally, and she began slowly to move: sliding the armchair as if just easing it back into its proper position, stooping to pick up the bottle that lay on its side, whisky draining into the carpet.

'What time's it on? Soon? Do *you* want a coffee? Robert, you can stay too, though I guess you may want to get going.'

The other two — first Natalie, then Robert — began to relax the frightening postures their bodies had adopted.

'Check the paper, see what time it's on, Nat,' Laura suggested, nodding towards the television in the corner to the left of the door.

Natalie looked at Laura questioningly. Laura nodded again. 'Over there,' she said. Natalie moved cautiously away from the doorway.

'Have you had enough coffee, Robert?' Laura now asked him. His gaze had followed Natalie and now turned to Laura; his drunkenness meant *his* confusion took longer to resolve.

'I'm going to think about what you said,' Laura told him. 'We'll talk about it again.'

Robert didn't respond, but then his body lurched from its immobility, and he marched towards and through the doorway. Laura and Natalie waited until they heard the sound of his footsteps on the stairs, and then the front door of the cottage opening and closing.

Natalie moved – to check Robert was gone – but Laura beat her to the doorway and rushed to Adamina's room. She was sure she'd find her cowering in her bed. But she didn't. Somehow Adamina had not been woken by either Laura's scream or Natalie's martial arts shriek; she lay asleep exactly as Laura had placed her.

Laura stroked Adamina's hair. 'My love,' she whispered, 'my heart, may nothing ever harm you.'

Laura returned to the sitting-room. Natalie had poured two glasses from what was left of Robert's whisky.

'That was brilliant, Laura,' she said, 'Jesus, that was so cool. Where did you learn that? I would have killed him.'

She passed Laura a glass. Laura took it, only to find that her hand was trembling, and she watched the glass fall from her fingers onto the carpet. Her whole body was shaking. Natalie hugged her tight.

'It's OK,' Natalie soothed her, 'it's OK. He's gone.' She held Laura, shaking, and stroked her back. 'I said I'd protect you, remember? I said I'd be here. It's OK now,' she said, as Laura shook for a long time in her arms.

One Saturday afternoon in August James stepped out of the camera shop on the High Street with a carrier bag full of film and paper. His bike was parked in a lane just round the corner. He pulled his keyring out of his pocket and as he flipped it through his fingers to select the bike-lock key he almost collided with a couple of pedestrians on the pavement.

'Sorry. Excuse me,' James said, as he looked up and into the eyes of Sonia.

'James,' she said. 'Hello. How are you?'

'Sonia. I'm fine. Good. You look good. You haven't changed a bit.'

'This is David. David – James.'

James shook hands with a smartly dressed, middle-aged man with translucent blue eyes.

'How's it going?' James asked.

'OK,' Sonia replied. 'You still dancing?'

'Not so much,' he said. 'You look good.'

They hadn't talked since he'd left her four years before. Now they exchanged uncomfortable, vacuous words. It was hard to believe that they were once lovers, that he had made love with this stranger. He looked at the man with a tanned face and translucent eyes and thought it could have been him.

'Well. See you around, James,' Sonia said.

'Take care,' he told her.

Robert came back to Laura's cottage sober and contrite, and with a wad of money that he offered Laura for Adamina's maintenance, as well as promises of regular payments in the future.

Laura was prepared. She'd thought it over and discussed it, not with Natalie but with Zoe: Natalie's anger, Laura reckoned, might have been useful against violence, but less so for the negotiations that had to follow.

So Laura explained the situation. Zoe agreed that, whatever the legalities of the matter, Robert's paternal rights could hardly be separated from Laura's position in the household, the cottage and the family. Laura *could* move out, she told Zoe, and make her living with her dinner-party catering, although even that wasn't certain: if the family were to close ranks against her and Charles Freeman and Harry Singh chose to hinder as they'd once helped her, her clients might rapidly diminish.

But, more important, there was Adamina herself. Robert *was* her father, she wouldn't be in the world without him, his genes were within her. Did Laura have the right to deprive her of a father's bond? Would he not give her things – quite apart from money, both now and as a future inheritance – that Laura could not?

Zoe listened with little interruption. 'Life is messier than legal clauses,' she said, finally. 'Why did he hit you, though? Why was he so angry now, after not saying anything for years?'

'I don't know,' Laura said. 'He never did anything like this to me before. I think . . . you see, he did come to see me, or her, when she was one, on her birthday. Came with a mountain of presents. I told him I didn't need him, and I didn't want her to need him either.'

'I see,' Zoe said.

'To tell you the truth, I wish he was . . . just not around. I mean, part of me still wants him, Zoe. At night. On my own. Oh, God, it'd be so much easier if he wasn't around.'

'Well, he is.'

'I know.'

And so Laura was prepared for Robert's contrition, his offers and claims. She took the money and they agreed that he could see Adamina one Sunday a month.

Laura sat Adamina down to prepare her for this new part of her life. She'd always known that there'd come a time when she would have to explain, that Adamina would ask questions that required an answer, and maybe in the end if was just as well that the time for such explanations had arrived like this. So she sat Adamina down and told her that Robert, yes, Amy and Tom's Uncle Robert, was her father, and that although he and Laura were not friends any more, he would like to spend time with her, take her out for the morning, and Laura thought it was a fine idea. She didn't have a clue what Adamina's reaction would be.

Adamina listened, impassive apart from slight frowns, minute gestures that flickered across her face; they seemed less responses to exactly what Laura was saying than outward signs of her mind processing the information.

'When?' she asked.

'Tomorrow,' Laura told her.

Adamina's eyebrows tightened, slowly, then abruptly relaxed. 'Where are we going?'

'He thought you might like to go swimming.'

Adamina laughed. 'I can't swim, Mummy,' she said.

'Would you like to learn?' Laura asked her.

She thought about it for a while. 'Yes,' she said, with a slight lisp.

Things went well at first. Robert picked Adamina up at the appointed time, and she came back happy. The Sunday mornings stretched to whole days: after the swimming pool Robert took Adamina to lunch in town, then on to a wildlife park or a funfair in the afternoon. But gradually a hostility came back into Robert's behaviour.

It wasn't easy for Laura, handing Adamina over; and Robert showed little inclination to *make* it easy. One morning he turned up an hour early and demanded Adamina be handed over right away, on the button, where's her swimming costume and towel and why was Laura fucking him around? The following month he wandered over from the big house two hours late, scornful of Laura's reproaches and even oblivious to Adamina's anxiety: she'd been sitting on the step outside waiting for him.

Robert took Adamina's hand and told Laura maybe they'd be back at the agreed time and maybe they wouldn't, he'd see what he felt like. Instead, he returned early, having taken Adamina to the swimming pool and then brought her straight back (Adamina silently nursing her disappointment at missing out on other treats.) But whatever hour he brought her home Robert was in a bad mood each time, treating Laura with resentment she found hard to understand and impossible to combat.

'I want to see her next week,' Robert demanded in his gravelly voice.

'The first Sunday of the month, as usual,' Laura replied.

'That's too long.'

'It's what we agreed.'

'Did she agree it? She'd like to see me more often, wouldn't you, pet?'

'Don't put her on the spot, Robert.'

'You don't give a fuck what *she* wants.'

Adamina stood between them, looking from one to the other in bewilderment.

'You go on inside, Mina,' Laura told her. 'Your father and I need to discuss this in private.'

'Give Daddy a big kiss.'

Adamina went in but watched through the upstairs window.

'I bet you'd like me to come in too, wouldn't you?' Robert asked her.

'Why do you treat me like this?' Laura asked him.

'Because you think you're so fucking superior,' Robert told her.

'I don't. That's so stupid. Of course I don't.'

'Just the way you say that shows you do,' he said.

'What do you *want* from me, Robert?' she cried.

'Nothing,' he said. 'I want nothing from you, Laura.'

What made it more complicated was how much Adamina enjoyed her days with her father. She turned out to adore swimming, and Robert was a patient teacher, content to spend hours in the smaller pool with Adamina, in her blue swimsuit and red armbands, kicking and splashing.

'I swam right across the pool without any help, Mummy,' she told Laura one Sunday afternoon, after Robert had dropped her off.

'Well done, Mina,' Laura told her. 'Clever girl.' She dutifully enthused over anything Adamina reported back, and took care to express nothing negative about Robert.

After swimming Robert usually took Adamina for a meal at McDonald's. That was preferable somehow, Laura thought, to his having her to Sunday lunch in the big house. Laura wasn't sure *why* it was preferable. It was such a delicate, confusing situation.

Laura hoped every month through that winter and spring that Robert would become more relaxed, would lose his incomprehensible hostility towards her. He seemed to spend more time in the house nowadays; he may have been antagonistic on Sundays, but when his and Laura's paths crossed in the company of others Robert was perfectly civil. Maybe the family would absorb his anger, she hoped; maybe his relationship with Adamina would mellow him. Whatever, it was at that time that Robert, in the house, threw a party of his own.

It was a Saturday when Charles was going to be away on business for the weekend. The expansion of the Freeman Communications Corporation was carrying on apace: Charles had taken over a computer hardware manufacturer in Birmingham and a software company in Coventry; but, no longer able to finance the purchases with money from the Freeman Company, he was securing loans from banks, and spending an increasing amount of time doing so.

'It's a bad time to borrow, with interest rates rising,' his accountant suggested.

'Nonsense!' Charles countered. 'It's never a bad time to borrow,' he laughed. 'Hey, I like that. Judith! Write that down.'

Charles was away, and Robert gave everyone else due warning.

'It may get a bit noisy,' he said.

'Is this an invitation?' Simon asked.

'I'm not stopping you,' Robert replied in a noncommittal way.

No one, though, made any alternative plans because they couldn't imagine Robert having enough friends to cause too much of a disturbance. They did begin to worry around midday when a lorry with the words HOUSE OF TROY emblazoned on its sides rolled up the drive, and men with goatee beards and baggy jeans carried batteries of lights and electric cables, consoles and speakers inside.

'Perhaps we should book into a hotel tonight,' Alice suggested.

'I'm sure there'll be no need for that,' Harry replied. 'I don't think they'll be a rowdy crowd.' He had heard rattling vans arrive and looked out of the window to see people unloading crate after crate not of beer and liquor but rather of orange juice, Coca-Cola and mineral water.

'I've a feeling they'll be a nicely behaved lot,' Harry opined complacently. 'Let's let the children have a treat and stay up late.'

It was a hot, dry day – which was just as well, since two hundred cars would end up parked on the hard, baked lawn. Many people arrived on foot as well, strolling along the drive towards the house. The three eldest Singh children mingled with them while Harry and Alice had supper alone together: it was a balmy June evening that reminded Alice of their honeymoon in Goa, and she and Harry felt at peace with each other and with the world.

'It doesn't get any better than this, does it, Harry?' Alice said. 'Does it ever strike you how lucky we are?'

'I know how lucky I am, my love,' Harry told her. 'But it can always get better.'

Their au pair put baby Mollie and the infant Susan to bed, while Harry and Alice sat in the comfortable silence of a couple who no longer had anything new to say to one another, and for whom such a state was a cause not of boredom but rather profound contentment.

And then, just before nine o'clock, the hazy peace of their house was shattered, when all of a sudden a juddering electronic beat exploded out of industrial speakers.

It might have been the very same disc that then played without cease for the next nine hours, because what thumped through the walls and into every single room, as well as out into the grounds of the house on the hill, sounded like the same 120-beats-a-minute din all night long.

Having let his small children roam at will, when they failed to reappear Harry had then to go in search of them. He walked downstairs to the ground floor of their east wing – whose emptiness felt eerie because the noise was already maddening him and the walls were quivering – and then he entered the main part of the house.

The large drawing-room had been miraculously cleared of its furniture, including the carpet, and refilled with psychedelic posters hanging from the walls, banks of speakers and multi-coloured flashing lights: the room looked like it could never have been used for anything else. Hundreds of people were crammed into it, dancing with epileptic gestures and startled eyes. Most were young, but exactly how old they were Harry couldn't guess, because he didn't recognize ever having been quite that age himself.

The house had been transformed into unfamiliar labyrinths of melting, kaleidoscopic colours. In other rooms people played drums or lay around watching computerized images on a video screen; in one bathroom the bathtub was full of ice (which seemed to be the only thing anyone was eating) and the cold tap in the sink was left running because a constant queue of people were refilling plastic mineral-water bottles.

Harry Singh stumbled through an unfamiliar world, where speech had been banished but strangers with dilated pupils smiled at him like old friends; one or two tried to hug him and he had to wrench himself free from their sweaty embraces.

'I'm not a violent man,' Harry told himself, clenching his fists, filled with hatred for these people who were blocking his way to wherever the children were. He had also to fight off the suspicion that this was less a disco than some kind of religious ceremony. He felt as out of place as he had when he followed Alice to her church one Christmas many years ago.

Harry wandered around the house looking for Amy, Sam and Tom, becoming increasingly disorientated by the remorseless music, thumping so loud it dispersed all coherent thought from his brain, until he'd lost hope of ever seeing them again. At that moment a woman took his hand and led him to a quiet room – which Harry felt almost but not absolutely sure was Charles' study – and rummaged under a mountain of clothes for where she'd stashed her bag.

'Look at you,' she said, with an Italian-sounding accent. 'You look exhausted already. You've got to prepare for these things if you want to keep going all night. Hold out your hand.'

Dazed, Harry did as he was told, and the woman explained as she placed a succession of tablets and capsules on his palm that she was giving him Vitamin E to help his kidneys, blue-green algae for energy, spirulina as a nutritional supplement, ginkgo leaf for peripheral circulation, and guarana, a sacred food from the Amazon.

'Swallow these,' she told him, handing him her water bottle, 'and you won't feel like a flattened hedgehog tomorrow.'

Harry complied passively.

'And this is a pure White Dove,' she said. 'It's for your *anahata*, the *chakra* of the heart.'

Harry obediently swallowed the white pill. 'I'm looking for my children,' he told her, on the verge of tears.

'Really? That's interesting,' she replied, and then she thought about it. 'I think I'm looking for my mother,' she conjectured. 'Just remember to drink lots of water. Come on. Let's return to the sauce,' she said, or words to that effect: Harry couldn't be certain, on account of the incessant ringing in his ears.

Harry made his way back to the drawing-room and resumed his search for the children. With huge relief he glimpsed Amy in a corner, but when he got there she'd vanished; then he saw Sam beside a speaker and rudely pushed frenetically dancing bodies out of his way, but in the time it took to reach him Sam too had disappeared. Harry went round and round the room in useless circles, unwittingly acting out the proof of Dr Griffin's hypothesis that if a person wants to find someone in a rave, the more desperately they search, the harder it becomes, at an exponential rate, because ravers behave in the arbitrary manner of subatomic particles, disappearing from one spot and materializing in another.

The only solution is to stay in one place, dancing, and then they'll come to you. So it would be with Harry: eventually, distraught and exhausted, he came to a bemused standstill in the middle of the drawing-room, crushed by the shuddering weight of sound. Repetitive electronic music seemed to have done what nothing else ever had: sapped the last remnants of Harry Singh's subterranean will.

Gradually, however, as he stood there, drained, Harry found his limbs twitching, in automatic imitation of the gyrations of those around him. A strange warmth manifested itself somewhere in his stomach and began to surge slowly up through his body. He felt his heart expand, his mind fizzle like crushed sherbert, and something happened in his ears: to his astonishment Harry realized that the indivisible noise that had battered him seemed to be rearranging itself inside his head. Its inner logic of repeated series of four bars, with four beats in each, was revealing itself to him: the music was making sense. At the same time, it was burning into his brain as it did so. He noticed with surprise that he was tapping his hands against the air to the time of this secret beat that he now heard, and was also aware that his legs were pumping to another, different rhythm from inside that aural maelstrom.

A young man was dancing beside him. He was staring straight at Harry with a wide grin across his face, and yelled: 'Yeh. Yeh.' It took Harry a moment to register that the man was not a mirror image of himself, since he knew he was doing the same thing himself. He had the uncanny feeling that whoever was making the music was reading his mind – or it could have been the other way round – and the smells of sweat, perfume, cigarettes, and something chemical from capsules odd people were sniffing entered his nostrils with a heady intensity.

Someone offered Harry their mineral-water bottle. He took a grateful swig and hugged the donor; he felt an abundant affection for all those around him, as well as something else he'd never felt before: a sense of total, unqualified acceptance.

It was there in the middle of the dance-floor that first Tom, then Sam and finally Amy found him, drenched in euphoric sweat and grinding his teeth, and they attached themselves like burrs one after the other until he had all three. With a great effort, they dragged and pushed their father back to the east wing. At the door he turned round. 'Look, children,' he said with a frightening smile, 'we just stepped out of the twentieth century.'

Alice and the other residents of the house stayed awake the rest of the night in their respective rooms, lying in mute, impotent fury. They were allowed to sleep finally when the music stopped abruptly at six in the morning, and so survived that siege from within. They wouldn't easily forget Robert's rave, though, and neither would many people in the town below: the house on the hill had looked like a spaceship, with lights flashing from every window, the roof and walls appearing to tremble and the repetitive beat reverberating forth.

Amy, Sam and Tom woke up around eleven and wandered back into the main part of the house, to find themselves in the aftermath of a strange massacre: most of the partygoers had driven away at dawn but many had danced and drugged themselves to a standstill and collapsed wherever they were. The morning silence was unearthly; sun streaming through the windows appeared not quite real.

Gradually, though, those people suffering from self-inflicted jet lags were resurrected, and, parched and hungry, they were led downstairs to the kitchen by the children, who ransacked the pantry and deep-freeze to provide them with assorted breakfasts and mugs of tea before they straggled away by car and on foot.

As luck would have it Charles returned home early in the afternoon, and was enraged, though whether at missing out on a party or by the last of those layabouts driving their cars off his lawn, having left the house turned upside down and taken advantage of his son's – and his own – hospitality, wasn't immediately clear.

Over the following hours Charles heard the complaints of the other members of the household, and neighbours, about the nightmare inflicted upon them, and he was hugely disappointed in Robert's naïvety. Until, that is, he confronted Robert himself and discovered that Robert had been charging entry, as well as exorbitant prices for orange juice and other consumables, and had made more money in one night than he ever had in a month of car dealing and antiques trading. Charles confided in Robert his approval, but for everyone else's sake they agreed the enterprise would remain a never-to-be-repeated one-off.

'Which is a shame,' Charles said, 'because I feel I've missed a hell of a ruddy shindig. I think I'd have had a marvellous time.'

To which Robert had to agree that his father was probably right.

James was at home when the phone rang early in October. The answerphone was set so he just stood there. When he heard Laura's voice he lifted the receiver, automatically cutting the answerphone off for the first time since he'd bought it.

'I'm calling to invite you out for my thirtieth birthday,' Laura explained. 'It's not a big party, just a few of us going to that Jamaican restaurant down the road from you. Where the man makes up the menu.'

'And the bill.'

'Really? Well, Simon's organizing it for me, that's his concern. Then on to some barn dance – Natalie's organizing that. I don't know where it is; somewhere else near you, I think.'

'I'd love to,' James replied. 'Sounds great.'

'You're going *where*?' Lewis demanded, when he dropped by the next day. 'People of our age are going to a barn dance? That's not right, Jay. It's immoral.'

'It's not my idea, Lewis,' James assured him. 'I've never been to one. Could be fun.'

'Fun? You must have seen morris men,' Lewis persisted. 'You're going to look like they look. I'm going to hire a video camera and then use the footage for blackmail.'

'Don't be so dogmatic, you bloody old disco codger,' James complained. 'You may not have noticed, Lew, but we're almost middle-aged.'

Laura's birthday group consisted of Simon, Natalie, Alice and Harry, Zoe with Dog, Laura herself and also three friends of hers James didn't know; he was glad, though, that none of them had silver hair.

The group were late at the restaurant and ate too much too quickly, but when they got to the Community Centre hall they dropped jackets and bags on chairs at an empty table and went straight onto the dance-floor, where the caller was beseeching more couples to tread, for the first dance of the evening.

James joined Harry at the bar. Harry had tried to make his excuses at the end of the meal, but Zoe and Natalie refused to let him go home.

'He won't dance,' Alice told them. 'Don't bother.'

'You've got a rod up your arse, Harry,' Natalie told him. 'Relax and enjoy yourself.'

'I'm quite capable of enjoying myself,' Harry protested, 'despite your vulgarity.' He almost asked whether anyone had one of those White Dove things on them, but held back.

Harry nursed his mineral water while James watched the dancers weaving clumsy figures of eight and making arches for others to pass through. The movements had a chaste gracelessness that was painfully English, James thought. Lewis was right.

When the first dance finished, however, Zoe grabbed him to partner her in the second, and by the time it was over James had discovered how different was the experience from the observation of it. The simple steps were explained by the caller and almost everyone got them wrong but that didn't matter, the music was a chugging train that didn't stop so you just had to jump back on it somehow, laughing.

At the end of that dance the group collected the drinks Harry had set on their table.

'Where *is* Harry?' Simon asked. They looked around but there was no sign of him, except for a half-drunk glass of mineral water on a beermat on the bar where Harry had stood, watching with mounting discomfort the flailing bodies before him.

'He's gone home,' Alice stated nonchalantly. 'I told you.'

The rest of the group stayed, and joined in most of the dances that followed. They swapped around partners but that didn't mean very much because as soon as a dance started you lost contact with the partner you began with anyway, and moved on to the next person in the line or the circle. James concentrated hard on carrying out the caller's instructions.

'You sure dance to a different drummer, James,' Natalie told him, but he didn't mind. It was clearly more enjoyable if you didn't know the steps and were always one or two behind the beat; James felt

407

sorry for the few experts there, who glided around with an elegant pomposity and a pained expression, trying to ignore the idiots bumping into them.

Those idiots didn't include Simon, who moved with an ease belying his 16 stone, nor Natalie, who explained during a breather that she never went to more than one or two ceilidhs a year, so as not to memorize the steps too clearly, because she didn't want not to laugh. As long as you *didn't* master them it was impossible not to have a good time. Only the experts looked like they didn't want to be there. Natalie also liked the fact, she said, that there were always more women than men; she took the male role, and asked women if they cared for this dance.

'You always get dykes at these things,' she whispered to Zoe, 'who don't know they are.'

They bought bottles of beer that Laura opened with a disposable cigarette lighter. She'd tried smoking once but given it up because it affected her tastebuds, but she kept a throwaway lighter in her bag just to impress people with this trick.

'Let me try,' James demanded, and missed two dances in the vain attempt to master it. He was left full of admiration for Laura's dexterity; she was on the other hand a surprisingly ungraceful dancer. It wasn't that she had no sense of rhythm, rather that the movement of her limbs was abrupt and stilted. Some people when they danced – like Simon, and Alice too – looked more comfortable than when walking: their bodies flowing gratefully into the motion.

The ceilidh lasted till midnight. The hall was bursting and everyone joined in the last dance and then they tumbled outside. James, who lived just up the road, hung around while the group dispersed. Zoe and Dog went off to look for a taxi back across town. Laura's three friends left together. The others got into Simon's car; Laura was the last to get in, but she stopped and said:

'Nat, could you possibly let the baby-sitter go? I feel like walking.'

Natalie frowned. 'You sure you want to walk on your own?' she asked.

'I'll be fine,' Laura assured her. 'I just feel like it.'

The car pulled away, leaving Laura and James on the pavement.

'Do you *want* to walk on your own?' James asked. 'I mean, I feel like walking too, so if you like . . .'

'That'd be nice,' Laura replied.

They strolled up Factory Road a way. 'Hey, Camera Man!' someone shouted out. The road was noisy still with cars crammed with people looking for parties and with loud, drunk youths, so they cut through residential streets up the hill to the park, and around the top of it towards the house. After agreeing what a good time they and everyone else – apart from Harry – had had, neither said anything for five or ten minutes. As they circled the park, though, as if realizing how close they were to the house on the hill, both James and Laura slowed their pace, and began talking at the same moment. Each laughed and apologized and urged the other to speak, but James said: 'Oh, it was nothing,' and Laura said: 'Me, too,' shaking her head.

'You know,' she resumed after a while, 'I was hoping we might do this. I wanted to talk to you.'

'Really?'

'Since we took those photographs, I've talked to you in my head, we've had conversations. Now I'm with you I feel there's a barrier between us.'

'What barrier?' James asked. 'I'm not putting up a barrier. Am I?'

'I don't know, James. You know, I saw you in the cinema some while back. You were sat a couple of places in front of me.'

'Was I?'

'I was going to say something at the end but you looked like you were really moved by the film. It was only afterwards I thought it wasn't the kind of film a person's moved by. It's one of my favourites. Maybe you were asleep!'

'Who were you with?' James blurted out. 'I saw you too,' he admitted. 'Is he a suitor?'

Laura laughed. 'What a quaint word. I suppose he is. Or was. A client I've done some dinner parties for; he's taken me out once or twice. A few times. *He* didn't like the film.'

They were slowing down as they talked.

'Do you like him?' James asked.

'He's been my lover. I've shared his bed. He treats me well, and gives me comfort. But I didn't want to talk about him. Damn it, it's that barrier, James, it deflects things.'

'I'm sorry,' James said, without knowing why.

'Do you remember,' she resumed, 'when we were really young, I don't know, I was twelve or thirteen, we all went swimming at the pool, you four and me? Simon had that car, an orange VW. Oh, you won't remember.'

'I remember,' James assured her. 'What about it?'

'Well . . .' Laura hesitated. They were hardly moving forward at all now. Laura coughed with nervousness. 'I remember clearly that day, for the first time, realizing I was attracted to you.'

'To me?' James gasped. 'You?'

'I felt guilty about it, though, because you were like my brother. Anyway, I've always felt you were special, somehow, and I feel it now, only now I know there's nothing to feel guilty about. Oh, God, I'm so clumsy. You don't have to say anything, you know. I just wanted to tell you.'

'I don't know what you *are* telling me exactly.'

'Neither do I. I've never said something like this before.'

'What about Robert?' James demanded.

'What about him? *He's* not like a brother. He's not like *your* brother, is he?'

'If you liked me, why did you go with him?' James asked.

'In the beginning? Because he went for me, I guess, and you didn't. Anyway, it was different. And that's all in the past, James. I just know I had to tell you, to get this off my chest.'

They had come to a stop, with the gates of the grounds of the house fifty yards ahead.

'I don't know what to say,' James said.

'Don't say anything,' Laura told him. Her eyes were gleaming in the darkness.

'I don't know what to think,' he said. 'The world is upside down,' he whispered as he stepped the half a step to Laura and kissed her. They kissed for a minute or two. It was like they were putting a seal on something, the end of something or perhaps the beginning, they didn't know, but either way there was no hurry. Then they hugged each other and they each knew that it was not the sad embrace of parting but that of two people, long separated, who have found each other. They walked to the gates.

'You're not going to come in, are you?' Laura asked.

'No,' said James.

They kissed again, this time without restraint.

'We should have done this when we were thirteen,' James said.

'Don't say that,' Laura replied. 'What are we going to do now?' she asked. 'Tomorrow?'

'Tomorrow,' James agreed. 'I'll call you.'

He watched her go through the gates and along the drive and then off left towards her cottage. Then he walked home but by a long, circuitous route, because he had no wish for the night to end. It was still warm and the town seemed to smell like a foreign city. James stopped to light himself a cigarette and strolled on. He raised his hands to his face, to inhale the scent of Laura's skin and perfume on his palms.

The next morning Laura drove down to James' flat and he led her straight to the bedroom, where they made love in fumbled haste as if afraid the long-postponed consummation might pass them by again. A dam of tense desire broke over them in one wave.

When they'd recovered, they then made love without hindrance or anxiety or desperation: each caress and sound felt less an exploration than a reaffirmation of what they already knew; their movements the concrete part of a puzzle that fitted together, which they had already solved in abstract in some other time and place.

Afterwards they found words beyond them and so held each other in silence until they fell asleep. Some time in the afternoon James awoke with the feeling that he was in a strange place, as if the contents and dimensions of his flat had subtly altered. He found that Laura was already gazing at him; she had the waxy look of someone who's just woken up.

'Hello,' she smiled.

After they'd made love again, they took turns to have a soapy bath – James' bathtub wasn't big enough for two people to fit in – scrubbing each other's back and giving a watery massage.

James and Laura were aware of their bodily imperfections, but made the other feel that every part of them was desirable. Laura seemed to have lost her self-consciousness about the stretch marks on her belly, her knock-knees and her small breasts.

'You should have seen them when I was feeding Adamina,' she told James. 'They were like melons.'

'I prefer avocados,' he assured her, carrying her back to the bedroom. 'And pears. Melons are ostentatious fruit,' he said.

'Is it possible for the erogenous zones to spread out and join up until they cover the whole body?' Laura asked him: she felt like she could hear her body humming, from the tips of her large toes to the split ends of her hazel brown hair.

While Laura had already begun to convince James that his thin legs, his fishbone scars and his slackening stomach, even his sticking-out ears, instead of diminishing him, added to his manhood; and because he believed it, so, bizarrely, they did.

They pointed out these and others of their own physical peculiarities, and found them to be comical without detracting from their

411

ardour, because they both discovered for the first time how shameless laughter could be transmuted into passion: the fourth time they made love they both came in a state of ill-suppressed hysteria, with giggles giving an added, dangerous rhythm to the thrusts of their love-making.

The fifth time, that evening, was just as funny, except that as the climax approached it was clear that they were both not only laughing at the stupendous absurdity of sex at the same time as moaning with pleasure, but also crying hopeless tears, in a mad journey into their equally hidden hearts. Shortly before the end, though, they emerged from those rapids of confused sensation and emotion into calm waters, and at the crucial moment James closed his eyes and murmured: 'This is it,' to which Laura grunted what could only be agreement.

To satisfy the hunger that made their stomachs rumble during placid intervals Laura walked off, naked, into the kitchen. James grabbed the opportunity for a cigarette, listening to scrapes and rattles that were followed into the bedroom by aromas that made his gut grumble all the more, while he wondered why it took her so long to collect the biscuits and cheese and maybe a tin of olives or gherkins that was all there was in his bachelor's fridge.

Laura reappeared bearing trays of tapas-style snacks of improbable variety and taste: fingers of grilled cheese on toast, with sun-dried tomatoes and marjoram, olives stuffed with almonds, boiled egg, anchovy and capers in mayonnaise.

They ate, and drank bottles of beer which James insisted Laura open with her cigarette lighter.

'You couldn't have made all these from what was in the kitchen,' James challenged Laura. 'It beats the loaves-and-fishes miracle. It's just not possible. You must have prepared them earlier.'

'No, I didn't,' Laura assured him. 'I've used what you had in the cupboard. People always have more than they think.'

'You must have smuggled the ingredients in about your person,' he persisted.

'Don't be silly,' Laura laughed. 'It's just a matter of imagination and practice.'

'I don't believe you,' James told her, putting the tray on the bedside table. 'We're going to have to search you for further contraband.'

'I'm naked!' she declared.

'I know,' he said sternly. 'I've sent for a sniffer dog. In fact, here I am: it's me. Don't move a muscle,' he murmured, licking his lips, adding: 'I'll be back in a while,' as he slid down her body.

It was late when Laura left. Her departure was a lengthy, extended operation because all the way across James' flat, down the metal steps, through the alley by the side of the chemist, onto the street, along the pavement to her car, and even getting inside it, James had to keep stopping her for a last goodnight kiss, because letting her go necessitated willpower greater than he possessed. When, however, with a heroic effort James allowed her to close the door and start the engine, and had raised his hand to wave her goodbye, Laura suddenly opened the door and jumped out.

James assumed she needed one more of his irresistible kisses, but instead she hugged him, tightly. She held him long enough for him to look over her shoulder at the roofs of buildings against the urban night sky, and to experience the rare conviction for a man that he is in the exact place on this planet he's supposed to be.

Finally Laura released her grip, looked at him for a moment, said: 'Thank you, James,' jumped into her car and drove away.

Laura came to James' flat on Tuesday evening, and again on Thursday – James wouldn't come to the cottage in the grounds of the house. Laura made her way down on Sunday too.

'What's happened to Sunday lunch up there?' James asked. 'I thought it was a sacrosanct institution.'

'It still is,' Laura told him. 'Only Harry cooks it. He used to make an Indian meal on Saturday evenings and it just got moved to Sunday lunch somehow. Fortunately.'

'You had an Indian last night,' said James.

'How do you know?' Laura demanded.

'Your armpits smell of pungent spices,' he told her.

'Oh, I'm sorry,' Laura apologized, retreating.

'No, come here, it's wonderful,' he assured her. 'Now I want to eat all of you.'

Without either of them planning to, James and Laura were slipping into a semi-secretive relationship. Laura didn't want any disruption of Adamina's universe: she'd seen how acquaintances, single mothers like herself, had brought into their home a succession of men, of surrogate father figures their children became more attached to than they did and then had to let go. Stability, she believed, was vital and she was determined to provide it for her daughter – especially now that Robert, the child's father, was part of her life.

Laura knew, though, that James was more than a passing lover, and she realized she was duplicating the stealth of her relationship with Robert; she must prove to herself that she didn't seek this furtiveness. There was also the danger of neglecting Adamina in the time she spent with James – quite apart from imposing upon Natalie on the Sundays Adamina wasn't with Robert, and having to find other baby-sitters in the week.

The fifth of November was on a Thursday that year, 1992: on Saturday, the seventh, the annual Round Table bonfire and fireworks display was held in the park on the hill between the house and the town centre. It had been an event fixed in the family's calendar and now a new generation was enjoying it. Harry and Alice were taking their bevy of children; Simon hadn't missed a single Guy Fawkes in his life; Natalie was going with her new girlfriend, Lucy. The one person who wouldn't be going was Charles, who despite his love of social gatherings had a positive dislike of fireworks and had been relieved when his children had grown old enough to go on their own.

Laura chose this moment for James and Adamina to meet. She brought her down for tea at his flat first of all, to introduce them properly.

'James is your uncle,' Laura explained to Adamina. 'He's your father's brother.'

'Why don't you live in the house?' Adamina demanded.

'That's a long story,' James told her. 'I'm too old,' he decided.

'Are you older than Uncle Simon?' Adamina asked him.

'No,' he answered.

'Why does *he* live in the house then?'

'Well, he's happy there,' James replied.

Mostly, though, Adamina was quiet. She replied tersely to James' solicitous questions about her school, and then she observed James and Laura eating, talking, gesturing. Reserved though they were, she saw their easy familiarity. When they'd finished and cleared away and were about to put on coats and scarves Laura went to the loo. Adamina watched James tying the laces of his boots.

'I don't like you,' she told him.

He looked up slowly. 'Well, that's OK,' he said.

'I know,' Adamina replied.

414

They walked from the flat. It was a damp evening with fog in the air that was dispersed by the streetlights and the heat rising from the urban surface of the earth.

The park, though, was a large, open field on the side of the hill, enclosed by iron railings. James and Laura and Adamina walked towards where the bonfire stood. They couldn't see it; they knew where it was because they'd each noticed it accruing over the previous weeks, a mound of tyres and pallets, furniture and timber.

It was dark, and thus difficult to tell how thick the fog was – it was surely inconceivable that it could sabotage the fireworks display, on this one day of the year.

Others were walking up the park around them: voices spoke as if from invisible people, who then appeared like apparitions and faded away as if into another dimension. Suddenly a technicolour porcupine passed before them – a girl selling battery-operated lit-up plastic quills; Adamina took the one James bought her and swirled it in the air. A man sold fluorescent headbands.

They came through the back of the crowd, already massed behind a rope-line, and pushed through near to the front for a better view for Adamina. It was to little avail. The fog seemed to thicken by the minute: they saw the first fireworks being lit and shooting upwards, but very soon they – and the rest of the crowd – waited for the whoosh of the fireworks rising and then gazed up at vague glows and will-o'-the-wisp colours in the sky above them through a thick blanket of fog; and they heard muffled bangs and explosions, as if a great battle were taking place not far away, there in the fog somewhere, another Battle of Britain of flak and blitz and dogfights in the skies.

Small children cried, whether through fear or simply disappoint-ment it was hard to tell. But they stayed where they were, the whole crowd, it seemed, enveloped in fog, imbued with a sort of stoic English optimism in the face of unfavourable nature. It would have taken little, James thought, for them to have started singing. As it was he could hear the odd quip thrown into the fog ('Guy Fawkes would have made his escape in this weather') that symbolized a kind of dumb defiance. James, who'd never felt patriotic, now (perhaps because he couldn't *see* the crowd he was a part of) felt a strange rush of glad emotion. He put his arm around Laura's shoulders, and kissed her – and then felt her pull away. A pang of disappointment saddened him, but it was dispelled as he looked down and saw Adamina glaring up at him, and realized she'd tugged her mother away.

The crowd's defiance was rewarded by the bonfire. It was so huge and so hot a blaze it seemed to burn the fog off and they saw it clearly. Flames swirled like liquid and showers of red sparks flew upwards. The Guy on top smoked, tottered and fell, to a great cheer. Adamina's enthralled face glowed orange.

James walked Laura and Adamina up the hill, to the door in the wall near to their cottage.

'Say thank you to James,' Laura told Adamina.

'Thank you to James,' Adamina addressed the ground.

James' grin pre-empted admonition from Laura. She kissed James lightly and whispered: 'It'll be all right.'

'It *was* all right,' he assured her.

Laura looked at him, and then said to Adamina: 'You go on ahead, I'll be right behind you, Mina. Pour us both a glass of milk.' Adamina stalled a second, then did as she was told. Laura turned back to James. 'I want to be with you tonight,' she told him. 'But I'm not going to leave Mina. Can you come back later?'

'I want to see you,' James replied, pondering. 'I don't want to go back in there. You know that.'

'I know, but don't you think it's worth it?'

'OK,' he decided. 'I'll come.'

A couple of hours later James cycled back up the hill and along the lane that ran around the outside of the lower wall, and chained his bike to a lamppost a hundred yards from the door in the wall near Laura's cottage. He almost tiptoed on the tarmac; he felt like a cat-burglar, creeping into his past.

'This is ridiculous,' James muttered to himself. He pushed open the unlocked door and slipped in. Two or three odd windows in the big house were lit, but he could see no movement nor hear any sound. The sky was overcast, the night dark; James was glad, not just because he couldn't be seen but also because *he* couldn't see much either. He could barely make out the whole outline of the big house itself. It seemed smaller than he remembered.

James knocked stealthily on the door of Laura's cottage and she let him in.

'Hi,' she said quietly.

'Hi,' he said.

She was smiling at him. 'That wasn't so difficult, was it?' she said.

416

'No,' he admitted. 'It wasn't.' They went upstairs, where Adamina was safely asleep.

'You know, I'm thirty-five,' James told Laura. 'I walked out of the house when I was eighteen. I haven't been back for seventeen years.'

'Hey, James,' Laura said, 'I'm impressed. I didn't realize you were a mathematician, too. I had no idea.'

'But I've been away almost as long as I was there growing up.'

'I can see that. Do you want a prize for your pig-headedness or what?'

'I don't want any prizes,' he said. 'Apart from you.'

They made love, and afterwards James felt a strong desire to flee: whether it was to get out of the grounds of the house, or to run away from Laura, he wasn't sure. He waited till she had fallen asleep, and then slipped out of her cottage.

10

THE RIVAL

IT WAS A GOOD THING IT WAS THE AUTUMN, WITH NIGHT FALLING ever earlier, since James refused to come to the cottage in daylight. He slipped through the gate in the wall in the evening, having waited for darkness all day, increasingly impatient. He arrived at Laura's door in a state of agitation so close to being bad-tempered that he shook himself to get rid of it before going in; only to find that Laura appeared to be in a similar condition, one that could only be dispelled with someone else's help.

During those nights Laura discovered that it was possible to carry James to the brink of climax and then hold him there indefinitely in a state of excruciating bliss by the most subtle means; even when she'd made him take a vow of silence, so that he wasn't allowed to give directions, or inform her as to the state of his innermost needs of the moment, she was able to discern exactly where he was.

While James sometimes saw that Laura was no longer with him, her eyes had glazed over and her skin was changing colour, and she'd gone off towards a distant planet in some other universe, some place that had nothing to do with him any more, except for the fact that he was steering her towards it.

Afterwards she leaned against him, and he said nothing so that she could come back to earth in silence, until she let him know she had returned to reality.

'This is Ground Control,' James whispered. 'We have contact.'

They'd discovered a shared propensity for love-making, to the extent that each doubted their own relative inexperience, never mind the other's.

'Who taught you that, James?' Laura asked. 'That Italian girl?'

'You did,' he assured her.

'How do you know what you know?' James demanded in turn. 'You said you never went to college, but I think you've done some Open University degree in pleasing a man. Was that man with the silver hair your tutor, or what?'

'It's you,' Laura replied. 'It's you and me.'

'Do other people have this?' James wondered. 'Is it normal?'

'No, it's unique in human history,' Laura laughed. 'People say they have. Now I know what they mean. At least I think I do. If it's the same as I feel. You never know with words.'

'You must have read things I haven't,' James told her.

'I'll read them to you, James, in the bath. Now stay there. Don't move. And don't say anything,' she ordered. 'Don't wake Adamina,' she added as she rose and proceeded to embark upon the leisurely process of covering James' body with tiny agonizing bites.

During the day Laura went about her work in a semi-conscious state, relying on recipes rather than her palate and the inspiration of the moment. It was a kind of relaxed exhaustion. In contrast to the dark months following Adamina's birth, though, she had no wish to escape it in sleep; instead she wallowed in a paradoxical languorous vitality, at one with herself and the world.

James had never photographed with such intensity and yet, at the same time, a kind of carefree abandon. He left his flat as soon as he'd had breakfast and stalked the town as if driven, as if time were running out, returning with rolls of exposed film he developed and then left in the darkroom for weeks, too busy to make even contact sheets. And yet the endeavour felt effortless. He sought and saw and clicked the shutter release.

James was spreading out from the road to chronicle the streets of the whole town, a mad enterprise except that he was no longer mad. He was simply doing what he now knew he had to do. He took pictures of traffic wardens and policemen, taxi drivers and street-cleaners, pensioners and children, people waiting for buses to come and parents waiting for school to finish.

He took only people: morose anglers like monks at prayer along the river; a young man with a tattooed face, and other hopeless drunks and dreamless beggars; acid-heads tripping through Shutterbuck Woods; Greens swimming naked in the gravel pit north of town; clerks and secretaries snoozing at lunchtime in the parks; stoop-shouldered barge-dwellers along the canal.

In addition to his restless activity around town, James had a new subject: Laura. His only previous attempt at photographing a woman as such had been a fuzzy picture of a blonde girl on a horse about to jump over his prone body. He hadn't taken more than odd snaps of his few girlfriends since then, but nowadays he had his camera to hand all the time, and first took nude photos of Laura.

'How come you're not fat like your mother, being a cook and all?' James demanded.

'I take after my father, of course,' Laura said.

James found that he could happily watch Laura reading or cooking – her almond eyes, small nose and mouth with slightly jutting teeth – engrossed for long periods in the changing expressions of her countenance and the movement of her facial muscles. Motherhood and time had thickened her waist and rounded her belly. When James flicked through a women's magazine left on her kitchen table for its recipes, he wondered why the fashion editors chose models who looked like dolls, when the only result was for ordinary women to feel compelled to try and look like mannequins themselves through cruel diets, punishing exercise and constricting clothes.

In a sudden illuminating flash James saw a complex conspiracy theory laid bare, one involving magazine editors, plastic surgeons, multinational make-up manufacturers, imperious supermodels and their millionaire paramours. When he tried to unravel it again, however, with Laura's help, she misunderstood what he was saying.

'You think I'm ugly?' she demanded.

'No, Laura,' James countered, 'that's exactly the point, I think you're just beautiful. They're the ones who've got it wrong. Those models are so perfect they're uninteresting.'

'It's my teeth, isn't it?' she suggested. 'Or is it my knock-knees? I know my joints crack.'

'No, you're adorable,' he assured her.

Laura nodded, in a way that showed she was offended. 'Well, if you don't like what you see, you know what you can do,' she told him curtly.

'Good grief,' James murmured. But quietly. When Laura was annoyed with him she bent back the little finger of his right hand at an angle once shown her by Natalie, which made him squeak like a stricken bat and drop to his knees, from where he begged for mercy and vowed to do anything in the world she wanted, damn it, anything at all, if she'd only release his little finger.

After he'd undertaken to iron Laura's clothes for the rest of her natural life and massage her feet with lavender oil every evening, and she had let him go, James said: 'That's some trick. It's a good thing I had my other fingers crossed.' Before she could grab one of his vulnerable digits again he threw them in the air and exclaimed: 'No, but you're right! I agree with whatever you said!'

Laura put her arms around him and held him tight against her, with a smirk at the sides of her mouth and a pressure against his lower regions that made desire swell down there, and said: 'Well, in that case you better prove it.'

His favourite photograph was of Laura laughing, her head thrown back, almond eyes shining, with two tiny dimples visible just above her cheekbones.

Adamina was the single child of a single mother, already, at the age of six, her mother's best friend. Laura asked Adamina's opinion about which clothes to wear; whether this dresser wouldn't be better in the kitchen than the sitting-room; what to get Natalie for her birthday; was it a good idea to pay to convert her VW Golf to unleaded petrol? Should they go to France next year or to Sweden to try the raw herring and reindeer meat? Adamina listened to her mother's questions calmly, considered them in thoughtful silence, and gave advice in a voice that combined the cadence of a child with the forbearance of a patient sister, and also contained a slight lisp.

When something was worrying either of them, a problem at home or school, they made a teatime appointment to discuss it properly. Laura shared her moods and hopes with Adamina; her small daughter was her confidante, her pal and her partner. But no one thought of Adamina as a spoiled child since petulance and whining were beneath her: Laura never gave her cause for immaturity, because she treated her as an equal.

They went shopping together in the superstore on the ring road as a couple: Adamina demanded not the sweets on sly display at the checkout, like other children, but rather pointed out toilet rolls which they were low on, Green washing-up liquid, a bottle of special-offer Bulgarian white wine, and not that red because, although it's cheaper, you know it gives you a headache, Mummy, and a bottle of fizzy mineral water, we shouldn't drink out of the taps, it's horrible and it's probably bad for you.

Despite the fact that her mother was a professional chef, Adamina herself lived on a diet of Heinz baked beans, oven-ready chips and Mars bars (plus McDonald's burgers on a Sunday) and the only times she ever threw a fit with her mother were when Laura tried to entice her into trying something new: on such matters Adamina was inflexible, and showed herself perfectly capable of starving rather than weaken.

Adamina recognized James as a rival from the very beginning, and James realized that he would have to court her as much as Laura herself. He organized an expedition to the ice-rink, but when they were there Adamina made it clear that he was enjoying it much more than she was (which was certainly true). Then he arranged a visit to Whipsnade Zoo, only for Adamina to refuse to go at the last minute, and they had to cancel the trip.

Despite Laura's warning that it was pointless, James brought fruit and sweets and drinks to the cottage, all of which Adamina spurned as if he were tempting her from a religious fast, until in a minor victory she sneaked a sip of sweet pear juice when no one was looking, finished off the bottle in one ecstatic splurge, and told him by the way that if he insisted on bringing all that stuff she might be prepared to drink a little bit of pear juice, now and again, just to make him feel better.

James sometimes came to Laura's cottage late only to find Adamina still up, prolonging bedtime by fooling around, getting stuck in her pyjamas, pretending she'd gone senile and couldn't find her bedroom. Laura told her off while laughing in the same breath, and said, yes, she could stay in Mummy's bed again tonight; then James and Laura had to sleep together on an improvised mattress of blankets and sheets on the sitting-room floor. Or else Adamina feigned sleeplessness or an upset tummy, kept coming through to the sitting-room, wanting to sit in front of the fire in Laura's arms, saying: 'I can't sleep, Mummy,' even when it was clear that it was only an extraordinary force of will that was keeping her awake at all. And while she lay there in her mother's lap she sneaked a look at James, a brief half-smile, just enough to let him know that she was the one in control of things around here, including her mother's heart, and he was an impostor.

James wanted to say something but he didn't know how to. Laura sometimes got annoyed with Adamina but in the end she always relented to Adamina's armoury of tactics, which were both persuasive and various, and if one looked like it might not work, then she changed gear abruptly and moved on to another, from insomnia to indigestion, bad dreams to existential despair, wailing: 'They told us in school, the universe is thirty billion light years across, Mummy, and it's *all* dangerous.' Until her mother succumbed.

It was worst after she spent the first Sunday of December with her father. She came back with both her language and her behaviour roughened, treated James with open hostility, ignored him, swore at him (which, to his consternation, made Laura laugh). Then she was surly with her mother but also softer too, asking if Laura liked having a day without her and why didn't they live with her father?

'Can't you and Robert live together because of me?' she asked. 'Is it my fault, Mummy?'

'No, honey, no,' Laura assured her, 'I love you, I adore you.' She hugged her daughter, who sneaked a look at James. The two of them drew closer together again, with James locked out.

James was perplexed by this little adversary. They circled each other, circled around Laura, looking for cracks in the other's resistance. But only Adamina jabbed forward. She scribbled his name in big letters with a bright felt-tip pen in library books he forgot at the cottage; one morning she hid his shoes under the sink in the bathroom and then while James was looking everywhere for them, cursing that he was already late to meet someone in town, she told Laura that that nasty dog of Sam's and Amy's had let himself into the cottage, he was up to his tricks, maybe he'd taken them.

When Laura dropped in to see James with Adamina the following Saturday he was in the middle of printing, and Adamina stayed in the darkroom with him, making him explain what he was doing and letting her help him. The infrared seemed to soothe her.

When he'd finished, Adamina ate the lunch Laura had been preparing in the kitchen, while James and Laura chatted in the sitting-room. Laura regarded herself as a woman free of sentimentality. Without realizing it, however, she had begun to utter endearments and whisper cute profanities in her lover's ear which, if she heard someone else use them, would have made her cringe. Now while they whispered and laughed louder than they thought they were doing Adamina in the kitchen emptied a bottle of whisky down the sink, rinsed it, and filled it with pear juice (which had incidentally relieved the constipation of her unhealthy diet) from the fridge. James flew off the handle and Adamina burst into tears, explaining to Laura through her sobs that she only wanted to make James feel that she appreciated his gifts.

She was an unpredictable opponent, spurning his approaches of affection yet also badgering him to play games with her.

'Tell me a joke,' she demanded.

'What tree smells?'

'Don't know.'

'A lavatree.'

To James' delight she laughed as loudly as he did.

'I've got another one,' he said. 'See if you can get this one,' he enthused. 'What fish is musical?'

Adamina shrugged, and sighed.

'A tuna fish,' James said, and started to fall about. Adamina, though, looked at him with a disdainful expression, raised her eyebrows, and said: 'What's so funny about that? It's stupid. Mummy,' she called, 'did you hear that? James' jokes are stupid.'

On the other hand Adamina cornered James and made him listen to rambling stories she made up as she went along that had neither point nor punchline, and asked him riddles to which there was no answer.

'How old am I?'

'Six.'

'No.'

'Five?'

'No.'

'I give up.'

'You can't!'

Nine? Twelve? Twenty-seven?

No, no, no.

'I don't know, I give up.'

'You're not allowed to!'

She was playing for time to invent an explanation for the riddle, but she couldn't, she didn't have the brainpower, so when even Adamina herself tired and said, 'Yes!' to James' weary 'Fifty-three?' and he asked her why, she came up with some nonsensical, unsatisfying answer. She reminded James of his sister Alice.

They circled each other, feinting, parrying, retreating; circling around Laura. Through those hurried weeks James and Laura – despite the interruptions – shared their bodies and their secrets, and James felt a mix of exhilaration and fear as he realized that their separate destinies were becoming intertwined, were being tugged forward and spliced together; and at a speed that was just out of control. The one thing they didn't share, the only thing James couldn't raise, was his suspicion that Adamina was an obstacle to their relationship.

The three of them went away for a long weekend to Devon in the middle of December. They took a circuitous route there, visiting farms mentioned in Patrick Rance's *Book of British Cheese*, and James discovered that Laura had a puritanical streak: she needed a reason for a brief holiday; once she was able to call it a research trip she felt less guilty about taking time off.
  'Curse of the self-employed,' James sympathized.
  '*You're* self-employed,' she replied.
  'I'm a workaholic *and* a lazy sod,' he said.
  'You take your camera everywhere,' she pointed out.
  'That's true,' he admitted.
  James said he hated cars but Laura persuaded him it was time he learned to drive: she put L-plates on her VW Golf and gave him lessons along the back lanes. It was a disaster. James was always braking, accelerating, lurching back and forth, an irredeemably jerky driver; as with his dancing, he observed, behind the wheel he responded to each junction, traffic light and corner as if it had just appeared unexpectedly in the road before him; he was for ever improvising. Whereas Laura, at ease in life (if clumsy on the dance floor, which was where the analogy broke down), cruised along the road. She registered obstacles well in advance and slowed down imperceptibly, or spotted an opening up ahead and accelerated smoothly towards it.
  'You remind me of your mother in her kitchen,' James told Laura, 'with her flowing movements. When you drive, the car floats.' Whereupon, feeling utterly safe while hurtling through space at 80 mph, James dozed off. When Laura braked, her left arm came across

in front of James, in barely conscious protectiveness, as she had once done with Adamina (who now sat in the back seat, belted in). While when she let *him* drive, Laura was unable to stop herself from scrutinizing the road more keenly than when she was behind the wheel, and emerged from the passenger seat with her clenched knees aching.

Eventually Laura plucked up the courage to tell James she realized she'd rather drive than be a passenger any day, she never got tired driving so she didn't even need a rest, and maybe it wasn't so important for him to be able to give Adamina lifts after all. She was as tactful as possible because she knew that the only thing people hate more than being told they're a bad driver is that they lack a sense of humour.

'Suits me,' James replied happily. 'If you're really sure. I'm a crap driver; I hate cars.'

It was the same on foot. James and Laura walked at different speeds, and had to learn to walk together comfortably, because at first James strode ahead without noticing: he'd done so much walking alone in his life, striding forward with his camera at the ready, eyes seeking rectangular compositions in the fluid world before him. Laura found herself forgotten in his wake and had to shout at him, 'Hang on, Harry Dean Stanton. What's the hurry, James? Jesus, we're not *due* anywhere you know, we're just walking out. We're on holiday.'

Sometimes she stopped walking and waited, arms folded, until James eventually recalled that he was one of a pair, and he turned round to see Laura's sardonic posture in the middle distance.

James carried Adamina on his shoulders when she was tired of walking across Dartmoor as the sun lowered to the horizon, and the shadows of a tor stretched across the sea-green moor. Laura's research continued with visits to the kitchens of National Trust houses at Saltram, Buckland Abbey and Castle Drogo: she checked out the menus provided in the eighteenth and nineteenth centuries, and they marvelled at what were once innovative labour-saving gadgets: mechanical spits and trivets on the kitchen range; tin-plated graters and peelers, corers and slicers.

'How on earth did they make such feasts with these?' James wondered.

'They had another labour-saving device,' Laura pointed out. 'Called servants.'

On meandering drives around the moors and along the coast they played car games, in which James and Adamina discovered an affinity

426

from which Laura was excluded: she was prosaic, choosing 'I spy' objects she knew Adamina could guess if she thought logically, regarding such games as educational. Whereas Adamina needed only the slightest prompting from James to fly off into her imagination: instead of thinking of objects, people or animals she thought of a joke James had told her earlier (Q: 'What's yellow and stupid?' A: 'Thick custard') or the look on Natalie's face a few days before when she'd taken a sip of Simon's camomile tea.

While James stretched his arms back behind the passenger seat for Adamina to slap high-fives on his palms Laura complained: 'But Mina, it's supposed to be animal, vegetable or mineral; it's supposed to be real, honey.'

'Natalie's face *was* real, Mummy,' Adamina told her.

'Of course it was,' James agreed.

A lot of the time, though, Adamina nodded off on the back seat – perhaps she hadn't entirely outgrown the days Laura got her to sleep as a baby by driving round the block. While Adamina snoozed behind them James and Laura continued the process of revealing themselves to each other, a car cruising through December afternoon darkness an isolated, intimate chamber.

'What do you want, James?' Laura asked.

'How? In what way?'

'What's your fantasy life? You know, if you won the Pools, or when we have this lottery they're talking about.'

'I'm happy now,' he told her.

'Oh, come on, play the game, spoilsport, now I've got one I like,' she pressed him.

The only thing James could imagine that he really wanted was Laura.

'Well,' he began, 'I guess I'd like a big house in the country, with a wood of beeches and birches—'

'In the country?' she interrupted. 'I thought you were a complete townie, James, and you were never going to leave the town. That's what Zoe told me. That *nothing* would make you leave.'

'That's true,' James admitted, 'but this is a fantasy game, isn't it? And I'm trying to play it.'

'OK. What else do you want?'

'Let me think. There's a football pitch in the back garden, not full-size, but five-a-side, with floodlights and vivid green grass and lime-white lines. And there are animals, lots of animals, not a farm but like a sanctuary, an Ark. And children, plenty of children, too.

427

I'd have table-tennis in a large room so that a bunch of people could play round the table without bumping into things. I'd want a bed so big I could get lost in it. Just for the pleasure of finding you again.'

James realized he'd got carried away and made a mistake – that maybe Laura didn't want it assumed that she'd be in the bed of his fantasy future; don't cramp her.

'A darkroom,' he added hurriedly. 'With the most modern equipment, of course. And a bathroom with a big sunken Roman bath, and shelves of smelly soaps and oils and foaming liquids. And flowers in every room, provided daily by the gardener.' James paused.

'Is that all?' Laura asked.

'No,' he answered. 'I could carry on,' he said, and he did, enumerating objects of desire that were no part of any ambition he had, not even of fantasy, really, it was simply a banal vision he was improvising on the spur of the moment, in order to avoid mentioning the one thing he did want. It was hard to avoid it, since he saw Laura lounging in the Roman bath, the photographs he was developing in his hi-tech darkroom were of her, and the flowers were meaningless unless she inhaled their scent.

'What about the kitchen?' Laura suggested. 'You haven't mentioned that.'

'Oh, no. No kitchen,' James replied. 'I'd live on take-aways.'

'In the country?'

'You said I was rich, so I'd pay over the odds. And tip the despatch riders generously, to make it worth their while.'

'A house is no home without a kitchen,' Laura said.

'Well, OK, I'll have a kitchen, but then I'll need a cook. Hey, you could apply for the job.'

'Thank you very much.'

'You'd need bloody good references,' he warned her.

'Fair enough.'

'I could give you one if you want. Don't know if it'd do you any good.'

'You're too kind, sir.'

'Let's change the subject,' James suggested.

'But it's my—'

'I know!' James cut her short. '*Desert Island Discs.*'

'You start then,' she frowned.

'Bach: *Goldberg Variations.*'

'Bach sounds like clockwork, James. No soul. My turn. The Pogues: "Thousands are Sailing".'

428

'They're drunken louts, Laura. They play out of tune. Kate Bush: "Running Up That Hill".'

'Well, she sounds certifiably mad to me. Miles Davis: *Concerto de Arunjuez.*'

'Jazz? I don't get it. I can't hear it.'

'It's your loss.'

'You're probably right. The Clash: I don't know which one.'

'That's just noise, all that punk stuff. What's it got to do with music? Maria Callas, singing . . . I don't know either. We can come back to those. Next.'

'Elgar: *Cello Concerto.*'

'Everyone chooses that.'

'It's beautiful, Laura.'

'It's too English.'

'Too English?'

'Robert Wyatt: "Shipbuilding".'

'That's OK.'

'Thanks, James.'

'I wouldn't choose it.'

James tried to put a Bach tape in the cassette player.

'You do, and you can bloody drive,' Laura warned him. 'And I'll put on earmuffs.'

'I want to *share* these things with you,' James complained.

Laura nearly told him that this overbearing need was a legacy from his father, but restrained herself. 'I love you for *you*,' she said, 'not for your taste in soporific music.'

'How can you *say* that?' James wailed. 'It's *brilliant*.'

It was the same with books, James dismayed that they hadn't matured, but rather argued now as they did over films as children after the Saturday matinées, many years before. Laura chose Yamuna Devi's *Lord Krishna's Cuisine*, but James insisted they limit their selection to novels. Not only did their tastes differ as widely in literature as in music, but as far as he could tell the only books Laura read were ones written by nineteenth-century white Englishwomen or late-twentieth-century black Americans: she alternated Jane Austen with Toni Morrison, George Eliot with Marsha Hunt.

'Why?' James asked. 'Is it on some kind of principle?'

'Only the pleasure one,' Laura shrugged.

James' spirits were lifted when Adamina developed a taste for the Beatles, and a live-concert tape they played in the car. They soon knew all the words, even to John Lennon's sardonic introductions ('Here's one for the older ones out there: it's a song that came out last year'). From the way the three of them sang along – in their own automobile karaoke – to 'Yellow Submarine', James thought they might *all* add it to their list of favourites.

'You're lucky, you can rediscover things through your child,' James told Laura. 'She'll probably move on to the Stones before she's seven.'

'And be into Dylan by the time she's eight,' Laura agreed. 'That reminds me, I forgot to include "Sarah" on my desert island.'

Adamina hated to miss out on anything. When she woke up from dozing in the back seat of the car the first thing she said was: 'You haven't been playing games without me, have you?'

'No, honey, we've been sitting here in silence,' Laura assured her.

'And you've only been asleep three seconds,' James lied.

'That's all right, then,' she said. 'I'm thinking of something.'

'Animal, vegetable or mineral?' Laura asked.

'I'll give you a clue: it's something I dreamed,' Adamina proclaimed.

'Nice one,' said James.

'I don't believe it,' Laura groaned.

Adamina wanted to be involved with everything. On their last night in Devon they stayed in a farmhouse B. and B. outside Moretonhampstead that had table-tennis set up in a barn. As soon as James and Laura had a go Adamina pestered them to let her too: for five minutes she missed and mishit the ball, and then she misjudged its flight towards her and the distance of things, or maybe she tripped – it happened so fast – because Adamina lurched forward to return a soft serve and thumped the bridge of her nose against the edge of the table.

Blood flowed but nothing was broken, and Laura administered arnica and soothing words and caresses till the shock and hurt had eased. The next morning, though, Adamina had a swollen nose, two black eyes and a blue bruise that was both awful in itself and also reminded James – and Laura herself – of the way Laura had looked after her father's beating, the day James saw her when he arrived home from the farm, the last time he'd ever been inside the house on the hill, seventeen years before.

*

When they came back from Devon James thought they had sailed clear of Adamina's resistance when she moved the last of her things from Laura's bedroom and made a nest for herself on the landing, where she proceeded to sleep soundly. James took it as a magnanimous if unconscious gesture, leaving Laura and him to enjoy unhindered evenings and relinquishing her last claim on Laura's bed.

But James was wrong.

It was the last Saturday before Christmas, cold and damp, and the three of them drove to an open farm outside town. They bought packets of grain and fed goats and chickens, scratched friendly pigs behind their ears, blew up horses' nostrils. They messed around for hours in the playground; Laura went into the café for tea while James carried on chasing Adamina in and out of swings and climbing frames.

They drove back into town together because that evening James' old friend Karel had the private view of his latest exhibition, in a gallery in Northtown. James and Laura rarely went out without Adamina. But tonight was to be spent with James' friends, sharing in their celebration, an evening of conversation, gossip, eating, drinking and maybe dancing later on that not even as precocious a child as Adamina could be expected to enjoy.

James had brought his evening clothes and while he and Laura got ready Adamina grew more and more silent. She and Laura had a bath together; then while Laura put on her make-up Adamina lay on Laura's bed, curled up in her pyjamas, staring vaguely into the distance.

'I'm not feeling very well, Mummy,' she whispered.

Laura, distracted in her preparations, said: 'You'll be fine, darling,' stooping to give her an abstract kiss as she passed by the bed on her way to the wardrobe.

James came in at that moment putting on his cufflinks; he still loved, despite his everyday scruffiness, to have the excuse of a special occasion for dressing up. He watched Laura stepping back to her dressing-table, dressed only in panties and a pair of sheer black tights, and he almost swooned with desire, felt his penis fill with blood and rise, Laura so unaware of her sexiness at that moment. He wanted her there and then, badly, quickly, but there wasn't time and anyway Adamina was there, curled up on the bed, pathetic, declining. James turned his attention to her. She looked so defenceless. James felt a ripple of anxiety pass through his guts; not at her weakness, but at her power.

By the time the baby-sitter arrived Adamina was sweating, her teeth were chattering, her nose running, and she was coughing a hacking, painful cough. She'd travelled from robust good health to death's door in the space of an hour.

'You go, Mummy,' she whimpered. 'I'm all right.'

Laura put a thermometer in her mouth and felt her forehead.

'We'll be late,' said James.

'She's got a fever,' Laura told him.

'She'll be fine, she just needs a good night's sleep.'

'You can be heartless sometimes, James. Look, she's got a temperature over a hundred. I think maybe I should call the doctor.'

'She's just been running around, she's tired, that's all. Let's not be late, Laura.' He felt his agitation ferment inside him. Laura was stroking Adamina's forehead.

'You go ahead,' Laura said. 'I'll follow you.'

'No,' he heard himself whisper. He wanted to go with her. He was going to go with her.

'What?' she asked absently. 'Go on, James, I'll be right along, honestly.'

Maybe it was his imagination: it was so fleeting. Maybe he expected or even wanted to see it, and it wasn't really there. But what he *thought* he saw was the sides of Adamina's mouth, just the edges of her lips, curl into a slight, slight semblance of a smile; of victory.

James' patience snapped. 'For God's sake, Laura!' he exclaimed, 'Can't you see she's feigning it? She does it whenever she wants.'

'What?' asked Laura, dumbfounded. 'A six-year-old child feigning a temperature of a hundred and two? Don't be ridiculous.'

'She *can* do it, that girl. She plays you like a, like a – shit, Laura, you fall for it every single time.'

Adamina lay shivering in the middle of the double bed, dark rings around her eyes in her pale face, tiny and shrinking, uncomplaining. Sally, the baby-sitter, stood in the doorway embarrassed, too young to know how, despite her discomfort, to simply slip away from this scene before her.

Laura stood up. 'How *dare* you!' she shouted at James.

Unvoiced suspicions and unmentioned defeats that he'd suppressed flew out of James' mouth: 'Can't you see, Laura? She's just doing it to keep us apart, it's the *one* night we're leaving her here. She's a cunning, manipulative little *fox*.'

'God, James, you are heartless *and* stupid,' Laura spluttered. 'And cruel and dumb! You don't know anything about children, how could you? You don't know anything about *people!*' she yelled. 'You don't know anything about *me!*'

The beautiful woman of moments before had been transformed into an angry, shrieking animal. James in his own anger wanted to grab her, except the idea of touching her was repugnant. His blood was raging around his body and he was scared as well. He didn't know whether he wanted to strike her or fuck her or fall at her feet.

Laura went back to the bed and knelt beside Adamina, a sick sparrow, huddled ever smaller and tighter. Laura half-turned towards James, as if only so that the heat of her fierce breath were directed away from the girl.

'Just fuck off, James. You're no help. Just get out.'

James felt weak, drained. In a faint voice he said: 'Are you coming?'

'Of course I'm not coming!' she said. 'Look what you've done. Now she's upset as well as ill.' She was stroking Adamina's feverish brow. 'There, there, Mina,' she soothed, her voice tremulous with anger still, 'it's all right, Mummy's here.'

James pushed awkwardly past Sally still standing in the doorway, and went to the gallery alone. He tried to cut off, to be a friend to his old friends but he drank too much too quickly, stumbled in the bright white rooms, became flustered and verbose in the tinkling, claustrophobic chatter closing in around him. He knocked into people, and stood stupefied and alone for long periods of the evening. At the end, James had to be pulled back from his own dumb aggression when the gallery owner asked the last of the crowd to leave so that he could lock up; and then he threw up outside on the pavement.

James' big mistake was in going back. He felt so bad and he thought he might redeem the situation if he acted before it had gone too far. He didn't have enough experience of lovers' quarrels; Anna Maria, all those years ago, had only been playing.

It was one thirty in the morning. He crept upstairs and into Laura's bedroom: he expected Adamina to be there, asleep beside her, but to his immense relief Laura was alone. He slipped off his shoes and tiptoed along the corridor to Adamina's room. She was sleeping, her breathing troubled by scraping inhalations and whistling exhalations.

James went back into Laura's room. He made a little noise, half on purpose, getting undressed, and then he slipped naked beneath the duvet. Laura lay with her back to him. He couldn't tell from her breathing whether she was asleep or awake. He whispered her name,

'Laura,' but she didn't respond. She was so still and silent he became convinced that she must be awake. He whispered her name again – 'Laura.' Again there was no response.

If she was asleep, then she was really sleeping soundly, and if James raised his voice and woke her from deep sleep she would be justly angry. And what would he say anyway? He'd disturb her and she'd come groping from the depths into unwelcome consciousness. She'd say: 'What?' in a voice half-dozy, half-irritated, and he'd say: 'Nothing.' And then she'd really be in a foul mood, she'd either say: 'Leave me alone,' or else she'd stir, turn over and say: 'What the fuck is it now? What the hell time do you call this?' He'd be in a hopeless position . . .

'Nothing.'

'Nothing? You woke me for nothing.'

'I just wanted . . .'

'*What?* You just wanted *what*, James? Jesus *Christ!*'

It was too awful to contemplate.

Or else she was awake. And that was even worse. It meant she was lying there, this very moment, ignoring him on purpose, making him feel as bad as he deserved to feel, but still, it was horrible. He lay facing her, facing the back of her head, his body inches from her body. Her body he loved, her body that fit his body, her body that moved easily with his.

Now she lay with her back to him, hostile, unwelcoming flesh. James felt wretched and he felt powerless. His mind was isolated. His head throbbed, his stomach was empty and acidic, his penis was small and rubbery, his feet were cold.

James tried to think but he didn't seem able to. He tried to turn his thoughts elsewhere, to visualize the photographs he'd taken that week, to distract his own attention. But no images would form in his mind's eye. There was nothing there but a faceless, characterless fog. He felt wretched and he realized that what it was was a terrible loneliness, but unlike anything he'd ever experienced before. There had been times he had felt cut off from the world with no comrades who understood him, no special friends who cared for him, and no lover in his life. At those times he had thought to himself: There is nothing worse than this. I will survive, it's only emotional, it's only emotion, it's my destiny. But there's nothing worse than this.

Now he knew that there was something worse, that the worst loneliness is to have found your lover and then to be estranged from her as she lies with her back to you. What he didn't realize was that he was making any noise, until Laura's terse, hoarse voice cut through everything:

'For God's sake don't snivel,' she said.

Slapped with shame and hurt, James rolled backwards and out of bed and pulled on his clothes. Laura didn't stir. James slipped from the room and down the stairs and cycled home, where he slept till the following midday.

The doctor came and diagnosed measles. Adamina spent a week in bed with a runny nose and eyes, sore throat and cough, trying desperately not to scratch the itchy red rash that covered her body and limbs, in a gloomy room with the curtains drawn because the light hurt her eyes.

James brought her supplicatory pre-Christmas presents — games, comics, tapes, dolls — that Adamina, weak and subdued, accepted graciously. He brought flowers for Laura, and apologized for his behaviour, and she too accepted his apologies but distractedly, because she was more concerned that Adamina didn't develop the secondary symptoms of pneumonia on the one hand or an ear inflammation on the other.

It had been a battle of wills, and James accepted that Adamina's was stronger than his; that although Laura did love him, her loyalty, of course, was to her daughter if her daughter should — as she had done — make her choose.

In some strange way James felt as much elated as dismayed; he felt like he had brushed up against some great truth of life. That he had lost to this small girl was absurd, that he and Laura should lose each other because of her childish whims was just ridiculous. So there must be some greater scheme of things: perhaps they were souls of vastly different ages, he was really a child and Laura was a woman but Adamina was old and powerful, and they each needed each other not how they *thought* they did, but for some mysterious profound effect; maybe James had to suffer in this precise way, he had to dwell in a desert of loneliness, maybe Laura had to accept a lesser choice, maybe Adamina was forced by her fate to cause others unhappiness and thus learn to curb her power.

This was all nonsense but the notion intrigued James and consoled him over those following days. He decided that just as Adamina had accepted her victory with good grace, so he should accept his defeat. The night before Christmas Eve he came late to Laura and they made love more gently than ever, more patiently. He lost count of the number of times he came close to coming and backed off, slowed down. They lay a while and changed position and started again.

They hardly said a word, and both knew that the other thought of many things. They screwed slowly till they were so tired they almost fell asleep with him inside her, but they withdrew from each other at the same moment, without having to say anything, neither of them satisfied and both exhausted. And they both sank into sleep beneath the sad weight of separation.

When he woke in the morning it took James a few moments to realize that it wasn't Laura whose limbs enfolded his: she lay a foot away from him. It was Adamina, squeezed between them. Both she and her mother were still sleeping. James didn't want to disturb either of them, and neither did he want to lose this sudden, unconscious intimacy. Adamina was naked as he was. She lay facing him, the top of her bent head resting against his chest, her arm on his side, one leg over his, the pale peach cheeks of her child's sex inches from his limp prick, in a pastiche, a mockery, of copulation. He bent his own neck down and inhaled the clean smell of her hair, and dozed off.

Laura woke them with a pot of tea and a plate of toast. The three of them sat curled up in bed together, crunching toast, licking jam from fingers.

'I'm better, Mummy,' Adamina told Laura. 'Look, the spots are nearly gone.'

Laura tickled her, and she tickled James, and they both tickled Laura in vain. They grew itchy in the hot sheets, prickly with crumbs.

Adamina jumped out of bed, ran over to the window and drew the curtains wide. 'It's sunny outside!' she exclaimed. She climbed shivering back into bed, snuggled up to James, and said: 'What are we going to do today, Daddy?'

Over lunch Laura told James that as well as looking after Adamina this last week she'd also been busy in the kitchen, practising old recipes and trying out new ones, because a few days before she'd been asked to do a special job: the day after Boxing Day Laura was to depart for a week-long visit to America. Two of her regular clients had a country house in the Cotswolds, where they spent eight months of the year, and an apartment in Manhattan. Their cook there had had to tend a sick relative and they had the inspiration of throwing dinner parties of English food for their New York acquaintances over

436

the new year. Laura had to provide a different menu for each of six evenings. It would be a working holiday, and a once-in-a-lifetime trip.

James' relief at being reconciled with Laura was instantly tempered by the awful prospect of her being lured to New York on a permanent basis. For the second night in a row they made love with James at least certain they were doomed to part, but this time it was with an energetic fury that left him feeling sated and detached from himself.

He woke on Christmas morning to the rustle of stockings at the end of Laura's bed, and the three of them unwrapped tangerines and apples and a great many more knick-knacks than physics would have allowed to fit into single large walking-socks. As James opened gifts of a camera that instead of taking photos spouted the subject with water, a hairbrush, a pair of cufflinks, a Zippo lighter, an Opinel penknife, bicycle clips, a wallet, and a bootleg tape of the Clash in concert from 1978, that Laura must have been collecting for weeks, it gradually dawned on him that the idea of separation had never entered her head.

He slipped away soon after because Laura had to make a huge Christmas lunch for the family over in the house, but afterwards she left Adamina there and came down to his flat. She fed him the most delicious results of her recent experiments, but they depressed James: the more wonderful they were, the more certain it was that at least one of the dinner-party guests would want to employ her singular skills.

'Everyone knows that Americans have a thing about English culture,' he moaned. 'I can just imagine those rich New Yorkers, what a social coup it would be. They'll be queueing up to beg you to stay there.'

'Don't be silly, James. It's out of the question. It's not on the agenda, and that's that,' Laura declared, omitting to mention that the more he went on the more she did consider such a possibility. The idea of starting afresh, away from the place she'd spent her whole life, away from the complications of Robert's and Adamina's relationship, had a real appeal.

A couple of weeks earlier, Laura had been cooking and Adamina, sitting bored at the window, was intoning to herself in the background:

> 'Last night upon the stair
> I saw a man who wasn't there.

He wasn't there again today –
oh, how I wish he'd go away.'

It was a drone in the background of Laura's concentration, when words suddenly focused in her brain and chilled her blood. She grabbed Adamina's arm.

'Who was there?' Laura demanded. 'Was your father inside the cottage?' In her panic she brought Adamina to the brink of tears before accepting that it was no more than a rhyme picked up in school.

'Have you ever thought of moving?' she asked James tentatively. 'As a purely hypothetical question. Does America hold any temptation at all?'

'What on earth would I do there?' James demanded.

'Take photographs. People are people, aren't they?'

'Laura, don't you understand? This is my town. I'm documenting my town. It's my life. I thought you understood.'

'Of course I do. It's just a hypothetical question.'

James went with Laura to Heathrow – they had to go by coach, since he'd failed to learn to drive – in a sombre mood. They checked in one suitcase of clothes and another of kitchen implements and sat in an air-conditioned cafeteria, surrounded by the throng of travellers from every continent; people who'd stepped out of different time zones and were eating anachronistic meals with an air of resignation or else sleeping stretched out across seats.

They squeezed into a photo booth and took a strip of four passport colour photos which James folded and cut in half with his Opinel penknife.

'I'm only going for ten days,' Laura said. 'And then I'll be back for ever.'

'There's no such thing as for ever,' James told her. She prodded him. 'I know I'm being melodramatic,' he admitted, 'it's this airport as well, all these people meeting and leaving loved ones: the place is clogged up with emotion. It's like some huge international wedding.'

James' melancholy may have been exacerbated, but his photographer's eye was enthralled. He was in a Tower of Babel, except instead of being destroyed, its inhabitants – Arabs, Asians, Chinese, Africans, in robes and veils, suits and ties, togas and saris, kimonos and djellabas – were about to fly out. Which helped him from dwelling on his lover's imminent departure.

'Your eyes will be worn out from staring,' Laura told him.

'Hey, come here, woman,' James urged her. 'I'm sorry. Listen, I hope you have a brilliant time out there. Make sure you have some time for being a tourist.'

Laura telephoned after a couple of days. The flight had been easy, although she'd kicked off her shoes early on and when they landed her feet had swollen up so much she had to walk off the plane barefoot; she didn't seem to have suffered jet lag, she said; she was discovering where to buy ingredients; and New York was a buzz.

'It's just like the movies,' she told him. She was in the penthouse apartment of a block on the Upper East Side. 'I look out across Central Park on one side,' she said, 'and the city on the other. Helicopters circle around the lit-up antennae of the skyscrapers, they're like lazy, luminous bees, James. Down on the streets whooping sirens of police cars swoop after their prey. And there's steam rising from the streets, there really is.'

James tried to welcome her enthusiasm. The line across the Atlantic was so clear it sounded like she was calling from around the corner, except that there were gaps, time lapses, between each side of the conversation.

'I miss you, Laura,' James said. There was a long pause, that made James' mouth go dry.

'I miss you, too,' she finally replied, as if forcing herself to. 'I'm looking forward to seeing you,' she said. This time there was a long pause at *Laura's* end. It was scary; it made her breath catch.

'So am I,' came James' reply eventually. 'Laura,' he said, his pulse racing, 'I love you.' He'd never said that in his life, to anyone: the words spilled out. A long, heart-stopping silence followed, like she was trying hard to make up her mind what *she* felt. Did she love him, did she not? A difficult question. What could she say? How could she put it? James nearly slammed the phone down in panic. Eventually he heard her voice.

'I love you too,' she said. And then they ended the conversation three thousand miles apart, both trembling from the strain.

While Laura was in America, James realized that he hadn't seen anyone else since Guy Fawkes night. For two months he'd had no need of the company of others, and hadn't missed them for a moment.

439

Not that anyone was queueing up to be with them: he and Laura radiated the exclusivity of new lovers that made a third person want to both pull them apart and run away.

Now that Laura wasn't there, James found he had to make up for her absence by telling Lewis all about her, so he cycled to the park that Sunday for Lewis's kick-around, and went back to his pad afterwards.

'I don't think a man should be alone, Lew, it's not really natural. A man needs a mate and I suppose I'm just lucky I've found her.'

Lewis groaned and escaped to the kitchen to make them a cup of tea, but James followed him to explain that Laura was one in a million in this town of two hundred thousand, so statistically he was even more fortunate than you might already think. He extolled the virtues of the woman who was Lewis's cousin – with whom Lewis and his sister had gone on annual holidays all through their childhood – and ended by admitting that as for sex, they'd been together two months and it wasn't getting boring, it was getting better, how about that?

'I mean I knew it could be fun, Lew, but I never knew making love was the best thing in the world.'

Lewis shook his head sadly. 'It's a temporary rearrangement of the chemistry of the brain,' he said as if to a third person.

'I don't need your diagnosis, you old cynic.'

'It's scientifically proven, mate, but the results have been suppressed. The trouble is people get hitched and the chemicals settle down and then they wake up married to strangers.'

'Married? Who said anything about married?'

'What's more,' Lewis continued, 'all the things they found most endearing and adorable in their lover are exactly what become most irritating and drive them bloody crazy. So to compensate they have kids, hoping that'll cement them back together. But it doesn't. It just creates new divisions.'

'Maybe you've got children,' James suggested. 'Do you know if you haven't?'

'I can't remember the last time I had sex without a condom,' Lewis told him. 'If you're not safe, you're stupid.'

'I can't remember the last time I used one,' James admitted.

'You are stupid.'

'And you're a misogynist, Lew, as well as a cynic.'

'That's crap, man. I just never fell for fairy tales. We're not meant to be monogamous animals. You know I love women. And you know they like me.'

440

Laura didn't phone again, except to confirm her flight home. Natalie drove Adamina and James to pick her up from the airport. They stood behind the Arrivals barrier and after an age and a multitude of strangers emerging as if from captivity with improbable sun-tans Laura came around the screen wheeling a trolley. Intimidated by the crowd of faces, she searched for the ones she knew, but they saw her first.

'Mummy!' Adamina yelled. She pulled her hand loose from Natalie's and slipped under the barrier, and ran over to Laura, who knelt and hugged her. James and Natalie waited till Laura had walked free of the partitioned area before embracing her.

Laura sat in the back with Adamina and did most of the talking on the way home. They dropped James off at his flat: Laura knew even now he wouldn't come into the grounds of the house in daylight.

'See you later?' she asked.

'Tonight,' he agreed.

'Oh, I wrote you a letter,' Laura said.

'I didn't get it yet,' James replied.

'I didn't send it,' she said. 'Here. Have it now.'

That afternoon James read and reread Laura's letter from America.

DECEMBER 27TH

Dear James

It's so cold here. New York is frozen. Derelicts are found dead in the mornings, on sidewalks, in Central Park. The maid (blue jeans and sneakers, mind) guides me by taxi to shops in the morning, and we return laden with extravagant food to this warm penthouse refuge. The top of this ivory tower.

Outside the city is numb; just concrete and tarmac on the frozen earth, as if the world's one big deep-freeze. There are no smells.

Then this kitchen becomes all the more lush and verdant for the contrast, a mini sensual world. The gas clicks aflame. Water, oil, butter heat up, and things are thrown into them, sizzle in the pan, and aromas are unlocked from inside the flesh of animals and plants, released into the air of this room.

In the kitchen I am absorbed, I lose myself. I chop onions running the cold tap close by, slice crisp ribbed stalks of celery, split open crackling peppers, crush cloves of garlic with the flat blade of a knife and already I am anywhere, nowhere.

441

Each vegetable has its own texture: take the skin of an onion off, it's followed by the outermost of those membranes between the layers like gold leaf, adding a viscous slipperiness to the crispness of onions.

They had turkey left over from their Christmas, so today I made one of my favourite soups, turkey and almond.

Simmered pink meat from the thigh in the stock for a few moments – just to reheat it. Then liquidized, and sieved it back into the rinsed pan.

Did you like those salted almonds in your stocking? Have you eaten them yet? Whenever I'm unsure about a meal I always salt almonds for an aperitif. We've been importing almonds for two thousand years, ever since the Romans introduced them; I guess we're hooked.

Almonds remind me of breast milk. Why? When I was suckling Mina I tasted my own, there was nothing almondy about it. It was pale and thin and sweet.

I remember being dragged up from sleep by her crying, hauled out of dreams, bemoaning my lot, yet my breasts already letting down milk in response to her cries: flowing down ducts into the aerola. Then her toothless mouth pressing, her tongue and throat sucking, and feeling milk pulsing out of my nipple. From torture to deep, tired contentment.

Now it is you at my breast; me sucking – my lips around you, my tongue – me a suckling child, bringing forth your milk, until it comes spurting albumen, tasteless, except for a faint aftertaste of blood, and of almonds . . .

I miss you already. Three thousand miles away. From across the sea, you tug at me; your absence pulls inside me.

DECEMBER 28TH

I made leg of lamb stuffed with crab yesterday. Yes, I assured them, it's an old English dish; although it fell out of fashion early in the nineteenth century, and was only revived by a French chef in London a few years ago.

(You know it's assumed that one of the earliest ways of cooking was to stew a slaughtered animal's stomach over an open fire: the stomach would contain semi-digested food, giving an unpredictable but rich, deep flavour to the meat. Whenever I make a gravy I always mean to try it myself; I still haven't.)

The crab gives not a fishy but a nutty-tasting piquancy to the meat. The guests didn't know what was in the stuffing; the hosts made them guess, and finally one of them did. Surreptitiously, I watched them.

Later I ate from what was left; when I tasted, I imagined your tongue not mine, your saliva not mine. I imagined you enjoying it, James.

DECEMBER 29TH

Every time I go out I apply lip-salve – and reapply it every ten minutes. I'm determined not to get cracked lips this winter, and I have to keep them safe till I get back, to you. Another person's saliva is the best way to keep lips in good condition through the winter. OK?

Hey, listing our favourite things, we never mentioned food, our favourite dishes. I assume it never occurred to you because – despite your vocal, demonstrative appreciation of what I give you – it means little to you. There's no use denying it, my love, I know you: the child is the man.

Or have I awoken your palate? I don't think so. It must be too late now, after all those cigarettes. Have you ever worked out how many you must have smoked? What chance do your tastebuds have?

Well, even your palate might have responded to the dessert I gave them tonight. I made a chocolate-cream pudding, from the seventeenth century, when chocolate was a rare luxury used mainly as a drink, in the chocolate houses of London and other cities.

The smell of melting chocolate is tantalizing. Have you ever been to Norwich? I bet you haven't, you who get the shakes if you pass beyond the ring road. I went there once, just a few hours: there must be a confectioner's factory near the centre, because the air smelled of chocolate that day. A whole tantalizing city.

Chocolate contains a chemical that's released in the brain when we fall in love. I didn't mean to fall in love. I never expected or even wanted it. I've seen friends reliant for their happiness upon men, and thought it strange. Not me.

I don't know yet whether I can afford that. I was impregnable; sufficient; safe. I was happy enough, too. Enough.

I shall phone you in the morning.

443

DECEMBER 30TH

I'm homesick.

Today they invited me, these Americans, to join them and their guests for dinner – as if I'd passed muster by now, had proved I could converse and so on. No, that's mean, it was nice of them. I made it clear I didn't want to, not even at the end of the meal; I hope they appreciated it was simply a question of etiquette. The fact is if I did the guests would be obliged to compliment me, and it's vulgar to pay too much attention to the food: to discuss nothing but the food one's ingesting is too much; gourmandizing. The point of a meal is conversation, communion.

Or maybe I just can't take a compliment. At least face to face. It's enough for me – it's the cook's prerogative – to listen from the kitchen door to guests' first responses. I need that, of course: a meal has little meaning if it's not tasted and enjoyed; otherwise we may as well be fruitarians, living in the woods on nuts and berries.

JANUARY 1ST

Sunday today: I went for a walk in Central Park this afternoon. Cold but sheer blue sky, and a stream of joggers, speed-walkers, cyclists and roller-bladers. Some looked like they were taking a painful cure, prescribed by a sadistic physician; others undergoing punishment for past misdeeds; or seeking redemption through pain, on a modern pilgrimage.

A very few looked beautiful, in their element, animals easy in their stride. All, though, somehow decadent, pursuing fitness as an end in itself – not walking a dog, digging a garden, bicycling to work, climbing a mountain, playing a sport. Not that I've done any of these things! I just cook food for the rich.

At least they kept themselves warm. I got back to the apartment with my toes dropping off, teeth chattering, fingers numb, ears aching, chilled through and shivering. I wished above all for you to be here and give me a massage. To knead warmth back into my body, revive the circulation of my blood, revitalize my skin from the outer stretches of my limbs all the way to the centre.

Have I told you how much I like it? The way you pull the curtains, turn on the heater, light a candle, put on music; choose a perfume to put in the oil; put your warm hands to my skin, and never take them off again. The way that sensation spreads out from where you're working the skin, until it's hard to tell where your hands actually are. Warm currents flowing out from your fingers, melting me.

I don't know if you're a great masseur. You're not trained, are you? You don't really know about anatomy. It's just instinct, feel. Well, it's good enough for me. I miss you in my body, James.

Sometimes I know what you've eaten the day before. We make love, you sweat, I smell cumin, coriander. Garlic in your armpits, ginger on your skin. I taste your sweat, it's not just salty but there's a flavour of rosemary, mint.

One's beloved – lover or child – becomes edible. Where love meets cannibalism!

You know there are cows reared for a particular sushi in Japan? They're fed beer, and given massages. Pampered flesh. Do you think cannibals fed their victims special food to make them tasty? I shall imprison you, feed you fantastic banquets full of spices for a week, and then eat you slowly!

Well, you weren't here, of course, No massage. Instead, a different kind of comfort, I made banana loaf. Mixed everything in a bowl with my hands: bananas are so mushy, they make for a great gloopy mess – which, of course, once the cake's baked keeps it moist. I love it when I have time to use my hands; feel like I'm getting my fingers inside the recipe, inside the process.

My mother used this recipe – you should remember it. It has to come out just right. Too dry and it crumbles in your mouth, the flavour's lost, it tastes old. Too gooey and it sticks to your teeth and each mouthful's a gummy ball you have to chew just to break up a bit. But get it right, and its texture's a sensual pleasure in itself, to bite into and feel on your tongue and play around the inside of your mouth, soggy and mulchy.

Then the flavour: bananas scented like a spice; walnuts, woody; tart lemon (why do citrus fruits make us salivate? Is it to protect the palate against the imminent arrival of sour juice?). Serve cooled, cut thinly, spread generously with butter. Winter food. Comfort food. The longer you keep it, the better it tastes. That's hard to do, though: you have to hide it away, or it disappears from any kitchen.

After supper was over and washed up and cleared away I wrapped up and went out on the balcony with a brandy. I remembered how I used to have nightmares, when I first took over the kitchen in the big house after I left school. I dreamed things like people finding shrimps or whitebait alive and jumping around their plates, or insects crawling out of vegetables. Or serving up and realizing I'd made enough for three people when there were twenty around the table.

I haven't had those anxiety dreams for years now. I have the confidence to know there's no disaster that can't be overcome. You know, I once made Jerusalem artichoke soup, before I'd found out you should boil artichokes for ten minutes before frying them. Your father had a number of guests for dinner. Afterwards everyone had to keep excusing themselves to rush to the loo, where they flushed the toilet immediately to cover the sound of breaking wind.

JANUARY 3RD

My last day today. The last meal has been cooked. You remember one of those Laurel and Hardy shorts you forced me to watch, when Ollie's wife gets a huge, heavy frying pan from the kitchen and comes storming through to the sitting-room?

'Are you going to cook something?' Stanley asks.

'Yes,' she says, 'I'm going to cook his goose.' And she's so short she has to pull up a chair and stand on it in order to bang the pan on Ollie's head. As he falls backwards unconscious – onto a conveniently situated settee – he flutters his hand waving goodbye, and there's the sound of birds twittering on the soundtrack.

Remember? I have to admit, that was funny.

This has been such a muted experience for me. I've enjoyed the work but seen so little of this city; partly because of lack of time if I was going to do a good job, but partly also because you are not here. It's so curious. I wanted to share it with you. Thoughts, feelings, sights, conversations, experiences of all kinds, good and bad, trivial or profound. I want to tell you about them; but more than that I want you to partake of them – just as I want to know what you think, feel, see.

Before, I had no need of this. I was content to live my life alone. Experiences were sufficient in themselves.

The thing is, now, because of you – and here, now, because of your absence – I notice more, feel more keenly, my own life, I suppose. At the same time, what I have seen, thought and felt is diminished without you here to share it.

446

Is this love? If so, how strange.

I fly home tomorrow. I will be with you soon.

Laura

That evening, after making love, they lay in each other's arms.

'Are you tired?' James asked.

'No, it's about seven o'clock in the evening in New York. The evening's just beginning,' she said, caressing him. 'The night is young,' she whispered in his ear.

They made love again. 'Are *you* tired?' Laura asked James.

'Yes,' he replied, 'but happy. I missed you so much, Laura. I'm glad you went, though. It made me realize how I feel. I said it on the telephone.'

'I know,' she murmured.

'I want to be with you. I want to share everything with you.'

Laura sat up beside him. 'You'd be prepared to move to New York?' she asked brightly.

A spasm of anxiety swam through James' guts. 'Are you serious?' he asked. 'You did get an offer.'

'No,' Laura admitted. 'I'm teasing. No one said a word.'

James breathed a sigh of relief. 'You're terrible,' he said, 'you're a horrible cow,' grabbing her and rolling her over. Laura fought back.

'You still antagonize me like a superior sister, you harridan,' James complained, as he pinned her down and tickled her.

Unfortunately for James, Laura wasn't ticklish. He was. After a prolonged struggle they'd both submitted once, only to attack again when the other's guard was lowered, and finally agreed a truce.

Laura made a pot of tea and brought it back to bed. They sipped in silence for a while, until James said suddenly: 'Laura, let's get married.'

Laura didn't react, for what was probably a few seconds but seemed like a lifetime; for a heart-stopping trans-Atlantic pause.

'Do people of our generation get married any more?' she asked.

'We're not people,' James said. 'We're you and me. We can do what we want. I've been alone for so long, and I've grown used to it; I'm aware of the freedom I have, Laura. But I'd like to share my life with you; I'd like to pledge myself to you. That's what I want, I don't care if it's old-fashioned.'

The words came out unrehearsed, following themselves like footsteps towards a precipice. James knew he was being both brave and foolish. Her letter had given him courage, but even so: he should

447

have inched forward, with Laura, negotiating every step; gauging the mutuality of their feelings. Instead he'd blundered on ahead, alone, until he ran out of words and firm ground and turned round to see if she was still in sight. James realized how little he knew Laura – *could* know her – because he had no idea how she would respond now. It was possible that she would come forward and join him; it was equally possible that she'd say, sorry, James, I have other plans, you're part of now, you're no part of later, I love you too but that doesn't mean for ever, James. There's no such thing as for ever.

James couldn't look at Laura; he looked down at his knees instead. *Speak!* his mind implored her. *Don't say anything!* his mind screamed. *Don't say anything!* He slurped some tea. And then he was aware, gradually, that beside him Laura was neither speaking nor silent: she was crying. James' first thought was that she was crying because she knew what she had to say would hurt him; she didn't *want* to hurt him. Or maybe because he had spoiled what existed between them. It was shocking, someone so strong crying beside you. He offered his arm and she leaned into his body and wept openly, profusely, with racking sobs and gulps that made James understand she was crying for much more than he'd feared, her tears falling on both their naked bodies.

James reached for tissues on the bedside table, and Laura blew her nose.

'I'm crying for my mother, I know it's crazy,' she sniffed. 'And for my father. And myself. See what you've started, James.'

'It's OK, you go ahead,' he soothed her.

'You think I'm this big sister,' Laura snuffled, 'responsible, sure of myself, in control of things. Everyone does, I know. I know it's true too, but it's not. I'm an orphan inside. I've only ever cried once since Mum died; just before Mina was born.' She took a deep breath. 'I had to keep myself aside, growing up with you lot. I wasn't one of you, I knew I couldn't be. And I've kept myself apart ever since. Oh, James,' she said, 'do you know what you're offering? Do you know what you're taking on?'

'Probably not,' he agreed.

'I would like to marry you very much,' Laura told him.

Simon's health group, which met in the drawing-room of the big house once a week, continued through that winter. One of the regular attendants was a forty-year-old anthropologist called Topper. He had horn-rimmed glasses, long hair and a thick beard and wore sandals made from car tyres. Topper had spent recent years in South America on field trips conducting research into the use of natural hallucinogens by natives of the Amazon rain forest, and regaled the group with intoxicating stories of journeys through the spirit world with his own spirit animal, a black jaguar. Now he was staying with his parents back in the town he'd grown up in, in the Northtown suburb near Lewis's house.

As chairman of the group, Simon tried not to let Topper take over the floor. Simon himself was seeing Mr Nakamoto at the time, a short, aggressive Shiatsu master who threw Simon around his treatment table with exclamations and grunts that sounded a little too much like pleasure for Simon's comfort.

Then one week Topper turned up at the group wearing socks and shoes, with a short-back-and-sides haircut, having swapped his spectacles for contact lenses, shaved off his beard and found work as a computer programmer. He had also, he said, started learning transcendental meditation, and Simon was so impressed by his transformation that he told Topper he wanted to learn.

'Actually, Simon, my name's John,' Topper explained.

'Oh, is that like a spiritual acronym?' Simon asked.

'No, it's my Christian name,' he replied.

And so one evening the following week Simon took a flower and a white handkerchief to an introductory talk given by a man in a suit and a woman in a Laura Ashley dress, and he began to meditate for twenty minutes in the morning and twenty minutes in the evening, using a personal mantra given by his teacher. Simon was bursting to tell people what it was, and find out whether theirs was the same.

John stopped coming to Simon's weekly group, but at the beginning of March he made a reappearance there and announced that he was their local candidate in the forthcoming general election, and would they like to make contributions to party funds?

The Natural Law Party had been founded overnight and submitted candidates in every constituency in the country. The basis of their manifesto was that if the square root of the population engaged in an advanced technique of meditation known as yogic flying, then certain principles of the natural law of the universe would be invoked, resulting in a reduction of crime and unemployment and an increase in health and wealth. This simple promise was contained in a manifesto of mind-boggling complexity, using Vedic science, quantum field theories of modern physics and statistical diagrams conveying the results of over five hundred research studies in two hundred and ten universities and institutes in twenty-seven countries around the world.

In fact it was already happening, John explained, on a housing estate on the outskirts of Liverpool. It was an outrageous claim – that would be verified by a chief constable and health workers after the election – but Simon and his friends pledged their support.

The major parties ignored the new one (as would most of the electorate) and resumed their usual gladiatorial struggle, putting most of their efforts into deriding each other. Charles spent more time than ever at the newspaper, much of it writing editorials. In one he bemoaned the Government's lack of vision and proposed a series of measures for the future that included privatization of the police, the army and the DSS, or the Department of Social Insecurity, as he thought it should be renamed, in order to discourage loafers and scroungers. He also advocated tougher punishments for criminals, especially those guilty of car thefts: the town was suffering a plague of 'hotting', in which youths stole cars and drove them onto the estate by the factory in order to perform high-speed stunts for a paying audience – they made Robert wish he was younger. Charles wrote that the opposition's idea of punishment was to give them their own car, whereas most intelligent people would rather drive them off a cliff; and furthermore, decent people should be allowed to fit their cars with traps that administered electric shocks to car thieves. It was one of his most popular editorials.

Charles didn't really understand the notion of media impartiality. He put up the money, so his was the loudest voice. No one quite had the courage to tell him the truth: that the money was running out.

The Freeman Communications Corporation, instead of realizing profit at the speed necessary to pay back the cost of its expansion, was leaking money in different places. The cable TV company had proved a dead duck; the computer programmes Charles had invested in were incompatible with the systems that had come to prevail in the global market; the radio station wasn't listened to by anyone. A good share of its advertising revenue came from other FCC businesses, using Charles' old ploy of moving money around within his various companies to suggest that things were healthier than they really were, a ploy that had worked before since, as he often declared, 'Confidence is as precious a commodity as gold.'

The trouble was, confidence alone couldn't pay off the interest on the loans he'd taken out. He had to take out further loans just to pay his debt burden, and he did so by handing over FCC shares as collateral.

'In a crisis, you have to keep money fluid,' he told his accountant. 'It'll turn out all right, it always does,' he assured everyone, as he slid deeper into debt. The more he borrowed – and the greater his debt became – so the more vulnerable grew FCC shares; but then he had to release more of them as collateral for further credit in a tottering financial edifice whose foundation was nothing more than the hot air of the man at its centre.

When Zoe bought a copy of the newspaper her uncle's views in print enraged her as much as they had at Sunday lunches in the past. She hastily arranged a week of special late-night screenings, in the run-up to the election, of films like *Comrades* and *High Hopes* and *The Ploughman's Lunch*. Every one was an enthusiastic sell-out (a rare event in those days, since a new multiplex cinema with ten screens had opened on Harry's land outside the ring road), which news happened to reach Charles via Natalie and Simon, and he found time to telephone Zoe from his office.

'I'm glad to hear you haven't lost your financial touch,' he goaded her.

'You'll be laughing on the other side of your face after polling day,' Zoe told him.

'I very much doubt that,' he replied.

James came to see *Paris by Night*, because Laura was cooking for some clients outside town that evening, and after a quarter of an hour he walked out and went upstairs, where he found Zoe doing her accounts on the miniature coffee table in her tiny sitting-room.

Zoe took off her glasses, did a double-take, and said: 'No, no, don't say anything. Don't tell me. I know the face. It's familiar. I've seen you before somewhere, haven't I?'

James held his arms out and shrugged sheepishly.

'Zoe, I'm—'

'No, don't, let me guess. We've met before, a long time ago . . . Hang on, it's coming to me . . . It's on the tip of my tongue . . . Yes, of course, I know who you are. You're James Freeman, the noted photographer, loyal friend and conscientious answerer of telephone messages. See, I did recognize you. Of course, you've changed, a lot actually, you're certainly older, but I recognize you all the same. Do I get a prize?'

451

Having successfully reduced James to a state of abject apology and fawning pleas for forgiveness for not visiting her for months, Zoe got up and gave James a hug, and made him realize that his cousin's embrace, the smell of her hippy oils, and the jangle of her bracelets, had provided the one constant reassurance in his life.

She poured them both a brandy, and he tried to explain what he'd been doing that excused neglecting everybody else. But she interrupted him.

'For God's sake, James, what do you think the whole family's been talking about all winter? It's all right, you're allowed to fall in love. I knew you would eventually. I never thought of Laura.'

'I don't know if I did,' he admitted.

'Is it true you're getting married?'

'Yes, we are. What do you think?'

'What do I think?' Zoe bowed her head. 'Well, sweetheart, I think . . .' She raised her head, and looked him in the eye. 'I think she's a lucky woman. It's wonderful, James. I'm very happy for you both.'

The final screening of that election week took place after the polls closed, and was a double-bill of both parts of *1900* followed by *Duck Soup*, which didn't finish until dawn. The capacity audience was imbued with a tremendous optimism, and emerged into the bright, realistic glare of a new day, to be met by the mild smile of the Prime Minister – who still looked like someone who'd wandered from the suburbs into Westminster by mistake – returned to power.

During that time James and Laura spent many hours discussing – in her car, in James' flat, walking across the meadow on Sunday afternoons, and at night when he crept into the grounds to her cottage – their wedding and plans thereafter. It was like another game.

They promised to both speak openly and honestly, to say exactly what they wanted, and only then to make fixed arrangements. The one thing they found they agreed on was to marry soon, early that summer. Everything else, as they might have expected with their contrary tastes, was up for discussion: James wanted a register office ceremony with a minimum of fuss, Laura preferred a church service with a hundred guests; James suggested hiring the largest hall in town for a brief reception followed by one humdinger of a barn dance, while Laura prevaricated; he fancied a honeymoon in Italy, she wanted to follow the East Anglian coast, from Felixstowe to King's Lynn, sampling dishes in the best fish restaurants.

'Good grief, it's a honeymoon, not a research trip,' James pleaded.

Laura made a list of the various options before them and, although they had to make up their minds soon in order to book places and print invitations, James made ready for convoluted negotiation. In fact when it came to it there was little: once Laura formulated what sort of reception she wanted, she conceded everything else to James, on condition he went along with her on that one element of the venture.

'We come back here for the reception,' she explained carefully. 'Not to the cottage: to the house. We have a marquee on the lawn. Games outside, then dancing later. Have guests to stay the night. We won't rush away, we'll stay the night in the cottage.'

James listened in disbelief.

'Guests can stay in the house,' she continued, 'and in the marquee, and even in their own tents in the garden if they want. We'll get up and stroll around and have breakfast with them. And *then* we can go to the airport on Sunday afternoon. And fly to Italy.'

'Is that it?'

'That's it,' Laura confirmed.

'You've gone completely mad,' James told her. 'You must know there's no way we can do this. How can you possibly suggest it?'

'Because, my love,' she said slowly, 'I've had enough. Of living in a kind of shadow world, in the shadow of that house; and of your family; of seeing Robert surreptitiously, in the dark, and now you too, just the same when it's so different, when I want everyone to see us together in the sunlight; of your obstinacy, James, and the rift between you and your father; of Adamina being the offspring of this shadow world and knowing that very soon she's going to have to start groping forward.

'It's got to stop, my love. I want everything up and out in the open. You've got to face your father. And you can do it, James; because I'm here beside you.'

453

11

CHINESE WHISPERS ON THE WIND

CHARLES FREEMAN, THE MAN-IN-CHARGE, HAD AN AIR OF INVUL-
nerability about him. There'd never been doubt about whether he'd
succeed, in any of his ventures; only to what extent. He gave succour
and strength to those around him, however much he also terrorized
them. Even his opponents over the years thought less of weak spots
he might harbour than of their own he might attack.

Despite rumours, the sheer force of Charles' personality and his
confident, exaggerated forecasts of growth and profit in the Freeman
Communications Corporation's annual reports (their figures ratified
by City accountants of unimpeachable reputation) had kept Charles'
standing intact, share prices inflated and creditors at bay.

When it came, the collapse of Charles' small empire in a town in
the middle of England, built up over forty years, happened in a matter
of hours. What triggered that collapse was the result of Charles' having
made the mistake of borrowing one sum of money from a Swiss
bank, and another from an American broking firm to whom he gave
FCC shares as collateral. While British banks remained convinced by
Charles Freeman's confidence and promises, the foreign ones had a
more distant and a cooler perspective. It was they who moved first.

In April the Swiss bank issued its first threat for loan interest repayment that was six months overdue; in May the US brokers gave an ultimatum: repay now or we'll sell the collateral.

Charles was unable to respond. On Thursday, 21 May, the New York firm sold a huge tranche of their FCC shares. Able to delay formal notification of the sale for two business days, they officially informed FCC on Tuesday, 26 May – that Monday was a bank holiday. Twenty-four hours later Charles' company secretary notified the Stock Exchange of the sale. At one o'clock on Wednesday a short announcement streamed across brokers' monitors stating that the American firm's percentage holding of Freeman Communications Corporation had declined. Within an hour FCC's share price began to plummet.

Afterwards, countless people announced to the world that they'd known all along he was heading for a fall, they'd seen it coming, obvious and inevitable, and what's more he was a bullying cheat, a shyster and a fraud; they'd known it all along.

In reality only one man in the town, Harry Singh, had the foresight both to diagnose his father-in-law's imminent demise *and* to prepare for it. Everyone else in a position to know what was happening had happily thrown more money at Charles when he asked for it. Then came that Wednesday afternoon, and the world turned. The figures that flashed across computer screens were like the whimpers of an animal in distress, and the hunters picked it up and came running; they knew he was in trouble and came for him in a pack; they knew *they* were in trouble. Charles' shield – the illusion of power – fell away. They came, the financiers, bank managers and brokers, scared and ruthless. To find that Harry had only just got there before them.

It was Saturday, 23 May (two weeks before James and Laura's wedding), and Laura cooked an early supper, on the table at six o'clock, so that adults could eat at home and then go out if they had plans and the children would have time to digest food before going to bed. Alice helped their au pair, Poonam, take the children upstairs. Sam dragged on his mother's arm and said: 'Can Grandad play a game?'

'Can Uncle Simon tell a story?' Amy asked.

'I'm sure Simon's got better things to do,' said Harry.

'I'll be happy to,' Simon said, and he asked what book he should read from; while five different requests poured forth, Harry took advantage of the hubbub to lean across to Charles.

'I think it's time we had a talk, Charles,' he said. 'I have a proposition to put to you.'

The two men slipped away from the dining-room, through the hall to Charles' study. He poured himself a bourbon and a mineral water for his son-in-law and, uncharacteristically subdued, sat down and invited Harry to go ahead.

They stayed talking in Charles' study through the evening, during which time Harry explained his rescue package: he proposed a way of separating Charles' private Freeman Company from his public one, protecting the albeit nearly worthless factory, and the house, from creditors of FCC. He was calm, pedantic, and reiterated each detail; Harry was irritating and irrefutable, and enabled Charles to come to terms with the fact that he was in a predicament from which he could no longer extricate himself with either bluff or bluster.

Charles was unsure whether his phlegmatic son-in-law was demon or saviour, as he signed contracts Harry had brought with him and handed over the property deeds for the factory and the house.

'I'd just like to recap, Charles,' Harry said.

'Yes, yes,' Charles responded.

'That this is a formal procedure between us, a piece of paper, and nothing will change here: as far as the family are concerned, you are the head and this is your house as much now as it always has been. You are simply bequeathing it a little earlier than is customary.'

'As you say,' Charles agreed. He felt a deep weariness seep into his bones, and he couldn't work out why he had no other response. The engine inside him had run down; he was all out of gas. That was the thing, he thought: Harry was so reasoned and respectful even as he cut your balls off. Impossible to combat, he imagined; he wondered why *he* hadn't used such tactics in negotiations over the years. Then he noticed Harry looking away, smiling to himself.

'What do you think you're laughing at?' Charles asked.

'Oh, nothing,' Harry replied. 'I was just looking at the curtains.'

'What about them?' Charles demanded.

'I never liked the colour, that's all,' Harry explained.

Laura arranged everything: the service, reception, marquee hire, catering, music, bridesmaids' dresses, even a bona fide wedding photographer found in the *Yellow Pages*. She arranged, too, a reconciliation in advance of the wedding: a walk the week before; a meeting on neutral ground.

Laura drove James, Adamina, Zoe and herself to the moor to the west of town, where they met the others: Charles, Simon, Natalie and Lucy, Harry and Alice and their children, as well as Dick the dog.

They left the cars and walked down to the moor, a marshy area, chequered with ditches, of scrub, poor grazing and some arable fields around its edge; a place appreciated more by ornithologists than farmers.

The adults present all knew that the main purpose of the exercise was for Charles and James to talk to each other, and so *they* talked more loquaciously than normal, both to avoid the awkward silences of so contrived a gathering and in the hope that such breeziness might be infectious.

Simon led the way, clutching an Ordnance Survey map he had no idea how to read, following instead whatever looked most like paths ahead of him. Natalie and Adamina dogged his footsteps, both telling him he was going wrong. Charles came next, surrounded by his older grandchildren, playing a kind of blind man's bluff as they strolled. Alice, Laura and Lucy were discussing arrangements for the wedding. James walked beside Zoe and Harry, who was carrying his youngest, Mollie, on his shoulders.

Zoe, James realized, listening to her, was goading Harry: the M40 motorway from London had recently been extended northward to Birmingham, west of the town. Its original route had been earmarked as cutting straight through the moor, and Harry had led a consortium that tried to buy the land off farmers in advance of the Department of Transport. They were beaten to it — in what was a celebrated victory for the Green movement — by a local environmental group who bought one sympathetic farmer's fields and then subdivided them into countless minute plots, which they sold on to friends and supporters all over the world. The bureaucracy required to obtain each and every one of these plots by compulsory purchase order turned out to be unfeasible, and so the motorway was rerouted further to the west, through land of less significance to wildlife.

'I really don't mind where the road goes,' Harry was saying. 'Anyway, I'm glad I didn't get involved in the end: I don't think the countryside suits me. I'm restricting all my future dealings to land within the ring road.'

'You're just saying that 'cos you lost,' Zoe replied; ''cos we beat you.'

'That may well be true,' Harry conceded. 'Although I don't see the need for your use of the royal we.'

'What are you talking about? We might be walking over my property. I *own* one of those plots of land.'

'Are you serious?' Harry asked.

'Sure,' Zoe told him. 'I'm one of the Two Hundred.'

'I didn't know that,' Harry said quietly.

James' attention shifted. He looked up ahead, and watched his father playing with the children. Charles was strolling along looking at the view, apparently unaware that the children were creeping up on him. But then he suddenly turned growling like a furious bear, and lumbered after the now shrieking infants fleeing rapidly away.

James knew by now, as did everyone else in the family, of Charles' bankruptcy, as well as the general drift of Harry's salvage operation – buying the house (and factory) at a nominal price to save them from Charles' debtees, and keep them in the family. James watched the children, how they enjoyed Charles' extrovert antics; a generation removed from his smothering paternal embrace, they were unworried and enthralled. James sensed how needless this resentment was, this hatred he had felt all his childhood and then stored up for his adult life. There was something monstrous about his father, but it was grotesque rather than cruel. He was a windbag full of hot air – there was no need to be burned by it. Not any more.

'How stupid I've been,' a tranquil voice said inside James' head. 'They're just people,' the voice said, echoing Zoe. 'They're just people, James.' He saw, too, for the first time since his own infancy, the advantage of his father's extrovert heart: in the midst of personal ruin, here he was playing an infantile game with his grandchildren.

Simon, meanwhile, had led them into an empty field. Except that halfway across it they discovered it *wasn't* empty: from around a corner came a dozen bullocks loping towards them. Or, to be more precise, towards Dick the dog who, disconcerted by these unknown beasts approaching, sought refuge among his fellow human beings.

Simon strode forward. 'Follow me, everyone,' he declared, aiming for a gate some fifty yards away. The bullocks seemed barely aware of the humans: they were fascinated by Dick. They lowered their snorting nostrils to the ground, breathing with an excited nasal huffing, and stared at him with wide-open eyes. The children huddled around their elders, infused with the same mixture of delight and terror as when playing with Charles a moment before, as if this were an extension of the same game.

To James' amazement, one person really *was* scared, the one he'd have least expected to be: Natalie was literally clinging to Simon as he strode along, cowering around him – as the bullocks moved around the group – for whichever side afforded her the most protection.

'Hurry up!' she urged Simon through clenched teeth. 'Oh, shit!' she cried. 'They're coming closer! Lucy!'

'No need to panic, darling,' Simon proclaimed. 'Let's not run, now. They're just dumb animals, they're more scared of us than we are of them, they won't come near us.'

'They *are* near us, dummy,' she hissed.

The person they *were* near was Alice, because Dick had sought safety with his mistress, had insinuated himself between her feet, causing her to trip and kick him as she walked.

'It's all right,' she announced, stumbling, to a bullock that had come within a few feet of her. 'It's all right, we're vegetarians,' Alice said, a remark which made James burst into loud laughter.

'What the bloody hell are you laughing at?' Natalie yelled shrilly at him, before deciding to make a dash over the remaining ten yards for the gate, which she clambered over with clumsy but effective haste.

The others followed her. By this time each of the children had become chaperoned by an adult, Tom and Susan scooped up in Charles' and James' arms, who reached the padlocked gate together. Charles handed Tom to James, who held him as Charles managed to surmount the gate without destroying it. James passed Tom over to Charles, who set him down and then took Susan.

Once they were all safely over, recriminations swiftly issued: Natalie had unaccustomed tears in her warrior's eyes as she rebuked Simon, which triggered sobs from Amy too, and then Tom, at which point Harry accused his brother-in-law of gross irresponsibility considering the number of young children in their care. Not that all the young children looked suitably scared: the bullocks had now aligned themselves in a crescent around the gate, upon whose middle rung Adamina stood, leaning over with her bared arms stretched out towards them. Losing now their obsession with Dick (who had retreated to the rear of his family), the boldest among them stepped forward and licked one of Adamina's bare arms with a brief sweep of his rough wet tongue.

'Look, Mummy,' she cried, and Sam climbed up beside her.

'You *know* I'm scared of the bloody things, I *told* you,' Natalie was sobbing.

'My God!' Simon exclaimed. 'Someone *else* can map-read. It's not exactly my idea of fun, you know.'

'There's no need to get huffy,' said Laura, 'you can see she's upset.'

'He's licking the salt,' said Zoe.

'I want to go home,' Amy wailed.

'Trust a man to get us lost,' said Lucy.

'Careful, Sam,' Harry counselled.

With all the confusion of tears and reproaches, of children and animals, Charles and James found themselves off to one side. They looked at the scene and at each other.

'I guess some things never change,' James said.

'Well, let's hope not, eh? It'd get ruddy boring if they did.'

'You remember that time you went out of the kitchen to get champagne with Stanley?' James asked. 'And came back to mayhem? Which for once you hadn't caused.'

'I think I do,' Charles replied. 'We all make mistakes, that's for sure. Are you all set for next week?' he asked James. 'Is there anything you need?'

'No,' James replied. 'It's all sorted, I think. We have what we need.'

'That's good,' Charles said. 'We're all looking forward to it, James. Well, I'm looking forward to it more than anyone.'

James nodded. 'Good,' he said, and then he was interrupted by more raised voices. Simon, Lucy and Zoe were arguing over the map.

'We can't be on *this* path,' Simon maintained, 'it's not red.'

'It's red on the map, doesn't mean it's red in reality, you buffoon,' Zoe pointed out.

'Good God!' said Lucy.

Then Amy stepped forward. 'Can you carry me, Grandad?' she asked Charles, and he did. And they set off again back to the cars, with Harry leading the way because from years of studying architectural drawings he stood the best chance of reading an Ordnance Survey map – though he wasn't helped by the fact that a blustery wind had blown up in the warm afternoon and crumpled the map every time he tried to open it out.

They walked across flat fields, with the wind swirling through and around them.

'Let's hope it's not like this next Saturday,' said Simon.

'No, the long-range forecast's excellent,' Laura told him.

James was walking between Zoe and Natalie, and he realized he was straining to catch what they were saying: the wind was blowing their words away. He could hear more clearly snatches of a conversation in front, and then a phrase uttered by one of the children behind him.

'Some people just have a healing energy, darling, they can't help it,' he heard Simon tell Lucy.

'You've got big red ears, Grandad,' he heard Amy say.

'One has to choose one's direction and stick to it,' came Harry's voice.

'They turn the lights off in the daytime just like we do, Sam,' he heard Adamina's lisping voice. 'That's why we can't see stars now. Everybody knows that.'

James couldn't hear what Zoe said beside him but the wind made him an eavesdropper on other, disjointed conversations; words, phrases being blown around, Chinese whispers on the wind. Is this what families are like? he wondered. We don't really hear what we're being told; we pick up unintelligible messages. Our attention drifts and scurries around, walking back to the cars on a late spring afternoon.

Laura didn't push the reunion further: the group got into their own vehicles and drove separately back into town. She dropped James off with Zoe at the cinema because she had a dinner party to cater for that evening.

'Are you OK?' she asked him. 'It went all right, didn't it?'

'It went fine,' James told her. 'I trusted you, anyway; I knew it would.'

Laura laughed as she kissed him. 'See you tomorrow,' she said.

Zoe made tea in her flat.

'How's Dog?' James asked.

'Who? Dog, oh, he's all right I suppose. You shouldn't get the wrong idea you know, James.'

'How?'

'Just because you and Laura are starry-eyed lovers, don't imagine everyone else is. God,' she said, 'do I sound bitter? That's awful. I'm sorry.'

'No,' James said, 'you're right, there's nothing more sickening than self-obsessed, cooing turtle-doves. Let's make a deal: you try not to be bitter, I'll try not to be nauseating.'

'It's a deal,' Zoe agreed. She sipped her tea.

'You know, I've never really thanked you,' James said.

461

'What for?' Zoe asked.

'Well, for always being here. For being patient when I've been an idiot. For being such a friend. You're a great woman, Zoe.'

'I'm losing patience now.'

'And I know you deserve better than Dog. Have you been in love, Zoe?' he suddenly asked, with a gauche timing he hadn't entirely lost.

'James, what a question,' Zoe responded. 'Yes, of course I have,' she told him.

'Who with?' he persisted.

'Jesus, James, give it a rest. Forget it. Look, finish your tea, *Urga* starts in three minutes. Don't miss this one, James. It's so beautiful.'

Dusk had gathered by the time James emerged from the cinema. He decided to walk home by a roundabout route via the meadow. Cows and horses were visible in the combination of town- and moonlight; James stood for a while imagining himself on a vast Mongolian plain, sharing a boiled egg and an apple with his wife in the darkness, before walking home through the Saturday night, loud and busy streets of the town.

Considering that it was the last Saturday night of his bachelorhood, James wondered whether he should go straight home so early. He'd decided against a stag party: pub-crawling with boozy mates had never been a part of his life. I could go on a one-man stag night now, he thought, go to Lewis's night-club alone as I once used to, in search of a last one-night stand. But he didn't hesitate or change direction as he considered the possibility: he carried on homeward.

By the time he got back to the flat James was looking forward simply to a glass of wine with the book he was halfway through: it was a book about jazz, which he was reading so that he could share Laura's taste for jazz, as if literature could open his ears to music as the music itself couldn't. And it seemed to be working, he'd told her, it really did, it was beautiful, and she'd raised her eyes to heaven.

A drink and a book: it's either love or age, James conceded. Instead of going round the back and up the metal staircase, he let himself in through the door beside the shop: he had been able to take over the erstwhile students' flat on the first floor; Laura and Adamina were going to move in. James had knocked out the partitions at the top and bottom of the staircase between that and his own flat, and he and Laura had already decorated, though they weren't going to move her furniture in until after returning from their Italian honeymoon.

James climbed through the empty flat to his own on the top floor and went straight to the kitchen: there was an uncorked bottle of white wine in the fridge. At least he *thought* there was. He opened the door and light burst out. The wine wasn't there. How odd, he thought; but then our daily life consists of hundreds of trivial, shifting calculations of memory, adjustments about food to buy, clothes in the wash, phone calls to make, prints to dry and so on and so forth. The occasional aberration is inevitable, he accepted. Especially with age.

Deciding to go straight back down to the street and the nearest off-licence, James closed the fridge door, blanking off the light, and headed through the dark flat back to the stairs. Just as he reached them a gravelly voice said: 'Wait.'

James' heart thudded. There was someone in the sitting-room, sitting in the dark.

James turned on the light and Robert, on the sofa, slowly closed his eyes − as if the light were a signal for him to go to sleep. The wine bottle − of course − lay empty on the floor by his feet, though he'd clearly drunk a lot more than that. After a few moments Robert opened his drink-deadened eyes, blinked, and focused loosely on James.

'How did you get in?' James demanded. 'What do you want?'

Robert smiled in James' direction, with a grin sloppily askew. 'How's our prodigal son?' he slurred.

'What are you talking about?' James said. 'What do you think you're doing here?'

'Decided to come home now, have you?' Robert continued. 'Come home to get the girl? Well, you're too late for the money.' He laughed, and then coughed, spluttering, before collecting himself. 'In case you haven't heard, there's nothing left. The old man's blown it all. There's nothing left for us.'

'I heard,' James said flatly. 'If that's what you came to tell me, you can go. If there's nothing else.'

Robert's eyes clouded. 'Yeh, there's one other thing,' he said. 'One other thing, you self-righteous cunt. She's my daughter, and you're not having her. I know you and Laura, you're both the same, you think you can do what you like, but you can't.'

'Of course Adamina's your daughter. Nothing's ever going to change that. Don't be stupid.'

463

'I'm not fucking *stupid*,' Robert exclaimed. 'I'm just letting you know, that's all.' He pushed himself up unsteadily. 'I'm just telling you, so you know. You're not going to get rid of me.'

Robert staggered past James and out of the flat the way he'd broken in – down the metal staircase at the back. James stood still, listening to the sound of Robert's uncertain footsteps ringing down the iron stairs. Then he lay a while on the floor smoking, letting his pulse calm down, deciding that he wouldn't tell Laura about this visit, wishing he was somewhere dancing into a brainless oblivion.

James dreamed that he came up the metal staircase to his flat in the dark. He could hear someone climbing behind him but every time he turned round there was no one there. He knew it was just the metal steps springing back from his own weight upon them but he couldn't help stopping and turning round, and he entered the flat with his heart thumping.

He went straight to the darkroom, took a sheet of printing paper that had been exposed earlier and slid it into the developing tray. It remained white for a long time, and he was about to give up when he saw an image begin to appear. He relaxed, but then the image suddenly shot through all the way to black in an instant, so fast he couldn't get even a glimpse of it.

James took another sheet of paper and put it in the developing fluid. This time he knew he had to take it out before it blackened, but then he missed it, it happened so fast: again he was unable to see what the image contained.

He tried many times, and each time the same thing happened. He tried to dilute the chemicals, to take the sheet out before it even began to show development, to switch the light on, but always the photo took ages to appear and then when it did rushed through to sheer black in a moment.

In the morning James lay in bed, wondering whether the images had registered somewhere in his brain: he had a vague sense of them, the feeling that he had seen them subliminally, that they were now stored somewhere in his head. He grunted with frustration, and rolled out of bed.

The wedding service was held in the local church at the bottom of the hill, despite both James' and Laura's agnosticism. The vicar, once a giggling young neophyte (at the first wedding James had been to), had become at fifty-five a popular, respected parish priest with a shock of white in his curly hair. He was both a High Anglican and a Nonconformist: he regarded the Virgin birth as a fairy story and thought of bodily resurrection as a metaphor, but his adherence to the rituals of worship was unwavering.

'I'm convinced of the subjective nature of human experience,' he told Laura and James when they met with him. 'We each have unique perception: the idea of life after death, for example, has a different meaning for every one of us. Which is precisely why the more formal, even ornate, our ritual is, the better; the more accessible it becomes to our own interpretations. At the same time, one should add, as affording the possibility of transcendent experience.'

James wasn't altogether sure he followed the vicar's logic, but he did suspect it meant that tradition was sacrosanct and that the form of their wedding service was not negotiable and was about to be dictated by him. In fact, the opposite proved to be the case. The priest elicited their thoughts about God, worship, marriage and family, and James and Laura heard each other say things it hadn't occurred to them hitherto to share. And then the three of them discussed the service itself, adapting vows and prayers and adding music and readings. The meeting lasted almost three hours.

'It seems to me,' the priest said as he saw them out, 'that there is the surface of things – which in itself gives us beauty – and beneath it a profound mystery.'

'To be honest, I find the surface pretty mysterious as well,' James admitted.

'I envy you your work, you know,' the priest told him. 'Rendering the invisible visible: a great endeavour.'

'Well, I wouldn't presume such ambition,' James laughed.

'But surely that's the purpose of art, isn't it?' the priest asked.

'Maybe it is,' James conceded, 'even when it's unconscious.'

'On the other hand,' the priest continued, turning to Laura, 'I wouldn't want *your* job for all the tea in China. I find few things in life as nerve-racking as cooking.'

'It's just training,' Laura told him, 'like everything. And I had a good teacher. But you must come round for a meal once we're settled in the flat.'

'Yes,' James agreed, 'you must.'

'I look forward to it,' the priest said.

'What a nice guy,' Laura told James as they walked home.

'You're right. Hey, what did you mean,' he asked, remembering

465

things she'd said, 'about praying? You've never told me that. How can you pray to a God you don't believe in?'

'I don't know,' she admitted. 'I just do sometimes.'

On Saturday, 6 June 1992, the church was half as full as it had been for Harry and Alice's wedding eight years earlier: there were no business acquaintances or civic dignitaries. Instead a dozen pews on each side of the central aisle contained photographers, footballers, artists and musicians, single mothers and a few of Laura's favourite clients who'd become friends, all behind family at the front. Pauline and Gloria Roberts sat with two vacant spaces beside them.

Her Uncle Garfield accompanied Laura up the aisle, followed by Natalie, Amy and Adamina, three bridesmaids. Natalie *had* tried to persuade Laura to let *her* give her away.

'I'm your friend,' she maintained. 'I'm the one who's losing you. You hardly ever see your uncle; let *him* walk behind with a posy of flowers.'

Simon read prayers. Zoe read 'He wishes for the cloths of heaven' by Yeats. They sang Psalm 121, 'I will lift up mine eyes unto the hills'. Alice read a prayer taken from the Brothers Karamazov: 'Lord, may I love all thy creation, the whole and every grain of sand in it.'

Lewis was best man, and produced the rings for the vows, the only change to those in the Prayer Book being that Laura pledged the same as James, omitting to obey and serve him but promising comfort instead.

'Wilt thou have this woman to be thy wedded wife, to live together after God's ordinance in the holy estate of matrimony? Wilt thou love her, comfort her, honour, and keep her, in sickness and in health; and, forsaking all other, keep thee only unto her, so long as ye both shall live?'

'I will,' said James.

'Those whom God hath joined together let no man put asunder,' the priest declared.

After straightforward photographs in front of the porch James and Laura left in a car provided by Harry, showered with confetti. Laura threw her bouquet back over her shoulder: by a freak coincidence (or curse, she said) it went straight to Natalie who, just as eight years previously, batted it back over *her* shoulder like a volleyball – to Simon, who accepted it graciously.

'What are you going to be, a Bride of Christ?' Natalie whispered to him as the congregation strolled to their own cars to drive up the hill in James' and Laura's wake. 'Or one of the Sisters of Perpetual Indulgence? By the way,' she added, 'if any more of you lot *do* get married, remember not to invite me next time.'

'Don't be sulky,' Lucy chided her, taking her arm. 'I don't know why you're so anti-marriage.'

Adamina had elected to travel the short distance with Zoe. She loved Zoe's old Morris Minor, and she was amused by Dog's thick beard. He didn't mind her crimping it from behind as he sat placidly in the passenger seat.

'How many fathers have you got?' she asked him.

'One,' Dog replied.

'I've got two now,' Adamina told him. 'When I was little I didn't have any. What about you, Zoe?'

'I've got a father; he lives in Scotland. I haven't seen him for ages. But it's a mother I haven't got, Mina.'

Adamina sighed. 'Just be patient, Zoe,' she advised. 'One might turn up when you don't expect it.'

'Thanks, Mina, I'll remember that.'

Lewis drove up with his family. He was in the front beside his father; Garfield sat stiff-backed behind the wheel; his hair was salt-and-pepper grey.

'Is it not about time *you* got married?' he demanded of Lewis. 'Or are you planning to mess around for ever with this disco nonsense and your football foolery?'

'Leave him alone, Dad,' Gloria appealed from behind.

'I'm coming to you, young lady,' Garfield said over his shoulder.

Gloria turned to her mother and rolled her eyes. Garfield scowled in the rear-view mirror.

'Don't encourage her, woman,' he said, 'she's twenty-eight years old, she's no spring chicken.'

'She's got a lot of patients,' said Lewis. Gloria and Pauline groaned.

'That will always be a pathetic joke,' Garfield pronounced.

The weather forecasters had been right: it was a glorious day, hot without being humid. Guests divested themselves of jackets as they drank champagne on the lawn before sitting down in a white marquee to a buffet lunch of coronation chicken, rice salads and cold meats, stuffed eggs and nut cutlets, followed by pavlova and summer pudding.

Coffee was poured and empty glasses refilled for the speeches.

Lewis spoke of people's mingled admiration and pity for James, for his single-minded pursuit over so many years of a deranged endeavour. He said James had little idea how many people in the town knew of and recognized the Camera Man – he'd become a well-known public figure. Lewis made the customary coarse jokes. And he confessed that neither he nor anyone else who knew James had any idea what kind of husband so selfish a man would make, but that they could only hope that Laura knew what she was letting herself in for, having known him all her life.

Garfield spoke with authority and conviction derived from his years addressing his trade-union members, and after embarrassing Laura with anecdotes from shared family holidays, he went on to sing her praises with such persuasion that every man in the marquee felt a personal sense of loss.

Laura spoke briefly, giving thanks to the vicar and the bridesmaids and others due them, including Charles, who then proved unable to restrain himself (despite Simon's earlier strictures that his words were not needed). Charles rapped his knuckles on the table and got to his feet.

'Oh, my goodness,' Alice hissed to Harry, 'Dad just cannot resist the limelight.'

'No,' Harry whispered, 'it's not that.'

Ten days earlier Charles had agreed the sale of the newspaper, to a Birmingham tycoon who already owned five other papers; Charles had written his last editorial. Shares in FCC had reached an almost worthless level and were fluttering around the Stock Exchange like so much confetti. A few days later Charles' bankruptcy would be formally declared. Thanks to Harry's deal, a string of creditors would discover their investment and loans evaporated into thin air: vilification and ignominy awaited him (much of it broadcast in what had been his own newspaper). Charles Freeman was living his last days as the man-in-charge. He stood up and tapped a fork against his champagne glass.

'Friends,' he boomed, 'I, sad to say, am the last surviving parent of these two young people. And I simply wish to say that I feel like I'm losing a cook, but gaining a daughter. And *regaining* a son. And that the people they've become, and their union today, fills me with enough pride and happiness for four people.' He raised his glass. 'To the bride and groom.'

'To the bride and groom,' came the reply.

*

After cutting the cake, there were a couple of hours before dancing. Languid from the food and booze and heat, adults dozed, played croquet, renewed acquaintance with seldom seen friends or relatives, while children dashed about the house and grounds, hyped up on sugar and emotion.

Natalie collared Laura. 'My promise is no longer binding, now you've got a man beside you,' she announced.

'What promise?' Laura asked.

'The same one I made to Alice: to protect you.'

'But James has only promised to love and comfort, and to honour and keep me. We didn't say anything about protecting each other.'

'Oh,' said Natalie, confused. 'I'm not sure, then.'

'How about we keep the pledge, but on an informal basis?' Laura wondered.

Natalie thought about it, then shook her head. 'No, I don't think so. You don't need it, Laura. There are other women in greater need. You know what?'

'What?'

'James is all right. He's soft. I don't think he'll treat you badly.'

'Well, thanks, Nat,' Laura said. 'I'll tell him he's got your seal of approval. He'll be chuffed.'

Natalie scowled. 'Just because you're a married woman doesn't mean you're safe from being thrown in the pond.'

James conversed with Jack and Clare, Garfield and Pauline. He tried to mix up the cliques at separate tables, introducing Natalie and Lucy to some footballers; Harry to photographers (he might employ one of them, after all); and his neighbours, who'd taken time off from café and grocery store, to Alice, who took over their children and introduced them to her own. Adamina wasn't with them: James had had the idea of giving her a camera, as he'd once been given one on such a day, and she was going around taking photos of people.

'I need to pee,' James told Laura, and he walked across the lawn, and entered the house.

Is this the last threshold? he wondered. Will I be coming here for Sunday lunch – for Indian Sunday lunches? Or have we simply signed a mature truce, a tired accord, so we can live free of canker and resentment? That's probably it, although Robert could have come, if only a brief appearance, the graceless bastard. Maybe that's it, James wondered, maybe all these years I thought it was my father I hated and really it was my brother. I'm resolving an Oedipal complex at the age of thirty-five and now I have to sort out Esau. Or is it me who's Esau and Robert Jacob? Fuck, I've had too much champagne.

He relieved himself and then snooped around. He looked at Harry and Alice's quarters in the east wing, their rooms furnished with antique furniture, the children's bedrooms with telephones and personal computers. Nostalgia induced his footsteps towards his old room, and the nursery, on the third floor of the west wing, but he only reached the second: he stayed a moment on the edge of what was now Robert's territory – looking up the dusty, dirty stairs, wondering if maybe he was actually up there now. Back on the first floor he met a gaggle of children playing hide-and-seek; Adamina ran round a corner and bumped into him.

'Hide in here,' James said automatically, opening the door to his old darkroom. He reached for the light, found and pulled it, and the room turned infrared. He saw at a glance it was just as he'd left it, if cobwebbed and mildewy, and closed the door behind him.

Apart from the darkroom everything upstairs had changed, but on the ground floor almost nothing had. Even the upholstery of the armchairs in the drawing-room seemed familiar. He found the same books on the shelves of his father's study – still, presumably, unread – the same unplayed piano, and the same portraits on the walls.

Amid so much the same the new stood out: which was James' own photographs, beautifully framed, hung here and there. The early ones that Charles had claimed were his by rights, since he financially supported his son's hobby, were in the corridor through to the kitchen: a set of four similar photos of apparently empty school classrooms, which closer inspection revealed to contain the ghosts of teacher and children.

In the study, behind Charles' desk, was the photograph Simon had bought from James' exhibition: of Charles being driven into work with, framed through the car window, the Wire on the picket line, his face contorted with fury, heaping abuse on Charles, who wore a smile of sublime indifference.

In the hallway were two other photographs James had taken for the newspaper when he worked there: either Charles had ordered prints at the time, or else he'd had them printed from the photographic archives once he was at the paper. One was of a crowd dancing at a Fun Day concert in the park on the side of the hill, with the house visible up high in the background. James hadn't noticed at the time that he'd got the house in the shot; he must have blanked it out of his mind. Although that was precisely, one assumed, the reason why Charles had bought and framed it: a photo of both a party and his house.

The other was from one of the very few assignments James had been given at the town team's football matches: a player was horizontal some three feet off the ground; for the briefest moment you might think he was levitating before you realized he was frozen in the act of diving from right to left to head the ball. On the left of the frame the goalkeeper made to save. The ball itself, however, was absent, and it was impossible to tell whether it was about to enter, or had just left, the scene. Had a goal been scored or saved? What *was* clear was the word FREEMAN directly beneath the diving player, on one of the advertising hoardings on the far side of the pitch. That, James recalled, he *had* been aware of at the time: Keith the printer had brought it still dripping from the darkroom into the office.

'This bloke's a genius,' James remembered Keith telling the others. 'He manages to sign his photos as he takes them.'

There were even clip-frames of his postcards of the town in the lavatory, hanging where newspaper cartoons of his father had once.

James went back outside, feeling slightly dazed, and foolish. Natalie passed him on the steps. 'I think your wife's looking for you,' she grinned. 'In trouble already,' she tutted. James made a lunge for her but Natalie ducked to one side and trotted into the house, chuckling. She found herself standing at the lavatory door, listening to someone moaning inside.

'What's up in there?' Natalie enquired after a while. 'Are we out of loo paper?'

The weeping abated into snuffles. Natalie heard there *was* plenty of toilet paper as the roll was spun round like a wheel in a mouse cage, and what must have been a long strip was torn off, and used to blow someone's nose. The basin taps ran, then the lavatory was flushed, and the door unlocked and opened.

'Are you all right, Zoe?' Natalie asked.

'Fine now,' Zoe replied.

'What's the matter?' Natalie asked her.

'Nothing,' Zoe assured her. 'Hay fever,' she said. 'See you outside.'

They danced for three hours to a ceilidh band in the white marquee. When the music began there were many reluctant, sceptical spectators, but by the time it had finished everyone was dancing — apart from Harry, which was just as well because someone had to take exhausted children to bed.

Adamina outlasted both her contemporaries and the band: they made way for Lewis and a one-off disco in which he mixed up Chic, Sister Sledge and the Bee Gees with pop House, combining Laura's taste for the Seventies with James' for the exuberant new. Adamina danced with James to 'Rhythm is a Dancer' and when it finished she stopped and said something to him.

'What?' he yelled over the first beats of the next disc, and bent down.

'I'm going to bed now,' she called into his ear, and she kissed him goodnight, went over to Laura and did the same, and walked across the lawn on her own, towards the cottage, miniature camera still in her hand.

Alice was dancing with Simon but grooving away in a world of her own. Natalie and Lucy were bumping bums with a couple of Arab footballers, who, James trusted, weren't setting their hopes too high. Charles was flailing around with one of Laura's clients. Harry's brother Anil and his wife danced timidly behind a tent pole. Zoe was taking a break at one of the tables; the smell of cannabis drifted. Pauline sat at another table, while Garfield was dancing calypso-style with his daughter. Not that *she* was: Gloria was an even groovier disco dancer than Alice; she'd had more practice (though rarely with her own brother as DJ). She and her father made a fine if incongruous pair, as did Dog and the vicar, who were close to each other at one side of the dance-floor and appeared to be competing for a prize for the worst sense of rhythm in the marquee. It was all they had in common: Dog didn't so much dance as wobble, yet managed to do that out of time, while the priest resembled a policeman on traffic duty in a Keystone Cop rush-hour.

'Let's slip away,' Laura suggested to James. When they'd almost reached the cottage they turned round and looked back across the lawn to the marquee. With the disco lights flashing it looked like the shell of some fabulous sea creature; or rather a whole family of creatures that they could see through the mouth of the shell.

'I don't believe it,' Laura said. 'Harry's dancing.'

James peered. 'I can't see him.'

'There on the right.'

'Is that Harry? It can't be. He's a great mover. It can't be Harry.'

'It is, I assure you. You enjoy it?'

'Mm. We didn't miss it, did we?' He put his arm around her.

'What do you mean?'

'When the astronauts came back from the moon they watched the

TV recordings, with all the reactions of people, and Buzz Aldrin said to Neil Armstrong: "We missed it." '

'You're crazy, my love.'

'I've missed things I've recorded. Trying to capture in images the essence of an event, not experiencing it myself. But not this time.'

Later James whispered: 'This time tomorrow we'll be in Italy.'

'This time tomorrow we'll be asleep,' Laura murmured back, snuggling closer to him. 'Hey,' she said, prodding him in the side, 'did you see Simon and your father doing the Basket with Pauline and Clare? They must have thought they were going to *fly*.' James could feel the ribs of her laughing lungs vibrate against him.

'Sweet dreams, love,' she whispered. He could sense her already falling away from him into sleep – into a separate world. As was his own, awaiting him, and that was incontrovertible. Or perhaps tonight, he wondered, we shall meet in our dreams, and that was his last conscious thought.

James woke abruptly, though not from a dream. He remembered no dream, had no lingering sense of that world whatsoever, even slipping through his fingers; he was wide awake. He and Laura had separated during the night. He looked over her shoulder at the alarm clock: twenty to seven, absurdly early. James closed his eyes: he shifted position, curling up, hoping to wrap sleep around him again, but it was no use, his body was restless. Wedding or no wedding, it was another Sunday morning, and, as usual, the one morning he could sleep in guiltlessly his mind wouldn't let him.

James eased out of bed, gathered clothes, crept downstairs, peed, pulled on T-shirt, shorts and plimsolls, opened the fridge and drank a mouth and throatful of grapefruit juice straight from its carton.

He wrote a note: 'Woke wide awake and happy. Gone for a run,' just in case, returned upstairs and put it on the floor outside the bedroom door. He looked in on Adamina: she slept, her mouth slackly open.

'Sleep on,' he whispered, and went back downstairs and outside.

There was a tentative glow to the June morning, as if the full glare of the day was being withheld, had to be earned by some unknown supplication of the earth. The aftermath of a party lent an air of pleasant desolation to the garden: guests had been invited to stay, so as not to have to worry about transport home and also to enjoy a communal breakfast, as Laura had requested. Two or three had put up tents around the edges of the lawn and among the fruit trees, others had simply laid sleeping bags on the floor of the marquee and now slept like chrysalides in the white light. James could see Lewis's dreadlocked hair sticking out of a red sleeping bag.

James jogged along the drive to the gates. He didn't particularly like running, because he felt the limitations imposed by his wonky hips: he felt slow and ungainly. Sometimes, though, he desired air in his lungs, sweat, pain and pain transcended, motion; either when the loneliness in his hollow centre needed to be dispelled by force or else, as now, when it brimmed over with happiness and needed release. He jogged down the hill, across the road and into the park.

There were few cars on the roads; one or two dog-walkers out already; birds; a squirrel scampered chattering away from him. Church bells began to ring, calling the faithful to early communion. Simon had told him that at the local church new bellringers couldn't be recruited to replace the old, and so tapes were broadcast. James now realized that was one of Simon's jokes, because the chimes pealing out were so haphazard: it sounded like inadequate apprentices. Or maybe this was a tape the priest used precisely for its awful authenticity. Thinking of the priest, he looked forward to seeing him again.

Two girls on horses clopped up the avenue by the side of the park, incongruous so near the middle of town, like lazy harbingers of a different – older – age approaching. A young red setter came bounding over, its owner wailing futilely, and James paused to stroke its eager, drooling face. He ran on, and a stitch seized him inside: determind to ignore it, he visualized footballers' celebrations (confusing the image of the players' bodies with his own): Hugo Sanchez's cartwheel, Ian Wright's robotic stance, Jairzinho's exultant falling to his knees, making the sign of the cross.

Natalie had woken early too, not long after James, over in the big house. She too had slipped away from her lover and gone downstairs. Unlike James she rarely had a problem sleeping in on Sunday mornings. She'd danced till Lewis stopped the music, some time between two and three; she had the stiff knees to prove it, as well as a thudding hangover.

James ran past the hideous college of further education, and a memory came to him of a childhood trip to Oxford – when he'd shrunk into

474

the middle of a punt, hiding from his father's bombast – and, walking past a castle-like college, his father had announced that this was where their great-uncle had been a brief scholar. 'Is there any chance one of you ruddy dunces will follow?' he'd asked plaintively.

Then his mother had told them that when the college was built a famous scholar considered it so ugly that he altered the course of his daily constitutional in order to avoid it. Yet time and weather had softened its vulgarity, healed its brashness. Would the passing of time do the same to this squat concrete brutality? Would it last long enough to be healed? Time, thought James – thinking rhythmically with his pounding footsteps – time wanders, time seals, time passes, time heals; until he lost himself once more running.

Natalie had offered overall responsibility for breakfast, and assumed that was what had compelled her from sleep so bloody early – hours before anyone would want to eat. She filled a big mug with mineral water and drank it in one long, gulping flow, then searched for Paracetamol.

James ran on the natural high his body produced, flew on a second wind, eating up the ground below him; not Hawkeye in the woods, no, I am James Freeman cutting a path through my town.

'You've been staring at the world so long,' Zoe had told him, 'maybe you've fallen in love with it.' He'd laughed at her. He thought of Laura still sleeping, her warm body, her smell, her flesh that he shared. 'Love isn't painless,' Zoe had said another time.

He heard a distant gunshot, and wondered if it had carried down from Shutterbuck Woods, full of rabbit warrens. He heard another one. Praying and hunting on a Sunday morning, James thought. And running. Sweat had greased his white body and beads of it flew off his hair; it stung his eyes and slid, salty, in his mouth. His stitch burned back. I'll run through it, he resolved, and began to try to lose himself in the rhythm of the morning.

Natalie prepared breakfast. Assuming people would want to eat outside, she stacked bowls, plates, knives, forks, spoons and mugs on the kitchen table, along with cereals and jams. Like a television chef demonstrating, she got everything ready within reach: bread by the toaster; croissants on a tray in the oven; coffee in a cafetière and teabags in a pot by the filled kettle; eggs and bacon, sausages, mushrooms and tomatoes, scrambled, separated and sliced, on the sideboard beside frying pans on the stove.

Such plenty, Natalie thought. What am I doing, living here? she wondered for the hundredth time, before acknowledging, again, that this wealthy family had given her a home with such ease, a refuge from which she had the strength to do the work she did.

Natalie looked at her watch: ten to eight. She laughed, for no one else would be up for at least another hour. The house was silent. Then she heard a sound. Only it wasn't occurring now: it was a memory of a sound; it was a *sound* that had woken her. Was it? She strolled into the back hallway. Dick, that neurotic little dog, was sitting staring up at the back door, his body tensed. Natalie opened the door, keeping Dick back with her foot, and stepped outside. It was just as quiet outside as inside the snoozing house. Something told her she hadn't been woken to make breakfast; she began running, towards Laura's cottage; and she heard the blast of a twelve-bore shotgun.

Natalie banged through Laura's front door and pumped up the stairs. She saw Robert emerge from Laura's bedroom. In a daze, he didn't hear her: he turned right, towards Adamina's room, and was almost there when Natalie reached the top of the stairs, and then he *did* hear her and turned round. They stood staring at each other. Robert held the gun loosely, with both hands, pointed at the ground. Natalie's mind raced: if Robert turned to go to Adamina's room, she might close the distance – ten to fifteen feet – between them and jump him. If she made for him now, he would kill her. He might decide to shoot her anyway, and if he made that decision she would have to rush him, no matter if it was suicidal. Her mind had no thought of Laura and James: whatever had happened to them was past.

They stared at each other for an age. Natalie felt like she was hovering. It occurred to her, fleetingly, that she might speak, rational, conciliatory, sympathetic, talk him down from his lonely psychosis; but that would be another person, not her. She couldn't do it. They stared at each other, unmoving. And then Robert's face began to change. Natalie's nerves shrieked on the verge of action. Then she realized that he was smiling. He raised the gun: Natalie made to throw herself forward, but he carried on lifting the barrel to below his own chin.

At that moment Adamina emerged sleepily down the hall beyond him, and gazed at the back of her father, standing rigid. Natalie felt

476

her eyeballs bulge with the effort not to look past him, at Adamina. Arms fully extended, Robert pulled the trigger, emptying the second barrel into his own head.

Natalie ignored the petrified child and the mess of Robert's body and ran into Laura's room. And then anyone in the big house who'd slept through the gun blasts was woken by a cry, a cross between a martial arts roar and the scream of an animal in agony.

James heard sirens wailing as he ran up the hill. His limbs were wearied and his lungs yearning; his T-shirt was soaked with sweat. He jogged through the gates. People were dotted around. Ambulances and police cars were by the cottage, and a knot of people. Startling blue lights were swirling: like a nightmarish vision of the party the night before, shifted from the marquee over to the cottage.

Lewis reached James first. James slowed, Lewis held him, began to urge him away from the cottage, towards the house. James was slippery with sweat: for the moment, though, he let himself be led, while gazing towards the commotion dumbly, waiting for clarification. Then Lewis sensed the first reluctance in James' body.

'Come on, Jay,' he said, 'come with me.'

'What's happening?' James asked.

'I'll tell you inside,' Lewis said. He exerted greater pull, one arm around James' shoulders, a hand on James' wrist. They were nearing the front door now: only twenty yards to go, Lewis judged. As long as James didn't bolt. Someone help me, he silently implored.

'What's happened?' James asked. 'Let me see.'

'You don't want to see,' Lewis said.

He felt James tense, but Zoe appeared. Thank God, thought Lewis. She distracted James enough, coming the other side of him from Lewis, to get him through the door and then into the drawing-room.

'Zoe, what's happened?' James asked, a bewildered boy sinking into a sofa. Someone brought mineral water: James had forgotten his thirst, he didn't feel it; he drank the water in one draught.

Suddenly James shouted: 'Fucking tell me!' He was trembling. Lewis, behind him, put a jacket round his shoulders.

'I'm going to tell you now,' Zoe said. 'I promise.'

A man entered the room, exchanged looks with Zoe, came to James.

'I'm going to tell you now what's happened,' Zoe repeated as James let himself be injected with what he knew to be a tranquillizer. He was burning, quaking, to know what had happened, and he wanted to put it off for ever, he wanted time to stop, to start rewinding, slowly, back into the precious past.

There was a bustle in the hall. Simon and Alice met from different directions, framed in the drawing-room doorway. The people in the room turned and watched.

'We can't find Mina,' said Alice.

'Has Nat said anything?' Simon asked.

'She's still in shock, they've taken her to hospital.'

'Damn it,' said Simon. 'Oh, damn it, Alice.' He looked like he might be about to collapse, but then took a deep breath and said: 'She *must* be in the grounds. Come on.' They vanished. This cameo had frozen the group on and by the sofa, which now came back to life.

'Let's help find her,' said James, getting up before anyone could stop him.

'No, sweetheart,' said Zoe, grasping his hand. 'Sit down. Let me tell you.'

'No,' he said, pulling loose. 'Give me details later.'

'You'll be asleep in a few moments,' said the doctor.

'Let's use them, then,' James replied. He marched out of the room, towards the kitchen, down a side corridor, and up the back stairs. No one followed: he'd lost them with the decisiveness of his actions. He reached his old darkroom and tried the door: it was locked, and he knew that could only be done from the inside. Without hesitation James put his shoulder to the door, which burst easily open, small screws of the catch splintering out of the door frame.

James closed the door behind him. The room was infrared. Adamina was sitting wedged in a corner under the bench, with her knees held up tight to her chest. She didn't seem to have heard or seen him. James sank to his knees; he had to anyway, he realized, he was so drowsy. He pulled himself over the floor. Adamina didn't look at him but squeezed herself tighter, shuttering herself more firmly in.

'I'm here now,' James slurred. 'Let's just stay here a while, shall we?' he managed, rolling on to his back a couple of feet from Adamina. His heavy eyelids closed themselves and he reached his hand towards her, letting his arm flop beside her leg before losing consciousness.

12

MAP OF THE HUMAN HEART

IT WAS MIDDAY WHEN ALICE OPENED THE DARKROOM DOOR AND found them: James laid out on his back and Adamina still crouched in the corner, holding his unconscious hand. She made no response until Alice tried to lift her up and then she clenched tight, like a limpet, to the wall and held fast to James' hand, although she made no sound. The doctor came and gave Adamina a tranquillizer, and when she too had lost consciousness they were separated and carried to adjoining bedrooms on the same floor.

Adamina had seen her father blow his brains out, and then she'd followed after Natalie into Laura's room and seen her mother's slaughtered body, beside which Natalie had broken down; and Adamina had turned and run without a sound.

Adamina would not speak, would refuse to say a word to anyone, through the weeks and months to come. That first day she woke in the evening, looked around her, ignored Alice, speaking soothing words, and struggled out of bed. She walked out of the room, turned left, and tried the next room: it was empty. She tried the next — empty, too.

'What are you looking for, dear? This is your Aunt Alice, Adamina, I'm here.'

Adamina reached the end of the corridor and then returned past Alice as if she was invisible. When she reached the room on the other side of hers she heard the sound of a man groaning behind the closed door, and she let herself in. James sat on the side of a bed, breathless, being comforted by Zoe. Adamina walked over and climbed onto the bed behind James, where he had slept, and leaned against his heaving back.

James alternated between a zombie-like state, in which he sat inanimate, and a furious, guilt-ridden grief. Zoe stayed close to him and was there to listen to his raving monologues, as he grappled with the awful puzzle of Laura's death, an apocalyptic riddle he turned over and over. Why had Robert done it? Was he mad always? Why had I woken, and gone for a run? Was Robert watching, waiting for me to leave? Or had he intended to kill me? Or us both? I went for a run and I'm alive. If I'd been there, could I have saved her?

James tried to contain the rawest eruptions of his grief until Adamina was asleep or absent. He stayed in the same room all the time, with the curtains drawn; Adamina slipped out from time to time.

'Let her go,' James told Zoe. 'She'll come back.'

Adamina wandered like a sleepwalker in search of someone in her dreams. She wandered through the house, in the garden, to the cottage, oblivious to those who crossed her path. Sometimes she stopped and sat and waited, patiently, for her mother to be returned to her. Back in the room with James, she knelt between the drawn curtains and the window – just the back of her kneeling legs visible in the dim room – looking out for her.

At night they slept together. Adamina cried only in her sleep, waking James with the dampness of her tears.

The family cleaved tight to itself. Zoe stayed in the house. Harry hired men to keep at bay the press and television crews. Natalie came home; she stayed in her room with Lucy, mostly. She'd saved Adamina's life but wouldn't admit it: only that she'd failed Laura. Natalie had seen so many women battered, had protected one or two of them when drunken spouses found the refuge, but she'd been unable to protect her friend, and sank into a despair as much of guilt as of loss.

480

Charles was broken. As if in imitation of Adamina, the youngest, the old man seemed to lose all inclination to speak, and sat around in a stupor. Alice took care of her children with efficiency and vigour, doing things the au pair usually did, then crumpling into tears without warning.

Only Simon was capable of taking care of both practicalities and emotions. He liaised with police, priest and doctor, answered door and telephone, but also provided broad shoulders for others to lean on.

James stayed in the house until the funeral. There were two funerals, of course, but only Simon accompanied Charles to Robert's. How to grieve for a son, a brother, who'd wrought such carnage?

Laura's funeral was private, almost secretive. James had been persuaded not to look at Laura's body, her face blown half away, beyond the restorative powers of the undertakers. Her coffin was buried in the churchyard.

The priest, knowing of James' and Laura's agnosticism, tempered the Christian hope of the burial service. Of what was left James took in every word: they fumed in his head, neat as pure alcohol, alternately consoling and enraging.

'Man that is born of a woman hath but a short time to live, and is full of misery,' the priest read out at the graveside. 'He cometh up, and is cut down, like a flower; he fleeth as it were a shadow, and never continueth in one stay.'

Yes, a shadow, that's all we are, James thought. Adamina held his hand tight the whole time. A shadow, my love, and I will follow. I will flee after you.

'In the midst of life we are in death,' the priest read. 'Of whom may we seek for succour, but of thee, O Lord, who for our sins art justly displeased?'

Her sins, what fucking sins? James' brain boiled. O Lord, you gruesome bastard, displeased, are you, you cunt-fucker God? Are you happy now to have your sinner home?

'Yet, O Lord God most holy, O Lord most mighty, O holy and most merciful Saviour, deliver us not into the bitter pains of eternal death.'

Simon stood on James' other side. He held his arm, and held him up from falling when he felt James' knees giving way.

'Thou knowest, Lord, the secrets of our hearts; shut not thy

481

merciful ears to our prayer; but spare us, Lord most holy, O God most mighty, O holy and merciful Saviour, thou most worthy Judge eternal, suffer us not, at our last hour, for any pains of death, to fall from thee.'

As they threw handfuls of soil onto the lid of the coffin the priest continued: 'For as much as it hath pleased Almighty God of his great mercy to take unto himself the soul of our dear sister here departed: we therefore commit her body to the ground; earth to earth, ashes to ashes, dust to dust . . .'

Afterwards they returned to the house – just the family and Garfield and Pauline, Lewis, Gloria and the priest – for a solemn, awkward wake made bearable only by Harry and Alice letting loose their children. The three youngest, insensitive to the pain of death, demanded to be dealt with normally, and so lifted the clammy weight of the occasion. Adamina, though, stuck fast to James, utterly aloof from them, silent and self-enclosed; the six-year-old child seemed as if she'd aged a hundred years.

And then at a certain point James, coming back from the lavatory, overheard Alice and Zoe in the kitchen.

'We can look after her,' Alice was saying. 'What difference will one more make?'

'You're probably right,' Zoe said. 'If you're sure. Are you sure?'

'We've got a ready-made family for her, she knows us all. With a bit of luck she'll just mesh in.'

James stormed into the kitchen. 'What the fuck are you talking about?' he demanded. 'How *dare* you discuss Mina like this?'

Alice paled.

'Easy,' Zoe said, putting her hand on Alice's arm.

'I'm her stepfather,' James exclaimed. 'I'm her guardian, in case you hadn't worked it out. I'm going to look after her. We're going to look after each other.'

'We're thinking of her,' Alice said faintly. 'Of what we can offer her.'

'Fuck off, Alice,' James said. He was already on his way back to the drawing-room.

'Let's go,' he said to Adamina, and she followed him. They went over to the cottage, where James blundered like a wounded bear, filling suitcases with Adamina's clothes.

'We'll come back for things we've forgotten,' he told her. He telephoned for a taxi, and they went to meet it through the side gate in the wall.

Over at the house the others sat and stood around, limp and useless, like marionettes waiting for a puppet master to pull their strings.

'Let him rage,' said Zoe, finally. 'He needs to.'

'She needs help,' said Alice.

'She needs more than that,' said Natalie. Lucy stroked her back.

'Look, I'll go and visit,' said Zoe. 'I'll see how they are, and I'll keep you all posted, all right?'

'I'm here, if there's anything you need, you know that,' said the priest, his eyes addressing Simon. 'I'll call on James anyway, in a few days.'

'I can arrange a social worker,' said Gloria. 'And I know one of the child psychiatrists, who's really good. I mean unofficially. However. OK?' She gave Zoe her home and work numbers.

Lewis sipped lukewarm tea. Each time he returned cup to saucer they rattled. Garfield, standing by him, put an arm on his shoulder. Charles sat quietly in an armchair in the corner.

When Zoe left, Harry caught up with her by her car. 'Money is not a problem,' he confided, slipping a wad of notes into her hand. 'James should know that. I'll leave it to you.'

Back in his flat, James made up a bed for Adamina on the sofa in the sitting-room. She spent the evening at the window, looking down at the busy street. James sat beside her, his back against the wall, drinking from a bottle of whisky. When it was empty she was asleep on his lap. He carried her, staggering, over to the sofa, then stumbled through to his bed.

James was woken in the middle of the night by thuds and scrapes, and gasps of exertion. Adamina had pushed and heaved the sofa as far as the doorway. James smiled drunkenly: she looked like a removals man struggling with a giant's furniture.

'Life is not a fairy tale,' he slurred. He wanted to help her but was told by himself it was futile to try. He fell back on the pillow.

In the morning Adamina was asleep on the sofa wedged in the doorway. James climbed over it and went to the bathroom. The hangover squeezing his head felt like appropriate pain; he relished it, even as he drank copiously from the tap and splashed water against his benumbed face.

In the kitchen James threw out bread, milk, fruit that had gone

483

stale or mouldy over those previous days. He heated up baked beans for Adamina, had black coffee and apples himself.

After breakfast Adamina wrote a note: 'Will we look for her today?'

'Yes, we'll do that,' James agreed. 'We'll look for her.'

And so they set out, walking through the town, looking for Laura. James walked in front, Adamina a shadow tucked into his footsteps. Occasionally he felt her hand in his and they walked side by side, and when she grew tired, in the afternoon, she tugged his arm and he lifted her up and carried her, on his back or shoulders.

'You can see better up there,' James said. 'That's your look-out position.'

They walked the streets James had walked before, with his camera, carving rectangular images from all that passed before his eyes. This was very different: they were searching for someone. James knew they wouldn't find her. He wasn't sure whether Adamina knew that too, but it was her game and it was a serious one, and he would play it as well as he could.

They returned to the flat around six, tired and hungry, to find the fridge and cupboards full of food: Zoe had let herself in with the key James had given her. He gave momentary thanks, and then took for granted the fact that he wouldn't have to concern himself with obtaining food. Except, he realized, that Zoe maybe didn't know about Adamina's limited tastes. He was looking through the provisions for baked beans, Mars bars and Coca-Cola when Adamina opened the fridge and helped herself to milk and cheese, and then – while James observed, amazed – a tomato, banana and peach from the fruit-and-vegetable rack: from that moment on she relinquished her exclusive childhood diet and ate whatever she was given.

They wandered the town each day, wherever the whim of their footsteps led them. The weather remained warm during those first days, allowing them to ease themselves into their endeavour. James bought a street map and traced their movements: each evening upon their return Adamina laid the map out on the table in the sitting-room and filled in the roads and lanes and avenues they'd freshly trod, with a red felt-tip pen, the map like a maze in a children's puzzle book.

James moved the sofa into the bedroom, and after they'd bathed and eaten Adamina soon slept. James remained in the sitting-room, drinking, whisky both loosening and anaesthetizing his mind into a strange kind of mourning, pathetic and inconclusive. 'What am I going to do?' he murmured. 'Why did you leave me? What do you expect me to do? I'm cracking up but I can't. Damn it, you must have known this might happen. Why didn't you prepare me? What kind of a mother were you, what kind of a lover, to leave me like this? What am I doing?' He drank until he couldn't hear or understand his own monologue, the words scrambling in his head and mouth, but he kept drinking till the bottle was empty; then he crawled to bed and instant, dreamless sleep.

They found their pace soon. It took an hour or two to reach the furthest parts of the town and often that's what they did, and covered the streets in that area for the day. Occasionally Adamina would see a woman in the distance and, pulling James' hand, run towards her: he responded eagerly, feigning hope, never prefiguring their imminent disappointment. If on his shoulders, when she spotted someone, Adamina pointed him in her direction and urged him faster like a jockey, and he stumbled towards the stranger until the resemblance faded. It seemed to them as if all over town were scattered women in disguise, Laura's more or less authentic doubles, or reflections, planted in their path.

Weekends, James decided, would be less strenuous, and they spent them in the town centre, making a bench their base. Sometimes a wino shared it, sometimes an elderly shopper, resting limbs and carrier bags, waiting for a bus. Adamina wrote on a card: 'were looking for my mummy have you seen her' and showed it to them, until she sensed James' disapproval and stopped.
    'You know, I lost my voice too,' James told her. 'I was older than you. I didn't lose it completely; I whispered. It's fine, you don't have to say anything.'
    Sometimes Adamina darted off into the crowd after a passer-by alone, but she always returned to the bench, as James knew she would.

James decided not to acknowledge anyone he knew. There were many who did recognize him, the Camera Man, but, if so, then they also knew what had happened – it had been in the papers, on TV, a scandalous local tragedy – and so avoided his eyes as he did theirs. A few were braver, kinder, stronger and pushed through the barrier around the bereaved. James hated it when they did. His grocer neighbour, Mr Khan, who'd come to the wedding reception, stepped

485

outside with a tray of vegetables as James and Adamina returned one evening. He put the tray down.

'I'm so sorry, my friend,' he said, reaching out a hand to James' arm. James nodded. 'It's so awful a thing, my wife and me, my friend, if you want—'

But James pushed on, his throat filling with air, nodding vigorously, the merest sound – 'Yep, yep,' – escaping his lips, pushing past Mr Khan for the refuge of the flat, unable to cope with kindness.

As Adamina hardened to their outdoor days, so she was less tired at night. She disappeared after supper one evening, and an hour later James realized that she wasn't asleep on the sofa in his bedroom. He went downstairs for the first time, into the empty, white-walled rooms below: it was too much like descending into a recently prepared tomb. But he found Adamina there, drawing on one white wall with felt-tip pens; she was drawing a feast of food, on a table seen from above, a meal her mother might have made. Adamina was too young a draughtswoman for James to identify all the shapes before him: he scrutinized them before hazarding guesses, which she confirmed or rejected with a nod or shake of her head.

'You're very clever,' he said. 'You've given me an idea. You do this room and I'll take the next one, OK?'

They now had an indoor project, for evenings and the wet days that came occasionally, at the beginning of August. While Adamina made her murals James brought his enlarger down from the darkroom, put an infrared bulb in the light socket, and blacked out the next-door room. He bought printing paper in liquid form that he painted in rectangles on the walls, and he projected negatives onto them. Each one took a long time: test strips had to be painted on, developed, painted over again. The developer, stop, wash and fixer chemicals had to be sprayed on using a plant spray, and the liquids streamed down the walls to collect in old newspapers and towels.

James began, following Adamina's example, with one of the few black-and-whites he'd taken of Laura's food that first time in his flat. 'You never know when they might come in useful,' he'd told her.

He sifted through his negatives of Laura and Adamina, and times they'd spent together, and laboriously printed them around the room, photographic frescoes almost, the images seeming to sink into the texture of the walls. Adamina standing on a Dartmoor tor; Laura sleeping; Laura dancing with Alice at the ceilidh on her birthday;

James and Adamina running towards Laura — who took this slightly out-of-focus picture — in a Somerset field, between cheese-making farms; Laura smiling, two tiny dimples showing above her cheekbones.

James locked the front door, and they only entered his flat by the iron staircase; and he locked the door down into the empty flat from above, too, whenever they went out.

James never answered the telephone. He let the messages accumulate until there were twenty-seven and the tape was full, and then without listening to them he turned the cassette over and let more build up on the other side.

Zoe delivered food twice a week, and finally she called one wet morning while they were still inside the flat. James came up from the empty rooms below to meet her.

'How are you?' Zoe asked. 'Are you OK?'

'We're OK,' James assured her.

'What are you doing?' she asked him.

'We're looking for Laura, of course,' he told her, realizing as he said it that he'd come to believe it too, in some way. He saw Zoe's anxiety. 'She can't be gone for ever,' James explained. 'I don't think that's possible, do you?' he said calmly.

'James,' Zoe said, 'you look terrible. Are you sleeping?'

'Kind of,' he replied. 'I *am* eating, thanks to you.'

'People have told me they've seen you and Adamina walking through town, just walking all day long.'

James nodded, smiling, smug.

'She's six years old,' Zoe said.

'Don't give me shit,' James warned her.

'I just need to know she's all right,' Zoe told him.

'I've told you all, I'm her guardian.'

'Yes and I'm yours, you idiot,' Zoe said. 'Aren't we allowed to care for you? Do you have to go through this alone, you stubborn bastard?'

Adamina appeared at the top of the stairs and came into the sitting-room in paint-splattered clothes.

'Hello, sweetheart,' said Zoe. Adamina walked over to James and stood by his chair, and gazed blankly at Zoe.

'Look,' said Zoe, 'I don't know what you're up to, but you must know it can't go on for ever.'

'Trust me,' said James.

487

'I'm trying to,' she said. 'I'll keep people off your back for the moment, anyway. Do you need money?'

James didn't reply, but lowered his eyes. 'Here,' said Zoe, passing over some notes. 'Here, take it. It's a loan, OK? Pay us back later.'

Zoe went up to the house. She found Alice clearing out Robert's rooms and recounted her visit.

'James is fine,' she lied. 'They're both doing well.'

'School starts next week,' Alice pointed out. 'Mina should be there.'

'They both need time. She can catch up.'

'Did she say anything?' Alice asked. 'Is she speaking?'

'A few words,' Zoe lied again.

Driving home, Zoe begged James in her thoughts: Don't let me down. Is this too great a gamble? Do I have the right to let you take it? I don't have children, what do I know? Don't let me down, James.

Her attention was diverted by finding herself stuck in an unmoving queue of traffic approaching the bridge over the canal leading to the High Street. Someone was tapping on her window. Zoe wound it down. A large man with an orange beard addressed her: 'Sorry if this delay causes you inconvenience,' he said, 'but this leaflet explains the reason for the demo.'

'Demo? What demo?'

'We're cycling around the roundabout by the bridge. We're campaigning for more cycle lanes and less cars coming into town.'

'How much longer are you going to be?' Zoe asked him.

'Another ten minutes or so, unless the police shift us before then. You're the woman from the cinema, aren't you? Well, I better get on with these leaflets.'

Zoe pulled her Morris Minor over and walked down to the bridge. A hundred or more cyclists were wheeling around the roundabout, transforming it into a merry-go-round. They were all ages on all sorts of bicycles: racers, tourers, mountain bikes, Dutch-types, children on tricycles, a couple of tandems and plenty of sit-up-and-beg bikes with wicker baskets. They were ringing their bells and Harpo Marx hooters, and the sound of irate car horns only added an appropriate freneticism to the carnival atmosphere.

Zoe watched them circling the roundabout and then at some unseen signal take off in a rolling cavalcade across the bridge and away up the High Street.

That evening Zoe rang the telephone number at the bottom of the leaflet she'd been handed. She introduced herself and offered to hold an evening of films to raise funds for their campaign. The offer was gratefully accepted and one of the organizers came to confer with Zoe: he turned out to be the orange-bearded man who'd tapped on her car window. His name was Matt and he owned the bicycle shop further along Lambert Street (not having a bicycle herself, Zoe had never been in). They considered possible films and their availability, to be shown on the earliest free date in the cinema's schedule, a month hence.

Matt dropped by again a couple of days later with a rough layout for a leaflet to publicize the event.

SPECIAL SCREENING
in aid of
CLEAN AIR CAMPAIGN

BICYCLE THIEVES
BREAKING AWAY
A SUNDAY IN HELL

SUNDAY 4th OCTOBER 1992
ELECTRA CINEMA
tickets £10

CYCLISTS OF THE WORLD UNITE!
YOU HAVE NOTHING TO LOSE
BUT YOUR CHAINS!

Zoe found a still from *Bicycle Thieves* in her office.

'Do you own your own shop?' she asked Matt over a cup of tea.

'It's on a twenty-five-year lease,' he told her. 'It's owned by some company, Meredith Holdings, in London.'

'Me too,' she replied. 'Well, the building was on a ninty–nine-year lease originally, but it's up for renewal next year, I guess we'll move on to a new twenty-five-year one. Though that should be plenty long enough: I doubt if there'll still *be* cinemas in twenty-five years' time. People will watch through this virtual reality gear; they'll live inside the films of the future. They'll become participants, protagonists, in the stories.' Zoe laughed grimly. 'What bull. As if they don't already.'

The evening was a great success, raising more than £1,500 for the campaign, except that not all those active in it were overjoyed to turn up on the night and find the event sold out in advance: the tickets had been snapped up by cycling aficionados never seen on the demonstrations. They came from miles around, triple-locked their gleaming bikes outside, and rendered the cinema foyer shocking with bright Lycra: it was a relief to Zoe and her usherette when they'd filed into the auditorium and the lights had gone down. Zoe slipped in to watch the films herself; her audience sat glowing in the dark.

James and Adamina didn't simply pound the pavements, as if on some military exercise. Often Adamina would stop in some nondescript street and for a while watch people entering and leaving houses and blocks of flats. James feared that she might take it into her head to go further, knock on doors and peer through windows, but she seemed to accept a mature compromise: lingering in a particular road with an apparent insouciance, like an animal waiting for the scent of prey to carry on the wind to her; as if, were Laura there, Adamina would know soon enough. And then at some point, apparently satisfied with the absence of clues, she tugged James' arm and they proceeded with their search.

Sometimes, though, they stayed too long. Net curtains would be pulled aside, faces appeared at windows, eyes watching *them*, the searchers. James made sure he and Adamina bathed daily, he shaved, and they had clean clothes; but they weren't new clothes, and walking and weather aged them. Occasionally vigilant house-holders approached: if polite, they asked if they could help, are you lost, are you waiting for someone? If not, they demanded to know what do you want, there's a neighbourhood watch scheme around here, don't get any ideas coming into our road, we've heard about men with child accomplices and kids can't be prosecuted, so clear off or we're calling the police.

One cold Tuesday afternoon a police car *was* called: it cornered them in a trim, uncluttered close. The cul-de-sac appeared eerily uninhabited, not a single car parked in a driveway, and maybe for that reason Adamina had been reluctant to leave: as if the place were odd enough for the extraordinary to take place there.

They were sitting on someone's wall. The police car drew up alongside them; James felt no fear, only irritation at the interruption of Adamina's shivering vigil. A policewoman asked Adamina to sit in the warm car while James was invited to explain what they were doing there. He said it was none of their business and asked if there was a law against being in a public place. The policeman said it *was* his business and there were a variety of offences concerning loitering with intent, and that was what he wished to ascertain: James' intentions for being where he was. James said he had his own reasons which were personal and the policeman told him he wasn't helping, either the police or himself or that freezing child. James said that was a real shame, wasn't it, and the policeman explained that there was another offence, obstructing the police in their line of duty, and from that point on it wasn't long before James and Adamina were being driven to the police station at Westbridge.

As soon as they were separated there James came to his senses.

'Don't take her away,' he panicked, 'she'll want to be with me.'

'You might have thought of that before,' he was told brusquely. So then he did explain their story. He was glad they responded with more annoyance than sympathy, demanding to know the name of her school, and they let him and Adamina go with a warning not to waste their time again.

James took Adamina up to the cottage. In contrast to the haste with which they'd stuffed Adamina's clothes into cases they took their time now, collecting things of Laura's: the collection itself became a ritual, as one of them lifted an object – earring, lipstick, hairbrush, shoe, kitchen utensil – and the other indicated yes or no or not sure, James entering Adamina's mode of silent discourse.

Back in the flat they arranged the things they'd brought on the floors of the empty rooms, again silently, making a secret shrine of small possessions.

'Her things will be ready for her,' James said when they'd finished.

On fair days, meanwhile, the red felt-tip pen filled in the streets of the town map as they trod them down. James could see an agitation in Adamina's demeanour as the blank avenues diminished, as hope implacably contracted. She began to slow him down, feigning weariness, slumping on park benches, pointing to grey clouds and

491

pulling him homeward soon after they'd set out. She marked just one or two new roads they'd reached and, satisfied, returned to her murals in the flat below.

On the last Saturday in October, James and Adamina made their base the memorial at the end of Queen Street, for the occupation of whose steps there was an endless battle between youths and winos. In summer the young predominated but as the climate cooled so the wizened drunks reclaimed their territory, from which to beg and mock early Christmas shoppers. James could stomach their company; he could talk knowing there'd be no undermining understanding from them.

'I lost my legs,' a man in a wheelchair told him. 'They chopped them off. I can still feel them twitching.'

'People live in the memory of those what loved them,' said another. 'I remember my wife like it was yesterday. What was her name? I forget that. I forget details. Can't remember what she looked like.'

'You've never been married, you queer cunt,' the legless man told him.

'I can't forget,' the man said. 'They don't let me. They give me drugs to make me remember and I see her, her hair black like a raven, a crow, black as night, long, black, satin hair.'

With James distracted, slugging cider, Adamina rediscovered her card crumpled in her pocket – 'were looking for my mummy have you seen her' – and showed it to a morose lady on the other side of the memorial.

'*I'm* your mother,' she said.

Adamina shook her head.

'I'm her rain carnation,' the woman insisted. 'I've been looking for you too, my darling. Come here.'

Adamina stepped back, returned to James and pulled him away.

The next day, Sunday, they spent in the park north of the town centre. James no longer joined Adamina in scrutinizing passers-by, but her attention was almost as quick as on the first day.

'You'll wear your eyes out, little bird,' James told her.

They circled the park, rested on a bench, strolled around again, ate sandwiches, walked more. In the early afternoon, after their seventh or eighth lap of the park, they found their now customary bench occupied. They carried on past but a voice said, 'James.' He turned without pausing, on guard immediately.

492

'James Freeman.'

He recognized her too, and relaxed. Her name was Jos and she'd once sung in a band for whom he'd taken publicity photos. They never got anywhere and he heard from other people that she'd given up music, drunk, drifted, become a junkie.

'It's nice to see you,' she smiled.

'You too,' James said. 'How are you doing?'

'I had to get out in the open,' she told him. 'You know how it is. You got any gear? Look, I brought my novel with me. I can't leave it in the B and B.' She gestured to a carrier bag at her feet, stuffed with exercise books and loose sheaves of paper.

James took hold of her hand, blue with cold. 'How long have you been outside?' he asked.

'Half an hour,' she replied. 'Sure you haven't got any gear?' Her pupils were like stars, like black snowflakes dissolving. 'I've got some acid, I don't want it. I'll sell it to you.'

James hesitated. 'I don't think so, thanks, but—'

'I need the fucking money!' Jos yelled at him.

He bought the four blotters she had and he and Adamina left the park.

After Adamina had gone to sleep that evening James let the blotters dissolve on his tongue one after the other, and he washed them down with whisky. After half an hour the patterns in the carpet began to dissolve and melt and flow. Particles of dust danced vividly around him. The windows changed shape, becoming holes that sucked and pushed and threatened him. The colour of objects in the room poured out of them, making him giddy with crazy laughter. 'This is what I'm going to live for,' he said or thought he did, 'for film that can show colour as it really is.'

He was high above the building looking down on his rooms, then he was plunged into the furniture, lost in the atoms of inorganic objects.

At some point he realized he was moaning through gritted teeth and sweating like a pig while everything became fluid around him and flowed through him full of poison, and he knew later that Adamina had woken and spoken to him then, and held him.

The next day he was blank; they walked the streets, and that night he returned to alcohol alone.

James drank so as not to dream, and it worked, mostly. Every now and then an image of Laura appeared on the far side of his stupor,

493

effortless, an image mundane and heartbreaking, and he awoke with hope only to be gutted by reality.

He would have drunk more, to obliterate even those few fugitive glimpses, to drown her deep down, but he had also to function for Adamina, and so it was a kind of controlled alcoholism. He waited till she'd fallen asleep before he hit the bottle, and in the morning he hauled himself out of the aching sludge of drunken sleep to run her bath, wash, shave, make breakfast.

No more dreams; and no more photos. James would take no more, and neither, it seemed, would Adamina: she had abandoned her camera. But then one evening at the beginning of November she produced it from a drawer and brought it over to James and mimed rewinding the exposed film inside, which James duly did. He sprang the catch on the camera and removed the film. Adamina tugged him towards the darkroom.

'It's late,' he said. 'It's your bedtime.' But she persisted. 'Why the urgency now?' he asked. 'This film's been sitting inside your camera for months.'

She made no response to his question, only walked to the darkroom and stood in the doorway with her hands on her hips. James felt irritation rise fast inside him.

'We'll do it tomorrow,' he told her. 'Bedtime is bedtime.'

Adamina didn't move, just glared at him from the doorway in a familiar posture, showing a side of her character that had been buried these last months of mutual support. Disobedience, obstinacy; a step towards a normality they would have to reach. She was a seven-year-old child. Of course he'd have to be a parent, strict on occasions. But maybe not yet.

'OK,' James said. 'We'll compromise. We'll make a deal. You go to bed and I promise I'll develop the negative this evening, and then tomorrow we can make prints. How's that? All right?'

Adamina considered his offer, and nodded her head. It was a deal.

James put his hands through the elasticated arms into the black changing bag. Snapped off the metal rim of the tiny capsule using his fingernails, extracted the film, attached the end to the developing-canister spool and wound it on. Pulled the film free of its old spool and peeled off the minute strip of sticky tape. Put the spool inside the canister and twisted on its lid till it fastened tight. Double-checked that it hadn't wound on askew; and unzipped the bag.

Pour in developer, turn it upside down and back again, shake it around, keep the liquid swirling, across every surface of the coiled film inside. Wash the canister out with water, and repeat the action for fixer. Then unscrew the lid and place the canister in the sink under a flow of water from the cold tap, rinsing it through thoroughly. Familiar smells; tedious and soothing ritual.

When James freed the strip of wet, developed negative he held it up to the light and studied it, not its inverted compositions but rather to check both that no part of it was undeveloped and that it was sufficiently exposed in the first place to offer decent prints. Then he hung it up to dry, with a weight pinched on the end so that gravity might uncoil its wound-up energy. He was already trembling for a drink.

An hour later James was on the sofa, placid, a third of the way through the bottle, watching TV as he did every evening now: his attention drifted towards it and nothing came back. Whether he had dreams the memory of which whisky erased or whether booze flooded the intricate nervous connections of dreams, he wasn't sure. But the TV he watched and retained nothing, a perfect anaesthesia.

He didn't know what moved him: he was surprised to find himself walking to the darkroom, already planning to surprise Adamina in the morning.

The negative was dry. He cut it into strips of six frames each. He put chemicals in their trays and switched the light to infrared; laid the strips of negative on a sheet of photographic paper, with a pane of glass to flatten them, and exposed a contact strip. It came up fast in the developer and he washed it and put it in the fixer, and then left it in the tray while he slid the negatives into the sleeves of a plastic page. The first, though, he placed in the neg-holder of the enlarger ready to print, and cut up a sheet of photographic paper into test strips. He put them back in their black plastic packet and switched on the main light, ran the contact strip under water for a while, then held it up to the light to have a good look.

They were the pictures Adamina had taken at the wedding. They began outside the churchyard, with James grinning while shielding himself from a cascade of confetti but only Laura's back, because she'd turned to get into the car. The photos progressed through the reception in and around the white marquee on the lawn; and ended with images of increasing obscurity, taken outside as night fell, until the last ones were entirely black.

James made a print of each of them. They were taken at odd angles, with people's limbs cut off by Adamina's eccentric framing, and some were out of focus, though that was difficult to determine because James laboured through a screen of tears. He made 10" x 8" prints of Laura laughing at something Natalie was saying, of Simon fooling with Alice's children, Charles making his impromptu speech, Laura dancing with Garfield. The last photograph James printed had been taken at dusk, from the marquee towards the house: the empty lawn and there beyond, standing at the sunlit window on the landing directly above the front door, was Robert, watching. James hadn't seen the figure on the contact sheet. Now the image came up on the paper in the developing fluid and James grabbed it clear of the chemical and held it up and stared at it until, without water washing it, the developer carried on working and drew the image into black. And so James had to make another one, his fingers fumbling with hatred. He wished more than anything in his life that he'd succeeded in strangling his brother all those years ago, when he came home and found Laura beaten.

James printed all the photos; and he wondered whether over the years he'd been dreaming of this moment, of standing in this darkroom, printing these photographs of his wedding, taken by Adamina. At four o'clock he went to bed sober for the first time in months, and the alarm clock woke him from a dream of a football game, stunning in its banality.

Charles Freeman put a brave face on things. He'd always regarded introspection as a recipe for mental illness, and saw no sense in looking backwards: he lived in the present and looked to the future. Unpleasant things happened in life and one had to ignore them and move on. How could a man cope with what Robert had done if he dwelled on it? You had to press on, find hope and cause for gladness in other things, he told Alice; like her children who showed us all the way ahead, he said: they didn't mope around, they knew they had their lives to live and brooding on what couldn't be undone would only hinder them.

As far as work was concerned, Charles was seventy-four years old and had taken, he claimed, early retirement: bankruptcy had come just in time, he declared, otherwise he might have spent the rest of his life as an overstressed workaholic and had no time for his garden, for his grandchildren, for the yoga exercises that Simon had recommended. Hundreds of people who'd worked for him had been made redundant, and now hated the boss they'd once admired, but if he felt guilty Charles refused to show it, urging everyone else to treat changed circumstances as a new opportunity, as he was doing.

'Life is just beginning,' he told Alice in a voice without conviction.

The truth was that something was happening to Charles, but no one could quite tell what it was. There appeared an unaccustomed gauntness in his features and a certain sluggishness in his once abrupt manner.

'Is your digestion functioning normally, Father?' Simon asked him.

'I don't know,' Charles replied. No one had heard those three words pass his lips before.

Charles began to weigh himself regularly, and he confided in Simon one evening that he weighed less than last week, and last week less than the week before. Was it possible, he wondered, that he was losing weight from inside, and was it connected to the weariness in his bones? He was growing no smaller: his tailored clothes still fitted him with flattering grace; belts were tightened to the same notch. He wasn't contracting, shrinking; he was emptying; he was losing substance.

Simon advised his father to stick to a diet high in carbohydrate while taking plenty of exercise.

'In fact, I'll join you, Father,' he said, 'let's go for a walk. Don't worry about your weight, it's normal for the metabolism to change with a shift in lifestyle. It'll all iron itself out.'

They strolled out of the gate and along the road out of town, taking by force of habit the customary direction they'd driven in each morning, and found themselves heading for the factory, which they reached after half an hour. Except that it wasn't there. The entire site was shockingly denuded, flattened rudely as a skinned animal. It stretched before them, a vast plain of mud and sand. In one far corner was a pile of rubble, the last evidence of the demolished buildings, not yet carted away. In the opposite corner, along the road, rebuilding had already begun, and they walked towards it past large noticeboards proclaiming *East Side Scientific Park*, and offering *light industrial units* for sale. Underneath was emblazoned HARRY SINGH DEVELOPMENTS, and the names of architects and building contractors.

Already three warehouse-type buildings appeared to have been completed, if not yet occupied. They looked impossibly new, plastic, unblemished; Simon couldn't imagine them as functional workshops of industrial production. He and Charles walked slowly through the deserted building site to where others were under construction. Two gigantic cranes loomed over them; a long heavy chain swung slowly, clanking. The workmen had packed up and left the site an hour or two earlier but something of the energy of their activity lingered; the din of construction could be imagined, faintly. Simon empathized with what his father must feel: the business he had built up, until at its height five hundred men and women worked here, the largest private employer in the town, exporting parts all over the world, was really gone; the manufacturing base of Charles Freeman's empire had been erased from the surface of the earth.

'You know, Father,' said Simon, 'an ancient Persian surgeon, Rhazes, sited the first hospital in Bhagdad by hanging carcasses at various points around the city. Where the flesh took the longest to putrefy, that was where they built the hospital.'

'If there was a market for ruddy useless information,' Charles replied, 'you'd be a rich man, Simon.'

Simon stood behind his father, looking across the site. He realized he was some inches taller than Charles, something he'd barely noticed before. He reached a reassuring hand forward towards Charles' sloping shoulders, and squeezed them; his father smelled like wood.

After a few moments Charles turned around, with a wry grin on his face.

'Well, old son,' Charles said, 'we had a fair crack of the whip, didn't we? It was fun while it lasted. And now it's some other bugger's turn.'

Simon shook his head, turned away from his father, gazed across the wasteland. He'll never change, Simon thought; stubborn old sod. When he turned back, Charles had sat down on a stack of bricks.

'Just need a rest,' he murmured. 'I'll be fine in a minute.'

Charles wasn't the only one in the family made redundant by the closure of his factory, of course. Simon, too, had lost a job. But he took responsibility – at Harry's suggestion – for the sale of all the computers (whose installation had caused all that trouble years before). He sold most of them to a small company that dealt in the burgeoning market for hard- and software; they asked if he had any more where these came from and so he got hold of some, and before he knew it Simon was making a new living.

He'd also discovered he had another gift. His weekly evenings of alternative health discussion had grown into something between a surgery and a seminar. Experts came to address them, like the American doctor who explained that most serious illnesses are caused by chronic dehydration, and if people only drank ten glasses of tap water daily they could cure themselves of osteoporosis, rheumatoid arthritis, migraines, high blood pressure, asthma and peptic ulcers.

'People think thirst is signified by a dry mouth,' he explained; 'but a dry mouth is the last, not the first, signal of a profound, chronic thirst.'

The group took his advice and found that it worked, except that the busier ones had to curtail the practice because they couldn't afford to waste so much of the day peeing. Until, that is, another guest expert advocated amaroli, the drinking of one's own urine, because it contains both melatonin to cure eczema and psoriasis and a naturally diluted homoeopathic dose of the body's illnesses, so that a regular draught acts as an auto-nosode to boost the immune system.

At the same time, Simon observed it was taking ever longer to say goodbye at the end of each session: people shook his hand and seemed reluctant to let go, they embraced him, and the boldest asked him to put his hand on some ailing part of their bodies. The bald woman wouldn't leave until he'd laid hands on her smooth skull; Mr Smith had Simon touch his stomach.

They finished their sessions with a group massage, whereby they took it in turns to lie down on a mat and have everybody's hands knead a different part of them, swapping techniques and feedback. Increasingly it happened that the others would cease their own ministrations to watch what Simon was doing, and to listen to the recipient of his restorative touch, who without realizing it was purring like a blissful cat.

At the beginning of November a psychic healer came to give a talk: her demonstration wasn't very successful, and afterwards she confessed to Simon that she'd been distracted by his aura, because it was a mirror image of her own.

'You've got the healing power,' she told him. 'You should use it.'

During the second week of November James and Adamina were walking the last untrodden streets of the town – inaccessible avenues and odd cul-de-sacs that could only be reached, now, via streets they'd walked before, some many times. Adamina pored over the map in search of them.

I could become a taxi driver, James thought. He didn't say it out loud; it sounded too flippant, and he knew that Adamina's game was becoming more serious the nearer they came to its conclusion. The map told the story, though how Adamina perceived it James wasn't sure: either hope was being squeezed out by the inexorable strokes of the red pen; or else they were getting closer to the centre of the maze – even if it was, finally, right out on the far edge of town, in Wotton: a dead-end lane that had been cut off, stopped, by the ring road.

That morning, Thursday, 12 November, they looked at the map before setting out.

'This is where we're heading, then,' James showed Adamina. She studied the map for a moment, turned and ran downstairs.

She doesn't want to go, James thought. She's hiding down there. I'll just have a cigarette, then I'll go and get her. We have to do this today. He sat down. Or maybe we don't; maybe we should pin the map to the wall and leave it with this one last lane unvisited.

Adamina, however, re-emerged a few minutes later, with a handful of Laura's things: a bracelet, earrings, driver's licence, a wooden mixing spoon with a circular hole in it.

'What do you want to do with those?' James asked her.

She shrugged: she didn't know. She stuffed them in the pockets of her coat.

When they got outside Adamina looked up at the grey sky and frowned.

'I've brought the umbrella,' James said, taking her hand. 'Come on.'

During the course of their journey across town James sang three or four songs, which he often did as they walked, songs from his own childhood that he'd long forgotten and then rediscovered through a tape of Adamina's that they'd kept in Laura's car and played on long journeys.

> 'I buyed me a little hen
> all speckled, grey and fair,
> I sat her on an oyster shell
> she hatched me out a hare,
> the hare it sprang a handsome horse
> full fifteen handsful high . . .'

James hoped that music might be therapeutic; that Adamina might find it easier to begin to speak again in sung rather than spoken words. An accompanying tune might render words less daunting. He held no great store by these intentions – he didn't want to put any pressure on her – James just sang and hummed them as he walked. James was tone-deaf; he couldn't sing in tune. With Adamina as his captive audience, though, as they walked along wide, airy Wotton Road – past the church; the DSS, tax office and driving-test centre in old Nissen huts set back from the road – he felt no self-consciousness. She was even appreciative: when he hesitated before a line then came into it with a flourish, when he did a quick jig on the wide pavement in time with the rhyme, she grinned, and even clapped when he bowed once. But she didn't join in: Adamina remained a mute audience.

They walked on, into Wotton village, as it was still called, though the town had long since spread out and absorbed it, another suburb but of old houses and cottages. They passed its small store. A shopper had tied a dog up outside, a wiry mongrel, and Adamina stopped to stroke it. It struggled to enjoy her attention while keeping an anxious eye on the shop door, from which its master or mistress should emerge.

They carried on, past thatched and wisteria-covered cottages, and reached the lane they'd been heading for. It stretched before them for some eighty yards, then turned a corner and, James knew from the map, continued for roughly the same distance as far as the ring road, whose rumble they could hear clearly. One house stood on the corner, and there would be a small cluster near the end of the next stretch.

'Here we are, Mina,' said James. 'Let's check it out,' he declared light-heartedly, but then he felt a pull on his sleeve and heard the word:

'Wait.'

'You want to hang on a sec?' he asked. 'Fair enough,' he added, before registering the fact that Adamina had spoken.

'Hey,' he said, turning to her, but she interrupted him.

'Let's go to the grave to see Mummy,' Adamina suggested. She spoke in a hoarse, rusty voice, without a lisp. James nodded, and they turned around and retraced their steps, James floored with relief that she'd spoken. Her voice had changed. It was tentative – understandable for lack of practice – and so sounded more serious, older, an impression completed by the lack of a lisp. Yet her new voice was, somehow, though different, *more* rather than less familiar. He ached for her to say more, but he didn't want to scare her voice away. Maybe the words had slipped past her defences and she would retreat inside her shell of muteness once more.

They walked back through the village suburb and onto Wotton Road. Adamina hadn't spoken again, but her one sentence echoed in James' mind. How come it was familiar? He was distracted, though, by his own utterances; when they traversed the stretch of road where he'd sung on the outgoing journey, so the association triggered melody in his brain, song on his lips, without him even being aware of its doing so.

> 'Hark, hark,
> the dogs do bark,
> the beggars are coming to town,
> some in rags
> and some in jags
> and one in a velvet gown.'

As they passed the municipal Nissen huts Adamina suddenly exclaimed: 'It's raining.'

'Is it?' James asked, and held out his hands. 'You're right,' he agreed, feeling spots of rain so light and intermittent it was hard to identify the sensation as coming from the outside rather than the inside of his skin. Drops became visible on the tarmac.

'Look,' said James, 'you can't really tell whether they're landing from above or seeping up from below, can you?'

Adamina frowned at him. 'Don't be silly, Daddy,' she said. And James suddenly knew that her voice was familiar for the simple reason that it reminded him of Laura's: the child's voice had begun to acquire something of her mother's intonation.

They came to the churchyard, and made their way to Laura's grave. The rain was beginning to drizzle.

LAURA FREEMAN
1960–1992
REMEMBERED

There were flowers, two or three days old, in a jar. Who'd put them there? Alice? Natalie?

'*We* should have brought flowers,' James admitted. 'We could go and buy some and come back.'

'I've got these,' said Adamina, emptying her pockets and producing Laura's jewellery, driver's licence, and the wooden mixing spoon.

'Do you want to bury them?' James suggested, and Adamina considered the idea and nodded. James produced the Opinel penknife he always carried.

'This'll have to do for a trowel,' he said. 'Where shall we put them?'

Adamina marked three places, and James hacked at the earth with the knife and scrabbled away loose soil with his fingers. The rain was falling. Adamina watched him from beneath their umbrella.

Rain fell into the three small pits that James had gouged. Adamina put in Laura's possessions, and James filled the holes in, scooping clogged soil with his hands.

'Mummy will like these, won't she?' Adamina asked.

'Yes, she will,' James agreed. He hugged her tight, feeling her sparrow's body through sopping clothes. 'We better get you home,' he said, 'or we'll both catch cold. Do you want to take the lookout position?' he asked, and he hoisted her up onto his shoulders. The rain drummed on the umbrella above her head.

It was only early afternoon but the sky had darkened. The rainfall intensified, from splattering to drumming to an indivisible roar around them. The rain collected in puddles and gushed thirstily along the gutters. Car headlights were turned on, people ran splashing for shelter, raindrops bouncing and dancing around their footsteps.

A shock of lightning lit up the town and a few seconds later thunder rumbled. James strode as fast as he could manage with Adamina on his shoulders.

'Are you all right up there?' he yelled.

'It's a flood,' she yelled back.

He couldn't see her face but could tell from the tone of voice that she was grinning.

'My name is Noah,' James shouted. 'You're my monkey, and we've got to get back to the Ark.'

They reached Factory Road a few streets down from the flat. The rain was so heavy many car drivers had simply pulled over to the side of the road to sit out the cloudburst. When lightning spat, thunder cracked immediately afterward, in hot pursuit. People sheltered in shop doorways. James crossed the road: his shoes sloshed through the water, as if he were crossing a ford from pavement to pavement.

Shop lights, traffic lights, car head- and taillights, windows, neon signs were dazzling in the pouring rain. Fuck, it's beautiful, thought James of this sudden alchemy of man and nature.

'It's beautiful!' he yelled up.

They had fifty yards to go to the flat. Halfway towards it Mr Khan darted out of his shop, grabbed a box of vegetables from the rack

503

outside and rushed back in with it. James had hold of Adamina's calves. He couldn't hear anything any more, with the roar of the rain and the traffic drone. 'Orange is the colour of the human soul,' he quoted from somewhere in his head. And then a car went out of control.

It was a Vauxhall Viva driven by an eighteen-year-old youth, who had two friends with him. He was trying to impress them (they said later) and they egged him on (he claimed). The police estimated his speed at forty-five miles per hour. The windscreen wipers swished lazily to and fro: the rain rendered the glass a fabulous screen of splashes exploding against a sheeting cascade. It was hard enough to see through the windscreen; it was also so hypnotic in itself that you didn't want to (the driver confessed).

The car glanced a parked van forty yards up from James and Adamina, and veered across the road. The driver wrenched the steering wheel down to the left and brought it careering back on to his side of the road, avoiding an oncoming bus by inches. James' hands gripped Adamina's calves at his chest. Mr Khan came out of his shop: looking to his left, he saw the Camera Man and the little girl, drenched, approaching a few yards away. He didn't see – and couldn't hear – the car screeching, back over his right shoulder, approaching very much faster. At that moment he assumed, sadly, that James was staring so fiercely away from him in order to avoid eye contact.

James was staring at the car. Coming too fast back to his side of the road the driver had again thrust the wheel down, this time to the right, and then as soon as the car responded swung it back to the left, twenty yards away from James. It was happening so fast, yet it was happening in slow motion: the car couldn't take another swerve, and locked into a diagonal slide. It came at an angle towards James, the driver's-side front corner pointing directly at him.

James' fingers gripped Adamina's calves. He pushed up his hands, lifting her body up over his head, and felt her haunches settle on the back of his fists. The car was ten yards away. The driver's front wheel lifted on to the pavement without being deflected a degree from its trajectory towards them. James had no time to swing back for momentum: he threw forward, hurling Adamina clear of the on-coming car, towards Mr Khan, who as the car struck James caught the flying child and cushioned the impact for them both by falling backwards across what remained of his crates of rain-soaked fruit and vegetables.

PART FOUR

THE HOSPITAL (4)

JAMES' PRIMARY INJURY WAS A DIFFUSE WHITE MATTER INJURY; THE diffuse white matter is fluid cushioning the brain within the skull. It was sheared by the impact of the accident, resulting in a number of haemorrhages, and the loss of brain function.

Zoe sat beside James, holding his hand tight as she read to him a memory from her notebook. She put it down and took off her glasses.

'It's better to be wrong in our watching than not to watch at all,' she said. 'You had to watch; you had to assess how things were before you acted. That's something I've learned, slowly, that's what self-confidence, or security, means: the ability to act spontaneously.

'Some people are born with it, or gain it. Others never have it, they fail to gain it; they know the lack of it.

'I always had it, I think — which is why it took me a while to understand what it was. I think you used to have it, James, and then lost it.

'If you feel good about yourself you can act. If you don't, then you have to watch, to discern what the rules are. You're convinced there *are* rules that everyone else knows. You don't realize there aren't any. You think all those self-confident people out there know the rules when really they just know they don't need them, that there aren't any.'

Zoe held James' hand tight and looked around the quiet, half-empty ward: there were no other visitors there, only two or three patients; machines hummed; distant clattering echoes sounded from the labyrinthine depths of the hospital.

'Can you hear me, James?' she said. 'Oh, God, I'd give my life to see you rise.'

Deep down inside a silent world James dreamed. He came through the gates of the big house on the hill and walked along the drive. He saw himself walking: his sandy hair bleached blond, almost white, by the sun, his sticking-out ears, the anxious expression of a boy wondering why the world is empty. He started trotting towards the house; his school satchel bumped against his backside.

It must have been the hottest day of that or any other summer: the whole world was dazzling bright, almost white in the glare of a huge sun that seemed to be hanging in the sky a few yards above him.

He began running towards the house, and as he ran he grew older but it wasn't strange because it was a dream, and he felt his anxious heart careering; then he saw someone in the garden with her back to him. She had on a long mac and her hair fell around her shoulders, and she was cutting dead heads off flowers or something, he couldn't see. He ran towards her, his heart thumping, crying, 'Laura!' only the word wouldn't come out of his mouth as he ran towards her. And the sun hung low in the sky and it was sinking lower, the heat was liquid and the world was bleaching out.

She was bending over flowers and her hair fell around her shoulders. 'Laura!' he cried as he ran towards her, and she turned, slowly, she turned towards him. But it wasn't Laura, it was Mary, his mother, and then he saw himself again and he wasn't older after all, he was an eight-year-old child. And his mother smiled as he ran towards her. The sun hung huge and low and was sinking, the world was bleaching into white, and he ran into his mother's arms.

Zoe felt her hand being squeezed. She jumped up and stared at James' body. Then she turned and called for a nurse. Gloria came to James' bed. She took his pulse. It was still.

'It's over,' Zoe whispered.

*

After Zoe had gone and the doctor had come to make out a death certificate, Gloria proceeded to lay out James' body: stuffing and binding his orifices; washing him; tying his mouth and weighting his eyes closed, and setting his arms across his chest, before rigor mortis set in.

Not for the first time in her nursing life she had the odd feeling she was doing more for a patient now than she had done when they were alive, in this final ritual. The sun was setting outside, and spread around the dim ward, soft as candlelight.

Gloria finished laying out the body, and telephoned down to the mortuary.

13

THE TRAVELLERS

ZOE COLLECTED ADAMINA FROM THE BIG HOUSE ON SATURDAY mornings through that winter, into 1993. They bought flowers and took them to the grave where James had been buried, his name added to Laura's on the headstone.

Afterwards Zoe took Adamina back to the cinema, treated her to lunch in the café, and got her to help putting up posters, passing ice-creams out of the freezer and issuing tickets for the children's matinée. Sometimes Adamina slipped away to the projection booth. The projectionist was a shy young man with long, blond, bandannaed hair and patchwork clothes, and he left Adamina to herself. She could have gone into the auditorium but preferred to watch from up here, through a small window close to the beam of bright light, beside the machine that threw it across the dark; every now and then she'd turn and watch the film threading its steady circular way from reel to take-up spool, as if to convince herself that this mechanical device really was casting those shadows onto the screen down there.

Adamina also explored the flat above the cinema, as James had once done; being, unlike James, even smaller than Zoe's grandmother Agatha, she felt at ease in its dimensions.

When Zoe told Adamina it would be time to get back to the big house in five minutes she disappeared, and Zoe found her sulking in the loos or crouched behind the popcorn counter.

'Come on, sweetheart,' she coaxed, 'Alice'll be getting worried.'

Adamina handed her a note.

I want to stay here, it said.

'Oh, honey, you can't stay here,' Zoe told her. 'I mean, I'd love you to, but there's things you need that I can't give you. Look, come up here, sit down. See, I'm on my own, plus I'm very busy, sometimes I'm on the phone all day, some days I have to go to London to see people in meetings.'

Adamina found a pen and scrawled another message on the same piece of paper.

'Take me with you.'

'Sweetheart, I can't do that. You need to go to school, and to be with people your own age. You know kids only come here to the Saturday matinée.'

Adamina's muteness, Zoe discovered, made *her* loquacious. She was forty years old, and was developing the growl of a middle-aged smoker.

'I know their kids are a little inert, but they're not bad. They're all Taureans, of course, a *herd* of Taureans, you might say, hey? They may be plodders but they're honest and kind, aren't they? You can always come and visit. Not just on Saturdays, either. We'll teach you to operate the projector, how about that? You can be my apprentice projectionist. Come on, I have to get you home now.'

Zoe was in no mood for celebration, but that was exactly what she was now planning: a celebration of a hundred years of cinema. The precise date of such a centenary had been a matter of debate, since the birth of cinema was a long series of experiments rather than a one-off invention. Some identified 1891 as the crucial year, in which Thomas A. Edison filed a patent for his kinetoscope camera and viewing device. Others preferred 1893, when the first public demonstration of the perfected kinetoscope took place, in New York.

The British Film Institute had finally settled on 1995 as the year in which to stage its official events, publications and screenings: the centenary of the Lumière Brothers' first films. Perhaps for that very reason, in a spirit of contrariness, Zoe had opted for 1994, a hundred years after the first kinetoscope parlour had opened in London: it made her think of her grandmother Agatha as a child at a demonstration of the kinematograph in the town hall. Zoe planned to screen a hundred great films throughout the following year, she told Natalie in January, explaining that she wanted to choose them herself, not be on an itinerary of regional cinemas all showing the same films.

'Not all the ones I want are available, needless to say; or else they are but in torn and tattered prints,' Zoe explained. 'As you can see from the list here.'

Natalie looked at Zoe's selection of films, with many deletions and additions, and the names of distributors beside them. Natalie didn't admit how few of the films she'd ever even heard of.

'Which are the ones directed by women?' she asked.

Zoe blanched.

'Relax,' Natalie told her. 'I don't expect you to know all of them off the top of your head. Just tell me some.'

Zoe grabbed the list off Natalie and scanned it. 'Shit,' she said.

'What is it?' Natalie asked.

'There aren't any,' Zoe confessed. 'I forgot to think about that. I just chose my favourite films. A hundred isn't actually that many.'

Natalie regarded her with scorn. 'You could start thinking about it now, I'd say.'

So, thanks to Natalie – who knew nothing about them – films by Larissa Shepitko, Margarethe von Trotta and Leni Riefenstahl were added to the list. A list of a hundred classics for a hundred years of cinema that would never be shown.

Shortly after Natalie left, Zoe received a phone call from her solicitor.

'It's about the lease,' he said.

'I thought we'd sorted that out,' she replied. 'You said our option for renewal is assured.'

'It was,' he agreed. 'But there's a new complication.' He hesitated. She heard him cough. 'The thing is, the agents have just informed me that the owners have obtained a compulsory eviction order.'

'Can you explain that?' Zoe calmly requested.

'The cinema is on the site of a proposed new inner ring road. Being considered by the council and the Department of Transport as part of a scheme to keep traffic out of the town centre.'

'I've not heard of it,' Zoe exclaimed. 'Sounds like bullshit.'

'Quite possibly,' her solicitor agreed. 'It appears the new owners suggested this route, north-west of the centre. They'll get a price above market value for their property; apparently they own quite a bit more along this proposed strip.'

'Jesus, I told you we should have bypassed the agents when we had a first hitch, last year or whenever it was,' Zoe told him angrily.

'Well, as I say, there are *new* owners now,' he pointed out.

'And who might they be?' she demanded.

'They're called Harry Singh Developments,' he told her. 'I believe they're something of a one-man show.'

'I know who the hell they are,' Zoe exploded. 'Oh, *Jesus!*' she exclaimed.

The brass nameplate was so small Zoe had to go right up to it to confirm that these were the offices of HARRY SINGH DEVELOPMENTS. She entered the Georgian building. The door closed behind her and the noise of traffic was instantly sealed off.

'Can I help you?' the receptionist whispered.

'I'd like to see Mr Singh's secretary, please,' Zoe requested.

'Who should I say is here?'

Zoe gave her name and was directed up thick-carpeted stairs to the first floor; her footsteps were cushioned but her bracelets jangled loudly, her flowery dress felt like a splash against the beige walls, and her patchouli perfume spread through air scented by pot-pourri. She was greeted by an elegant woman with porcelain skin.

'I'd like to see Mr Singh, please,' Zoe requested.

'I don't believe you have an appointment,' the secretary said. 'Perhaps you'd like to make one. If you could leave your details with me, I'll tell Mr Singh the nature of your business and get back to you as soon as possible.'

'Just tell him I'm here,' Zoe said.

'I'm afraid Mr Singh's busy all day today,' the secretary smiled.

'OK,' Zoe said. 'Which is his office?' There were a number of doors off the landing.

'Would you like a seat?' said the secretary, flustered now.

'Not really,' Zoe told her, and she strode to a door and opened it: inside, a draughtsman bent over an architect's drawing-board.

'You can't possibly do that,' the secretary told Zoe. 'Please, either sit down or leave, or else I'll have to call our security.'

'Shove it,' Zoe told her nonchalantly. She tried another door: a small kitchen. The secretary had retreated. Or maybe she was still hovering behind Zoe, beseeching restraint, Zoe wasn't sure and she didn't care. She tried a third door. There was Harry on the far side of a large desk, gazing at a computer screen. It illuminated him in a sickly blue light.

Zoe banged the door shut behind her. Harry looked up. It took him a moment to emerge from his hypnotized state.

'Just explain, Harry Singh,' Zoe demanded before he even had a chance to greet her, 'how you could do this to me.'

Harry frowned. 'You mean selling the cinema, of course,' he surmised. He shrugged. 'It's just business. It's a good move.'

'What about my cinema?'

He frowned again. 'Build a new one,' he suggested. 'It's a good business, I know. I might consider investing myself if you need venture capital. Think of it: a new cinema, entirely modern facilities, to your own design.'

'I *live* there,' she exclaimed. 'It's my *home*.'

'Funny: I never imagined you considered that cramped flat anything other than temporary accommodation. You can buy your own place now.'

'Worst of all,' Zoe continued, 'you're helping to carve a new road through the middle of our town. Don't you give a shit? You've got *children* growing up here, for God's sake.'

The door behind her burst open, but Zoe didn't turn round; she saw Harry wave someone away and then lean back in his chair. His body stiffened and his eyes narrowed.

'I think you know, Zoe, that I'm an easy-going man, but one thing I can't abide is a holier-than-thou attitude. There is a demand for a new road; I shall play a part in supplying that demand.' He stood up. 'We're not children, Zoe. In fact, to be blunt, you're a middle-aged, successful businesswoman. And this is business.'

'It is, is it?' she laughed. 'I thought you were a believer in nepotism, Harry Singh.'

'I don't think it applies, precisely, to second cousins-in-law,' he said.

Zoe looked incredulous.

'That's a joke,' Harry explained. 'I admit I never have been noted for the quality of my humour.'

'So much for a hundred years of cinema,' Zoe said off the cuff.

'Your ninety-nine years are up,' Harry noted. 'I do see the irony.'

'I'm going to fight this,' Zoe told him.

'As you wish,' he accepted. 'You won't win. If I were you, I'd put my energies into a new cinema and a new home.'

'I don't *want* a new place,' she exclaimed.

'As you wish, Zoe.' Harry shrugged.

The children's au pair, Shobana, went to pick them up from school: first Mollie at kindergarten, then the boys, and finally the three girls, Amy and Susan, and Adamina, for whose private education Harry was paying.

One Tuesday Shobana rang Alice from a telephone in the headmistress's office. 'Adamina's disappeared,' she said.

'She's probably wandered off somewhere,' Alice replied. 'Look in the empty classrooms.'

'We've done that,' Shobana explained. 'We've looked everywhere.'

'You'd better bring the others home,' Alice told her, 'and we'll take it from there.'

Alice spoke to the headmistress; she rang Zoe, in case Adamina was at the cinema, but there was no sign of her there; then Harry. He went to meet a policeman at the school, where they established that Adamina had attended all her afternoon classes and then vanished before meeting Amy and Susan at the school gates.

Natalie came home from work. A policewoman was there, questioning the girls, obtaining a photograph of Adamina. Shobana was in tears, sure she'd done something wrong. Simon came through to find out what the fuss was about and found them all in the kitchen.

'Adamina's been abducted,' Natalie told him.

'We don't know that yet,' Alice rebuked her.

'When are you going to get a search party together?' Natalie demanded of the policewoman.

Harry came home. 'How about someone getting some of these children to bed?' he suggested, but they were too excited for that. Susan began to sob and Tom told her to stop showing off.

'I don't like standing here chewing my fingernails,' Natalie said to Simon. 'Let's drive around and look for her.'

'Where would we start?' he asked.

'It'd be better than stewing here,' she exclaimed.

'Can I go with them?' Sam asked.

'And me!' said Susan.

'Why don't you blow your nose and take the younger ones upstairs?' Alice asked Shobana.

'There's almost always a logical explanation for these things,' the policewoman tried to calm them.

'Yes, a pervert,' Natalie replied abruptly.

Just then they heard the back door open and close, and all froze.

A few moments later Adamina appeared in the kitchen doorway, carrying a stuffed-full carrier bag. She assessed the huddle of stalled faces, and turned on her heels.

'I'll go,' Alice said quickly, and she followed Adamina to her room. She found her there removing items – crayons, gloves – from the carrier bag.

'Where have you been, Mina?' Alice asked her firmly. 'The cinema?'

Adamina unpacked the rest of the contents of the plastic bag: a photograph album, her passport, a pullover.

'Did you go to the flat to collect these?' Alice asked.

Adamina nodded.

'You went on your own, and came back on your own?'

She nodded again. Alice sat on the bed beside her, sagging with relief.

'You must not do that again. Go off without telling anyone. Ever. Do you understand?'

Adamina shrugged, and got up and took the jumper over to her chest of drawers. Alice went over and took her hands in her own.

'Listen to me. You must promise me not to do that again,' she said.

Adamina nodded peremptorily, and pulled her hands free.

While James had been in hospital Harry had continued to pay the rent on his empty flat. He knew it was futile, but he also understood that Alice – and everyone else – needed such gestures of hope. It was Alice, though, who now told Harry she'd drive down with Sylvia, her cleaning lady, to clear the flat; the two of them had already cleaned out the cottage.

They climbed up the two flights of the metal staircase and let themselves in. The flat smelled surprisingly clean and fresh, as if its occupants had been away for the weekend rather than months.

'This should be easier than the cottage was,' Sylvia said, 'apart from those iron stairs. I don't want to be going up and down those too often with my knees.' She'd already begun unwrapping bin-bags from a tight roll, and entered the small kitchen, where straightaway she set to filling one with half-empty jam jars, cereal packets, and other boxes and cartons.

'Looks like a trip to the bottle bank later on,' she called out to Alice, having found a box of empty whisky bottles under the sink.

Sylvia plunged into her task, with no curiosity about the flat, or

516

indeed what it contained that required their efforts to remove or clean: that would have been a waste of time. The kitchen needed attention, and the rest would await her arrival, no doubt. Her daily repeated phrase, putting down a coffee cup, was: 'Well, Alice, it won't get done by itself.'

Alice was prompted by Sylvia to adopt a similar attitude. She scanned the flat as she opened the windows to let the spring air blow through; pulled an old street map of the town covered in red lines off the wall, and scrunched it up; and looked around the bedroom while she stuffed James' – and Adamina's – old clothes into bin-bags. On the bedside table under a pile of scuffed paperbacks she found a slim volume of poetry in which was inscribed in faded ink: *To my little man, who helped me speak out loud*. Alice put it in her pocket.

They cleared out the junk and stacked bags in a mound by the back door, and broke for a coffee and, in Sylvia's case, a cigarette: a smoke was her reward for hard work and she couldn't bear to be interrupted in the middle of one. She made delivery men at the big house wait until she'd stubbed it out before seeing to them.

'What next?' Alice asked when she'd drained her mug. 'Shall I fetch the Hoover up?'

'What's this door here?' Sylvia wondered, opening it. 'Look, there's stairs.'

'Of course,' Alice realized. 'The first-floor flat. Laura was going to move in. I don't know what's down there.'

'You have a look,' Sylvia suggested, 'I'll get some of those bags out. They won't shift by themselves.'

Alice ventured down the stairs. There were cobwebs here, dust on the skirting boards. At the bottom she crossed the small landing, passed a bare kitchen and bathroom; she wasn't surprised to find it empty. Then she entered the room where Adamina had scrawled and painted on the walls. Alice stared at the six-year-old's chaotic murals of unidentifiable figures and multi-coloured shapes, lines, swirls. They covered the walls, from floor to ceiling: James must have fixed up some kind of scaffolding for her.

Laid out on the floor were objects and clothes Alice identified as belonging to Laura. She picked her way through them for a closer look at the walls. There was no pattern that she could discern, only shapeless marks made over others. Did they hold any meaning for Adamina? she wondered. Surely not. But then there was one explicable figure, low down on one wall: a body lying with much red felt-tip on and around it, its head disfigured, though whether by

Adamina's lack of draughtsmanship or by injury only someone who knew the story would have been able to tell. Alice was someone who *did* know the story. And maybe the haywire mosaic around the rest of the walls told more, for one able to read it.

Alice stepped through to the other room, where all was uncluttered and perfectly clear. Looking at the photographs, she didn't feel sad, but was rather struck by the strange beauty of this room: neither gallery nor any longer domestic space, but twenty photographs on the walls – *in* the walls – of a rented flat above a busy road. She saw herself in one, standing behind Laura at the barn dance in the community hall on Laura's thirtieth birthday. She had no idea James had taken any that evening; but then he carried his camera everywhere, took pictures like blinking, and you didn't notice. It's true that black-and-white's more realistic than colour, she thought, except, look, it doesn't show what people remark on about me: my one blue and one green eye.

So what should we do, she wondered, with this private shrine of love and grief?

A memory came to her: she and Laura were being taken by her big brother James to their great-aunt's cinema. They were maybe seven, James eleven (she couldn't imagine letting *her* children do that now). They walked down the hill to a bus stop at the bottom. Perhaps it was their first such expedition, because Alice could recall – could *feel* now its memory – a knot of anxiety in her stomach; there were no boundaries, only brittle rules they might ignore or forget, and who knew what might happen? But then the bus arrived and they got on and James paid and they sat down, and that is how the memory burst forth – for that bus ride across town. The groaning rhythm of the bus; the smell of its upholstery and of other passengers; watching the town slide by through the window with Laura and James beside her and feeling both that she was on an adventure with them but also that she was protected by them – her virtual sister and her older brother.

Alice's reverie was interrupted by the sound of Sylvia's heavy footsteps on the metal stairs outside the window (and their echoes on the stairs behind) and her shadow passing across the opposite wall. Sylvia entered the flat above.

'All right down there?' she called down.

'Fine,' Alice responded. 'Only,' she added, 'we're going to need to buy plenty of white paint.'

As she climbed the stairs she thought: maybe one day some future tenants will begin to see those photographs, those faces will peer through fading paint; or they'll be found, like church frescoes from before the Reformation, by domestic archaeologists of the future.

'This tomb is empty. Seal the tomb,' Alice heard herself murmur, as she reached the top of the stairs.

Alice and Sylvia had cleared out the top flat, making two trips to the dump in Alice's Volvo, another to the animal-sanctuary shop, by the time Sylvia finished work; they'd paint downstairs tomorrow. Alice stayed on, and a couple of hours later Harry came by the flat on his way home from the office. He took off his jacket to help Alice finish cleaning the bathroom, and, watching him, she was surprised by her husband's energy: despite years as a desk-bound executive, he launched into physical labour with a bodily relish and the apparent efficiency of habit.

'Don't forget all the work I did, those houses I renovated,' he told her as he scoured the bath. 'It's like riding a bicycle, I suppose: once you've done it it stays with you.'

'You can't ride a bicycle,' Alice pointed out. 'Which reminds me of an old university joke: a woman without a man is like a fish without a bicycle.'

'I don't get it,' Harry responded. 'Sounds like one of Natalie's to me.'

They worked in silence for a while, and then Alice stopped. 'This makes me sad, Harry,' she said. 'Why am I putting myself through this?'

'Someone has to do it,' he replied.

'It's always us, though, isn't it?' she said. 'I mean, I volunteered. But we do the clearing up. Why should we have to do it, Harry? I'm just musing. And taking Adamina, too; I mean, I don't resent it, you know, I take it for granted. I just wonder why it's always us. Do you know what I'm saying?'

Harry didn't stop what he was doing – polishing the taps of the sink with scouring pad and cleaning cream. 'Because we, my love, are the strong ones,' he puffed. 'With our feet on the ground. We're normal and boring, but we're strong. We can carry other people. It's our duty, isn't it?'

He stood up. 'Well, I think that's just about finished in here. Spick and span. Is it just painting downstairs now? Why don't I get a decorator in to do that?'

'There's one other thing,' Alice told him. 'Come and look.'

She led him to James' darkroom, opened the door, and turned on the light: the walls of the small room were entirely covered with shelves crammed with boxes and folders.

'Negatives,' Alice explained. 'And contact sheets. In chronological order, each sheet marked with month and year, and nothing more. As if he'd remember everything that was in them. Thousands. What on earth should we do with them all?'

Harry pondered. 'I tell you what,' he suggested. 'Let's ask your father.'

The next morning Alice brought Charles down to the flat he'd never been invited to before. While she and Sylvia took paint and plastic sheets, brushes and rollers downstairs, Charles occupied the dark-room. With the aid of a magnifying glass that he found on the work-bench he studied contact sheets, replacing each one where he found it. He spent all day in there: by the end of it he had no more than a cursory idea of the full extent of James' labours, but was already amazed. While down below Alice and Sylvia covered the walls of James' and Adamina's mourning, Charles sifted through the work, and explored the life of the son he had never really known. These photographs of what James had seen, had witnessed, became in turn the evidence – each one in part a mirror – of his life.

It was Charles' idea to sort and classify the collection and to donate it, whole, to the Centre for Local Studies on the top floor of the public library in the middle of town. He was going to call it the Freeman Archive, but then just in time changed it to the James Freeman Photographic Archive.

The collection was deposited in the library early on and then most days of the week Charles went in and helped the categorization process. Sometimes James *had* scrawled information – people, places – on the back of contact sheets, but more often they were bare. Charles went through them slowly, with whatever local experts he could persuade to join him, identifying buildings, streets, shops and as many of the people as possible.

It was a painstaking process, but Charles became absorbed in it over those months: it became his project; it revived him. He became something of a local expert himself, inevitably, and friends with others. Friends with the humble men who frequented the library: bent over microfiche screens, lost in branches of their family trees;

checking facts against oral histories of their streets; or going through back copies of newspapers for news of people long departed.

Gradually it became clear to Charles that his son's name would outlive his, and he even came to savour the irony – considering the anonymity of James' life and the publicity of his own. In truth, though, most of the time he was actually unaware that the photographs were James's; these photographs of people and places in this town, his town, in their lifetime. And then occasionally he pulled one out and it would be of someone in the family, or its orbit, and Charles said to his companion: 'Ah, I recognize her, yes, don't worry. I know this one.'

'I'm going to get the old man an anorak for his birthday. He's becoming a train-spotter,' said Simon one evening.

'What have trains got to do with anything?' Harry demanded.

'You explain, Alice,' Simon gave up. 'He's your husband.'

Harry woke up the next morning first, as usual. He performed his ablutions in the en suite bathroom, poured tea from the Teasmade for Alice as he woke her, and set off to make some phone calls before breakfast. Alice stirred behind him.

'Don't let it get cold,' Harry advised as he opened their bedroom door, stepped forward, turning, towards the stairs, and found himself about to tread on a jumbled heap before him. He jerked his leg up again over the obstacle and kicked off with the other foot in order to clear it. His forward foot, though, also cleared the landing: Harry projected himself down the stairs, and such was the momentum created by his instinctive evasive action that there was nothing he could do about it. He tumbled head over heels down the eight steps to the next landing, where the stairs turned, and lay in a stunned pile-up of limbs, groaning.

Alice rushed to the bedroom doorway. Harry was untangling himself gingerly.

'I could have broken a bone,' he moaned, rubbing his elbow. As it became clear that he hadn't, Alice let go of the laughter she'd been suppressing.

'I saw you *leap* down the stairs, you dotty loon,' she said.

'Some bloody idiot left that duvet lying there,' Harry complained. 'I don't regard that as a joke.'

'Well, it was very considerate of you not to step on it,' Alice said. 'Come here, boo-boo, let me rub it better.'

Harry looked up, his wounded expression fading. 'There was no

521

direct hit, actually, but you could rub it better anyway,' he suggested, limping up the stairs.

'I wonder what to use,' Alice smirked. 'Vaseline? Or a ginger and turmeric compress?'

'Honey from the honey pot,' Harry growled, stepping onto the top stair but one. At that moment the duvet on the landing between them shifted and rustled. As if there were some nocturnal animal – a hedgehog, perhaps – hidden beneath it. Alice took a step back into the doorway, Harry took a step back into space: he clutched the banister rail and just saved himself from tumbling, backwards this time for variation, down the stairs again.

The duvet shuffled once more, and Adamina's sleepy head emerged. Before Harry could speak Alice said: 'Don't say anything, Harry,' and he frowned, shook his head, turned on his heel and clumped down the stairs. Alice knelt down. 'What's the matter, Mina, did you have a bad dream?'

Adamina looked confused. She shook her head.

'Do you not like your room?' Alice asked. 'Or the things I put in it?'

Adamina didn't respond, only looked around, unsure of herself.

'I remember your Mummy used to tell me you slept on the landing sometimes. Maybe that's it,' Alice concluded. She helped Adamina up. 'Time for breakfast in a minute. Let's get this bedding back to your room and get dressed, eh?'

For the next few mornings Harry opened the bedroom door cautiously checking that Adamina hadn't rolled herself into a land-mine to throw him up in the air and down the stairs again. But there was no sign of her, and he looked in her room and there she was still sleeping in bed. A few such reassuring mornings later Harry went straight downstairs. The others had joined him for breakfast and started without Adamina – Shobana had knocked on her door – when Simon walked into the kitchen from his part of the house bearing Adamina's duvet with the child still asleep wrapped up inside it.

'Look what I found outside my room,' Simon explained. As the family gazed, Adamina stirred, and looked around from Simon's arms like a newborn animal.

'I'll take her upstairs,' Simon suggested, and as he left the room he added: 'You never told me she was a sleepwalker, Alice. Must have inherited it from our mother.'

But that she was. Every few days they'd find her bed empty – of

Adamina and her duvet – and Shobana and the children would search everywhere before breakfast. She made nests for herself all over the house, but always in a hallway or on a landing, never inside another room, so that it wasn't hard to find her, in her linen chrysalis, her soft down shell.

Zoe had hired a new solicitor – an Irishman whose tongue worked faster than other people's brains – and instructed him to fight the sale of the cinema with every possible legal means. In the end, they came to nothing beyond a succession of brief postponements of the date by which she had to vacate the premises; eventually there came a final deadline beyond which there was no legal appeal, but by that time Zoe had helped to found Gath Against the Ring Road, and they were prepared to employ other means.

The proposed inner ring road came north from the bus and coach station, along Lambert Street the half mile to the cinema, and a further two hundred yards or so before turning right up Barnfield Road to join Stratford Road, the main artery north out of town. According to the proposal, the stretch of road-widening that necessitated demolishing buildings began just short of the cinema and extended along Lambert Street. Most of the street, and Barnfield Road, were already wide enough for the simple expedient of double yellow lines to be sufficient.

The buildings to be demolished included the pub next door to the cinema, a piano shop, a Chinese take-away, a small grocer, a burger joint and about thirty houses, some of which were by this time already boarded up and empty. Most of the other owners or tenants had employed the same stalling tactics as Zoe, pooling their legal advice, but all now had similar final notices to quit.

The rumour was that by agreement between the owners – Harry Singh Developments – the road-building contractors and the Department of Transport, the cinema was to be made an example of: on the due day of eviction, demolition would commence. The cinema was the most prominent building, both physically and symbolically, in the way.

The campaign group was composed of inhabitants of buildings due to come down, other local residents, some of the film buffs of old and environmentalists against the building of the road on principle. The cinema, they agreed, was to be their battleground.

Not *all* local residents joined in the campaign. Some had willingly sold their houses or shop premises for hefty sums and moved elsewhere. Others lived in side streets and were glad of a road that would deter drivers from nippy short cuts down *their* narrow streets. Still others professed a certain sympathy for the campaign in general but less for the cinema in particular: they remembered those shiftless hippies Zoe had once sheltered (many of these current protestors, come from God knows where, resembled them) and anyway they never went to the cinema these days, it's all sex and violence and bad language nowadays, isn't it, who'd *want* to go?

The day approached, Wednesday, 15 September 1993. Zoe knew that on that day she would be forcibly evicted, the cinema taken over, demolition begun. All that was left was a final protest, and it was agreed that they would occupy the cinema the night before.

'We'll have an all-night screening,' Zoe had suggested at a campaign meeting in Gath Community Centre. 'They'll have to drag us out of the auditorium.'

Zoe cleared the things out of her flat, but she hadn't found a place to move to: she sold or gave away her possessions – her Makonde carving, voodoo mask from Haiti, Tibetan bells, even her books, which Simon helped her transport to the Oxfam shop on the High Street.

'Why don't you move into the cottage?' Alice suggested on Saturday morning. 'Just until you've made fresh plans. I can't stand it empty and I can't stand the thought of someone else living there. But if it was you, Zoe, it'd be different. It would lay the ghost somehow.'

'You know I couldn't,' Zoe told her. She wasn't able to even look at Harry without a rage swelling inside her, and she arranged her visits to pick up Adamina so that she wouldn't have to meet him.

'Anyway,' she added, 'I do have fresh plans. I just haven't told anyone yet.'

That wasn't quite true: Zoe *had* told someone; she'd told Adamina the week before.

Adamina had become so reluctant to go back to the big house on Saturday evenings that Zoe let her stay at the cinema all weekend. She slept in Zoe's bed, helped her make breakfast, did drawings while Zoe read the Sunday papers, a silent, undemanding companion. And then when it was time to go back she sneaked into the cinema and hid between large spectators, so that Zoe had to wait for her eyes to become accustomed to the dark before hauling Adamina out.

The previous Sunday, after having her help sell tickets for the afternoon performances, Zoe had taken Adamina upstairs. The girl sipped her Coke, apparently not listening to what Zoe had to tell her – deaf as well as mute – but Zoe had learned to identify evidence of her attention, even though it was hard to pin down: something in the tension of her shoulders, the odd flicker of her eyes, revealed she heard and responded to what Zoe said.

'I'm going to tell you something,' Zoe began, 'I haven't told anyone else. And I don't want you to tell them either; don't be a blabbermouth, Mina,' she joked, and wondered if that was a smile suppressed she saw.

'I'm going away,' Zoe continued quietly. 'You see, there's nothing left for me here – apart from you, sweetheart. My cinema's going; my home, too.' Adamina's face betrayed nothing. Zoe reached a hand to her shoulder but Adamina twitched away and Zoe withdrew it.

'You're very precious, Mina, and I want to see you again. I'm going to travel a while, and when I settle down somewhere I'm hoping you might come and visit me. Come and stay. You'll be welcome, you know, any time and . . . You'll be OK, sweetheart, I know you will. Alice will be a great . . . aunt for you, and you've got brothers and sisters all ready-made. There's just nothing left for me here, I'm forty years old, that may not mean much to you and maybe it's not that old but I never meant to stay, that's the weird thing, I was just going to help my father through college and I just kept staying on and . . .'

She broke off. I shouldn't be telling her, she admonished herself: a seven-year-old child; you self-indulgent egotist. But Adamina's silent, solemn presence brought forth more than she deserved to hear.

'You know, another thing I never told anyone else: I loved James very much. Even he didn't know. He didn't think anyone *could* love him. That's why your mother and him – it was a miracle. Not a big God miracle, I don't mean, but a little human miracle. I wasn't jealous of Laura, that was strange. I was happy for them.'

Adamina sat, hunched, listening and pretending not to, looking away. Zoe blew her nose, and felt Adamina press against her side. This time she didn't flinch as Zoe cupped her arm around her and hugged her tight.

'Come here,' she said. 'We're a pair of orphans, aren't we? I haven't cried in years. Not outside the cinema, anyway; not in daylight. You'll be OK, I know you will. You'll survive. You must do.'

Although Zoe couldn't separate Harry's actions as a businessman from her own loss – indeed was *glad* she couldn't; she had no wish to – she didn't want to cause a rift in the family, or the household in general: she didn't ask anyone to join in the protest. But Natalie found out about it and told Zoe she wouldn't miss it for anything. And when she popped in on Sunday afternoon, Simon was with her.

'Nat's told me all about it, darling,' Simon explained. 'You can keep a seat for me. In fact, if you're overbooked already, you can give me *her* seat. My bulk will come in handy in a situation like this, Zoe. *She's* too skinny, they'll carry her out by the scruff of the neck.'

'You can piss off,' Natalie bristled. 'If anyone tries to move *me*, I'll deck them,' she claimed, and had to be reminded that this was supposed to be a non-violent demonstration.

'What about Harry?' Zoe asked Simon. 'You're friends as well as brothers-in-law; won't he be upset if he finds out about your participation?'

'He already knows I'm offering my services,' Simon declared. 'He said—'

'Yes, I know,' Zoe interrupted. 'It's only business.'

'No,' Simon corrected her. 'He said he'd join in too, except it might be legally ambiguous.'

'Plus I wouldn't let him through the bloody door!' Zoe exploded.

'Well, he doesn't own it now, he's sold it, it's Department of Transport property. Also,' Simon continued, 'Father wanted you to know that if you're short of numbers, he'd like to lend his support.'

'What? Are you serious?'

'He's lost weight, he's not as heavy as he was, but he's still a big man.'

Zoe looked at Natalie appealingly: 'Am I crazy or are they?' She turned to Simon. 'Tell him thanks, but, you know, Charles is not the most popular man in this town. I don't think his presence would help the campaign.'

There was someone else who would, though: Lewis had heard about the occupation and offered to improve Zoe's sound system. Since she was only using one auditorium, he said he'd wire up the speakers from the smaller screen to provide quadrophonic sound for the occasion.

'Also, with my long legs, they might find it difficult to get me out of one of your seats in the morning,' he told her. 'I find it hard enough myself. They're squashed too close together, you know.'

Zoe's other concern was deciding on the films to show at that valedictory screening. She thought protest films of one kind or another would best fit the mood of the event, except that it might not be such a good idea to inflame the audience's emotions; they should be resolute, but peaceful. And so she settled on a self-indulgent, severely edited version of what *would* have been the following year's programme of a hundred classics from a hundred years of cinema. Or, to put it another way, Zoe was going to bow out with half a dozen of her own personal favourites.

'I'm going to be on the road,' she told herself. 'I may not see the inside of a cinema again for years. I need a strong fix to see me through.'

The evening would commence at ten p.m. on Tuesday, with *L'Atalante*, to be followed (with fifteen-minute intervals for caffeine and nicotine fixes in the foyer) by *Duck Soup, La Règle du Jeu, Some Like It Hot* (for more laughter in the dead of night). They weren't, in the end, her very favourite films, but there were other considerations, namely the need to keep people awake; there would only be a few film buffs like herself, who'd trained themselves to watch gloomy masterpieces without falling asleep.

Amarcord would carry them through to dawn and then, she figured, they could enjoy something heavier, although she refrained from inserting her very favourite, *Mirror*, made by the man who'd opened her eyes twenty years earlier. This audience would be in no fit state for that one. Instead she selected another made in the same year, *Days of Heaven*, shot mostly in the magic hour and appropriate for the dawn they wouldn't see.

Zoe also decided against *Tokyo Story*, in case it should make the audience too sad and render them unfit even for passive resistance: *Time of the Gypsies* would be next, then *Shadows of Our Forgotten Ancestors*, and by then the bailiffs would be knocking on – battering down? smashing through? – the glass doors at the front of the cinema.

How long, though, would it take them to carry the occupying audience, the protesting viewers, outside? Perhaps another hour or more, in which case – provided they could keep the projection booth battened up and powered by the generator they planned to install – they should have more to watch. Zoe wanted *The Piano*, which she had just seen an advance print of, in London, but she feared that if she were torn away in the middle *she'd* turn violent. So she plumped for *Koyaanasquatsi*, with *M. Hulot's Holiday* a first reserve, glorious laughter for the last vulnerable stragglers. She realized that she was back to a collection without women directors, but decided Natalie would have to make do with the extraordinary women up there on the screen: Dita Parlo, Margaret Dumont, Marilyn Monroe, Linda Manz, the grandmother in *Time of the Gypsies*.

Sam, the elder Singh boy, was Harry's favourite. He was the only one allowed to interrupt Harry at his desk in his study at home. Harry would pick him up and sit him *on* the desk.

'How are you today, Samuel? You're looking moony. Are you in love?'

'Yes,' Sam unwisely admitted.

'Really? Who with, I wonder? One of the girls in Susan's class?'

'I'm in love with Shobana. I'm going to marry her.'

'You can't possibly marry her,' Harry told him. 'Don't you understand? She's a country cousin, a village girl, she's practically illiterate.'

'She *said* I could marry her. I watch her doing her dancing practice.'

'Well, maybe I should watch this dance too,' Harry suggestly slyly.

'No! You're not allowed to,' his son told him.

At supper Harry teased Shobana by asking whether she was prepared for the devotion of her charges, and was she aware how she inflamed their desires further with her dancing? Shobana blushed, Sam stared furiously at the tablecloth, the other children crowed. Only Adamina ignored the proceedings.

Harry bent down to Sam beside him and whispered something in his ear. Sam looked at Adamina across the table, turned back to his father, and said: 'She's *dumb*.'

Adamina picked up her dessert spoon, leaned over and whacked Sam on the forehead: it sounded like hard wood. Sam's face went rigid with surprise – as if he'd witnessed something astonishing but not yet recognized it'd been done to *him* – and then his face shattered and he howled. Bedlam erupted. Shobana leaned across the table to grab Adamina but she'd already jumped back.

'Go to your room this minute, girl!' Harry yelled.

She scooted past Alice, who was making her way from the end of the table to comfort Sam: he was bawling, and a small round bump was already preparing to protrude from his skull.

It was Dog's idea to use locks. It came to him while helping Zoe clear out old posters and finding one for the bicycle films screening.

'Let's chain ourselves to the seats!' Dog suggested. 'That'll slow them down.'

'Great idea,' Zoe agreed, and he said he would take care of it. She wondered whether she should tell him she was leaving, but decided not to. He hadn't asked; and they were seeing less and less of each other.

On Tuesday morning Dog turned up with hundreds of long, U-shaped graphite bicycle locks.

'Matt at the bike shop said we should have more than one each,' he declared. 'See, we'll clamp our hands and feet to the seats, like electric chairs, I've tested it out already. These locks are made of carbon steel. If they try and saw or weld through all of these, it'll take *days*.'

She'd never seen Dog animated like this: the excitement of protest.

'And they won't know what they're going to release when they *do* succeed: like Frankenstein monsters.'

'Damn. *Spirit of the Beehive*,' Zoe murmured.

'A beehive?'

'No, nothing. It's too late.'

Lewis moved and rewired the speakers from the smaller screen in the large auditorium, and during the afternoon other helpers brought the generator; the projectionist prepared the numerous reels; copious quantities of coffee, popcorn and ice-creams were made ready.

There were no public showings that day, although people had heard about the occupation and came to ask about tickets for the night's screenings.

'It's all sold out,' Zoe told them. 'Come along in the morning if you can, though. The more the merrier when they cart us out.'

Later on, those with tickets arrived: neighbours; Green activists; one Labour councillor; dreadlocked anti-road protestors, young veterans of such dissent; film buffs, looking more mournful than at Agatha's funeral, more washed-out than ever; Natalie, and Simon. They took their seats. The chair of Gath Against the Ring Road gave a short speech, the lights went down, the screen flickered with life, the first titles for *L'Atalante* appeared, and they were off.

It *was* like a journey, Zoe thought, sitting at the back by the aisle

– and later on they'd even be strapping themselves into their seats. A journey through cinema history. She should have chosen a road movie. *Alice in the Cities*, maybe. She thought about Adamina, and felt ashamed at lumbering the child with her own tears. She thought about James, and tried to remember if she knew whether or not he'd ever seen this strangely beautiful poem in black-and-white celluloid, made by a man who'd lived a life nearly ten years shorter than his. And then she forgot about James, as she was drawn back into the images on the screen before her, in her own and her grandmother's cinema.

The night progressed, the films unwound. Helpless laughter at the Marx Brothers' manic satire; absorption in a French aristocratic society breaking up from within; more sporadic laughter at Jack Lemmon and Tony Curtis in drag. People fell asleep, dribbled onto their chests, woke with stiff necks and slipped out to the foyer for coffee. Pills of various kinds were taken. It was clear, though, that the audience as a whole were flagging during *Amarcord*: snoring could be heard in the few quiet moments and people were wandering out to the loo with the slow, swaying gait of sleepwalkers – or the hypnotized actors in *Heart of Glass*, Zoe thought. She was worried. Only the film buffs were watching with all their attention glued to the screen, the mad uncle in the olive tree crying: '*Voglio una donna!*' Peering like captivated vampires who received their sustenance not from blood but images.

Zoe met Simon at the popcorn counter, and confessed her anxiety.
    'They just need a good breakfast,' he told her.
    'Shit! I'm stupid. I completely overlooked that,' she admitted.
    'Is your kitchen still set up upstairs?' he asked.
    'Well, yes,' Zoe replied. 'But there's no *food* there.'
    'Good. Fine. Leave it to me, darling. Just let me out of here, and I'll be back in an hour.'
    Simon returned from who knows where with boxes of food.
    'I'll provide breakfast,' he promised, 'although I'll need an assistant.' He found a Donga warrior who'd slipped into the empty smaller auditorium and was sleeping peacefully there, and woke him rudely with his foot.
    'Come on, you,' Simon demanded. 'Come and make yourself useful.'

*

530

What Simon then achieved, while the audience were immersed in the epic triangle of *Days of Heaven*, was a miracle. Not a little human miracle, Zoe would later tell Adamina, but a big God one. When the film finished and the house lights came up, Simon's dreadlocked, dragooned assistant announced that during this interval breakfast would be served in the flat, at which precise moment people became aware of the mouthwatering odour of fried bacon entering their nostrils. They filed and shuffled impatiently into the foyer and upstairs, where Simon and George provided paper platefuls of English breakfast.

'Not one or two or half a dozen,' Zoe would recall, still incredulous, 'but all two hundred, Mina. It was tiny, you remember, and people ate off their laps on the stairs and everywhere. But these meals kept coming, half of them for carnivores, eggs and bacon, and alternatives for vegetarians, soya protein sausages with beans on toast. With coffee *and* fruit juice. I didn't get a chance to ask him how he did it – in the rush he mumbled something facetious about microwaves and army training and that really it was all due to his young friend George's improvisational genius – and I never have been able to work it out.'

Fortified, refreshed, the audience returned to watch *Time of the Gypsies*, to be transported by that operatic cinema. It would have taken longer than the interval that followed for them to come back to reality if it wasn't for the fact that those who went out to stretch their legs saw from the foyer the beginnings of activity in the street outside. The first police car was parked, passers-by were pausing, a large yellow van pulled up.

'It's starting,' someone returning to the auditorium announced. Before the next film began the bicycle locks were distributed and Dog, a big, shy man, explained to the Campaign chair how they should be attached, and he repeated the instructions at an audible volume: the locks were clamped into place, people imprisoning themselves, after last-minute dashes to the toilets and amid nervous laughter, as each realized that the person sitting next to them would have to click shut the last lock. Simon's assistant chef, George, came and sat beside him, and sent Natalie to where *he'd* been sitting.

'WHAT ABOUT THE KEYS?' someone shouted out.

'What about the keys?' the chair asked Dog.

'Yes,' he replied. 'I'll go around and collect them and pass them up to the projectionist.'

'HE'LL COME AND COLLECT THEM OFF YOU!' the chairman announced.

The operation took longer than planned. People in the middle of rows found themselves surrounded by comrades already locked securely in position while they still had an arm free, so someone else had to climb over seats and bodies to reach and shackle them. Dog began to do it but provoked cries of pain from those his big and clumsy limbs squashed, whereupon Natalie, who'd not yet fettered herself, volunteered.

As the last people were locked in place ('ALL ABOARD THE STARSHIP ENTERPRISE!' someone shouted out) Dog realized he wouldn't be able to lock him*self* in: the very last person would have to have one arm free.

'Just put it in position, and they won't notice,' Zoe advised him.

'An illusion!' he replied. 'It might just work. I'm going to get rid of these keys now. Let me lock *you* in, Zoe. You're the penultimate one.' He shackled Zoe in her seat and passed a bucket on string up through the projectionist's small window.

'Signal to him to start,' Zoe called to Dog, and he did. The next film began, *Shadows of Our Forgotten Ancestors*, and as the audience gradually forgot themselves, the activity *outside* the cinema was building up. A besuited bailiff rang the bell and knocked on the glass doors, and when no reply was forthcoming he ordered a workman – with assent from the senior police officer present – to use a sledgehammer.

It was 8.30 a.m. and by this time a hundred or more people had already gathered along the street: they were on the opposite pavement, pressed against barriers put up that morning, as if for some royal gala performance, waiting for the glittering stars of a Hollywood première to roll up in limousines; when in fact they were waiting for other, humbler kinds of stars to come *out* of the cinema.

Inside, the shattering glass of the front doors could be heard clearly, and although one or two of the incorrigibly imaginative spectators assimilated the noise into the film's soundtrack, as in a dream, it made most blanch with anxiety. Some at the back heard also the booing from the crowd that greeted it.

Moments later the bailiff and security guards in yellow jackets entered the back of the auditorium.

'Find the lights,' the bailiff ordered. 'Switch them on.'

When this was done the image on the screen was washed out but still visible; as had been agreed beforehand, the viewers kept their

532

attention on the film, ignoring (or at least pretending to) their evictors. Like two hundred adult Adaminas, Zoe thought.

'Bloody hell,' the security foreman told the bailiff, 'they're locked to the seats.'

'Well, get some saws in here then.'

'They're graphite locks. It'll take hours.' The foreman scanned the cinema for an approximate body count. 'Days,' he corrected himself.

'A locksmith, then,' the bailiff suggested.

'They're virtually unpickable, these Trelocks. My lad's got one.'

'I can't think straight with all this noise, damn it. Go and turn off the projector,' the bailiff ordered.

'We can't get into the booth. It's all boarded up: the projectionist's barricaded himself in.'

'Well, cut off the power, then. Just shut that bloody film off, and get some torches in here.'

An electrician found the fuse box and switched off the mains supply. The film wound to a halt; the soundtrack groaned to silence. The audience sat in total darkness. But there were more sounds from the projectionist's booth up above and those who craned their necks could see light in there. And then the generator came on, humming, and the projector cranked into motion, the screen came alive once more, the soundtrack found voice.

'That's all we need,' the bailiff exclaimed. 'They've got a damn generator.'

'We're back to where we started,' the foreman pointed out.

'Very perceptive,' the bailiff told him. 'Where are those torches?'

Zoe and Dog, Simon, Natalie, Lewis and the rest of the audience were left in peace for the next few minutes as the managers of their eviction retreated outside to work out what to do. The security men in their yellow jackets stayed inside but, with legal cases for assault pending from previous incidents, had strict orders to avoid physical confrontation, and so instead of adopting intimidating tactics they huddled in the corridor.

The bailiff conferred in the foyer with the chief police officer, an executive of the demolition company and an official from the Department of Transport, while the crowd outside continued to grow. The road had been blocked off by now, traffic diverted. A crane with a huge ball on the end of a chain arrived and some people jumped the barrier and lay down in the road to block its path: it stood thirty yards from the cinema, while police carried away the floppy bodies of protestors; newspaper photographers and a television crew filmed them and also the crane operator, sat high up in his cab, smoking.

The bailiff and the other officials re-entered the auditorium with torches – which was where an extra element of farce entered proceedings: since a generator was powering the projector, they might as well have turned the mains power back on and had the house lights up, but it didn't seem to occur to anyone to do so. Zoe had to bite her lip to stop herself suggesting it. Not that the scene really *needed* more absurdity, with four men discussing the removal of two hundred immobile people who mutely ignored them, watching a film instead.

'There's only one thing for it,' the demolition company executive declared at length. 'Unbolt the seats. Carry them out *in* their seats.'

'I'm not so sure,' the Ministry official opined.

'We'll have to sort out what to do when we get them outside,' the police officer said.

'We've got spanners and mole-grips,' said the foreman.

Outside, rumours of people being beaten up in there swirled through the crowd: now that the bailiffs had forced entry, why were they *keeping* the protestors inside? Why didn't they let them *out*?

Inside, men unbolted seats from their fastenings, having to squirm around the feet of the seats' occupants, while their colleagues shone torches.

The first of the cinema occupiers emerged, to the relief and consternation of the tense crowd, and that person was, fittingly, Zoe herself, who'd sat at the back beside the aisle. Strapped to her seat, she was borne aloft on the shoulders of four security guards in yellow jackets. The crowd pressed against the barriers and noisily clapped and cheered her, photographers clicked their cameras, news crews filmed her, as she left her cinema for the last time, carried out as if in tribute. Zoe felt disappointment that she couldn't wave back. She wasn't smiling: clamped in position, overcome suddenly by the bright daylight, lack of sleep, the large crowd and her imminent departure, tears spilled down her cheeks. She was unable to restrain or hide them, and they were caught in close-up by a battery of cameras.

Zoe was followed, in surprisingly quick succession, by the rest of the audience, similarly carried out: militant protestors shouting, 'NO MORE

534

ROADS! NO MORE ROADS!'; film buffs with their nocturnal eyes tight shut; Simon, beaming, carried by six huffing and puffing men terrified of dropping him; Lewis, his long legs dangling before him; local residents, bemused at finding themselves the centre of attention; and Natalie, with a look of a warrior's readiness on her face that made those who knew her glad she'd been rendered immobile.

None of them could salute the applauding crowd. Except, that is, for Dog, who perhaps recognized that at this moment he bore a certain responsibility. He slipped his free arm out from under the bicycle lock that had been merely resting on his wrist, and waved; but then, feeling rather foolish, he shyly lowered his head, balled his hand into a fist and held it high above him.

Once the yellow-jacketed security guards had carried the protestors out of the cinema they gladly passed them over to the reluctant custody of the police, who in the absence of a better plan had them carried around the corner into Branagh Street and set down on the pavement.

A couple of hastily hired locksmiths began the laborious process of unpicking them. Back inside, though, the projection booth was broken into, and the projectionist came out with the box of keys: by now the locks had served their purpose.

Even before she had been released Zoe was pounced upon by the press, and interviewed on the pavement, still strapped to her seat. Besieged by jostling men and women with notebooks and microphones before she'd recovered her equilibrium, she gave an incoherent interview, before being freed and willingly making way for more practised spokesmen.

As people were unlocked from their seats, so they joined friends on the other side of the barriers. Some of the hard-core protestors, though, doubled back and lay in the path of the crane as others had earlier – to Zoe's surprise Simon was among them, joining his assistant chef, George, on the tarmac – at which point the police lost their patience and began making arrests, showing less restraint than before as they manhandled them into waiting vans; reinforcements arrived to hold back the growing crowd.

A banner was draped from the windows of the flat above the launderette opposite that said: SAVE OUR CINEMA.

A bit late for that, Zoe thought. She mixed in the crowd. People patted her on the shoulder, said things like 'Well done', and 'It's a crying shame.' She saw that all around her strangers were talking to each other and offering cigarettes; pensioners were joining in the chant that youths had started: NO MORE ROADS! NO MORE ROADS!; a couple of waiters from the Indian restaurant next to the launderette had come out and were contributing to the chorus of boos for the workmen disconnecting the mains supplies of electricity, water and gas.

This is what they mean by community, Zoe thought, surprised. Not that it makes any difference now. I am a traveller.

Shortly before midday the crane finally got into position, and the operator started up his machine. The massive, heavy ball began to swing, very slowly at first, only gradually gathering momentum: swinging out into the yawning space above the street, then back towards the façade of the Electra Cinema, a little closer each time; and suddenly Zoe had a flash of memory, something she'd long since forgotten. It must have happened when she was incredibly young. She'd been sitting on her father's shoulders when she saw it: in a church, no, surely a cathedral, filled with people; a censer was being swung on a chain through the nave, trailing smoke of burning incense and making a great whooshing noise as it swung. She could sense again the pungent smell of the incense in her nostrils.

The huge demolition ball made first contact with the front of the cinema with no more than a kiss, like some ritual pugilistic greeting before destruction. It swung away and returned with a sluggish thud that made little impact: a few flakes of paint and plaster fluttered down as the ball swung out. The third strike made another dull thud and still did no more than superficial damage. For an illogical moment Zoe wondered whether this might really be a kind of combat, an assault the cinema might actually withstand and the crane retire, defeated. But the next blow put paid to such fancy, sending cracks shooting out across the façade like embodied shrieks of pain; and the one after brought bricks loose and falling.

Each impact was greeted with tumultuous boos from the crowd, that swelled into an eerie accompaniment. The crane operator, Zoe noticed, had on a pair of earmuffs: he couldn't hear the disapproval of his actions. Maybe he was even connected to a Walkman; maybe he was listening to music while he demolished the cinema. She felt a tap on her shoulder, and a voice in her ear.

'We're all ready,' the voice whispered, and she turned. It was Joe the Blow, her old friend Luna's man.

'OK,' she said, and she followed him, slipping out of the

536

crowd, away from the scene, along the road, the thud and rumble of the demolition and the crowd's loud indignation receding behind her.

Zoe didn't turn around: she was walking into the future. She didn't realize she was being followed; she didn't hear the footsteps echoing her own.

Joe the Blow's new van was parked up a side street, in front of two others, each with the words ELECTRA TRAVELLING THEATRE on the side. Luna was inside the van with two of her children. She opened the door.

'How did it go?' she asked.

'Well, it was something, Luna,' Zoe replied. 'I'll tell you all about it on the road.'

'You've tied up your loose ends?' Luna asked.

'All except about a hundred,' Zoe laughed. 'Hell, let them sort it out.'

She made to climb into the van when she felt a tug at her skirt, and looked down. Adamina was standing there. She was holding a carrier bag. She looked up at Zoe with a resolute, expectant expression.

'Mina! What on earth . . . ? How did you get down here?' Zoe asked, but Adamina said nothing and neither did her expression change.

'Did you walk across town?' Zoe asked, and Adamina nodded. 'You crazy girl,' Zoe said. She knelt in front of Adamina.

'This is it, sweetheart,' she said. 'I'm going away now. We've been through this. I can't take you with us.' Zoe tried to think of how to explain why not. 'We're going abroad,' she said. 'We're driving down to Dover now.'

Adamina looked inside her carrier bag and produced her passport.

Zoe couldn't stop herself laughing out loud. 'You think of everything, don't you?' she said. 'I'm sorry about this,' she told Luna and Joe. 'This is Adamina, she's my . . . I don't know what exactly. What are you?' she asked Adamina. 'My best friend's stepdaughter. My cousin's niece. What else have you got in there?'

Adamina produced two or three items of clothes, and two photograph albums, which Zoe opened: one with black-and-white pictures Adamina had taken of Laura and James' wedding, which James had printed for her; the other with James' photos of his family. Zoe flipped briefly through. Even if she had time, she wasn't sure

537

she was ready to look at them; and now there wasn't time. She closed the second album.

'What are we going to do with you?' she asked, and Adamina pointed at the van.

'We may never come back, you know,' Zoe told her.

Adamina nodded gravely. Zoe looked at Luna, and at her two children: a boy of about eight, a girl a little older.

'Oh, God, I don't know,' Zoe exclaimed, and sat in the side-doorway of the van. She looked up and took in grey clouds in the warm sky.

'I don't want to rush you, Zoe,' Joe said, 'but if we're going to get that ferry, if we need to drop her off or anything . . .'

'No, we don't,' Zoe decided. 'We're taking her with us. Come on, Mina, get in. Let's go.'

Adamina climbed into the van, Zoe slid the door shut behind them. Joe signalled to the drivers behind and the small convoy pulled away. Zoe stepped forward into the passenger seat, wound down the window and rolled herself a cigarette. Adamina got up beside her and strapped herself in. She lifted the end of Zoe's seatbelt and offered it to her.

'Not just yet, thanks,' Zoe said. 'God, I'm tired,' she murmured.

'It's a pleasure to drive, this beast,' Joe told her, changing gear. 'It's a good investment, Zoe.'

'I hope so,' she replied. 'Does the phone work?'

'Of course it does.'

'I ought to tell Alice Mina's all right.'

Zoe didn't know what lay ahead, but she was glad that she was leaving. She'd telephone Alice again when they reached Calais, although she'd *say* she was calling from Dover: having made the decision, she didn't want any trouble erupting at Customs. She did know Adamina's legal guardianship hadn't been sorted out, and maybe Alice and Harry would be relieved to let Zoe take her.

She put her arm around the mute child beside her. 'Shall we adopt each other, then?' she asked, as they drove along Stratford Road, out of town.

Owing to their travels, it has taken over two years (during which time they've kept in touch with Alice with weekly phone calls) and a convoluted adoption process, for Zoe to become Adamina's legal guardian; but in time Adamina has become somewhat less of an

538

orphan. As has Zoe herself. Harry administers a trust fund. In this instance Zoe agrees they shouldn't let feelings interfere with business: there's little doubt that under his stewardship Adamina will come of age with a helping financial hand.

Zoe Freeman misses her cinema; she's made the troupe stop so that she could spend a couple of hours in out-of-the-way fleapits and at outdoor screenings in warm town squares across the Continent. It's been some compensation to Zoe that images of people being carried out of her cinema locked to their seats (in particular a picture of Dog, the least militant of men, with head bowed and defiant fist raised in dignified protest) played a large part in mobilizing protest against an inner ring road in the town. Receiving national coverage, the campaign swelled overnight, drawing large support, and vilification for the scheme; no more buildings were demolished. The Transport Minister blamed the scheme on Whitehall incompetence and three months later announced new plans for a showpiece pedestrianized area in the town centre; an enlargement of the existing park-and-ride system; and a widening of the *outer* ring road – his one tactical error. Within the space of a sentence he quelled one protest and inspired another. He'd missed the point.

Harry Singh, on the other hand, doesn't miss a thing. He isn't sorry the inner ring road was scrapped: he'd already sold the properties he owned to the Department of Transport; he even bought some of them back again at reduced prices. Harry has achieved what he set out to achieve. He's a contented man. He's wealthy, he owns the house on the hill, he loves his wife – a distracted woman who's dispensed with the services of all but one of the three gardeners and spends much of her time in the garden. Their children are still well-behaved models of decorum. The eldest, Amy, is ten years old; adolescence awaits her (and the others too) and who knows what rebellion may stir even now in their burgeoning hearts?

As for Charles, his world – as well as his weight – continues to diminish. He's a little-seen figure, and few of those who do see him recognize the man-in-charge, Charles Freeman. He doesn't shout at people any more, and he doesn't greet them with his suffocating bear-hugs. Alice says her father walks with a stick, slowly, as if feeling his way through fog. Charles isn't unhappy, he's just lost his energy, he's a tired old man who fills his days with habitual activities, in the solitude of forsaken power.

His work identifying photographs is completed. The James Freeman Photographic Archive, in the Local Studies section of the public library, is used regularly, both by individual browsers through local history and for commercial purposes. There's talk of a book.

Simon isn't at home much these days – and when he is he's shut in a room a lot of the time, staring at a computer screen; it's very different, though, from that brief period he once wasted in front of the TV, in his teenage oblivion. For Simon was galvanized by the cinema sit-in, and by his arrest: nowadays he communicates through E-mail with environmentalists around the world for a group called Earth Action.

It may also be that Simon was galvanized by love. His assistant chef of a miraculous breakfast is now his partner, and they make the oddest couple in both their circles: with the fastidious hypochondriacs of Simon's health group, with the rainbow warriors of George's acquaintance. They make fine spontaneous breakfasts, too – in the house on the hill as well as in a tepee in a Welsh valley that George calls his home.

The rest of his time Simon spends at a surgery he set up in Northtown with three of his colleagues from the health group. It's called the Back Clinic, and they treat exclusively disorders of the spine: sciatica, slipped discs, rheumatism, lumbago, fibrositis, pulled muscles, osteoarthritis and the common backache. Which, they soon discovered, covered just about everyone over the age of thirty in the town. The other three are a chiropractor, a practitioner of the Alexander Technique and an osteopath; Simon refers to what *he* does as Greek massage, but everyone knows that's just an excuse to have him lay his fat hands on their skin and feel the hot liquid heat that flows like honey through their body.

Simon has given Natalie Bryson a computer for the refuge. She said they had no use for it but he pressed it on her anyway and now the children there play computer games on it. He also gave her a fax and a photocopying machine, which are more useful. Natalie moved into the cottage in the grounds last year. She told Zoe the last time Zoe telephoned that she wouldn't mind doing something different, if only there was no call for the refuge she offered. That need would always be there, though; and having failed the friend she'd promised to protect, she wasn't planning to fail any more.

Lewis Roberts no longer DJs. He'll be forty next year, and figured either his credibility or his hearing would be damaged if he carried on. He owns a bar, in partnership with one of his old footballers, and he's doing fine.

Gloria is now a ward sister in the town's hospice. She's writing a book about nursing care of the dying patient and hopes she'll finish it before the hospital trust privatizes the hospice, as is rumoured. If and when that happens, she's planning to quit nursing. She says marriage is a good moment for a career change, anyway: Gloria's engaged to Nick, a probation officer, and their wedding is set for next summer. Her father, Garfield, is glad and tactless at the prospect of grandchildren; he's already announced that he's sure there'll soon be another decent cricketer in the family, because *he* can't be expected to play on much longer.

Zoe didn't know any of these things back then. 'Shall we adopt each other, then?' she asked Adamina.

The convoy drove along Stratford Road out of town, and round the roundabout. A few hundred yards further on, the road crossed a bridge over the river.

'Hey, stop the van, Joe,' Zoe exclaimed.

Joe did as he was asked; the other vans slowed to a halt behind him.

'This won't take a minute,' Zoe explained, as she opened the door, jumped down from the van, and began to undress.

'You drive over and meet me on the other side,' she said.

'What are you *doing*, Zoe?' Luna asked. Her children stared.

'I'm leaving, and I want to do it properly,' Zoe replied. 'See you in a minute,' she told Adamina. 'It's a good thing there's not much traffic,' Zoe added, as she stripped naked and set off down the bank to the water. They watched her scramble down.

'You'd better get a towel ready,' Joe suggested to Luna. 'Your aunt is bonkers,' he told Adamina.

Adamina, who'd been watching motionless, suddenly sprang to life. She jumped out of the van and threw off her clothes, and scurried after Zoe, reaching her just as she was treading gingerly into the cool water.

'Mina, what do you think you're up to?' Zoe demanded. 'Go back to the van, this is too dangerous for you.'

Adamina shook her head. Zoe scowled at the grey sky, and back down at Adamina, but the child stood her ground. A soft, warm rain began falling, speckling the surface of the river.

'Look: let's not kick off with an argument,' Zoe pleaded. 'I'm not a strong swimmer. I'm certainly not a lifesaver. And I'm *not* standing here, naked to the world, arguing with you. Now go *back* to the van this minute!'

Adamina looked across to the far bank, then back at Zoe, and smiled. It wasn't such a long way; the river wasn't so wide. And, as she'd later tell Zoe, someone had taught her how to swim; a good teacher. She plunged forward into the water and began a smooth breast-stroke towards the other side.